SPARKING

THE

INFERNO

SPARKING THE INFERNO

Circle of Origin
Book 1

Brandon Carter

Substratial Press | Oklahoma City, Oklahoma

ISBN: 978-1-962268-01-1 (Paperback)
ISBN: 978-1-962268-00-4 (eBook)

Any references to historical events, real people, or real places are used fictitiously. Names, characters, and places are products of the author's imagination.

Cover design by Merrily Rivera Chaykin.
Book design by Substratial Press.

First printing edition 2023.

Substratial Press
www.SubstratialPress.com

Https://CircleofOrigin.blog

DEDICATION

To my mother and step-mother, for always believing in me no matter what strange new hobby I decided to try from week to week, for never pressing me to finish this book, and being infinitely supportive once I finally picked it back up.

To James, for reading over that first TERRIBLE draft and not instantly disowning me, and for reminding me year after year that I needed to finish it.

To my wife Hanna, for patiently letting me chase whatever hobby caught my interest over the years. I'm so blessed to be taking this journey through life together with you.

And finally . . . to an amazing community of authors who welcomed me in, showed me the ropes, and continually believed in me when I didn't believe in myself.

Moose Trackers for life.

ACKNOWLEDGMENTS

Thank you to anyone and everyone who picks up my book and gives it a read. Hell, I'll just be happy to have it gathering dust on your shelf!

A HUGE thank you to all the supporters of my Patreon, those who believed in me and this project, but an extra special thanks to the following:

To **Karen Mize**, my first *Everyman Hero*, and someone who has supported everything I've done for as long as I can remember,

To **James Sandmann**, my very first patron and *Dark Warrior,* another long-time supporter,

To **Donald and Tia Justice**, two wonderfully supportive human beings and *Dark Warriors*,

And to **Laura Schile**, the family I didn't know I needed and *Dark Warrior*!

Each of you deserve all my love, and without you, I would never have made it this far.

"Fire burns naught without a timeline of preparation. The common eye sees only the conflagration, oblivious to the path stretching out behind that single, instigating spark.

Then again, it's hard to see much of anything when the flames are clawing at your heels."

—The Keeper of the Tomes

Prologue

The young man buried his mouth in the crook of his elbow—less to stifle the reek of sodden earth and the coppery scent he was desperately fighting not to think about, and more to prevent his panicked breathing from alerting the pair of road-scuffed boots on the other side of the overturned wheelbarrow from pinpointing his hiding spot. In the utter darkness beneath the barrow, he couldn't be sure of the boots' location, but they were close enough it didn't matter.

"There's nothing back here," said the boots' owner, a husky male voice tinged with disappointment. "Just some baskets, rusted tools, and some rotten equipment."

A soft kick rocked his hiding place, and a brief flash of daylight stung his eyes before the barrow shifted back into place. A burning ache in his right side ebbed with every breath, and he struggled against the urge to reach back and comfort his wounded ribs.

Another voice answered from the other side of the hovel, too far to make out what was being said.

"Nah," the boots responded, and he could hear someone rooting around in the pile of empty wicker baskets. "Just a buncha provincial junk. The whole lot wouldn't fetch half a shil back home."

The boots sighed, and a rock bounced off the wall of the barrow. "Been waving these stupid hunks of glass 'round all day without seeing so much as a sparkle. Not gonna be any townsfolk left if things keep on like this."

A distant chuckle, followed by more incomprehensible speech.

"For these hicks?" An incredulous snort. "They're barely even people."

He swallowed back the growing lump in his throat and closed his eyes. Picturing the area around their hovel, he searched for his best shot at escaping the two strangers without getting grabbed. To the east, the edge of the Traagen

Woods butted up against the rim of the property, but a tangle of wild blackberries made escape in that direction nearly impossible without a lot of luck and a bevy of shallow tears in his skin and clothing.

The north and west weren't much better. The organized spacing of the apple orchard lent itself toward ease of access, making it practically impossible to lose anyone in the wide open groves. With little to no hiding places among the manicured apple trees, he doubted he'd make it far before one of the two men ran him down.

That left the area on the south side of the house, where the forest encroached on the barn. Problem was, the house itself stood between him and the small grove of balsam fir that would mask his retreat. He'd either have to go around or through the little hovel, and without knowing the location of the second stranger, either way risked a calamitous face-to-face encounter.

The leather strap cutting into his wrist was slowly leeching the feeling from his right hand, but he didn't dare shift his weight to relieve the pressure. Hunched over within the wheelbarrow's bucket as he was, the wooden handcart mounted his back like a turtle shell, and would mirror even the slightest adjustment to his position.

He tried not to think about that strap, but his thoughts betrayed him, following its length down to the object wedged between his hip and the base of the wheelbarrow. As if summoned by his mental attentions, the metallic tang of blood tickled his nostrils once more, and a soft whimper unconsciously slipped through bloodless lips.

The seconds passed in strained silence.

His forearm tightened around his clenched jaw. He flexed his thighs, preparing to burst out from beneath the barrow to make a mad dash for the trees. Navigating the brambles would be a small price to pay for escape.

He was no stranger to pain.

The distant voice sounded again, more forceful now but no closer to being understood.

The boots didn't respond. Soil crunched against moving feet.

A thin line of sunlight blinked into existence as fingers wiggled through the muck to grip the rim of the barrow.

"Someone hiding there in the dark?" The curious whisper set his heart to pounding, and his breath froze in his throat.

With a creak of aging wood, the barrow shifted and a blinding light stole away the protective black.

Chapter 1: The Young Man

Nevin sprinted headlong through the sea of ferns.

The why of the running, whether he was running toward or from something, never occurred to him. All he knew was that he *had* to run, but as the forest whipped past at dangerous speeds, and hidden roots and uneven terrain threatened his footing, the surrounding serenity ate away at the urgency empowering his feet.

He slowed his pace through the reaching ground cover, gazing almost absently up into the flickering sunlight. A thin smile parted his lips as he walked. As the adrenaline pumping acid through his veins evaporated, the familiar surroundings warmed him in a way the exertion and terror never could.

Dappled sunshine filtered through the threaded canopy, stealing through the burgeoning greenery in angled, glowing pillars. A heady mixture of crisp juniper, woodsmoke, and cedar wafted in on a breeze thickened by a predawn shower that still lingered on the finger-like leaves of the ferns obscuring the ground. The cavernous shade beneath the treetops echoed with wren song and the gravelly cry of ravens, the shadows magnified by a distant haze that had stubbornly refused to dissipate with the arrival of the morning sun.

His true home, and one where injury only arose from his own careless actions.

How did I get here?

He stumbled almost drunkenly as he walked, supporting himself on errant branches and passing trunks. Sticky mud caked his shins and the undersides of his forearms. He smelled faintly of apple pulp, of fresh sweat, of fear.

Is this a dream?

The shifting light beams steadily penetrated the pillowy fog stuffed between his thoughts, and a deep frown eventually stole away his smile. He looked around, confused. The Traagen Woods stretched out in all directions, without a single sign of civilization to mark his position in the untamed wilderness. He could be anywhere, though the relative flatness of the terrain told him he was likely somewhere in the vicinity of Elbin.

I don't remember coming here, he thought. He rubbed his aching thighs. *What was I running from? I know better than to run in the woods.*

Fingers probed his aching head, brushing the ragged edges of a gash residing mere inches above his neck. The brief touch released an electric jolt of pain that twisted his guts into queasy knots. The hand came back covered in blood and flecks of what looked like bark.

Squinting, he raised the hand for a better look, feeling his shoulder complain in return. Warm light peeked through swollen fingers. Wincing, he fanned them wide, noting the strange bruises spiraling around his tender wrist and more bits of bark embedded in his forearm.

"What have you done to me this time, Dalen?"

As though summoned forth by his question, a sharp pain lanced through his skull, and with it arose an unfamiliar image.

A memory.

Wilted silver-backed leaves and drooping branches crowded in on him from all sides. His right arm extended awkwardly overhead, disappearing into the tangled greenery. He hung by his wrist, the weight of his upper body straining his already sore ribs and making him gasp.

The images faded, and Nevin was surprised to find himself sitting in the dirt, the hungry overgrowth leaning in to paw at his torso.

He stretched his jaw to dispel the hurt, but the sharp pain vanished just as quickly as it had appeared, leaving behind nothing but a dull ache to mark its passing. In return, the troublesome fog filling his mind weakened further.

He took a moment to gather himself, choosing to enjoy the breeze as it sapped the residual heat from his flushed skin. While the Waking months were finally drawing to a close for the rest of Stragus, the Traagen Woods would enjoy the cooler temperatures and intermittent storms into the heights of the Tending. The residents of Elbin—a village of roughly five hundred souls scattered around the southern reaches of the forest—would often claim the favorable clime as the sole reason their ancestors choose to settle the forested peninsula.

But in truth, it was the seclusion that drew them, and in his current state, Nevin was grateful that the chances of someone stumbling upon him in the cavernous depths of the woods were practically zero.

An intrusive root in his backside finally inspired him to return to his feet, and as he rose, an uncomfortable heat blossomed in the ribs. He pressed on the spot but didn't rub, now remembering the rude awakening the ornery drunk had served him before sunrise.

"Must have been existing too loudly for the hateful prick's taste this morning," he said, wincing. "Gonna have to work on that."

Despite the truth of his upbringing, Nevin refused to claim Dalen as his father. The years had only served to deepen the old apple farmer's depression and anger, with the negative aspects of his temperament often exacerbated by the large quantities of homemade apple wine he regularly imbibed.

As his wounded ribs proved, it took very little to earn the ire of the man who raised him. A bad harvest, a broken tool, even an interrupted nap—Dalen frequently turned his temper on Nevin, and when he felt unable to eloquently express his displeasure in a verbal tirade of insults, he expressed it with the back of his hand or the heel of his boot. Few were the days that Nevin hadn't hidden bruises from either Aidux or Ishen, and he'd grown quite adept at silently bearing the pain—both mental and physical alike.

And while Dalen didn't need to be drunk to be cruel or abusive, one of the quickest ways to a beating was to refer to the man in any way other than his name. Still, Nevin would gladly call him 'papa' before touching the old drunk's bronze canteen.

Only once had Dalen ever beaten him into unconsciousness, and never again had Nevin dared go near that forbidden metal flask.

Now that he was back on his feet, all his various aches and pains fought to make their presences known. His swollen hand throbbed to the beat of his heart. His thighs burned. Tiny cuts on his bare arms oozed blood. His tender lower lip kept catching on his teeth. His right shoulder felt stretched, overextended almost, probably a result of the same situation that had injured his hand.

"It's fine. I'll just tell Aidux I was mugged by a dryad." He plucked some bark off his cheek. "Wouldn't be the first time I blamed something on wood fairies."

His fingers trailed down his arm, grazing the bruises encircling his wrist, the damaged flesh presenting almost like a burn on his sun-darkened skin. The bruised edges were unusually straight, and about two fingers in width. The result of an item he should be carrying, but was somehow missing.

My pack?!

His hand flew to his shoulder, feeling for an object that wasn't there.

"No, no, no, no, no!" Nevin bent over and swiped at the ferns, hoping he'd dropped it nearby. The immediate area gave up nothing to his frantic search, but a growing wave of nausea soon forced him to straighten. His head swam and the world listed precariously. Reaching out, Nevin braced himself against a gnarled oak and waited for the nausea to pass.

Though he remembered nothing beyond Dalen's sharp kick to his ribs, all signs pointed toward an unfortunate early encounter with the man. Mornings were the worst, and Nevin had quickly learned to rise before first light to tackle his chores before heading to Ishen's cabin for the day. His mentor—a bookish older gentleman living off by himself in the more secluded reaches of the Traagen—had always applauded his initiative, though the young man kept his true reasons for rising before the sun to himself.

Today, though, Dalen had beat him to the punch and ambushed him while he slept.

He nodded to himself as he thought. A fight with Dalen *would* explain why he'd be out in the middle of the forest with his pack in tow. With his seventeenth birthday just over the horizon, the desire to finally set out into the world and leave his abusive home life behind occupied his thoughts in nearly every waking moment.

Hard to do without supplies, he thought, turning around to retrace his steps. A fissure of bent and broken ferns greeted him as he walked, evidence that he'd been moving through the woods at a carelessly rapid pace.

Soon, a hulking shadow emerged through the distant haze, lying directly across his intended path. Looking at it made his skull throb.

A silver maple, uprooted by a recent Waking thunderstorm. With their shallow, meandering root structures, such trees were notoriously weak, making for a dangerous choice of temporary shelter during the unpredictable early year storms. A gap in the canopy caused by its absence bathed the fallen tree in a warm glow, its trident-shaped leaves still vibrant despite its unfortunate future. The wilting leaves shifted with the breeze, and a metallic glint drew his gaze before being swallowed up in the variegated greenery.

The fissure of broken ferns disappeared right into the heart of the maple's drooping branches.

Nevin stopped, eyeing the fallen tree in an effort to gauge its height. It didn't actually matter, he knew, but his mind scrambled for any explanation as to why he would chance vaulting a downed tree instead of just going around.

"Aidux is never gonna let me live this one down," he grumbled.

According to his best friend—his only real friend in Elbin—jumping a fallen tree was quite simply idiotic, especially one of this size. The tangled branches could be hiding any number of dangers: holes, roots, broken sticks, even animal burrows. The chances of escaping injury, serious or otherwise, were low enough that Nevin, given the option, would have chosen to circumvent the hazard.

He eyed the broken path through the ferns. *So why didn't I?*

Nevin immediately regretted pulling at that mental thread. The pain in his skull returned once more, drawing out another series of images from the darkness of his mind.

He stumbled as he ran, skidding across the soggy earth left behind by that morning's rain, carried forward by momentum and adrenaline. He pumped his arms and legs until they burned. His joints screamed, but fear had taken control of his senses and his only concern was the two armed men who were likely only moments behind.

"Armed men? But wasn't Dalen the one—"

Beads of sweat sprang from his brow as his headache sharpened, piercing his thoughts like a knife thrust to the beat of his heart, over and over and over. A disjointed replay of the morning's events flashed across his mind's eye, and the resulting agony nearly brought him to his knees.

Raiding the hovel to stuff cheese and apples into his pack. Being roughly awoken by a sharp kick to the ribs. Pillars of smoke rising up from various points on the horizon. Cowering beneath the overturned barrow.

Two soldiers emerging from the trees, armed with blood-stained cudgels and overeager smiles.

Somewhere nearby, a dry stick snapped, and the raucous banter of songbird gave way to a pair of muffled voices.

The pain filling his skull evaporated, and Nevin's focus snapped back to the present.

"Watch your step, fool," a voice barked. "Twist your ankle and I swear, I'll report you to the captain as 'missing in action', you hear me?"

Soldiers. Without hesitation, Nevin leapt forward and was swallowed into the heart of the silver maple.

Chapter 2: Hidden in a Tree

Nevin hunched forward as he waded through the curtain of leaves.

Why are there soldiers in Elbin?

Ishen had always warned him to give the baron's military a wide berth should they decide to show themselves on the peninsula. Elbin *was* a province under the barony's jurisdiction, but only just. Its distance from the capital and difficulty in reaching the little town meant practically no ruling body wanted anything to do with them, leaving them mostly to their own devices. It took a special circumstance to draw any authority out to the Traagen, and Ishen had explained that many of them didn't appreciate being sent so far from home, sometimes taking advantage of Elbin's seclusion in questionable ways.

"Sorry, I jus—OW!" began a second voice, punctuated by the crack of splintering wood. "How are you so good at this? The ground keeps moving 'round on me 'fore I can get my foot on it."

"It's not magic. Just use your bloody eyes."

Nevin carefully backed through the reaching branches, his eyes following the sound of rustling underbrush and voices even though he couldn't see through the layered foliage. Sound traveled strangely in the woods, the uneven ground and haphazard arrangement of plant life gathering noise in stagnant pools and focused streams like stones in a river. The branches of the fallen maple made for effective camouflage, but that effectiveness was a double-edged sword. The men wouldn't find him without wading in themselves, but the relative dryness of the leaves also meant that any careless movement on his part would be broadcast through hundreds of natural wind chimes.

He'd trapped himself again, and now all he could do was wait.

He frowned. *But . . . why 'again'?*

The first man continued, close enough now that Nevin could hear each bumbling footfall through the brush.

"Wouldn't need to be stumblin' around out here had you just listened to me about that suspicious wheelbarrow in the first place."

The stranger's familiar voice scratched at Nevin's mind, stirring up vague recollections of claustrophobia and darkness. He backed even further into the tree, his shoulders bumping the ribbonesque bark covering the tree in strips.

"Let's just hurry and find him so we can get back to it, Biggan?"

Biggan grunted. "One of the others can find him. Where's he gonna go?"

"Then what are we still *doing* out here?"

The crackle of underbrush silenced. "Something over here caught the light funny. A patch o' metal, maybe."

Metal? Nevin's eyes slowly inched upward. A wide leather strap swayed gently on the breeze. From his current position, the strap was out of reach, but had he been standing, he could have simply reached up and grabbed hold of it.

A dull ache swelled between his temples, and fresh beads of sweat leaked from his pores. The sounds of the forest faded, replaced by the forceful thud of his heart. The creases furrowing his brow deepened as his eyes followed the strap skyward.

A small voice begged him not to look, to stay his gaze, to spring free of the fallen maple and dash out into the woods without looking back. But his eyes moved of their own accord.

"There!" said Biggan. "Are my eyes playin' tricks or is that a bit of gold I see?"

Nevin buried a gasp in his hand.

At the end of the wide leather strap, wedged between the silver maple's trunk and a particularly thick branch, was Dalen's bronze canteen.

All the blood evacuated the young man's body.

The drooping branches shuddered, and Nevin could hear someone trying to push their way in. He instinctively slid his feet closer, hoping the abruptness of the motion didn't give away his presence. They didn't move far before the tangle of branches got in the way.

"Whoa, whoa, hold on a tick. Better leave it be, Biggan."

A short pause, and the rustling stopped. "That's the first thing of value we come across out here and you just wanna leave it?"

The first voice grew serious. "Come on, we've got a job to do. Let's get back to the team."

"Oh, Vincht can wait, and yer crazy if you think I'm leaving this worthless forest empty-handed."

"Look, I don't want to be out here any more than you. These woods are not a place for men. Not . . . normal men at least. These country bumpkins make me just as nervous as this trackless forest. They're nothing like the people back home. The things they pray to out here . . ."

"What, like the turnip god?" Biggan chuckled.

Not-Biggan spoke again, his voice low and brimming with agitation. "Watch your words, fool. These old woods aren't just filled with trees and game and uncultured hicks. There are things . . . *listening*. Things without a sense of humor. Things that care very little for the needs and dreams of men. Spirits. Ghosts. Forgotten gods."

"Yer eyes are as brown as that crap yer spewing, Widge."

There was a deep sigh from someone, and Nevin imagined the man named Widge putting his hands on his hips and regarding his partner with a troubled look.

"Few years back, the baron sent a small group of us soldiers into Elbin to investigate a rumor. A trapper had taken some pelts into Comelbough to trade, and during a conversation with an off-duty constable, he mentioned running into a strange man out in the deepest parts of these woods. See if this sounds familiar. All black garb, wooden mask, glowing eyes . . ."

"Oh, get off it," Biggan scoffed. "Now I *know* you're just busting my—"

"Hey, I'm just telling you what the guy said. Was a fool's errand from the get-go, anyway. Anyone with a half a brain and a tick's knowledge of the land could vanish out here, and we knew it when we set out, but when the baron gives an order, you pack your bags. We made the trek, set up camp, and spent a few days half-ass combing the woods for any sign of this guy.

"It wasn't until the last day that we stumbled upon the altar."

Altar? Nevin leaned forward. *But worship is outlawed in the barony.*

Biggan apparently had the same thought. "What do you mean, 'altar'?"

"We'd hired a guide for the first two days," Widge continued. "A scrawny old goat with what looked like guinea moss growing in the gaps between his rotten teeth—but the field commander got a bad vibe off the guy, like he was leading us in circles and deliberately keeping us from certain areas.

"On the third morning, we set off without him. Again, we found nothing, and feeling confident in our efforts—wasted as they were—we turned back south as the sun began to set.

"Heading up, I don't know how we missed it. Every trail turned directly into this clearing. The trees and underbrush thinned as we got closer. Even the ground itself seemed to funnel us in that direction, rising up on each side like it wanted to ensure the easiest path available led to that opening in the trees. A focal point."

He sighed. "I don't know. Maybe I'm crazy, but it just felt . . . purposeful. Like there was no other way it could have happened."

"Like Fate?" Biggan asked, the energy missing from his voice, forgotten at the feet of a growing trepidation.

"Maybe, maybe not." Nevin pictured Widge shaking his head. "Fate can be a cruel bitch, for certain, but this . . . I don't know.

"The clearing itself was nothing special. An open field. A barely noticeable slope leading down from the mountains. A pile of old stones and rotting planks where an old tower once stood.

"But the altar . . . It stood right at the center of it all, ringed by clusters of these delicate white flowers no bigger than your pinkie. A grizzled ram's head monument carved from a chipped stone the color of stagnant water. Bits of animal and plant matter in various stages of decay occupied any surface flat enough to hold them.

"The whole of it reeked of death, of decay, and a hint of something . . . else. Like the air surrounding a smith's shop on a windy day. Metallic. Acrid. The kind of smell you *feel* in the back of your throat."

Nevin cocked his head as he listened, growing more and more disconcerted as the story wore on. The Traagen Peninsula stretched out for well over a hundred square miles west of the Hyret Gorge. Not a small area by any means, but having spent nearly a decade of his life exploring the tangled woods and open fields, navigating the quiet streams as they meandered south from the mountains to gather in shallow ponds teeming with speckled trout and orange-fin perch, and dozing beneath the drooping boughs of tower pines and ageless elms, Nevin felt at home in these woods.

Safe, and at peace in ways that living in Dalen's barn had never provided.

When he could, he and Aidux would spend days at time lost in the wilderness with nothing but each other's company, before slinking regretfully back to the meager civilization that Elbin had to offer. He eventually grew into a comfortable familiarity with the layout of the peninsula: the places frequented by local trappers, fishing holes, the hidden groves of wild pears and blackberry bushes, abandoned animal dens, areas of unusually stunted or blighted growth, even places so deeply removed from the touch of man that the air literally vibrated with the raw energy of unbridled nature.

And in all of those excursions, in all those days spent combing the woods, the two had never once happened upon a clearing with a ram's head altar.

It made him question how much he really knew about the lands he called his home.

Someone shuffled their feet. It was Biggan that spoke. "A ram's head? That doesn't sound like one of the old religions. Not from Comelbough, at least."

Nevin recognized the symbol. As the god of the harvest and the struggle of existence, some of Elbin's older residents still quietly venerated Ivvilger. Their dogged insistence that it was their responsibility to cull the weakness from the village in order to overcome the terrible and unforgiving nature of reality was pulled straight from Ivvilger's tenets, and often placed them at odds with the more relaxed mindsets of the younger generation. According to the elders, the youth of Elbin didn't understand the hardships the original settlers overcame in those early years, and by forgetting their roots, they were dooming Elbin to an uncertain future.

A group is only as strong as its weakest member, Ishen would say. *But does Ivvilger ask too much? Is it not human to care for and protect those who cannot do so for themselves?*

"That's exactly my point," said Widge. "It takes a certain kind of weird to willingly plant yourself out here in the middle-of-nowhere and survive. A certain strange kind of thought process, a way of thinking that calls out to the wilds, the shadows, the emptiness.

"And sometimes, when you call out to the emptiness long enough, loud enough . . . things . . . *answer.*"

The brush crackled as someone shifted uncomfortably.

Telling the story was getting Widge worked up, and the fervor of his words only increased as he continued. "A number of trinkets were scattered atop that crude altar, mixed in with the rotting plants and carcasses. Handcrafted bits and bobbles that likely had little more than sentimental value to their owners. Polished rocks, crystals, animal carvings, that sort of thing. Offerings to whatever being that ram's head supposedly venerated.

"Now, I wanted precisely *nothing* to do with that forsaken block of stone, and had *I* been leading that particular excursion, I would have immediately ordered my men to eyes forward and haul boots out of the Traagen. Some things are better left ignored."

A soft rustling of leaves tickled the edge of Nevin's attention. For a moment, his focus shifted away from the two men and magnified that fleeting interruption in a way that only a mind tuned to the unique nature of the woods could.

The three of them were no longer alone.

Widge's tone darkened. "But I wasn't the leader that day. I was just another soldier, and in truth, that altar made me feel things I didn't understand, not until after . . ."

"After what?"

Again, the soft crackle of leaves. Closer now. He supposed it could simply be a curious squirrel, or a small bird rummaging through the moist detritus for a hidden earthworm, but instinct told him otherwise.

That's when he realized the woods had gone completely silent.

"His name was Charles, but everyone just called him Bags. Had a number of these little pouches strapped to his belt, his vest, tucked down in his boots. Each one holding something different. He called them his 'memories'.

"You see, Bags wasn't exactly . . . whole. Took a blow to the side of the head when he was a kid. Spooked a horse. Was never the same after that. He could still function, mind you, still talk, walk, shit by himself. Aside from the jagged scar he tried to hide beneath an unruly mass of curls, he was about as normal as they come. He wanted to be in the military since he was a little kid, and despite the accident, that never changed as he grew up."

He paused. "Maybe even *because* of the accident. See, unless you got to know him, really sat down and talked to him, you'd never be able to suss out exactly what broke inside him when that horse kicked.

"People are naturally forgetful, especially about the little things. Where you left your shoes the night before, whether you cleaned your pipe last time you used it, those sorts of things. But Bags didn't just have trouble with the little things. Bags couldn't remember the specifics of a conversation he'd had five minutes ago. Didn't matter what you told him. In one ear and out the other."

Biggan scoffed. "Come on. This was a *soldier?* How could he learn to fight? Learn procedure? The names of his crew? How could he do his job?"

"He had a lot of help. Friends he leaned on, followed around, depended on for direction. The captain made sure they came up together, ended up in the same units. And despite his disability, Bags wasn't stupid. Somehow, he figured out that the knowledge was there, in his head, floating around like a dinghy on troubled waters, masses of them just jostling about in that broken gourd of his.

"He needed an anchor, something real and tangible to connect this world to that. Any time he had an experience he wanted to remember, he took something from the environment, familiarized himself with it, and added it to one of his bags. Dozens of bags, each one connected to a specific moment in time through an object with a unique scent, texture, or design."

"Wait . . ." Biggan whispered, realization washing over him. "He took something, didn't he? From the altar, I mean."

Widge cleared his throat, but failed to steady the emotion in his voice, though Nevin wasn't sure if it was excitement or apprehension he was hearing.

"Later that night, after the squad settled back into base camp, Bags shuffled out of the trees, straight out of the darkness, cradling his right arm tightly against his stomach . . . this dazed, faraway look in his eyes.

"We hadn't even realized he was gone, not until he reappeared, that is."

He grunted. "He only paused for a moment before crouching down by the fire and dumping a handful of random items in the dirt. He started picking through them, one by one, muttering to himself, getting increasingly loud and agitated. We slowly gathered behind him, the whole troop, watching over his shoulder as he threw bits of forest trash into the fire.

"And that's all they were! Just pine cones and acorns and sticks and rocks. He kept checking each one, sniffing it, rubbing it on his face, even tasting some of them. He quickly broke into tears and started throwing them into the fire more and more rapidly. Finally, the field commander shoved past us, jerking Bags to his feet and demanding to know what his problem was."

Nevin had to lean forward to hear the end of Widge's story, he'd grown so quiet. "Our commander let him go almost immediately, stumbling back from Bags like the guy had struck him. I won't repeat the string of profanities that escaped his mouth as he tried to get a handle on what he was seeing, what we were *all* seeing."

Biggan's words were all breath and wonder. "What . . . what did you see?"

"Bags was drenched in blood, from his stomach to his knees. How we didn't see it when he walked out of the woods, I'll never know. Blood looks black in the night, even with a roaring fire up against it. The man lifted his right arm, his hand, and just stared at it, only . . . there *was* no hand. Just a bloody stump, still wet and oozing.

"I don't know how he had the strength to stand, let alone speak, but he kept saying the same thing over and over and over, growing louder every time he said it until he was screaming at us, screaming so forcefully that strings of spittle dangled from his trembling lips."

"Dammit, Widge, what was he saying? Yer killin' me here!"

Nevin nodded unconsciously.

Widge took a steadying breath. "He said, 'If I burn them, will I forget? How many do I have to burn before I forget those terrible eyes?'"

Nevin choked down the lump in his throat. While he'd never himself come upon the altar Widge had described, the man had hit upon Elbin's connection to Ivvilger in a way that lent some weight to the tale, enough so that Nevin was like to keep one eye over his shoulder in future trips through the Traagen.

Nothing moved beyond the tangled branches. Nevin held his breath, knowing even the smallest of movements would call attention to him in the tense silence. He prayed the story had done the trick, had dissuaded Biggan from wanting to retrieve the canteen, and any moment now, they would—

"Oh, that's some *good* hogshit, Widge." With an amused chuckle, he offered his companion a slow clap. "You can't actually expect me to believe that just because some half-wit gets his hand chewed off in the woods after stealing some worthless bauble from a goat-shaped hunk of rock . . ."

"I'm serious!"

Biggan ignored him, and the branches ahead of Nevin began to shift. "You really had me goin' there for a minute, but you should save your campfire tales for some wet-eared cobble-dogs. Kid's'll eat that 'forest god' crap right up.

"But as for me? I'm gettin' my treasure . . . hand-eatin' monsters be *damned.*"

Nevin had about ten seconds before the man waded into the tree and revealed his hiding spot. Despite his memory issues, these soldiers were an unknown quantity, strangers to the area with an agenda all their own, but he remembered the blood stains on their heavy cudgels, he remembered hiding from them, he remembered the fear the sound of their voices invoked, and every instinct he possessed told him being found would end poorly.

Too bad he had no choice in the matter.

The leaves parted, and a man's face—all nose and slack jaw—peered down at him in blatant surprise. Nevin pressed back against the maple's trunk.

Widge's annoyance was obvious. "What is it now?"

"I found that kid we're looking for!"

"Oh, now your pulling *my—*"

A rumbling growl cut him short, deep and menacing and from somewhere above. Biggan's eyes jerked up, widening instantly in fear.

Twigs and leaves rained down on Nevin's head and the length of the fallen maple jerked as a streak of golden fur collided with the soldier's face, and Biggan disappeared just as suddenly as he appeared. Both men screamed, first in surprise and then pain, and Nevin could only imagine the scene unfolding just a few feet in front of him by the furious cacophony that followed.

He wasted little time taking advantage of the rapid change in circumstance.

Chapter 3: Only a Small Dumb

Nevin fought to stand, struggling against the pressing reach of branches and the disorienting rush of adrenaline.

Biggan's words pulled on his thoughts. *That kid we were looking for.* First they show up at his home, then they chase him through the woods. What could a pair of soldiers want from him?

Beyond the curtain of leaves, the crackle of underbrush and human squeals of pain had ceased, quieting nearly as suddenly as they began.

He cocked his head and listened. Blood pounded between his ears, magnified by the taut silence of the forest.

After a moment, a small voice, not unlike that of a young boy, finally broke the silence.

"Are you coming out? Or do I need to come in and get you?"

A carefree grin broke out across Nevin's lips.

Sweeping aside the drooping branches, the young man stepped out into the dappled sunlight. There was no trace of the two soldiers from just moments before, but in their place, resting on its haunches and peering up at him with a set of wide silver peepers, sat the biggest wild cat Nevin had ever laid eyes on.

"That was some otherworldly timing, Aidux."

The massive golden lynx responded to his name with a quiet purr.

With the charcoal tips of his tufted ears just passing the three foot mark, Aidux struck an imposing—if not downright terrifying—figure. Pointed ears like horns, giant paws hiding claws built for ripping and tearing, and a cry like that of a frightened child . . . qualities that would curse your average farmer with a lifetime of twisted, sweat-soaked sheets.

Yet Nevin only saw the face of his closest friend.

Eyes like puddled mercury peered up at him, wide and curious. Rising to his feet, Aidux arched his back and stretched. "Welp, I still had a bit more nap left in me, but something told me I should come see where you were in your chores. Good thing I did."

The cat continued, sniffing the air. "So *you* smell like blood, and the *tree* smells like blood. Did you do a dumb?"

Nevin balked. "What . . . that's not . . . I didn't 'do a dumb'."

"Oh?" Aidux looked past him. "That wasn't your *scalp* I sniffed all over the trunk of that tree? Or are you gonna try and blame wood fairies again?"

With a lopsided, self-conscious grin, Nevin wiped a hand across the back of his neck. The blood was practically dry at this point, but it crusted a wide swath of bare skin and hair. He felt okay, considering he'd knocked his head hard enough to blackout most of the morning. Just a headache that seemed to come and go with his memory.

"Okay," he conceded. "Maybe a small dumb."

With a shrug, he turned around and waded back into the fallen tree.

Aidux groaned with disapproval. "Nevin, I do the cat things in this friendship—the jumping, the running, the hunting. You do the boy stuff—the planning, the picking of campsites, the cooking of . . ."

The cat twirled a paw. ". . . things. You're too delicate to do my job. You'll break, and then where will I be? Alone and bored, that's where."

Aidux grumbled incoherently under his breath. "I hate being bored."

He tested the strap, yanking it down and then sideways, putting as much weight into his pulls as he could using one good arm. The canteen wiggled only slightly. "You *can* entertain yourself from time to time. You don't always need my input."

Aidux was having precisely none of that. "I'm a talking cat, Nevin. You think many deer say hi on the way back from grazing? What about moles? You think they get particularly chatty after spending the morning tunneling through solid rock? And how about the squirrels? You think the squirrels have a lot to say with a mouthful of nuts?

"No, Nevin. They don't. They're *moles* and *deer* and *squirrels* and none of them are talking cats. It's lonely in this forest. I would literally *die* without you."

The young man wrapped both hands around the strap and pulled with all his might, but the canteen refused to budge. Wincing, he shook his swollen hand. "Little help?"

The cat didn't immediately respond. "You aren't mad at me?"

"Mad? For what?"

"For scaring off those soldiers. Didn't I just break the carnival rule?"

"The 'cardinal' rule."

Another pause. "I just said that."

He rolled his eyes and smiled. The cardinal rule, as Aidux mentioned, was in truth the only rule, put in place by Nevin years ago as a way to protect the curious feline from wandering into trouble with the locals. 'Stay away from people.' Predators were not tolerated within the bounds of Elbin, and should the villagers discover that a lynx had made the surrounding woods his hunting grounds, it wouldn't be long before some overzealous hunting party tracked him down and made a rug from his pelt.

Aidux's unique nature wouldn't protect him. In fact, Nevin suspected the superstitious locals would view a talking cat as some sort of fell omen, a divine harbinger of future strife that could only be circumvented through both drastic and terrible means. Normally, Nevin *would* have cause to be upset that his friend had picked a fight and revealed his presence in the woods.

But today was shaping up to be anything but normal.

"All things considered, I think a faceful of angry lynx was *exactly* the right response." He shuddered to think what those two soldiers might have done had Aidux not come along precisely when he did.

The leaves rustled as the cat ducked through the drooping branches, skirting Nevin's position to find an easier route to the trunk. Within moments, he could hear claws scrabbling against bark. The leaves rattled overhead and the leather strap went slack as the canteen tumbled free of its perch.

"What is it?" The cat worked his way down through the branches to stand at his side.

"A canteen," he said morosely. *And the last thing I wanted to see today.* At nearly a decade old, the bronze container had seen better days, but its simple, rounded design meant it could withstand some fairly careless treatment. The dingy metal was scratched and foggy from years of rough and regular handling.

To his surprise, the cork had recently been replaced, appearing fresh and blemish-free. He popped it out. Empty, though the canteen still bore the sickly-sweet stench of apple wine.

"Did you hit your head on it, too?"

"What gives you that—" Curious, Nevin flipped the canteen over.

What he found made him choke on his words.

A sizable dent marred the flask's outside edge, a drying splotch of what could only be blood darkening the dent's deeper crevasses. A chill crept up his spine, and a sharp pain built up in the back of his skull.

You would have to hit something pretty hard to damage it like this.

"Blech." Aidux's nose crinkled. "Can't smell anything past the stench of rotten apples."

Nevin flinched, and the canteen tumbled from his numb fingers. The battered ferns and branches greedily swallowed it up. With its disappearance, the pain in his head vanished as well.

He pondered, momentarily, the idea of bending over to retrieve it, but with the prospect of leaving this life behind lying just beyond the immediate horizon, he found himself grateful to be free of any souvenir capable of reminding him of the pain-filled upbringing he was leaving behind to rot in the moldering detritus of the woods.

Good riddance, he thought, adjusting the hang of his belt.

The cat, wandering off into the surrounding branches, appeared not to notice. "What's this over here?"

Wiping his hands on his shirt, Nevin backed out of the tree. He emerged to find the lynx pawing at a bulging leather pack that had been partially obscured by a combination of both leaves and ground cover.

"You found it!" He knelt down, elated to find the pack none the worse for wear. The bulging satchel was practically bursting with food stuffs and clothing —exactly what he'd need for an extended journey toward freedom.

The lynx looked up at Nevin, then back at the pack in confusion. "Were we supposed to be going camping today?"

"Not camping," he said, cinching down the pack's flap. "We're leaving Elbin."

"Aww, not this again." The cat visibly deflated. "We did this last week, and again the month before. I don't *want* to spend another day watching you from the bushes, and you always yell at me for falling asleep!"

"You snore like a lumberjack! Any random passerby would hear you and come investigate."

"It's not my fault I'm darkturnal!"

Nevin rolled his eyes. "It's 'nocturnal', goof. And I don't have a choice this time. Those two soldiers you attacked? I don't know why, but I think they were looking for me. And by the way they were talking and the blood on their cudgels, I don't think their intentions were honorable."

The cat cocked his head quizzically, his tufted ears flopping to the side. "But . . . what would they want with some nobody apple farmer?"

Good question.

Because of its distance from the capital, the Baron's constabulary weren't like to make the long trip to Elbin without cause, and 'some nobody apple farmer' wasn't a very strong draw. Still, the two soldiers had admitted to chasing him through the woods, but whether it was him specifically they wanted, or whether they were just reacting to the presence of human life in general, he couldn't be sure.

He cast a sidelong glance back into the heart of the fallen maple, feeling a sharp pain once again blossom in the back of his skull. A stream of memories flashed through his mind in a chaotic stew of mismatched images, images of him scrounging up various items of import from the main house, going room to room in rapid succession, moving with such speed and urgency that he had never once looked up to make sure Dalen hadn't caught on to his actions. Packing and leaving was so important in those moments that he hadn't cared about the devastating consequences of being discovered.

Running through the forest? That was just dangerous. He knew better than that. Rummaging through the house? That was a beating. As he'd grown up and bigger than Dalen, dealing with the man's violent outbursts had become far more manageable, though he dreaded the days when the man was sober. He was especially cruel when his mind was clear, and he had a knack for catching the young man off guard. The smartest move Nevin could make on what he called 'dry days' was to just disappear into the woods and camp.

But the ultimate sin in Dalen's eyes, the one thing he knew *never* to do, was to so much as touch that battered bronze canteen. The old drunk had made it painfully clear on a number of occasions just what it would mean for their relationship should Nevin ever cross that line. And for as long as he could remember, he had held that warning as sacred above all others.

Nevin's heart threatened to break from his chest. That bronze canteen had always hung at Dalen's side, so as far as Nevin was concerned, the two weren't separate entities. So when he'd found the canteen hanging from the fallen tree's branches, he immediately realized that nothing good had transpired in the morning's missing moments.

The line of broken ferns told him he had been running, but was he running from the soldiers, or was he running from Dalen?

Slinging the leather pack over his uninjured shoulder, Nevin came to his feet. "It doesn't matter. We're trying it again, even if it takes all damn day. We're finally doing what we always talked about. We're finally leaving Elbin behind and starting a new life somewhere out in the world."

The cat reluctantly followed along behind him. "Welp, looks like I'm getting another nap way sooner than I thought."

Nevin ignored the lynx, grinding his teeth in anticipation. Aidux was right to be skeptical. For years, the two friends had talked about setting out for the greater world, leaving the confines of the peninsula to find a new life in some distant corner of Stragus. One where people wouldn't treat the presence of a talking cat as something to be solved with murder. One without the looming threat of physical and verbal abuse without cause. One where they could both be themselves and be happy.

Only one thing stood in his way.

A thirty foot stretch of rope and wood dangling precariously over the Hyret Gorge to the east, and the heart-stopping terror inspired by the prospect of setting foot on the bridge's aging slats. As the only way onto or off of the Traagen Peninsula that anyone in Elbin knew of, Nevin had thought to brave the bridge on a number of occasions.

He'd never made it within a dozen feet.

Chapter 4: Death in the Traagen

Still reeling from their encounter with the feral cat, the two soldiers didn't react as the shadow materialized in the clearing, growing directly out the surrounding trunks and appearing in their midst without a sound.

At first, Widge had thought it a simple trick of the light—a sharp breeze spinning figments as it realigned the tightly threaded branches overhead. As the choked light sputtered and vanished, the shadow had taken its place among them like the specter of death itself.

Hot blood spattered a gruesome line across Widge's lips before he could part them in warning.

His companion, a foul-smelling cooper named Biggan, clawed at his throat and stumbled to a stop. A neat red line split the clean, hairless part of his neck away from his close-cropped beard. The front of his tunic darkened almost immediately as he dropped to his knees and disappeared beneath the ferns.

Just like that, the shadow had materialized from nothing, from nowhere in particular, and in a blink Widge found himself alone, his lone companion wholly consumed by the woods' prolific ground cover.

It wasn't supposed to go this way.

A fairly straight-forward find-and-retrieve mission, Vincht had said. Some searching. Some threatening. Some strong-arming. As far as their commander was concerned, nothing was off-limits when it came to their mission. If that meant leaving the peninsula with naught but trees and dirt and smoldering piles of ash and bone in their wake, he had a feeling that Vincht was the type to not even look back over his shoulder as they rode away.

And if the man was to be believed, there wasn't a single person in the whole of Elbin who could stand against them. Farmers and trappers, the lot of them. Putting the hurt on some dirt-necked hicks didn't bother Widge in the least. As a career soldier for the Lancowls, he'd learned long ago that the people at the economic bottom only cared for the barony when they stood to gain. Rarely did they respect or even recognize the sacrifices made by the constabulary in their name, reacting to simple attempts to maintain peace and order with rudeness and outrage. Their lack of gratitude disgusted him, so he'd jumped at the opportunity to join a mission where he might relieve some of his pent-up aggression.

But this . . . he hadn't signed up for this.

Reflex brought his cudgel up before him, a knotty oaken rod wrapped in fraying leather strips and notched from use. In response, the shadow jolted forward, and something unseen lashed out and struck his weapon hard enough to rip it from his grasp and leave his arm ringing and numb. He sucked air in surprise, and just in time, as the shadow jolted forward again.

Fingers tightened around his throat and the ground disappeared beneath his boots.

"Why have the baron's soldiers come to Elbin?" the shadow barked, its voice all gravel and malice.

Widge struggled to breathe around the unyielding grip. He clawed at the man's arm, but he may as well have been pawing at solid rock. Blackness crept in from the edges of his vision.

At least I'll die sleeping.

Sensing the man's wavering attention, the shadow slammed him into a nearby tree trunk. The collision brought down a shower of leaves and splintered bark. A reflexive squeal of protest broached his lips, silencing what little wildlife had been brave enough to vocalize their presence during the slaughter of his companion.

"Did the Baron learn nothing from his last attempt to corner me? Or was the fact that I left most of his men alive to tell the tale too subtle a warning?"

The grip on his throat relaxed and the blackness receded, but the blow to his back had paralyzed his lungs. His lips went through the motions but no sound emerged.

The shadow leaned in, and Widge realized that this being of solid darkness was little more than a man in a hooded cloak. Dull black leather covered in jagged stitching and misshaped patchwork encompassed the stranger from head to toe, an impenetrable sheath of lusterless hide. In the darkness under the trees, he still couldn't see into the hood.

Widge strained against his uncooperative lungs, struggling fruitlessly with his body's inability to bend to the frantic urgings of his mind.

"Breathe," the man whispered. "Or join your friend in the dirt."

A welcome rush of air poured down his throat, and Widge heaved and coughed, fighting to find at least one word to give the man, one word to delay his death for another moment or two.

"P—" he choked out, succumbing to another coughing fit.

"Yes?"

Widge frantically shook his head, pointing to his throat. "P-p-ple—"

Fingers like five individual steel bars tightened once again around his neck. "Had better start making sense, and quick."

"Please," he spat, squeezing the shadow's leather-wrapped wrist with both hands. The tension on his throat loosened, but only just. "I'll tell you whatever you want to know! Just don't kill me."

A low growl reverberated from within the drooping cowl. "Think I don't know what you've done today? Think you deserve better than those you've wronged?"

"I don't know." Thick tears streamed down Widge's face. "I . . . I didn't mean it."

"Didn't *mean* it?" The pressure on his throat increased, and Widge's leaking eyes bulged in their sockets. "Meant every bit of it, cur. Knew exactly what you were doing, just didn't expect the consequence. That you could tap into your dark side and nothing bad would come back to you. Thought you could get away with it out here in the middle of nowhere.

"Thought you could draw me out by hurting them that have nothing to do with your leader's vendetta."

Widge violently shook his head. "I'm sor—"

"Save it." The man slammed him against the tree again. "Only reason you're still alive is so someone can once again tell your foolish baron the consequences of not leaving me be."

"But . . . we're not looking for you."

As soon as the words left his foolish lips, Widge knew he'd screwed up.

The drooping cowl cocked to the side. "Of course you're looking for me. Why else would a Lancowl send soldiers to Elbin?"

"We're l-l-looking for this," he said, the words forced out through snot-coated lips. Fumbling beneath his leather cuirass, Widge withdrew a crumpled vellum swatch. "We've been searching all morning to no avail."

The shadow snatched the vellum sheet from his grasp, dumping him into the ferns and turning away to examine the slip of paper. Widge squeezed his eyes shut and coughed uncontrollably, rocking back and forth as he massaged his tender neck.

The shadow poured over the small drawing like it was a riddle to be solved. Something bathed the paper in a faint blue glow, but Widge was more concerned with saying whatever he needed to say in order to survive the day. "Who gave you this? The baron?"

Widge shook his head, fighting the urge to cough some more. "He said his name was Vincht. He's no soldier, not one of ours, at least. All I know is, we were explicitly ordered to do everything he says, and he said we weren't leaving Elbin without . . ." He waved to the slip of paper.

The man in black crumpled the sheet of vellum into a tight ball. He lifted his head but didn't turn. "Then why are you . . . *here?*"

Widge frowned, his worry increasing. "I . . . I already told you."

"No. Why are you *here?* In this spot? The town's half a mile in the other direction. What are you doing out here in the woods?"

The fallen soldier nodded emphatically. "Some of us were sent out in search of outlying farms. Vincht wanted us to make sure we found every single member of the town, to not leave a single homestead unsearched. We were just over at this apple orchard, and Biggan thought he—"

Faster than thought, the shadow twisted toward him, and something cold entered the tender flesh just above his belly button.

All feeling left his legs, as though the ferns coiling about his midsection had finally made a meal of his lower half. His mouth opened and closed over and over again in confusion. An intense tingling sensation crawled up his chest. He looked down, his trembling hands sliding over the hardened leather cuirass protecting his torso.

A thin, curved blade reached out from beneath the folds of the leather cloak, its lethal end effortlessly penetrating his inadequate armor and the helpless flesh beneath. Blood, black as pitch, oozed from the wound in a steady rivulet.

I'm stabbed.

He's stabbed me.

"Wha—" he mumbled, but the words died in his throat as he stared up into the shadow's hood for the first time.

Eyes like twin blue suns stared into his own, burning with a cold indifference to the suffering their owner had caused.

Widge's final words were an awe-struck whisper.

"You're . . . real."

The blade in his gut twisted sideways, and Widge arched his back against the tree. Hot agony replaced the growing tingle, exploding outward from the wound until it was all he could feel, all he knew, and all that existed was white-hot fire. He stared into those terrible blue eyes as the shadow withdrew his narrow blade and stood.

Widge quietly slipped beneath the hungry ferns, and the clearing was empty once more.

Chapter 5: Hoppy Things That Sneak

Shaking boots ground against packed earth and gravel as Nevin inched painstakingly closer to the yawning mouth of the Hyret Gorge. Fear distorted the facts, adjusting his reality until the terrible slit morphed into something else entirely: jagged rocks became bared teeth, rushing water an angry growl, the rising mists a saliva-infused exhalation.

It wanted him.

Hungered for him.

Yearned to swallow him whole.

"Don't forget," Aidux whispered encouragingly from beneath the nearby brush. "It's just a hole in the ground, not a monster! Don't be dramastic!"

Nevin's jaw tightened. "It's 'dramatic'."

The cat grinned, his lips peeled back in a terrifying snarl of razor-sharp teeth.

"It's dramatic, you're dramatic . . . just cross the bridge!"

Nevin adjusted his pack. *You make it sound so easy.*

A visit to Elbin's suspended bridge ranked near the bottom of Nevin's list of fun ways to pass the time, wedged solidly between eating raw pine cones and sleeping in a wet ditch. He could count on both hands the number of times he'd even caught sight of the bridge in his lifetime, and not one of those times had he rustled up enough courage to actually set foot on its creaky, aging planks.

The thought alone was enough to summon an unconscious whimper from bloodless lips.

Stupid, he thought, closing his eyes and trying to gain control over his rapid breathing. *A stupid fear for a stupid kid.*

Ishen had never thought it was stupid.

A phobia, his old teacher had said after Nevin approached him for advice, *is but a survival mechanism taken to an unhealthy level. Fear, you see, is one of the mind's most powerful tools, and while the mind normally uses fear to focus our attention on situations capable of doing us harm, a phobia turns the mind against itself, robbing us of our will until the object of our irreconcilable fear has been removed. A phobia represents a form of mental injury, and, like any other injury, it hinders our interaction with reality until we allow it to heal.*

He felt a pang of guilt for leaving without telling his old mentor goodbye, a man he'd grown to view as a sort of stand-in for the father Dalen had proven himself incapable of being. Worse still, the thought of checking in on Ishen hadn't even occurred to him until he stood within spitting distance of leaving. Had he not been so addled by his head injury and the appearance of Dalen's canteen, he might have stopped by Ishen's secluded cabin on the way, might have warned him of the armed men with questionable motives skulking about the woods.

But now that he was on the brink of escape, traipsing about the forest seemed an invitation for trouble, and even though it meant leaving Ishen unaware of the day's dangers, Nevin found himself unwilling to re-enter the woods and chance another unexpected encounter.

The young man opened his eyes. A faded road stretched out beneath his boots, pushing carelessly forward toward open air as if expecting the gorge to be some sort of twisted illusion. The faint wrinkles of cart tracks struck unnaturally straight lines where none should exist in nature, ending where a tight band of sun-bleached planks began. Four ropes, each thicker than the meaty part of his forearm, hugged the same number of posts and supported the bridge.

He raised a hand to block the morning sun. The distant road and surrounding woods seemed impossibly far away, like a mountain peak viewed through passing clouds. Still, he could clearly see the small encampment erected on the banks of the dirt road – numerous horse-drawn wagons, a handful of flysheet shelters stretched between trees, a collection of square tents, and the shadows of men moving among them.

Nevin frowned. Only two types ever made the trek through the Traagen Woods to little Elbin: traders and tax collectors. The final days of the Waking made for comfortable travel, if one could forgive the occasional shower and be lucky enough to dodge a full-fledged thunderstorm. Now, and again when the Fading set the Traagen Woods' verdant foliage ablaze, spelled Elbin's busiest days of the year.

But he doubted this group was either.

Almost as though summoned forth by his mental appraisal, the flap of the nearest tent peeled back and a stern-looking woman in a high collared tunic stepped out. Even at a distance, Nevin could clearly see a gold-and-crimson emblem emblazoned across her chest. Tugging at the frilled hems of her forearm-hugging leather gloves, she slowly appraised the state of the camp.

Aidux shot him a funny look as he dove into the bush beside him.

"Are we . . . are we napping together today?"

"No napping!" Nevin spat out a leaf. "Those soldiers you attacked? Their camp is just on the other side of the gorge."

The cat's nose went to work. "If so, they haven't made it back yet. You should cross now while the camp is empty."

He crawled forward on his forearms until he could peek out through the brush. "The camp *isn't* empty. Someone just came out of one of the tents."

Aidux crawled up beside him. "Then we'll just wait until someone goes back *in* one of the tents and we can sneak across all quiet-like."

Nevin nodded absently, watching the stern-looking woman storm across the road and tear aside the flap of another tent. She jabbed an arm toward the bridge and yelled at someone inside, but he couldn't make out what was being said over the din of the melt-swollen river.

Four more soldiers emerged from the tent and jogged toward the bridge. The boy and his cat hunkered down in the brush, but the soldiers stopped short of crossing, bending down to hastily untie the ropes securing the bridge to the lip of the gorge.

"What are they doing?" Aidux whispered, his ears and eyes trained on the men.

"I'm not sure."

Within moments, the men had loosened each rope and were straining against the weight of the unsupported bridge. Nevin watched as they lowered the creaking planks into the throat of the gorge, only stopping to tie them off once the sole method of exiting the peninsula lay completely out of sight.

Aidux flicked an ear. "That doesn't seem like a design improvement."

"Because it's not." Keeping his eye on the stern female soldier surveying the gorge with her arms crossed, Nevin backed out of the brush and shoved to his feet.

The air chilled his sweat-drenched face as he retreated back into the questionable safety of the trees. With the gorge disappearing behind him, his heart calmed to a less-noticeable thrumming. Wren song replaced the roar of water, while cedar and the faint sweetness of apple blossom filled his nose. A thorn-eared hare watched him from atop a tangle of roots, ready to bolt should he amble too close.

Aidux loped up beside him, and the hare remembered it had important business elsewhere.

"Look at it this way," Aidux began. "At least you don't have to be mad at yourself for failing to make it across again."

"That's . . . very reassuring, thank you."

"You're welcome."

The cat cocked his head, his silver peepers narrowed in thought. "What I don't understand is the why. I mean, bridges are meant to get you from here to there so you can make the there here. Why would anyone want to take it down?"

Those wheels had already turned in Nevin's head, and he wasn't overly fond of where they'd arrived. "For the same reason we were there, Aidux. That bridge is the only way onto or off of the Traagen Peninsula. Without it, no one new can visit Elbin, and no one from town can leave."

"No one was coming or going anyway, so—"

"So they're looking for something. Those two soldiers searched the farm and chased me through the woods. I don't know why, but they wanted *me*. Problem is, there's a lot of places to hide out here in the trees, a lot of nooks and crannies where someone who knows the land can hide. The Traagen is vast, but with enough time and men capable of following a trail, every member of Elbin would eventually be rounded up."

The lynx clicked his tongue. "Unless they could just cross the bridge and leave."

Nevin nodded. "Control the bridge and you control the only path of escape for whatever you're looking for."

His chest tightened with worry. How many of the townsfolk knew what was happening? How many homesteads had already been visited by groups of soldiers? How much of the blood staining the cudgels wielded by his pursuers had belonged to someone he knew?

Then again, maybe he was overthinking this. What evidence was there that the Baron's soldiers had committed any actual violence on the townsfolk? Sure, there was some blood on their weapons, but he hadn't actually seen them attack anyone, and as far as he could remember, nothing he had overheard them saying gave him cause to expect lethal intent. Perhaps this was all just a simple misunderstanding.

And yet, that little voice of instinct shouting at him from the shadows of his mind told him otherwise. Though he had little evidence to back it up, a part of him was certain the soldiers possessed nothing but ill-will toward the residents of Elbin, and he had been lucky to escape Biggan and Widge with his life intact.

A furry paw pressed up against his thigh. "Are you alright?"

Nevin blinked. Without realizing it, he'd come to a stop, a sharp pain drawing a hand to his temple. As his wits returned, the pain receded, but Nevin was beginning to worry his skull's encounter with the fallen maple had done more damage than he thought.

The twitter of songbird surrounded the two, but the playful quality had been replaced with an odd tension, a hesitancy to turn their full attention to one another and ignore the day's unusual events. Nothing moved beneath the endless sea of ferns, but considering the close proximity of one carnivorous feline, he expected nothing less from the forest's more timid denizens.

Then again, the young man thought he felt something else out there in the haze. An unwelcome presence separate from the invading soldiers, silently observing the drama unfolding around him and waiting for its—

"Umm . . . Nevin?"

"Sorry." He nodded, forcing himself to smile for the cat's benefit. "Just my head. Thinking about all this isn't doing me any favors."

Aidux relaxed, sinking back onto his haunches. "So, now what? Without the bridge, there's really nowhere to go. Wanna head into the foothills and camp out until the soldiers leave? I'll keep us in rabbits if you promise not to cook the whole thing."

"It's still too early in the year for the foothills. Lassiter's Pond on the other hand—"

"No!"

The lynx sank beneath the ferns until only his eyes and ears poked through. "You are NOT dragging me out to that pond again. That stupid place is filthy with frogs and toads and tadpoles and other gross, hoppy things that gribbit and croak and sneak up on cats when they aren't paying attention!"

"Okay, okay!" Nevin waved his hands in mock defeat. "No frogs."

The cat eyed him suspiciously. "You promise?"

"I promise."

Aidux inched out of the grasping ferns. "Well, if the foothills are too cold, that doesn't leave us many opinions."

"Options."

"Those either."

Nevin agreed. Hiding was only a temporary solution, and not one he put a lot of faith in. Even with his knowledge of the more secluded reaches of the Traagen, a truly committed tracker would find them eventually. The frequency of rain this time of year made it practically impossible not to leave a trail, and at least two of the soldiers already knew he was out here, somewhere.

"I think we need backup."

Aidux looked over his shoulder. "I mean, okay, but we'll probably trip over a root or something."

"No, goof, I mean 'help'. We need to talk to Ishen." Adjusting his pack, the young man set off through the trees, the cat swishing through the undergrowth at his side.

Nevin knew full well it had been Ishen who assured him of the bridge's sovereignty as the only means onto or off of the peninsula, but they had to do something. If nothing else, Ishen needed to be warned before a group of soldiers showed up at his door and added his blood to their cudgels.

But even then, even if he knew what was coming, where would he go? Where would any of them go?

Chapter 6: The Value of a Name

The point of Vincht's shortblade rested on the exposed neck of the frumpy old woman kneeling in the dirt before him. Though she only whimpered quietly, he imagined her crying, imagined the rivers of briny liquid pouring from too wide eyes as she struggled to find the words necessary to stay the hand of the man holding sway over her life. He pictured lips coated in sticky yellow snot and dripping with frothy saliva, the three mixing together in a revolting river of bodily excretions that drizzled in rubbery strings from the chin and soiled her already grimy frock.

The sour stench of fear seeped from her every pore.

As he'd done for much of his life, Vincht displayed a mask of calm observation to hide his revulsion.

Your ugliness only makes my own beauty more pronounced.

With his jet-colored plume of hair, chiseled facial features, and piercing eyes, Vincht often found himself the recipient of admiration from both men and women alike. As time passed, he began to notice the privileges afforded him by his extraordinary features, but the most surprising source came from his parents.

As the second son born to a politically powerful family in Vadderstrix, Vincht was initially confused when he usurped his brother's position as the favored son shortly after his fourteenth birthday. He finally grew to realize it was neither love nor pride they were showing him, but rather coveted his usefulness as a tool in the great political machine of the city, as not even the learned arrogance of the aristocracy could withstand his boyish charm.

With age, he eventually recognized the endless attention for what it really was—a natural and necessary consequence of universal law. Within beauty, power. As such, Vincht spent a considerable amount of time grooming and adorning his body in ways that would accentuate his Fate-granted talents.

Vincht ignored the old woman's simpering, turning his attention instead to the muffled shouting and rhythmic thudding coming from inside the nearby cabin. He couldn't imagine what was taking so long. He'd begun to suspect that Baron Lancowl had dredged the absolute bottom of the barrel when he'd begrudgingly agreed to honor their organization's alliance and loan him a team of soldiers.

"You want me to help?" asked the soldier standing off to his right.

A faint sneer cracked his otherwise cool composure. "No, Rowen. You've already proven your incompetence when you lost your horse. I want you to stay where I can see you."

Rowen shuffled his feet but didn't protest.

"You don't have to do this," whispered the older woman.

Vincht leaned in, cocking his head in mock curiosity. "And who are you to tell me what I do and don't have to do?" he teased, his resonant voice deep like distant thunder.

"We don't have what you're looking for. On Ivvilver's name, you have to believe—"

"The invocation of your false god has no bearing on my beliefs, I assure you." The dead god's name brought a hot rush of blood to his face, and it was all he could do not to skewer her where she sat. "It's Liddy, am I correct?"

Rowan practically choked. "You know her?"

"Of course not," Vincht spat, breaking his composure to glare. "Her husband said it when he called for her to answer the door."

"Oh, right." Rowen blinked. "I just can't believe you remembered it."

Vincht's scowl returned. *Of course a man like you would have no understanding of the power of a name.*

Never forget a name, his mother would hiss as the little boy rubbed his stinging cheek. *Remembering a person's name is one of the highest compliments you can pay them. It is not something they easily forget.*

A person's name is the sweetest music to their ears, his father would lecture, raising his voice to be sure he was heard over the sound of the little boy's sobbing. *Remembering someone's name garners their respect, commands their attention, and ultimately, weakens them to your will. In the myths of old, men gained power over spiritual entities through the invocation of their true name, and for good reason. A name is a singularly important piece of a person's identity, despite how utterly meaningless it is to anyone beyond the named themselves.*

The sharp crackle of splintering wood proceeded a cry of fear and protest from inside the little cabin. *Finally.* Vincht turned back to the woman, lifting her chin with the tip of his blade.

"Now then, Liddy. One of my cohorts is about to bring your husband out here to join us, and I'd very much like to know what to call him. Can you tell me his name, dear?"

"M-M-Marion," she said, her wide eyes taking in the full length of steel.

A hunched figure tumbled out the open door, landing hard against the moss-draped cobblestone walkway with a yelp. Clad in a mismatched bundle of moth-bitten clothing, the heap of a man would appear as little more than a pile of discarded fabric if not for the dirt-stained fingers and balding pate poking out. He made no move to rise when a potbellied soldier stepped out the door behind him, rotating a shoulder as he dabbed a blood-soaked swatch of cloth at his rapidly purpling nose.

"He clocked you harder than I thought," Vincht said flatly.

The soldier nodded, spitting a mixture of blood and saliva down the old man's back. "Only reason I couldn't grab him before he barricaded himself in the room."

He gestured to the kneeling woman with the head of his cudgel. "See that one didn't give you any problems."

"She's twice my age, Arik. How much trouble you think she could give?"

Arik's already exertion-flushed face bloomed a deeper shade of crimson. He lashed out with a sharp kick to the crumpled pile of old man, catching him somewhere in his ribs.

"Stop it!" Liddy cried, and Vincht tapped her shoulder with his sword to remind her not to move.

Marion scrambled to his feet and bolted for the trees, but Arik was faster. His bulbous cudgel slammed into the old man's bicep with a wet pop, adding a new joint to his arm and bearing him back to the ground.

"I'm losing my patience," Vincht said, sighing. "Bring Marion over and place him in front of his wife."

The pot-bellied soldier grinned, tossing aside the bloody rag and plunging a meaty hand into the layers of fabric bunched behind the old man's neck. He barely protested, cradling his broken arm with a hand like twisted roots as Arik dragged him across the cobbles.

Rowan made no move to help, having shown little stomach for the 'freedom' Vincht had promised the other soldiers, despite assurances from the garrison commander in Comelbough that he'd selected some of the more troubled men and women under his watch. Vincht regretted not personally vetting the commander's selections, having instead fallen victim to the excitement of his mission and the desire to quickly put as much of the countryside behind them as was humanly possible.

Had he been made aware of Rowan's incompetence and reservations toward violence, Vincht would have taken another in his stead, but he had a sneaking suspicion the garrison commander had kept that information to himself for precisely that reason.

Arik deposited the whimpering old man at Vincht's feet, jerking him aloft and slamming him onto his knees across from his wife. He groaned, slumping forward and cursing weakly beneath his breath. Liddy started crying again, fighting the urge to reach out and embrace her husband.

A third soldier emerged from behind the house, holding aloft a hexagonally shaped wafer of what looked like quartz with a shake of his head and a shrug of defeat. Vincht nodded. He pointed at his own eyes, then swept his hand out to indicate the forest. The other soldier brought a fist to his chin in salute, hefting his cudgel and stepping off into the trees to sweep the area.

"Now, then. Liddy, Marion," he began, gesturing to each in turn. "It's been a long day for me and my men. I'm getting tired. They're getting tired. I'm sure you are both eager to be rid of us."

Marion spit, earning him the back of Arik's fist.

"Come on, Arik," Rowan protested.

Vincht produced a single sheet of folded vellum from a hardened leather pouch on his hip. Sheathing his blade, he carefully unfolded the worn sheet of paper. The page was soft from regular handling, but in relatively good shape aside from an angular tear indicating the page had once belonged to a larger sheet of paper.

"Now, Marion, I hope you'll be just as forthcoming as your wife. She's been so kind as to answer all of my questions, and with a refreshing level of honesty, I must say. But then, the point of a blade has that effect on people."

Vincht bowed his head. "My apologies for that. The people of this province haven't been particularly cooperative today, and the strain on my patience has caused me to approach relations with an unpleasant level of haste."

"You pushed your way into my house, you stu—" Marion's outburst was cut short by a quick jab to his wounded arm by Arik's cudgel. The old man howled in agony, sweat erupting from the flaking skin of his bald head.

Arik squeezed his shoulder and leaned in close. "Speak again, and I'll give you a jaw to match your arm."

To his credit, Marion nodded in agreement.

"Let's start over," Vincht continued. "My name is Vincht Morfren. As the three of us are already on a first name basis, I won't object to you calling me by mine. I generally prefer to conduct my initial interactions with people from a certain position of respect, patience, and understanding. Regretfully, that was not an option in your case due the immediately unpleasant attitude Marion here presented my man before we could truly introduce ourselves. I hope you understand why the rest of our interactions must now proceed with a certain level of necessary . . . hostility, if you will."

Vincht twirled his hand. "To business. My companions and I have made the long journey to Elbin not out of pleasure, but of necessity. Some time ago, an item of import made its way to this peninsula. It is my hope that said item was not lost to the trackless wilderness, but instead, found itself in the hands of one of your fellow citizens.

"However, I am growing less hopeful of this with each passing hour. Too many of your neighbors have been unhelpful, to say the least, and many were outright . . ."

He cocked his head, considering his words. "Rebellious, if you will. I've lost at least one man since beginning this morning, and it's possible more will follow before the sun sets on Elbin."

He sighed, peering down at the two in pity. "But the toll on your little hamlet has been far greater. You may never see some of your family again. You may never know what happened to some of your friends. Thus is the plight of those who give succor to false gods instead of placing their faith in their own two hands."

Kneeling, Vincht tapped the sheet of vellum. "I will make you a deal. You help me to find what I'm looking for, tell me who has it, and I promise you this: whichever of you gives me what I ask, won't stain these cobbles with your blood."

The silence was palpable. Rowen opened his mouth to protest, but a single withering glance from Vincht made him reconsider. Arik just kept grinning, shifting excitedly from one foot to the other like a child surrounded by piles of Namesday gifts. The husband and wife exchanged helpless looks, but it was the wife who spoke up first.

"But . . . I told you already, I—"

"I know, I know, my dear," Vincht interrupted, resting a comforting hand on her shoulder. "But you can't even begin to understand the importance of my task. What I'm looking for could change everything . . . everything, for everyone. The world itself. I'm just not willing to take the chance of not recovering it because I didn't insist hard enough.

"What do you say, Marion?" he said, grinning like a hungry wolf. "Tell me something good, something helpful, and you get to walk away from this with naught but a busted arm. Or do the noble thing; say nothing, and your loving wife gets to spend the rest of her days in the quiet safety of your little hovel over there."

He shrugged. "Alone, of course, but no one said life was fair."

He turned the sheet of vellum around and tapped the crude ink drawing with a finger. The item in question was long, with rounded edges like an oval stretched to its breaking point. One end was slightly narrower than the other, and on that end, a tubular grip was embedded on the bottom edge. Jagged lines crisscrossed the object from tip to tip, breaking off the main tangle of lines at various points to terminate along the edge opposite the grip.

To Vincht, the lines appeared to have some sort of mathematical significance, but the truth of the matter was that he had no real idea what he was looking at, or even what the item was. All he really had to go off of was the enigmatic drawing, and the meager descriptive details the other half of the letter had provided him.

Marion's eyes drank in the picture, not noticing his wife's quiet sobs and increasingly defeated posture as a feeling of utter helplessness crept over her. Vincht's free hand moved to the hilt of his belt knife, unseating it enough to be certain of smooth, unrestricted draw. Rowan chewed his thumb and shifted his attention to the little cabin.

The longer Marion stared, the more annoyed Vincht became, and the more annoyed he became, the more he wanted to visit harm upon the old man. His fingers tightened against the soft vellum, crinkling the already worn paper further. His frown deepened into a scowl, but still Marion looked, eyes darting from side to side as he studied the simple drawing. His darkening mood made even Arik uncomfortable, and the soldier had to take a deliberate step back away from the increasingly tense scene.

"Wait . . ." Marion breathed, stroking the indentation above his lip with a finger. He bowed his head, mumbled quietly to himself. "I've seen this, I know it. But where have I seen it . . . ?"

Liddy stared at her husband and shook her head, fighting back a fresh wave of tears. Vincht studied Marion's scrunched face, but a growing disgust kept him from getting a read on the old man's sincerity.

"You're wasting my time." The jet-haired swordsman came to his feet, stuffing the paper back into its case with little regard for its integrity.

"Arik, cave his head in."

The pot-bellied soldier hefted his cudgel, but a frantic burst of energy from Marion caused him to hesitate.

"Please, I know this!" He scrabbled forward, pawing at Vincht's belt.

"Marion, he'll kill me!" Liddy wailed, hyperventilating.

The old man ignored her. "It was over a decade ago. This . . . awful storm had blown in. A mighty strong one, and possible the worst storm we've ever seen out here. A merchant had swung through town the day before. A rare treat, and I was able to trade away some of my private tobacco stash for a bottle of Toddleton's saffron mead. I owed a friend for a tincture he'd made to hel—"

"Get to the point." Vincht hissed.

Marion swallowed. "We was sittin' on his covered porch when the storm blew through. A little rain at first, but it picked up fast. The trees' is pretty dense 'round his cabin, so we just took the whole of it in as we drank.

"We were scraping the bottom of the bottle, and I couldn't hardly see straight. Suddenly, somebody just comes marchin' right outta the trees, a bundle of something draped over each shoulder. Late night caller. He's good with fixing people, my friend is. I figured what, with the storm and the time, whoever it was musta needed him something urgent."

"Please, Marion," Liddy reached out, but the man shrank from her grasp.

"Now, I could barely stand at this point, and the whole world was spinning, but my friend just hopped up like he'd been sipping water all night. Leaves me sitting there clinging to my chair like I might float away. I could hear them, mucking about just inside the door. Shoving things about. Talking.

"I don't even know how I stood up, let alone how I made it to the door, but when I looked in there, there was this . . ." He paused. "Thing."

"A *thing?*" Vincht jerked him to his feet by his collar.

"I don't know! I was drunk and it didn't look like much! Just odd, ya know? Out of place."

"By all that is good, you'd better give me some details and quick. Something more than you can figure out from looking at that picture I showed you, or so help me, Marion . . ."

"Metal!" Marion screeched, flinching as if expecting to be struck. "It was made of metal!"

Vincht held him there, face-to-face, pondering the possibilities. The old man might have been able to guess that detail. He might have gotten lucky. He might have reached out into the ether and pulled out the one descriptor that would keep Vincht from having Arik spill the man's brains all over the cobblestone walkway.

Then again, he could very well be telling the truth . . . but there was another detail described in the remaining piece of the vellum letter that would confirm the veracity of the man's claims, a detail that would not be so easy to guess.

He released his grip on Marion's collar, and Arik helped him back to his knees. Vincht crossed his arms, adopting a mask of cool indifference, an expression that stood in stark contrast to the storm of emotion raging within.

"If you are lying to me, I'll have Arik break your remaining appendages before I personally disembowel you here, right in front of your wife. But if you *are* telling the truth . . . then answer me this.

"The object . . . it has a grip." His eyes narrowed into slits. "What color was it?"

Marion nodded frantically, breaking into a desperate smile. "White! Some sort of grainy white stone! I saw it, plain as day, plain as the nose on my face, I saw it!"

Vincht's heart practically stopped. *He's really seen it.*

"WHERE. Where is it?!"

"Don't," Liddy said so weakly Vincht wasn't sure he actually heard her.

"Ishen has it! His name is Ishen!" Marion pointed off to the east. "He has a cabin out in the forest. The ol' boy isn't much for village life, so he lives off by himself, off the beaten path and out of the way. I-I could show you! I could take you there right now!"

Vincht nodded. Most of the homesteads they had visited throughout the morning had resided directly on the overgrown path the village considered a road. If a cabin existed deep within the Traagen, it was unlikely any of his men would have stumbled upon it already.

"Liddy, look at me." Vincht gently cupped the woman's face in his hand and turned her to face him. The woman met his gaze with teary eyes, but remained silent. "Do you know of this Ishen person? Is Marion making things up so I don't kill him? Answer me honestly.

His tone hardened. "I do not want to have to hurt you."

Liddy nodded, eyes vacant.

"Do you know where he is? You could find him if you had to?"

A flit of confusion in her gaze. She nodded again.

Vincht grinned. "That's my girl."

In a flash, Vincht buried his belt knife to the hilt in Marion's throat. A river of red poured down his neck, blossoming across the front of his mismatched clothing. The old man's mouth spasmed, opening and closing like a fish snatched from the water. Vincht tore his knife free, cleaning it on Marion's shoulder before the man collapsed face-first onto the cobbles.

Liddy never even blinked.

Sheathing his knife, Vincht whistled to the third soldier. Rowen leaned against a nearby tree and retched. Vincht pointed at the woman. "Arik, get her on her feet. She's going to lead us to this Ishen's."

"You killed him," said Rowen, clutching his stomach. "He did exactly what you asked and you killed him. Why? Are you mad?"

Vincht could only sigh. *A never-ending disappointment.* "He gave up his wife to save his own skin, Rowen. Twice. Once in the house, and again out here. I was never going to let such a dishonorable coward live. He was dead the moment he called for his wife to answer the door."

Rowen shook his head in disbelief. Arik pulled the woman to her feet. Vincht was all smiles. Soon, their journey to Elbin would pay off and he would finally get his hands on his order's most sought-after artifact. Everything was falling into place. Fate was truly on his side.

The third soldier appeared from the trees. Vincht lifted a hand and wiggled four fingers, gesturing to the house with his other. The soldier nodded begrudgingly and made his way toward the hovel, disappearing through the open door.

Vincht rested a gloved hand on the older woman's slumped shoulder and squeezed.

"Alright Liddy. Time to be useful."

Chapter 7: Out of Place

Towering blue pines speared skyward through an interlocked canopy of greedy elm and silver maple boughs, fighting for their share of the Waking afternoon sun. A fine layer of composting detritus quietly languished in the false night. In a shallow earthen cleft, a narrow creek stumbled along, swollen from snow melt and seasonal rain, roiling over exposed root and jagged rock and any marginal undergrowth either unlucky or foolish enough to thrive on yesterday's shore. The birds didn't even attempt to compete with the raucous grumbling of the miniature river. They, like the owner of the cabin situated there in the middle of it all, came to this part of the woods to be alone.

Nevin sometimes marveled at how much the area had changed in the last two decades. Staring out his study window during a lesson on Fen Quarry's near constant rain, Ishen had once told him how he'd had to work out a special arrangement with Martha Chandler, Elbin's resident candle smith, to keep him in ample supply during the warmer months. With each passing year, the canopy overhead only grew denser, the trees thicker, and the sunlight increasingly scarce.

Life is unfathomably covetous, Nevin, he had said, his gaze unfocused, distant. *It wants things it cannot have, hungers for things not rightfully its own, and above all, yearns for more, more, more. It's never content. Never happy. Never fulfilled. It's why trees can reach such lofty heights, spread their roots through solid rock, and persist the countless eons.*

Life strives for nothing short of everything. It's only man who chooses to settle for 'enough'.

It had been a small part of a much larger discussion, but that snippet of conversation had stuck with Nevin like a poisonous barb, infecting the few moments of contentment he so rarely experienced with doubt and self-loathing. More and more, he'd come to wonder if he was truly the victim of unfortunate circumstances, or if he was the victim of his own unwillingness to brave uncertainty to escape the meager pleasures his circumstances occasionally afforded him.

At least here, he was alive. He had Aidux. He had Ishen. He had a roof over his head, food for his belly, relative—though sporadic—safety. What right did he have to want for more?

The world across that terrifying stretch of rope and wood and beyond the Hyret Gorge held no such promises. He'd spent his life submitting to the evil he knew over the possibility of being master to the evil he didn't. And now, as the traumas of the morning piled one on top of the other, he hoped his lack of foresight and complacency hadn't damned him to being crushed beneath the boots of both the evils he'd feared for so long.

Standing frozen on the stoop of Ishen's cabin and pondering the ramifications of the darkened window and partially open front door, Nevin prayed to whomever or whatever might be listening that those evils hadn't now come to damn one of the only two people in the world he cared about.

The whole situation felt strange. Dangerous, yes, but *odd*, in the way that coming home to find out someone had moved your things, but only just enough that it was possible *you* had left them there, but hadn't remembered doing so. Nevin's attention flitted about the scene before him, absorbing it all before allowing his feet to take the lead.

With its numerous rooms and precise construction, the secluded cabin bore little resemblance to the other structures scattered around the province. Most of Elbin's families made their lives in little more than a one room hovel; sharing a bed, an outbuilding, and generations of clothing, tools, and a lack of personal space. Few homes had secondary rooms, and those that did were often add-on afterthoughts of absolute necessity. Sheds and barns were far more common, with some homesteads presenting like miniature towns themselves.

Simply put, Ishen's cabin broke the mold. Built from interlocking arrow-straight pine logs, Nevin often marveled at the sheer geometry of its construction. Perfect right angles, gapless joints, inset doors, interior walls, a covered *porch* of all things . . . Maybe the village carpenter Mikael possessed the skill and knowledge—not to mention the patience—necessary to accomplish those feats . . . now . . . twenty years after the fact, but back then?

He wasn't so sure.

Nevin carefully slid the pack from his shoulder and lowered it to the leaf-strewn earth. His weak arm shook with the effort of staying quiet, but the moist dirt made no protest as the pack settled at his feet. Everything seemed louder here due to a general lack of noise, but luckily for him, the small creek behind the cabin was working double time.

He cast a wary eye to the bronze lantern resting at the foot of the porch. A small flame burned weakly within, only moments remaining until the end of its life and usefulness.

Not one of Ishen's. Had someone come calling in the early morning hours, ushering the old scholar from his home and into town? If so, why had they left their lantern behind? The people of Elbin weren't rich, so what meager possessions they had were coveted and treated with care. Had its owner been in a rush, out of urgency or maybe fear?

Or had someone come in the night, someone with dark intention, turning low the flame as they approached so as not to be seen, and traded lantern for blade at the door?

Nevin grit his teeth in frustration. He could stand here all day pondering possibility and stalling, but he knew that having answers didn't equate to solving problems. He already had enough problems. He certainly didn't need more catching up with him while he stood out here, failing to act.

The lantern weighed light in his hands, but a gentle shake revealed a wealth of oil still remained in its reservoir. A quick flick of a small lever on its domed hood widened a series of narrow vents, and the dying flame burst to life. Resigning himself to whatever answers lie within—good or bad—Nevin extended the lantern before him and stepped inside the cabin.

Normally awash with the glow of scattered candlelight, the shadowed interior felt cold and unwelcoming beneath the harsh glow of the lantern. A sturdy square table rested in the room's center, marred by countless divots and gouges that stood out like bloodless wounds in the light.

Along the surrounding walls, rows of clay jars and straw baskets squatted on shallow shelves and crowded the floor, most displaying a dried version of whatever lay within pasted to its front or woven into the straw. Few had written labels. The floral aroma of dried herbs and marinating unguents had always pleasantly tickled his nose, but today he could scarcely detect their presence. A brick stove languished in the corner.

Only rarely had Nevin been allowed to sit in when Ishen treated one of the locals, watching from the corner, perched atop a three-legged stool. Most of his visitors would stand, explaining to Ishen some discomfort or chronic malady whilst the older gentleman nodded thoughtfully and paced back-and-forth between the many jars and baskets, plucking one-by-one a series of seemingly unrelated ingredients and gathering them on the table. He'd interrupt with the occasional question, sometimes returning one ingredient in favor of another, sometimes waving off an answer as irrelevant.

Nevin would watch in fascination as he muddled the collection together using mortar and pestle, or bound them into a tight bouquet, or steeped them into a murky, fragrant tea. After instructing the visitor in the mixture's use, Ishen would express his desire for some item or service, before quickly ushering them back into the woods.

And out of our lives, he'd say with a wink.

Frowning, Nevin set the lantern down on the spacious tabletop. A number of jars and baskets had been moved from wall to table, their lids removed and their contents all but missing. Pottery shards crunched beneath his boots. They were all over. Dried lemongrass stalks and blue monkshood blossoms mingled together on the floor, their baskets overturned along with a handful of others.

Ransacked? Nevin hoped he was wrong, but he couldn't imagine a circumstance so dire that Ishen would treat his collection with so little care. Had the soldiers already come and gone, and if so, what use would they have had for a collection of dried plants? What were they looking for?

Nevin popped a morsel of willow bark in his mouth and chewed, eager to be free of the steady ache Dalen's boot had left in his ribs.

There were two other doors. One led to Ishen's bedroom—the only part of the house Nevin had never seen—and the other to his study. Alarmingly, that second door was flung wide.

Eyeing the study warily, Nevin cracked the bedroom door and appraised the space with a hasty glance. A modest room, it held no decoration and only two pieces of furniture: a pine chest and straw-stuffed mattress draped in a drab woolen blanket. The chest's lid hung open and appeared empty but for a moth-eaten robe, balled up and shoved into the corner. The bed was perfect, the blanket tucked neatly beneath the mattress and smoothed flat with an almost military precision.

Probably always fell asleep in his chair, Nevin hoped. He tried not to think about the alternatives. The cramped room was otherwise empty, leaving him with but one final room to check.

In the stillness, Nevin's heart counted out the seconds in double time. Part of him wanted nothing to do with that final doorway, hanging open despite Ishen's continual insistence that it always remain closed. After all the times the old scholar had admonished him for failing to secure it behind him, Nevin actually felt a pang of guilt for not rushing over to immediately press it closed.

But compared to the fear of what the contents of the study might reveal, that guilt was but a raindrop swallowed up in a sea of worry.

Something bumped his leg as he turned, something hard and round and unexpected and wrong, but as he reached down to determine its source, hot pain seared his brain, stealing his breath and welding his eyes shut.

Strange images flooded into his mind. *A pair of boots, soles worn smooth and cracked with age, sticking out from the base of the furthest stall. Broken bits of straw dusting the soil. One pant leg, stained yellow at the hem, bunched up around a pasty calf muscle. A leather strap wound tightly around his wrist.*

His jaw stretched to its limits in a silent scream, Nevin reached out to steady himself, but found only air. He sank into a crouch, sitting on his heels. He squeezed his head against the pain, but as quickly as it flared, the pain vanished, and the images evaporated like candle smoke on a gust of wind.

"What was *that?*" he whispered, rubbing the lingering ache from his temples. A faint ringing tickled his hearing, but all was otherwise silent.

When he opened his eyes, he realized with some concern that he had migrated during the unexpected episode, and was now crouched a number of feet *inside* the study.

The room stood empty—devoid of life and any signs of it, but its disheveled and chaotic appearance did nothing to alleviate his concerns.

Ishen's study accounted for nearly half of the cabin's footprint, and justifiably so, as the older scholar spent the bulk of his time within; lounging, book in hand, or hunched over the angled writing desk pushed up against the side wall. Matching upholstered armchairs sat opposite one another at the room's heart, sharing a circular pine end table mounded with creamy pools of hardened tallow. Of the two, the chair facing the door bore deep impressions in its faded green seat cushion—Ishen's favorite reading spot.

Lines of stalwart shelves covered any available wall space, stretching from polished floor to vaulted ceiling and displaying books and artifacts of both a curious and valuable nature. Waxed skulls of unfamiliar carnivorous fauna, detailed sketches of ancient battles and temple structures, wooden figures and marble busts, and even the occasional polished gemstone decorated the shelves, but their number was paltry compared to the volumes of leather-clad journals clustered in their midst and the loosely rolled scrolls arranged carefully in the lattice style shelves at knee level.

Meager in comparison to the amount of books I've read in my lifetime, Ishen had said, a self-satisfied smile plastered across his lips as he gazed lovingly at his collection. *But some of the most important I've encountered. I dare say these books are just as much a part of me, of who I am, as they are a part of this tiny library.*

On his right, one more feature split the wall between the shelves, and out of all the inconsistencies and wonders of the cabin's construction, Nevin placed this one at the top of the list—Ishen's glass window.

Ishen often expressed the importance of maintaining a healthy environment for the care and safety of his books, a collection he bragged contained a number of original scrolls and tomes the likes of which the world may never see again. He regularly swept the cabin for warm drafts, the roof for leaks, and put a kettle on the stove to adjust the humidity in the room.

But it was light, he asserted, that posed the most danger, if only because combining light with books was practically inevitable. It was a double-edged sword. One could not study bereft of ample light, but light also faded ink, yellowed paper, and made brittle the already delicate edges. Sunlight caused the most damage the quickest, so books and scrolls were often kept in windowless buildings for their protection, and dedicated scholars single-handedly kept the local chandlers in business.

There were some days I wondered if I'd forgotten what the outdoors looked like, Ishen had mused, peering out into the forest. *The trees block out the sunlight, and this window helps me remember the world I'm part of. It actually pains me to draw the curtain closed when the leaves fall in the Fading.*

A single pane of smooth, clear glass. Nevin had never seen its like. Every stitch of clear glass in Elbin was no larger than the palm of his hand, and the few windows not made of paper were tiled together using said smaller pieces. He'd witnessed the process necessary to form the individual panes, and Nevin would sooner slap Dalen on the mouth than be convinced the same process capable of reproducing Ishen's favorite window.

Yet, in that moment, the narrow window was the sanest part of the entire study. Books stood in precarious stacks on the floor, like the columns of some forgotten henge unearthed by cautious historians. Still others lay scattered almost carelessly about. Scrolls filled the seat of Ishen's favorite chair, while its twin lay upside down against the far wall. The sloped writing desk had been moved from its place, angling awkwardly out into the room in a way that made traversing the space difficult.

Even with the state of the study, Nevin could tell a number of books were missing, but whether that meant Ishen was robbed, or had packed up in the middle of the night and vanished, Nevin couldn't tell.

Nevin carefully picked his way around the jumbled furniture, trying to remember all the little tips about tracking that Aidux had taught him over the years. What would he reasonably expect to find in a space where a fight broke out? He scanned the floor, the chairs, the desk, the shelves. No blood, as far as he could see. No gouges in the wood either. Misplaced furniture, in that the chair had been moved across the room and the desk was out of place, but nothing looked damaged or roughed up.

He peered out the window and into the quiet forest, wondering where Aidux had hidden himself. Outside, all was still. Even the burbling of the creek could barely be heard through the precisely adjoined pine logs.

"How could you go missing *today*? And here I thought it impossible for you to be a bigger pain-in-the-ass than you already were."

He scratched his blood-crusted neck and took a second look at everything. With the bridge out, Nevin and Aidux would need another way off the peninsula, and quick. Aside from wanting to make sure he was okay, Nevin needed to pick the old scholar's brain for any possible means out of the Traagen that didn't require a rope bridge. But while all the evidence appeared to point to Ishen having left the cabin voluntarily, assuaging Nevin's concern for his safety, his old teacher's untimely disappearance had only worsened his own situation.

That left him with two options. He could stay, digging through Ishen's remaining books, scrolls, charts, and whatnot, hoping the means and method of escaping the woods lay hidden within. Problem was, he was fairly familiar with Ishen's collection by now, and doubted anything new would materialize. In addition, if they hadn't already, a team of soldiers was bound to show up sooner rather than later, and he did *not* want to be up to his knees in literature when that happened.

The only other option was to run for the hills. Put as much countryside behind Aidux and himself as possible. Stay out of the open. Head into the foothills and climb the Nimmons, if at all possible. Brave the wolves, the snow, the altitude, the Narlocs.

Nevin cocked his head, leaning slightly to the side. A black-stained ironwood box sat on the floor behind the writing desk, barely visible but for his position by the window. He skirted the book piles and crouched beside it. The box was barely the length of his hand and was possessed of a rather austere design. A single narrow keyhole decorated its front, but there wasn't a key in sight.

"Never seen you before," he said, picking the box up for a closer look. He barely made it a foot from the floorboards before something jerked it right out of his hands.

Nevin blinked in surprise, cautiously reaching for the box again. This time, his fingers brushed something taut and almost invisible running horizontally across its face. He ran a fingertip over it. *A thread?* The bit of string matched the box's stain perfectly, and its thinness only added to its utter invisibility.

"What . . . ?" He raised the box until the string went taut, then firmly tugged.

One of the boards popped loose from the floor. Eyes widening, Nevin lifted the box higher still, bringing the board with it. Under the added weight, the thin string finally snapped. The three foot long board clattered to the floor. Nevin flinched, losing his balance and setting him on his ass.

In the clamor, Nevin had failed to notice the sound of men's voices approaching the cabin.

Chapter 8: Being Watched

"Quiet," Vincht barked, stopping so suddenly that Rowen collided with Liddy, nearly sending them both careening face-first into a tangled knot of brambles. Arik snickered and shook his head, anxiously twisting his hands around the pommel of his cudgel. Off to his right, the third soldier looked to Vincht for further instruction.

Rowen carefully plucked a hooked barb free of his tunic before turning to Liddy. "You alright?" he asked, but Liddy's unfocused gaze hadn't wavered since departing her homestead some thirty minutes prior. Rowen studied her face while he untangled the brambles from her blood-crusted shawl. Red and swollen from the steady stream of tears leaking from the corners of her eyes, he wondered if she could even see, or if she'd simply been guiding them based entirely on instinct.

"Don't be such a *pish*." Arik slapped Rowen's hand away. "Your bleedin' heart's makin' me stomach all gibbly."

"Back off, Arik. No one asked you."

Vincht scanned the vegetation, ignoring their exchange. The trek toward the cabin had imbued him with a feeling of shrinking, as the trees swelled in girth and height, and the hungry ferns brazenly advanced up his legs until they clawed at his belly with every step. The quantity of brambles had increased as well, as though the woods were warning them off delving any deeper.

The cabin's appearance wasn't what gave him pause. Lurking beneath the protective boughs of a hulking elm, their destination stood apart from the rampant vegetation on all sides, as though an invisible barrier blocked all comers but those what were invited. A faint orange glow outlined a single narrow window. As he watched, the glow waned and shifted, giving way to a vaguely human-shaped blob of darkness that briefly paused at the window before disappearing within.

No, something else had drawn his focus. Out there, out beneath the trees, something had shifted. Something had moved. Something, he sensed, watched them as they watched the cabin.

Arik waved a calloused hand through the old woman's blank gaze. "You see? May as well be buttons. She's whiffed, friend."

It was Rowen's turn to slap Arik's hand away. "We should have left her behind. She's in no state for travel."

The pot-bellied soldier rolled his eyes. "Are you hearin' this? Pish thinks he knows best, now. Got balls like ripe melons, this one. Can't keep track of an 'orse, but thinks himself smart enough to earn some yups."

His brow furrowed in concentration, Vincht swept the scene. He saw only shadows—nature's vibrant patchwork of greens, yellows, and browns muted by the artificial curtain of night the impenetrable canopy drew across the sky. His blade hand drifted to rest on the ivory pommel of his shortblade, taking comfort in its proximity.

Rowen raised his hands apologetically. "Hold on, that's not what I'm getting at. I merely meant—"

"I said *quiet.*" Vincht hissed. The two soldiers nodded obediently. Vincht's sword arm returned to his side. Perhaps he was just being paranoid, but either way, a hidden observer was not likely to move again, not while he watched. He decided it best to go on like he hadn't noticed, with the hope whoever it was would reveal themselves when they thought his guard down. He cast one final look into the shadows before facing his men.

"For the foreseeable future, I don't want to hear *either* of you so much as clear your throat without being asked to do so. Stand there and choke, if you must."

The two nodded again, and Rowan tugged at the collar of his tunic.

Vincht raised a finger and drew a circle in the air. Slipping a red-fletched arrow from a quiver belted to his hip and nocking it in his bow, the third soldier nodded and waded through the ferns in a wide arc in front of the cabin.

The black-haired soldier then pointed to Arik. "Sweep the woods behind the cabin. If there's a back door, post up nearby. Should this . . . Ishen make a run for it, I want to make sure we're nearby to grab him. The forest here is too dense to let someone who knows the area get far. Too many places to hide."

His attention shifted to Rowen. "Find a tree trunk within line of sight of the front door and watch it. I'll be going inside alone. With any luck, this man will be alone and incapable of putting up of a fight.

"But in case he slips past me and makes a run for it, whatever happens, do . . . not . . . kill him. I don't care if he sprouts a wing and comes out spewing fire and swinging a ten foot long blade with one hand. Knock him out, break his legs, cut off his arms . . . stop him, however you can, as long as he's alive. Stephen can treat nearly any wound, but we'll get no answers from a corpse."

Arik's hands tightened around his cudgel, the wood creaking faintly beneath his grip. Liddy twitched, fresh tears welling up in the corners of her dead, swollen eyes.

Vincht stepped up to Rowen, lowering his voice to a whisper and making a show of adjusting the man's vest. "Keep your guard up. I've a feeling we're not alone out here."

"What about her?" Rowen asked before slapping a hand to his mouth. The dark-haired soldier regarded him coolly, picturing the fool trying to speak with a mouthful of blood and a handful of tongue.

Instead of answering, Vincht simply nodded to Arik. A wicked smile broached the pot-bellied soldier's lips, and the last thing Vincht saw before he turned toward the cabin was Arik extending his cudgel high above his head.

Chapter 9: Cold and Dark, and Also Cold

Nevin blinked, staring slack-jawed at the three foot long gaping hole in the floorboards and the unyielding blackness within. His thighs ached from the strain of crouching, but he was too concerned with the hidden compartment to care. The rim of the hole and edges of the loose board were chipped and cracked from what he assumed was regular placement and removal, and the wood around it glossy and discolored from handling. Had the curious ironwood box not kept his attention before, Nevin imagined the removable board would have stuck out like an ink blot on a blank page. How had he managed to overlook it for so many years?

The desk, he thought, running his empty hand along the floor. He saw them now, the scratches in the wood left behind by the angled writing desk's balled feet. Even running perpendicular with the wood grain, the faint gouges were almost invisible, but where his eyesight fell short, his fingertips prevailed. With the pine desk in its normal position along the wall, the removable board would be both inaccessible and hidden, and with the other decorative objects displayed prominently around the room, he doubted many people would think to move a desk in search of further valuables.

Nevin looked around. If Ishen's bragging was to be believed, any would-be thief could retire happily on just a fraction of the study's contents, and his old mentor had boldly insisted on placing them right out in the open.

Had it all been a distraction?

"Ishen . . . what were you thinking?" He rolled the broken bit of black thread between his fingers. "You wanted someone to find this."

He sank to his knees, leaning forward until his free hand rested on the floor beside the gap in the floorboards. Maybe the unrecognizable box had been chosen as 'bait' in order to draw his attention. Maybe Ishen had squirreled away an atlas or travel journal of some kind, something that Nevin and Aidux could use to escape the peninsula, but as to why the old scholar would hide such mundane knowledge away from the world, he couldn't know. Maybe Nevin was just desperately clinging to any hopeful possibility that popped into his troubled mind.

"Question is, did you want me to find it . . . or someone else?" He took a deep breath.

Only one way to find out.

He set the wooden box beside the hole and plunged his hand into darkness, mumbling a soft prayer that no hungry animals or poisonous insects lay hidden within. To his surprise, something soft and coarse instantly enveloped his hand. He grabbed a fistful and pulled. A ratty woolen blanket emerged from the hole, stained and faded and stinking of mildew.

"Ugh!" Nevin grimaced, tossing the foul-smelling blanket aside.

Undeterred, he tried again, sinking his arm up to the elbow, but finding only cold air. His wounded shoulder complained, shaking from the effort as he sank ever lower. The stagnant air chilled further, but still the hole gave up nothing.

"I know you're in there," he grunted, dropping onto his chest and squashing his cheek against the worn pine planks to stretch as much reach from his arm as he could manage. He could see under the desk now, could see all way across the study and through the door into other room.

As for his searching hand, it felt like he'd shoved it into bank of fresh snow. He stirred his arm about, reaching in every direction he could think of, inching farther and farther, feeling the muscles in his upper back cramping from the strain . . .

A pair of calf-length black boots stepped into view, pausing in the doorway.

Nevin flinched, nearly calling out in surprise. His grip faltered, and he slid deeper into the hole than intended. The back of his head knocked against the rim of the hole, and a bright light bloomed across his vision. Waves of hot pain and nausea wracked his body. He abandoned the search, flailing and grasping about before finally attempting to brace himself against the underside of the floor.

And that's how he found it.

His hand crashed into something hard. Hard and unfathomably cold. His mind screamed at him to breathe, to instinctively suck air from surprise, to jerk his hand away from the brutal cold, but it was too late. All heat abandoned his body, torn from his extremities, through his center mass, and out through his frozen hand.

Everything stopped. A thick cloud of breath hung in the air before his parted lips. Beyond the writing desk, one black boot hovered over the floor, frozen mid-step.

All feeling vanished, replaced not with numbness, but with an utter lack of existence. Each of his senses failed, one by one and all at once. His sight failed last, as the floor, the desk, the study itself just faded away, evaporating into nothingness.

Chapter 10: Et Clothas Travta Nevin

The moment stretched out before him, an endless plane of curious absence.

Where did I go? The question, the thought, echoed through the void—a thought spoken without voice.

Am I dead? Is this what death is like?

With his being dissolved, the nothing penetrated his mind. He gave himself to it, welcomed it in, opened all his mental and emotional doors to the sweet emptiness. He felt his worries bleed away . . . his needs . . . his fears. All gone. Running from Dalen. The soldiers in Elbin. His friendship with Aidux. His desire for more. For a family. For meaning. For love.

The nothing accepted it all, consumed it readily, dispersed it out into the infinite.

Devoid of his being, stripped of his trauma, free of his emotions and baggage, all that remained of Nevin was a single undulating pinprick of prismatic light, shining at the heart of the void with all the brilliance of a thousand suns.

No more running. No more pain. No more worry. No more regret. Just simple, unburdened being.

For the first time in his life, Nevin was at peace.

The link . . . is established.

The voice, feminine and soothing, called out from the nothing. It existed apart from him, from somewhere beyond, but as the words washed over what little was left of him, Nevin experienced a strange familiarity. He recognized the voice somehow. An old friend, perhaps, from a past life, a repressed memory, a faded dream . . . forgotten, but still part of him.

There was something else too, some other presence, hidden out there in the dark. Smaller, but somehow more real, more substantial. He could sense it, out there in the distance, faint but growing more distinct with each passing moment.

Approaching.

We each are connected. Can you feel us?

"I think so," he answered back, even before he realized he could speak. "Who are you?"

I am the Arbiter. I execute that which has been initiated.

"I don't understand."

You have initiated the process. As such, I have established the proper links. This is my duty.

Nevin paused to think. What did she mean he 'initiated the process?' The last thing he remembered was searching Ishen's study, finding that strange box and digging around inside the hidden compartment. He remembered the cold encompassing his hand, of touching something hard and frozen and having all trace of warmth ripped from his body.

What could possibly do that? Had he stumbled on something he shouldn't have?

Could he have possibly fallen victim to some sort of magical effect?

That's impossible, he thought aloud. Ishen detested magic, refusing to even speak on the subject. Every time it came up during a lesson, the older man would grumble to himself, running his bony fingers up and through his tangled salt-and-pepper beard as he shifted to a new topic. Nevin had grown increasingly curious over the years, but the more he pushed, the more evasive his old mentor had grown.

Magic is not a solution, Ishen had told him the last Nevin had pressed him for answers. *It masquerades as an all-powerful force capable of rewriting reality and overcoming any obstacle, but don't believe the stories. It's a tool, no different than a sword or shovel. But where the effects of a sword are immediate and obvious, the effects of magic are often nuanced and invisible, and rarely without cost. Some things in this world create more problems than they solve.*

Be grateful you live in a part of the world where the practice of magic is strictly forbidden. You're better off without it, you have no need of it, and if you're very lucky, you'll never encounter it, so let's just agree to leave the subject be.

No, it was far more likely he'd slipped into the hole and knocked himself out again. "I'm dreaming," he said to himself. "This is just some terrible head injury hallucination. It has to be. I'm not even here."

A few seconds passed before the voice responded.

I find your confusion . . . unexpected. Allow me to alleviate it.

Breath rushed into Nevin's lungs, unbidden but welcome. His eyes fluttered open, coming into focus as the nothing withdrew, leaving him standing alone in a shimmering circle of white light. His bare toes curled against an unidentifiable coarse white stone. He flexed his fingers, rotated his shoulders, wiggled his jaw.

Nothing hurt. All his aches had vanished, his strained shoulder displaying none of the tightness and tenderness he was worried would persist for weeks. He felt new, reborn free of a body wracked by a life of hard labor and painful lessons. He even wore a new outfit: a simple linen shirt and pant ensemble, both light and comfortable.

He thought he should be more surprised, more confused by these events, but all his emotions seemed trapped beneath the frozen surface of his mind—tiny bubbles breaking against an unyielding sheet of ice, visible but just out of reach.

"I have to admit, this all feels so real. All of my injuries—"

I have discarded them. They are not necessary.

He nodded unconsciously, not really understanding but grateful none-the-less. "And the rest of me? My . . . feelings? Were they discarded, too?"

Your emotions will return once you return. Unlike your physical maladies, they are an integral part of your being, and cannot be discarded.

"Then why are they gone? I mean, not having a body may have freaked me out, but was it really necessary to block me from feeling altogether?"

They have only been temporarily dampened for your protection, though you should be feeling their return now that we are approaching the final steps of the process.

The voice wasn't lying. During the last few moments, Nevin could sense a spiderweb of narrow cracks forming in the frozen barrier between his consciousness and the impatient emotions churning below. He didn't understand why he would need protection from them, but he wasn't going to object to the brief reprieve.

He shook his head. *Strangest dream ever.*

Out in the darkness, a rhythmic plodding echoed quietly all around him. Footsteps, moving ever closer.

Nevin folded his arms across his chest. "Look, I don't know what's really going on or what you're doing to me, or if this is actually happening—"

It is.

He held up a hand. "Okay, but even if I believed what you're saying—"

Your belief is unnecessary to the process.

Had his emotions not been dampened, Nevin suspected he would have been exceedingly annoyed at the woman's constant need to interrupt each and every one of his thoughts.

I'm literally arguing with myself here.

He took a deep breath before continuing. "What exactly *is* necessary then? Can you at least tell me that?"

You are not an active participant in the process. Though you are a subject, it is I that executes and completes the changes necessary to prepare you for dilation. Once the process has been initiated, all that is required of subjects is to endure.

"But I didn't agree to whatever you're doing to me."

That statement is factually incorrect.

The plodding echoed through the cavernous space, growing louder and more distinct with each passing moment.

Regardless, any form of continued agreement is, ultimately, unnecessary. The process cannot be safely interrupted once phase-locking of the souls has begun. Attempting to do so has a chance of generating an inverse pattern, an event which would likely end in the complete cancellation of all spiritual entities involved, and possibly even, in a worst case scenario, the creation of one or more verdant husks.

"I don't . . ." Nevin slumped forward. "I don't have even the slightest idea what you're talking about."

Your understanding—

"—is unnecessary, yes, I'm starting to get that."

To ensure your safety, the dilation process will be performed incrementally, over an extended period of time. To ensure the safety of others, it is imperative that you stay within five meters of the Sharasil for the duration of the dilation process.

Dilation process? Phase-locking? Sharasil? Nevin couldn't tell if the voice was pretending to be obtuse, or if she simply didn't understand his overwhelming confusion.

"You say this isn't a dream, but here I am, standing in the middle of nothing, listening to an invisible woman spouting what sounds like nonsense and telling me nothing I say or think matters. I got enough of that from Dalen, thank you. If not for the fact that you 'discarded' my wounds, temporarily or not, I'd say this was feeling more and more like a nightmare."

With a final clap of wooden sole on coarse stone, the footsteps stopped, somewhere just beyond the tattered edge of the circle of light.

"Is that you, walking around out there in the dark?" Nevin searched the darkness pressing in on all sides. "Why won't you show yourself? Come out."

Regretfully, our next meeting is not scheduled to take place until the hour of your death.

All around him, the shimmering circle of light wavered and shrank, his tiny island in the sea of blackness losing integrity as emotion flooded his thoughts. The shadows crept forward, inching and stuttering as they consumed the steadily weakening light. With the darkness came a stinging cold, one he couldn't have noticed before, when he didn't have a body.

He hugged his chest and stepped back from the encroaching darkness. "Wait! I still have questions!"

A different voice responded. "Questions? And here I thought you were just dreaming, Nevin."

Nevin flinched in surprise and took another step back, the edge of the circle of light right on his heel. The voice that responded wasn't female, and it didn't come from all around him. The voice that answered was just outside of reach, mere steps ahead of him somewhere out in that blackness, and spoke with a hint of amusement in its words.

But strangest of all . . . the voice sounded exactly like him.

The ice shattered beneath his feet, and emotion overwhelmed him. He could feel everything again. His heart pounding on the walls of his chest. Blood screaming through his ears. The dryness in his throat. The tears welling up in the corners of his eyes.

The terrible, inescapable *fear*.

He felt it all, all at once, and it was too much.

May you go forth with both wisdom and temperance.

The circle of light vanished, and darkness washed over him.

Chapter 11: Missed Opportunities

Nevin jerked his arm free of the hole in the floor and away from the unknown source of the vision. Numbness stiffened his fingers, and thin streamers of fog escaped his lips as he struggled to control his rapid breathing.

What was THAT? The vision was already beginning to fade from his mind, even as he turned its contents over and over in his thoughts. He'd slipped while reaching around in the hole, banged his head again, he was sure of it. A concussion dream, that's all.

Still . . . it felt like I was in that strange space for hours . . .

Somewhere else in the abandoned cabin, a door opened, and Nevin suddenly remembered what startled him into the hole in the first place.

The boots!

Lowering his cheek to the floorboards, Nevin peered beneath the angled writing desk, but the doorway to the study was empty. He strained his ears, ignoring the adrenaline-spiked blood racing through them to try and hear any further movement from the other room. Pottery shards crackled beneath careless boots as someone walked about Ishen's treatment room.

Nevin cast an appreciative glance at the writing desk. Due to the way it had been shifted into the middle of the room, the desk mostly obscured his body from the view of anyone standing in the doorway. It had been the only reason Nevin wasn't immediately discovered by whoever was creeping about the cabin.

"Hello?" called a man's voice, deep and authoritative. "Your door was open. I was hoping someone could help me."

With its distinct, smooth baritone, Nevin quickly realized he wasn't familiar with the voice. And while that didn't necessarily guarantee the man wasn't from Elbin, the fact that he had barged in uninvited—open door or not—did.

No one in town was *that* brazen. Not since the Milton Winslow incident.

Cradling his tender ribs, Nevin inched to his feet, watching the door with unflinching eyes. There was no going out that way, he knew. The chances of slipping through the treatment room unnoticed were practically zero, and depending on where the intruder was standing, he doubted he could even make it to the door at full sprint before getting grabbed.

His only option was the window. He silently cursed Ishen for his insistence on framing the edges of the glass within the wall itself. *No leaks that way,* he'd say.

No way to sneak through it, either, you old goat.

Breaking the glass was sure to cause a racket, but with any luck, the intruder would simple charge into the study to see what had happened, allowing Nevin time to disappear beneath the overgrowth. All he'd have to do from there is wait until the stranger found what he was looking for or gave up, and Nevin could slip away to join up with Aidux.

His only concern? Would the glass break easily, or would he simply bounce off, knocking him flat on his ass and giving the intruder all the time he needed to rush in and grab him?

"I wouldn't, not if you value your skin."

Nevin flinched, jerking his head toward the source of the words.

Too late.

At half a head taller than Nevin, the stranger filled the doorway, the golden skin of his chiseled arms nearly brushing the frame on either side. Dark eyes bore into him from beneath a prominent brow, their intensity lending a certain ferocity to the toothy white smile he offered. Waves of black hair fell onto a pair of three-piece polished leather pauldrons, and his matching vest did little to disguise the corded muscle beneath. One hand rested on the ivory hilt of a straight sword, the scabbard tilted to point behind him like a tail.

From his pauldrons all the way down to his calf-high boots, the man was a picture of utilitarian fashion, purposeful and meticulously maintained.

The stranger twirled a finger as he spoke. "I've seen that injury before. Glass doesn't leave particularly clean wounds, and the shards are ferociously sharp. Digging out the pieces with your fingers tends to either shred the hands or drive the bits even deeper. I wouldn't chance it, not without some longer sleeves and some sort of face covering."

Faced with the unexpected stranger, the young man took a small step back. The man spoke with an odd sort of musical quality, one that stood opposed to the vaguely threatening nature of his message.

"That's . . . I wasn't . . . ."

The stranger ignored his stammering. Instead, he took in the length of Nevin, his gaze sweeping the younger man from head to toe and back again. "My, my. You're not at all what I expected to find out here. Not of the typical inbred village stock, are you, friend?"

"I . . . uh . . ." Nevin trailed off. Hot blood rushed to his cheeks.

The man knuckled a small smile. "You'll have to forgive my forthrightness. Most of the men and women I've encountered today were but a pair of horns or pointed tail away from being hunted for sport. To come across someone even moderately good looking . . . well, it just caught me off guard is all. I hope I've not made you *too* uncomfortable."

Something about the way the man spoke, his tone, his careful inflection, not to mention that bit about injuries from broken glass . . . Nevin couldn't help but wonder if discomfort was precisely his intention.

"I'm sorry, but . . . what are you doing here?"

"Introductions, yes, of course." He placed a hand on his chest and offered a modest bow. "My name is Vincht Morfren, consul to the Origin Knights and ally of the Lancowls of Comelbough. Forgive me for barging in unannounced, but the door was open and thought it prudent to inquire on the state of the cabin's inhabitants. Imagine my surprise to find its contents in disarray and its owner absent."

Nevin folded his arms across his chest. "What makes you think I'm not the owner?"

The man called Vincht chuckled. "I've been told the owner, a man named Ishen, is quite a bit older than yourself, and unless you share a bed with him, I'd wager you live elsewhere.

"Now then." He cocked his head. "You still haven't told me *your* name."

"It's Nevin."

He bowed again, deeper than before, and swept a hand in the air before him. "Well met, Nevin."

Vincht adjusted his leather vest, turning to take in the disheveled study as he strolled into the room. "On the topic of unexpected . . . I would have bet thirty Faulken shils on there not being a single book in this whole backwoods village, let alone an entire library."

A little over three feet separated the stranger from the now empty doorway. If the man moved any farther from that door, Nevin might be able to slip by. Then it was only a matter of making it to the trees. While the man was visibly stronger that him, muscle itself didn't dictate speed, and Nevin was willing to bet his life on the chance of outrunning him.

He inched his leading foot a half-step closer toward freedom.

"I am confused, though," the stranger began, pausing to toe one of the unstable pillars of books. He tugged at his gloves as it wobbled. "With treasures like these, this Ishen must have been a very rich man. Why, the contents of this room alone are worth more than the lives and possessions of every man, woman, and child in Elbin, as far as today has shown me, and this is what he left behind! Either he left in such a hurry that he was unable to take such a prized collection with him, or what he did take was far more valuable that what we see here.

"I also didn't notice a stables or pen for a horse or mule outside, and no cart tracks leading to or away from the cabin. It's likely he made off with only what little he could carry."

With a sigh, Vincht turned again and approached the angled writing desk. He ran a finger down its surface, grunting his approval at the apparent lack of dust or grime. Craning his neck, he casually ruffled a stack of papers strewn across the desk. He snorted and shook his head, mouthing a word he must have seen written on the papers, but Nevin couldn't make out what.

While Vincht's attention was focused on the writing desk, Nevin crept ever closer to that open door. If he could just again another foot or two without Vincht noticing, he should be able to sprint past him before the man could react.

Biting his lip, Nevin carefully slid his leading foot over the polished floor and slowly shifted his weight to keep the wood from creaking and giving him away. *One more step.*

Vincht lifted his short blade free of its scabbard and slammed it back into place without turning. The sudden motion caused Nevin to freeze, his raised foot hovering in place.

"I will sever the tendon separating your leg from your foot before you even cross the threshold, and that's me being polite."

His speech had lost that contradictory musical quality from before, replaced by one that exuded absolute malice. Nevin found himself frightened more by the effortless change in tone than by the threat of violence.

The black-haired soldier turned his head, gauging the young man's reaction from the corner of his eye. When Nevin simply nodded and lowered his foot, Vincht flashed a toothy smile and turned to face him.

"Excellent," he said, his tone once again light and melodic.

Nevin suppressed a shiver.

"Now, where was I?" He snapped his fingers and nodded. "Of course. Ishen is no longer here, and it's likely he made off with his most valuable items, though only those he could carry. No horse, no cart, and a three day walk to the nearest settlement, two if one really pushed themselves. As a man of advanced years, it would surprise me if he didn't take his time, especially weighed down with a pack of consumables and valuables."

He looked around, frowning. "Considering the state of the room, it appears as though he picked through everything he owned in order to gather the pieces he wanted most. Otherwise, why the piles? Why move everything off the shelves? If you were really only taking one or two things, why go through everything? Why not just grab what you need from the shelves and leave?"

Nevin shrugged. "I don't—"

Vincht interrupted him. "And then there's you, skulking about his empty home in the light of day, surrounded by items whose value could quite literally buy you a comfortable life in most major cities, and yet . . . your hands are empty. Either you're a terrible thief, or you're a friend of the man and were surprised by his absence."

Nevin straightened self-consciously. "Like you said. The door was open. I thought it was odd."

The soldier opened a small pocket on his vest and produced a folded sheet of vellum. "You're not much of a liar, Nevin, but I'm willing to overlook your rudeness and give you another chance. You see, I'm looking for something . . . unique. Maybe you've seen it, maybe you haven't. I only ask that you take a look. Answer me honestly, and maybe our little encounter here will come to an agreeable ending."

He presented the charcoal drawing to Nevin. "For the both of us."

The odd oblong-shaped sketch had little in the way of detail aside from a few jagged lines crisscrossing a curiously shaped object, and an inset handle positioned at the narrow end. Nothing else was written on the worn page that granted any sort of context to the item's features—size, weight, material, intent. Nevin studied it carefully, hoping he could give the man something useful so he'd leave him alone, but in the end, he could only shrug.

Vincht grimaced, smoothing down the front of his vest with his free hand. "I know, it's not much to look at. Fortunately, through my interaction with the locals here, I've learned that the item in question was at least *here* at some point in the past, and I have a few more descriptive details not found on this drawing that may help.

"First, the bulk of the object is metal, but you see little cylindrical bit here?" He indicated with a finger. "This is a grip or handle made of white stone."

Nevin stared back at him. "I swear I haven't—"

"In addition, it's rumored to lower the temperature of the area around it. It's even said to freeze anything it comes in contact with."

Nevin flexed his fingers, his mind back inside that frigid gap in Ishen's floorboards, feeling around in the emptiness beneath the cabin until his hand brushed against something wholly unnatural. Something hard. Something metal.

Something unfathomably cold.

Vincht must have picked up on the change in his expression. "You *do* know something, don't you?"

When Nevin hesitated, the soldier glided forward and grabbed the young man by the shoulders. Nevin tried to shrug him off, backing up until the window pressed against his bottom, but Vincht simply followed, squeezing to the point of discomfort. All trace of civility had vanished from his countenance, replaced by a mixture of controlled fury and poorly contained elation.

He suddenly wished he'd jumped through the window when he had the chance.

Chapter 12: Shadows in the Woods

When Nevin didn't immediately respond to Vincht's question, the soldier shoved him against the window, causing the back of the young man's already wounded head to bounce off the stalwart glass.

Pain and light exploded in his brain.

Dalen dug his bony fingers into the meat of Nevin's shoulders, his sour breath reeking of stale wine and rotten teeth. "You think I'm stupid, boy? You think I wouldn't find out?"

The image flickered out of existence, and Nevin found himself face-to-face with the eager soldier.

"Let me go," he mumbled, turning his head away.

"Where is it, Nevin? It was the cold, wasn't it? You've run across something far colder than you could explain, something that didn't make sense."

He craned his neck, trying to pull as far away from Vincht as he could, but the window pushed back. Cool glass fogged around his hot skin.

"I almost can't believe it. That old fool was actually telling the truth." A relieved smile flashed across the man's taut face. "Tell me where, Nevin. Where did you find it? Tell me where and I'll take it and be gone."

Nevin's hands quivered in the air beside Vincht's, wanting desperately to grab the soldier and pry him off but worried the situation would grow even more physical if he did. "I don't—"

Vincht shoved him against the window. A spiderweb of jagged cracks spread out from the back of his head, threatening to tear the whole panel down, but the window held firm. His vision swam momentarily, and another burst of light overwhelmed his mind.

Dalen caught Nevin across the face with the back of his hand, the sudden blow knocking the younger man off balance and off of his feet. Straw crunched beneath him as he landed flat on his back.

He brought a shaky hand to his lip. Blood.

The old drunk wobbled on his feet, tilting his canteen back for a deep swig of yellow wine. Streamers of liquid drooled from his chin and into the dry earth. He wiped his mouth with a stained sleeve and shoved the cork in place, gesturing to Nevin with the canteen.

"I seen where you get off to when I ain't lookin'. You a little sneak, you know that?"

"You still with me?" Vincht slapped him on the cheek. "I asked you a question, Nevin."

He looked around the disordered study, confused. "What?"

Vincht spun him around and slammed his face into the window. Nevin gasped. Tiny sharp edges ground into the tender flesh of his cheek. The cracks spread wider, but still, the window somehow held.

Vincht pressed a hexagonally cut sliver of crystal against the fractured glass before his eyes. The clear stone exuded a soft white light, waxing and waning from its core like a series of measured breaths.

"I've been looking for that glow all day, and now I have it. What I seek is here, somewhere nearby, likely in this very room. And I will find it, Nevin, with or without your help, but I'd much prefer not to have to hurt you.

"You're a good looking young man, a rare find amongst the inbred cretins infesting this forsaken forest. It did not pain me to visit harm on those who willfully stood between me and my mission here in Elbin. Misfortune comes to us all: rich and poor, good and bad, ugly and beautiful. No one mourns the worm that is crushed beneath the boot. But crush a flower, and the world is lessened by that loss.

Nevin could feel the man's hot breath against his cheek as he continued. "You and I, Nevin? We're the flowers. The worms exist to feed the flowers, to prop them up, to help them bloom so the rest of the world can revel in their beauty and be all the more for it. A flower, Nevin . . . a flower is worth a *thousand* worms."

Nevin struggled against his captor, but Vincht dug his shoulder into his back, grinding his face against the glass. His eyes widened in pain, bringing the whole of the forest outside the cabin into sharp focus.

Surrounded by a darkened halo of wet earth, a pot-bellied man lay face-first atop Ishen's approach. His shoulders spasmed, releasing a burble of fresh blood from a wound in his side with each involuntary jerk.

Nevin's eyes bulged in their sockets.

In the distance, a shadowy figure stepped out from the trees and into view. Its measured, unhurried pace in the midst of all the violence confused him, like whoever it was somehow couldn't see the person bleeding out in the dirt or the terrified young man pressed up against the cracked glass window.

Something about the distant figure unnerved him. In the dark, he couldn't discern who it was or even what it looked like, but he could *feel* the gaunt figure staring into him.

"I do not *want* to hurt you, Nevin," Vincht repeated, unaware the boy had stopped listening. "One can correct ignorance with knowledge, weakness with hardship, poverty with labor. But one *cannot* correct ugliness. We can cover it up, disguise it, hide it away from the world but no more. We are simply born with beauty, or we are not. Because of this, beauty holds incalculable value and must be preserved if at all possible."

The soldier spun him around, this time grabbing a fistful of his shirt and holding him at arm's length.

"Don't make me do to you what I have done to so many others today, Nevin. There is no compromising my mission. I will go to any length to find this object, whatever it is, and return it to those I serve. And if that means ripping every flower out of the ground from here all the way back to Comelbough, then that is what I will do.

"So if you do not tell me what I need to know, understand, though it would pain me deeply to do so, I will not hesitate to visit such pain and disfigurement upon your person that even the worms will pity your fate."

Vincht was so involved with the sound of his own voice that he failed to realize that Nevin's dumbfounded stare was not for him, but for the someone that stood behind him. Someone that wasn't there a moment ago.

Someone with blue eyes that shined like torches on a moonless night.

A gravelly voice cut the tension like a blade.

"Maybe you'll have a better opinion of the worms once you spend a little time with them."

Chapter 13: The Man in Black

Vincht whirled around, drawing his ivory-handled blade in one smooth motion and extending its gleaming edge toward the intruder.

Nevin didn't budge from his spot against the window, his adrenaline-honed attention lost in the sight before him. Radiant blue eyes considered them both from afar, shining out from beneath the darkness of a drooping cowl, still and piercingly serious. The figure presented as little more than a hulking shadow, draped in floor-dragging black nubuck, the fabric soaking up the lantern light like a hole in reality. The southern edge of a mahogany mask covered the cinch at the cloak's throat, a simple horizontal mouth slit the only visible decoration.

"You're actually *real* . . ." Nevin whispered through bloodless lips.

The blue orbs narrowed, and the cowl dipped in a shallow nod. "Been hearing that a lot today."

There's no way. He couldn't have heard that.

"That's a pretty sword," the man in black said, cocking his head in amusement. "And you're even holding it right. Daddy must have paid for some private lessons, I see."

Eyes like slits, Vincht glared at the man in black, caught off guard by both his unexpected appearance and backhanded compliment. He glanced out the window and then back to the newcomer. "How did you get in here, Wizard? I have armed men surrounding this cabin on all sides. Someone should have signaled me."

The cloak parted, and a wooden cudgel and broken reflex bow clattered to the floor. The cudgel skidded across the floorboards to stop within inches of Nevin's boots.

Vincht muttered profanities under his breath, cursing a person named 'Rowen' emphatically. "Both of them?"

"All three." The man in black chuckled. "Not exactly surrounding."

Nevin cast a furtive glance at the club. His exit was blocked, and Vincht stood too close for him to get a running start at the window, but putting a weapon of any kind between himself and the two men had to be a better alternative to playing defenseless farm boy.

Still, if it came to violence, and the man in black decided he was an enemy, Nevin knew there wasn't a weapon in the world that would prevent him from joining the other body currently spilling its lifeblood into the ferns in front of Ishen's cabin.

When he raised his eyes again, the man in black was staring straight at him. The cowl moved side to side, a silent warning.

Don't try it, it said.

Nevin swallowed, offering his own nod of understanding. *Message received.*

The black-haired soldier slid back a step, keeping Nevin in his peripherals as he put some distance between himself and the newcomer. "A grave mistake, Wizard. Those were the Baron's men you killed. You play at being a hero, but what do you think he'll do to this town when he discovers one of its members murdered a number of his guard?"

Wizard? Was it possible Vincht had no idea who he was dealing with?

The man in black shrugged. "No worse than what you and yours have done today."

Vincht tugged at the hem of his vest and cleared his throat, his sword tip wavering. "I've done what's necessary."

Unrelenting anxiety twisted Nevin's guts into knots. He couldn't remember the last time he blinked, his eyes dry and stinging as they darted back and forth between the verbally dueling men. Each time he thought Vincht wasn't paying attention, he shifted ever so slightly away from him, hoping the opportunity to dive through the study door and into freedom would eventually present itself.

"Necessary," the man in black spat the word from his mouth like so much rotten meat. "Necessary means breaking into an old man's house and terrorizing a helpless boy? Necessary means the murder of countless innocents?"

Vincht stilled. "Whatever it takes to ensure man's ultimate dominion over false gods and the charlatans they empower."

His empty hand lashed out, bridging the space Nevin had built between them and grabbed the younger man by the back of his shirt. He jerked him from his feet, sliding deftly around behind him and laying the flat of his gleaming blade along the tender skin of Nevin's exposed neck. Its light touch drew a painless line of crimson on his skin. A single drop of blood scuttled down the length of the sword to dangle precariously from its tip.

"Now, Nevin," Vincht said into his ear, sneering. "You're going to finish telling me where I can find the object I'm looking for. You're going to tell me, and we're going to go get it. We're going to get it together. And after I have it safely in my possession, the two of us are going to take it back to Comelbough.

"And if anyone gets in my way," he continued, pointing his sword directly at the man in black, "will have his blood of their hands. Have I made myself clear, hero?"

"Stop calling me hero," the man in black growled, edging forward.

Nevin could hear Vincht gnashing his teeth in frustration. "Did you not hear me? I will quite literally tear this boy in half if you don't *back off*!"

I'm dead. Tears gathered at the base of his eyelids, blurring his vision as they prepared to make a run down his cheeks. How he envied their freedom.

The darkness behind the man in black flickered and shifted, and Nevin thought he could see the outline of a gaunt figure materialize in the doorway. It watched him silently, drinking in his fear and helplessness through unseen eyes. A pale hand reached out to him from the shadows, its fingertips glistening black in the modest light.

Nevin felt his own hand lift of its own accord, reaching out across the open space of the study to accept whatever help the gaunt figure could offer.

And that's when the window finally shattered.

Jagged shards of glass careened past him. Pieces hit the wall, the floor, the shelves, Vincht, himself, tinkling like chimes in a windstorm.

A whirling ball of teeth and fur slammed into Vincht's exposed back, throwing Nevin free and bearing the surprised soldier to the floor.

Nevin covered his face with his hands and dove to safely, slamming against the wall. A groan fluttered through his pursed lips. The impact jarred loose an amethyst geode, and Nevin rolled out of the way as it thunked to the floor right where his head had been.

Vincht's sword spilled from his grasp as he tried to fend off the snarling whirlwind of pain. The man in black lunged backward, his cloak flung wide with the arrival of a sicklesque blade.

Screams of surprise rapidly gave way to squeals of agony as the soldier struggled to fight off the tenacious lynx. Claws met flesh as the cat raked into

Vincht's face again and again and again, retaining his grip by latching onto the man's skull with his toothy maw. Realizing his fists weren't doing the job, Vincht's blood-slick hands fumbled at his belt.

"Aidux, he's got a knife!" Nevin screamed.

Metal flashed in the weak light, but Aidux was already gone.

The cat skidded across the floor, every hair on end as he placed himself between the wounded soldier and his closest friend. Red-tinted saliva dripped from his teeth, and the whole of his front was matted with blood. The cat's shoulders raised and lowered in rapid timing with his breath.

Shivering uncontrollably, Vincht rose to his knees. Chunks of meat dangled from long gouges where his cheeks and forehead had been, showing white where claws had met bone. His eyes had miraculously survived the attack. To his credit, Vincht made no sound as he stared slack-jawed into his shaking, blood-drenched palms.

He fumbled through the glass, struggling to gain purchase on the hilt of his sword. Aidux bristled.

The man in black stepped forward, raising his sword high overhead.

"Wait!" Nevin screamed, throwing up a hand.

The man in black shot him a smoldering glare, but didn't advance.

Vincht cradled the sword in his open palms, peering down at the gleaming, mirror-like blade. He tilted it this way and that, adjusting the surface until the wreckage of his face looked back at him.

An agonized wail burst from ruined lips. Nevin cringed at the sound, burying his face in Aidux's side.

Vincht squeezed the bare blade in his hands, spilling fresh blood down his wrists and forearms. He grit his teeth, still screaming, pain morphing into rage. Nevin peeked out beneath the cat, locking eyes with the shredded soldier one final time.

"That's enough." The man in black brought his sword back up, prepared to finish the job the lynx had started.

Vincht's screaming abruptly ceased, and he dove head first out the broken window and into the open forest beyond.

Chapter 14: What's a Little Talking Cat?

Through the broken window, the man in black cut a dark silhouette against the backdrop of the forest. The near night conditions beneath the tangled canopy appeared bright and welcoming in comparison. His telltale glowing eyes panned the overgrowth, twin blue searchlights burning for some sign of the quarry whose lifeblood stained the wood throughout the study.

From inside, Nevin crouched beside the lynx and watched the man in black vanish around the outside of the cabin. He turned away from the broken window, fighting to ignore the dead body growing cold just outside the reach of the sea of ferns encircling the rustic cabin. His stomach was already twisted in enough knots, and he knew if he looked too long at the soldier's corpse, he wouldn't be able to stop the day's steady accumulation of acid and bile from rising up to fill his mouth and throat.

Something else was bothering him. He cast a sideways glance at the study's now empty doorway. When Vincht had pressed him up against the window, Nevin was certain he'd seen another figure approaching the cabin. The same figure had appeared again in the moments after Vincht had threatened his life, but no one else in the room had seemed to notice its presence, and the figure had completely vanished by the time Vincht dove out the window.

He chewed his lip thoughtfully. In the stress of the moment, had he been imagining things? Were the hallucinatory dreams caused by his head injury now bleeding over into the real world? Nightmares of being tortured by Dalen and dreams of disembodied voices confusing him were one thing. Now he had to worry about shadow people?

The light glinted weakly off something resting on the floor just beyond the study's entrance. He suspected it was little more than a bit of broken glass, but his mind welcomed the distraction, and he soon found himself crossing the disheveled room to investigate.

Sitting on the floor, just out of reach of the halo of lantern light, was Dalen's bronze canteen.

Nevin stumbled in surprise, bowling over a nearby pillar of books.

That's not possible. I lost that canteen back at the silver maple. How could it have made its way here!?!?

He rubbed his eyes, thoroughly convinced this new development was little more than another unfortunate symptom of a suspected concussion. Blackouts, memory loss, weird dreams, and now full-blown hallucinations. What other explanation could there be for the sudden appearance of a shadowy figure and the canteen he had purposefully left behind?

Aidux rested on his haunches, casually wiping away the blood drenching his golden fur in long, patient slurps. Had Nevin not been so distracted, he may have been disgusted by the scene playing out before him. The cat, though, barely acknowledged the devastation all around, content to silently bathe away all evidence of his participation in the day's violence.

"What do you think he wants?" the cat mused between licks.

"He?" Nevin asked, forcing himself to focus on something other than the obvious hallucination crying out for his attention just beyond the door.

"Yeah, 'he'. Him? The guy with glowing eyes." The cat flicked an ear. "He seems nice."

"Nice?" Nevin poked him in the neck. "He nearly murdered that guy. If I hadn't stopped him . . ."

Aidux shrugged, running his tongue between the toes of a paw before answering. "He doesn't like the soldiers. We don't like the soldiers. The way I see it, that makes us friends. That's like . . . math, I think."

He waved a hand toward the broken window. "He just glared at me and stormed outside. Do you think he's angry?"

"About what?"

"I don't know. I don't think he's happy that Vincht got away."

Aidux glanced up from his licking and sniffed. "He smelled pretty calm to me."

"Can't believe I let you stop me," the man in black growled, stomping through the cabin toward the study. Bits of glass jostled and bounced on the floor, reflecting geometric bolts of lamplight along the walls and ceiling.

Cocking his head, Aidux wiggled his nose. He pressed a paw to his muzzle and took a long draft through widened nostrils before shrugging.

"That's . . . weird."

"Be quiet." Nevin hushed him with firm hand to the muzzle. Shuffling around the cat, he placed his body directly between Aidux and the study door. His legs were all river foam and cold sweat, and justifiably so, considering the identity of dark swordsman heading their way.

The man in black stopped just inside the doorway, plopping Nevin's leather satchel on the floor between them without a word.

Nevin swallowed the rocks in his throat before speaking. "I know who you are."

"Gathered as much," he grunted, nodding slightly. "Be more surprised if you didn't."

The lynx gingerly padded through the scattered glass to stand beside Nevin and frowned, clearly unimpressed by the young man's chivalrous protection efforts. "Can someone gather me as much? 'Cuz I have no clue who he is."

Nevin shot him a withering look. "Aidux!"

"He's got glowing eyes, Nevin! Like his head's filled with starflies or something." The cat sank gingerly onto his haunches, careful not to get a shard of glass in his rear. "Next to that, what's a little talking cat?"

Nevin opened his mouth in protest, but the man in black cut him off.

"Stop. Both of you. I don't actually care."

He leaned against the door jam, crossing his arms beneath the cloak with an annoyed sigh. "Not actually the first talking animal I've seen. Not even the first talking cat."

As the dark warrior tilted his head back, the lantern's glow fully penetrated the drooping hood, giving Nevin a clear look at the mahogany mask beneath. Carved from a single piece of tarnished wood, the mask completely covered the man's face, aside from one narrow mouth slit and a pair of oval cut-outs for eyes. A ridged brow and exaggerated cheekbones granted the piece an elongated skull-like appearance. A prominent diagonal gash split the right cheek and mouth hole in twain, with a small wedge of chin missing where the gash ended.

The lynx huffed, squirming in place. "Will one of you *please* tell me who he . . . you are?"

The man didn't respond, looking to Nevin to answer the cat's question.

"This—," he began, sweeping a hand toward the dark warrior before them. "—is Theis Bane. The most wanted man in the Lancowl Barony, and probably the most infamous swordsman that ever lived."

The lynx flicked an ear. "Why 'infamous'? Why not 'the most *famous* swordsman that ever lived'? That sounds nicer."

Theis grunted. "Because famous people are *liked*."

"Oh, okay then," Aidux said, appearing inexplicably relieved by that introduction. "Well, Mr. Bane—"

"Theis."

"—Mr. Theis, my name is Aidux. I'm a cat. Well, a lynx, specifically, if you couldn't tell by the ears. It's the tufts. Dead giveaway. I'm pretty much the sneakiest thing in the forest. Been here my whole life and the only person that knows about me is Nevin here. And you, I guess, since you're also in the forest."

A wave of pressure bubbled up to fill the space between Nevin's ears, somehow both pushing outward and pulling inward all at once. Eyes wide, he worked his jaw open and closed, taken aback by the chaotic blur of images springing out from the shadows of his subconscious.

"Give it back," spat the sneering Dalen, wobbling on his feet. The barn stank of stale body odor and sulfur, a side effect of the fermentation process. Dalen hefted a naked ax handle, batting aside a tattered rope dangling from a low girder.

"Give it back, or things are gonna get real bad for ya."

"This here's Nevin." He placed a paw on the young man's thigh. His touch banished the visions and with it, the sudden, overwhelming pressure. "He's a boy. Or . . . maybe a man? I don't get how that works, yet. Cats are just cats, unless they're cubs, and then they're cubs until they get their first kill. Nevin's still a boy then, because he hasn't made his first kill. That's always been my job."

Aidux shrugged. "Then again, maybe it's not the same for peoples."

"Is where I come from," said Theis grimly.

Nevin waved the cat into silence. "This doesn't make any sense. Yes, I've heard of you. *From books.* Books older than me. You're more fairy tale than person. And hasn't it been . . . I don't know . . . almost a decade since the Baron put a price on your head?"

Theis simply nodded, allowing Nevin to continue without interruption. "I mean, even if everything I've read was true, even if you were a teenager in those early stories, that was . . ."

He tossed his hands up, pacing the floor as he spoke. "Half a century ago? You're telling me you're in your seventies? Your eighties?"

The man in black snorted derisively. "And you're what . . . twelve? Seen more hair on a trout than you've got on your chin."

Scowling, Nevin bit his tongue.

"I'm eight," chimed Aidux, happy to be included.

Theis pressed his fingertips to the forehead of his mask and took a step into the study, cursing under his breath. "We've no time for this. More soldiers are bound to come here sooner or later. Isn't much town left, and some already know about this little cabin. Probably stumbling this way as we speak."

"What do you mean, 'there isn't much town left'? Elbin's pretty spread out. I don't know that half a day is enough time to even *find* every homestead, let alone search them."

"Saw their camp. Brought enough eyes with them to cover the area in short order." Theis shook his head. "What I mean is, there isn't much of *Elbin* left to search."

"I don't understand. You just said the same thing, again. You're not making sense."

The man in black balked. "*Khek,* boy, can you not feel it in your chest?"

"Feel . . . what?" The cloistered atmosphere within the study suppressed all but the scents of dried herbs and smoky tallow—Ishen had made sure of that. He shot a quizzical look at the lynx, but the cat was already sniffing the air. The blacks of his silver eyes ballooned until almost no color was left.

"Smoke?" the cat chirped.

Theis nodded. "They aren't just going house to house, getting pushy with the locals. What happened here, in this cabin, was mild compared to what's happening elsewhere. Been ghosting them all day, and at every single farm I've visited, been the same story."

Nevin shook his head, still not understanding. "Elbin—"

Theis slammed his fist down on the desk's angled surface hard enough to crack the wood. "Elbin doesn't exist anymore! When they didn't find what they were looking for, they burnt down the farms and killed their owners. Can't see it from here, but there are fires raging all over the woods.

"By day's end, all that will remain of Elbin is smoldering ash . . . and this vacant little cabin."

Chapter 15: Fate, or . . . ?

Nevin's eyes narrowed until his eyelids nearly touched. He studied the expressionless mask of the man in black and quietly chewed the evidence.

Could I have really been so clueless?

Thinking back, he remembered the persistent haze hanging over the woods at every turn, but the strangeness of his predicament—added to the proximity of two of the baron's soldiers—had distracted him away from prying too hard into its source. A growing ache penetrated his skull, boring its way into his brain and threatening to tear away the present and replace it with some questionable image masquerading as a moment of missing time.

"No," he almost shouted, shaking his head so hard his neck muscles ached in protest. "That's not possible. Elbin's a part of the barony. We might be way out here in the sticks, barely worth sending a tax collector to every few years, but we're still a province under the protection of the Lancowls. Why would the Baron, *our* Baron, send his men to torch a village he's responsible for? That doesn't make sense."

"Does if you assume the Baron didn't send them."

Nevin hugged his chest, careful not to exacerbate his injured shoulder. The muscles were a little stiff, but didn't otherwise complain. He was impressed by how quickly it was returning to normal. "No, but . . . but I heard them talking myself. One of them specifically made mention of being the Baron's soldiers."

Theis nodded. "Some are. Some are conscripts I'm sure, or even soldiers in training. Mercenaries too, possibly. Not the Baron's best though, but sufficient enough for the area. Ran into a pair out in the woods less than an hour ago. One told me the Baron assigned their group to a man named Vincht, a man he claimed wasn't a soldier in the Lancowl's employ.

"Now, I don't know who this Vincht really is, but after dealing with him here, listening to the way he spoke and how he carried himself, I have my suspicions. Doubt the Baron had any idea what he was sending his men to do. Likely owed a debt to either Vincht himself or an organization he's a part of, and was obligated to offer support when requested."

Aidux picked his teeth, his silver peepers moving back and forth between Theis and his friend. Nevin did his best to ignore the pointed slurps, not wanting to add the idea of the lynx casually dining on human flesh to his already troubled thoughts.

Theis matched Nevin's stance, folding his arms beneath his cloak. The motes in his eyes swirled tightly around their pupils. "It's the 'why' that really concerns me."

"Why what?"

"Why they're *here*, boy. Or more specifically, how they knew what they were looking for was here. Been trying to figure that one out all day."

That got Nevin's attention. "You know what they're looking for?"

The man in black nodded, slowly, deliberately. "Man I interrogated showed me a drawing. Crude, but unmistakable. They all carried one."

The younger man took a hesitant step forward, glass crunching underfoot. "And you think it's here?"

"Mmm."

"Like . . . *here* here?"

Again, he nodded. "Problem is, the old man could have hidden it anywhere. Buried it beneath a tree. Stuffed it in a hollowed out log in the walls. Tucked it under the cabin itself."

He sighed, annoyed. "It's here, I just don't know where."

"What makes you say that? Why here, in Ishen's cabin, and not anywhere else in Elbin?"

Theis stared long and hard at Nevin, the motes in his piercing blue eyes jerking this way and that as he considered his next words carefully. "Because I'm the one that brought it here."

Ishen, what did you get yourself into?

Nevin glanced down at the gap in the floorboard, trying to picture just exactly what was hidden inside that shadowed hole. Something was down there alright. He could still feel that cold, an unbearable chill that burrowed through the flesh and blood and bone to freeze him to his very core. A wave of gooseflesh tore down his arms at the memory.

Whatever it was, Vincht wanted it, and badly enough to kill. And now Theis wanted it too. Ishen had gone to some lengths to keep it hidden, and for how long? That mold-crusted blanket bore stains and fungal growth likely years in the making.

And then there was the method of its discovery. A box he'd never seen before, tied to a set of loose boards with a single strand of black thread. Those boards had fit perfectly into the gap in the floor, flush and functionally invisible to the naked eye. Only someone who already knew of the hiding place could possibly have found it without methodically dismembering the entire room, one piece at a time. Ishen had tied that book to the floor for only one reason he could think of: so that whoever picked it up would also reveal the hole.

As Nevin suspected he was the only other person his old mentor had ever allowed in his study, the only other person allowed to handle his precious collection of books, maybe the only other person in the whole of Elbin that could even *read*, he could only surmise that Ishen had orchestrated the discovery of the gap in the floorboards—and whatever lies within—specifically with his young student in mind.

Nevin closed his eyes, pinching the bridge of his nose with his fingers as if using the pressure to anchor his swirling thoughts. Then again, maybe he was confusing coincidence for causation.

Bad days happened. *Really* bad days, days stringing one unfortunate occurrence onto the next, happened less often . . . but on a long enough timeline, a truly disastrous day—one capable of fundamentally altering a person's path or direction in life—was bound to come along for a certain percentage of the population.

But this day . . . Nevin felt it would be *more* foolish to blame such a terrible confluence of events on bad luck or simple happenstance. The timing of it all just didn't add up. So much had happened in but a few hours; his problem with Dalen, the Baron's constabulary, the burning of Elbin, the sudden return of the 'infamous' Theis Bane, Ishen's disappearance, and now this.

No way, he thought. *Not even coincidence was this . . . coincidental.*

"What's wrong?" Theis said, studying Nevin's face closely.

With a sigh, the younger man brushed aside the scattered shards of glass dusting the floor with the sole of his boot. Aidux hopped up from beside him and padded over to the corner of the room, turning about in a circle before stretching out in one of the few clear spaces remaining in the decimated study.

"Do you believe in Fate, Theis?"

The man in black snorted. "A catch-all for the foolish and the impotent to blame their problems on. My destiny is mine to control, through my strength and intelligence, not some glorified librarian and his magic books, half a world away."

Nevin placed two hands on the angled writing desk and planted his feet. He hadn't really noticed it before, but a number of flattened scrolls were spread across its surface. He recognized the top most slip of paper; a crude map of the peninsula, illustrating only the region's most recognizable features—the Traagen Woods, the town of Elbin, the Hyret Gorge, the southern road and bridge, the Nimmon Thrust to the north, and an uppercase 'I' no doubt referencing Ishen's own cabin.

In a small space to the north, where the river emerged from the Nimmons, Ishen had drawn an irregular circle, notating the spot with a single familiar word: Narloc.

I already know about your stupid mountain chimeras, Ishen. Not helpful.

Grunting, Nevin shoved the desk aside. It warbled like a snow goose as it ground against the polished floor. Its relocation revealed the gap in the floorboards to the man in black, who couldn't have been aware of its location from his position in the doorway. Like the desk had been placed there expressly to shield it from casual view.

Wiping his sweaty hands on his shirt, Nevin peered down into the hole. "You're talking about the Keeper, right? The man charged with reading the Tomes of Fate and directing world events. I always thought he was just a story. He's real, too?"

"As real as any other charlatan." Theis moved up beside him, staring down into the darkness as well. "Why are you asking me these things?"

"Because I'm beginning to suspect that either someone or something has orchestrated today's events to bring the three of us here. You, me, Aidux. Standing right here next to this hole in the floor. It's just too much to be coincidence.

"And if it's not, if everything that's happened *isn't* just the result of random chance and bad timing, I'd rather believe it the work of some emotionless force of existence like Fate. I'd rather believe that the slaughter of innocent farmers is somehow the will of the cosmos, or some hateful god, or even some distant librarian, than to consider the possibility that the only person I know smart enough, patient enough, and with enough inside information into my life, Elbin, and whatever it is that everyone is looking for . . . is the true perpetrator of the day's events."

Nevin dropped to his knees, the muted thud of bone on wood reverberating through the empty cabin. "Because if I thought for a second that Ishen had put this whole thing together, I don't know if I'd ever want to get up off this floor again."

Chapter 16: The Sharasil

"You think . . . *Ishen* . . . is responsible," the man in black said almost rhythmically, obviously taken aback by what he thought was a statement of absolute absurdity.

Nevin ignored him, absentmindedly rubbing his chin and staring down into the three-foot long lightless gap in the floorboards. He wasn't actually looking though, not really. In truth, his mind was lost in a jumbled replay of the day's events, wading through a churning mashup of mishaps and missteps whose unfortunate sum yielded far greater dangers than an appraisal of the individual instances would belie.

None of it made any sense, and the timing of it all . . . Why would the Baron's soldiers go out of their way to set fire to the town? Why would Ishen vanish in the middle of the night, leaving behind his invaluable collection of books—books he claimed were gathered over a lifetime of careful and intentional searching? Why would his old teacher arrange his study so that Nevin, and likely *only* Nevin, would stumble upon an object hidden beneath his cabin for who-knows-how-long?

Theis shook his head and kicked a shard of glass into the hole in the floor. It disappeared without protest, wholly consumed like so many other things that day. "Ishen may be many things—prideful, condescending, an insufferable know-it-all—but he's just as much a victim of the day's events as you and everyone else."

Nevin grunted. *Seems Theis really DOES know my old mentor.*

"So it's just coincidence he managed to escape right before the killing started? You want me to believe that?"

Theis shrugged. "Don't much care what you believe. But if you actually thought Ishen capable of orchestrating, to whatever degree, the destruction of Elbin and the massacre of her residents, I'd begin to wonder how you made it this far in life without tripping over your own feet and caving your skull in on a rock. Have to be a witless moron to believe that."

Nevin's teeth squeaked from grinding them so hard, but he held his tongue. He liked to think that years of being subjected to all kinds of emotional and psychological abuse from Dalen had hardened him against condescension and insults, but the truth was, it never got any easier to hear.

Theis took a breath before continuing, but changed his mind when Nevin stretched out onto his stomach and gingerly dipped his hand into the darkness beneath the cabin. The man in black slid forward half a step and leaned in over him, the motes in his eyes spinning circles around his ballooning pupils. Even Aidux took notice, his tufted ears perking up as he lifted his head to watch his friend.

"That's odd," Nevin pulled his arm out of the hole, frowning.

"What is?" said Aidux, beating Theis to the punch.

"When I reached in here earlier, it was like sticking my hand in a snow bank, but now . . ." He laid back down and continued searching. ". . . I don't know. It's about the same temperature as the rest of the cabin."

Aidux flicked an ear. "Maybe the cold was trapped? Like some snow got under the house and the hot air from up here finally melted it? And then, when you opened the floor, the cold *whooooshed* out and now its gone."

"Maybe . . ." he lied, remembering how the depthless cold had overcome him at the same moment he hit his head and passed out. Could he really have just imagined it? Could the cold have just been a precursor to the strange dream that followed, a remnant of his unconscious imagination that somehow spilled over into his conscious memories?

His palm brushed something different, something smooth and cool to the touch. *Metal.* He bumped it with his fist, hoping it wasn't somehow mounted in place and therefore inaccessible without crawling around in the cabin's foundation, but to his pleasant surprise, the object moved.

He wiggled it around a bit. It was loose.

"Alright you two, back up."

The object, whatever it was, was bulky enough that Nevin could barely get a sufficient grip on it with his fingers, but the surface had an unusual, almost gritty quality that stuck readily to his skin. Grunting with effort, Nevin dragged the object off its perch, tugging and tugging until he could grab it with both hands and awkwardly maneuver it up and out of the hole. He gently placed it on the angled writing desk and stepped back.

Nearly three feet of lusterless metal the shade of thunderclouds during flood season stretched from one end of the oblong object to the other, rounded at the edges and crisscrossed with dozens of thin, arrow-straight grooves. The grooves struck out from an oval-shaped indentation near the center of the object on both sides, splitting into numerous smaller lines that terminated perpendicular to its longest edge. The opposite edge was inset at one end with a white stone handle, visibly coarse and long enough to fit both hands around. Judging by its composition and how thick it was, Nevin would have expected the mysterious object to weigh somewhere north of forty pounds, but in truth, the young man would have had little trouble hefting it with only one hand.

It didn't look like anything he'd ever seen before.

"You removed the blanket?" said Theis, more accusation than question.

"Not intentionally. It was the first thing I touched when I reached in the hole. I would have pulled this out too, but Vincht sort of interrupted me."

"That blanket was there for a reason," he said ominously.

"What . . . is it?" Aidux pawed the air but didn't approach the writing desk.

"The Sharasil," Nevin said without skipping a beat.

Theis whipped his head around. "The *what*?"

Nevin blinked. Both Theis and Aidux were staring intently in his direction. ". . . what?"

"You called it the 'Sharasil'."

"Yeah . . . is that not what it's called?"

"Don't actually know, but a better question is, how would *you* know? Isn't this the first time you've ever seen it?"

Nevin opened his mouth to answer, but the words didn't come. How *did* he know? The name had just popped into his head when Aidux asked what it was, and it hadn't occurred to him to question it, he just blurted it out like he'd known it his entire life.

The word felt awfully familiar, though. Like he'd heard it somewhere recently, but try as he might, he couldn't place it.

"Maybe Vincht said it. I don't know." Nevin wiped a hand down his face and walked over to a plush oaken desk chair propped upside down against the wall. He righted the chair and sank gratefully into it, staring out through the open window to ponder the hulking trees beyond.

The level of Ishen's involvement in the day's events still weighed heavy on his mind. Was Ishen out there right now, hiding away from everything that had happened that morning? Maybe he had successfully made in across the Hyret Bridge before Vincht and his crew had set up camp. Or maybe he was on the run, picking his way through the less hospitable areas of the Traagen Woods, trapped like Nevin and Aidux but protected by the safety of distance.

Or maybe . . . none of those were true. Maybe the truth was far darker than Nevin wanted to admit or even imagine. Maybe the truth would put into question over a decade of trust and friendship and—

STOP HIM!

The voice boomed out from the depths of his subconscious, shattering his previous thoughts into a million pieces and propelling him unwillingly to his feet.

Theis was already in the process of reaching out to grab the white stone handle of the mysterious object. Nevin didn't pause to question the voice, he simply acted, willing his feet to move and parting his lips in preparation for the single word of warning that was rising up from the base of his throat.

That was as far as he made it before the world erupted in a scorching red light.

Chapter 17: Get Smart or Die Stupid

An angry crimson glow washed over the storm-tinted metal object, bathing the shadowed room in various shades of piercing red light. The object blurred and shifted, like it was vibrating wildly atop the angled writing desk, but it neither fell nor changed position in the slightest. Beads of sweat sprang to the surface of Nevin's arms and neck, and his eyes burned in their sockets.

A faint ringing filled the disheveled study, not heard so much as felt, reverberating in the back of the skull, sounding distinctly from inside the object in question. Aidux recoiled in pain, his mouth stretched wide in protest, but the quiet ringing somehow drowned out his plaintive, high-pitched yowl.

Suddenly, a clap of thunder.

A flash of orange light.

Theis flying backward, his body crumpled forward, a trail of smoke in his wake.

The flash blinded Nevin, and the thunderous boom both deafened and disoriented him. White enveloped his sight as he stumbled toward the spot he last saw Theis, unaware that the man in black was currently half-way across the study, steaming and smoking and balled up at the shattered base of one of Ishen's bookshelves. Nevin frantically grasped at the air, tears of panic forming in the corners of his wide, unblinking eyes.

But, almost as rapidly as it arose, the blistering heat faded. The terrible ringing quieted. The white film occluding his vision slowly began to clear.

As a welcome chill washed over him, Nevin fought to gain control of his rapid breathing, hoping it would in turn still his racing heart. He squinted, searching the study through the dissipating haze of white smoke.

Theis was in the process of extricating himself from the rubble of the bookshelf, brushing aside fragments of shattered wood and stepping over an engraved fox skull that had somehow survived their calamitous encounter. His right arm still smoked, the outer layer of his leather glove a tattered mess. He appraised his steaming hand and gingerly flexed his shaking fingers.

Nevin shook his head in amazement. Despite the force of the explosion, the man in black appeared none the worse for wear.

Is he even human?

It took him a few seconds to find Aidux. All he could see of the cat was the tops of his ears and his wide, silver peepers, poking up over the southern edge of Ishen's now broken window from the safety of the cabin's front approach. Nevin sighed in relief.

"*Khek*, boy. Have you lost your wits?""

Theis was frozen in place, his eyes vibrating with an alarming intensity as he stared down the younger man.

Nevin could only frown.

A single gloved finger pointed to the contents of his hands. Confused, Nevin looked down. To his horror, the young man found himself standing right beside the angled writing desk, unwittingly cradling the mysterious object across both arms like a newborn babe. A cloud of visible mist exited his lips with each breath.

"When did I . . ."

His arms jerked apart, dumping the metal object at his feet. Instead of bouncing as it settled into place, it hit the floor with a dull, lifeless thud and immediately stilled. His breath returned to its normal, invisible state, but Nevin kept both hands overhead, unsure what the pair might do if left to their own devices.

"Nearly blew off my hand," Theis mused, barely loud enough to be heard in the quiet study. "But it didn't react to you at all."

Nevin shuffled back from the discarded object, quickly putting as much space between him and it as he could before his backside collided with the wall. "I didn't mean to. Grab it, I mean. I didn't mean to grab it. I wouldn't. I couldn't even *see* it, what with all the smoke and light."

He shook his head and nervously rubbed an arm. "I must have just bumped into it and picked it up as it fell. Not on purpose. That . . . that wouldn't make any sense, right? That thing blew you across the room! If I could have seen what I was doing, I wouldn't have gone anywhere near it."

Through the broken window, the cat's ears flicked off to one side before Aidux vanished beneath the sill. His departure barely registered in Nevin's mind, startled as he was by his own out-of-place actions. He hadn't even felt the cold metal stealing the warmth from his hands, hadn't even felt the oblong object pressing against his midsection as he cradled it tightly to his body, not really, not until the man in black had pointed it out to him.

Theis crossed the room and sank into a low crouch, hunching over the object like a vulture come to roost. He thoughtfully rubbed the gouge in the chin of his mask. Nevin slid along the wall away from the two, expecting another strong reaction to his proximity and wanting to be as far away as possible when it happened.

But the object just sat quietly.

Theis tentatively extended a gloved hand, holding it level with the top of his head. He slowly lowered the hand, wiggling his fingers as he inched closer and closer. He paused every few seconds, his blazing eyes never lifting from his target, continually accessing its storm-gray surface for any change, small or large.

Nevin, though, watched him, mesmerized not only by the possibility of another dramatic end to the man in black's actions, but also by his apparent lack of fear in the face of what could only be described as an overtly destructive magical force. The man nearly lost a hand before. How could he be so casually curious?

When Theis' passed within a foot of the object, its surface abruptly changed. The gray metal exuded that piercing red light, as though someone had just pulled it from beneath a smoking heap of glowing coal. The man in black moved his hand no closer, holding it still and observing the reaction.

"O-Okay, Theis," Nevin's face scrunched as a high-pitched ringing filled the room. He shoved a finger in each ear, but it didn't help. The temperature in the study rose a few degrees with every passing moment, but Theis held fast.

"I t-t-think that's enough. Please."

He squeezed his head between trembling palms, but the ringing pushed through. The heat washed over him and beads of sweat bled from his pores.

"Theis!" he screamed, and the man flinched, returning his hand to the darkness beneath his leather cloak. The object quieted, and the room was still once more.

"*Khek.*" Theis straightened with a heavy sigh. "Can't be sure if the weapon is responding negatively to me, or if it will do so in response to anyone but yourself."

Nevin blinked. "Weapon?"

Theis ignored him. "What's your plan here, boy?"

"Don't call me 'boy'," he managed through a tightening jaw.

Theis gestured out the window without turning. "Elbin's gone. Vincht and his men have effectively wiped it off the map, and if the fires continue to grow, the entire Traagen is in danger of the same. Might be that this little cabin is the only dwelling still standing, and it's already empty. Soldiers are combing the forest, and it's only a matter of time before more find this place."

His tone soured. "And, because of you, because of your interruption, Vincht—the leader of this band of soldiers—was allowed to escape, and from the little I heard as I arrived, he seems convinced that you know exactly where what he seeks is hidden.

"I know his kind. Men like that don't give up, not when things get difficult, not when they get hurt, not when there's even the smallest chance they might succeed. They keep coming, over and over again, until they win . . . or they're dead."

Nevin's fists vibrated against his thighs. "Then he can have it! Why would I want anything to do with it? I'll even leave it by the gorge so he doesn't have to search anymore."

"And when he realizes he can't touch it without losing an arm?"

"Well, life sucks, doesn't it? That's his problem, not mine."

The man in black chuckled. "Can't seriously be this stupid, *boy*."

Fire swelled in his chest, and Nevin lashed out with a boot, kicking the angled writing desk back to its rightful place against the wall. Already damaged by its proximity to the Sharasil's violent magical reaction, the wooden desk couldn't withstand the blow and broke apart mid-slide.

A stabbing pain in his ribs stole his breath, and Nevin sank to his knees. He clutched at his side and scowled at the floorboards. As his anger gradually cooled, his eyes sought out that shaded hole in the floor, wanting nothing more than to drag himself beneath the cabin to be forgotten about.

The man in black's drawn out sigh was laden with disappointment. "Spent enough time in the Traagen to know there's nowhere to hide, not from someone who really wants to find you, and once Vincht realizes he doesn't have the means to transport the Sharasil, you'll be the next person he goes looking for. And he *will* find you, make no mistake.

"You're just a wet-behind-the-ears farm boy. You've no shelter. No food stores. No supplies. No weapons. No allies but a talking cat. And Vincht? He has men, time, resources, training. And the advantage always lies with the tracker, not the tracked."

Nevin refused to look at him, refused to raise his head and meet the man's eyes, refused to let the callous stranger see the twin streams of tears running down his flushed cheeks. As frustrating as it was, he had to admit the man was right. About everything. He was completely out of options, and completely in over his head.

Without the bridge, Nevin was as good as dead. Be that at the hand of Vincht and his soldiers, the harshness of a Traagen Languor, or hiking through the unforgiving Nimmons to the north in search of some means of leaving the peninsula behind. If he could sneak into town to gather some equipment—some dried meat, potable water, a few tools—maybe he'd have the *smallest* of chances, but if Theis was right about the fires, even that was off the table.

The man in black cocked his head and stepped toward him. "Didn't catch that. Come again?"

Nevin rose to his feet and cleared his throat before repeating himself. "I don't have a plan, and I don't want to die."

Twin blue eyes burned into him, the white motes scattered in the sea of light. "Then pick it up and follow me. We're leaving."

Nevin recoiled from the discarded object. "No way. I want nothing to do with that thing."

"Not giving you a choice, boy. Came here to get it. Not leaving without it."

The younger man folded his arms across his chest defiantly. "I don't care what you do, but I'm not going anywhere with that thing."

"Want to die on that hill? Fine then. Stay behind and that'll happen. How's that for an option?"

Nevin chewed his lip and let out a long, frustrated sigh. As much as he hated to admit it, Theis had him cornered.

There was only one problem. "It doesn't even matter. There's still only one way off the peninsula, and unless you've got a pair of giant wings hidden beneath that cloak, you're just as screwed as I am."

From the darkness of the kitchen, the lynx emerged, slinking into the room with his ears laid back against his skull. The way he sheepishly looked back and forth between his oldest friend and his newest, it was clear he could sense the tension in the room.

Theis shook his head. "There's one other way, but it's a hard walk through trackless forest."

Nevin's eyes narrowed. "Bullshit. Where?"

"Through the Nimmons to the north."

The younger man paused momentarily before responding, carefully watching the motes in Theis' eyes as they swirled lazily around their pupils. If the man was lying, he couldn't tell. "Ishen told me long ago that the Hyret Bridge is the only way into or out of Elbin. I have a hard time believing you know something about the area that he doesn't."

Theis shrugged. "Don't give a shit what you believe, boy. But I'll make you this promise: come with me, and I'll keep you alive for as long as I am able. Make sure you met the old woman in one piece."

Finally, unable to wait any longer, the cat swallowed the lump in his throat and spoke. "Would now be a good time or a bad time to tell you there are men out in the woods, a big group of them, heading this way? I think maybe being here isn't a good idea anymore."

Theis nodded in agreement. "Time to get smart or die stupid. What's it gonna be, boy?"

Nevin's jaw tightened until his teeth squeaked.

Not much of a choice.

Chapter 18: Lucky

Yawning, Nevin forced his eyelids open, straining not only against the weight of exhaustion, but also to see the nearly invisible form of Theis against the darkness gathered beneath the treetops of the Upper Traagen. How the man in black could so easily pick his way through the increasingly hilly terrain without slowing to find his footing made Nevin jealous. It felt like the ground threatened to sweep him from his feet if he took more than five steps without pausing to look down, and each time he did, he lost sight of the constantly moving man in black.

The ceaseless murmur of cicadas chased them as they fled north, rising and falling in intensity as the three maneuvered their way through the creatures' midst. The effects of that morning's rain lingered, the soft dirt sinking beneath his boots in places where it should crumble instead. A gust of chill wind swept past them, thick with the crystalline scent of melting snow.

Nevin hugged his chest and shivered. Like he'd told Aidux that morning, the season was still too young for late night treks into the northern woods, but the day's events had stolen any choice he'd had in the matter. Still, it wasn't the cold that chilled him. Something else had him on edge, something other than the soldiers chasing them, something . . . intangible.

Wincing in pain, he loosened his grip on his wounded ribs. Maybe it was the heavy curtain of night. Maybe it was the threat of who may or may not be following them, but Nevin couldn't shake the feeling the three of them weren't alone.

"You okay over there, Aidux?"

"Ready for a nap," the cat said, his child-like voice no more than a breathy whisper as he wadded through the swishing ferns beside Nevin. "Which is super weird being as how I'm supposed to be nightural."

"Once again, the word is 'noctural'."

Aidux flicked an ear at him. "It sounds funny when you say it."

"That's because I say it right."

"Well, my feets are singin' and my eyes are droopsey, but I'm okay if you're okay." He turned and looked up at his friend. "How *are* you doing? Legs getting all itchy by now, huh?"

"Uncomfortably so, but I'm making do." Nevin scratched at the tops of his thighs, the constant thrum of blood pouring through his muscles creating an odd tickling sensation that always showed up during long treks through the woods. Scratching never helped, but it felt weird not to try. "Can I ask you a weird question?"

"All of your questions are weird."

"When you were outside the cabin, before you jumped through the window, did you happen to see anyone else out in the forest? Someone dressed in dark clothing, maybe?"

"Someone like Theis?"

Nevin mixed a shrug with a nod. "Yeah, kinda."

"In that case, no."

That settles it. If Aidux hadn't spotted the shadowy figure approaching Ishen's cabin from the forest, then there was no way it could have been real; an unwelcome holdover from a particularly nasty head injury. That meant his current itchy suspicions regarding a hidden voyeur were likely little more than a combination of stress and a healing brain.

He shook his head at his own silliness and chuckled. *Which meant the canteen wasn't there either.* Then again, what was the alternative? That a ghost had plucked it from the silver maple and lugged it all the way to Ishen's to torment him?

Pretty stupid, he thought, the smile wilting on his lips.

His overloaded belt pouch bit into his side every now and then, the soft leather stretched around the pointed corners of Ishen's unfamiliar ironwood box. The container's mystique persevered as a result of the untimely arrival of additional soldiers outside the cabin. There had been no time to search the upended study for a key that fit the lock, and even if Theis grew a heart and let them rest for a moment, Nevin had no tools capable of picking the lock, and the near-total blackness beneath the trees meant he'd be operating on feel alone as it was.

He turned his eyes to the canopy above, uttering a quiet curse at Theis for forcing him to leave behind that simple shielded lantern.

It'll slow you down, he'd said dismissively, snatching the lantern from Nevin's hand and jamming it down on Ishen's kitchen table. *And anyone with an eye will see you in the dark. Can't protect you from everything, boy.*

Nevin made a face. *I'd have argued harder if I'd remembered tonight was a null moon.*

The closer their group got to the northern timberline, the fewer trees there would be. Already, the weaker silver maples had ceded their territory to the narrower and hardier tower pines, an exchange that would eventually thin the canopy and allow more light to fill the forest floor than many places in the lower elevations. And yet, if Nevin remembered correctly, the two rings of Etro were in descent; they wouldn't be visible again for at least two days, and their absence would greatly reduce the moon's pale blue radiance.

Up ahead, he heard the man in black bark a curse.

"Been a long day for everyone, I guess."

He adjusted his pack for the hundredth time, but nothing would alleviate the awkwardness of the bulky object strapped across his shoulders. The oddly cool metal brushing against the back of his bare neck with every step added to the already chill evening, but it was the uneven distribution of the item's weight that wore on him. Most of the object's weight was gathered near the coarse stone handle, and because of that, he found himself listing awkwardly to one side as he walked.

Like having one leg longer than the other. His thighs burned not only at the effort of stumbling up and down the uneven terrain, but also from constantly working to even his gait.

A part of him wanted to reach over his shoulder and loosen the two leather straps holding the object in place, letting it slip quietly off his back and onto the leaf-strewn forest floor. The Traagen could be its final resting place, another remnant of mankind reclaimed by nature. Over time, the Fading would steadily bury it beneath layer after layer of decaying plant matter, forgotten by all but the trees and the spirits that walked between them.

And now that Elbin was little more than a name on a map, who would be around to stumble across it?

About an hour before sunset, Theis had led the three of them up the southern-facing side of a steep hill. The rocky ascent limited the number of trees, and as they neared the top, the canopy cleared enough for him to finally get a good look out over the whole of the Traagen Peninsula.

Nevin remembered his jaw going slack as his eyes drank in the scene.

Plumes of thick, black smoke blanketed the southern sky. Orange flames licked at the treetops, belching ash and soot into the air. High above, flashes of red lightning briefly illuminated the folds of a monstrous cloud as it spread across the darkening sky. The low angle of the setting sun only served to magnify its oppressive appearance.

Nevin searched the fire line, trying to find any evidence of his hometown —a roof, a chimney, anything—but the flames had advanced too far north. No recognizable landmark remained, all of Elbin gone, and with it, dozens upon dozens of people and their storied histories.

The cat crowded up against the young man's leg. He took a single sniff of the air, then stilled. One sniff was enough.

"Do you think the fires have reached Ishen's yet?"

"I don't know. It's hard to tell." Nevin rested a clammy palm on Aidux's head, earning a barely audible *mrow* from his companion. If the flames hadn't overtaken the hard-to-reach cabin yet, he knew it was only a matter of time. Elbin's destruction was nearly complete. The cold truth that he and Aidux may be the sole survivors of Vincht's assault on his hometown wrapped its fingers around his heart and squeezed.

Theis planted his foot atop a small boulder and leaned over his knee as he gazed up at the growing cloud of smoke.

"We're lucky," he said bluntly.

Nevin wiped the tears from his cheeks, a wry chuckle bursting from his lips. "Lucky isn't a word I'd use to describe any part of this day."

Theis dragged a gloved finger along the outer heel of his boot, scraping free a glob of sticky, black mud. He lifted it to his face, rubbing it slowly between his thumb and index finger.

"Made it here, didn't you? Don't think that makes you lucky?"

Nevin hugged his chest and scowled. "By whose metric? I'm here because I was driven from my home, a home that doesn't exist anymore. Everyone I've known my whole life is dead or missing. Everything I've known is on fire. You may not believe in Fate, Theis, but it sure seems like the universe, the gods, and maybe even random chance is completely against me."

He shook his head, brushing a new batch of tears from his eyelids before they could gather the strength necessary to run down his face.

"I sure don't feel very lucky."

Theis let out a long, disappointed sigh and straightened. One by one, he pulled his gloves tight around his fingers. At some point, he'd replaced the shredded right glove with a fresh one, and the virgin black leather squeaked as he flexed his singed fingers.

"Try pulling your head out of your ass. Might could see things a bit more clearly then, boy."

Stunned, Nevin's mouth dropped open.

Theis shoved a finger his direction, piercing the air like his hand was a blade long enough to stick the younger man in the gut. "You're *lucky* I came along when I did, otherwise you'd just be a stain on Ishen's floor right now. You're *lucky* to have made it out, not just alive, but with your friend over there in tow."

He took a few steps toward the young man, raising his hand to show the thin layer of mud coating his gloves. "And you're *extra* lucky it rained this morning, otherwise, that fire you see, off in the distance? Likely would have been on our heels the whole way out. And with the way you've been trudging along behind me for the past few hours, feeling sorry for yourself, it may have even overtaken us before we could escape.

"So if you want to feel bad, fine. You want to cry? Go for it. Mourn the dead. Mourn your past. But don't lose yourself to it. Focus on what you can control, what you have going for you. We're not out of this yet, boy."

Theis pulled away from the overlook and headed for the treeline. "Now let's go, before the wind shifts north and takes away our head start."

Light and pain flashed behind his eyes, and he heard Dalen's voice once again. *You can run if you want, but we're gonna get ourselves a little huntin' party together, and then we'll see, won't we, boy?*

A small part of him was relieved to be free of the old drunk, but despite the violent invasion of Elbin, despite the all-consuming inferno raging across the whole of the southern Traagen, the larger part of him suspected that Dalen was somehow still out there, that escape wouldn't be so easy as all this.

When Nevin looked out at the smoking woods below them, he could almost feel the old drunk staring back at him.

Chapter 19: A Forgetful Nose

Another curse from Theis pulled Nevin back to the present.

"Why do you keep cursing?" he called up to him, wiping his cheeks. The specter of Dalen faded into the shadows of his subconscious, but didn't vanish entirely.

"You should try it sometime." He snapped an errant branch unlucky enough to cut across his path, breaking it in half again for good measure before dropping it to the side. "Be good practice."

"What's that supposed to mean?"

"Forget it," the man in black grumbled. "Keep walking."

Nevin rolled his eyes. Despite the man in black's harsh words on the overlook, Nevin found it hard to stay angry with him. What he lacked in tact and diplomacy, Theis made up for in bald-face honesty and logic. Things really could have been quite a bit worse for him, for Aidux. Maybe a measure of gratitude wasn't uncalled for, if nothing more than to keep his mind off of the horrors behind him.

Focus on what you can control.

"So, are you gonna tell me how you plan to get us out of here?"

"Didn't plan on it, no."

"No? What do you mean, 'no'? What if you fall in a hole, or off a cliff, or the soldiers find us and you get killed in battle?"

Theis actually chuckled at that, only serving to annoy Nevin further.

"I'm serious! What if you get lost? I mean, it's pretty dark out here. You have to admit it's possible the three of us could get separated at some point tonight."

"I admit to nothing."

"But what if we run into trouble? Soldiers or monsters or . . . or . . . I don't know! I'm basically defenseless over here!"

"Not defenseless. You have a weapon."

Nevin held up a hand in confusion. For some reason, his first thoughts went to the canteen he'd left behind. "What are you talking about? I don't even have a belt knife."

A soft grumble floated back along the breeze. "What do you think the Sharasil is? Already told you that. Pay attention."

"I'm not gonna hit someone with this! It might look like a big club, but it doesn't weigh anything at all. But I guess that's good, because I don't want to hurt anyone, anyway."

He rubbed his sore ribs. *Good people don't look for reasons to hurt other people.*

The seconds ticked by with no reply from their trail guide, and Nevin felt his irritation growing as Theis' silence stretched taut.

"How I am supposed to know you're even telling me the truth, and not just stringing me along so I'll mule this stupid thing around for you?" He smacked the weapon slung across his shoulder. While he expected to hear the wet clap of flesh on metal, the impact was silent as the grave.

He finally caught a glimpse of the man's bright blue eyes as the warrior turned to glare. "Your status as mule is the only thing you've got going for you. Think I have any other use for some obnoxious child and his mouthy cat? And last I checked, boy, you didn't have any better options, so maybe just save your questions and stop lagging behind."

Theis snorted. "Idiot."

Hot blood filled his cheeks. "Stop calling me 'boy.'"

The man had a point, but then . . . what did he really know about Theis? Other than the stories, the legends of an unparalleled warrior traveling from province to province, challenging to martial combat any who would accept? No one knew where he came from, and until today, no one had known what happened to him. He was practically a ghost. Within the patchwork leather cloak, beneath the carved mahogany mask, the man could be anyone.

He could also be *no one*. The stories could just be stories. After all, Nevin hadn't seen him fight. Aidux had been the one to take down Vincht. It was entirely possible the myths surrounding the legendary Theis Bane were nothing more than rumor and hot air.

"How do you know?"

"How do I know *what*?" Theis sounded annoyed, but Nevin couldn't tell if it was from him or whatever the man kept cursing at.

"How do you know there's another way off the peninsula? Is that where you've been hiding all these years? Or is it the way you came to Elbin from Comelbough? I just—"

"Not gonna shut up about it, are you?" He kept walking, crunching innocent undergrowth beneath his boots and batting aside low-hanging branches. Nevin watched him, the outline of his black leather cloak fading into and out of existence like a blotch in his vision.

Theis finally sighed, grumbling to himself in a language Nevin had never heard before. He turned to face the boy and his cat, the motes in his eyes swirling with barely restrained agitation.

"Catch your breath while I look around."

Nevin crossed his arms. "You're not gonna answer me, are you?"

Theis turned back to the trees. "Don't wander off," he called over his shoulder before vanishing into the surrounding foliage.

Aidux sank onto his haunches, patting aside an overly friendly fern that had leaned in to tickle his whiskers. His stomach grumbled, loud enough for Nevin to hear over the screaming cicadas.

The young man cracked a small smile and rubbed his friend's head. "Someone's hungry."

The cat yowled quietly, clearly annoyed. "Don't even get me started on food. We've passed more rabbits in the last few hours than I've smelled all week."

Nevin grinned, sliding his pack off his shoulder and stretching before plopping down in the dirt beside the cat. "I might have some jerky hidden away in here if you're really hungry."

"Ewww . . . no. I'd rather starve. I'd rather eat skunk. I'd rather a snub-nosed groflin gnaw off my paws and then I'd rather eat the groflin."

He shook his head and laughed. If he thought the cat would eat it, he'd offer him whatever food he had. Nevin himself hadn't had much of an appetite all day. Probably a symptom of all the stress he was dealing with.

"What do you think Theis' problem is? He seems really agitated."

Aidux yawned. "I dunno. I'm kinda dealing with my own confusion right now."

"Oh?"

Dragging his pack along the ground with him, Nevin scooted back until he could recline up against a nearby tower pine. The long metal object bound to the top of the satchel prevented access to the supplies within, but Nevin was in no mood to fiddle with it. Instead, he maneuvered the pack to his side and took a deep breath, resting the back of his head against the pine's scaly bark.

"What's on your mind?"

The cat curled up beside him, resting his chin on Nevin's knee. "Well, do you remember that time I got in a fight with a badger, and you told me I smelled so bad you couldn't stand to be within thirty feet of me?"

He made a face. "Gods, you were ripe. I thought we were gonna have to shave you."

"You weren't coming near me with a razor, I can promise you that. Anyway, Ishen could smell it on you, so he gave you some soap and made you go take a bath in the creek behind his cabin. You cleaned me up too, but no matter how much we scrubbed, we couldn't get rid of the smell.

"You said that, after a few minutes of being around me, you didn't notice it anymore, but for the next few days, every time you went away and came back, you could always smell it again. And then, after a few minutes, you'd stop smelling it again. It was almost like, if you spent enough time around me, your nose would forget that smell."

Nevin cocked an eyebrow. "I guess, but what's your point?"

"Well, cat's don't work like that. If it's there to be smelled, I smell it. And I keep smelling it until it goes away. It might get weaker, but I always know it's there. My nose never forgets, not once it gets hold of a smell. So while you stopped smelling it after a few minutes, it kept bothering me, and it bothered me for weeks."

"That sounds . . . really annoying."

"Oh, soooo really." The lynx paused, considering the next bit carefully. "I think . . . I think I'm smelling something and forgetting about it and then remembering it. And then forgetting. Again."

"You just said it doesn't work that way for cats."

"It shouldn't. But I keep smelling the exact same smell, over and over and over again, since the sun set. It keeps going away and popping back up."

"Why is that weird? There's lots of the same things spread out all over the forest."

Aidux waved a paw. "No, that's not what I'm saying. Not the same things, Nevin. The *exact* same thing, over and over and over and over . . ."

That got the hairs on his neck to stand on end. "Like something's following us?" He leaned forward, cautiously taking in the darkness around them, but all was still.

Aidux shook his head. "No, it always starts in front of us and then we pass it. Like we're going in circles, but we're not. I'm sure of it. Us cats know our directions, and I'd definitely know if we were going in circles. And we aren't, because we've been heading north all day. You can't go in circles if you're heading in the same direction!"

The inky form of Theis trudged out of the trees, grumbling quietly to himself as he approached. "Cat's right. Think we're going in circles."

Aidux leapt to his feet with a huff. "Hold on, no, I'm not right. I said we can't be going in circles. *Can't*. I've never been so not right!"

Theis shrugged. "Don't understand it either, but we aren't making any progress toward the mountains. Haven't been for over an hour now. Maybe longer."

"And this one," he began, pointing a gloved finger toward Nevin. "Needs some real rest. Not just a break. Spent most of the night breathing so hard he's bound to wake the rocks."

Nevin scowled. "I haven't eaten, and we've been walking almost non-stop since this afternoon. Not to mention I'm the only one carrying a pack and a huge chunk of metal."

He gestured to the man in black. "How do you even plan to survive out here? You've got no supplies."

Theis ignored him.

"He's right," said the cat, bumping him with a shoulder. "Not about the circles though. We're both wrong about that, him more than me. But you do need to rest. How's your head feeling?"

He shrugged, lightly rubbing the faint divot in his skull. Dried blood peeled off in flakes, and he could feel a rough scab had formed over the wound. To his surprise, the lingering pain had all but vanished and the area wasn't even tender to the touch. "Good enough, I guess."

"Get some sleep, both of you." Theis vanished back into the darkness as he spoke, his fading words slowly consumed by the incessant murmur of cicadas. "Be back to wake you before first light."

Nevin shifted his pack behind him, propping it up on the tree trunk and sliding down into the foliage until he could rest his head on the soft leather. Despite his exhaustion, he didn't imagine sleep would come quick or easy. He closed his eyes and reached out a hand to ruffle Aidux's fur.

The boy was fast asleep before the lynx could even settle in beside him.

Chapter 20: Healing Magic

The world moved beneath him, a violent jostle that shook him awake and roused the dormant agony; a burning, angry pain that sleep had helped him forget. Like a scream in the silence, it pierced his senses, a thick blanket of heavy flame that smothered every thought. He could feel the wail growing in his chest, pushing back against the weight of the pain and clawing up his throat and out his mouth.

And then, it was all gone. The pain vanished faster than it appeared, and the scream withered and died on his lips.

Vincht wrenched himself upright, shaking and confused. A thick sheen of sweat coated his furrowed brow and bare chest. Beads of the salty water stung the corners of his eyes. His chest heaved as he sucked in breath after breath of dry, dusty air.

Blinking in the dim light, Vincht found himself reclining on layers of crag wolf pelts that were spread out on the bed of a moving wagon. The sun bullied its way through the thin sheet of brown leather stretched across an arched wooden frame, barely enough to illuminate the cramped interior but still managing to sting his sleep-weak eyes. A jumbled cluster of deep green curtains covered both ends of the wagon, preventing Vincht from discerning front from back. Piles of blood soaked rags and empty unguent pots were scattered around him. A fresh pile of clothes, along with the majority of his equipment, awaited him atop a small crate in one corner.

"You are awake," said the woman sitting on her knees in the corner. She dutifully smoothed the ruffles of her blue dress before sliding over to his side.

"Willa," Vincht whispered, unsure of the strength of his voice. "How lo—"

The wagon jumped as it encountered some unknown obstacle, and Vincht braced himself against the floor. The strain elicited a painful groan; the muscles in his arms and chest were sore and stiff. He flexed them cautiously.

Willa shushed him, wiping his sweat-soaked face with a lace-trimmed cloth and forcing him to lay back down. At nearly ten years his senior, the aging beauty carried herself with an unbreakable composure. That fortitude had cleaved him to her back in Vadderstrix, in the days following his parent's untimely deaths. With her characteristic frilled blue dress cinched just beneath her breasts by a wide black ribbon and her gray-streaked brown hair pulled up in a tight, spiral bun, Willa stood out among the sweaty, unkempt soldiers like an iris in the desert. And yet, the dark stains coloring her wrist-length sleeves added a touch of violence to her beauty—the dried blood of the wounded and dying.

He silently wondered how much of that blood was his.

Vincht closed his eyes, relaxing his troubled face until calmness smoothed the skin into an emotionless mask. He'd been so close to achieving their goals today. Mere moments from success, he was certain. But, as it does, Fate had stepped in and snatched victory from his grasp.

Why it had chosen to let him live despite his dramatic failure, he could only guess. Maybe it wasn't time. Maybe his moment of victory was yet to come.

He chuckled—a strained, unnatural sound. He found it odd how little he could remember after the fight with Nevin and his pet cat. The shattering of glass, a ball of fur and claws and teeth, the look of his decimated face in the reflection of his blade. So much blood—his blood—dripping and oozing from ragged strips of torn flesh. The trees rushing by as he stumbled past . . . the noises of the forest fading in and out as he fought to remain conscious . . . the endless, burning agony driving him to run harder than he'd ever run before . . .

Yes, that was what he felt as he woke. A memory of pain. He looked down at his arms and chest, fingers trailing along the faint depressions in his skin where the cat had torn into him. Only scars remained now, the wounds almost completely healed over.

Anger swelled beneath the forced mask of indifference as his hands swept over his face, tracing the numb lines over his left eye and down his right cheek, the jagged impressions in his scalp and forehead. His fingers stopped at a divot in his left jaw about the length of his thumb. The bone felt unusually close to the skin.

Anger vibrated in every molecule of his body. *I'm hideous.*

The wagon overflowed with light as the front flap was yanked back, and a squat man stumbled inside. Vincht shielded his eyes with a hand, shoving the anger down until it roiled in his gut and his features smoothed once more.

"Oh, I thought I heard you moving about in here." The man waddled over to Vincht and crouched down awkwardly next to him and Willa. He had a scholar's skin—pale and blemish-free from a lifetime of ease and sloth. His squinting eyes and finger tips darted across Vincht's bare skin. He chattered quietly, pausing occasionally to wipe the sweat from his bald head. Vincht suspected his perspiration was less a symptom of the heavy brown robe he was wearing, and more a result of the man's permanently nervous disposition.

"How are you feeling? Still a tad sore, I imagine?"

Unsure if he had enough control over his anger to prevent it from coloring his tone, Vincht simply stared at the ceiling and nodded sharply.

"I can help with that." Stephen closed his eyes and spread his open palms across Vincht's chest. Within moments, the soothing tingle of magic spread out through his torso and into his extremities. The tightness in his muscles vanished. His residual soreness disappeared. Any lingering grogginess faded away beneath the warm rush of energy that wrapped itself around his body like the gentle embrace of a loved one.

Vincht fought the urge to squirm and shift. The invasive nature of spirit magic always made him deeply uncomfortable.

"That's enough, Stephen," Vincht said, shorter than he would have wanted. He took a calming breath and gently pushed the man's hands away. "Between you and Willa, I'm grateful to live."

Stephen smiled shyly. "W-well, I did my part." The faintest flicker of light retreated from his eyes as the man released the mental grip on his soul.

Vincht sat back up, patting Willa on the shoulder and waving her off. With a brief nod and a solemn look in Stephen's direction, Willa faded back into her spot in the corner.

"You definitely did part of it, Stephen, that's for sure," she said, a disingenuous hint to her words.

Stephen visibly relaxed, failing to catch the subtle barb. Vincht placed a hand on the robed man's bony shoulder and changed the subject. "Bring me up to speed. I remember very little of today after being injured. How long have we been traveling?"

"Um, well, we've been back on the road for over half a day now. It was barely afternoon when you appeared on the far side of the gorge, screaming and covered in blood. We raised the bridge, but by the look of you, I wasn't sure you were long for this world."

He bowed his head deferentially. "Without my help, of course."

Vincht ignored that last comment, leaning forward. "Who gave the order to break camp? Milo? Frick?"

Stephen shook his head and met Vincht's gaze. "I've not seen either of them. Not since everyone struck out into Elbin. In fact, you are the only one who came back. When I saw your wounds—"

"Who gave the order?" he interrupted, his tone insistent.

Stephen chewed his lower lip. The wagon lurched again, and he yelped in surprise. Vincht had always thought the old mage was a bit high strung, but his current attitude was beyond the pale.

You're right to be nervous.

"Well . . . you did, my lord. You told us to break camp and return to Comelbough with haste."

Vincht frowned unconsciously. He turned his attention to Willa, earning a quick nod of confirmation from the one person in the wagon he actually trusted. He didn't remember the order, but he had to have had good reason. Leaving the area should have been the last thing on his mind, wounded or otherwise. Nevin and his glowing eyed companion knew the location of the object in question, Vincht was sure of it. He'd seen the truth in the boy's eyes.

But he had them cornered, trapped on the Traagen Peninsula with no way out aside from the bridge his team controlled. Why would he not choose to press his advantage? Hunker down across the gorge until his wounds healed and then return in force? Had he learned something, something that made him decide it more advantageous to break camp than to remain?

The writing desk.

Vincht chuckled to himself. Turns out that those childhood language lessons his father had forced him to endure weren't entirely useless after all. Ilwarin had never been his strong suit, but it seemed enough of those lessons had made a useful impression on his young mind.

Still, that would necessitate a slight deviation from this current course of action. "How many returned with us?"

Stephen scratched his head. "Four . . . no, five soldiers, aside from the three of us."

Vincht waved him off. "Sorry, I meant, how many horses?"

"All of them. Jayla didn't feel comfortable leaving them behind, what with the fires popping up all over the western woods."

Vincht usually didn't care much for Jayla's bleeding heart philosophies, but in this instance, it had served him well. Extra horses—ones not pulling wagons—could be enlisted to provide him with the means to rapidly return to town ahead of the wagon train. With a two or three in his possession, he could ride hard for many hours, regularly trading steeds to spread the strain of bearing a rider and prevent him from running them to death.

He flexed the fingers of each hand in turn, cracking his knuckles as he squeezed. "Willa, considering the state I arrived in, would you say I'm healthy enough for some serious physical exertion?"

Willa nodded. She wet her lips and responded, her monotonous tone strong and unhurried. "Aside from the visible marks left behind when Stephen attempted to heal you, you are in otherwise perfect health."

"Not quite," interrupted Stephen, wringing his hands. "You had very little muscle damage, and somehow, the wounds on your face avoided damage to either eye. That would have been catastrophic, but you were quite lucky in that regard.

"Still, infusing the body with healing magic strains it in unique and sometimes unforeseen ways. For the next few days, you may experience mild fatigue, difficulty concentrating, increased emotional response and susceptibility to infection, nightmares, and you'll likely hunger more frequently. Your body needs to replenish its spiritual stores after all the work it had to do to regenerate your wounds."

"I'm well aware of the side effects of healing." Vincht flexed his arms, his shoulders, rotated his ankles. Truth be told, he felt fine. Better than fine, actually. All of the typical aches and pains associated with travel and hiking through uneven terrain were gone.

He ran a finger along the depression of a particularly wide scar on his arm. The unnaturally smooth scar tissue's paleness stood out in stark contrast to the surrounding skin's bronze luster. "But what of these? How long until they fade?"

Stephen cleared his throat, tugging at the collar of his robe. "That's uh . . . only time will tell, my lord."

Vincht frowned. "What's that supposed to mean? I thought you said the wounds were only superficial."

The balding man dragged a sleeve across his forehead, leaving a wet stain on the fabric. "Superficial yes, but none of the wounds were cleanly made. More tears than cuts, you see. The body can heal them, but large chunks of flesh were missing completely, and in order to fill such gaps, the body must generate brand new tissue, and it doesn't always fill in properly."

"No, that doesn't make any sense, Stephen. I've been healed before, from wounds far worse than this. Pierced here, through the lung."

Vincht crossed his legs beneath him and straightened, circling a finger around an unblemished patch of skin just above his right nipple. "A barbed arrow, went right through a gap in my chest plate. The medic pulled it straight back out. Pulling an arrow out that way doesn't exactly leave the cleanest wound behind, but after she healed me, there was no evidence I'd ever been wounded."

"A skilled healer, indeed," said Willa from her corner.

"Y-yes. A Shaman, I'm sure." Stephen nodded emphatically. "But I'm just a Dabbler."

Vincht's frown only deepened. "Magic is magic. Aren't you a Wizard?"

"Not quite, my lord. While I have a working knowledge of how to manipulate and direct each of the five elements, I don't have the natural skill necessary to specialize and master one element specifically. Healing magic—true healing magic—is a complicated process. I can only energize and accelerate the body's own regenerative efforts. Manually creating new flesh and bones from nothing is not within my capabilities."

Stephen took a small step back, wringing his sweaty hands together and bowing. "I'm sorry, my lord, but I'm afraid your scars may very well be permanent."

Chapter 21: Ruined

Vincht's debilitating stare set the man on his heels, and Stephen sheepishly cast his eyes to the floor. Willa sat quietly. The jet-haired soldier wondered if she'd known exactly where this exchange was headed from the beginning, even if *he* was just now wising up to the ramifications of Stephen's incomplete healing. Her subtle, backhanded remarks gave her away, though he could never tell if she was helping guide him to the truth, or attempting to goad his temper.

"Willa," he began, softening his gaze but keeping his attention focused on the nervous, balding mage. "Did I ever tell you of my older brother?"

A sly smile colored the corners of the older woman's lips. "You have, but I'm certain Stephen should like to hear of him."

If he did, the man didn't say, but Vincht didn't particularly care what Stephen wanted at that very moment.

"My brother's birth name was Garrett, but outside the inner circle of the aristocracy, everyone called him Dex. A nickname given by his rivals in the sword ring. Get trounced enough, and hate has a way of morphing into respect, even admiration. He eventually gained a reputation as one of the most skilled young swordsmen the city had ever seen.

"You see, Garrett had a way about him. A natural grace, a litheness, an agility. Supernaturally so, some would say. A rare gift that granted him the ability to pick up nearly any blade within reach and become almost instantly deadly with it. Curved or straight, long or short, for cutting or for piercing, it didn't matter. He had true talent, and worst of all, he knew it. Garrett was always involved in some form of scandal, usually involving some of the other noble families' daughters."

Shifting his legs until he rested on his knees, he clicked his tongue. "And in some cases, their sons."

"My lord—" Stephen started.

Vincht waved a hand dismissively and continued. "The man was infuriating. At two years my senior, Garrett's idea of good sport was to publicly humiliate me—his younger, less experienced brother. As members of the upper class, it was nothing for us to draw steel and spar in the streets, so when Garrett found himself in a foul mood, he'd often seek me out. Knowledge of the sword was a requirement for men of both wealth and privilege, but I hadn't a single drop of the god-touched talent my brother possessed.

"For the first few years, he took it easy on me. A bloody nose, a bruised rib. Nothing too serious, but as his accolades and reputation grew, so did his cruelty and the frequency of these . . . 'lessons'.

"The first time his blade pierced my flesh, I knew things had changed."

Vincht gestured to a narrow, diagonal scar just above his left hip. The glossy patch of flesh was about the length of his palm and had faded considerably since receiving it years ago. "My parents thought it a waste of money to employ a proper healer, even going so far as to imply the wound was a badge of my personal incompetence as a swordsman. Garrett never apologized either. He simply promised that the days of going easy on me were long behind us."

"A scar," Willa began, pausing dramatically before continuing, "never truly fades."

"Indeed."

Vincht slowly rose to his feet, flexing his toes against to floor to get a better grip on the constantly shifting wagon bed. *Worse than sailing.* He drew back his shoulders and cracked his neck.

"Garrett rarely practiced. He had no need of it. I, however, threw myself into my studies. I hired an expensive tutor with some shils I'd squirreled away. I invented reasons to accompany my father's associates to nearby towns in order to interact with their warriors, to learn from their scholars.

"I ate, drank, and slept swordsmanship. None worked harder than me. None worked longer than me. None hungered to grow stronger more than me."

He ran a hand through his tangled, wavy locks and took a deep breath in through his nose. He closed his eyes and flexed each arm in turn, finally arching his back as he released a long, deliberate exhale.

When he opened his eyes, Vincht shot forward and snatched Stephen by the collar of his robe. The man recoiled, but Vincht held tight, dipping his head to bring the two face-to-face.

When he spoke again, his voice was a low, menacing whisper.

"On my fourteenth birthday, my parents presented me before the nobility of Vadderstrix as a man of House Morfren, and made public their decision to name me—and not my brother Garrett—as heir apparent to our esteemed family. The news created chaos amongst the nobles, and rightly so. Usurping the eldest son in favor of a younger sibling wasn't just scandal, it was practically heresy. Garrett's many indiscretions had earned him a reputation as somewhat of a loose cannon, and many were relieved to know he wouldn't be in charge of leading such a storied house down a similar path."

His wry smile did nothing to dispel the glimmer of violence shining in his eyes. "And embarrassing them all in the process."

Vincht poked at Stephen's plump nose. The man flinched, but didn't retreat. "But Garrett, you see, he blamed me. *Me.* As if I was somehow responsible for our parents' decisions. I pleaded with him, tried to get him to listen to reason, but my brother was having none of it. In his mind, I was the orchestrator of his downfall as favored son.

"For well over a year I'd successfully avoided him in public, but it took less than a month after my Namesday for he and his . . . cronies to catch me alone at the edge of town. He drew his sword and, with little fanfare or grandstanding, challenged me to duel. Not for sport, mind you. This time, Garrett challenged me to a duel for the position as heir to the House Morfren."

He smirked. "To the death, of course."

Stephen pressed his shaking hands together. "W-why are you telling me all this, my lord?"

Vincht ignored the question, reaching out to squeeze the man's shoulder until he winced in pain. "Garrett entered into the duel thinking that nothing between us had changed. He'd never truly been challenged by another warrior, not really, not once in his entire life. People recognized in him this god-touched talent and simply . . . gave up. They practiced, sure, but not enough to overcome that which came naturally to Garrett, and everyone that entered into combat with him did so expecting to lose.

"But I possessed something greater than talent—an unshakable resolve. Unlike Garrett, I could manifest my own destiny through sheer force of will. My brother never stood a chance. He lacked the vision necessary to even compete.

"Within four moves, I had him on his knees. I gave him only enough of a break for the full extent of his defeat to register in his feeble, undisciplined mind . . . before I ran him through."

Stephen finally peered up into his eyes. "You killed him? How could you do such a thing? He was your brother."

"Oh, no no no. You misunderstand." Vincht looked on him with pity. "Garrett killed himself. He choose his death when he refused to evolve beyond his talented birthright. Had he given himself over fully to his craft, none could have stood against him, but because he lacked the will necessary to embrace discomfort, to steep himself in uncertainty . . . he doomed himself to death."

In an instant, Vincht lashed out and gripped Stephen by the throat. The balding man's eyes bulged in their sockets. As he wrapped his hands around Vincht's wrist, a glimmer of light flashed within his dilated pupils, and the air vibrated with an intense, burgeoning energy.

Vincht increased the pressure on Stephen's windpipe, his smile vanishing in the wake of a furious scowl.

"Release your soul, you worthless cretin, or I'll tear your throat clean from your neck."

The man's eyes widened considerably, but the tingle of magic shivered, then vanished.

Vincht's smile returned. "Good. Now we're getting somewhere."

He continued. "You see, talent is wasted on those without purpose. It breeds hubris, and stunts a person's true, organic growth. Force of will, you see, is ultimately superior, as one can overcome the few individuals blessed by the gods through measured, intentional practice. I overcame my brother through intensive training, though sheer force of will.

Vincht pulled Stephen close. "But your own lack of will has ruined me."

Stephen blinked. "What? No! That's not fair! I healed you, my lord. You live due to *my* efforts, *my* capabilities. Without me, it's likely you wouldn't have survived the night."

Vincht nodded. "That's true, yet *without* you, this form would not be cursed to walk the face of Stragus covered in grotesque and inhuman scars. While I'm grateful to not be dead, you have doomed me to a life of hideousness, due solely to your pathetic lack of will."

"No, I—"

"*No!?*" Vincht buried his fist in Stephen's stomach. The older man folded into the blow, slinging drool across Vincht's taut bicep. "Did you not say it yourself? You're a Dabbler. You don't possess the natural skill necessary to generate flesh anew. You can only fortify and empower the existing regenerative systems. You lack the will necessary to repair me completely."

"No will, no talent," Willa mused from her corner. "How valuable can such a man truly be?"

Stephen coughed, his shaking hands cradling his midsection. "I'll try again! I'll do better this time, I promise! Just give me the chance!"

"You've already proven you don't have the skill or strength necessary to finish what you started, and I'm not giving you free reign to use your stunted magic on me now. You're more like to harm me than heal me now.

"What incentive have you to grow, what need have you to improve? As it sits, you're likely the only mage in Comelbough the Breathers allow to exist due to your relationship with the Baron. Without competition, why would you strive to better yourself? I suppose I *could* threaten your life—"

"Don't kill me! I'll do better, I swear!" Thick tears rolled down the man's blood-swollen cheeks as he begged, dripping off his chin and onto Vincht's wrist.

"—but we both know the Baron would skin me alive if I deprived him of his one and only mage. And you've no family to speak of, so I can't even hold *that* over you."

Smirking, Vincht kicked Stephen's legs out from under him, slamming him onto his knees. There was a wet popping sound, and Stephen cried out in pain. He tried to reach down and comfort his injured knee, but Vincht tightened his grip on the man's throat and tilted his head back until the whimpering mage was forced to look him in the eye.

"You see," Vincht began, gently brushing the tears from Stephen's cheeks with a finger. "When I trained to beat my brother, I had incentive. I had a purpose. I had a goal. What incentive do you have to grow stronger, to hone your craft, to become a better version of yourself?"

He shook his head sadly. "None. Your life is filled with the comforts of success, and only discomfort inspires growth."

A wildness filled his eyes, an insanity the likes of which Stephen had never seen, but when he spoke again, his tone was as flat as a sheet of parchment.

"So allow me to provide you with said discomfort."

Before Stephen could protest, Vincht lashed out with a fist, sinking his knuckles into the soft flesh beneath his left eye. Stephen yelped and covered his face with his hands, shrinking away from the attack.

In the confines of the wagon though, the man had nowhere to go.

Vincht responded by going to work on the man's ribs, sinking blow after blow into his midsection until the man gasped for air and hugged his chest. Vincht then turned his attention back to his unprotected face.

Every time Stephen slumped to the side, Vincht renewed his grip on the man's throat and jerked him upright before continuing his barrage. Strings of blood arched through the air between them each time he drew his fist back for another punch, and the whimpers of pain quickly changed into cries for help before ceasing altogether.

And still, Vincht poured his fury into the man's limp, disfigured body.

Willa watched quietly from her corner as the black-haired soldier's chest and arms grew redder and redder with Stephen's warm blood. The wet squelch of each blow drowned out the ceaseless noise of the road, but no one appeared from the front of the wagon to put a stop to the violence.

Finally, the mage's motionless form collapsed into the pool of his own fluids, burbling intermittently as he attempted to breathe through his ruined face. Vincht cleaned himself up with one of the fur pelts that made up his pallet, carefully watching the pile of Stephen to make sure he hadn't gone too far.

To make sure he hadn't accidentally killed him.

"Willa," he began, tossing the soiled blanket aside. "Wake him. Focus him. Put him to work on himself."

Willa smoothed the ruffles in her blue dress and rose to her feet, as graceful and controlled as if she were standing on solid ground. "I will do as you ask, but I'm not so sure he won't yet die from the beating he just received."

Vincht shook his head. "Damned Wizards don't die that easily. He's likely begun healing already, even without conscious effort."

Retrieving her lace handkerchief from a small pocket on her dress, Willa dabbed at a small collection of blood droplets on Vincht's shoulder. "You surprise me, young one. Something I'd thought unlikely after so many years."

He shrugged her hand aside and began sifting through the pile of clothes set aside for him on the small wooden crate. He needed something rugged, resilient, an outfit that could stand up to the rough treatment he was about to subject himself to over a period of days.

"How so?"

"You showed him mercy."

Vincht barked a laugh. "Mercy."

He pulled a shirt over his head. "You misunderstand. He cursed me to the life of a cripple through his own incompetence. I merely returned the favor. Now, should he fail to rise to the challenge I issued, he'll spend the rest of his life subject to the horrified grimaces and whispered curses his image engenders. Wherever he goes, revulsion will follow."

Willa simply nodded, unphased. "And what will you do now?"

The black-haired soldier ripped aside the green curtains at the back of the wagon, flooding the tiny enclosure with early morning light. He winced at its suddenness, but faced the light head on, forcing his eyes to adjust on his schedule. "I'm heading to the capital on my own. Those who remain know to follow you in my absence. Push them, but not too hard. I'd rather the Baron finds out what I did to his mage after he does me one final favor."

Vincht stared down the road behind them, reveling in the vast plume of inky black smoke stretching out across the western horizon. He ran his fingers through the gouges that ruined his perfect face, imagining those same fingers slowly peeling away the skin of Nevin's pet cat. His trembling fingers curled at the thought, his nails digging into the still-fresh scar tissue, raking hard enough to draw fresh blood from their passing.

Watching him from his side, the generally unflappable Willa failed to suppress a shiver.

Chapter 22: Left Behind

Nevin's eyelids wrenched open and he jerked upright. Swallowing a mouthful of air, he choked on the acrid smoke drifting in on a firm southern wind and squinted against the false brightness created by his sleep-weak eyes. Daylight had finally given form to last night's anonymous woodscape, but the smoky haze and an overcast sky painted the whole of it in shades of dreary, emotionless grays.

The fading specter of a disconcerting nightmare weighed on his thoughts, and as he put a hand to his sternum and coughed, he half-expected to find Dalen's moldering fingers digging into his flesh. Instead, his nearly numb digits bumped something hard and smooth and wholly unexpected.

Resting atop his heaving chest was the old drunk's tarnished bronze canteen.

He cried out unintelligibly, slapping the canteen and sending it tumbling into the surrounding foliage.

The exclamatory irritated his already parched throat, and was cut short by a string of ragged coughs. A few steps in front of him, a section of ferns swayed as though something had barreled through them just moments before he opened his eyes, but they quickly settled back into the rhythm of their wind-swept brethren.

"Aidux!" He pulled himself to his feet, dragging the awkwardly packed leather satchel along as he stood. He rubbed his eyes again and peered up through the canopy. A featureless blanket of storm clouds had fanned out across the sky while he slept, and not a speck of blue showed through.

What time is it? Theis was supposed to wake him before first light, but by the look of things, morning had come and gone and the man in black was nowhere to be found. Aidux, either, for that matter. He couldn't imagine the cat would have wandered far from him while he slept, but to get beyond earshot?

Then there was the matter of the canteen. He shook his hand, the sting of having slapped aside the canteen still ringing in his cold fingers. *That didn't feel like a hallucination.*

"What in the Numbra is going *on?*"

A gust of stinging wind ripped through the understory, and Nevin protected his face with his arms. To the south, the slow groan of cracking wood broke through the quiet, but the smoky haze was far denser downhill, and it masked the sound's source like an impenetrable wall. The distant glow of fire was not so distant anymore, and an orange glow bled through the smoke as it crawled up the hillside. More sharp cracks could be heard within the approaching haze, no doubt boiling sap bursting in the hearts of trees old enough to remember a time before men threatened their peace with fire and greed.

Aidux . . . Theis . . . where are you two?

A distant peal of thunder sounded from farther up the hillside, and a fine mist wafted down through the branches overhead. The rain couldn't come soon enough, he thought, but even if the sky opened up and dumped a small ocean on the Upper Traagen, Nevin doubted it would do little more than temporarily forestall the advances of the inferno eating its way toward the Nimmons.

Satisfied that Theis and Aidux were neither unconscious nor hiding beneath the sparse undergrowth, Nevin heaved the leather satchel in place on his back and prepared to hoof it away from the steadily approaching smoke. He didn't make it far before something tangled around his right arm jerked him to a stop.

A familiar leather strap encircled his bruised wrist, trailing off behind him to disappear beneath the ferns.

Nevin felt his spirit exit his body.

"No no no!" He wrenched on the strap, but his efforts only tightened the soft leather until it choked off the flow of blood to his hand. Wood creaked beneath the ferns, but refused to give.

Remnants of his forgotten nightmare bubbled to the surface, and Nevin's eyes stretched wide as he imagined Dalen's skeletal hands reaching up through the overgrowth to drag the young man down to join him in death.

Would you deserve any different?

Nevin froze. The voice had come from downhill.

"Theis?" he asked the empty woods, the finer hairs on his neck and arms rising up at the behest of a growing trepidation.

Out of the corner of his eye, a dark figure lurked at the edge of the curtain of smoke, motionless and unaffected by the bursts of flame-heated wind whipping past it through the trees.

His heart rapidly slammed the blood through ill-prepared veins.

"Theis, is that you?" he whispered. He knew full-well his words were too quiet for the figure to hear him, but the urge to speak up and repeat himself was conspicuously absent.

The figure's shadowed head twitched side to side in response.

That man can't save you.

The voice reverberated through his mind like an underwater scream. His insides twisted against themselves and Nevin coughed against the wave of bile rushing up his throat.

The figure shifted its weight forward and took a single step uphill.

Choking down the ick in his throat, Nevin didn't wait around for the second step to fall.

With a sharp crack of wood, the canteen ripped free of the undergrowth and the young man bolted uphill, kicking up loose dirt and trampling ferns as he passed. He leapt over a squat evergreen bush, stumbling briefly as his feet landed atop a collection of exposed roots. He steadied himself on a passing tree trunk, glancing over his shoulder before rounding a moss-crusted boulder.

The figure now crouched in the place he'd taken his nap, its gaunt head turning to follow Nevin's frenzied escape. Though the smokey haze was much lighter where it now stood, interminable shadows enveloped the strange figure wherever it went, as though reality was somehow ashamed of its very presence and sought to hide its mistakes.

The young man jerked his head around in time to avoid tumbling through a patch of brambles, turning his body northward to clamber up a narrow gully of exposed granite filled with pine needles and loose stones. Pebbles squealed beneath his boots as he fought his way up the slope.

A thorn-leaved holly bush guarded the only exit to his ascent. Nevin clutched the unwanted canteen to his chest and dove ahead, shoving his way through the foliage with a guttural cry of pain and determination. The tightly-threaded branches and jagged leaves dug into the exposed skin of his arms as he struggled to protect his face, and a number of shallow cuts oozed hot blood as he burst free from the other side.

And suddenly found himself running through a fully realized Waking thunderstorm.

So surprised was he by the unexpected shift in weather, Nevin tripped over his own feet and slammed into the sodden earth. His momentum sent him surfing across the soaked grass. He jumped almost immediately to his feet, shrugging off the bulky leather satchel and wiping a hand through his sopping hair as he took in his surroundings.

A strangely familiar clearing greeted him.

An almost perfectly circular lapse in tree growth brimmed with wild grasses and flower blossoms that shouldn't be blooming so early in the season. At the far edge of the clearing, a pile of sun-bleached stones and termite-eaten pine supports hinted at a long abandoned building of some forgotten purpose, languishing beneath a tangle of creeper vines and opportunistic weeds.

Between brief flashes of lightning and through a curtain of rain, Nevin paid particular attention to the odd structure at the center of it all. Ringed in low clusters of white hemlock, a circular stone platform bore a grizzled ram's head statue in its midst, its curled horns holding a single oak leaf aloft between their sharpened tips.

He recognized the symbol immediately. An effigy to Ivvilger, patron of nature and the struggle of existence.

Bleached animal bones and meat in various stages of decay surrounded the mottled gray figure, their presence staining the stone platform with oily puddles of long-dried viscera. Though he couldn't smell it in the rain, looking at the mess was enough to set his stomach churning uncomfortably.

Utterly confused, Nevin wiped the rain from his face and looked back the way he'd came.

The holly bush was gone.

The narrow gully? Missing.

Nothing behind him bore any resemblance to the forest he'd just sprinted though. Not a single wisp of the nearly omnipresent smoke had followed him here.

It was almost as though he'd burst free from the brush . . . and set foot in an unknown clearing, miles away from where he'd started.

Chapter 23: The Morbid Effigy

"*Nevin!*"

The cat, his voluminous fur laid flat by the downpour, leapt through the bushes crowding the limits of the clearing and bound full-speed through the calf-high grasses toward his friend. Each time a paw left the ground, a rooster tail of water kicked up behind him.

Nevin scooped up the frantic lynx in a tight, grateful embrace.

The cat savored the wet hug for a moment before pulling himself free. A hint of fear colored his over-wide silver peepers, and his ears twitched as if attempting to frighten off an invisible cloud of flies. "Something's really wrong. I don't know what—"

"Where did you go?" The young man reached down and grabbed his friend by the mane with both hands, pulling their faces together. "I woke up and you were gone, and the fires were so close I could see them."

"No, Nevin, listen—"

"Why did you leave me there? Why didn't you wake me with the sun?"

Aidux shook free of his grasp and stepped back. "You don't understand! I *tried* to wake you. When I finished my nap, the sun was already up and smoke was creeping up the hill. Theis didn't answer my calls, so I yelled and screamed and jumped on your chest, but no matter what I did, you just kept sleeping."

The cat clawed at an ear and shook his head in agitation, spraying water in every direction. "I thought about giving you a little love bite, but I didn't want you yelling at me, so I jumped off to try and find Theis again."

"So you just ran off into the woods without me?" Nevin swept aside his sopping hair, feeling the warmth of his run through the woods being steadily sapped by a combination of chill air and rain. He could tell the storm's strength was ebbing. With any luck though, it would stick around long enough to slow the advance of the fire line, giving them the time they needed to outrun it.

But without the man in black to show them how to escape through the Nimmons, outrunning the fire wouldn't do them much good.

The lynx flinched when a peal of thunder followed too closely behind a flash of orange lightning. "No, that's just it, I *didn't* leave you. When I jumped off your chest, I turned to look out into the forest, but instead of landing in the ferns, I was just . . . I was . . . well, I was *here*. In this clearing.

"I was confused at first, sure, but I knew I had to get back to you as soon as possible, so I turned right back around and ran right back into the forest. I don't think I made it more that a hundred feet or so before I burst right back into this clearing again! I did that three more times before you showed up." He pawed at his other ear and yowled in irritation.

Nevin turned to look back the way he'd came. While the trees framing the clearing were too tall for him to get an unobstructed view of the approaching fire, the billowing cloud of inky smoke stood out starkly even against the backdrop of storm clouds.

Nevin rubbed his eyes in disbelief.

The fire line had to be more than a half a mile away. There was no possible way he could have cleared that much distance in the fifteen seconds he'd spent running from the unknown figure.

Aidux plopped down on his belly, shoving his front paws in place over his wilted ears. The cat closed his eyes and released a long, plaintive mrow.

Nevin quickly knelt at his friend's side. "Hey, are you okay? What's going on with you?"

He tugged at the lynx's front leg, but the cat pulled away, scooting back through the soggy grass using only his rear paws like some sort of furry crab.

"It won't stop, Nevin, and it's so loud it hurts my ears."

Nevin cocked his head. All he could hear was the rain. "I don't hear anything, buddy."

"It's calling them in. They don't want to come but they don't know what they're doing." The cat yowled again. "I could hear it in the woods. I didn't want to listen, but it made me listen and it made you listen and now it's making them listen, too."

Frowning, Nevin lifted his hands in confusion, but as the storm continued to wane, the interminable patter of falling rain gave way to a previously undetectable high-pitched squeal. The young man looked back at the weapon bound to the top of his discarded satchel, remembering the painful ringing the weapon had seemed to emit before violently reacting to the man in black.

Surprisingly, the mysterious object was sheathed in a thin layer of ice, but was otherwise still.

He scanned the clearing, and when his eyes came to rest on that morbid effigy emerging from the earth like a corpse called back from death, the squeal intensified. As he stared, wide-eyed, the air around the statue seemed to shake and warp, distorting the trees beyond until they appeared to squirm grotesquely in its presence.

"Ugh," Aidux whined. "Make it stop."

And just like that, it did.

As the rain dwindled to little more than a fine mist, the otherworldly squeal faded and the distortions surrounding the stone effigy stilled, bathing the clearing in a welcome silence. Aidux peeked up from his spot on the ground, tentatively peeling his paws away from his ears one toe at a time.

Nevin, though, was focused on the trees lining the edge of the clearing, squinting as he stared into the heavy shadows lurking beneath their boughs.

Something moved within.

"Aidux," he began, his voice barely more than a whisper. "What did you mean when you said 'them'? It's calling 'them'?"

The lynx rose to his feet, his silver eyes trained on the distant trees as well. He placed himself in front of Nevin and growled.

"I think we're about to find out."

Chapter 24: A Voice in the Head

Aidux's low growl drowned out the dwindling patter of raindrops on the water-logged grass. Had the cat not been soaked through by the seemingly brief and unexpected deluge of water, Nevin wouldn't have been surprised to see every hair on the cat's body standing at attention as the two apprehensively searched the shadows moving beneath the pines on the opposite side of the clearing. And while the cat stood stiffer than week old bread, Nevin shifted uncomfortably on his feet, clawing at the tangled leather strap as he waited for whoever was moving about in the dark to finally step out and reveal himself.

Or 'itself', he thought, shuddering.

The pair didn't wait long. As the disturbances surrounding the goat-headed effigy stilled and the high-pitched squeal faded, a number of tall figures emerged from the bush line at the clearing's edge. While each appeared at nearly the same moment, they did so from different points along the circumference of the meadow—actors unwittingly answering the cue of an unseen playwright. Sharing looks of confusion and uncertainty with one another, the group stumbled into the muted sunlight and brought the already troubling day to a dangerous crescendo.

The group consisted of eight soldiers, a mixture of men and women alike, dressed in rugged travel garb and sporting an assortment of clubs, axes, and bows. One—a middle-aged man whose dark, close-cropped beard mirrored the hair on his head—had a long, curved blade strapped to his right hip and wore a cuirass of interlocking leather plates. He strode into the clearing with a level of confidence his companions lacked, and when he slowed to gather his wits, the rest of the pack gravitated in his direction.

If the group had noticed the boy and his cat sharing the clearing with them, they didn't immediately react, and Nevin wasn't going to give them the chance.

"Aidux, run!" he shout-whispered, scooping his discarded satchel up with one arm.

Nevin's boots slipped on the wet grass as he dashed for the tree line, threatening to dump him on his face with nearly every step, but safety took precedence over stability, and the thought of twisting an ankle or worse never even crossed his mind.

The young man covered his face as he breached the clearing's edge, but didn't slow. Tree branches and pine saplings reached for him as he passed, clawing at his bare arms and snagging on his possessions. He hugged his pack to his chest and ducked around a crooked boulder.

Eyes going wide, Nevin tried to plant his feet, but it was already too late.

The slope rapidly degraded on the other side of the half-buried boulder, and Nevin found himself listing backward as his feet slid out from under him. Sucking air, he dropped onto his backside and unwillingly rode the avalanche of rain-slick pebbles, soft mud, and pine needles down the embankment.

A tangled web of roots rushed up to met him, and thinking quickly, Nevin drew his boots together and planted his feet. The gnarled wood complained beneath his weight, but held strong. A downward slide became forward momentum. Nevin curled around his pack and braced himself for a mid-air somersault.

He closed his eyes, held his breath, and leapt free from the ground.

Empty air rushed over his damp body as the world rotated around him.

Without the grinding cacophony of tumbling rock drowning out the noise of the forest, Nevin thought he could barely detect a faint, high-pitched squeal digging its way through his brain.

Countless grass stalks surrendered beneath him as he rolled across his back, the soft ground hugging his body as he passed, thankfully free of any obstacles capable of cracking a rib or worse. As his heels came down, he opened his eyes and grunted the air from his lungs and stood, leaning into the momentum and preparing to sink right back into a full-on sprint.

Instead, he immediately slid to a stop.

Somehow, Nevin found himself back at the edge of the clearing, with Aidux peering dejectedly in his direction.

He stumbled back, nearly losing his footing on the wet grass.

This can't be happening.

Across the clearing, the soldiers had gathered together in a tight cluster around the bearded man, their raised voices an incoherent tangle of fear and anger as they argued. The bearded soldier stood silently among them, gazing out past the goat-headed effigy to appraise the flustered young man who had just tumbled out of the woods.

Unable to accept that something had drawn him to this strange clearing and didn't want him to leave, Nevin turned once again to the trees and broke into a run.

Beneath the darkness of the trees, a gaunt figure took shape, and Nevin once again skidded to a stop.

"What are you?!" he called out, his voice shaking.

Wreathed in shadows as it was, Nevin could barely make out the mysterious figure extending a pale hand in his direction. Palm up and fingers wide, the hand beckoned for him to take it.

It tempted him to reach out and accept its silent offer.

It urged him to pull it close and surrender himself completely to its embrace and—

Nevin shook his head, squashing the strange thoughts. His intestines wrapped around themselves in tight, queasy knots. His legs shook. The satchel dropped to the ground as he clutched his aching belly, fighting the urge to spill his insides onto the grass.

You can't run.

The words came at him from every direction at once, vibrating against his skin like a swarm of insects. Again, he jerked his head side to side, drawing short, ragged breaths through the coiling pain in his guts. He pressed his hands to his ears, hoping to drown out the intruder's voice and the growing high-pitched squeal, but the sounds ignored the meager barriers of flesh and bone.

You need me.

Nevin sank to his knees, his vision swimming as the words reverberated through his mind.

The voice was right. He couldn't run. Gods, he was so tired. Exhausted even, from too little sleep, from hiking, from hiding, from all the stresses of running for his life. He'd never wanted to rest so badly in his life. Just sit back, close his eyes and—

Give in to me.

He nodded. He didn't know what the strange figure wanted, who it was, or even what would happen if he gave in to its urgings, but as the energy bled from his body, he felt his arm lift of its own accord and his hand reach out to grasp the figure's own and just—

Fingers like iron bands wrapped themselves around his forearm and jerked him to his feet. Nevin's eyes fluttered open, and found himself looking up into a drooping black leather cowl.

An army of dazzling white motes swam tight circles within a pair of shining blue eyes.

"Are you hurt?" The voice, deep and gravelly, dragged Nevin back from the brink, and he felt his energy returning. The darkness receded, and the knots in his gut unraveled, finally allowing him to catch his breath.

Theis steadied Nevin with a hand to the shoulder. He took in the full height of the young man, checking for any obvious wounds.

"Are you hurt?" he asked again, softly this time, and Nevin thought he detected concern in the man's tone.

"I'm . . . okay." Nevin pulled his forearm free of the man in black's grasp. He leaned to the side and peered around Theis, but the gaunt figure lurking beneath the trees had seemingly vanished.

Aidux loped up beside them, all of his razor-sharp fangs on display in an excited grin. "Theis! Am I glad to see you!"

Theis grunted, offering the lynx an awkward pat on the head, a gesture Aidux gladly arched into.

Nevin fumbled with the tangled leather strap and shot the man a dirty look. "Where have you been?"

"Got lost. Turned around in the dark."

Aidux nodded up at him. "Yeah, the voice got us, too."

"Voice?"

The cat glanced over his shoulder at the stone effigy. Theis followed his gaze, then looked past the ancients stone monument to the group of soldiers milling about beyond.

Their dark-haired leader gestured to the two archers and directed them to fall into position at opposite ends of the clearing. The pair each nocked a single arrow and split off from the group, with one hopping up on top of a termite-eaten stump and the other navigating through the rubble of the collapsed hovel to overlook the clearing from a pile of soot-stained stones. The remaining soldiers readied their weapons and turned to approach.

"Something's really wrong," Nevin said, wringing his hands. "I've tried to leave the clearing, but I just ended up back here. Aidux, too."

Theis nodded, his attention back on the goat-headed effigy. "Think I know why. And what to do about it."

He toed the leather satchel with a boot. "Gonna need that weapon. If someone makes it past us, just keep it between you and them until one of us can get to you."

"What? You're gonna fight them?"

"Not if I can help it." Cracking his neck, Theis strode into the heart of the clearing.

"Cat, guard the boy."

Aidux offered the man an exaggerated nod and stepped protectively in front of Nevin. "He's safe with me!"

Dropping to one knee, Nevin gave up trying to disconnect himself from Dalen's canteen and hastily went to work on the frozen straps securing the metal object in place. Nearly the whole top flap of the satchel was coated in a thin sheet of smooth ice, but it shattered easily beneath his hands. Wrapping his fingers around the coarse stone grip, Nevin knocked the tip against the ground until the majority of the ice cracked and fell away.

Hefting the object with both hands, Nevin stood. How little it weighed, this storm gray metal 'weapon'. Would it be able to do any damage, should push come to stab?

When the time came, could he really hurt another to save himself?

Chapter 25: A Wanted Man

The man in black offered a pair of empty hands to the soldiers as he approached, the rhythmic squick of his boots on the water-logged soil accompanying each step. He visibly stumbled, slowing his stride to regain his balance on the slick grass. Aside from the two archers to his far left and right, the five other soldiers had fanned out beside their apparent leader—the bearded man wielding the only sword in the bunch. None had drawn weapons yet, but Theis knew that could change in an instant.

A stiff wind swept across the clearing, bending the wild grasses and white hemlock toward the ground in undulating waves. The soldiers, drenched as they were, cringed as the gust further sapped the heat from their bodies.

Good, he thought. *The cold will make you clumsy and slow.*

As he neared the goat-headed effigy, Theis turned his empty palms up in a show of peace. Despite their numbers, Theis had no misgivings over fighting them all by himself. He'd faced larger groups before and escaped unscathed. Of the eight, the two archers posed the greatest threat, especially perched above the rest of their companions as they were. There would be no sneaking up on them either, not like he'd done with the archer hiding in the trees outside of Ishen's cabin the day before.

The real question, though, was whether or not the two possessed any training or skill, or if they were just window dressing.

He trained his eyes on the man to his right. A low grip on the bow, quiver on his right hip, no wrist guard on his left forearm, no arrow in sight.

Theis snorted. *Amateur.*

The woman standing in the rubble of the overgrown hovel was different, reminding him of a girl he'd trained beside. A leather wrist guard—its once waxy sheen worn to the consistency of nubuck by years of being scraped by the returning bow string—protected her left forearm. Her quiver was slung over her right shoulder, allowing for the quick retrieval of ammunition. She already had an arrow nocked and ready to go, the index finger on the hand holding the bow hooking the shaft to keep it in place while her drawing arm relaxed.

The man in black resisted the urge to look back at the boy and his cat. Things were different now. He couldn't go into a fight with only himself on his mind. Once his blade tasted sunlight, who knew what these soldiers would do? In the time it took him to reach and neutralize the first archer, any number of soldiers could have crossed the clearing behind him. And while he had faith in the cat's ability to take care of himself, the boy was another story.

Theis knew he would need every advantage he could muster to keep *that* one alive.

Feigning an audible groan, the man in black stepped up on the circular dais, careful not to disturb the grotesque assortment of animal parts and rotting plant matter with a boot. As he crossed the platform to place a hand on one of the effigy's curved horns, the vibrant glow of his eyes subtly strengthened, painting his view of the world in a faint layer of translucent turquoise. An electric tingle spread through his body, suffusing his muscles with the need to act, to move, to perform.

To fight.

"Greetings, stranger," said the dark-haired soldier with a nod, unfolding his arms to rest a hand on the scabbard behind the hilt of his saber. Theis noticed his thumb pop the blade ever so slightly free, ensuring a smooth draw should it be necessary. "I am Grobin, an officer of the Lancowl constabulary."

Theis bowed his head. "Bit far from home, aren't we?"

"I serve at the pleasure of the Baron." He half-shrugged, a complex expression crossing his face. "Work is work. Who am I to question?"

The man in black appraised each of the soldiers spread out before him in turn. None had moved to surround, and had instead formed a handful of paces in front of the stone dais. A few eyed the effigy warily, while the rest seemed equally struck by the mysterious black-clad stranger addressing their leader.

Grobin simply appraised him coolly, his steely gaze never wavering. The man in black felt his soul flicker in the shadows of his subconscious, reaching out to paint the dark-haired soldier in a faint white aura that made him stand out from the scene like a torch on a moonless night.

Pay attention, it told him. His eyes narrowed slightly. He thought he saw something in the way the man watched him. A hint of recognition or concealed intent, maybe. He couldn't yet tell.

"Your men seem tense," said Theis. "Rough morning?"

Grobin sucked his teeth and frowned. "Of a sort. It seems none of us know where we are or how we came to be here. Fact of the matter is, we each set out in separate teams of three this morning, yet somehow arrived here together at precisely the same moment. And short a man."

The dark-haired soldier shot a dour glance at a buck-toothed man to his right. The soldier scratched an arm nervously and cast his eyes to the trees.

Theis nodded thoughtfully. "These woods are tricky. Easy to get lost out here if one isn't careful."

Grobin spit off to the side. "Lost is one thing. Popping out of the woods in a clearing miles from where we started, and right in the middle of a storm? That's of a different sort."

The man in black idly rubbed the stone horn beneath his glove. "Might be that woods like it that way."

"And what's that supposed to mean?"

"I mean, the Traagen is not a friend to the careless, the disrespectful, or the stupid. The people of Elbin have lived in relative harmony with the woods for coming on a hundred years now. Done well to keep the Traagen in its original state, too, taking only what they need and replacing it when they can. I imagine the god of nature makes for a fairly pleasant bedfellow when one shows the proper deference in his domain."

Theis' tone darkened. "As opposed to those who set fire to his home."

The small collection of soldiers murmured nervously at that, exchanging dubious glances as each stepped back. A few put weapon to hand, as though a chuck of hardened wood or sharpened metal could somehow fend off the vengeful whims of the supernatural.

Grobin didn't retreat. "I don't know much about that. Comelbough has had little use for neither gods nor magic since before I became a man. Baron Lancowl saw to that. After his father was murdered, the young baron did everything in his power to cut both from the flesh of the barony, no matter who's blood was spilled in the process.

"It's an unfortunate thing, too. Our crops could benefit from the occasional prayer to this nature god of yours, but, as it sits, open worship and deific symbolism have been outlawed within the bounds of the barony, no matter how far we find ourselves from the capital."

He pointed not at Theis, but to the effigy beside him. "As it sits, I'm obligated by oath to set this one to rubble once I've got you in order."

Theis removed his hand from the effigy and returned it beneath his cloak, his soul flaring in the darkness of his mind. *There's my opening.*

"Got *me* in order?"

"Mmm. It occurs to me . . ." Grobin began, raising an eyebrow and taking a deep breath before continuing, ". . . that you've yet to introduce yourself, stranger."

"Didn't realized you'd asked."

The dark-haired warrior flexed his fingers on the grip of his sword. "I had the strangest idea when I left Comelbough and set out for these woods. Working for the Baron pays the bills, yes, but . . . what *couldn't* my family and I do with three thousand gold shils? Why, we'd practically be nobility in our own right, with money like that filling our pouches. I could buy a ship. Sail the world. Show my son the mythical Chapel in Repose. Take my wife for a walk along the White Crystal Shores to hunt for quartz crab.

"We could *live,* free to do as we please. No more barons. No more commanders. No more rainy, freezing treks into the mountains. No more burning forests. Just comfort and freedom.

"All I'd have to do is cross paths with an aging swordsman with glowing eyes said to have disappeared into the woods over a decade ago. The chance was infinitesimal, I knew, but it seems your forest gods *do* favor me today."

The grate of metal on wood announced the arrival of his saber.

"You're a wanted man, stranger." A triumphant grin split his face. "And that bounty is *mine.*"

Chapter 26: Baiting the Trap

Theis took a small step back, his hand floating over to the pommel of his sword, out of sight beneath the folds of his cloak. Now that the dark-haired soldier had recognized his value to the barony, things would escalate quickly.

A small smile tilted the corner of the man in black's mouth.

Now for the next step.

"Careful, friend. If you know who I am, then you also know what I'm capable of."

Grobin scoffed. "Maybe ten years ago, old man. Life out here in the sticks couldn't have been easy on you, and from the way you carry yourself, I can't imagine you'd stand much of a chance against a soldier in his prime."

Though the man didn't say it, Theis recognized the 'like me' was implied.

Arrogant little prick . . .

From the corner of his eye, Theis caught a flurry of movement as one of the soldiers jogged to Grobin's side. He pointed out past the man in black while he whispered something to the bearded soldier. Even as good as his hearing was, Theis couldn't quite make out what the man was saying, but he had a pretty good idea.

Grobin's eyebrows crawled their way up his forehead as the other man spoke. "You're certain?"

The soldier nodded emphatically, and Grobin actually barked a chuckle, shaking his head in amazement. He gestured, and the man returned to his position.

"Well, well. My luck continues. Not only will I earn the bounty on the most wanted man in the barony, but I'll also be the one to find the object our commander is looking for. Seems this little detour was even more of a boon than it first appeared."

Time to set the trap.

Theis extended a finger skyward.

"You're forgetting one thing."

"Am I? Seems like I have everything well in hand."

The man in black pointed back at the monstrous plume of black smoke that consumed the southern horizon. "The way home lies back through there. Wouldn't last an hour breathing in all that smoke, let alone a full day's march. More, if you get lost again."

Grobin's expression was unreadable. "I'm sure we'll manage."

"You'll *manage?*" Theis barely got the words out before a harsh, wheezing laugh took over. "Couldn't find north if I pointed the way. If the fire doesn't get you, the crag wolfs will, you street-soft wetfoot."

The dark-haired soldier's blade leapt to the ready, extending outward from his waist like he might, at any moment, charge forward and skewer Theis through the chest. The rest of the soldiers reached for their own, their eyes darting back and forth between their leader and the man in black.

Theis stood still as a statue, the motes in his blazing eyes vibrating frantically in their orbit around his pupils. He could almost hear Grobin's teeth squeaking against one another as the man's jaw tightened in irritation.

After a moment, Grobin relaxed his sword arm, and the saber's tip dipped back to the ground. Derision stained his words. "I suppose you're going to tell me you know an alternative route."

Dangle the bait.

Theis nodded. "Was just heading there myself, leading the boy and his cat behind me to safety. Let us go, and I'll tell you how to find it yourself."

"And let a three thousand shil bounty just walk out of my life? Not gonna happen, friend." Grobin shook his head and raised his blade until the tip was level with Theis' throat. "How's about you tell us the way out of these woods and we won't torture it out of you and then kill your two friends while you watch?"

Theis shrugged nonchalantly. "You really want to take the chance that one of your men doesn't accidentally kill me in the exchange before you get the chance to pry the information out of me? After all, I'll be fighting to protect the boy and his cat. Don't know that I'd want to live knowing my failure cost them their lives."

A short breath of wind whipped through the clearing, and Theis made a of show of hunkering down and drawing tight his cloak. A number of soldiers had begun to shiver, with a few hugging their chests and shifting uncomfortably in place while they watched their leader verbally spar with the newcomer.

Theis snapped his fingers, pretending at an idea.

"Adasi Shuur."

Grobin cocked his head, but didn't lower his blade. "Adasi . . . what?"

"A rite," he explained, resting a gloved hand on the effigy's grizzled head. "Or rather, a promise, of sorts. Agreed upon by all those in the presence of this symbol of Ivvilger. A duel. Just you and me."

"A duel."

Theis waved his hand dismissively, stepping away from the stained statue and down off the dais. "The details of the rite are unimportant. All that matters is the spoken oath, and the knowledge that if either side violates said oath, they tempt the ire of Ivvilger himself."

Grobin moved to speak, but Theis cut him off. "I'll make it simple. You win, and you get everything you want. The way out, the object you're looking for, and me. I'll come quietly, as long as you promise not to hurt my companions."

A pregnant pause. "And if you win?"

The man in black gestured to the trees. "You let us go."

Murmurs of objection arose from all around. The nearest soldier took a small step in Grobin's direction. "Sir, you're not seriously—"

"Shut up," he barked without looking.

"We'll be stuck out here—"

"I said shut up!" He swept his blade to the side, and the soldier jumped back in surprise. The murmurs around them died down abruptly.

Sneering, Grobin turned his head and spit. "Not good enough. We have you outnumbered. You don't stand a chance against all of us, and even if it did come down to an all-out brawl, we'd still be making off with the item in question and your corpse. Half a bounty is still better than no bounty at all.

"If I win, we'll let the other two go, but you're coming with us."

He doesn't actually care about the object they're looking for. He just wants his money.

He shook his head. "You aren't getting me, but, to appease your comrades, if I win, you can have the item your group came here to find. At the very least, your commander will be pleased with what you accomplished out here today, and no one will have to die.

"If everyone behaves, I'll even tell you the way out." He shrugged. "After I take up all your weapons, of course."

Theis could see the wheels turning behind Grobin's eyes as he weighed and compared every possible outcome of the situation. The soldier was right.

From where they stood, if they chose to press their advantage, there would be little an aging swordsman could do to stop them. The archers alone sealed his fate.

But there could be no victory if winning only served to bring them a horrible death at the hands of either a raging forest fire or the sub-freezing temperatures higher up in the Nimmons. Their only chance at escape rested in their cocksure leader's ability to best the man in black in one-on-one combat.

A trap works best when your quarry wants to step in it.

"Agreed," the dark-haired soldier said suddenly, sliding a small pack from his shoulder and tossing it at the feet of his young, buck-toothed companion.

"First to surrender?"

"Or first to blood." He pointed his blade at the man in black. "And watch yourself. If you kill me, my crew will take you down so fast you won't have time to wonder if your little friends back there will survive the day or not."

Theis merely nodded.

Grobin raised his voice and turned to address his team. "Everyone clear? No one will interfere. If he wins, we let them go and they leave behind the object we're looking for. If we win, we take their weapons and take them into custody. Is that understood?"

Solemn nods and somber yups answered back.

Grobin slashed the air in an x-shaped pattern and put some distance between himself and his opponent. The nearest soldiers fell back, clearing the space for the battle to come. The dark-haired soldier offered Theis a modest bow and flashed a toothy sneer.

"Well? That good enough for your forest god?"

Theis closed his eyes and bowed his head.

"Adasi Shuur is struck. May Ivvilger be pleased."

Concealed behind his skull-like mahogany mask, Theis' lips parted in a triumphant grin.

And now you're mine.

Chapter 27: Adasi Shuur

Nevin watched the man in black negotiating with the dark-haired warrior through unblinking eyes, his attention trained so intensely on their conversation that he failed to notice his hands trembling from the effort of squeezing the coarse stone handle of his weapon for so long. The object's tip quivered in the air a scant few inches above the ground before him. Blood thudded through his head to the rhythm of his apprehension.

"He just walked right up into the middle of them," Nevin grumbled, his words breathy and short. An hour had passed in the minute since Theis had left their sides.

What could they possibly be talking about for so long?

Aidux glanced back over his shoulder, his silver peepers landing on the quivering Sharasil and following it up to rest on Nevin's clammy face. "Why are you standing so hard? Nothing is happening yet."

"I'm not . . . standing hard. I'm ready, just in case."

The lynx turned and placed a paw on Nevin's hands, pushing down until the tip of the weapon came to rest on the rain-soaked earth. The grasses nearest the storm-gray metal stilled as a thin coating of ice crept outward from its surface. "You're gonna wear yourself out. Loosen up and breathe. We'll be okay."

Swallowing, Nevin nodded. He took a few deep, calming breaths and relaxed his grip on the pommel. His hands immediately stopped shaking.

The cat rolled his toes on Nevin's hand. "That's better. Now, wiggle your arms, your butt, your head. Get all that nasty tension out."

Nevin did as he was told. He flapped his elbows and tilted his head this way and that. He rolled his left shoulder in both directions, then did the same with his right, feeling the tension in his neck and back partially relax.

He paused as he flexed his right shoulder, cocking his head to the side. He flexed it again.

His shoulder barely complained.

That's weird. I was certain I'd really hurt it.

"Huh." Aidux flicked his ears in the man in black's direction.

Nevin reflexively tightened his grip once more. "What's wrong?"

"I think they're gonna fight."

"What?! *All* of them?"

Aidux shook his mane, spraying droplets of water all around. "No, just him and the talking guy. Sounds like they'll let us go if he wins, but we'll still have to give him your Shaffodil."

"Sharasil."

The cat frowned. "That doesn't sound right."

Nevin blinked incredulously. "That . . . no, he can't do that. As soon as one of them tries to touch it, it'll blow their hand off. Then all bets are off!"

The object's tip rose up off the ground, snapping free of the thin membrane of ice. It made no sense. The man in black claimed he had come to Elbin specifically to retrieve the strange weapon. Why offer to give it up even in the case of a win?

As the soldiers spread out to frame the would-be arena for Theis and their bearded leader, Nevin's apprehension only increased.

What are you up to, Theis?

Theis flipped his cloak over his shoulder, and in a careful, deliberate motion, eased his sicklesque blade free of its scabbard and into the light.

Grobin's mouth turned down in appreciation. "That's some of the highest quality steel I've ever seen. Where'd you find it?"

Theis ignored the question. "It isn't steel."

"Well, what about the cloak?" He drew a circle around Theis in the air with his sword. "You're not planning to fight me that bulky old thing."

"The cloak stays." His words dripped with condescension. "Take me longer to remove than this fight will last."

Light chuckles arose from the gathered soldiers. Grobin shot the crowd a scowl. "Cocky bastard," he spat. "What makes you so sure?"

Theis closed his eyes, taking a moment to crack his neck on both sides and arch his back until a satisfying series of pops ripped their way up his spine. Exhaling a cloud of warm mist through his mask's narrow mouth-slit, he opened his eyes and stilled.

"Because no duel ever has."

There was a sadness in Theis' quiet response that wouldn't have gone unnoticed in a less tense situation, but Grobin's ego was far too focused on the man's casual disdain to catch it.

The dark-haired soldier offered a quick salute, bringing the back of his fist to his chin.

"Well . . . a first time for everything, I suppose."

Then, he lunged.

The man in black's soul blossomed out from the darkness of his mind, rising up to paint the snarling warrior stretching out across the space between them in targeted auras of hazy white light. Each glowing point told him something about his opponent, some detail that might assist him in battle.

In Grobin, there were three.

His boots, failing to properly gain purchase on the damp grass, limited his speed and ability to maneuver.

His grip, white-knuckled and rigid around the leather-wrapped hilt of his saber, would make disarming him comically easy if timed correctly.

His free arm, drawn close to his hip, would make regaining his balance at end of the lunge more difficult than if he held a more open stance.

Theis sighed quietly to himself as he easily sidestepped the attack, backing away from the circular dais and out into the open space among the other soldiers. Grobin tried to plant his feet and turn, but the wet grass refused to grab onto his boots and the man slid farther than intended.

As Theis put some distance between them, he quickly looked in Nevin's direction. The boy and his cat were right where he'd left them, enraptured in the unexpected fight playing out at the center of the clearing. To his credit, the boy looked more angry than scared.

Spurred on by the cheers of encouragement around him, Grobin found his feet and whipped around, cutting the air in a wide, whistling arc. He lunged again, more sure of himself this time, but Theis shuffled back, just out of reach.

"What are you, a dancer?" he growled. "Fight back!"

The curved edge of Grobin's saber cut x's through the air as he pressed his attack, forcing Theis back in a constant retreat. A weathered stone brushed the man in black's boot, and as he stole a glance behind him, he realized how close the dark-haired soldier had driven him toward the ruins of the old hovel. A few more steps and Theis would find himself wading through piles upon piles of similar bulky stones.

Not a good place to be during a sword fight.

Jerking his hood around, Theis caught the triumphant grin plastered across Grobin's face as he leveled the flat of his blade at his opponent's head.

Metal flashed, and Theis slammed the back of his sword against Grobin's so hard the unprepared soldier stumbled gracelessly back. A sharp ringing pierced the air, and Grobin paused to move his saber to the other hand.

"*Gods*," he grunted, shaking his sword arm to relieve the bone-vibrating sting left behind by the lightning-fast parry. His hand quivered as he flexed his numb fingers, his confidence faltering at Theis' show of strength.

Theis let his own sword hang at his side. "Little shame in yielding to your betters."

The silence was palpable. Somewhere in the clearing, one of the soldiers chuckled. No one cheered anymore.

Grobin's seething expression could melt glass. Grabbing the hilt with both hands and with a feral cry, the dark-haired soldier lifted his saber high overhead and rushed headlong into the readied form of Theis.

Flipping the blunt side of his blade forward, Theis took a breath and ducked out of the way of Grobin's downward cut and spun around to his side. Metal hit stone behind him, filling the narrow gap between the two men with a fan of white-hot sparks and peppering his cloak with stone chips.

At the crest of his rotation, Theis exhaled and sent the back of his sword crashing into both of Grobin's legs above the ankles. Without the traction of dry ground to stabilize him, the sheer force of the blow ripped the warrior from his feet and propelled him horizontally into the air.

"Shiiii—"

Theis clapped his palm onto the man's chest and slammed him down into the grass, stealing the curse from his lips.

Straightening before Grobin could gather his wits, Theis planted a boot on the man's sword arm. He nudged the tip of his sword against the soldier's plate leather cuirass, keenly aware that, should he decide to put any weight behind it, he could easily pierce the hardened leather and end the man's life.

"You're done, soldier," Theis said, no hint of malice or insult evident in his gravelly baritone. "Time to call it."

Fury flickered in the man's eyes as he tried in vain to yank his sword arm free of Theis' boot. He looked around, but none of his men dared move to help.

Then, his gaze sank to his belt, catching on a small knife sheathed at his left hip.

Theis shook his head, moving his blade to hover just over Grobin's cheek. "Don't do it."

But the man didn't listen. The soldier ripped his knife free and swung it awkwardly toward his opponent's leg. Bounding backward, Theis danced across the heap of stones making up the remnants of the hovel until he was safely out of reach.

With a flourish, he flipped his cloak over his left shoulder and bowed his head. "Adasi Shuur is complete. Time to pay up."

"Bullshit," Grobin spat, glaring daggers. "I didn't yield."

Theis flicked a hand across the left side of his mahogany mask, then pointed at Grobin's face. The man wiped the back of his knife hand over his cheek and winced. A tiny smear of blood colored the skin of his hand.

"First to blood." Theis jabbed a finger at the fuming soldier. "An oath struck to an oath fulfilled. Like I promised, we'll leave the object behind when we leave."

Grobin jammed his knife back in its sheathe. "And the way out?"

Theis paused briefly before answering. "Considering your poor form just now, I *should* just leave you here to burn. But I'm not going to punish all for the mistake of one.

"Once I've collected everyone's weapons, one of your people will accompany us as we leave. When I'm comfortable with the distance we've put between us and the rest of you, I'll tell your man the way and send him scurrying back to save you. Won't get you rich, but it's the best deal you're going to get."

He shrugged. "But hey, work is work, right?"

Grobin planted his hands on his hips and fumed. After a number of seconds passed with no signal from their leader, the soldiers surrounding the two reluctantly began pulling out their weapons, many of them shaking their heads in astonishment at the surprising outcome of the fight.

"Not good enough," Grobin grumbled.

Everyone stopped.

The man leveled his blade once more at the man in black. "I don't care about the object. It's nothing to say we couldn't find it. I don't much care for this Vincht anyway.

"But you? You're coming with me."

Theis crossed his arms beneath his cloak. "That wasn't the deal."

"We still outnumber you. I don't care how fast you are or how good you are with a sword, you can't possibly beat eight soldiers in a fight."

"You would willingly violate Adasi Shuur?"

Smirking, Grobin faded back toward the circular stone dais. "Oh, I don't give three polished shits about your stupid nature god. I'll take my chances. Damned or not, I'm not letting a three thousand shil bounty just walk out of my life.

"Throw down your blade or your friends won't survive the day."

Chapter 28: Oath-Breakers

Behind him, Theis heard the archer's bow string draw taut, but it was almost imperceptible over the faint, high-pitched ringing that had spread out across the clearing while Grobin broke their pact. Each of the soldiers cocked their heads in turn, wincing as the piercing sound burrowed its way into their brains with increasing ferocity. Groans and whimpers abound, and the two closest to the goat-headed effigy sank to their knees, clutching their skulls and rocking in place.

A thin line of blood dripped from Grobin's left nostril. He swiftly wiped it away, but was unable to hide the look of alarm that flashed across his face.

Theis, unaffected by the shrill ringing, could only shake his head. "Give it up, soldier. While you'll leave just as poor as you arrived, you and your men will at least leave with your lives."

Grobin's lips curled in an angry sneer before raising his voice to address everyone in the clearing.

"Take him alive!"

He spat in the grass.

"And kill his friends."

Nevin's blood ran cold.

For a moment, no one in the clearing moved. A low growl built up in Aidux's throat. Soldiers looked to one another as if waiting for someone to make the first move and grant permission for the rest of them to act. Theis watched the bearded soldier from the rubble of the collapsed hovel, still as stone despite the intermittent bursts of chill wind.

Nevin brought the long, bulky metal weapon to bear. While its uncharacteristic lightness made maneuvering it a simple affair, too many tense minutes left his arms sapped of energy, and just holding the object at the ready set his arm muscles trembling fiercely.

The canteen dangled awkwardly from his wrist.

Finally, Grobin whipped his head around. "Don't just stand there! Take them *now!*"

But it was Theis who would make the first move.

Pivoting on his back foot, Theis ripped his blade through the space between him and the nearby archer. Realizing her mistake too late, the archer leaned away from the incoming blow, but his brief duel with Grobin had succeeded in bringing the man in black within reach. His sword's sharpened edge exploded through the thickest part of her bow, propelling jagged bits of wood into her chest and face.

As the woman reeled back, Theis jolted forward and kicked her square in the breastbone. The blow drove the breath from her lungs loud enough for Nevin to hear it on the other side of the clearing. The woman crumpled like a cloth doll and flew backward, clearing the pile of rubble to disappear beneath the tall grasses.

Grobin lunged, seeking to catch the man in black unprepared, but his feet failed to gain purchase on the damp soil and he fell on his face. This seemed to wake the rest of the soldiers up, and the group sprang into action with scattered cries of determination.

This is really gonna happen.

Two men turned to approach him and Aidux—one spinning a bulbous wooden cudgel at his side, and another twisting his hands around the extended haft of a rust-speckled hewing ax. The uncertainty clouding their eyes during Theis' verbal exchange with their leader had vanished, replaced with gleeful expectation and the lust to do harm. Their leathery-bronze skin bore all the hallmarks of a life toiling in the sun, and callouses decorated their chapped palms and fingers.

"Okay," Nevin whispered to the cat as the men drew closer. "What do we do here?"

Aidux coiled into the grass. "Well, for starters, try not to get hit by—"

The ax-wielding soldier rushed forward, pulling his weapon high over head and yanking it down with a feral grunt. Nevin and Aidux leapt to either side as the blade sank into the damp soil where they'd both been standing with a muffled plurrf. Losing his footing, Nevin skidded through the grass on his shoulder, the metal weapon leaving a trail of frozen grass in its wake.

Aidux was more nimble. Bounding forward as soon as his feet found the ground, the lynx flashed past the attacking soldier with claws spread wide. The man yelped and grabbed a handful of thigh. Blood seeped out around his fingers where three of the cat's claws had made it through the fabric of his trousers.

Without slowing, the cat drove his shoulders into the other man's knees, barely sliding underneath a swinging cudgel. The pair collapsed in a pile of flailing limbs and animalistic cries.

Stumbling to his feet, Nevin stood just in time to see the second soldier stick a boot in his friend's chest and hurl him to the side. Aidux's paws scrambled at the air before landing hard on his back. The soldier rose and dashed toward the cat in the hope of catching him before he could stand.

Fear gave way to anger, and Nevin pushed himself to act.

Digging his boots into the soft earth, Nevin charged forward, hoping beyond hope that he could reach his friend's side before the soldier did.

In his hands, the Sharasil jerked and spasmed, its smooth metal surface rippling at the behest of some unknown internal pressure. Cold light flashed through cracks in its exterior. A faint hissing—

A rusty ax cut a wide, horizontal arc before him. Nevin barely brought the weapon up in time. The two objects collided, ripping the Sharasil from Nevin's hands to send it hurtling end-over-end behind him. At the same time, a sharp crack overwhelmed the muffled clank of metal on metal as the ax's extended haft snapped in twain.

The ax head, now free to move as it pleased, caught the surprised soldier in the shin as it fell. Though the blow was softened by his boot's leather shaft, the sheer weight of the iron head was enough to elicit another yelp of pain from the already wounded man and send him backpedaling to safety.

In the meantime, Aidux had somehow gotten to his feet to latch his maw around the other soldier's forearm, effectively preventing him from swinging his cudgel. The man tried punching the lynx, but the blows hardly did more than annoy the cat.

Nevin spun around, quickly searching the tall grasses nearby for any sign of the storm-gray metal. *What in the Numbra was that?* The weapon's otherwise unbroken surface had changed for a moment, emitting light and briefly revealing another shape hiding underneath.

He set his jaw. A detail that wouldn't matter if he couldn't find the weapon in time to keep himself from being killed.

Theis ducked beneath another arrow. His opponent wasn't so lucky. The arrow caught the man in the shoulder, his woolen over-shirt offering no protection against its sharpened iron tip. A puff of red spray filled the air and he dropped his club to grab at the wound.

The man in black didn't waste the opportunity. Twisting to deflect a swing from Grobin's sword, Theis buried the tip of his own blade in the wounded soldier's neck. His cry of pain was instantly silenced and his eyes glazed over as his soul channel collapsed and retreated.

And so seven became six.

Theis wrenched his blade free and shot between Grobin and another soldier in a bid to take out the remaining archer. The man was performing just as badly as expected, but despite Ivvilger's temporary assistance, the man in black didn't want to push his luck.

As he crossed the clearing, he slid around another incoming arrow and turned to check how the others were faring. The cat had his opponent on the ropes, the soldier trying in vain to fight off the lynx's snapping maw from the flat of his back. Blood drenched the man's right side, and a number of the fingers on one hand were missing.

He was more worried about the boy. His opponent fumbled with a long, straight bladed dagger, finding it difficult to hold in hands slicked by blood. The boy eyed his opponent while he swatted the grass in search of something.

Theis scowled. *He's lost his weapon.*

The man in black jerked his head forward. With another arrow already in place, the archer pulled back on his bow, but ended up stumbling from his perch atop the termite-infested stump when his bowstring unexpectedly snapped. The frayed string sliced into the flesh of his face—cutting a neat line from his jaw to his temple—but the wound didn't even have time to bleed before Theis cut short his life.

And so six became five.

Theis flicked the blood from his blade, tilting aside as Grobin's thrust pierced the empty space beside him. The man's attempts to wound him were beyond sloppy. Overzealous and fueled by rage, not to mention under-trained.

More dangerous to himself than to me.

The other two soldiers were hot on Grobin's heels, circling around either side of their leader to surround. Theis knew he needed to handle these final three quickly. The soldier attacking Nevin might be wounded, but he was both armed and willing. The boy was currently neither.

Grobin smirked at the man in black, caught in the midst of a ring of bared weapons with nowhere to go. "You're good, old man, but I don't care what they say about you, you can't possibly make it out of *this* alive.

"Give it up now, and I'll let you keep your legs."

"You should have paid closer attention to those stories, soldier," Theis' eyes narrowed. "Then your boy wouldn't starve while you rot in these woods."

The man's smirk vanished, and anger flashed in his widening eyes. Swinging wild, he aimed his blade for the meat of Theis' thigh, but the man in black was more than ready.

Theis stepped inside Grobin's reach, spinning around as he moved to drive his hip into the man's crotch and hooking his bicep under his opponent's armpit. A club and an ax caught only empty air where Theis had stood but a breath before. He shifted his weight and pulled hard, bearing down on Grobin's arm as he would the overhead slice of a sword. The soldier's boots left the ground, his body rotating around and over the man in black's hip.

He slammed head-first into the unyielding ground.

Bone crunched in his neck, and the dark-haired soldier went limp.

And so five became four.

"Where ya off to?" chided the wounded soldier, waving Nevin closer with one hand while he brandished a vicious looking dagger in the other. Despite the gouge in his thigh and the blow to his shin, the unshaven brute was rapidly regaining his stride, but, in his rush to find his missing weapon, Nevin had failed to notice how close the soldier had actually gotten.

Metal flashed in the muted light, and Nevin cried out in pain.

Steel disappeared into the unprotected flesh of his torso just below his rib cage. The young man stumbled away, clutching the wound with shaking hands. Warm blood seeped through clenched fingers.

Nevin felt his head swimming almost immediately. A cold sweat burst from the pores on his face and the ground seemed to sway beneath his feet.

The soldier sneered triumphantly. "Next one's in your throat, boy."

Nevin pressed a blood-soaked hand to his suddenly throbbing temples, smearing the warm fluid all across the side of his face and through his hair.

Light exploded in his brain and the clearing melted away.

Dalen, wobbling on his feet, reached down into the straw dusting the bare dirt floor and hefted an old ax handle. He smacked it three times against his empty palm before he spoke, the wet clap it made against his sweaty flesh echoing between the walls of the barn.

"*Give it back, or the next one's against your head, boy.*"

Dalen's voice and the unshaven soldier's threat grated against one another over and over in his mind. ". . . in your thro*Next one's* next one's *Give it back* in your *against your head* throat *head* throat *boy* boy *boy* boy *BOY!* BOY!! *BOY!!* BOY! *BOY!* BOY!! *BOY!!!*

The image flickered out of existence, and Nevin felt himself swinging Dalen's tarnished canteen with all his might at the wounded soldier's stupid grin.

Chapter 29: The Aftermath

Distant peals of retreating thunder and the occasional burst of mist-laden wind intermittently brushed aside the quiet reigning over the woodland clearing. Nevin sat cross-legged in the damp grass, elbows on his thighs and head in his hands. He rubbed his temples in wide circles, hard enough to occasionally send a sharp ache back behind his ears and down through his clenched teeth. He barely noticed it when it happened, his unfocused eyes directed into his lap while he tried to make sense of the confusing emotions battling it out in his mind.

Sprawled out on the grass before him lay the motionless body of the wounded soldier, his unnaturally loose jaw dangling from his bruised and swollen face. A mixture of drool and blood oozed from the corner of his slack lips. Beside him lay the discarded bronze canteen, an impromptu weapon that now bore two sizable dents along its southern edge.

One dent for each of the men I've laid low in the past two days.

Aidux licked away the last vestiges of blood coating his paws and approached. As caught up as he was in his own internal drama, Nevin hadn't noticed the cat watching him intently as he cleaned himself up, and he didn't react when the concerned feline rested one of his considerable paws on the young man's shoulder.

"Are you okay?" he asked, an uncertain edge to his child-like voice.

Nevin pulled away from the cat's touch. "I wish you two would stop asking me that."

The cat's ears wilted.

"Either of you hurt?" called the man in black, wiping his blade clean with a faded red handkerchief procured from a pouch on his belt. Nevin gritted his teeth and turned away. He wrapped a hand over the still seeping wound in his side, more concerned with hiding the cut from Theis than he was about stopping the bleeding. The narrow gash burned something fierce, and Nevin fought to keep the pain from coloring his facial expression.

Aidux padded around to his other side and nosed at his hand. "Come on, lemme see."

"Leave me alone, Aidux."

He draped a paw over Nevin's wrist and tugged. "Just let me make sure your stomach isn't gonna fall out."

"My stomach isn't—" He sighed. Arguing took too much energy. He lifted his arm overhead to give the lynx what he asked for.

Blood soaked the fabric of his gray woolen over-shirt like sealing wax all the way down to his hip. It glistened even beneath the overcast sky, the day's humidity preventing it from hardening and losing its luster. Wincing, he raised the shirt high enough for the lynx to get a good look. Aidux closed one eye and leaned in close, his tongue hooking over the corner of his upper lip in concentration.

"How's he look?" asked Theis as he strode across the clearing to join them.

"Well," the cat began. "He's lost a good bit of blood, but he's lucky. Looks like the knife hit bone. With a little clean water, I don't even think we'll have to ampatit."

Nevin shot him a dirty look and yanked his shirt back down. "You're not funny."

"I'm pretty funny."

"It's 'amputate', you dolt," Theis grumbled. Aidux rolled his eyes, but Nevin could hear the click of fangs as he mouthed the word over and over again.

The dark warrior shoved his blade home in its scabbard and knelt beside the slack-jawed soldier. His shining blue eyes searched Nevin's face as he probed the man's neck for signs of life.

"With a dented canteen, no less." Theis shook his head, amazed.

Nevin surveyed the carnage scattered across the forest clearing. Nearby, a soldier laid on his side, facing away. Though he couldn't see how the man had died, Nevin had witnessed Aidux take down enough big game to know his methods. He wouldn't want to see even if he could.

The trampled grasses on the far side of the stone dais did little to conceal the bodies Theis had left in his wake. No blood. No visible wounds. At this distance, they may as well have been sleeping. Five dead, with a questionable sixth hidden somewhere beyond the ruined, crumbling hovel.

He hugged his legs to his chest, resting his chin on his knees. He couldn't understand how the day had come to this. The chances of encountering any of Vincht's soldiers in the wilds of the Traagen were so slim he'd stopped worrying about it. Even if a group did wander this far north, Aidux would have sniffed them out in time to easily avoid crossing paths. And with the legendary Theis Bane as chaperon, a small group wouldn't stand even the smallest of chances should worse come to worst.

But this . . . something had orchestrated this day. Something had brought each of them here against their will and set them against one another. Something with a lust for conflict. Something with a hunger for blood.

He squeezed his eyes shut and shivered. Something, he suspected, not of this world.

Still, the thought of some near-forgotten deity manipulating the two groups into a confrontation bothered him less than what he'd done with Dalen's canteen, and the memories the act had brought screaming back.

Theis straightened with a huff. "Where's the thing? The weapon."

Nevin shrugged. "Dunno."

"Figure it out. We're leaving soon."

"Then go." He buried his face in his knees.

"You know I can't touch the . . . " Theis twirled a finger before dropping his hand and shooting the young man a seething glare. "What's wrong with you? We won, you're alive. Get up."

"I don't want—"

"Don't care what you want, boy." Theis stormed over and grabbed Nevin by the arm, but the man's touch inspired an unexpected wave of emotion, and Nevin ripped free of his grip and shot to his feet.

"You're not *listening*." The intensity of his vicious, tear-stained scowl surprised Theis enough to drive him back a step. For a moment, the motes in the man's bright eyes practically vanished.

Nevin's chest heaved from the anger and despair competing within. Tears dripped from his chin. He loathed being seen this way. Weak. Vulnerable.

But as much as he hated feeling this way in front of the most callous, unfeeling person he'd ever met, he hated himself in that moment even more.

"I didn't—"

His voice caught, so he closed his eyes and breathed. When he spoke again, his quiet tone had taken on a weary edge. "I've spent so much of my life reading about the terrible things people go out their way to do to one another, and for what? Precious metals? Land? Spices? It's . . . it's just *stuff*. There's not one thing I've ever owned or wanted that was more valuable to me than my friendship with Aidux, that was more satisfying to me than getting to spend the day talking with Ishen. The only thing I've ever really wanted was my own life, a life away from . . ."

He stopped, shaking his head against the sting welling up in his eyes.

Theis watched him, still as death. "Away from what?"

"It doesn't matter. I just . . . I didn't want this. I didn't want *any* of this. I just wanted to leave Elbin, to surround myself with people who don't get off on hurting others. *Good people*, Theis. I wanted a life for me and Aidux that didn't involve fear and pain and constant disappointment."

"Then why stay?"

"I didn't have a choice!" he snapped, his clenched fists shaking against his sides. "I grew up in an apple orchard. Farming is really all I know. Sure, Aidux and I could hide out in the woods, scavenging and hunting for food, but that's not much of life. What about a family? Kids? Love?

"And the city? I *might* be able to eek out a living as a scribe or scholar, but what about Aidux? The farmers of Elbin would have skinned him alive if they ever learned he was out there in the woods. I can't imagine city folk would be any better. What sort of person would it make me if I was willing to trade away the life of my one and only friend for the *chance* at having some sort of normal existence?"

He sighed, kicking at the grass. "But that's getting ahead of myself. I'd have to get up the courage to actually leave the Traagen first. I'm not brave. There's things in this world that scare me so much my mind and body literally shut down in the face of them.

"I'm not like you, Theis. I'm not a warrior. I don't go looking for fights. I don't want to hurt anyone."

I'm not Dalen.

He winced, pressing a hand over the still bleeding gash in his side.

"Even if I am a killer."

"You didn't kill anyone, boy."

"I know what I—"

"He's still alive," he barked, jabbing a gloved finger toward the motionless soldier. "You shattered his jaw and knocked him out cold, but he'll yet live."

The cat cocked his head, listening. "He's right, Nevin. I can hear his heart, thunk-thunking away."

Nevin squeezed his head. They didn't understand, and he couldn't bring himself to explain. "What even happened? There's no way we should have lived through that fight. Eight armed soldiers? And they were practically tripping over themselves trying to get at us. *Actually* tripping."

Theis snatched the feathered tip off a nearby grass stalk and crushed it in his fist. "Can thank Grobin's greed and complete lack of honor for that."

"It was like they each suffered a streak of the absolute worst kind of luck." He extended a finger with each point he made. "Grobin slipped and fell. That archer's bowstring snapped. Mine broke his ax against the Sharasil."

Aidux raised a paw. "Mine got eaten."

"Like they were cursed," he continued, ignoring the cat. He pressed a hand to the wound on his side and groaned softly. "This wound could have been a lot worse, too. A little higher or lower and I might not be talking to you right now. I can't explain it, but it's almost like we had some . . . magical assistance."

Theis shook his head. "Not magic. Deific influence. Might seem magical, but it's no less real than you or I."

"Deific influence?" Whether it was his imagination or something else, the young man thought he could feel the goat-headed effigy watching them from atop the mottled stone dais. Listening. "Ivvilger . . . helped us?"

"The god of the living struggle doesn't help. At best, he ignores you. At worst . . ." He trailed off suggestively. "Just be grateful we were on the side that got ignored."

Aidux raised a paw. "Is that the name of the goat? The statue thing? That's Ivvilger?"

Theis nodded.

"That's who was talking to all of us. The one that made us all come here." The cat bared his teeth. "And you want to us to be grateful?"

"Do what you like," he grunted, waving the cat off. "I don't really care."

A faint humming filled the air. Theis froze in place, his body positioned as though gazing off the edge of some vaulted cliff side. He carefully backed away until the humming ceased.

"Over here, boy."

Nevin snatched up his pack and trudged over to Theis' side. He bent forward and ripped the missing weapon from the midst of a thin patch of frozen grass. Sinking into a crouch, he went to work binding it to his pack.

"I need to dry off," he said, shivering in his soaked clothes. Without fear driving him forward, the morning's chill was finally starting to take its toll.

"Not here. Once we've put this place behind us, we'll see about making a fire."

He nodded, looking forward to the prospect of a fire that wasn't chasing him. While they were too high in the mountains to find any white oak, he was certain he could gather some leaves from a demon's crook shrub if he paid attention while they walked. It wouldn't take much to throw together a simple poultice.

Rubbing his tender wrist, Nevin glared down at the discarded canteen. Now that Theis had verbally confirmed its existence, he could no longer write its reappearance off as hallucination. It was as real as the bodies littering the clearing, and despite his efforts to be rid of it, it refused to be left behind.

Even more troubling was the cursed flask's seeming connection to his shadowy pursuer. The canteen had resurfaced both times in close proximity to the strange entity, and though that was enough to cause concern, Nevin wasn't quite ready to claim the two related.

Or maybe he just didn't want them to be.

Nevin waited until his companion's back were turned before lifting Dalen's battered canteen by the strap and hurling it deep into the forest.

With any luck, the approaching fires would save him from having to see the damned thing ever again.

Chapter 30: The Narloc

Within an hour's hike from the clearing where Vincht's soldiers had attacked them, Theis had directed Nevin and Aidux to take a break against the hulking remains of a fallen tower pine. The storm had broken just to the south, leaving their resting spot mostly dry and sheltered from the cutting wind by the pine's trunk and a pair of bushy viburnums. Unlike the uncharacteristically verdant blooms scattered around Ivvilger's clearing, it was still too early for the bushes' spherical white blossoms to emerge, but only just.

With a bundle of leaves plucked from a demon's staff shrub they had passed not fifteen minutes prior, Nevin had set about to constructing a crude poultice. In his haste to flee the farm, he'd failed to collect much in the way of first aid supplies, but a loose stone and a divot in the surface of a nearby boulder made for a decent mortar and pestle, while strips from an old shirt stood in for a bandage. Aidux had watched him curiously while he worked, asking at different points in the process if Nevin would let him taste the smelly concoction.

He did not.

Theis had built a passable fire using a dab of pine tar while Nevin doctored up the cut to his left torso. Aidux had been right; it wasn't particularly deep, but its location would make it difficult to avoid exacerbating. Just swinging an arm while he walked would be enough to continually brush against it, especially with the extra padding the poultice provided. He'd need to be mindful of its presence for at least a few days.

By the time he'd finished dressing the wound, his clothes had dried, prompting Theis to impatiently usher them back en route. While the sun began its western descent, the omnipresent ferns slowly vanished as the rocky soil climbed skyward. The gorge ran beside them on their journey north, growing shallower with every mile they put behind them until Nevin could hear the rush of melt-thickened waters in their push toward the ocean.

Broken storm clouds crowded the eastern sky, having emptied their contents on what little remained of the Traagen earlier in the day before drifting apart as they fled. All that remained were wispy strands of translucent fabric hanging high above the reaching Nimmons, painted in shades of vibrant pinks and oranges from a sun that had long vanished beneath the snow-capped western peaks. Scattered pines and stocky grasses supplied the only touch of color to the otherwise rocky landscape, spread so thin by the increasingly harsh terrain that the three had little worry of the fires chasing them further.

The young man couldn't have known they were but moments away from their destination when he spoke up.

"You about ready to tell me where we're going?" he had asked, fully expecting the man in black to ignore him, but hopeful none-the-less.

To his surprise, Theis had actually responded.

"You ever heard the word 'narloc' before?"

Making a face, Nevin nodded. "Some monster hybrid Ishen tried to sell me on. Said to be part goat, part wolf, part frog or some other nonsense. I'm pretty sure he just made them up to keep me from wandering around in the mountains."

The cat's ears perked up. "I'm sorry, 'part frog' what?"

Thinking back to Ishen's cabin, the young man nearly tripped over his own feet. "Tell me you didn't see that crude map on his desk and think 'narloc' stood for . . . I don't know . . . 'mountain pass' or 'road'."

Theis chuckled softly. "Actually, that's almost exactly what I thought."

Anxious knots twisted up his insides, and Nevin cradled his stomach with an arm. Aidux padded up beside him, anxiously watching the horizon for monsters. The two followed Theis up the slope of a squat hill, picking their way around girthy pines large enough for them both to hide behind.

Theis continued, the pace of his words unaffected by the meager slope. "Where I grew up, our elders required all members of the tribe to learn what we called the pariah tongue—the language of outsiders—alongside our own language, what I've come to understand to be a watered-down version of ancient Ilwarin."

Nevin scratched behind an ear. "I've heard of that. Presumed to be the basis of all modern speech. But it's a dead language, right?"

"Sort of. About the only times you'd hear it spoken is by historians, and practitioners of certain forms of magic. Other than that, you're right. About as dead as can be."

He waved a hand dismissively. "My native tongue shares a number of words with base Ilwarin, and many are so similar that it's easy to make the connection between the old and the new. 'Narloc' is actually one of our words, but it's very similar to its Ilwarin root, 'anarloketh'."

Oh, that's great. Ancient goat hybrids are an actual thing. He absently reached over his shoulder to brush the coarse stone handle of the Sharasil with his fingertips.

"That being said," Theis continued, cresting the hill and coming to a stop. "The word 'narloc' has nothing to do with monsters or creatures of any kind."

"Oh thank goodness," Aidux gushed, relieved. "Half-frog creatures are where I draw the line."

Nevin looked up at the man in black, only a few steps behind now. "Then what the heck is it?"

"It has several meanings." Theis had pointed down the hill, to a spot lying just beside the Hyret Gorge. "But most often, the word is used when referring to a connection or crossing."

About a hundred yards away, the gorge cut a zigzag into the stony earth, butting up against a series of stair-like cliffs and stopping the three from progressing northward without climbing higher into the mountains themselves. In the empty space on this side of the gorge, strings of pallid smoke crawled skyward from the darkened heart of an abandoned campfire. On the far side, shallow snow banks, massive boulders, and the occasional tower pine broke up his sight line, but the terrain opened up enough for comfortable travel in the shadow of the mountains for as far as he could see.

But it was what lay across the gorge that had caused Nevin to backpedal from his two companions.

A lone tower pine stretched out across the fifty foot gap, a makeshift bridge offering the promise of escape to anyone brave enough to trust in their own dexterity and challenge gravity.

The aging pine felt sturdy enough beneath his feet as he stepped out over the thirty foot drop. It didn't sway like the rope bridge that spanned the two sides of the Hyret farther south. It didn't sink into the yawning earthen cleft at the slightest touch of additional weight. It didn't even creak in protest. And while those differences were enough to get him this far, the similarities stoked his anxiety and spurred his heart into a frenzied gallop.

Aidux had made crossing look easy. Without a moment's hesitation, the lynx had leapt onto the arrow-straight tree and bound across, turning to offer the two men on the opposite side a fangy grin as soon as his paws touched solid ground.

Nevin shook the feeling back into his fingers. He stomped once. Twice.

Nothing. No reaction. His heartbeat slowed until he could no longer feel it smashing against his breastbone.

"What's the hold up?" Theis grumbled impatiently behind him. "You're wasting daylight. Get to it."

He shifted uncomfortably, feeling the chill metal weapon sliding along the skin of his bare neck. "I'm trying, Theis. Just . . . give me a second."

The man in black crossed his arms. "Tell me you're not afraid of heights."

"Not exactly," he mumbled, taking a tentative step forward and fighting the urge to look down at his feet. The last thing he wanted to do was catch a glimpse of what awaited him below. "I've never had a problem climbing trees to get to out-of-reach apples. I think it's bridges that scare me, honestly."

He felt his way forward with the tip of his boot, stepping around the pointed stump of a broken branch without looking. The gorge exhaled a gust of chill mist, but adrenaline kept him warm. He took a deep breath and kept going.

Theis reached out and plucked a clump of dry earth from the upended roots of the tree, squeezing it between his fingers until it broke apart. "Dirt's still here. Tree couldn't have fallen more than a few days ago."

From across the way, Aidux's grin hadn't faltered, all razor-sharp fangs and nightmares. "It's okay, Nevin. Just put one boot in front of the other. As long as you don't fall, you'll be fine!"

"Not helping, cat," Theis yelled from behind.

The cat's smile wilted. "You're right, that's my fault."

About twenty steps across the fallen tower pine, a strained crackle echoed along the walls of the gorge.

Nevin stopped when he felt the tree shudder beneath his feet.

Theis straightened, his shining eyes widening considerably. "Boy, if there was ever a time to grow some balls, it's right now."

Blood pounded through the young man's skull. He fought to still his trembling limbs, but for all his efforts, waves of shivers tore through his frozen, unresponsive body. He forced himself to blink, training his gaze on Aidux to keep from accidentally glancing down and peering into the hungry throat of a gorge that wanted nothing more than to open up and swallow him whole.

There's no other way, he told himself, working his tongue and lips to get some saliva flowing in his bone-dry mouth. *Get to Comelbough. Get rid of the weapon. Live your life. The only way out is forward. You can do this, Nevin.*

No, you can't.

The spectral voice rolled over him in an undulating wave of sickening pressure. Startled, Nevin's balance faltered. He crouched to steady himself and relieve the twisting pain in his gut. Bits of loose bark tumbled off the sides of the tree to disappear below.

Refusing to turn from the concerned face of his friend, Nevin could none-the-less see a dark figure lurking at the edge of his vision. At the end of a branch, perched atop a frail finger of needle-laced wood, a gaunt shadow watched him struggle to maintain his composure nearly thirty feet above the surface of a swollen, roiling plane of turbulent water.

You can't do it, and you know it.

"Just keep moving," Theis urged, leaning toward the young man but not stepping up onto the tree for fear of making things worse. "You make it across, we make camp. The final challenge in an already trying day."

Nevin nodded, gritting his teeth as he tried to force himself to stand up straight. Tears of frustration spilled down his cheeks. His legs twitched and trembled, but for all his efforts, they wouldn't listen.

The gaunt figure glided closer, navigating the delicate branch with no more difficulty than someone walking on solid ground.

This gorge will eat you alive.

Nevin pressed his hands to his ears. "Stop it."

The figure took another step.

It's going to choke on your limp, dead body.

Each breath came in short, heaving gasps. "Shut . . . up."

Aidux cocked his head. "Nevin? Who are talking to?"

Can they not see it? Is it all in my head?

The tree shuddered again, shifting slightly in place and groaning. Theis searched the fallen pine for signs of weakness, instability. "You have got to move. Tree's not going to hold much longer."

"I . . . I can't." The pine tree lurched with a resounding crack, sending up a cloud of rock dust and splintered wood as the narrower top of the pine bent and split. He grabbed hold of a branch stump and hunkered down further.

"This is bad, Theis!" Aidux yelled, every inch of his fur standing on end. "I think he's stuck! You're gonna have to go get him!"

The man in black jerked his head side-to-side. "If I go out there and grab him, this tree will break in half for sure!"

The shadowy figure advanced to Nevin's side. It leaned in and extended a pale hand, its fingertips glistening black beneath the day's dying light.

Give in to me. Let me be your strength. I can save you.

Nevin gasped as the fallen pine dropped a few more inches. "I don't . . . want . . . to die."

The gaunt hand reached for his own.

Then just take my hand.

The young man nodded. He didn't know what would happen if he gave in to the dark figure, but it had to be better than this.

"*Khek*," Theis spat, taking a few steps back. He sank into a tight crouch. His eyes narrowed. Then, with a huff of hot breath, he launched forward in a dead sprint.

With a single leap, the man in black cleared the edge of the cliff and landed without stopping on the sheath of rough bark encompassing the fallen tower pine. The crumbling bridge jolted downward, but Theis neither stumbled nor slowed as he ran, his black leather cloak billowing out behind him like a trail of smoke.

They can't save you.

I know.

And you can't save yourself.

Nevin could only nod. The hand spread its glistening fingers wide beside his face, inviting him to merely reach up and grasp it.

No pain. No fear.

His hand trembling, Nevin reached out.

Just endless, comforting black.

Somewhere, deep within the shadows of his subconscious, Nevin felt a tiny voice screaming out in alarm, but in his current state, it took nothing for him to brush it aside.

"Nevin!" Aidux screamed.

The crumbling tree dipped again, and Nevin's eyes rolled back into his skull. The last thing he felt before slipping into unconsciousness was the sickening sensation of weightlessness.

Chapter 31: Intent to Kill

Theis sank to his knees, leaning forward until he had to prop himself up with one arm to keep from falling face-first onto the bare stone. Clouds of hot breath burst through his mask's narrow mouth slit. Closing his eyes, he cracked his neck with a grunt before gesturing to the cat without looking up.

"He's okay, I think." Aidux reached out and spread a massive paw across Nevin's chest, visibly relieved to feel his friend's chest rising and falling beneath his toes. "Still asleep, but it looks like he's coming around."

Behind him, nearly all evidence of the temporary bridge had vanished, swallowed beneath the yawning lips of the gorge. Only a matching pair of vertical scars on either side of the cliff face and a scattered collection of wood chips hinted that something had once been there. Theis had his suspicions about the origin of that unstable, makeshift bridge, but for the moment, he was simply grateful to have made it across alive and intact.

An odd feeling, that.

The boy stirred, sucking air as he raised a hand to grip his head. Aidux rested his chin on the boy's chest and peered up at him with wide, silver eyes. Nevin glanced down at the cat before reaching out to scratch between his tufted ears. A soft, rumbling purr filled the air.

"Can you hear me, boy?"

Nevin nodded without taking his eyes off the darkening sky. Deepening reds and purples dominated all but the western horizon, and mere moments separated them from an emerging sea of shy, twinkling stars.

Theis pushed to his feet, adjusting his leather cloak until it draped about him like a shroud. He walked over and knelt at the boy's side. The motes in his eyes barely moved. When he spoke, all trace of the usual harsh edge to his rumbling baritone was absent, softened by an uncharacteristic sympathy for the troubled youth lying supine before him.

"Them that raised you," he began, reaching up to adjust the hang of his wooden mask. "Never asked you whether it was the fires or the soldiers that took them."

Nevin chewed his lip and swallowed before answering. "Frieda died when I was very young. I don't really remember much about her."

"Frieda," Theis said thoughtfully. "And your . . . ?"

The boy looked away. "I've never had a father."

Aidux moved to speak, but Nevin silenced him with a firm pat.

Content with his head scratch, the lynx returned to the comfort of his friend's chest. The boy watched the sky, his eyes unfocused and brimming with painful memories. Theis knew that look. For the first time in a long time, the man in black had something to say, but that little voice in the depths of his subconscious bade him remain quiet. And he always listened to that little voice.

With a sigh, Theis tugged down on the hem of his cowl. "Been through more in the last few days than many people deal with their entire lives. And against all odds, you survived."

"Thanks to you." Nevin rubbed the lynx's head once more. "And thanks to Aidux. Without the both of you, I'd be little more than another victim of Vincht's search for the Sharasil."

"Without you, the Sharasil would have likely ended up in the hands of the wrong kind of people, or been lost forever. Don't know why it's important to keep that from happening, but that old woman in Comelbough seems to think neither option would be good."

The boy slid his fingers beneath Aidux's chin and gently nudged the cat off his chest, before sitting up and shrugging the satchel from his shoulders. He pulled the top-heavy pack into his lap, the storm-gray Sharasil stretched out before him like a pair of welcoming arms. Hesitant to be so close to the mercurial and dangerous weapon, Theis and the cat each slid back a step.

His fingers traced the engraved lines zigzagging out from the strange indentation at the object's center. "Something strange happened in the clearing. In the middle of the fight, I thought I saw it . . . change? It didn't last long, but there was this bright light and a weird hissing sound, like when you throw cold water in a hot pan. Then it was gone and it looked like this again.

"I know there's more to it than what we're seeing. It's not much of a weapon in its current form, but I don't know what I did to make it change."

Lying beside the gorge, minutes away from night, Theis knew that now wasn't the best time to get into this discussion, but after what they'd just been through, he wondered if maybe an intellectual discussion was just the distraction the young man needed.

The man in black thumbed the gouge in the chin of his mask. "At the lowest level, all magic functions off of something called 'intent'. What you mean to do, your goal, the direction you've chosen to take."

Nevin scratched his head. "Like a thought?"

"Not exactly. Thoughts have no weight behind them, no real substance. Intent is the mental component of physical action. A precursor, if you will. A wise man once said, that everything that's created or built is done so twice. Once in the mind, and once in the world. The clearer and more precise the first, the better the quality of the second."

"I don't see how that's any different from a thought. I think about a house and then I go build it. Intent, thoughts . . . same thing."

Theis cocked his head, thinking about the best way to make his point. Then, with little hesitation, he reached out and slapped the young man on the side of the head. The dry clap of leather on flesh pierced the quiet.

"Ow!" Nevin said, rubbing the sting away. "What was that for?"

"Thought about hitting you for a few seconds there, but nothing happened until I made a decision. Then I formed an intent in my mind, and my hand followed suit. Years of combat training forced the two to work together at a high level, and the result was a hard slap placed precisely where I intended."

"Next time, just tell me," he said with a scowl.

"I like it better when he smacks you," Aidux said, grinning.

"Point is," Theis continued. "Thoughts don't get you anywhere. Wishing, daydreaming, hoping . . . pointless. Action is the goal, but without a clear, focused intent, the resulting action will be sloppy, half-assed, disappointing.

"Magic works the same way. If I had to guess, the Sharasil waits until the right intent acts on it, then it . . . does whatever it does. Do you remember what you were doing or about to do when it changed?"

Nevin shrugged. "Just trying to survive. Aidux was fighting a soldier, and it looked like he needed some help, so I moved to protect him when the other soldier knocked the weapon out of my hands."

Theis held up a finger. "Aidux was in trouble?"

"He was in a bad spot, and I was worried he wouldn't be able to defend himself."

"Now hold on," the cat protested. "I had everything under control—"

Theis cut him off. "You wanted to kill that soldier, didn't you?"

Nevin looked insulted. "That's ridiculous. Good people don't choose to hurt others."

Theis crossed his arms as he stood. "A man is about to kill your only friend, and you didn't want to hurt him? What were you planning on doing? Charge over there and talk him out of it?"

The boy waved a hand, obviously taken aback by the man's ludicrous view on the situation, but if he wanted to argue, he couldn't seem to find the words. Theis watched him struggle, but didn't interrupt. A person needed to come to certain conclusions on their own.

After a moment, the boy dropped his hand and shrugged. "Honestly, I couldn't tell you. I wasn't really thinking. I was just acting."

Theis nodded. "Intent unrealized is still intent. The subconscious mind acts on intent all day long. Moving the heart, the lungs, hearing, seeing, breathing . . . each action performed due to unconsciously generated intent. Wouldn't surprise me if your subconscious formed an intent to kill when confronted with the prospect of losing a friend . . . and the Sharasil reacted."

"So you're saying that, if I want it to change again, if I want it to reveal what it really is, I have to want to use it to kill?"

"It's possible."

"All the more reason to get rid of it sooner rather than later."

Nevin sighed, resting a hand on the object and exhaling an unnaturally dense cloud of fog. "It's just . . . it's so strange. You have to know *something* about it, Theis. Anything. You wouldn't just come out to the middle of nowhere looking for something you know nothing about, right?"

The man shrugged. "Never seen it's like."

"But, you're the one that gave it to Ishen. How can you know nothing? Who told you to take it to him? Why did it need to be hidden?"

"Was just the messenger, boy," he said, turning to face the southern wilds. The rain had weakened the inky smoke's hold on the sky, but it could be weeks before it vanished completely.

He awkwardly shifted his cloak about his shoulders. "The past is the past. Doesn't matter *how* we got here, just what we do now that we're here. We've a long way to go before we reach Comelbough, and with any luck, it will be uneventful from here out.

"Can't promise you things will get better when we get there, but the old woman should have some answers. And trust me boy, I'm just as curious as you are."

Nevin ran a finger along the upper edge of the Sharasil. "You think . . . you think maybe she'll be able to sever the link? Disconnect me from this thing?"

Theis' vibrant eyes waned purple. "Let's set up camp. We've a long road ahead of us, and you two need your rest."

Chapter 32: Demanding an Audience

Gripping his belt with both hands, the nervous page scurried along in front of Vincht, his short legs a blur of motion beneath his gold and crimson tunic as he fought to stay far enough ahead of the focused soldier to keep from being trampled. Given the option, Vincht would have forgone the company of his guide; a boy with broom chopped hair barely old enough to be trusted with a whittling knife. The scar-faced warrior had committed the layout of the Baron's modest estate to memory on his first visit, though that wasn't saying much. Nearly the whole of Comelbough would fit snugly inside his hometown's slums, and likely wouldn't have appeared out-of-place.

He idly scratched the fresh scab covering the dimpled scar on his chin. Baron Lancowl had always been one to stand on ceremony. Everyone had a place in his service, and everyone adhered strictly to the jobs they were given. Servants, few as they were, dutifully maintained and organized the spartan manor grounds, though Vincht had never so much as laid eyes on one, as the Baron preferred them to accomplish their tasks without drawing attention. Conversely, armed guards stood at attention at strategic points within the corridors, tucked into small, out-of-the-way, arched alcoves and armed with man-catchers and short swords.

Vincht looked down at his hand. Fresh blood glistened on his fingertips, and his nails were packed with scab dust. He brushed them against his dusty leather vest, smearing the mixture atop a darkened swath of crusted fluids from dozens of previous wipes.

Truth be told, Vincht was in no state to seek an audience with the leader of Comelbough. Three days of hard, non-stop riding had left him with only one of the three horses he'd left the caravan with, and an accumulation of road filth and dried sweat whose scent was sure to pucker the sheltered nose of even the least pampered aristocrat. But since Stephen's incompetence had taken from him the one thing he could never get back, Vincht found himself increasingly less concerned with the specifics of his personal appearance.

"Move it, Geldon," he said to the back of the page's head. "I only have so much patience today, and I've reserved none of it for you."

The boy picked up the pace and barreled through an arched doorway, skidding to a stop at the foot of an elongated stone dining table. Vincht followed him in. Late morning sunlight poured into the spacious room through a series of soaring, open windows, framed with sets of bunched crimson curtains emblazoned with the Lancowl coat-of-arms. To one side, a low fire simmered within an ornate brick fireplace. On the other wall, a pair of armed guards silently appraised his arrival from within two of three recessed alcoves. A dense pair of crimson curtains hid the contents of the third alcove from sight.

The polished white dining table was mostly bare but for the space at the head of the table. Bowls of dried sand plums and mulberries, a torn loaf of speckled rye bread, and a half-eaten roast quail sat before a surprised aristocrat. Hunched over his meal, Baron Caviil Lancowl considered Vincht from beneath a protruding brow, sucking loudly at a morsel of food lodged between his upper incisors.

"Caviil." Vincht flashed the young leader a comfortable smile, feeling the scabs on his cheeks and forehead cracking painfully. "You look well."

Baron Lancowl wiped his mouth and leaned into his high-backed chair. The man's eyes flicked across Vincht's face, quickly taking in each of his scab-encrusted scars before speaking. "Deacon Morfren. Your expedient return was unexpected, nor was the condition of . . ."

"Of what, your lordship?" Vincht edged forward, resting his hand on the ivory hilt of his sword. "The condition of what?"

Clearing his throat, the Baron popped a mulberry in his mouth and averted his eyes. "The southern woods are not always kind to travelers. It's good you made it back in one piece, and only mildly the worse for wear."

Despite his youth, the baron's long face and cheeks displayed a sunken, almost corpse-like quality that had always disgusted Vincht, but what the man lacked in physical attractiveness, he made up for in style. His stark white hair was pulled tight against his skull in a high ponytail. A number of polished brass buttons adorned his crimson, low-collar jacket, with a charcoal scarf tucked neatly into its lapels.

But what bothered Vincht the most was the piece of the man that wasn't present. The left sleeve of his jacket was folded and pinned neatly to his shoulder, his missing arm a remnant of the event that solidified his position as patriarch of the family name. In the interest of maintaining decorum, Vincht had never pressed the man for the details of that day.

If the Baron wished to discuss the circumstances of his father's death, the man would need to bring it up on his own.

"That will be all." The Baron wiped his mouth with a tasseled napkin and gestured toward the door. With an exaggerated bow, the young page scampered out of the room.

The Baron straightened with a resigned sigh. "Now then. What more do the Origin Knights require from the Lancowls? I can only assume your presence means you need some additional assistance, as I doubt you'd come before me again had you found whatever it was you were looking for."

By the man's irregular pace and uncertain inflection, Vincht could tell he wasn't used to sustaining such a careful tone. A problem unique to intelligent people who don't regularly interact with those in power over them. Vincht found it endlessly entertaining.

"Things did not go exactly to plan, but I am confident the outcome will ultimately align with our interests."

"I am pleased to hear it." The Baron forced a tight smile, leaning forward to rest his hand on the tabletop. "Might I inquire on another matter, momentarily? In your exploration of the Traagen Peninsula, did you come across anyone . . . unusual?"

"Unusual?"

"A man. A warrior with unnaturally blue eyes. Burning with some internal, infernal light. Did you happen across anyone like that?"

Vincht clasped his hands together behind his back and strolled around the room, coming to a halt before the pair of curtains drawn tight across the opening to the third, central alcove. The weighty fabric drifted in and out, manipulated by the currents of some undetectable breeze. Slowly, the man leaned forward, turning his head to point an ear at the covered alcove.

Though he couldn't be certain, he thought he could barely detect the whisper of raspy breathing coming from behind the twin curtains.

"I have no interest in playing a part in your personal vendetta, Caviil. It's been ten years. If you haven't yet solved it, you likely never will. Best you should focus on what you've gained, and put to rest the thoughts of what you've lost."

The Baron slumped back into his chair, frowning. "Of course. Thank you for your insight, Deacon Morfren."

Vincht grinned. How easily the weak give in. Years of failure had apparently eaten away at the man's hope, and Vincht refused to reward his lack of persistence. If the man had pressed him even a little . . .

"How do they work?" he asked softly, trailing a fingertip along the laced edge of the curtain.

"Who?" The Baron halfheartedly picked at his quail. "You mean the Breathers?"

"Mmm. For someone who hates magic as much as you do, you've certainly found a unique way to turn it against those who use it."

"So I've been told." Caviil pushed his plate away and reached for a clay jug, filling a simple cup with a deep burgundy wine. He swirled it idly, but didn't drink. "The way I understand it, the human body only pulls as much spiritual energy through its soul channel as is necessary to operate its systems. In truth, most people live their lives deficient in the amount of spiritual energy required to perform at their highest levels. What they lack is then supplemented in part by the sun, the food they eat, and the company they keep."

"Really. The company they keep?"

The Baron nodded. "Some people give. Others take. Unconsciously, mind you, but I'm sure you've met someone who left you feeling drained after long bouts of their company."

Vincht grunted in agreement. *Rowen.* He was even more glad to be free of that one.

"Users of magic are of a different sort. As willful manipulators of their own spiritual energy, they seem to suffer from a natural excess. They bleed this extra, unused energy into their surroundings wherever they go. The Breathers track that excess, sniffing it out and honing in on its location."

"Ah." He scowled, disappointed. "Little more than glorified trackers, then."

Caviil scoffed, taking a sip from his cup before returning to his nervous swirling. "You insult me. How foolish I would be to create a tool capable only of locating, but not of dispatching.

"No, Deacon Morfren. The Breathers are much, much more. They are single-minded beasts existing only to find and destroy sources of spiritual manipulation. They are possessed of a hate matched only by my own, yet where mine is impotent, theirs manifests in the strength to tear limb from limb any user foolish enough to come before them."

The smile returned to his scarred lips. "They sound magnificent."

"They are nothing short of a necessary evil. A poison masquerading as the antidote. Given I could, I'd have them all put down just to be free of their detestable wheezing and horrifying countenances."

Vincht turned to face the man full-on. "Are they truly so hideous?"

The baron ceased his swirling, staring down the table to keep from meeting Vincht's glare. Finally, he took a long drink before setting his cup down, a slight tremble in his hand.

"Speaking of users, where is Stephen? I must say, I was surprised to see you return to the capital in such a wounded state. Surely my man would have tended you had he been offered the chance."

Vincht returned to his examination of the crimson curtains. He scratched at the scab covering his cheek, picking at the clot until fresh blood drooled down the side of his face.

"He'll be along, in time."

"In time," he repeated flatly. "I trust nothing tragic has befallen him?"

"I can promise you he fared better than most." Vincht reached into a small pouch on his belt and produced a small, glass sphere. It was perfectly round and smooth to the point of slickness, and no larger than a field mouse. A mote of what appeared to be spent coal rested at its heart.

"As you suspected, the item we sought eluded us, but if my instincts are correct, it's likely heading this way as we speak. I rode out ahead of everyone else in order to prepare for its arrival."

He raised the sphere to his lips and blew gently across its surface. Orange light rippled out from its core before the blackened mote burst into a single, unwavering flame encased entirely in crystal-clear glass.

In the space behind the twin curtains, something gasped, an extended inhalation that sucked the heavy fabric deep into the recessed alcove.

The soldiers to either side shifted nervously, lowering the blunted tips of their man-catchers and edging out into the open. The Baron slowly stood, his wide, sunken eyes trained on the glowing object clutched in Vincht's fingertips.

"Have you lost your mind?" he said, his harsh whisper echoing in the cavernous dining hall. "Bringing unauthorized magic within the walls of this estate is strictly forbidden, and for good reason. Have you any idea of the danger to which you expose not only yourself, but the rest of us as well?"

The trapped flame blinked out, and the mote fell dark once more. "The only thing you need worry about is failing to help me secure what I seek before it leaves your city."

As Vincht watched, the twin curtains slowly bulged outward as something pushed forward to press its bulk against the walls of its fabric prison. Nearly a foot above his head, the curtains shuddered as the unseen creature sucked in a lungful of air. He resisted the urge to reach out and touch what he could only assume was the beast's face as it sought the source of its brief taste of magical energy.

Smiling, Vincht idly picked at the scabs on his forehead.

"Magnificent."

Chapter 33: Shadow and Stone

For the third time in so many minutes, Nevin reached out and knocked tentatively on the stalwart three-panel door.

"Do you suppose we're at the wrong place?" Aidux danced uncomfortably atop the low stoop, unable to keep his paws still on the mist-slick cobbles. His hindquarters sank briefly every few seconds, his tired mind urging him to sit, but the thought of plopping his butt onto the hard, slimy stone kept him upright.

He shrugged, peering out over his shoulder and into the night. "I can't tell. It's got the sign, though Theis never mentioned an engraving."

Compared to Elbin's scattered homesteads and winding dirt roads, the seaside city of Comelbough was a labyrinthine mess of cramped, hulking buildings and congested thoroughfares. To make matters worse, a gluttonous fog loomed at every turn, constricting their world to a repeated series of bowed cobblestone streets and overbearing shopfronts.

The ponderous haze, empowered by the night, had trailed them closely as they attempted to follow the man in black's directions, giving ground only reluctantly as they soldiered forward. All trace of life had presumably retreated to the safety of the darkened buildings, leaving Nevin and his feline companion alone to navigate the hauntingly empty corridors of shadow and stone.

The pair stood beneath a tattered canvas awning, its color indeterminate after years of sun damage and the darkness of a fog-shrouded night. Clumsily interlocking stones matching those paving the drab streets framed the lower story like every other building on the block, with the overhanging second floor trading heavy stone for a wood-framed stucco facade. Murky water dripped from the angled edges of clay shingles, smelling faintly of brine and soot.

Nevin craned his neck to look around the awning. Suspended overhead, a decorative sign advertised the purpose of the business before them; three polished bronze spheres suspended beneath a wrought iron bar.

He recognized the sign from his studies with Ishen. The three spheres were the universally recognized symbol of a pawnbroker—a collector of non-specific items of value from both locals and travelers through the city. He squinted, trying to read the single letter engraved on the side of each sphere.

"D-O-N? What is that? Is that a name or a title?"

"Maybe internals?"

Nevin eyeballed the cat, always surprised by his friend's tenuous grasp of the language.

". . . initials?"

Aidux eyeballed him back. "How come when you repeat what I say it always *sounds* different?"

"Because it *is* different?"

Somewhere out in the pervasive fog, the sudden clatter of metal silenced the pair. Nevin spun around, ushering the cat behind him as he stared out into the gloom. He remembered thinking how strange it was that they hadn't crossed paths with any of the locals as they traversed the city, but had chalked it up to the late hour and eerie weather. Still, no stray animals, no vagrants, no city guard . . . the emptiness was both complete and unsettling.

"Eww," said Aidux, suppressing a gag. "Your breath *stinks*."

"Shh." Nevin stretched his eyes open, but beyond roughly fifteen feet in any direction, all he could see was gray. Theis had sent to the two of them into the city with no source of light despite the young man's protests, citing a complete inability to see in the dark. Etro had only just entered its waxing phase, and wasn't yet bright enough to pierce the dense, low-hanging clouds.

Nevin wondered if Theis' glowing eyes afforded the man some measure of night vision he'd failed to mention.

Now, though, the absence of any sort of light felt beneficial, as being spotted out in the open like this could be more troublesome than blindly wandering the streets.

Chain rattled on stone, closer than he would have liked, and Nevin quietly backed Aidux up against the storefront's door, hoping whatever lurked in the fog was just as blind as him.

Nevin held his breath. He reached over his shoulder, trying to feel for the Sharasil's coarse stone grip, but Theis had made him hide the weapon within a sheath of burlap, and Nevin's fingers found only cloth.

"On the left!" Aidux whispered, sinking into a crouch.

Nevin flinched in surprise, and nearly fell backwards off the low stoop.

A faint orange glow peeked around the corner of the pawnbroker's shop. As he watched, the glow listed ever closer, until a tall figure rose up through the fog and lumbered into view.

With no other option, Nevin raised his fists defensively, feeling like a child next to the burly shadow growing ever larger as it approached the pawnbroker's storefront.

"Is that you out here, banging on the door of a closed shop at this ungodly hour?"

The figure extended a glass-shielded candle overhead, revealing an aging bald man in a pale blue robe and matching night clothes. Even with Nevin standing atop the raised stoop, the white-bearded stranger gazed down at him through a cumbersome pair of thick spectacles. Concern, not annoyance, colored his hushed tone, and Nevin found himself quietly hoping that this was indeed the man they had come looking for.

The stranger squinted first at Nevin, then turned his attention to Aidux and started, stumbling back a step. "Whoa! You know you keep the company of fanged horse, young man?"

Aidux cocked his head in confusion. "You've got your four-legged animals confused. Clearly, I am a cat."

Nevin shot the lynx an icy look. "*Aidux.*"

"What? The rules only applied to Elbin."

The old man dug a finger around in his ear. "And a talking one, to boot! Obolvia take me, my mind is finally giving out from all those years of cheap whiskey and baccy rolls!"

Somewhere in the dark, the unseen chains rattled again, and the old man whipped his candle out toward the street, a serious expression wiping the surprise off his face. He squinted nervously into the mist, but nothing moved.

"Don't you two know there's a curfew in place?" The man shuffled forward, quickly sizing him up. "The benighted streets are no place for children and their pets, especially considering the horrors that now patrol the dark. Have you nowhere to go? Speak fast."

"We're looking for the home of an old pawnbroker."

The man nodded, adjusting his spectacles. "Well, you've found one. What's your business?"

Nevin licked his lips. He wasn't sure how much trust he should place in the stranger, but remaining out in the open felt increasingly unwise.

"Theis Bane sent us."

The man's untamed eyebrows reached for his non-existent hairline. "Better then we get you inside before something unpleasant this way comes."

He squinted into the gloom once more as he turned, gesturing for the boy and his cat to follow behind. The two shared a quick look before stepping down from the raised stoop and circling around behind the fog-wrapped building.

The bald man raised his candle high as he approached an unpaved alley running alongside the shop. A weathered hand-cart emerged from the mists like a silent sentry as they stepped single-file beneath the arched opening. Their leader carefully picked his way around it, grumbling to himself about needing to find a new place to store the blasted thing.

Behind the building, warm light spilled through an open door and into the night, pushing back the gloom to frame a small wooden porch decorated with a reinforced rocking chair. The man rested a hand on the door and beckoned them both to enter. Nevin flashed a weak smile as he passed, the lynx trotting along at his heels.

The cozy living space reminded him of Ishen, and Nevin experienced a pang of longing as he acclimated to the abrupt change in scenery. A hodgepodge of scents drifted about the still air: a balanced mixture of spent tallow, vegetable broth, wood smoke, and mint. Assorted lamps and candles of every shape and size decorated the peeling maroon walls, the gentle light touching nearly every nook and cranny of the common room. A single round tabletop, empty but for two porcelain cups of cold tea, waited in a domed niche beneath the open banister staircase leading up to the second floor. A pair of plush lavender couches faced a crackling fire, and a small cast iron pot belched out puffs of stewed cabbage and potatoes. In the far wall, another door stood closed, the only secret the open room allowed.

The bald man gingerly placed the shielded candle on a small table beside the entryway and closed the door behind him. He paused, sinking into a long sigh of relief. "I have to admit. A boy and his talking cat were not the visitors I had expected to darken my door on this night. And in such dangerous times. The Fates, they toy with you, young one."

Nevin slid his pack from his shoulder with a groan of relief. "You don't know the half of it."

The man chuckled. "A story better shared on a full belly and wrapped in dry clothing. I can address both, if you'll grant me the pleasure."

The young man nodded gratefully. Uninterested in conversation, Aidux padded across the room to stretch out on the floor before the welcoming fire.

Nevin shook his head. "Just like that, huh? Someone invites you into his home and you immediately find the nearest fire and curl up for a nap?"

The cat shrugged. "You haven't let me sleep during the day since we started. At this point, I'm not even sure I'm still knockturnal."

They each stared at the other through narrowed eyes until Nevin slowly shook his head.

"Somehow, I still don't think you're using that right."

The cat stuck out his tongue before covering his muzzle with his paws.

"Before you sit," said their host, extending an open hand in greeting. "My name is Donald Iustus. You may call me Donald or Don, though never Donny. The rights to that name will be forever reserved by my late wife, and even then, I only tolerated it because I loved her so."

Donald placed his other palm to his chest, thumbing a rigid lump hidden beneath the fabric of his nightshirt. The young man shook his burly hand. "I'm Nevin. Pleased to meet you, Donald."

The larger man smiled. "And your friend? I heard you call him Aidux?"

The tired lynx had rolled onto his back, his massive paws floating limply in the air. A faint grin parted his toothy maw. The two men shared a laugh at the sight.

"Come," he said, releasing his grip on Nevin's hand to take him by the shoulder. "Drop your things over by the table and I'll take you upstairs. My clothes might be a touch large on you, but they'll suffice until we can clean and dry your current set."

Few things sounded better to Nevin in that moment. Comfort was a long forgotten luxury. How many days had come and gone since the tragedy in Elbin had put them on the run? How many miles of unmapped wilderness had passed beneath their feet? How many hours of sleep had been disrupted by near-constant nightmares? Nightmares of fire, of spiteful gods, of Dalen's cruel and twisted face?

He dropped the satchel in the seat of a dining chair as Donald gathered the tea cups from the table and placed them in a water-filled washtub in the corner. Unstrapping the burlap-shrouded Sharasil, Nevin moved to place it at the center of the table, but quickly thought better of it. It would be safer for everyone if the weapon never left his side.

"What have you got there?" said Donald.

"That's what I hope to figure out. In the meantime, just make sure you don't touch it. It apparently doesn't like it when anyone but me gets near it."

Donald's eyebrows reached once again for his non-existent hairline, but he didn't argue.

"Very well," he said, smiling. "Let's go see about those clothes, shall we?"

With a final glance at the snoring lynx, Nevin followed the man upstairs.

Chapter 34: My Name is Nevin Walker

Nevin tugged the knit sweater over his head and frowned. His hands fell well short of the arm holes, with a good half a foot of extra material brushing his knees.

He shrugged. Warm. Dry. Things could be far worse.

Shoving the loose sleeves up to his elbows, Nevin gathered his old clothes and travel supplies together at the foot of the bed. He picked up his belt, pausing to run a hand over the overstuffed belt pouch containing the strange ironwood box he hadn't found the time to unlock.

He sank down beside his pack and carefully removed the box, turning it over and over in his hands. The lid fit the base almost seamlessly, and no amount of prying earned even a sliver of movement. Tongue dangling out the side of his mouth, Nevin lifted the box to his face and peered into the darkened key hole.

Ishen always has to make everything difficult.

Somewhere below, a door creaked open, then quickly creaked closed. Muffled voices drifted up the staircase, too quiet for him to make out.

He straightened. *Theis.* Dropping the box atop the quilt-covered bed, Nevin shouldered the burlap-sheathed weapon and bolted down the stairs.

And came face-to-face with the most beautiful human he'd ever seen in his life.

"A friend of yours, Donald?"

The young man started at her unexpected appearance, the breathy silk-wrapped voice belonging to the flawless face of a middle-aged woman. With her steepled hands clasped at her waist, her almond-shaped brown eyes regarded Nevin through wavy strands of chestnut hair. The faint traces of a self-assured smile touched the corners of her pale, wispy lips. A gauzy yellow dress hung loosely about her diminutive form, appearing as though the slightest hint of wind might sunder the delicate cloth and carry it like a cloud toward the horizon.

He swallowed, painfully aware of how he must look in Donald's giant-sized hand-me-downs. In all of Elbin, there hadn't been a single woman to match her beauty. The way she stood, her back straight as a wooden dowel, chin tilted slightly toward the ceiling, one foot leading the other, she reminded Nevin of a dancer posing before an adoring crowd in the moments preceding a show.

Donald, sporting a knowing smile, reclined back into the plush cushions of the couch. He hoisted a glass of dark liquid to his lips and sipped.

"I'd be careful there, young man. Better not to let your heart get out in front of your head. Especially with *that* one."

The woman rolled her eyes. "As if the heart was ever a man's problem organ, Donald."

She grunted in amusement, gliding over to the dining table and sitting. She crossed her ankles and sat perfectly straight, ignoring the chair back like it might stain her dress. "Taking in strays now, are we? You always were a gentle soul with a soft spot for the less fortunate."

"Be a rich man if not for that." He shrugged. "But I get by."

Nevin blinked, slightly put off by her 'stray' comment. "I'm sorry, I wasn't trying to stare. It's just . . . I thought you were someone else."

A door clicked shut, and the young man turned his head to see the inky form of Theis standing in the entry way of the common room. With his simmering eyes trained on Nevin, he pulled back his cloak and slid his sicklesque blade home.

"Surrounding block is clear, far as I can tell. Blasted fog didn't make it easy." He pointed a finger at the woman in the yellow dress. "Long as you can control yourself, old woman, we shouldn't have any visitors tonight."

"Wait, 'old woman'?" Nevin wrinkled his brow in confusion. "This is who you kept telling us about? The woman who sent you to Elbin?"

"I prefer to be called Aurnia, if it pleases you both."

Aidux stretched from his place in front of the fire before rising from his brief nap. "Mister Theis isn't one for names, so I wouldn't get your hopes up."

"Drop the 'mister', cat. It's just Theis."

The lynx padded over to Nevin's side. "See what I mean?"

Donald raised his glass. "Point of interest? The cat talks."

Aurnia turned an icy gaze to the man in black. "My patience has worn thin on this, Theis. You told me this fetch quest of yours would take no more than a week, but by my count it's been nearly ten days, and unless I'm confused, you've returned with little more than this . . . scrawny provincial and his pet."

Scrawny provincial? Irritation crept into his voice. "I prefer to be called Nevin, if it ple—"

Theis cut him off. "Criticism comes so easily from those who spend their days drinking tea by the fire."

Aurnia shrugged. "You're the one who refused my company. Can't say I didn't offer."

"Would have been even more useless in a fight than that one." With a derisive snort, Theis waved a gloved hand in Nevin's direction.

And with that condescending remark, Nevin's pent up frustrations overflowed.

"How about you both just shut up already?"

The seething young man had everyone's attention now. Silence fell over the room, interrupted only by the occasional crackle of burning wood. Nevin was gripping the bundled weapon so tight his knuckles were white. He stared at the floor, gritting his teeth in the throes of a sudden surge of anger. Aidux placed a comforting paw on his thigh, but it didn't help.

The man in black reclined against the door, the motes in his eyes vibrating against their swollen pupils. "Something to say, boy?"

Nevin shot the man in black a withering look. He strode over to the empty table and slammed the Sharasil flat. Aurnia didn't flinch, watching the young man like she was really seeing him for the first time.

He started first with Theis. "You know, I've about had it with this 'boy' crap. You've yet to use my name once. Even Vincht, the man who nearly killed me, treated me with more respect, with more consideration. You act like I'm some stupid child that needs to be dragged around without being given a reason or purpose."

He turned next to Aurnia. "And you. I don't even know you, and you don't know me. So where do you get off calling me scrawny or . . . or . . . a stray? You don't know what I've had to endure to get here. In the last week, I've watched my entire village burn to the ground. I've lost my home and everyone I've ever known has been murdered. I've faced men who wanted nothing more than to bludgeon me to death to take something I can't give and didn't even want in the first place.

"And for what? To bring it to some ungrateful stranger? Someone without the decency to at least introduce herself before she starts talking down to me?

I've half a mind to just walk out of here and leave all this and all of you behind. Then where would you be? Considering the damn thing's bound to me, and trying to move it would cost you an arm, sounds like you'd be out of luck."

Exhausted, he plopped into the chair beside her. "But frankly, I'm just sick of all the abuse. I've been called everything *but* my name since I found this stupid weapon, and I'm done. I am *done*.

"My name is Nevin Walker. Call me Nevin, or go screw yourselves."

Overwhelmed, the young man slumped back in his chair. Life had been out of his control for so long that it felt nice to snatch a measure of it back. Still, history had taught him that standing up for himself often ended with him not being able to comfortably sit for a few days. He had eventually learned to just ignore or avoid Dalen when he fell into one of his drunken binges.

Theis, still as a statue, regarded him from beneath the hem of his hood. The motes in his eyes were still, their glow a light but strong blue. Nevin just stared back, fuming.

After a moment, the man in black offered him a slow, deliberate nod.

Donald polished off the remnants of his glass and stood. He clapped his hands together and smiled, apparently unfazed by the tense exchange that had just taken place in his living room. "Well then, Nevin. You're warm and dry. All that's left now is to get you fed. What would you say to a warm bowl of stew?"

Running a hand through his messy hair, Nevin could only nod. That brief outburst had sapped what little energy he had left.

"This stew was my late wife's creation." The tall man lumbered over to the mantle and retrieved a pair of wooden bowls and a spoon. He crouched beside the bubbling pot and gently swirled the mixture with a long iron ladle. "Life has not always been so kind to us. Before I had this shop, there were many days we went to bed with empty bellies and little hope, with no idea where our next meal would come from.

"Was she who taught me how to spot the treasure among the trash. She'd often set off early in the morning, leaving before I'd even opened my eyes, to rummage through the alleys, the rubbish heaps, comb the beaches for anything the ocean might have given up overnight.

"When she found something that might find value in the right hands, she'd take it home and clean it up. She'd take it vendor to vendor, shop to shop, seeing if she could convince someone to trade it for a meager sum of shils. More often than not, though, she'd be happy leaving with table scraps—leftover vegetables, herbs, bones, the less appetizing cuts of meat."

He filled the bowls with a generous helping of stew and straightened. "She called it 'pauper stew'. I didn't know if that was a real thing, or something she'd come up with on the spot. All I knew is, we were hungry, and every spoonful was bliss.

"But the strangest thing happened. One pot of stew seemed to last and last and last. At first, I thought the gods had blessed us, that all of our struggles had earned our little family a modest boon, but the truth was far simpler.

"You see, every time the wife would get hold of new ingredients, she'd just toss it in the pot. Didn't matter what it was, as long as it was edible, in it would go. The longer it cooked, the better it tasted. Dense as I was, it took me forever to figure out what was happening. I was just so happy we had something to eat. So many different flavors, disparate as they were, coming together thanks to time and heat and proximity."

Donald set a bowl on the table and squeezed Nevin's shoulder. The hearty aroma roused him from his near slumber, and the young man wasted little time.

"Wow," said Nevin around a hunk of potato. "This is amazing."

With a smile, Donald pat him on the shoulder before kneeling to set the other bowl in front of Aidux. "Glad you think so."

The bald man turned to Theis and gestured to the pot of stew. The man in black shook his head. With a shrug, Donald refilled his glass from a tall decanter and happily returned to his spot on the couch.

Aidux pawed at his bowl, but it was obvious to Nevin that the cat was only interested in it for its entertainment value. Fishing the last substantial chunk from his own bowl, he switched the rest with the cat's. "Just drink the broth."

With a defeated grumble, Aidux bent forward and lapped up the gooey broth while Nevin went to work on the other bowl of stew.

Aurnia hadn't take her eyes off of him since the moment he started his rant. Even as he devoured his stew, she watched him, pointedly appraising his every move without so much as shifting in her seat. He pretended not to notice, but as the minutes and the silence dragged on, Nevin began to grow increasingly uncomfortable beneath the weight of her scrutiny.

The moment he pushed his second bowl away, the woman in the yellow dress chose to speak.

"It appears I've misjudged you," she began, smoothing the fabric draped across her knees. "It's not often my initial impressions of someone are wrong, but in your case, I'll admit I was incorrect. I'd like to apologize and, if you'll allow me, start over. Is that something you think we could do . . . Nevin?"

He crossed his arms and nodded. An apology was as good a start as any.

"Good." She wiped a hand across the tabletop as if clearing it of dust, then turned her attention to the burlap-sheathed package waiting at its center. He could tell she wanted to reach for it, to loosen the ties securing the wrap and reveal the strange object hidden beneath, but instead, she folded her hands across her lap and leaned back into her chair.

"This is it, then? This is the sword?"

"Sword?" It made an odd kind of sense. The shape, the length, the placement of the grip.

She nodded. "You warned me, a moment ago. Not intentionally, mind you, but you said the sword is 'bound to you' and that attempting to move it would 'cost me my arm'. When I sent Theis after the sword, I was aware that it possessed some unique properties, but I never expected it would require a dedicated bearer.

"Is that why you're here? Why you and . . ." She cast her eyes below the rim of the table.

The cat grinned up at her. "Hi there. I'm Aidux."

"Aidux then." She dipped her head, but didn't smile back. "Is that why you and Aidux made the journey to Comelbough? Did Theis escort you here because, for some reason, the sword bound itself to you in a way that makes it dangerous for anyone else to touch?"

"That's right." A odd realization struck him. "It's . . . it's probably the only reason why we're still alive."

The significance in his tone caused Donald to look up from his glass.

Aurnia pursed her lips thoughtfully. "My name, young man, is Aurnia Celine Mistral. I'm afraid you're in this mess because of me, but if we're going to get you out of it, I'm going to need details. Tell me everything that's happened since the sword came into your possession.

"Do that, and I'll share with you what I know. Maybe together we can figure out what to do next. Can you do that?"

Nevin searched her face. "I can try."

She brought her hands together in a pointed steeple and rested them on the tabletop. "Then start at the beginning, wherever you feel that may be."

Donald slapped both hands on his knees and stood.

"Sounds like we're in for a long night." He winked at Nevin. "I'll make the tea."

Chapter 35: Answers?

Nevin sipped at his tea, stopping just short of a bitter mouthful of mint and lemongrass sediment. He made a face, remembering the unpleasant surprise at the bottom of his first cup and decided to cut his losses. Despite that final sip, Donald's tea was fantastic—tart, slightly sweet, peppery and energizing. The first two cups had woken him up, had given him the presence of mind necessary to make it through his story from calamitous start to gloomy finish.

Aurnia ignored her tea, her eyes elsewhere as she gazed toward the still wrapped Sharasil. Neither she nor the previous hour had been easy on him. The woman's attention to detail rivaled his old mentor's, only she didn't let up and give him time to gather his thoughts like Ishen would. Question after question passed through her thin lips, and sometimes she failed to give him the proper time to answer the first before throwing out a second or even a third. At some point in the exchange, Nevin had wised up and begun using his tea as a means of getting a break, however small.

To his annoyance, Theis had completely opted out of the discussion, even going so far as to vanish upstairs with Donald right about the time Nevin got to the part of the story where the man in black showed up at Ishen's cabin. The tall pawnbroker had returned alone a few minutes later, offering Nevin an overly hard pat of encouragement before refilling his glass from that tall decanter of dark liquid and dropping gracelessly back down on the couch. He'd spent the last hour staring into the waning fire and fiddling idly with that small lump hidden beneath the chest of his nightshirt.

Aidux hadn't exactly been much help either, but at least he was present. A handful of quips and misused words led quickly into back-to-back yawns and finally some light snoring and twitching paws. Nevin envied his friend. Stress just wasn't a word in his limited vocabulary. The past week's events had rolled off of him like water off a duck's back.

He smiled, reaching down to brush the top of the lynx's head. Maybe, in some strange way, the cat really was the wiser of the two.

Aurnia straightened in her chair, the small adjustment to her posture returning her to the present and magnifying her aura of self-control. When she spoke, no emotion painted her words, and every uttered syllable was precise and purposeful. "And that brings us to the present. You and Theis split up as you entered the city, and eventually, you found your way here."

She tilted her head. "Why *did* Theis set out on his own? Did he say?"

Nevin shrugged. "As usual, he wasn't specific. Just that he needed to pick something up, and he might not get another chance if he waited."

"I wonder why not." Frowning, she pressed a thin finger to her bottom lip. "Of course, he's not here to tell us himself. Still, there's nothing that can be done. I'd be surprised if he did more than dance around the topic if pressed, anyway. That man has more secrets than a retired streetwalker.

"But what of you, Nevin? Is that the whole story? From start to finish, you've left nothing out?"

"Not that I can think of," he lied.

Of course he'd left things out. He'd left plenty out. His encounters with the dark figure for one, and the battered canteen that seemed intent to follow him wherever he went. It would do him no good to have her think him crazy.

He had also kept to himself the dream of talking to the disembodied voice in the dark. He still wasn't entirely sure if the whole experience actually pertained to coming in contact with the Sharasil, or if it was little more than the consequence of untreated head trauma and coincidence. He couldn't remember most of it anyway, and with the way Aurnia had dissected every detail of his story, he dreaded the idea of spending the next hour or more lost somewhere between frustrated and confused.

She opened her mouth, no doubt preparing to assault him with more questions, but Nevin beat her to the punch.

"Look," he began, leaning forward in his chair. "You asked me to tell you my story. I've done that. You told me I'm in this mess because of you, and I think it's time you told me why."

"Couldn't have said it better myself," said the man in black from above, trailing a gloved hand down the banister as he sauntered down the stairs.

Nevin scowled up at him. "Now you show up."

"Were there for just as much as I was. What's wrong? Don't think she'd believe you unless I was there to grunt in agreement with everything you say?"

Donald craned his neck. "Get what you needed?"

Theis nodded, circling around the dining table to lean against the wall opposite Nevin. He crossed his arms and set his burning eyes on Aurnia. "Alright, then. Let's hear it."

Her face smooth as stone, the woman stared at the Sharasil as if trying to mentally unwrap the burlap cover to glimpse at what lay beneath. He could tell it was frustrating her, the object of her desire within reach but wholly inaccessible. It was the only leverage Nevin had in the situation, and he had no qualms with making her wait until he was satisfied by her side of the story.

Finally, she wiped a hand across the tabletop and began her tale.

"For hundreds and hundreds of years, man has depended upon a varied pantheon of gods to guide them through troubled times, with those who devote themselves fully to religious service being granted positions of both power and prestige. Entire nations have formed around specific spiritual ideals, and over time, some have grown to become major players on the world political stage. The theocratic state of Volludon on the Delphine Continent is likely the most well-known of these, but throughout history, there have been and still are many others."

Nevin rested his arms on the table. "Volludon . . . that's Empyria, right? The god said to be responsible for creating mankind and gifting us with language."

She nodded. "Among other things. She's also known as the Dreaming God, as it's said the act of creating us took so much of her energy that she fell into a deep slumber, leaving her physical form to float on a bed of wind until the day she wakes and ushers in an era of absolute truth and peace."

"I heard she's in the highest tower in Volludon, a hard-to-reach temple called The Chapel in Repose. Only the most devout are allowed to see her."

He shrugged. "The devout and the rich."

Aurnia shot him a look of genuine surprise. "Correct on all points. Where did you come by such knowledge? Surely they didn't venerate Empyria in a remote farm town like Elbin."

"I spent a few days a week being tutored by one of the locals. Most of our discussions revolved around world history and the different religions. He had quite the extensive library." A pang of longing stabbed him in the heart. He hoped Ishen was alright.

"Seems odd to invest such knowledge in someone who would never use it. What other topics of discussion did—"

"Where is this going, woman?" asked Theis, twirling a finger in the air. "You already asked your questions. Now's the time for answers."

She rolled her eyes. "I liked it better when you were gone.

"As I was saying, religion has become a keystone in nearly every pillar of mankind's development, but the world is changing. Too many powers in too little space meant conflict was eventually inevitable."

She chuckled—a soft, brief sound that barely touched her narrow shoulders. "Not that the gods got along with one another when there were few, but they thrive on religious fervor, and a man has only so much energy for worship when he's trying to feed and shelter his family. The more gods there are, the less worship there is to go around.

"The gods can be petty. Vengeful even. But most of all? They get jealous. They are the very definition of attention seeking, and as the pantheon grew bloated and man's attention spread ever thinner, their envy only intensified."

Nevin held up a hand. "Wait, what are you saying? I thought we were talking about religion, but now it almost sounds like you're talking about the gods themselves, like they're people with wants and flaws and feelings."

"On some level, Nevin, the gods and their followers are indistinguishable from one another. Every leader is like that. Their power, their authority, what they represent, what they stand for . . . this is all an extension of their followers' wants and needs. The closer they adhere to the interests of those who lift them up, the more power they are granted. The gods are the purest form of that process, though whether that power lies in mind of the believer, or in some otherworldly figurehead, is a discussion for another time.

"Gods, followers, it doesn't matter. What matters is that when the fighting began, followers died, and their gods vanished with them. Little ones at first. The Church of La'Rei, The Fog Templars, Totero Alunveh, to name a few. Many more have been lost to history."

Nevin shared a look with Theis. "Ivvilger."

She nodded. "Elbin was originally settled by the last surviving members of the struggle against the unforgiving wild. Ivvilger fell near the final days of the religious wars. One of the few major religions to lose that fight.

"They called it 'The Hallowed Schism', as if anything about genocide could be hallowed. Men with pens are always looking for ways to polish clean the rough, ugly patches of history with fancy words that reframe the truth. But the cold fact they often gloss over, is that, while the resulting war between the gods was ultimately inevitable, it was started by only one.

"Heddaster."

"Wait, *Heddaster*? The Living Hearth?" His final lesson with Ishen was a study on the church of Heddaster, god of family and civilization.

Nevin suppressed a shiver. The coincidence gave him the creeps.

"Weren't they known for building a network of hostels along major thoroughfares? I thought they took in the homeless, the weak, the sick? You're telling me *that's* the religion responsible for starting the great war?"

A small smile tilted the corners of her lips, pushing her confident aura to the brink of smugness. "Benevolence can be an effective mask for malicious intent. Take the hunter's snare. Works well enough when placed along a game trail, sure. But the smart hunter learns to bait it with food, draw in his intended prey with promises of a full belly.

"And then . . . *snap*." She punctuated the word with her fingers.

Donald snorted in his sleep. He squirmed, sinking deeper into the plush cushions of the lavender couch.

Aurnia waved off the tension and sat back in her chair. "As the war entered its final act, the armies of Heddaster were naught but unrecognizable hordes banging on the walls of Volludon. The largest and oldest religion in the world was practically on its knees. In some accounts, the Empyrians were but days away from extinction.

"And then . . . the war ended."

"Just like that? What happened?"

She shrugged. "That's where the history books go quiet. No one really knows. Empyria survived where others didn't, Heddaster included. Within a decade, the Living Hearth had all but vanished from the face of Stragus. For all their strength and reach, they may as well have never existed."

"That's enough." Theis barked, pulling the third chair from the table and tossing it aside in frustration. "Know you well enough to know you've got a point to all this, so how's about you get to it?"

Aurnia pinched the bridge of her nose and nodded. She reached beneath one of the folds of her yellow dress and retrieved a worn letter. The edges were blunted from regular handling, and the surface was yellowed with age.

A blot of red wax colored one of the folds—the remnants of a broken seal.

She didn't open it. She didn't remove the letter from the confines of the envelope. She didn't read its contents aloud to the men gathered around the small dining table. She simply held it, turning it over and over in her hands like a puzzle with no solution.

"Five months ago, a young man I'd never met before delivered me this letter. He sought me out in a place only one other knew me to be, recognized me on sight, and called to me by name."

She rolled her shoulders uncomfortably. "Scared the wits out of me, if I'm being honest. I think about that moment every time I read this letter, and believe me when I say, I've read over it more times than I can count."

Gone was her aura of self-control. Aurnia was nervous, and for some reason, that made Nevin nervous, too.

"Gonna read it to us this time?"

"No," she barked, a little too quickly. "And it wouldn't matter if I did. The letter wouldn't make any sense. Most of it doesn't make sense to me and it was *meant* for me."

The letter disappeared back into the folds of her wispy dress. Out of sight, but decidedly not out of mind. "Had it just been a fetch request, I could have ignored it. But the letter knew things about me, and it claimed to know the real reason for the Hallowed Schism and what caused the war to end so abruptly. It said that, and I quote, 'The children of Heddaster will soon rouse to make real the dreams of truth, but the light they shine will only burn.'"

"Prophecy." Theis snorted with disgust. "Just a waste of ink."

"Prophecy is the sole reason our civilization survived to become what it is today. Only a fool discounts divine revelation. It is the purest form of truth."

"It's horseshit, is what it is. Life is a bowl of snakes and silver; you reach in and hope you don't get bit."

Nevin scooted to the edge of his seat. "Wait, you said the letter knew what really caused the end of the war. What did it say?"

Aurnia turned her chair until her back was to Theis. The man in black mumbled something under his breath, but the young man couldn't make it out. Something unpleasant, he suspected.

"We've always assumed the war ended because the Empyrians successfully fended off the armies of Heddaster, but according to this letter, their forces were in the process of breaching the walls and razing Volludon to the ground on that final day. Their leaders though, the heart and soul of the Heddaster invasion, were elsewhere, protected by elite warriors and a powerful cabinet of magicians. They were practically unreachable."

Her eyes turned to the Sharasil. "Until someone wielding that came along.

"The letter claims that someone, and it isn't clear who, single-handedly took the battle to their leaders, breaking through the perimeter and killing each and every guard, mage, and commander. Somehow, word quickly reached the front lines, and with no one to lead them, Heddaster's armies simply fell apart. And just like that, the Hallowed Schism came to an end."

"Seems awfully convenient."

"Agreed. Which is why I looked into it." Aurnia finally took a sip of her tea, unconcerned by the fact that it had gone cold an hour ago.

"You see, historians have always wondered at the identity of the mastermind behind Heddaster's war campaign. Nothing could ever be definitely proven, and the list of potential candidates is a long one. But the letter spoke of a citadel hidden in the upper reaches of the Pelasik Mountains, indicating it as the hidden base of operations for the Heddaster forces. The location wasn't on any maps I could find and none of the more well-known historical compendiums referenced it.

"So I went there. It took me a few weeks and a fair amount of shils to locate it, and when I did, I could tell that fire and nature and time had reduced it to little more than overgrown rubble. But there were skeletons, and many bore evidence of being killed in battle."

She shook her head. "It didn't perfectly wrap the letter's claims up in a bow, but it was enough. Add in the rest of its contents, and I was sold. The letter continued, informing me that the blade was now in the care of a particularly infamous warrior, and that in order to find it, I first had to find him. No mean feat, considering no one had seen him in a decade, and he didn't want to be found.

"Turns out the letter was correct about that, so maybe it's right about all of it. The world *is* changing. It's not felt as strongly in small, out-of-the-way provinces like the Lancowl Barony, but even here the ripples are felt. Deific symbolism has been banned in this province since before the current baron, and magic not long after.

"Similar things are happening elsewhere, all over the world. The rumblings of war. In some places, it's already started. The person who wrote this letter seems to think that sword will be an integral component to the coming struggles. Or, at the very least, important enough to be kept out of the fight.

"And yet . . . the letter bears no signature. No instructions on where to take the sword once I'd gotten hold of it. No indication whatsoever of who sought my help or what I'm supposed to do once I complete their mission. Only that I must do everything in my power to figure out what the sword is, and to keep it out of the wrong hands."

Nevin picked at the tabletop. "Do you think maybe . . . maybe you failed even before you started? There's no way my hands are the right hands. I've got no combat training. My best defense in a fight is to let Aidux fight in my stead. I don't know what I'm doing here."

Aurnia reached out and took hold of his hand. "Nevin, you're here because you have a part to play in Fate's plan. Trust in that."

"That's a great excuse for being full of shit," said Theis, striding briskly toward the door. "I'm going out. Maybe when I get back, you'll have something worthwhile to say."

He slammed the door behind him as he left, causing both Donald and Aidux to jerk from their slumber with a snort of surprise. Aidux quickly laid back down, but the tall man looked around in confusion for a moment, rubbing his eyes as he fought to center himself. As the room came into focus, a slow smile broached his lips and he pushed to his feet with a groan.

"I could use a cup of tea. Any takers?"

The woman in the yellow dress sipped at hers, watching Nevin over the rim of her tea cup. The young man answered with a silent, numb nod. Had Aurnia answered his questions, or had she only raised more? There was so much left unexplained, but Nevin got the impression that no matter how well he understood Theis and Aurnia's intentions, no matter how much he learned about history or the origins of the Sharasil, nothing would change the fact that sword was bound to him and him alone.

Setting his jaw, Nevin placed his hands on the table and stood. "I think it's time I finally showed you what you came here to see."

With trembling hands, he went about undoing the burlap ties holding the sword's cover in place.

Chapter 36: Examining the Sharasil

"Well?"

Nevin's patience with Aurnia's unflinching look of intense focus was wearing thin. She stood at his side, leaning over the table with her chin in her hand as she tried to wrap her mind around the strange weapon's equally peculiar construction. She hadn't moved in nearly five minutes, mumbling incoherently under her breath and ignoring him the entire time.

Inhaling sharply, she straightened. "What was it you called it again? The sword?"

"The Sharasil."

"Interesting. And how did you come up with that?"

Nevin squirmed, twisting out an awkward shrug. "I didn't . . . come up with it. That's its name. I don't know how I know, and I don't know when I learned it, but I'm sure that's what it's called. It just sort of came to me in a conversation, like I'd known it the whole time and it was weird that no one else did."

She tapped a finger to her lower lip. "Likely a side-effect of the bond. An instinctual transference of necessary information. Honestly, that makes more sense than you coming up with it on your own.

"'Sharasil' is a constructed word in the dead Ilwarin tongue. It's two words, in point of fact. The first part, 'Shar', is an uncommon word in the language, one that doesn't show up but a handful of times across the breadth of Ilwarin texts and carvings documented by historians. It was adopted by early magic users as way to reference the spiritual energy generated by and directed during incantation.

"'Shar' means soul or spirit or energy, depending on context. However, without more than a name to go on, it could be any one of the three. 'Sil', though, is an interesting one. See, Ilwarin has these bilateral suffixes that it uses to

denote opposing concepts. The suffixes are always three letters long—two consonants framing a single vowel. The suffix is written in one direction when indicating one side of the spectrum, and the other direction when indicating its opposite."

"So, 'Sharasil' and . . . 'Sharalis'?" Nevin frowned. "Wait, where did that 'a' come from?"

Cringing, she twisted her mouth. "The rules get murky in a few places. It actually would be 'Sharlis', but don't ask me to explain why. My understanding of Ilwarin might be above average, but considering there are practically zero living experts on the language, average might not be saying much."

Nevin scratched at his hairline. His old mentor had possessed a number of different artifacts decorated with Ilwarin script, but the details of the language had only rarely come up during their lessons.

I really hope I don't need to become an expert in a dead language in order to be free of the sword, but I'm willing to try.

"Okay, so what does 'sil' mean in this instance?"

She continued fiddling with her bottom lip, playing it with her fingertip like the string of a lute. "Well, 'Sharlis' is used to indicate a glut of spiritual energy, so in that case, 'lis' might mean 'abundance' or 'full'. If we flip it, 'sil' likely means something along the lines of . . . 'empty' or 'scarce', maybe? I can't be sure. It's not a configuration I've run into, nor would it be one I would have ever thought to put together. It's a terrible name for a magic sword, though."

"How so?"

"One feature of a magical object is either a reserve of magical energy, or a soul channel of their own. An apt translation of Sharasil? 'Spiritless'? 'Dead'? 'Inert'? Seems like the exact opposite of what you expect to find."

She started to reach for the Sharasil, but thought better of it. "A little off topic, but . . . when it reacted to Theis, when it nearly took off his arm as you put it, he was approaching it?"

He scratched his head. "It happened really fast, but that sounds right."

"He was going to take it? Pick it up?"

"Yeah, I guess."

"Hmm." She pursed her lips. "Maybe it reacts to intent."

There's that word again. Back at the gorge, Theis had mentioned something about magical objects reacting to intent. He still didn't quite understand it, but hearing Aurnia say it now made him wish he'd asked more questions.

"You think the sword can read our minds?"

"I hope so," she said, taking a deep breath in and slowly releasing it over a number of seconds. "Or this is really going to hurt."

"Why would it—"

Without hesitation, Aurnia stepped forward and reached out for the Sharasil.

Surprised as he was by her choice of action, Nevin barely had the time to raise his eyebrows in alarm before the unprotected flesh of her palm slapped down on smooth metal.

Nothing happened.

No red light. No high-pitched squeal. No blinding flash of energy. Aurnia closed her eyes and sighed with relief. She retracted her hand, flexing away the thin coating of frost that now coated her palm. The spot on the sword where her hand had been glistened like diamonds in the firelight.

She grimaced. "By the Numbra, that's cold."

Nevin covered his mouth with his hands. "Are you *nuts*, lady? You could have—"

"Lost an arm, yes. You've mentioned that. Still . . ." She folded her arms across her chest and leaned over the table to get a closer look. "Sometimes one must engage in a calculated risk in order to make progress. I've been mulling your story over, and something in the details bothered me. At the gorge, you told me you nearly fell when the tree you were crossing became unstable.

"I initially didn't think much of it, but it nagged at me. You say the sword reacts negatively whenever someone other than you comes near it. If we assume that's true—"

"It *is* true."

She waved him off. "If you kept it strapped across the top of your satchel, why then did it not activate when Theis leapt onto the tree and carried you across?"

Nevin opened his mouth to speak, but nothing came out. She had a really good point.

"I don't know. That didn't even occur to me."

"Even if he tossed you over his shoulder, the blade had to have been no more than a few inches away from the back of his head, and I doubt he would have even been able to grab you without inadvertently brushing against it at some point. So why didn't it react?"

"I'm guessing it has something to do with intent?"

A smug smile broached her lips. "I think the sword can read not just its wielder's intentions, but anyone within a certain range. I think it listens for certain queues and reacts based on some sort of internal directive. Just wanting to touch it isn't enough. I suspect only attempting to interact with the sole purpose of moving or wielding will activate its latent defense mechanisms. It makes sense, otherwise the whole system would react each time you struck an opponent, a situation that would likely be just as dangerous for the wielder as it would be for the target.

"Of course, that means if someone knocks you out while the sword is strapped to your back, they might just be able to carry you off and take the sword that way."

Her smile faded. "Then again, the sword might be smart enough to read THAT intention and literally decide to blow up in their face."

Nevin took a small step back. If the sword really *could* read minds, he didn't want to be anywhere near it in case Aurnia accidentally thought the wrong thing.

Aurnia placed her hands on the edge of the table, and with a soft grunt, slid it closer to the wall. She stepped back into extra space and appraised the sword from a distance, occasionally checking on Nevin from the corner of her eye.

Donald shifted in his spot on the couch, and a rolling snore ripped through the quiet room. In his nervous state, the unpleasant sound startled Nevin. With an audible scoff, he shot the tall man a dirty look.

"Problem?" Aurnia said, following his gaze to the sleeping giant.

"It's nothing." He crossed his arms.

"Oh, yes, it seems like nothing."

Nevin could almost feel Dalen's canteen banging against his leg. "He's drunk."

"If he was aiming for sober, I imagine he would have stuck with tea."

"This is *funny* to you?"

Aurnia's perplexed look caught him off guard. It was almost like she didn't understand the problem. "You don't approve. The man took you in, gave you his clothes, fed you, and you take issue with his means of relaxation?"

Nevin fumed in silence. He didn't owe this stranger any sort of explanation. Truth was, he didn't owe her *anything*, not yet at least. Not until he'd gotten some real answers. Answers beyond a cursory examination of a dead language.

When he didn't respond, she turned her attention back to the sword. "One of alcohol's greatest gifts lies in its power to temporarily suppress the brain's ability to dwell. Regrets, embarrassments, lost loved ones . . . for those in pain, numbness is often a preferable alternative. It's not as effective as mastering one's emotions, of course, but not everyone possesses a will powerful enough to eliminate emotion in its entirety."

A slight frown cracked her cool composure. "Nor do most want to."

He looked back at Donald. The bald man had folded his hands protectively across the lump hidden beneath his nightshirt. "It's his wife, isn't it. The reason he wants to be numb. He misses her."

Aurnia nodded.

"I know what alcohol does to people who lose the ones they care about most," he said.

Eager to change the subject, he extended a finger, pointing to the oval indentation near the center point of the sword. A number of angular channels struck out from that odd structure, each one terminating on the object's southern edge.

"This is an odd feature. And these channels? What do you suppose they're for?"

She frowned in concentration. "I'm not sure, but I doubt it's purely decorative. A focal point, of some sort? Might hold the power source, and it could use these lines to transmit spiritual energy throughout the blade. Then again, the lines may just be the seams that retract to reveal the true form underneath. Could be this entire metal shell is just a housing for the real weapon. A sheath, if you will. But . . . until we can activate it, I can really only guess."

Nevin tossed his hands up. "So you've got nothing. Great. That's really great. What *can* you tell me?"

Aurnia rubbed her eyes and sighed. "This isn't something I'd planned for, Nevin. I had expected Theis to return with naught but the weapon I sent him after, but instead he arrives saddled with two unintended stowaways whose Fates are more intertwined with that of the blade than I can hope to unravel from here. Magical problems require magical solutions, and Comelbough provides neither the resources nor the safety necessary to attack the problem. Even a superficial examination would require manifesting a goodly amount of spiritual energy, an act that would surely attract the magic-hungry creatures currently prowling about in the fog."

Magic-hungry creatures? He looked toward the door apprehensively. This was the first he was hearing of it.

Aurnia tapped her lip. "If I could just get a glimpse . . . Nevin, will you do me a favor and pick up the sword? I'd like to try something."

Without taking his eyes off the door, Nevin nodded. He reached out and grabbed the coarse stone handle and dragged it close without lifting it clear of the table's worn surface. It made zero sound as it glided across the wood.

"Good," she said, sliding over to his side. Her hand gently came to rest on his bare forearm. The soft touch made him immediately uncomfortable. He looked down at it and tried to pull away, but she wrapped her fingers around his wrist.

"It's okay. This is a very simple thing. I'm going to try to help you, but I need your trust and cooperation if this is going to work, alright?"

Nevin searched her flawless face, but it gave up nothing. Reluctantly, he nodded again. "If you think it might help."

"It will," she said, tilting her chin up and staring deep into his eyes. He couldn't help but stare back, lost in the rich, honey-brown rings surrounding her depthless pupils. An electric tingle climbed his arm as her fingers kneaded his wrist. He felt his breath quicken.

"Now. You told me the sword reacted during your fight in the clearing. Tell me again, briefly, what you were experiencing in that moment."

He didn't understand how going over it again was going to help, but he didn't figure it would hurt. "Well, two soldiers had just broken off from the group and were coming toward us."

"Us?"

"Me and Aidux. The one with the ax attacked, and we both dove out of the way. Aidux fought back, wounding the ax-wielding soldier before charging the other. They wrestled each other for a moment and—"

"The two soldiers were threatening your life. Before now, nothing really dangerous had happened, but as they approached, it suddenly became very real."

His eyebrows reached for each other. "Yes, I mean, I was definitely afraid. I didn't know how to fight and I didn't want to hurt anyone. I didn't want Aidux to get hurt, either."

Aurnia was nodding along to his speech, and as her head bobbed up and down, so too did his own. Her pupils shrank and grew in time with her breath, and Nevin found himself matching each inhalation and exhalation.

Something stirred in the darkness of his mind.

"What a terrifying ordeal. You had nowhere to go, no idea what to do, and little hope of survival." The warm tingling sensation crawled up his arm, spreading through his bicep and mounting his shoulder.

In the shadows of his subconscious, a tiny voice cried out to him, but as he stared ever deeper into the woman's enchanting eyes, its call went unheeded.

"Was that what it was like, Nevin? Can you remember the details for me? Think hard, remember how it felt to hold the sword in your hands, to feel the fear rushing through your veins, your damp clothes clinging to your skin, hear the wind whipping through the clearing . . ."

He *could* hear it. The stillness cut down by a chill wind, tearing through the open clearing to sap the warmth from his bones. He shivered, the edge of the sword bouncing soundlessly against the surface of the table.

She took a step closer, trailing her fingers up the skin of his arm. The tingling crawled up his neck, past his hairline. It finally enveloped his entire head, growing in strength until the sensation shook his vision into a disconcerting blur of light and color.

Aurnia leaned in, her words melting directly to his brain. "Go there, Nevin. Find that fear. Find that hopelessness. Step into it."

His eyes fluttered closed as the uncomfortable feeling washed over his entire body.

When he opened them again, a flash of light erased the quiet common room and replaced it with a cold, grassy clearing.

Chapter 37: An Uninvited Guest

Nevin stumbled forward, bringing the sword up protectively before him. The rapid shift in location muddied his thoughts, confused him, shutdown his ability to think clearly all while ramping up his survival instincts.

Faceless soldiers rushed toward him across the forest clearing from every possible angle. Weapons of every sort imaginable pointed at him threateningly. Exaggerated plumes of water rose into the air with every thundering step they took forward.

"Fight back, Nevin." A unknown feminine voice echoed through the scene. "You'll have to protect yourself if you want to survive."

"Leave me alone!" he screamed, backing away from the soldiers. One of them lunged with his club, his wild swing grazing Nevin's shoulder. Pain, both sharp and dull all at once, erupted down his left arm. Crying out, the young man swung his blunted sword at the soldier, but his body absorbed the blow like it was made of cotton, folding over the storm gray metal as he danced back to safety.

"Summon the blade! It's your only chance."

An ax blade clipped his leading leg, and it was all he could do to stay upright. Blood arced, evaporating into a weightless red mist before it could fall to the ground. He swung the sword again, but caught only air.

The faceless soldiers formed an undulated ring of flesh and aggression all around him. Their feints kept him off-balance, and the constant spinning to keep them at bay left him dizzy and breathless.

He shook the Sharasil, willing it to do something, to become something more than the useless hunk of metal he'd always known it to be. But the cold metal resisted his mental urgings, and the Sharasil remained as it was.

"You know how to do it! You must! You have to kill if you want to save yourself!"

Nevin gripped his sword tighter, preparing for the fight of his life.

A familiar chill ran down his spine.

He jerked his head around, searching between the shifting bodies encircling him. A shadowy form paced the perimeter, fading in and out between the constantly moving soldiers. He could feel its rueful grin as it watched him struggle. A pale hand dripping black ichor reached out for him, offering to rescue him from his own inadequacies.

"No!" Nevin stumbled away from its extended hand. He dropped the sword to clutch at his swimming head and lost his footing, the dizziness finally getting the best of him. He landed hard on his backside at the base of Donald's stairs, his chest heaving from fear. The Sharasil settled in silently beside him.

Aidux jerked to attention, keeping one eye closed as he blinked in Nevin's direction. He flicked an ear toward the door.

Wiping a thin coating of gray dust from her palms before folding her arms beneath her breasts, Aurnia wordlessly looked down her nose at him. Her dark brown eyes were dulled by disappointment.

Nevin dragged an arm across his face and took in the room from his lower vantage point, half-expecting a team of bloodthirsty soldiers to burst through the walls and attack. "W-what did you just do to me? I was . . . there were . . . how did you do that?"

She gave a disinterested twirl of her hand and returned to her chair. "A little infusion of Vellis, a bit of auditory guiding. You did the rest yourself."

"Vellis?" He stood, leaving the sword where it lay at the base of the stairs.

"Magic, Nevin. I told you already. Magical problems require magical solutions." She patted the tabletop across from her. "Come sit, and tell me what you saw, what you felt. Maybe we can figure out where we went wrong."

Magic. Barely a week away from home, and he'd already met his first Wizard. Still, the revelation didn't exactly surprise him. "Are you serious right now? You use magic on me without my permission, without warning, and you just expect me to just sit down and talk you through my feelings?"

He rubbed his shoulder, his thigh, still suffering phantom sensations of pain despite the illusory nature of his vision. With a simple touch, the woman had somehow tapped into one of his most traumatic moments in some misguided attempt to summon the Sharasil. But the blade hadn't changed, hadn't so much as flinched during the whole ordeal.

A vision of combat, constructed from fragments of both remembrance and imagination. A strange marriage of reality and dream. Even now, he could feel his memory of that fabricated world slipping away, eroding beneath the weight of a repeated mental review of its contents and meaning. Aurnia claimed she had only guided his thoughts, that he had done the rest himself. But why would he want to revisit that moment? Why would he want to put himself through that again?

Aurnia pressed her fingertips together in an exaggerated steeple and rested them in her lap. "I needed your defenses down, needed you willing. If you knew what I was about to do, your instincts would have formed a mental barrier to protect you from the process, and the amount of magical energy needed would have increased ten-fold."

He shook his head, unable to comprehend her presumption, how she could violate him in that way and believe everything would somehow be okay. To her credit, there was no malice in her actions, no ill intent, no desire to make him suffer like Dalen had always made him suffer. She simply wanted answers, nothing more.

In some ways, knowing that made it better. In others, it made it so much worse. At least Dalen saw him as a person worth hurting.

Did Aurnia only view him as a tool worth using?

The front door swung open, and in burst a clearly agitated Theis, spinning on his heel to ease the door shut behind him. His blue eyes burned into the woman in yellow as he strode across the room.

"You've really done it now, woman," he spat, his voice no more than a harsh whisper. "Caught one sniffing about outside, but it was leaving."

He slapped the couch, gesturing for Donald to stand. "Not anymore."

"What do you mean, 'caught one'?" Nevin asked, but a blazing look from the man in black set him to silence.

With some effort, Donald lurched to his feet, drawing his blue robe tight about his bulky form. Theis wasted little time. He grabbed the back of the couch with one hand and dragged it in front of the door like it was made of straw. He jammed his boot against the foot of the couch and eased his sicklesque blade free of its scabbard.

Aidux leapt to his feet with a hiss of alarm.

An unseen weight collided with the exterior of the building, and the whole structure shook.

Dust fell from the rafters, and hairline tears appeared in the peeling maroon wallpaper. The fluted glass protecting a dying candle tumbled loose, snuffing the flame and shattering into a million pieces on the floor.

Theis raised an empty hand. Everyone froze.

In the sudden quiet, the sound of metal jostled against the outside wall. Nevin crept protectively in front of Aidux. He had heard chains rattling around in the fog before Donald invited them inside. He wondered if the two were connected, if someone or something had been out there in the dark all along.

Searching.

The building shook once more as the massive weight dragged itself along the stone facade. There was a terrible creaking of old wood. Silence stretched each passing second taut before succumbing to another drawn out creak. Theis cocked his head and looked to Donald. Their host mouthed the word 'porch' and backed up beside the smoldering fireplace. The creaking continued, growing louder and louder as whatever it was drew closer to the front door.

Aurnia eased toward the man in black, carefully sliding one foot forward and pausing, before carefully following up with the other. Theis shook his head and motioned for her to stay put, but Aurnia didn't listen.

The door shuddered as the unseen weight pressed up against it. Hinges crackled against their moorings, the corroded metal plates shifting to reveal a hidden patch of bright wallpaper the color of fresh blood. The door bowed inward at the top, and through the narrow crack, a number of wiry black hairs poked through.

Aurnia scooted up beside Theis, pressing her diminutive form against his floor-dragging cloak. His eyes flashed with understanding. Leaning forward, he braced himself against the couch. Aurnia followed suite.

The creaking stopped, and the front door stilled. The rattling chains went quiet.

Nevin held his breath, and as his ears finally acclimated to the utter silence, he almost thought he could make out the faintest sound stealing its way through the crack above the door.

Wheezing.

Theis held his hand high once again, but no one dared move. There was a rough snort from the door, and a cloud of spittle erupted through the crack. Aurnia pressed herself as close to the man in black as physics would allow and held her breath.

The door loudly complained as it bent and warped.

Nevin slowly sank into a crouch. The Sharasil was just out of reach, but if worst came to worst, he wanted as little distance between it and himself as he could muster.

The wiry black hairs vanished back through the crack, but the door didn't return to its previous shape. Instead, a wriggling red blob pushed through and began feeling about, leaving a blotch of viscous slime wherever it touched.

Horrified, Nevin clapped a hand over his mouth to suppress a gag.

A tongue.

It was a tongue.

A long, sinuous tongue.

Theis raised his sword, preparing to lash out and sever the invading appendage, but Aurnia stayed his hand.

After a moment, the tongue carefully retracted through the narrow crack and the door creaked back into place. Chains rattled softly and the raised deck groaned as whatever lay beyond the outside walls moved away. Soon, only the faint groosh of crumbling firewood broke the tense silence, and the group collectively heaved a sigh of relief.

Theis shoved his blade home. "*Khek,* woman. What were you thinking?"

She propped a hand on her hip and shoved a finger at the man in black's face. "Don't you dare invoke that name at a time like this. You know better."

He slapped her hand aside. "As should you. You know what's sniffing about in the dark."

"It was a small thing. The boy was willing and unaware, so only a sliver of magic was necessary. How was I supposed to know one of those things would be walking by at precisely that moment?"

Theis dragged the couch back into place. "This night has had enough wagging tongues, friendly or otherwise, so pack it in. Can talk more tomorrow in the safety of the light."

Nevin leaned back against the banister, exhaustion finally getting the better of his need for answers. Still, he had to ask. "What was that thing?"

"A Breather," Donald said, taking him by the shoulder and gently leading him upstairs. "A twisted creature bred to hunt down magic users."

"Hunt them? What for?"

"To kill, of course." He shrugged. "Bad luck, that was. Had it wanted to, that Breather could have torn the door off its hinges just as easily as open it. I'm not pleased that her actions nearly cost me my home, but I knew what I was in for when I allowed the two of you to stay. I trust her, and though she isn't one to show it, Aurnia is likely kicking herself for drawing one's attention."

Donald squeezed his shoulder reassuringly and gestured toward a wide four-post bed layered with a menagerie of colorful quilts. "We're quite safe, for now. Our two friends downstairs will see to that. You'll take my bed tonight. Don't hardly use it much myself anymore. Only when my back is acting up."

Aidux curled up on the floor, his twitching ears still on the prowl for intruders. Nevin scratched at an arm, but didn't approach the bed.

Donald adjusted his spectacles. "My wife made the quilts. Every single one. Roughly thirty five years of sewing, right there in one place. Just didn't feel right packing them away after she passed. We can take some off if you think you'll get hot."

"No, no," he said, waving his hands. "It's . . . it's not that."

"Not tired then?"

"Actually, I'm exhausted. I can't think of anything better than sleep right now."

The bald man frowned, obviously confused. "Well, what's wrong then? Figured you'd be neck-deep in blankets as soon as I offered."

"It's just . . ." Nevin chewed his lip. "I've never slept in a bed before."

Donald stared at him, searching his face as if trying to decide if the young man was putting him on. Nevin smiled sheepishly and turned away, watching as the lynx stretched out on his side and sighed. The cat had the annoying ability to fall asleep instantly.

His hulking host finally removed his glasses all together to rub at his eyes, hiding the heartbreak evident on his face behind his broad hand.

"Well . . . first time for everything I suppose." He pat the young man on the shoulder. "Take your time, but get some rest, young sir. I imagine things will grow ever more complicated come daybreak."

Donald left him there with his thoughts, but for as tired as he was, it wasn't long before he found himself curled up beneath a mountain of quilts, lulled off to sleep by the weight of years of lovingly crafted fabric embracing his tired body.

The last thought on his mind before sleep claimed him was to wonder what his life would have been like had Donald Iustus been his father.

Chapter 38: The Gift of Memory

Donald's barrel-shaped chest rose and fell in time with his soft snoring. He'd only sunk further into the plush couch overnight, the purple cushions now wrapping around his sides like it would eventually subsume him into its bulk. One of his hands rested protectively over the lump hidden beneath his blue nightshirt.

The candles along the wall had long since burnt away, the metal collection cups below their mounting spikes filled with hardened spent wax. In the dim light, Aurnia peered down at her hulking host, taking a moment to gather her wits. Today would mark the third time in so many years she'd entered into negotiations with Donald, but no matter the outcome, this time would have to be the last. Considering the current climate in Comelbough and the contents of Nevin's story, it was becoming increasingly clear that she couldn't afford to fail again.

Aurnia flicked her hand toward the fresh candlestick she'd placed on the side table next to Donald. Her soul flashed briefly through the darkness of her mind and the candle's curled wick burst into flames. The flash of light startled her host awake. Blinking and rubbing his sleep weak eyes, Donald extracted himself from the clutching cushions and sat up straight.

"Aurnia?" He stretched an arm overhead and yawned. "Is it morning already?"

She nodded, sinking into the dining chair she'd strategically placed across from him.

"Sleep well?" she asked, folding her hands in her lap.

"A might better than you, I'm sure." Aurnia's expressionless stare only spurred his chuckling. He scratched at his curly white beard. "Dreamless and brief, but I'll manage."

"One of whiskey's finer qualities."

His child-like grin out-shined the candle. Slapping his thighs, he leaned forward to rise. "I suppose a good cup of tea is in order. Warm these old bones before I go wake the boy."

"One step ahead of you." Aurnia retrieved one of the two steaming cups of tea she'd placed on the end table and took a sip, gesturing to the other cup with a thin finger as the warm liquid flowed through her in a rejuvenating wave.

Donald pursed his lips and raised an eyebrow, scrutinizing the cup of tea like one would a coiled adder. She sipped her own and waited. Behind her, the soft glow of dawn peeked through the latched shutters, highlighting the fine motes of dust floating unnoticed in the still air of the common room. They loomed just over her shoulders, hundreds of shapeless figures listing about as they closed in around her.

"So," he started, the jovial tenor of his voice shifting to a more somber tone. "It's finally time for this discussion again. Truth be told, I was beginning to wonder if you'd forgotten about it."

She scoffed. "You know me better than that."

"That I do," he mumbled, nodding into his lap. "That I do."

He picked up his tea, wrapping his burly fingers around the circumference of the cup and, closing his eyes, took a long sniff. The cup trembled in his hands, and when his eyes flew open, he stared at Aurnia with such intensity that it took every ounce of her considerable will not to squirm uncomfortably in her seat.

The cup vibrated against the tabletop as he slowly set it down, his piercing stare never wavering from her expressionless face. Once the cup rested securely on the end table, Donald rose to his feet and flew to the kitchen with a speed that seemed contrary to his considerable size.

Aurnia watched in silence as the man tore open a cupboard and shoved aside its contents, pulling from its depths a small yellow tobacco tin. He pried the circular lid free and peered inside.

He looked up at her, confused. "Where did you—"

"I'm not so callous as to raid your stash, Donald."

He snapped closed the lid and replaced the tin at the back of the cupboard, his shoulders slumping as the worry fled his muscles.

She inhaled the tea's floral aromas as she awaited him to return to his seat. Hibiscus, lavender, cardamom. Whether she'd ever encountered a more interesting blend in her travels was likely a subject of personal taste, but Donald's fondness for this particular mixture extended far beyond its effects on the palate.

He returned to his place on the couch, eagerly lifting the aromatic tea to his lips with both hands. He didn't drink though. He simply existed in the flavorful aromas, a soft moan rumbling from the base of his throat.

"Forgive me. It's been years since the last merchant came to town with more of this unique tea. I've been saving what little I had left for a special occasion. When I realized what you'd given me, I was certain you'd stumbled upon my reserves and . . ."

Aurnia tossed a bulging leather pouch into his lap. "I remembered it was your favorite from our last visit. Crossed paths with a merchant who had some on my way through Trovel last Fading. She told me the batches made after the leaves started turning enriched the flavors, but the blend had proven too much for her. I bought the whole lot at a discount. Been carrying it about ever since."

"Thank you. I mean it." He smiled down at his cup. "It's not *my* favorite, though. Much like that merchant you purchased it from, I've always found the flavor to be a bit cloying. I prefer a more delicate brew. Something subtle. Something you really have to think about to appreciate."

"I don't understand," she lied, knowing full well what he was getting at.

Donald wiped a hand down his bald head. "It was Tia's. The only tea I could ever get her to drink. She hated tea. 'Dirty water', she'd call it. I'd practically have to guard my cup, because if she got hold of it and it wasn't steaming hot, she'd dump it in the wash basin with rest of the 'dirty water'.

"I bought some of this tea on a lark, but right away, I knew I wasn't going to like it. Tia though . . ." He chuckled, memories glistening at the corners of his eyes. "The woman had a bit of a morbid streak. The walls were her idea. The color, I mean. Blood red. She took one look at the color of this tea and fell in love. Used to stare at me, grinning like a demon while she sipped it."

Aurnia peered down into her own cup. In the relative darkness of the room, the tea appeared almost black, but as she tilted the cup around, she thought she could make out a deep burgundy color around the edges.

"Is this—" he started, his voice catching. "Is this just another ploy to get me to let go of her necklace? Butter me up in the hopes I'll finally give in?"

She set her cup aside and folded her hands in her lap. The tea really was a bit much. "And here I thought I was just doing right by a friend."

"Don't blow that smoke up my pampered rear, missy. We both know every action you take is carefully calculated."

He reached beneath his shirt and drew a delicate silver chain up and over his head. A small pendant emerged from the collar of his night shirt; a silver lace filigree framing a small cube-cut citrine the size of her pinkie nail. The yellow gemstone was utterly clear, sans a single visible fracture running diagonally through its heart. The way the candlelight played through its facets made it look like it was fluttering on a gentle breeze.

"It's quite beautiful, isn't it?" He held it up between them, allowing it to rotate slowly at the end of its chain. "I'd never allow her to wear it in public, mind you. A cut purse would have slashed her throat for something like this even if it wasn't Orlicite. First thing she did when she walked through that door was to slip this over her head, and it stayed there until she decided to leave again."

"I need it, Donald."

He nodded, clutching the pendant to his chest. "I thought you might try that," he said, fighting against a rush of emotion.

She reached out and laid a hand on his knee. "I mean it. Things are different this time. Having that may mean the difference between escaping this bigoted city and suffering a horrible death at the hands of the Breathers. To the right person, there's a value in that little stone beyond money, greater than sentiment. Power, my friend. A real, substantive, undeniable power."

She leaned back. "And one that's wasted if it follows you to the grave."

"I can't, Aurnia. I can't give it up." He brushed the tears from his flushed cheeks. "You don't understand. When I hold it, I can feel her warmth. I can smell her hair. She's with me. It's like . . . it's like a small piece of her soul somehow transferred into that little gem when she—"

He choked up at that, turning away from her to clear his throat.

Aurnia's face was stone. "You know it doesn't work that way."

"I don't care. It's getting harder to remember her face. As much as I appreciate the tea, it's not going to work forever. My Tia's there, hiding in the shadows of my mind, but every day she steps further back into darkness. I'm worried one day I'll wake up and she'll just be a blur of grays . . . or a mashup of familiar customers and the strangers I pass on the streets."

His mouth contorted in anguish, so he covered it with a hand. "That when I eventually leave this life of mine behind, I'll spend the rest of eternity wandering the luminous fields of Obolvia, alone and unable to recognize her when she finally crosses my path."

Aurnia looked at her hands, uncomfortable in the face of Donald's intense display of emotion. This discussion was not heading in a positive direction. She was beginning to doubt the wisdom of replenishing the stores of his late wife's tea. An unforeseen misstep, and one she hoped wouldn't keep her from her outcome.

Her host squeezed the necklace to his chest and sobbed. Part of her could empathize with Donald, with his fear of forgetting the one he valued above all others. But where Donald's loss was only six or seven years in the past, hers had surpassed two decades. She wondered how painful his lack of memory would be when nothing in his life reminded him of Tia, when a week would pass by without a single thought of his missing wife, when he would wonder if that part of his life was truly real . . . or just the tattered remnants of a half-imagined dream.

Her brow tightened in thought. *Memory.*

"Donald."

The hulking man wiped his nose on his sleeve. He smiled at her apologetically. "I'm sorry, my dear. There's nothing you can offer that's worth more to me than than this pendant. I'd sooner give you my life than give up on her memory."

She nodded, pressing her fingers together in a tight steeple. "What if I could give you that? What if I could give you her memory? Vivid? Immaculate? Obdurate?"

He waved her off, retrieving his teacup from the side table. "Save your silver shil words. You're reaching."

"I'm serious. You know what I'm capable of. The skill to impress a thought or feeling or image on the mind is well within my capabilities as a Vellurgist. In point of fact, it's the very thing that drew the Breather here last night. So answer the question."

She eased forward, perching on the edge of her seat. "If I could give you an enduring memory of Tia, a memory of your choosing, if I could draw that memory out and bring it so thoroughly into the forefront of your mind that you forget where you are and experience the past as though it's the present . . ."

She pointed to the silver pendent pressed against his chest. "If I can do all the things I say, would you then at least *consider* the idea of trading me that bit of Orlicite?"

He stared at her for a good while in silence, searching every inch of her expressionless face as if the truth of her words would emerge and paint a story across her flawless skin. She gave him nothing though, nothing beyond her spoken message and the time it would take to digest it. Time was something she had little of, but if she rushed him now, she knew she'd lose him.

But if he gave her the chance to do as she said . . .

. . . that Orlicite was as good as hers.

Finally, Donald released a drawn-out sigh, allowing himself to relax back into the cushioned couch. He removed his spectacles and rubbed his eyes, taking the time to pick the mung from their corners. Once clean, he placed the glasses on the table beside his forgotten cup of tea. "Any memory I'd like?"

Aurnia straightened. "And you don't even need to tell me what it is."

He nodded into his lap. "If I say yes to this, I can't promise you I'll give you what you want."

"I'm aware."

"And you'll be able to accept that?"

Her lips stretched into a thin smile. She wasn't about to tell him she had little worry of that happening.

"I will."

He wiped his palms on his wrinkled night pants.

"Then tell me what I need to do."

Chapter 39: No Goodbyes

Theis shook his head and crossed his arms beneath the folds of his heavy cloak. "Boy's not gonna like it."

"We've no other choice in the matter." Aurnia wiped a hand across the surface of the dining table. "And I don't care whether he likes it or not."

"Whether or not I like what?"

Nevin forced himself to take a deep breath as he and Aidux descended the staircase. Dawn was still a memory on the horizon and already they were making decisions without him. Donald was nowhere to be seen. At least their generous host had seen fit to make himself scarce while Theis and Aurnia rearranged his future.

Despite its relative bulk, the Sharasil rested comfortably atop his right shoulder. If pressed by his two companions as to why he hadn't left the mysterious blade upstairs, he probably couldn't give them a satisfying answer. It just felt . . . odd, to leave it behind.

"Nevin," Aurnia said with a manufactured brightness, parting her lips in a shallow smile. A single plate of rye bread and creamy white cheese awaited him at the table. Aidux licked his lips and trotted over to a bowl of raw meat one of them had left for him to find.

"Have a seat. We've much to speak on." She gestured to the chair across from her. With her other hand, she fiddled with a small yellow gem, spinning the cube-cut stone in a slow circle on the tabletop with the tip of her index finger. Despite its size, Nevin could plainly see the darkened crack running straight through its core. The stone was pretty, but with such an obvious defect, he couldn't imagine it would be worth much.

He locked eyes with the woman in yellow and took his seat, sliding the blade across the empty tabletop beside his breakfast plate. Aidux ignored them all, sinking onto his haunches and laying into the bowl of meat with abandon.

"Sounds like you two have *already* been talking."

Theis chuckled at that, an odd sound from the normally stoic warrior. Aurnia shot him a dirty look as she spoke. "The city wide curfew was initiated the night before the three of you arrived. Given the distance from Comelbough to Elbin, it would be safe to assume this Vincht returned just in time to convince the Baron to activate the Breathers in an effort to catch the sword once it crossed the town's borders. That you managed to find your way here without encountering one of those monsters is nearly inconceivable. You must have caught Fate in a generous mood."

"Then let's just kill Vincht," said Theis, twirling a hand like he was suggesting a leisurely hike. "Solves more problem than one."

Aurnia shook her head. "The city's on alert, and there's no way a man with your features would go unnoticed in broad daylight. You're a walking legend, Theis Bane. You wouldn't make it twenty minutes before the guard caught wind of your presence. You can't fight the entire city."

The man in black snorted, half-drawing his sicklesque blade from its scabbard before dramatically slamming it home. "Think you're grossly overestimating these country rough necks."

"Maybe, maybe not. Still, I'm not entirely convinced Vincht's death would end the threat. He strikes me as an agent of a much larger agenda. I doubt the Baron would go to such lengths to assist him without either having a mutual interest in the outcome, or being strong armed by some external power. In both cases, killing Vincht would have little to no effect."

"So . . . what do we do?" asked Nevin, tearing off a hunk of bread with his teeth.

Aurnia folded her hands in her lap. "The fact is, Comelbough doesn't possess the resources necessary to unlock the secrets of the blade, and I'd rather not earn the enmity of an entire province on my way out the door."

Nevin shifted the hunk of rye into his cheek so he could talk. "Wait, you're leaving? When?"

"The sooner the better. With any luck, I'll find a boat heading in the direction of Montes au Buel or even Vadderstrix, and this horrible city will be little more than a stain on the horizon by noon."

Nevin leaned back in his chair. Both destinations were on the far side of the Sea of Calor, days and days of travel by boat. And since the sword wouldn't follow her without his help, that meant . . .

"You want to take me with you."

She nodded. "It's not ideal, but Vincht's actions have left us with little in the way of options. We can't stay here, not with Breathers walking the streets. It would only be a matter of time before one got a good enough taste of me or the sword. Besides, I can't properly examine it here. I need books, tools, and an unfettered access to my full repertoire of spells. Even the weakest ritual I know would draw the attention of every Breather within a mile's radius.

"I've no contacts in this province save Donald, and I've already strained him more than I have any right to. I have friends in the Tichoor Province, a family of commoners who made a fortune mining precious ore during the reformation period in the years after the Hallowed Schism. They're basically the de facto leaders of the town that popped up around the mines."

"So what?" Nevin raised his hands, frowning. "How is a family of miners supposed to help me?"

"One of those miners has spent most of his adult life studying magic and its effects on our world. He has access to literature and equipment and spaces designed specifically for containing and directing the type of spells I would need to use in order to analyze the sword. And, if it turns out the best option would be to just lock the blade away to keep it from falling into the wrong hands, he has the resources necessary to see that through."

If everything he'd learned since arriving in Comelbough was true, he couldn't find the fault in her logic. The Sharasil was clearly a magical object, which meant no amount of non-magical inquiry would yield the answers needed to free himself from the bond. And if these 'Breathers' could really sniff out magic, and were as dangerous as everyone made them out to be, it would only be a matter of time before they discovered their hiding place.

He chewed the skin of his lip. Theis and Aurnia. How much could he really trust them? Despite laying down a good story about ancient wars and mysterious letters, Aurnia had done very little to answer the question of why she was really doing this. Vagueness and conspiracy wrapped up in a history lesson, with a dash of misdirection for good measure.

And Theis . . . Theis had hidden the sword with Ishen for a reason. Why then, after over a decade, would he retrieve it at the request of some woman he'd never met? Now that he'd done as he was asked, why hang around?

While Nevin didn't think they were openly lying to him, he suspected they weren't being completely honest, either. At least he knew one thing for certain; as long as he and the blade were bound to one another, his two companions would keep him safe.

For the time being, that would have to suffice.

He shot Theis a knowing look. "Then I guess it's time to get smart or die stupid."

The man in black shrugged. "Got somewhere more important to be?"

No. I guess I don't.

Nevin reached out and scratched Aidux between his tufted ears. The cat arched gratefully into his hand and purred. "Let me be clear on one thing. I'm not going anywhere without Aidux, so whatever plan you have in mind, it had better include him as well."

Aurnia plucked the yellow gemstone from the tabletop and deposited it within one of the myriad folds of her dress. "I hadn't even considered the alternative. Donald is loaning us a wagon. We'll have to keep the cat hidden until we make it onto whatever ship will have us, but I don't foresee any problems with him tagging along. Greater Delphine is a much more understanding place than the Lancowl Barony. His presence will be viewed more as a curiosity than a threat."

She stood. "As long as he doesn't stray too far from your side, that is."

Nevin followed suit, leaving most of his breakfast untouched. "Wait, are we leaving *now*? What about Donald? I need to thank him for all his help."

"The sooner the better. By the time we arrive, the harbor will be filled with merchant and shipping vessels. Many will be making the final preparations for a long voyage. They won't dawdle. It's perfect sailing weather and the seas are calm. They'll be eager to make water, and I don't want to miss an opportunity to join them.

"And don't worry about Donald. In his mind, he got far more from our visit that we did from him. He was glad to help."

Nevin nodded reluctantly. He wished he could give the big man a warm hug before they all set out, but he understood that time was of the essence. He'd need to grab his pack, but beyond that, he was ready to leave at a moment's notice.

"Do you think they'll be okay letting two people and a cat—"

"Three and a cat." Theis stepped out from his place on the wall. "I'm coming, too."

Aurnia's yellow dress billowed outward as she spun around, a furious scowl distorting her normally expressionless face. "Oh no you are not. We have enough against us without the company of a wanted man attracting even more of the wrong kind of attention."

The man in black shouldered past her to stand by the door. "And what makes you think you can stop me?"

She followed right on his heels, standing on her toes to shove an accusing finger into the warrior's chest. "You're not a stupid man, Theis Bane, but you're fooling yourself if you think you can tag along without bringing the entire might of the Lancowl constabulary down on our heads before we even reach the port.

"Frankly, I was surprised at your return this morning. You've done as I've asked and brought me the sword. You have no further obligation to remain. Why not just go back to wherever you've been hiding? The world forgot you once. It can do so again."

Theis slapped her hand aside. "You won't last the day without my help. Barely survived the night. Had I not been here when the Breather—"

"Yes, and had you retrieved the blade before some random child stumbled upon it, I would have made it out of this horrible city long before Vincht and the Baron could have rallied their forces. I wouldn't have needed to make special accommodations for a boy and his cat. I would have no one to worry about beyond myself.

"You're a walking complication, and one that's outlived its usefulness. Don't make this harder for us than necessary."

The man in black turned to Nevin, his eyes vibrating angrily.

"Well? You want me gone, too, boy?"

Nevin's jaw tightened reflexively. "I told you to stop calling me 'boy'."

A reaction, spoken in haste and without thought. As soon as the words left his lips, he regretted not saying something different.

With an incredulous snort, Theis shook his head. "That's about to be the least of your problems."

He ripped open the door and strode out into the morning. Aurnia took a step back and placed a thin hand to her chest.

Aidux crowded up against Nevin's leg. "He didn't even say goodbye."

The cat mrowed plaintively, his ears wilting like flowers in a drought.

Aurnia smoothed the ruffles of her dress and pulled back her shoulders. "Gather your things, Nevin. We leave in five minutes."

And just like that, Nevin knew he'd traded one chaperon for another. Swallowing back the rising lump in his throat, the young man begrudgingly ascended the stairs in search of his pack.

Goodbyes were beginning to seem a rare gift.

Chapter 40: The Misanthrope

David Williams, captain of the Misanthrope—a three-mast caravel rigged with the squared sails preferred for long-range ocean voyages—shook his head at Aurnia for the third time in so many minutes and folded his dark, leathery arms across his bare chest.

"Look, lady. My crew and I just don't care for outsiders that much. They make us uneasy." He spit to the side. "It's nothing personal."

Situated behind a serpentine strip of bare sand that stood but a few feet above the ocean's surface, the town's port wrapped around the edges of the wide, slow-moving river that split the town in twain. Two-story stucco warehouses crowded up against an open cobblestone field bordering the shore line, and multifarious finger-like docks reached out into a murky blue-green lagoon. Scattered boats marred the horizon like clumps of dirt on a blue tablecloth, boats that would eventually reside at the docks come nightfall, but their present absence left room for the moored transport ships and their crews to move about with freedom and ease.

Only a handful of the docked ships were both large enough and rigged properly for an extended voyage. Out of those handful, all but Captain Williams were heading in the wrong direction. But the man apparently had no use for gold.

The day was not progressing as she'd hoped.

Captain Williams was beginning to seriously irritate her. *Since when could an obscene amount of money not buy transportation?*

She forced a friendly smile. "And I'm willing to soothe your unease with a commensurate amount of gold. With a ship as large as yours, you must have taken on passengers at some point in the past."

Scratching a hand through a dark tangle of chest hair, the man directed a troubled stare back to his ship. Three pairs of men hastily transferred an assortment of sacks, barrels, and crates from an open top wagon onto a wench-operated lift, their attentions everywhere but on the task at hand. Despite their strenuous pace, Captain Williams scowled with obvious dissatisfaction.

"Never felt the need," he said without turning back to her. "The Misanthrope trades in the ports of seven different kingdoms, specializing in the acquisition of such rare commodities as Tottleton's saffron mead, dried Ledodis mushroom from Fen Quarry, and rock toad oil from Crag Orten. We do well enough for ourselves that we don't have to suffer the company of stone-leggers like you."

Aurnia tried not to frown. *Stone-legger.* A crude seafaring term used to describe those who have spent the majority of their lives constrained to land. As silly and innocuous as it sounded, in David William's mind, he had basically slapped her across the face.

Realizing she wasn't just going to go away, he finally afforded her the whole of his attention. His eyes dipped south from her face, taking in the full height of her lithe form in slow, greedy sweeps. A lecherous grin split his sun-cracked lips.

"Then again, we just might be able to work *something* out. My crew does get lonely on those long, cold ocean nights. It's not often a woman as . . . comely as yourself wishes to share our company." He rubbed his hands together, licking his lips as he gawked. "You're not shy, are you?"

Aurnia straightened reflexively. Were she anywhere but Comelbough, a crude bastard like Captain Williams would quickly come to regret his disrespectful tone, but she had to be extremely careful here. Considering the tense state of the city and the looming shadow of both Vincht and the Baron's Breathers, it seemed the scales of Fate were already stacked against her. Using anything other than the conventional means of negotiation to secure transport would only tip them further.

Besides, that little voice in the darkness of her mind told her his attitude was all show. Everything about him—from his crossed arms to his stand-offish tone to his blatant misogyny—screamed 'go away.' And had he not been their only hope of getting out of Comelbough today, she might have listened.

But one way or another, Aurnia Celine Mistral always got her way.

A pair of silver peepers stared out from a series of wide holes cut into the sides of a long wooden crate, darting from man to net to cart as fish of all shapes and sizes paraded past the wagon. A soft whine wafted along the damp ocean air as a fisherman carrying a two-foot long silver-blue fish walked by. Nevin shushed the crate, reaching out to adjust the heavy woolen blanket draped atop the hungry lynx's hiding spot.

"Just one, Nevin." Aidux whispered through one of the hastily cut air holes. "I just want one of those tasty looking fish. Just *one*."

Nevin leaned in close. "You can have all the fish you want once Aurnia finds us a boat."

The cat squinted out at him. "All I want? You promise?"

"I promise."

He looked around nervously, checking to make sure none of the locals had spotted the strange young man conversing with a wooden box and decided to come investigate. Despite the cat being locked up in a crate for transport, he was worried people might react poorly to his friend's presence in the port. Ideally, the three of them would make it out of Comelbough without anyone ever knowing Aidux was here, but as long as the guard specifically never figured it out, Nevin would count that as a win.

Appraising the wide-open staging area at the port's heart, he was grateful to see that no one was paying him and his mule-drawn wagon any mind. Sailors hefted crates of goods up wooden ramps. Fisherman gutted their hauls by the shore, tossing the unwanted bits into overflowing tin buckets. Gulls waddled in to pick at the piles, pecking and screeching at one another as they fought over scraps. A vagrant squatted against a nearby warehouse, swaddled in stained rags and picking at the dirt with a crooked stick. Small bands of soldiers conversed beneath scattered canvas pavilions, relaxing against their iron-tipped spears and generally ignoring the locals.

Nevin's fingers nervously brushed the cloth-wrapped Sharasil bound across his back. Had Aurnia gotten her way, the mysterious blade would currently be packed away inside a crate in much the same manner as Aidux, but Nevin had vetoed that plan before she could even finish speaking. The idea of being disconnected from the blade in that way had sent his anxiety soaring. A strange reaction, considering he'd been keen on dropping the blade off a cliff not but a week prior.

The cloth sweater had been his compromise. This way, curious onlookers wouldn't see anything particularly odd about the young man in their midst, and Nevin could still take comfort in the Sharasil's proximity.

A lot of good it will do if things get violent, he thought.

With Aidux secreted away and the man in black absent, Nevin prayed that Aurnia would find them a boat, and soon. Every minute out in the open was one more minute for the soldiers to take interest and wander over. One more minute for a Breather to catch a whiff of the blade and run him down.

One more minute for Vincht to wander out of some side alley and take his revenge.

"Nevin."

The unexpected voice ripped him from his dark thoughts. Aidux stared intently out at him from within the confines of the crate.

"It's gonna be okay. You'll see."

He offered the cat an uncertain smile, but couldn't hide his shaking hands. "I want to believe that. I do. But without Theis . . ."

"You still have me. And Aurnia too."

"I don't get it. He just left. He dragged us through the mountains and into this stupid town and just . . ." Nevin tossed his hands in the air. "Walked away."

"But he *did* get us here. He told us he would, and he did."

"I shouldn't have let him go. I should have argued with Aurnia."

The cat pressed a paw up against a circular air hole, the smooth pink skin of his footpad tasting the late morning sun. "I miss him, too."

Nevin balked. He didn't miss him. How could he? The man was infuriating. Grumpy. Stoic. Harsh. He should be happy to be free of him. At least Aurnia took the time to explain things to him. At least Aurnia spoke to him like a person.

And yet, there was an odd honesty to the man in black's actions. He didn't sugarcoat his thoughts and didn't dance around his points. He said what he meant and didn't care if the truth hurt. And while it might be painful to hear in the moment, Nevin realized he always knew where he stood with the man after he took the time to think about his message.

No, he didn't miss him, but that didn't mean he was happy he was gone. He pressed his hand up to the crate until the skin of his palm rested against Aidux's footpad.

"Now can you please go get me a fish?"

Aurnia pressed her lips together in a thin line. It was time to go on the offensive.

"Captain Williams, might I ask what sort of cargo you're transporting?"

Stepping forward, the captain trailed a finger down her arm and grinned. "Oh, a little of this, little of that. Quite a bit of brandy, if you're interested. You can have as much as you like, if that will help loosen you up, get you in the mood for a little fun."

She ignored him. "It's just that I couldn't help but notice how attentive your crew is to guarding the ship, especially with the reputation of Comelbough as one of the safest ports in all of Stragus. One would think that the captain of a ship like the Misanthrope would feel at ease in such a secure and quiet city."

Captain Williams glanced back over his shoulder. Three rough-looking men stood watch beside a wide ramp leading up to the ship's deck. Each held a wicked-looking cudgel in one hand. They were completely silent, avoiding becoming engaged in conversation to pass the time. Their eyes darted furtively from one passerby to the next.

"What can I say?" He shrugged. "Me and my crew are suspicious people by nature. The Misanthrope's our home, and we don't appreciate strangers snooping around our home."

She shuddered to think what Captain Williams and his crew would do to someone they caught snooping around their ship. Out at sea, a ship was practically a country unto itself, and it wouldn't be hard for a snooper to 'disappear' once a ship broke port. And Captain Williams, with his broad chest, thick arms, and unsavory attitude, would have little trouble exacting his own personal form of justice once the Misanthrope hit open waters.

"A completely understandable sentiment. I wouldn't want people sneaking around my house either. But something else is bothering me. It's rare I run into someone who doesn't appreciate a heaping bag of gold shils. It's just not natural. In my experience, there are generally only two reasons why someone won't take a job when I offer them as much money as I've offered you.

"The first reason is if I've asked them to do something that directly puts them or someone they care about in a life-threatening situation. It seems a man's greed is only out-weighed by his self-preservation instinct, though there are times when a sufficient amount of money can overcome even that. And as my request for passage won't take us near any dangerous territory—and I'm fairly certain that you, despite your general distaste for outsiders, don't *actually* feel threatened by me and mine—I doubt you've turned down my money out of fear for your life and property."

Captain Williams thumbed his nose. "And the second reason?"

"The second reason is something I wasn't convinced existed until I met a man some months back. You've heard of Theis Bane?"

"Sounds familiar." He twirled a finger impatiently. "You gonna get to your point before the tide comes in?"

Aurnia bowed her head. "Of course. As I was saying, until I met Theis, I had never confirmed the other reason why money wouldn't buy results. You see, some people just don't need the money."

The man crossed his arms once again. "There you go. We don't need your money, woman. We're doing just fine without you."

She held up a single finger. "Everyone needs money, Captain Williams, no matter how much they already have. Greed is in our nature, and the more money we have, the more money we want.

"Now, I've been at this game for a long time, long even before your eyes first glimpsed the ocean." Captain Williams cocked an eyebrow quizzically. "And in all my years, I've only ever met one person who *really* didn't need the money. I understand his reasons, but yours . . ."

Aurnia waved a hand at the Misanthrope. "I can only assume you don't need the money because the amount I've offered doesn't compare to the value of your cargo, and you're afraid that by giving me and mine passage, we'll find out what you're hauling."

She paused, her stare penetrating deep into the man's steely eyes.

"And that would only be a problem if you and yours are smugglers."

Captain William's face flushed a bright red as he took a quick step forward and grabbed her upper arm with a burly hand. "Now you listen here. If you think I'm gonna stand by and be threatened by some trollop, you've got another thing coming."

A cruel grin sprouted on his lips as he leaned closer, his breath hot on Aurnia's face. "Maybe a personal tour of the Misanthrope is in order. See the lower decks. You won't need any brandy for *us* to have a good time."

Aurnia just smiled pleasantly. "Threatened? You misunderstand my intentions. I only wish to offer my help. In exchange for passage, of course."

The warm glow of her soul blossomed out from the darkness of her mind, crawling down through her arm to concentrate at the tip of her thumb. She placed her hand softly atop the man's unfriendly grip, strumming his knuckles with her magically infused digit.

After a moment, the captain's eyes went wide and he jerked his hand back, retreating a step in the process. "Bragga's brow, lady, wha—"

"There's no need to invoke the ocean god's name for my sake, Captain. A frivolous act like that might earn you a spat of foul weather in the near future, and we wouldn't want rough seas to damage your cargo, would we?"

Captain Williams just stared at her, rubbing his hand as if to ensure it was still attached. She didn't wait for his retort. "Tell me, what do you know of the Calorthian Void?"

He answered by spitting on the cobbles. "A windless region of the sea blocking a clear run at Greater Delphine. It costs us a week of travel getting around it, but it's a heap better than the melancholy two days of constant rowing instills in the men. Ernal Rumsley hung himself from the crow's nest the last time we made the crossing, and ol' Bodger hasn't been the same since."

"Do you and your men have a fondness for rowing?"

He grunted.

"What if I told you that having me on board will save you over three days on the water, and you won't need to touch an oar at any point in the journey?"

The captain shrugged. "I do it all the time. What's a few extra days?"

"The problem with dangerous cargo lies in the carrying. The longer you have it, the more time it has to cause you trouble. I'm sure your employers would appreciate it if you happened to show up ahead of schedule. And should circumstances take a turn for the unfortunate, wouldn't it make sense to have someone around with the ability to remove you from those circumstances? They say the best defense is a good offense, but I'm of the opinion that no defense is greater than the ability to strategically remove one's self from the conflict altogether. Am I right?"

He stared at her in silence, searching her face for a tell, any sign of a hidden agenda. But her countenance was that of chiseled granite, a bulwark of placid haughtiness that left him little choice but to take her words as she spoke them.

Overhead, a flock of pigeons tore through the air, but as the two weighed themselves against the other, they hardly noticed.

"You aren't wrong." Captain Williams admitted with a sigh, and Aurnia knew she had him. "Alright lady, explain your plan. Maybe we can work something out."

Chapter 41: The Inferno Rekindled

Vincht stared down into the quiet black dot resting at the center of the glass sphere clasped in his fingertips. He'd been waiting for something worth calling up the sleeping flame, something worth communicating to the man whose soul channel resided within, but the constant march of time had been eating away at the day, and dragging with it his ever-eroding patience.

But now, finally, he was merely a handful of moments away from victory.

He sighed, unconsciously peeling away a barely congealed strip of scab from his flushed cheek and cast it onto the wooden roof tiles. Despite the coolness of the day, thick beads of sweat coated his brow and stained the pits of his shirt. He barely noticed it anymore, barely recognized the acrid miasma occupying the air around him, barely felt the thickening husk of grime coating every inch of his body.

Returning the glass sphere to its pouch on his belt, Vincht leaned out over the twenty-foot drop and surveyed the bustling port below. Everything was in place. Soldiers had taken up strategic positions, covering all avenues of escape, ready to bear arms and move in on his signal. He had more waiting just out of sight, if it came down to it.

A sneer cracked his mangled lips. *I almost hope it would.*

He crouched at the edge of the rooftop. The woman in the yellow dress seemed to be making headway with her negotiations. He'd noticed her earlier, moving up and down the line of moored ships, and made note of her exquisite beauty long before he'd connected her with his quarry. He hated knowing that the blood of someone so physically perfect would be on his hands, but that was the price one paid when they fell in with the wrong crowd.

"*Nevin.*"

He hissed the word through shaking lips. Rising from his spot at the edge of the roof, Vincht cast one final, hateful glance at the oblivious young man tending a wagon below before striding purposefully toward a cage of pigeons. He slapped the side of the cage and flung wide the door. Six pigeons burst through the exit, their wings beating at the air like it might fight back if they gave it enough chance. Their flight path cut down into the open plaza before turning to head west along the coast.

Tilting his head as he watched the startled birds vanish into the distance, he peeled free another thin strip of hardened scab, this time from his neck. The reddened flesh oozed a pinkish fluid that pooled into the collar of his vest.

An uncontrollable shiver wracked his body, but whether it was a shiver of agony or of ecstasy, he'd long lost the ability to discern.

The finer hairs on Aurnia's neck jerked to attention when Captain Williams' eyes tore from hers to examine something just over her right shoulder. It was the first time since he had agreed to hear her out that he didn't watch her intently, didn't scrutinize her every word and move.

With his attention now turned elsewhere, a growing discomfort twisted knots in her stomach.

The rhythmic pulsing of wooden soles on cobblestone announced the approach of three men. She knew without turning they were city guard.

Things are about to get very unpleasant.

A slight breeze ruffled the folds of her delicate yellow dress as the three men came to a halt. *They must have lowered their spears.*

"By the order of Baron Lancowl," spoke a stern, monotonous voice, "I order you to relinquish your weapons and surrender. Comply, and you will be taken into custody. Any failure to comply will result in lethal action."

Captain Williams turned his attention back to her through a pair of narrow, questioning eyes. "What have you gotten me into, woman?"

"Too late to back out now, Captain. We have an agreement." She lifted a single finger, slowly tilting it forward until it pointed directly at the man's sunburnt nose. "Welch on it now and I'll drag you down with me, understand?"

The man flinched like she'd slapped him. Swallowing hard, he nodded.

"Comply," repeated the soldier, impatiently.

Aurnia reached down into the folds of her dress and wrapped her delicate fingers around the small yellow gemstone she'd received from Donald. She took a deep breath, turned to face the small group of soldiers, and allowed the gentle warmth of her soul to spread out and suffuse every inch of her expectant form.

Somewhere, not far from where she stood, a misshapen creature sucked a lungful of air through its gaping mouth hole and stirred.

"Hey," Aidux whispered, barely loud enough for Nevin to hear over the bustle of the plaza. The cat nudged the steadfast lid with his nose. "Undo the latch for me. It's getting stiffy in this box."

"The word is 'stuffy'." Nevin grinned, tugging aside the wool blanket to reveal a half-moon shaped iron latch.

A familiar baritone voice addressed him from behind. "It *is* a bit on the warm side, isn't it, Nevin?"

His blood turned to ice, a frozen river of terror that brought his heart to jerking halt.

Even without looking, he knew exactly who the words belonged to. Forcing himself to turn, he prayed he was mistaken, prayed his stress-addled mind had finally snapped and was spinning delusions out of his darkest fears.

The black-haired Vincht smiled down at him, his hand resting casually on the ivory hilt of his short blade. Taking a step back, Nevin covered his mouth to hide his revulsion.

The man was a shadow of his former self. Gone was his meticulously maintained external appearance, replaced with a set of filthy, blood-stained clothes and a gruesome face split by thick, pus-swollen gouges. The wounds were open and oozing, their edges red and swollen with unchecked infection. Thick gobs of milky sweat clung to his clammy flesh, and uncontrollable convulsions occasionally wracked his body. The cloying scent of dried sweat and rot permeated the air.

A trio of spear-wielding soldiers spread out behind him, their presence likely only a secondary precaution in case Nevin decided to run. The young man looked past them for help, but it seemed Aurnia had her own soldiers to deal with, and more were rapidly approaching from both sides of the plaza. Within moments, the empty space between the docks and warehouses would be filled with armed men.

He cast a sideways glance at the crate. Aidux knew to keep quiet. With any luck, no one would ever know he was there.

"You're quite a long way from home." Vincht scratched at the bloody divot in his chin, staining his already darkened fingertips a fresh shade of red.

"You left me no choice. It was either this or burn to death."

He shifted his weight to step away from the cart, but a terrifying thought stopped him. Aidux was stuck, the crate lid latched to keep it from popping open as the cart bounced along the city streets. If he ran off without unhooking it, Aidux would be as good as dead if the soldiers found him.

I could pop the latch, but then all these soldiers will now about Aidux's hiding spot.

All over the plaza, sailors and commoners alike were abandoning the open ground, fleeing to their ships or disappearing down alleyways. With no one to scare them off, hordes of screaming gulls descended upon the discarded fish guts, fighting among themselves over the bloody remains.

The jet-haired warrior looked around, frowning. "You're oddly alone. Where are your friends? The man with glowing eyes? That infernal cat?"

"They're dead," he lied, hoping the manufactured quiver in his voice sounded convincing. "The fires caught us before we could make it to the mountains. I barely made it here myself."

Vincht's lower lip stuck out in mock sympathy. "I'm so sorry to hear that. That must have devastated you. I suppose now you're going to tell me you left the object I'm looking for back at that old man's cabin, too?"

"It burned along with everything else."

A sinister grin split the man's devastated lips. "Then explain the fog on your breath, Nevin. Nothing magical about that, right?"

Nevin looked down. A fine mist swirled in the air before him. He hadn't realized it, but his right hand had shifted behind him and found its way between the folds of the wool blanket to grip the bare metal of the Sharasil.

"You really are a terrible liar." Vincht shook his head in disappointment. "I'll let you keep it, for now. At least while you're helping me find the cat. You can't imagine how eager I am to—"

A sudden blast of briny wind battered the group with a wall of dust and debris, and the bodies of three screaming soldiers flew past them overhead. They slammed into the warehouse wall before dropping limply to the cobbles. Vincht and his men covered their faces protectively and turned.

Aurnia stood with an arm stretched forward, a strange yellow light shining out between the fingers of her closed fist.

Vincht sneered through clenched teeth. "*Witch.*"

The scar-faced warrior waved a hand overhead and called out to the soldiers scattered across the plaza. "The woman in yellow's a user! Take her down with as much force as you can muster!"

Nevin only took a moment to gawk at his female companion's surprising show of magical force before he realized everyone's attention was trained elsewhere. He lunged toward the crate, slapping open the latch holding the lid closed on Aidux before sprinting down the nearest alleyway.

As the warehouses rose up around him, he heard the distinctive ring of steel as Vincht's short blade emerged from its home.

Chapter 42: Losing Ground

Aurnia shoved her hand forward, willing her soul down through her arm and into the tiny yellow gemstone. She could feel its reserves of solidified power, feel the bonds shattering beneath the force of her will, feel the rush of energy growing around her in the split second before her intent manifested physically before her as a violent burst of cutting wind.

The small band of surprised soldiers careened up and backwards, losing their weapons as they slammed against the wall of a nearby warehouse. She knew the blow wasn't enough to kill them, but neither would any be eager to regain their feet.

Behind her, Captain Williams mixed orders with obscenities in his rush to prepare the three-mast Misanthrope to break port. By the tone of his voice and the frantic sounds of people dashing about, she had no doubt the man would be ready in record time. She only hoped she could withstand the constabulary's assault long enough to retrieve her two companions.

She looked back to where she'd left Nevin and grimaced. *Bad luck.* The boy was in a dead sprint down a nearby alleyway, a team of soldiers hot on his heels.

More soldiers swarmed the plaza like flies over rotting meat, but she still had a few seconds before they were close enough to cause her problems. Calming her turbulent mind, she clapped her hands together at her breastbone with the Orlicite between her palms, then shoved them forward and spread her fingers.

Across the plaza, halfway down the alleyway between the boy and his pursuers, a shimmering ball of air coalesced, swirling tightly around a gleaming yellow core of barely visible light.

The band of soldiers didn't even have the time to balk at its appearance before the entire mass erupted. The narrow alley amplified their cries of pain and surprise as the wind knocked them prone. Three of the men slid across the cobbles toward the alley's entrance, while the fourth somehow managed to wedge his blade between the stones to hold his ground.

Breathing heavily, Aurnia nodded to herself and prepared for the soldiers rushing her from every angle.

You're on your own for the moment, Nevin.

Bits of wood and debris peppered his back as a frighteningly powerful blast of wind erupted behind him, but Nevin ignored it in his rush. Ahead of him, the alley split left and right in a t-shaped intersection.

Equal and opposite. Gotta get lucky some time.

Setting his jaw, he took the left-most path, only to skid to an immediate stop.

A gaunt shadow emerged out of the cracked cobbles, a pale hand reaching out to offer help, an unrecognizable dark liquid coating its finger-tips.

Trust in me, Nevin. Give in and survive.

Nevin lost traction on the stone and landed hard on his hip, radiating pain up his right side. He wasted little time though, scrambling back to his feet and sprinting down the alternate path and hopefully out into freedom and safety.

Unfortunately, the second alley was only about thirty feet deep, ending in a pair of metal reinforced doors secured with a rusted iron chain and lock. Swollen barrels and chipped crates lined the stucco walls on either side, covered with layers of cream-colored bird droppings from years of neglect. With a grunt of frustration, Nevin shoved the doors with both hands. The chain rattled noisily but held fast.

"Guard the entrance," called Vincht from somewhere at the far end of the alley. "Let no one in or out but me."

Panting, Nevin looked back over his shoulder. The gaunt figure had vanished once again, but he could feel it—feel *him*—somewhere nearby. Waiting for its moment.

What *was* this thing? He had nearly accepted its offer on the fallen tree just days before, but for some reason, its presence still terrified him. The more rational part of him wanted nothing to do with the being only he could seem to see and hear, but another part of him—the part of him responsible for fear, for uncertainty, for despair, for hopelessness—longed to reach out and grab hold of that pale hand, consequences be damned.

He shook his head. *No time for thoughts like that now.*

He looked up, scanning the soaring walls for a ladder, a window, anything that would allow him to climb up and out of this dead end, but even if he stacked the crates and barrels one atop the other, they wouldn't come close to reaching the roof line, and that was assuming they could hold his and their combined weight without crumbling to bits.

"This is ridiculous, Nevin," yelled Vincht from nearby, but still around the corner. He almost sounded bored. "You don't think I've memorized every inch of this port? You don't think I know exactly where each one of these streets and alleys lead? You don't think I've planned for every possible contingency, every possible route you could take to get away from me?"

He grabbed the rusted chain and pulled. Flakes of red rust shook free, and the doors cracked open slightly. He cursed under his breath. There was no way he could squeeze through that gap. He'd have to remove the chain first, but despite its superficial appearance, he doubted he had the means to sunder it.

Nevin slung the woolen bundle off his shoulder and hurriedly unwrapped the Sharasil, allowing the blanket to collapse in a heap at his feet. He gripped the coarse stone handle with both hands, set his feet, and took a deep breath.

With one fluid motion, he brought the Sharasil crashing down on the iron lock with all his might.

Nothing. Not even a spark for his efforts. The chain itself barely even rattled.

He should have known better. The weapon weighed practically nothing, and without a cutting edge, he had little hope of it doing any sort of appreciable damage.

"It's a sword," he whispered down to the useless cylinder of metal. He twisted his hands along the grip and closed his eyes. "She said it's a sword. Somewhere, hiding beneath all of this is a sword. I just have to call it out."

The man in black's voice filled his mind.

You wanted to kill that soldier, didn't you?

He nodded. "He was gonna hurt Aidux. I did. I wanted him dead."

It was the first time he'd admitted it. Even in his own mind he'd denied wanting to cause the man harm. He had lied to Theis, but more importantly, he had lied to himself. Owning up to his darker urges scared him, but it also left him with a feeling he hadn't experienced for quite some time.

A feeling of control.

The voice of Theis continued. *And the Sharasil reacted.*

Could it be that simple? He squeezed his eyes closed until little white stars danced in the blackness behind his eyelids. *I want to kill. I have to!*

The weapon shook in his hands, not from some internal magical process, but by the sheer force of his grip on the handle. Grimacing, Nevin's head slumped forward and the tip of the weapon relaxed to the cobbles.

With a painful swallow, Nevin realized he was on his own, fighting with a bladeless sword, in an alley with but one way out.

Aurnia threw her arm out once again, and once again a pair of surprised spearmen went flying, but she was beginning to feel the strain. The warmth of her soul was starting to burn, and not just from the effort of casting such involved and draining magic.

The yellow gemstone wasn't shaped properly for such magic. For sustained spells, the cut was perfect, but forcing these bursts of energy through the cube-cut Orlicite was akin to trying to shove an entire lake through a single channel dam. Each time she cast her soul through it she could feel its internal defect cracking further. At this rate, she wouldn't have much left to get them across the Calorthian Void, and the soldiers were still coming.

Her soul suddenly screamed in warning.

Down the plaza, a metal reinforced door set into the side of a tall warehouse shuddered as some unseen bulk hammered into it from the inside. Soldiers all around flinched at the impact, looking at each other uncertainly and tightening their grips on their spears.

Soldiers are about to be the least of my worries.

A second hit tore the door from its hinges, sending it cartwheeling across the plaza with the terrible scream of ripping metal. The jagged projectile barreled end-over-end through the nearest group of soldiers, cutting two down with a spray of blood and shortened cries of pain and anguish. The rest scattered in every direction, abandoning their weapons to the cobbles.

A nude mass of pallid flesh and unimaginably corded muscle leapt into the sunlight, loping forward on bone-bare knuckles and gulping lungfuls of the briny ocean air. At some point in its forgotten past, the creature was a human man, but maturity and some unknown magical process had engorged its muscles and enlarged its frame to absurd proportions.

Had it been able to stand upright, it might have cleared ten feet in height, but its overdeveloped musculature bent its upper body into an awkward hunch.

The skin of its face was pulled tight over its skull, and a fan of wiry black hair jutted out in every direction from the top of its head.

That's a Breather.

Aurnia backpedaled, but quickly realized she couldn't outrun the creature, not on her best day. While its arrival wasn't entirely unexpected, its abrupt appearance unbalanced her.

Like a snake before a big meal, the creature's jaw was unhinged and hanging, nearly grazing its swollen chest muscles. Over a foot of slimy, pinkish tongue snaked out of its horrifically slack mouth to taste the air before being sucked back inside the toothless hole. Its labored breathing ceased and it jerked its head in Aurnia's direction, staring at her with wide, bloodshot eyes.

And then, holding its breath, the Breather charged headlong across the plaza.

Caught by surprise, an unprepared group of five soldiers tried to get out of its way, but the beast charged right through their midst. The impact struck them like a runaway wagon, sending four of them tumbling end-over-end. The fifth wasn't so lucky. The Breather took hold of the middle-aged spearman by wrapping an over-sized hand around the man's thigh and hoisting him overhead.

The man's skull split like an overripe melon when the creature slammed his body to the cobbles, all without the beast breaking stride.

Aurnia quickly looked around. The Misanthrope was the closest shelter, but she knew that even a bevy of strapping sailors would be no match for a Breather after a scent. That thing could tear a hole through the wall of a boat with its bare hands. Luckily, the rest of the soldiers had slowed their approach, not particularly eager to be nearby when the Breather reached its mark.

She extended the fingers of the hand holding the Orlicite into a blade and took a hard step in the direction of the charging creature, slashing her hand diagonally through the air while she focused her intent. Stone exploded from the cobbles in a razor-sharp line ahead of her. The line raced forward toward the Breather, peppering the air with shards of grayish rock dust.

The Breather wailed in agony as the invisible blade of air collided with its midsection. It stumbled forward, limbs flailing in the air.

A slow smile spread across Aurnia's lips.

Soldiers froze or backed away, wary to face off against a magic user that could stand up to their province's answer to magic users.

But the beast would not be put down so easily.

When it couldn't regain its balance, it rolled along its back and came to its feet. A neat line of blood revealed a thin gouge in its flesh from thigh to shoulder, but the damage was minuscule compared to what the cutting wind had done to the stone. The Breather slowed to a stop, allowing the dust to settle before sucking in another lungful of air and extending its worm-like tongue once more to taste the air.

Aurnia's smile vanished.

The tongue retreated back into its home with a wet schlurp, and the Breather galloped toward her once more.

Chapter 43: Cursebreaker

Aidux peered out through the crate's hastily drilled air holes, waiting until the soldiers moved deep enough in the alley before he made his move. He had to get to Nevin. Vincht's voice was unmistakable, and now he had his friend on the run, maybe even trapped.

Unable to wait any longer, he bumped the crate lid with his noggin.

Thunk. "Ow?"

The cat blinked. He pressed the top of his furry head to the lid again and shoved.

It refused to budge, refused to give him even an inch of play.

"No, no, no, no, no," he whispered, frantically craning his neck to peer out one of the air holes in search of the crate's latch, ignoring the fact that there was no possible way he could see it from his position within the sealed wooden box.

Panic set in. He'd seen him do it, seen Nevin reach out and slap the latch open before running off down the alley. He'd heard the thing click free. The troubled cat stretched his legs, grinding his head, his neck, his arched back against the lid and pushed with all his might.

"Come on . . ." he groaned, straining. The wooden crate groaned back, fighting to maintain its integrity as the lynx enlisted more and more muscle with each passing second of resistance.

The scream of tearing of metal echoed down the open plaza, and the sheer violence of the sound caused Aidux to flinch.

That extra bit of oomph snapped one of the crate's hinges loose.

Aidux dropped to his stomach, staring out through the air holes toward the source of the noise, but all he could see were soldiers and two-story buildings. He frowned. The noise wouldn't matter if he couldn't free himself from the crate. But this time, when he rose and pressed the full length of his frame against the lid, it gave.

Only an inch, but an inch was a start.

I'm coming, Nevin.

The cat's muzzle peeled back in nightmarish grin.

Just hold on.

Vincht cocked his head, gazing back down the alleyway and past the growing throng of spear-wielding soldiers guarding the sole entrance to the narrow corridor of stucco and stone. A wild grin split his scab-crusted lips.

"You hear that, Nevin? That terrible ruckus?" He twirled his sword playfully and sauntered toward the t-shaped intersection. "That, my terrified little friend, is a Breather. An absolutely abominable creature, but effective none-the-less. I wanted one in the port district in case you happened to pass through with the sword. I thought maybe it would sniff out what I might have missed. Never thought it'd catch wind of a tried-and-true magic user, but sometimes Fate looks out for you in ways that preparation can't.

"The Baron didn't like that part of my plan. He doesn't like the Breathers out walking around in broad daylight. He said it makes his citizens nervous to see such hideous creatures, especially considering they were once people."

He crushed a morsel of stale bread beneath the heel of his boot, twisting his foot to grind it to dust. The volume of his speech rose until his words shook the dust from the cobbles. "I asked you if you were hearing me! They were people, Nevin! The Baron figured out how to take a person and warp them into something unspeakable, breaking their minds as much as their bodies in a process that turns them from man into magic-hunting monster.

"The most ironic part? It's not that the Breathers were once people . . ."

He rounded the corner, stopping to stand at the dead-center of the intersection, his ivory-handled short blade tap-tap-tapping away at the side of his leg. The boy called Nevin backed away until a pair of metal-reinforced doors stopped him from retreating further, a mixture of fear and frustration glistening in his wide, watchful eyes. He clutched an oddly-shaped metal object the color of storm-tossed waters with both hands, extending it protectively out before him.

And there it is. That's what I'm here for.

His feral grin widened further. ". . . but that the Breathers were once the very magic users they were created to hunt."

A distant cry of guttural agony drew Vincht's attention from the boy for a moment, but when he turned back, the cornered youth had neither moved nor responded to his speech. Instead, Nevin's eyes appeared to flick back and forth between Vincht and something else, something Vincht couldn't see, something just as important and unnerving to the boy as Vincht himself.

Then again, in his fevered state, maybe he was just imagining things.

The jet-haired mercenary scratched his face before waving his blood-soaked fingers at the young man impatiently. "You're not putting it together, Nevin. You're not . . . hearing . . . what I'm telling you. I need you to hear me.

"A man only has two paths he can walk in life, two real choices in front of him as he grows into the person he'll one day become. It's not a choice of *who* he will become, but the choice of *how* he will become. You're not hearing . . ."

Vincht trailed off, rubbing his aching temples. The world swam in his vision, the alley lilting first one way then the other. He flexed his jaw and squinted until reality stilled around him.

"You see, a man is either the 'maker', or he is the 'made'." Vincht awkwardly punctuated each option with a stab of his sword. "One either takes responsibility for choosing who one becomes, bringing forth the full brunt of his considerable will to guide himself toward a manufactured vision of his future, or one submits himself to the greater will of another, and is forced into an unrecognizable future beyond the realm of his choosing.

"These Breathers? They're the 'made'. Users who weren't strong enough to withstand the will of the Baron, who weren't strong enough to protect themselves from his twisted machinations. These Breathers? They were 'made' into his monstrous tools. An ugly addition to an already ugly world, but sometimes you have to destroy in order to create, I suppose."

"Stop it!" Nevin cried out, shaking the metal object at Vincht. "Are you just trying to torment me? Why are you telling me these things?"

"Because this moment is a focal point for you."

Vincht took a step forward, thumbing his chest as he continued. "I'm a 'maker', Nevin. I've spent my whole life shaping my skills, my body, my skills, my personality to fit the vision I held for my future. I will do whatever it takes to get what I need from life. No matter the price. No matter the pain. No matter who I have to crush beneath me to get there.

"Despite the terrible wounds inflicted on me, despite the horrific countenance your cat has cursed me with, I am still the maker of my future. Out of the two of us, my will shall overcome, because yours is too weak and unfocused and confused about what you want and what you will need to do if you want to survive. You're weak."

"You don't have to do this, Vincht. You don't. You can stop. Just walk away and stop."

Tears glistened on the young man's quivering cheeks, but the black-haired warrior was completely without sympathy.

"I cannot. I will not. It's the path I've set myself on, a path that ends with the item I seek resting in the palm of my hand. And the only way you're going to escape the path I've laid out for us, the path I've *made*, is if you step up and *make* a new path for us both."

Vincht pulled a simple chain necklace over his head. The chain looped through a number of jagged iron keys. He rattled them teasingly at the younger man.

"The key to that lock behind you lies somewhere on this chain."

Nevin stuttered his response. "What do you want from me?"

"What do I want? I want you to lift my curse, Nevin."

A sad smile was all he could offer in response to the young man's confusion.

"I want you to kill me, if you possess the will."

Aurnia dove out of the way, sending a small cushion of Vellis before her to soften the fall.

And not a moment too soon.

Flailing its limbs with a hungry fervor, the Breather tore past, scrabbling at the patchwork cobbles for purchase but finding none. Its momentum carried it into a stack of crates brimming with dried corn. Like beads from a broken bracelet, the shattering crates littered the open space with thousands upon thousands of the tiny, hardened kernels. The frenzied Breather slid down on its back and away from the woman in the yellow dress.

Captain Williams appeared atop the sterncastle of the Misanthrope, leaning out over the rudder to yell down at her."Get moving, woman! The Baron's ships will soon choke the lagoon. This won't end until Comelbough disappears behind us!"

Shooting the man an incredulous look, Aurnia struggled to her feet. "How about a little help?"

"Help?" The captain gestured to the plaza behind her. "Looks like you got all the help you need."

With a frown of confusion, Aurnia quickly turned.

For the first time in a long time, a child-like grin spread out across her face.

All the help, indeed.

Theis' scowl was as lethal as his sword. Too bad no one could see it behind his mask.

With a quick slash of his sicklesque blade, another soldier yelped and collapsed. By his count, that made seventeen. Seventeen dead, and still they came. Their spears hadn't so much as nicked the edge of his cloak, and still they pressed after him. They fought like they *wanted* death, rushing him like water before a cliff, and they fell much the same. But still they poured in, relentless and foolhardy and doomed.

He was a whirling cloud of death sent to pass judgment on those stupid enough to seek him out.

Two iron-tipped spears reached for him at once. Theis rolled beneath their polished tips and severed the leading legs of the soldiers. They toppled over, erupting in a chorus of agony and clutching at the emptiness below their knees. Vaulting to his feet, his upward slice caught another man beneath the chin, and Theis finally made eye contact with the pompous old woman at the center of all this nonsense.

Bet you're happy I'm here now.

Their reunion was short-lived. The fumbling Breather finally found its feet among the slippery corn and hesitantly rose. It panted like a dog as it stretched for the sky, reaching up with a monstrous hand to grip itself by the forehead and yank its skull to the side. Theis felt the resulting crack deep in his bones.

"Lovely," he growled, wasting no more time among the dying. He leaned into a headlong dash, his curved sword dragging behind him like some sort of lethal tail.

For the moment, the Breather's attention was on Aurnia, and that was all the opening he needed.

The man in black hit the spilled corn at full tilt. The Breather had his back to him, preparing to charge the woman in yellow, but Theis didn't give him the chance. He dropped onto his hip and slid between the monster's splayed legs.

He twisted into the slide and lashed out twice with his blade. As he cleared the Breather's legs, he rolled deftly to his feet and continued toward

Aurnia with no further consideration for the magic-seeking giant he'd left behind.

With a look of surprise, of utter confusion, the Breather collapsed to the stone. Its disembodied feet stayed right where it left them, having been severed in passing by the razor-sharp edge of the man in black's blade.

The woman gripped her wrists inside the sleeves of her yellow dress and straightened. "You're late."

"Late?" Theis snorted. "You sent me away."

She shrugged. "I didn't actually expect you to listen."

Pompous, old . . .

"Where's the boy?" he demanded, changing the subject to something that actually mattered.

"Cornered." She pointed across the plaza. "In that alley. I've been trying to clear a path, but between the soldiers and old wheezy over—"

Theis pushed her aside to confront a spearman brave enough to approach on his own. His spear immediately lost its tip, and the soldier lost a hand. As the man stumbled backwards, Aurnia instinctively lashed out over his shoulder with an open hand, but nothing happened. To Theis, everything was briefly awash in faint blue light.

"Dammit, Theis. I'm useless with you around."

With an effortless flick of his sword, Theis finished what Aurnia failed to, and another body dropped lifeless to the cobbles.

She put the Misanthrope to her back and planted her feet resolutely. "I'll keep the riffraff away from the boat. Go and fetch the boy."

"And him?" He nodded toward the mewling Breather, writhing in the corn not twenty feet away.

"I'm only concerned with the foot soldiers now. The threat of that one has passed."

Theis shook his head and dashed through the heart of the plaza, toward the alley and the small contingent of men awaiting the pleasure of his company.

Foot soldiers? That woman has an awful sense of humor.

Chapter 44: Yes

"You're crazy," said Nevin, pushing back against the chained doors like he might somehow be able to melt between them if he tried hard enough.

From the other end of the alley, the jet-haired warrior laughed, a full-body cackle that spattered droplets of milky sweat and blood across the interlocked stones beneath his boots. His fingers raked at the gouges in his face, tearing pieces of discolored flesh from their ragged edges until they exposed the muscle beneath. Fresh blood coated his claw-like fingers, and the bright red fluid drizzled off his wrist in a long, gelatinous line.

The laugh quickly morphed into a series of wet, wracking coughs, and Vincht hunched over his knees. He fought against the powerful fit, struggling to catch his breath, wheezing and choking and clutching his throat.

Now is our chance. Give in to me, and let me save you.

Nevin ignored the disembodied voice and straightened, cautiously stepping off the doors.

"Vincht . . . you're sick," he said softly, his tone morose.

"I'm not sick, you foolish child." His voice was hoarse, but still he smiled. "I am *driven*."

"No, I mean you're *sick*. Feverish. Your wounds, the cuts to your face . . . they're infected. It's making you—"

"Nothing makes me!" Vincht screamed. His sword flew to attention and he jerked forward a few steps. "*I* am the maker! It is *my* will that creates, *my* will that moves, *my* will that . . . that creates! I . . . I am the . . . the . . ."

He swayed on his feet, cradling his head between shaking palms.

He's weak, distracted. With my help, we can end him.

"I am trying, papa," Vincht whispered, so quietly that Nevin had to lean in to hear. "Please don't be cross. I just need . . . I just . . . a moment to catch my breath. A moment, papa. Please."

The sounds of battle echoed down the alley, the sharp ring of steel and the clatter of wood punctuated intermittently by the terrible cries of death. Nevin tuned them out, the entire breadth of his attention honed in on the fragile yet life-threatening situation playing out before him.

Vincht was a man on the precipice of madness.

Twenty two.

As his opponent dropped, Theis caught a brief glimpse into the heart of the alley before another soldier took up his fallen comrade's place. A black-haired warrior stood near the farthest wall, only a few feet from stepping forward and disappearing around the corner. In the man's right hand, an ivory-handled short blade gleamed in the late morning sunlight.

Theis scowled. *Vincht.*

The man in black lunged, slicing through the air with his blade before springing away from the reaching spear-points, too slow to catch him.

Twenty three.

A blast of chill wind from behind ripped at his cloak, and his eyes burned a few shades hotter. The four other spearmen squinted to keep from being blinded by dust, and wildly jerked their spears this way and that to keep the seemingly untouchable swordsman from sneaking through their defenses while they couldn't see.

It made little difference. *Twenty four.*

Infused with energy, Theis quickly surveyed his opponents to identify his next target. However, the hollow slap of wood on stone gave away the rapid approach of reinforcements, and the man in black begrudgingly rolled aside to prevent himself from becoming surrounded.

He grabbed a reaching spear with one hand as he straightened and sundered the shaft with his blade before hopping backward. From his new vantage point, he could no longer get a clear view of what was happening in the deeper reaches of the alley. Luckily, Vincht hadn't appeared to be in any kind of hurry, but every moment Theis allowed himself to remain caught up by these poor excuses for soldiers was another moment for Vincht to change his mind and put the defenseless boy to the blade.

The rear deck of an open-topped wagon jammed into his lower back. The aging contraption creaked at the impact, but Theis was most surprised by the faint groan of effort he heard inside the large crate atop the wagon's bed.

His sword raked through the air in a wide, whistling arc, sending the soldiers back on their heels, and he used the brief opening to glance through a bore hole in the crate's front.

"Cat?" he practically yelled over his shoulder, returning his attention to staying alive.

The lynx pressed a silver peeper to the hole. "Theis! Am I glad to see you! Nevin's trapped down the alley and Vincht—"

"I'm aware!" he barked, batting aside a spear and wrapping his fingers around its owner's throat. Grunting, Theis hefted the wide-eyed soldier into the air in time to block a different soldier's spear with the man's body. The surprised man arched in the blow, his mouth stretched wide in a silent scream. Theis shoved him into his companion, and the two went down in a tangle of limbs.

Twenty five.

"Okay," the cat mewled. "But can you stop playing around?"

"*Khek*, cat, I'm not—" He ducked just in time to avoid being skewered.

More soldiers weren't far off. Theis wasn't making nearly enough headway to enter into the alley without chancing serious injury, and if Vincht was half the swordsman Theis expected him to be, he couldn't risk engaging him at anything but full strength.

"Let me out, Theis! The latch is stuck, but if I can get out, I should be able to—"

Theis whirled around, and with otherworldly aim, wedged his sicklesque blade between the lid and the crate and twisted. With a sharp crack of wood, the lid burst from its hinges, and a streak of golden fur burst from its depths and sailed over the group of warriors. One soldier yelped and spun on his feet, landing in a heap on the cobbles, a sizable chunk of flesh missing from the side of his neck.

"Now, then." The man in black leveled his blade at the remaining warriors. "Who here knows how to count to thirty?"

Nevin couldn't fathom how Vincht had survived since his escape from Elbin. All that blood and shredded flesh . . . it seemed unreal. The remnants of his confrontation with Aidux were evident all over his face and arms—ragged gashes oozing blood and pus and deep enough in places for a hint of white to show through.

It's not possible. He should have bled out days ago.

But the man's otherworldly constitution wasn't his biggest concern. Vincht was barely holding it together, his self-righteous speech on the makers and the made having devolved into mumbling pleas of mercy toward an invisible father figure. In his fevered state, Vincht was as unpredictable as a Waking storm cloud, but Nevin knew one thing for sure—he wasn't going to talk his way out of this.

He looked down, taking in the full length of the enigmatic object he gripped with both hands. Maybe the Sharasil *could* save him, just not in the way he'd initially hoped.

The muffled grind of metal on stone barely registered in the narrow alleyway as the cylindrical object tumbled across the cobbles and came to a rest between the two men.

A gaunt shadow seeped out of the cobbles and rose to its full height beside him.

What are you doing?!

Not now!

Nevin held his hands high, hesitantly stepping away from the two metal doors. "I'm not going to fight you, Vincht. I couldn't win, even if I wanted to. Even if you were unarmed."

Shivering uncontrollably, the jet-haired warrior jerked his head in Nevin's direction. His facial expression seemed caught between a scowl and a grin, twitching back and forth as he took a step toward the unattended weapon. "Of course you couldn't. Couldn't fight me, couldn't win. *Nevin.*"

The young man chewed his lip. In his weakened state, the Sharasil's magical defenses might just be enough to incapacitate the man. All he had to do was bend over and pick it up.

Vincht picked at his face and squatted, tap-tap-tapping his short blade on the stones. "You'd give it up? Your only defense?"

Nevin shrugged. "Won't need a defense if you just take it and go."

Vincht nodded, the fingers on his free hand folding inward like they had already reached out to grip the Sharasil's stone pommel.

Come on. Nevin slid forward another half-step. *Just take it already!*

Down at the other end of the alley, someone screamed. A man, Nevin thought, not a woman. Not a cat. Not a friend.

He suddenly missed the stoic man in black more than he could put to words.

"No."

Shaking his head in disappointment, Vincht closed his eyes and ran a hand through his thick, black hair. "You're weak, Nevin. You not the one to help me. You're just another one of the pathetic 'made.' Tools of the makers, victims of Fate, pawns in the great game. The walking dead."

The gaunt figure took its place by Nevin's side, leaning in to rest a pale hand on his shoulder. He could feel its touch through the fabric of his shirt, drawing the heat from his flushed skin.

"If you won't take responsibility for your own life, for that which has been entrusted unto you . . ."

Vincht stood, running a bloodied finger down the length of his spotless blade, leaving a small trail of red in its wake.

". . . then it's up to me to take it from you."

With a gruesome grin, the blood-covered warrior readied his sword.

The two metal reinforced doors rattled against Nevin's backside, shedding flecks of rust like red smoke. The gaunt figure pressed up against his side, sensing his sudden spike of fear, of desperation, of hopelessness. Its chill breath hissed against his ear.

Just . . . say . . . yes.

He pulled his head away, recoiling from its touch even as he wanted to give in to its singular desire. He knew from their dialogue at the gorge what giving in would mean.

His lips trembled, from fear, but also from fighting the urge to answer, to open his mouth and speak that one simple word, and then . . .

Darkness.

"Just wait!" he yelled instead, holding his hand out to stop him. The force of his outburst drove the tenuously sane warrior back a step, and he looked at Nevin as if seeing him for the first time.

And that's the exact moment when a whirling ball of teeth and claws collided with the man's torso.

An involuntary smile broke Nevin's trembling lips.

Aidux!

Just like before, his best friend had arrived at the last possible moment to save him. Vincht cried out, new wounds rapidly appearing on his arms and face as the lynx tore into him with abandon.

There was a faint yelp of pain, and before Nevin could process what had happened, Aidux collapsed at the base of the alley wall, motionless.

"Wait your turn, demon," Vincht growled.

Nevin stared, tears welling up in the corners of his eyes and rocks filling his throat. A thin line of blood trickled from his best friend's ear.

Oh no.

Time slowed to a crawl, then stopped all together.

Is he even breathing?

Somewhere in Nevin's mind, beyond the furthest shadows and darkest corners of his consciousness, something died. Something he could never get back. Something precious, priceless, but as he turned his murderous glare to Vincht's shredded face, Nevin hardly noticed.

Death was all he could see. It burned in his mind like a shard of the sun, driving back the shadows and consuming everything in its path. His fear, his uncertainty, his idealism . . . everything fell before the all-consuming light.

Only his intent, pure and impervious, was left unscathed.

Say it.

The word resounded through his entire body, and a pair of icy cold hands wrapped his shoulders in a frigid, unyielding embrace.

"Yes."

And that's when everything went black.

As the final soldier fell before Theis' blade, a brilliant light flashed deep within the alleyway, and the temperature in the open plaza plummeted. His breath crystallized into a small white cloud before his face.

Then, just as suddenly as it departed, the world returned to normal.

With the path before him clear, Theis darted down the alley, only to come to a skidding halt. Behind the cover of his mahogany mask, the man's jaw hung slack and his burning eyes searched for an explanation. Aurnia rushed up to his side, inhaling sharply at the sight before them both.

"*Khek*, woman. What—"

"Fool!" she hissed. "How *dare* you invoke that name at a time like this."

He shot her a sharp look, but kept silent. *You're not wrong.*

Aurnia hiked up her dress as she stepped through the scene. "Grab the boy and the cat. We were lucky only one Breather joined this fight, but that luck will only hold for so long. Captain Williams awaits, and I'm afraid he may leave without us if we don't make haste."

A million questions blazed through Theis' mind, questions he knew would have to wait, questions with elusive and complicated answers.

With the boy over one shoulder and the cat over the other, Theis chased Aurnia through the field of dead bodies clogging the alleyway entrance as they raced off to catch their boat.

Chapter 45: A First Time for Everything

Pale slices of orange light infrequently mar the roiling storm clouds, briefly illuminating the inky black trees and under-traveled cart path passing hurriedly beneath his feet. The humid night air weighs heavily with the wet scent of impending rain. Each breath irritates his parched throat, but he doesn't have the energy to cough. Too much of it is going into putting one foot in front of the other.

Must be a dream, Nevin thinks. *Strange. I don't remember going to sleep.*

He tries looking around, but quickly finds that, despite the almost immediate realization that this is a dream, he has no means of controlling anything but the thoughts floating around in his head.

The trees disappear behind him one by one, but neither notice the other. The first is too concerned with the approaching storm, while the second is too concerned with the approaching men. He barely hears them over his own labored breathing, but their intermittent hoots and teasing calls help him ignore the burning in his lungs and legs. His fear of them, of what they might do if they catch him, of what he's already seen them do, drives him ever forward.

Fear, and the unwavering grip of the darkly dressed man pulling him along behind.

Nevin pictures himself frowning, aware that his dream body isn't reciprocating. It's an odd sensation, feeling as though he is a guest in his own body, an unwilling passenger to an unknown destination, but while he doesn't know where he's headed, he does know the dark figure before him.

At least, he knows he *should* know him. His brain twists and strains, but nothing comes. There is a name there, beyond his thoughts, ephemeral and teasing and whispering nonsense from the forgotten corners of his mind. How could he not recognize someone who feels so familiar, so integral? Nevin feels safe with him, protected, comforted. Not at all like the feelings engendered by his pursuers. This man is his salvation, his only hope of survival.

And he can't even remember his name.

He pulls on the man's arm and urges his legs to move faster, drawing his partner close, searching him for a spark of recognition. Strangely, his legs move at almost twice the speed of the other man's, but he doesn't pass him. The man is much taller too, nearly twice his height.

The yelling and screaming gains. Even in the heavy darkness, he knows he'd be able to see their hateful, leering faces if he turns. Their lofted torches. Their well-maintained weaponry. Their lust for his blood.

But the shadowed silhouettes behind mean nothing in comparison to the depthless void guiding him forward.

Beside the colorless form of his partner, the overcast night shines with all the dazzling brilliance of the rising sun. He can't imagine why he didn't notice before, why the details of the man had escaped him, but now . . . the black outline garners his attention to the exclusion of nearly everything else. The man has no features save darkness.

Who *is* he? Why doesn't he know?

The figure suddenly speaks, and Nevin feels the words ripping the dream asunder.

"Just a little farther, Nevin."

The man's voice is the voice in his head.

"Don't give up now."

His own voice.

"Wha—" Nevin started to say, but the words got stuck in a mouth drier than salted bone meal. The briny air was thick with moisture, but it felt good in his lungs and breathing it in got the saliva flowing. Sweat glued his shirt to his chest, and the pillow beneath his head was soaked through.

Groaning from an entire body's worth of stiff muscles, he pulled himself up on the simple cot until he could sit and rubbed his puffy eyes.

"What did you say?" he asked again, not completely understanding yet that he wasn't dreaming anymore.

A gravelly, unexpected voice answered.

"Told you not to give up. Would have said it hours ago if I'd known it would finally wake you."

Glowing blue eyes appraised him from beside the cot. The man in black leaned against the wall of the small storage room, positioned atop a squat crate like a king pining for his missing throne. A globe-shaped glass lantern hanging from an iron hook cast an eerie glow over the dark folds of Theis' cloak and the stacked assortment of sacks and crates. On the far wall, a moth-eaten wool curtain dangled across a narrow opening in the vertical oak planks. Along with the heavy scent of salt, the moisture-dense air carried the smells of cinnamon and kerosene and sweat.

Nevin rubbed his sticky face, flicking the sleep mung from the corners of his eyes. He was surprised to find the sword still gripped tightly in his right hand. The fingers of that hand were blanched and sore. He relaxed but didn't fully release the coarse stone hilt. He couldn't imagine why he hadn't let go of it in his sleep.

"Theis," Nevin said, finding himself genuinely glad to wake up to the familiar—if not so friendly— face of the stoic warrior. "You left us. When did—"

"We're on the boat, headed to Greater Delphine," the man in black interrupted. "You've been out for nearly two days now."

Two days. No wonder his muscles felt so rigid. He ran a hand through his damp, matted hair and allowed relief to overcome him. *We made it. A hometown in ashes, a raging forest fire, hundreds of miles of wilderness, and an army of men out for blood, but we made it through it all.*

The relief was short-lived. His eyes stretched wide and he nearly leapt from the cot. "Where's Aidux? He had blood—"

Theis hopped down from the crate and put a firm hand to Nevin's shoulder, forcing him to sit. "Save your energy. Cat's fine. Woke up about two hours into the trip, and none the worse for wear. Spent most his time laying next to your cot, waiting for *you* to wake up.

He snorted. "Whining, mostly."

Nevin breathed a sigh of relief. "Where is he?"

"On deck, if I had to guess. The crew has taken to stashing fish up there, to get him to come topside. Didn't much like having a giant predator on board at first, but that all changed around the first time he opened his mouth."

A wide grin brought the spark back to his eyes. "I know the feeling."

Nevin glanced up at the hanging lantern and scratched at the twisted snatch of wet hair irritating the nape of his neck. The lantern was still as the dead, not an ounce of sway in its dangle. "Doesn't much feel like we're on a boat."

"No complaints from me. I hate sailing. Was bad the first day and a half, but now . . ." He cocked his head, a thought occurring to him. "Hadn't even noticed the change."

"We must be close to the Void."

"The Void?"

Nevin nodded. "Ishen taught me about it. Ships don't generally sail directly from Comelbough to Greater Delphine across the Sea of Calor. They tend to take a more circuitous route along the coast, even if they aren't planning on stopping in any of the smaller ports along the way. The Sea of Calor has an anomalous stretch at its heart that, while it isn't exactly dangerous, can be problematic for the unprepared.

"They call it the Calorthian Void. It's supposed to be next to windless, and without wind, the sea is as still as glass. Don't think anyone has ever figured out what causes the Void, and I don't know why the captain would sail close enough to it to lose the wind. That seems like a bad idea."

He remembered a lot more than that brief explanation, but he doubted the man in black would be interested that the Void may be the remnant of an ancient seafaring civilization lost to a powerful curse, or that a stray cloud may have blocked the rays of Empyria's holy light at the dawn of creation, or any of the other unproven theories of how an unremarkable stretch of water was somehow bereft of naturally moving air.

The crate creaked beneath Theis as he leaned forward to rest a forearm across his knee. "Want to tell me what happened back in that alley?"

Different moments from that morning flashed through the forefront of Nevin's mind, summoned not by his own desire to know, but by the man in black's query. Aurnia's argument with Theis. Aidux in the crate. Aurnia talking to various ship captains.

He visibly flinched when he remembered how Vincht and his men had cornered him. Theis watched him, unmoving, as he closed his eyes and struggled to stitch the events together that followed.

He shook his head, frowning. "We got away safely. Does it really matter?"

"It does. What do you remember?"

Nevin slumped over his knees with a resigned grunt. "Things happened fast once Vincht showed up. I ran into the alley, and Vincht started ranting about . . . I don't know. The man was losing his mind. I remember being cornered, trapped on the wrong side of a locked door. I dropped the Sharasil at some point. Then Vincht came at me and—"

Visions of Aidux slamming into the warehouse wall replayed over and over again, the sickening thud of flesh on wood a sadistic drum roll that urged his heart to match the beat. A wave of bile burned his throat, and he had to squeeze his eyes closed to banish the thoughts.

After he composed himself, he took a deep breath and shrugged. "And then that's it. I don't remember anything else. I woke up here."

"That's all?" Theis pressed him. "Nothing else?"

Nevin bowed his head and shrugged. "Thanks . . . uh . . . thank you for the company."

Theis turned away, the bright blue light within his drooping cowl shifting suddenly to a dim violet glow. He reached up and adjusted his mask before taking a single, awkward step toward the cramped room's narrow exit. He stopped there, his back to Nevin, the faux starlight dancing across his matte black cloak as the moth-eaten curtain swayed. He only half-turned back, and when he did, he tossed an odd-looking leather strap onto Nevin's lap.

Raising one eyebrow, Nevin lifted the object to his face. The thin double-layered strip of brown pig leather was easily long enough to wrap around his waist a few times. A traditional belt buckle adorned one end, while a pair of dissimilar c-shaped pieces of metal were attached to the strap about two feet apart near the middle of its length, each designed in a way that reminded him of some sort of custom pressure clasp.

As far as he was concerned, it may as well have been a purple tentacle.

"It's a baldric," Theis said, reading his mind with a hint of annoyance.

Nevin continued to stare at the leather strap like it had three heads. "You got me a shoulder belt?"

Theis twirled a finger as he spoke, his normally biting tone replaced by an uncharacteristic diffidence. "Don't know how you manage to keep hold of that thing, even while unconscious, but you can't keep carrying it around the way you do. You need your hands free. Wear that, and the sword can rest on your back while you travel. The clasps should secure it, but since I couldn't hold the weapon during the baldric's creation, they might need some adjustment before they work perfectly."

He blinked, holding the baldric to his chest. "You made this for me?"

"Don't make a big deal of it." Theis grabbed the hem of his cloak and jerked it tight around his form, hard enough to elicit a whip-like snap of leather that startled them both.

Somewhere on the ship, beyond the tattered curtain, someone coughed.

"How did you do it?" he asked quietly, still facing away from Nevin.

The young man ran his fingers along the burnished leather, its oiled surface as yet unmarred by use. He had a hard time believing Theis had gone to such lengths for him. "Do what?"

"Survive." He planted his hands on his hips, the action broadening his stance until his cloak absorbed every pinprick of light cast by the ratty curtain. "The state of that alley . . ."

"I'm think I'm gonna go find Aidux." Nevin struggled to his feet, flexing muscles frozen in various stages of petrification due to his extended rest on the cot. "Thank you, Theis. Really. For the baldric, for keeping me and Aidux safe. And for coming back. You've been a good friend, and I don't think any of us would have lived through the fight had you not been there."

Theis snorted, regarding Nevin from the corner of his eye.

"You would not have."

Drawing the cloak about his lean form, the man in black shoved the ratty curtain aside and paused. He spoke one final phrase before disappearing into the underbelly of the ship.

"You're welcome, Nevin."

With a warm smile painting his face, the young man set to donning the baldric and learning how to mount the Sharasil on his back.

That was the first time Theis had ever used his name.

Chapter 46: The Moments Before

Aurnia sipped at her tea, the unexpectedly cold brew twisting her lips in a reflexive scowl of disgust. She closed her eyes and focused the tiniest sliver of Ignolis into the heart of the metal cup, and an aromatic puff of steam instantly arose from the dark liquid's surface.

Though she was grateful to have made off with a small container of tea from Donald's collection, Aurnia's stomach regretted not picking a mixture heavy in either ginger or chamomile. Their rapid escape from Comelbough had found them plying choppy waters within minutes of setting foot on Captain William's ship, and the Misanthrope's constant ups and downs hadn't much improved until the vessel had neared the edge of the Calorthian Void the night before. While her supernaturally bolstered constitution protected her from seasickness, she wasn't entirely immune, and the faint stirrings of nausea had made a temporary home in the base of her belly.

The wooden slat stairs groaned overhead, and she groaned along with them, bringing a hand to her lips to mask a soft belch. Relief was brief, but she was grateful nonetheless. She would have thought her stomach accustomed to the roiling motion of the sea by now, especially considering the relative calmness of the waters inside the Void.

Old crates and burlap sacks formed impromptu rooms and corridors in the hold just below the Misanthrope's deck, and at the captain's behest, Aurnia had staked her claim on one of the larger empty sections just beneath the stairs. Globe lanterns protected by iron husks hung as if affixed permanently in place, undisturbed by the unwavering wind and still waters. Night had fallen with little fanfare, though tucked below deck as she was, Aurnia likely wouldn't have noticed its arrival anyway.

In the center of the 'room', a trio of rickety stools crowded against a low, long crate. Gouges, deep and narrow, marred the make-shift table's surface like someone had used it for knife-throwing practice. In her gauzy yellow dress, a woman of Aurnia's effortless beauty appeared completely out-of-place in such crude surroundings.

Her honey brown eyes turned to the table's centerpiece, a cube-cut yellow gemstone shining with a serene golden effulgence that appeared to waver as if disturbed by a gentle breeze. At the direction of her soul, the Orlicite had been glowing uninterrupted since their flight from Comelbough, but a brief flicker in its shine stole her attention and made her forget about the growing discomfort in her gut.

"Careful, Theis," she admonished, certain the man was lurking somewhere just beyond the wall of crates.

His boots gliding silently over the pitch-stained floorboards, Theis' inky form emerged from the shadows, cautiously skirting the outermost edge of the glimmering gemstone's aura. "Easier said than done, woman. Not much room for me to maneuver down here as it is."

Aurnia sighed in reluctant agreement and stood, taking the tiny gemstone in hand as she rose. The stone was warm against her already flushed skin, and it vibrated ever so slightly. She repositioned herself against the wall of the ship and leaned back, folding her arms beneath her breasts.

"I'd sit, but I'd hate to interrupt your little spell." His skull-like mask failed to disguise the sneer evident in his voice.

"You've been scarce."

"You complaining?"

"Not really," she answered, an edge of boredom to her voice. "Makes my job easier, to be honest. I'm concerned the Orlicite may not last the trip. It has a fairly substantial flaw cleaving directly through its heart, and my inelegant application of its power back in Comelbough did little but exacerbate that problem."

"Inelegant?" His shining eyes were burning brighter than usual, leaving the meager space awash with crawling bands of living jade.

A sour look crossed her face. "Such straightforward spell casting is the domain of spellswords and initiates. Manifests, they're called. It's a class of spell resulting in a flashy, direct outcome of spiritual intent. Throwing fire, directing wind, moving earth . . . They lack subtly, efficiency. The magical equivalent of bashing a problem's head in until it stops moving."

Theis gestured to the glowing gemstone nestled in her fingertips. "Is that not what you're doing now?"

She had to give him that one. "In essence, yes. I'll admit, Manifests do have their place in every caster's toolbox, as sometimes a two-handed club turns out to be the proper tool for the job at hand. Still, the energy investment for such quick and powerful effects scale poorly against the desired outcome, requiring more and more input for less and less output."

"Diminishing returns."

"Indeed."

He thumbed toward the ceiling. "So how's the constant breeze you've summoned any different?"

"In the case of its effect on the Orlicite, it's an issue of magnitude. Imagine the stone is a wool blanket. Picture yourself reaching out to tug at an errant thread. As you pull, the blanket slowly unravels, one stitch, one knot, one bit at a time. If you keep a slow, steady pace, you might eventually find yourself with one long, unbroken pile of thread, but during the process, the blanket itself holds its shape. The damage you are doing constrains itself to the area connected directly to that single thread. That's the spell keeping the ship moving through the Void."

"And the ones back on the dock?"

She thrust her empty hand forward. "Akin to shoving a knife straight through the center of the blanket and out the other side. Do it enough and the whole thing falls apart, the remnants both tattered and useless. I'm just hoping I didn't shove the knife through the Orlicite more times than it could handle."

There was a cough from somewhere deeper in the ship, and Aurnia turned to look despite being unable to see beyond the line of stacked crates. "I thought I heard voices before you showed up. Did Nevin wake?"

Theis nodded. "Doesn't remember much about what happened though."

Aurnia bumped the inner wall of the ship with the back of her head and sighed again, this time in relief. "Thank goodness. I was beginning to worry. The cat alone draws enough unwanted attention without also having to explain the transport of an unconscious boy across national boundaries, not to mention the scrutiny of the port authority."

With a snort of derision, Theis jerked his cloak closed. The woman in yellow cocked an eyebrow and pursed her lips. "Something on your mind?"

"Just glad his unconsciousness isn't going to hinder your little plan. Be a shame if his health got in the way of whatever you hope to get from him."

"Well," she said, clicking her tongue. She hadn't expected such a passionate response from him. "You're in a mood. For someone who abandoned the boy mere hours before the Lancowl constabulary nearly ended his life, you seem awfully protective of him."

"Didn't abandon him. Was there when I was needed,"

Theis paused, turning away. Without the contribution from his glowing eyes, the space was once again awash with the Orlicite's golden light. "No sense remaining somewhere I wasn't wanted."

"Spare me your false indignation." Aurnia brushed off his retort with a wave of her hand. "I've heard the stories about you. No allegiance but to the promise of mortal combat. Public duels, but only to the death, enticing victims to their demise with an offer of gold. Whispers even of regicide. If but *half* of those rumors are true, you might just be one of the most selfish people I've ever met."

"Noble by contrast," said Theis under his breath. He straightened, pacing just beyond the rim of the Orlicite's glow. "Interesting tactic."

"What's that supposed to mean?"

"It means I see through your shit, woman. We both know you're only in it for the sword. You'd bet the kid in a game of Pauper's Pledge if you thought it a good chance to get some answers. Skin the cat for a rug if you were short a single shil for passage. Can call me selfish all you want, but from where I stand, you wrote the book on it."

Aurnia pinched the bridge of her nose and reclined her head back on the inner wall of the ship, feeling the rhythmic slosh of water gently beating against the hull as the ship cut across the ocean's surface.

There was little sense arguing with him. The man had made of life of winning, at any cost. Besides, he wasn't exactly wrong. Her main focus *was* on that of the sword, not on the boy inadvertently attached to it. She had little desire to protect someone incapable of protecting themselves, little desire to play mother to some helpless, hapless child. Not again.

She closed her eyes instead, pressing a palm against her gurgling belly. A wry smile tilted the corners of her lips.

"The cat *would* make for a magnificent rug, would he not?"

A steady breeze greeted Nevin's damp face as he emerged from the stairs and stepped out onto the Misanthrope's expansive deck. Shimmering blue stars pierced holes in the night sky in every direction, obscured only by the ship's three towering masts and taut sails. In the northeast, the outer ring of Etro encircled the pale azure moon in a silver-blue halo, while the faster-spinning inner ring had faded from sight yet again. The ocean's motionless, mirrored surface perfectly reflected its heavenly voyeurs, allowing the stars a rare moment to personally appreciate their nightly contributions.

The baldric fit perfectly, and the sword had slid into place on the first try. The hang of it on his back felt good, felt right. It wouldn't take long before he'd stop noticing the tightness of the leather belt across his chest or the odd weight on his back. He'd have to thank Theis again when next they spoke.

Two deckhands, bare-chested and shoeless, conversed in low voices at the back of the ship. One rested his lean forearms onto the wheel, holding a compass in one hand and wooden mug in the other. The second man lounged on a bed of tangled nets, flipping the lid of a worn wooden compass. They laughed softly together as he looked the deck over.

Nevin hardly noticed. All he cared about was finding Aidux.

The golden-haired cat watched him approach from the bow of the ship, his silver eyes shimmering in the pale light and his lips pulled back in his characteristic snarl-smile.

A rush of unexpected emotion flooded Nevin's mind, and he was surprised to find that happiness wasn't the most prominent. Tears welled and trickled down his cheeks as the memory of Aidux being dashed against the warehouse wall played over and over in his mind's eye. His lower lip trembled as he remembered seeing that thin line of blood leaking from his best friend's ear.

Sobbing, Nevin dropped to a knee and caught the surprised lynx in a spine-crushing hug.

"Uh . . . Nevin?" Aidux strained to speak, craning his neck away from the embrace. "Can't . . . um . . . breathe so good . . ."

Nevin pulled back and grabbed the cat by his shaggy mane with both hands, pulling their faces together. "Are you okay? That bastard didn't do any permanent damage, did he?"

"Nope. I had a headache yesterday, and my shoulder feels bruised, but nothing I can't handle. What about you? What happened?"

He shook his head. "One minute I was about to make Vincht pay for what he did to you, and the next . . ."

He hugged Aidux again. "I'm just glad you're okay."

"I'm fine, Nevin. Really. Are *you* okay? You're kind of a lot right now."

He pulled back and wiped the tears from his eyes and cheeks. As happy as he was to see his friend alive and healthy, he couldn't ignore the crushing weight of the week's terrible events. So much had changed. His homeland was gone. Ishen was missing, and likely dead. His life was no longer his to control. He and his best friend had almost been killed. Nothing was okay.

"I don't know, Aidux. Despite all we've survived, it feels so hopeless. Like it's all just going to end badly."

Aidux placed a comforting paw on his shoulder. "Why would you think that? Vincht is gone. Ships don't leave footprints on the water. We're free. All we have to do is drop the sword off and people will stop chasing us."

Fresh tears burst forth from his reddening eyes. He could hardly breathe. Why was he feeling like this? Why was he feeling so sad, so depressed?

"It won't. They'll find us again. They keep finding us, no matter what we do. They'll find us, and they'll kill us. All of us.

"And there's nothing you or I or Theis or Aurnia can do about it."

Theis folded his arms across his chest. He hated being below deck, in a cave of wood and pale light and still air. He much preferred the open, limitless skies of the world above. Beneath the sun and stars, there was nowhere he couldn't go, nowhere he couldn't be alone.

Not like here.

With *her.*

He glared at Aurnia through the faint blue haze encroaching on the edges of his vision. Easing back a step didn't improve his sight, and he could already feel the rough texture of an unfinished crate grinding against his heel, leaving him no more room to retreat in the maze of boxes and barrels.

He'd handled the ever-present haze for the last few days with zero problems. Why was it suddenly bothering him now?

"This is all your fault, you know," she said, pressing her hands to her stomach as if trying to keep her insides from spilling out. "If you had just done as I'd asked—"

The man in black buried her tired complaint beneath a drawn out groan. He paced the edge of the space, each step deliberately placed as if traversing an invisible line, one foot in front of the other.

"Be careful where you swing the pendulum of blame, old woman. Your Fate gods might not appreciate shouldering fault they haven't earned."

She rubbed her eyes and sighed. "Fate is not a god, Theis Bane. It's an indiscriminate force. It doesn't care upon whom the fault lies."

"Like blaming the clouds for the rain?"

"Precisely. The clouds don't care what we think, and blaming them won't change the fact we're wet."

Theis rubbed the chin of his mask and nodded. "Then, if Fate doesn't care, I guess that means your conscience is clear."

Her head jerked up. "And just what is *that* supposed to mean?"

"Don't play the fool. You dealt Nevin the Fate card the first night you met him. 'Fate's heavy hand' and all that crap. And he ate it up, because he's too scared to understand what's really going on."

"Tell me, then." Ice coated her focused gaze. "Tell me what you think is *really* going on."

He stopped, facing down the hall of crates toward Nevin's room. "You blame me, you blame Fate, you blame the Breathers . . . but it isn't their fault we're headed half-way across the world. That blame belongs to you. You manipulated the boy's need for safety in order to satisfy your own curiosity."

"I seek answers, ones that can't be found in the Lancowl province."

He scoffed. "Those answers are less pertinent to Nevin than being free from the sword and the danger surrounding it. He isn't a tool to be paraded around in order to fulfill your own personal agenda."

Aurnia's icy glare was replaced with surprise. "You're actually defending him. Do you . . . do you *care* about him, Theis?"

The man in black shot her a hard look over his shoulder. "He's young, foolish, and painfully naive. The only feelings I have for him are annoyance."

"*Really*. Then tell me, why are you still here? Why follow us to Vadderstrix? What's in it for you?"

Theis folded his arms and returned his gaze to the corridor of crates. She couldn't understand his reasons, not without having lived his life. And it wasn't any of her business anyway.

The blue haze coating his vision still hadn't abated. He supposed it could just be the presence of the charged Orlicite, but something told him it wasn't. And it was getting worse. What had begun as a faint hue of color lining his view like a picture frame now covered everything he saw. The world presented itself through a thickening pane of stained glass.

Something tickled the back of Theis' mind, teasing his awareness with feelings of discomfort, of alarm.

Then, everything went completely blue, and Theis couldn't see.

"*Khek.*"

"Theis, what did I tell you about invoking—"

"I just went blind."

A moment of silence. "You don't . . . A Pool? That's impossible. In the middle of the ocean?"

Her voice broke, her words brimming with rising fear. "Nevin! Who knows what that sword will do in the midst of a Pool!"

Wind tugged at the hem of his cloak as the woman rushed past. He heard her shuffle quickly through the maze of crates, followed by the groan of wood as she ascended the stairs to the Misanthrope's upper deck.

Theis crept along step by cautious step, blindly aiming for the stairs. The itching clawed at his thoughts, screaming warnings that he could put no words to. All he knew was that he had to reach the boy.

Cursing the existence of magic, Theis stumbled after the woman in yellow.

Aidux growled in disapproval. "Don't talk like that, Nevin! I won't let anything happen. I'll protect you!"

Nevin violently shook his head. "Just like you protected me back in the alley? Vincht nearly killed us both. There's nothing we can do. We're all going to die."

"What's gotten into you? This isn't like you!"

Nevin shoved his fingers into his disheveled hair and squeezed, yanking at the strands like he was trying to tear the images from his mind. This wasn't right. Something was wrong, but he couldn't stop the painful images from playing over and over again, magnifying his depression and feeding the growing queasiness in the pit of his stomach.

The barn catching fire.

The bloody canteen, hanging from the fallen silver maple.

The mercenary's corpse, bleeding out in the overgrowth beneath Ishen's window.

The fire stretching across the horizon.

The bodies of soldiers scattered across Ivvilger's clearing.

The crumbling tree bridge.

The Breather pushing through Donald's front door.

Vincht cornering him in the alley.

Watching as Aidux slammed into the warehouse, a line of blood flowing from his ear.

Not knowing if Aidux was breathing.

Not knowing if Aidux was dead.

His mouth parted in a silent wail, anguish driving his heart into a pounding gallop. His lungs burned from lack of air. He was drowning, choking on the deluge of emotion, emotion with no source and no end and no relief in sight.

The sword hummed in his mind, radiating an odd warmth that drew him back to the present.

When he opened his eyes, a fine blue mist had settled in over the deck, flickering with luminescent spots that reminded him of Theis' eyes. Aidux had backed away, his silver eyes saucers of uncertainty, his hackles raised in alarm. The two deckhands had disappeared, though he could hear their frantic shouts calling out to the other sleeping sailors.

A silent hum rolled over his skin in waves. The finer hairs of his neck and arms danced with each pulse, and the queasiness flared and subsided to its beat.

The warmth at his back grew hotter with each humming pulse, the sword reacting to this disturbing and unknowable phenomena.

As he reached back to grab it, Aurnia dashed up the stairs.

"*NEVIN!*" she screamed, stopping short when her eyes found him.

He started to respond, but the images flooded back into his mind, destroying all sense of time and reality and consciousness. He dropped to his knees and wailed at the overwhelming sadness, filling him to the point of bursting. His nails bit painfully into the skin of his palms until blood dripped from his hands.

The more he watched, the more distance he gained from the images, until all he saw was a suffering stranger, a victim to all the world's injustices.

Terror clouded the woman's flawless face. He fought to keep his eyes open. He knew if he closed them, he'd drown under the weight of the images.

"*BREATHE, NEVIN! IT'S THE POOL! IT ISN'T YOU!*"

Nothing the strange woman said made any sense.

Only the sadness held meaning.

The mist crackled with gathering energy, swelling and thickening and threatening to consume the entire ship. The hum pounded with every beat of his racing heart, sending ripples out through the shining mist.

A dark figure stumbled up the stairs. He didn't know who it was, but two bright spots of blue shone like the sun from its head. The mists circled and swirled around the figure, funneling towards it like water down a drain.

The strange woman screamed words that never reached his ears. An unfamiliar animal shoved him with its furry head, but he couldn't move. The sadness was a lodestone, and he was crushed beneath its fatal weight.

The whole world screeched in agony, and Nevin fell into blackness.

More than twenty miles away, lounging on the prismatic sand of the White Crystal Shores, a young woman with strawberry-blond hair enjoyed the last bits of a perfectly cooked sole and a handful of wild blueberries. She'd squelched her fire as soon as her meal was done cooking, preferring the faint light of Etro and her million sisters to the harsh glow of firelight. Staring out across the ocean, she smiled warmly, pleased with life's little simplicities.

A high-pitched screech shattered the calm and brought the woman to her feet in a rush.

Far out to sea, a vivid blue sun was rising, erasing the colors from the landscape and replacing them with varied shades of sharp, harsh azure. Swirls of fog gathered around the light, vaulting into the black sky in a pillar of shimmering motes. It had to be miles high, and climbed as though reaching out to the stars themselves. Streamers of energy circled the pillar in alternating orbits.

With an influx of wind, the pillar and azure sun collapsed in upon themselves in a blinding flash. The woman shielded her eyes with the back of one hand. When she removed it, the horizon was gone, hidden behind a bank of impenetrable fog. The low-hanging cloud billowed out along the surface of the sea, and at its current speed, it would cover the shore in but a short few minutes.

A peal of thunder rolled over her, resounding in her chest, but soon the only sound she could hear came from the waves lapping gently against the shoreline.

Retrieving her fishing spear from the sand, the strawberry-blond woman turned down the beach, carefully picking her way through the soupy fog and back to her little fishing village. She wondered what people were already saying about the event. She had no idea what it could be, other than it had to have something to do with magic.

And where there was magic, there were people.

And out on the open ocean, where there were people, there was a boat.

Two days after the explosion . . .

Chapter 47: Raiya

"Finally," Raiya said with a relieved huff.

Threading her toes through the immaculate white sand, the young woman crouched at the water's edge and squinted through the fading fog. Tugging her strawberry-blonde ponytail over her shoulder, she idly stroked the tightly woven rope of hair, waiting impatiently for her first glimpse of the horizon in days. The fog had persisted since that violent explosion two nights ago, and she was past tired of being unable to see more than twenty feet beyond her nose.

She reached out and plucked a jagged sliver of swollen wood from the water before the waves could drag it back out to sea. A bit of crate or floorboard maybe. She twisted her mouth and tossed it back. Always the same. No matter how far she traveled from Calibri Grotto, splinters and wood chips followed. Occasionally, larger and more recognizable pieces of a ship and her cargo languished in the shallows, the hollow jostling of wood on stone announcing their presence beneath the heavy blanket of fog.

Raiya chewed her lip. Bodies had been discovered as well, though thankfully she hadn't seen any herself. Rumor had it that the broken corpses discovered along the shoreline hardly resembled humans, their flesh left shredded by the blast and picked upon by opportunistic sea creatures. She couldn't imagine what the passengers had experienced, but by the state of the wreckage and the whispers of mutilated bodies, she imagined those last few moments of their lives must have been absolutely horrifying.

It made her think of her mother.

Raiya shook the thought from her head and stood. This wreck had been like nothing the town had ever seen. That few substantial pieces had washed up, and that no returning fishing boats had brought news of remnants of the vessel told her that finding anyone alive, especially so many days after the explosion, was highly unlikely.

Still, part of her refused to accept that. When she told her father she didn't think the town should give up looking for survivors, he'd smiled and expressed that hope was one of her more admirable qualities, but the town's people would likely adopt a more pragmatic attitude towards the event.

He was right. Whoever had been involved in the wreck was a stranger to the Grotto, and the chance of finding survivors was slim. Despite the fog, fishing was best this time of year, and most of the residents couldn't spare a boat to scour the ocean for something that might not even exist.

Raiya sighed and walked down the beach, away from Calibri Grotto.

I understand it, but I don't have to like it.

As the waning light eagerly devoured the weakening fog, glimmering white sand greeted her for as far as she could see. The retreating sun warmed her lean form, sending her gaunt shadow scouting ahead. The light felt good against her golden skin. A sleeveless pale green shirt stopped short just above her rib cage, giving her taut stomach room to breathe. She fiddled idly with the drawstring of her calf-length breeches, the hem frayed and the cloth bleached white from the salt and sun. The sand hardly bothered her weathered feet, and her thin fishing spear helped steady each step through the shifting grit.

An unconscious smile lit up her face. She'd spent almost two full days in Calibri Grotto this time, and the visit had made her antsy. It felt great to be away from everyone again, alone with the waves, the sand, the sun, her thoughts. The townspeople treated her differently than everyone else, treated her like some fragile doll. Not a day spent in town went by without at least one person bringing up the past.

A past she'd rather not dwell on.

She couldn't fault them. Her father always said she was the mirror image of her mother, and in a small town like Calibri Grotto, everyone knew everyone. Watching Raiya walk the winding stone paths must be hard on them. Fiall had been a friend to everyone, and Raiya couldn't find the will to ask them not to bring her up.

Her grip tightened subtly around the perfectly smooth ash pole of her fishing spear. Five feet of wood ended in a double hand-length strip of flat, blue steel. The triangular tip was mounted atop a y-shaped split in the wood, a curious gap shaped so as to hold something else, something currently missing.

A single charred branch floated lazily at the brink of the water's edge. This was where she'd been camping on the night of the explosion. Two days of the changing tide had nearly erased all evidence that she'd been there. The site itself was underwater now, and wouldn't be revealed again until the sun set in a few hours.

Time was something she had in abundance. She needed time to cut more kindling from the squat shrubs dotting the grassy hills, and time to skewer a fish or two. Maybe she could hunt down some more wild blueberries as well.

Her eyes automatically returned to the ocean after nursing a swig of water from her sheep's bladder. Detached wisps of fog still clung to the water's gently rippling surface, now but a shadow of its former strength not thirty minutes prior. She searched the waves, the shore, the distant yet still partially obscured horizon, but the sea held nothing. No boats, no debris, no one in need of saving. Just endless, comforting blue.

As she started to turn away from the empty waters, a gust of hot wind kicked a plume of fine sand into her face. Her eyelids slammed shut, too late.

"I can see you're glad to have me back," she grumbled to the beach, rubbing the grit from her teary eyes.

Her hand froze on her cheek.

The empty waters were no longer empty.

Taking a hesitant step forward, Raiya stared into the blue, ignoring the urge to blink. She stabbed her spear into the yielding sand and shielded the sun from her face with one hand, pulling the strap holding the water skin over her head with the other.

A brown spot, there, in the distance. She squinted, wondering if the spot was real or just a simple trick of light refracting off of choppy waters.

She didn't budge for a full minute, watching the brown spot like a rabbit startled by rustling grass, too afraid to move. No, the spot was real, and it was getting bigger. Floating closer to shore. It wasn't shaped right to be a boat, but it was too large to be driftwood.

A flash of muted light, like sunlight catching on a piece of metal. The glint faded and returned as the object sloshed back and forth on the waves. Each time it flashed, the light consumed her entire field of vision like a lighthouse on a foggy night.

A strange urgency washed over her, welling up from the pit of her stomach, urging her heart to prepare for action, and before she knew it, she was diving headlong into the coming waves, beating her arms against the warm waters and kicking up curtains of mist behind her.

It wouldn't be until later that evening, lying in bed and failing in her attempt at sleep, that Raiya would question her unflinching decision to swim half a mile out into open waters. But now, as she sluiced through the balmy, cresting waves, she had no time for questions or doubts, no time to wonder what she was thinking, and no time to wonder what she'd find once she reached the brown spot.

She was at the mercy of instinct.

Of hope.

A school of high-finned yellow fish scattered like leaves in a gale. The world above and the world below alternated with each gulping breath. The farther she moved from shore, the harder it became to determine if she was making any headway against the churning water. After a few minutes of constant swimming, she pulled back, treading water as she blinked away the stinging brine, searching the swells for her target.

About a hundred yards out, a hefty chunk of sundered wood drifted along with the current. Even at this distance, she could clearly see a body lying prone atop the floating plank.

Raiya plunged forward, kicking up a plume of water in her wake.

By the time she finally reached the shattered plank, the muscles in Raiya's arms and legs had just begun to burn. Gripping the splintered edge of what appeared to be a piece of a ship's deck, she pulled herself up out of the water and wiped the water from her face.

A young man, somewhere around sixteen to eighteen years of age lay face down on the pock-marked wood. He was unconscious, but the constant rise and fall of his shoulders told Raiya he was still breathing. His clothes were in tatters, and tiny cuts and dried blood covered his chapped, sunburned skin in multiple places, but she didn't immediately spot any worrisome injuries.

Sinking back to the water's surface, Raiya clamped her fingers around the deck's threshold and kicked her legs, driving the makeshift raft toward the distant shore.

After what seemed like an eternity, Raiya's feet finally connected with the soft sand of the shore and the plank ground to a stop. The skin of her palms stung from being pressed against the jagged wood for so long. It surprised her to find they weren't bleeding.

She crawled atop the plank beside him, placing a hand on the small of his back. "Hey, are you alright? Can you hear me?"

Aside from his shallow breathing, the young man didn't move.

She sat up to examine his condition. No sign of fresh blood, no open wounds, no apparent broken bones. That was good. What wasn't good was fiery red sunburn covering his bare extremities and the bevy of blisters giving his skin a toad-like appearance. She probed his arms and legs, alarmed to find extensive swelling as a result of his extended time in the sun and from a case of severe dehydration.

"Well, stranger," she whispered, folding her legs beneath her and stretching her fingers out across the small of his back. "You're about to be very grateful that I'm the one who pulled you from the water."

She closed her eyes and focused her intent, drawing her soul into the body and willing it down her arms and into the injured young man.

When she opened them, she found no trace of reddened skin, and all his blisters were gone.

"Hey!" she said, louder this time. When he didn't respond, Raiya reached up and pinched his earlobe.

Hard.

"Gaaaa!" he grunted sleepily, flinching away from the attack. "That hurt, Aidux. What did I tell you about biting in the morning?"

The young man stretched his arms and legs, blinking and yawning like someone waking from a relaxing nap. A hand casually drifted to the sword handle hovering over his back, and, once he had assured it was still in place, he continued to stretch and pop his joints.

"Gods, I had the weirdest dream-"

He froze, arms straight out over his head. His head jerked around, eyes connecting with hers briefly before jumping about their surroundings. With a quick shove and deep groan, the young man pushed up to his knees, searching frantically for something that wasn't there.

"Whoa, slow down." Raiya squeezed his shoulder. He flinched at her soft touch, but didn't pull away. "Try not to move too much. You weren't in the best shape when I found you, and it might take you some time for your body to acclimate."

His brown eyes locked onto hers. Wide. Penetrating.

Afraid.

"Where am I? Where's Aidux?"

"Well, these are the White Crystal Shores, a few miles east of Calibri Grotto. I spotted you floating around on the current, so I pulled you ashore." She bit her lip anxiously. "I don't know an 'Aidux'. Is he a friend of yours?"

He nodded, concern written in bold letters on his face. The rumors of shredded and half-eaten bodies washing up in town flashed through her mind. She wondered if this 'Aidux' was among them. She sincerely hoped not.

"Calibri Grotto?" Thought lines creased his brow. "That's a fishing village built on top of a system of ocean caves, right?"

She nodded.

"Then that means . . . is this Greater Delphine?"

Raiya nodded again. He must be from Lesser Delphine, as most of the inhabitants of Greater Delphine simply referred to it as 'Delphine'. "How do you feel? Any pain, numbness?"

The young man took a deep breath, his eyes darting back and forth as if consulting some mental inventory sheet listing the status of his limbs and torso. "No, I think I'm pretty much okay."

"Can you stand?"

His lips quivered in an uncertain smile. "I'm not making any promises."

Chapter 48: An Unearned Sense of Peace

Raiya squeezed the young man's hands and slid backwards, pulling him up as she stood. He wobbled for a moment, teetering on stiff, shaky legs. After assuring himself that he wouldn't topple over once he stopped concentrating, he beamed a white crescent of perfect teeth at her.

"Actually . . . I feel great. A little stiff, but really and truly pretty good."

He released an exasperated chuckle and shrugged. "Which makes zero sense, considering the things I've been through in the past two weeks."

Raiya's eyes filled with wonder. "You really were on that ship, huh?"

The young man's smile withered. It made her sad to see it go. He really was quite cute, handsome even. Her cheeks warmed when she realized they were still holding hands. She released her grip and hid her hands behind her back.

"Has anyone else been found? A man in a cloak? A woman in a yellow dress?" He swallowed hard. "An unnaturally large cat?"

Raiya twisted her hands together and shook her head. "Pieces of the ship have been washing up for days, but so far you're the first survivor."

She prayed he wouldn't ask about the deceased.

"Did you say 'days'?" he asked, stretching out the word. "What day *is* it?"

"Corsun, the eighteenth of Veet."

"*Corsun?* Last I remember it was the evening of Tharsun. That's two whole days!"

He dragged his fingers through his hair. "Four days now, lost to unconsciousness . . ."

Raiya explored the old wounds scattered down his bare arms with her eyes. Yellow splotches and flaky scabs told her they were well on their way towards healing. Based on the fact that her healing session hadn't completely eliminated them, she wondered how bad they had been before.

"Are you sure you're feeling alright?"

He nodded, a smile creeping slowly across his face, and Raiya couldn't help but return it. "No, no. I feel . . . good. Unusually so. Not at all like a guy who's just been rescued from the sea by some pretty girl whose name he doesn't even know."

As if realizing what he just said, the young man blushed furiously and lowered his head.

Raiya chewed on her lip to hide a grin, extending an open hand to the stranger. "Well then, sailor, I suppose it's time we introduced ourselves. I'm Raiya Callicade."

"Nevin Walker." The two exchanged a friendly handshake. "Thank you for pulling me out of the ocean. If I'd woken up and seen all of that water around me, I would have died of fright."

"Come on." She tugged on his hand and turned up the beach. "I'll take you back to town. We'll ask around, see if any of the fishing boats have found anything of your friends, get you some food, and maybe if you're really nice we can get you something other than a piece of wood to sleep on tonight."

Nevin followed without protest. "*Gods*, I don't even want to think about sleep right now. Feels like I've been asleep for weeks."

He rotated his shoulder, swinging his arm around and around, trying to work out some of the residual stiffness. His hand brushed the white stone grip of the blade hanging off his back and he stopped, pulling it from its clasp and slipping it around in front of him. He cradled it like a child, running his eyes up and down its foggy gray length.

Raiya frowned. The dull metal hardly reflected any light, barely more reflective than polished stone. It couldn't have caused the glint she saw from the shore. She searched him up and down, her eyes finally settling on the tarnished bronze canteen strapped to his hip.

"Well, you can thank that beat up canteen for your rescue. The sunlight must have caught it just right while I was walking by. You'd probably still be floating around out there on the water without its help. Kinda makes it the real hero of today, huh?"

He looked down at the canteen in surprise before shaking his head and chuckling. "Yeah, I guess so. Imagine that."

Nevin turned his attention back to the sword, spinning it around his right, then his left side. Raiya took a cautious step back. "I don't have to worry about you, do I? I mean, I didn't rescue some sort of professional killer or wanted murderer, did I?"

With some effort, he returned the sword to its place on his back and shook his head. "I'm not really the killing type."

"No?" It didn't make any sense, but something in his tone convinced her, beyond any words he could have possibly spoken.

Their path eventually led them to where Raiya had left her spear in the sand. She plucked it from the ground without stopping. "I suppose you're going to tell me you use that big sword to fish?"

He smiled at that. "I wouldn't even know where to begin."

The warm sun slowly took its toll on her damp clothes, but she knew it would be quite a while before she was dry again. Every few steps, a droplet of water would rush down her bare arms or legs, threatening to unleash a shiver in response. She didn't mind. After so many years spent in the ocean, she almost preferred being wet. Maybe she was finally becoming part dolphin like her father predicted.

"So, you're not a fisherman."

He grunted. "Not even a little."

"And you aren't a professional killer, or so you say. That really remains to be seen." She eyed him, but he quietly avoided her gaze. "And by your fear of the ocean, I'm guessing you weren't a member of the ship's crew."

"Very perceptive."

Raiya playfully shoved him with her shoulder. "Are you gonna make me guess?"

"Why not? You're doing great."

"Alright, alright." Raiya tilted her head skyward and pulled her strawberry-blonde hair over her shoulder. "Well then, let's start with your hands."

Nevin self-consciously looked down at his bare palms. "What *about* my hands?"

"Well, you have the hands of a working man. Calloused. Strong."

He wiped a hand across his ragged shirt, as if the act would somehow cleanse the hardened flesh from his palms. Raiya tried to stifle a giggle and showed him her own calloused hand. "I spearfish. Rough hands are a natural side effect of manual labor."

He laughed. "Okay. So far, so good. What else?"

"Wellllll . . . you've got a good tan and don't burn easily, so that tells me you work outside. And you've got that huge sword or whatever it is, so regardless of your denial, I'm guessing you're some sort of trained warrior. You're young, but well-spoken and knowledgeable, and a good education is generally a sign of nobility.

"But then there's your clothes. Simple, straightforward." She paused, scrunching her nose with distaste. "And barely wearable at this point in their lifespan. Every time a tax collector comes into town, he's in a horse-drawn carriage and wearing all this superfluously puffy clothing. Like someone took thread to a bunch of clouds.

"But you? In that outfit, combined with everything else? Maybe some sort of estranged peasant knight? I can't tell."

Incredulous, Nevin shook his head and stopped dead in his tracks. "Hold on a second. 'Superfluous'? 'Estranged'? Those are some awfully big words for a fisherman."

She hid a grin with her hand. "Sorry. It's just nice to talk to someone with more than a twenty word vocabulary. Other than my father, I mean. The uncanny ability of fishermen to butcher our language makes me want to pull off my ears at times."

"Please," he said, waving his hands. "Don't apologize. I know exactly what you mean. Growing up, the only person I knew capable of carrying on a conversation outside the topics of farming or weather was about fifty years older than me. And Aidux just stumbles over big words like he's walking through a rockslide with his eyes closed."

He started walking again. "What about your father? Is he a scholar or something?"

She nodded. "That's exactly what he is—a sage. He moved here with my mother before I was born. You should see how many books he has. A whole room full of them."

"Sounds familiar," he mumbled cryptically. "And your mother?"

Raiya's mouth twitched, but no words emerged. Instead, she bent forward and scooped up the top half of an oyster shell, only to discard it a few steps later.

"What about you? Did I get anything right?"

He raked a hand back through his hair, smoothing it down hastily when he realized how ragged it must look. "Honestly? You started out strong, but that bit about the peasant knight lost you a few points. I was raised on an apple farm in a secluded forest town called Elbin. My parents . . ."

He hesitated, barely, before continuing. "I studied a few times a week with an old man named Ishen. He was sort of a sage himself. He wasn't from Elbin, though he never told me where he came from. He always acted like living there was beneath him, like he was somehow better than the locals. I got the feeling that he didn't want to be there. Never made any sense."

They passed the minutes in a comfortable silence, strolling through the glimmering sands as if hoping the beach would never break free from the horizon. Raiya couldn't help but worry for him, worry that he might be the sole survivor of the shipwreck, that his friends might be lost to him forever, leaving him stranded, alone and far from his home.

And yet, despite the awful state of his circumstances, he seemed to be handling it quite well. Almost too well, she thought. Maybe the seriousness of the situation had yet to impress itself on him, or maybe he had simply chosen not to dwell on events far beyond his control.

Maybe that was just his way of trying to cope, but something about his attitude nagged at her. He was almost too carefree, too nonchalant. Almost like he was refusing to feel. Raiya knew from personal experience the dangers of burying emotion. Everything buried eventually rots.

Nevin stopped, craning his neck to peer inland. "What's that?"

Raiya stood on her toes and looked past him. She frowned, muttering a curse under her breath. "Braga's brow, it still burns. I'd almost forgotten about it on account of the fog."

"Fog?"

"Come on," she begged, taking him by the arm and directing him back down the beach. "That's a bad place, and it'll be sunset soon."

Nevin shrugged off her grasp. "You come on. I want to see."

Nevin crouched over the floor of the smoking ruins, his fingertips tracing a series of scorched lines burned into the blackened floorboards. He tugged the ruined collar of his shirt over his mouth again in the hopes that the thin fabric might block the lingering haze from entering his lungs, but a burning itch clawed at the walls of chest with every breath regardless.

Sweat glistened on his furrowed brow. "This doesn't make any sense."

A misshapen lump of melted flesh and warped bone sat at the center of it all, the macabre focal point of whatever calamity had befallen the ruined cabin. Dying sunlight streamed through scattered holes in the roof, barely illuminating the hazy interior. All furniture and decoration had been shoved against the walls, unseated forcefully enough from their rightful places that most presented as little more than piles of soot-stained scrap.

Black smoke oozed from nearly every surface, from wood to stone alike.

Nevin straightened, his eyes still trained on the oddly organized lines burned into the floor. Concentric circles, too perfect to be accidental.

Raiya watched reluctantly from the doorway, occasionally leaning out to take a breath of clean air. She hadn't wanted to approach even this close, but had followed behind him out of concern. The young woman hugged herself and shifted uncomfortably.

"I don't like it here, Nevin. There's something . . . I don't even know. It just feels like we're not alone."

In the corner of the room, a familiar gaunt shadow watched him, making no effort to speak or interact. He did his best to ignore it. "I know the feeling."

He turned his attention to the walls. A fine layer of soot blanketed the stone in all but three places—vertical patches of clean limestone roughly five to six feet in height. No smoke bled from these patches of stone, almost as though they had been shielded from whatever had caused the persistent and disconcerting effect.

Curious, he ran a finger down a stretch of still smoking stone.

"Ow!" he cried out, jerking his hand away.

"Are you alright?" Raiya took a half-step into the cabin, covering her mouth with an arm.

He nodded, scowling down at the reddened circle of skin on the pad of his index finger. A faint blister had already started to form, the skin raised and puffy.

What could cause stone to burn? He rubbed the scalded fingertip against his thumb. *And why, after so many days, was it still so hot?*

"It's weird, right?" she asked, as if sensing his confusion. "Three Wizards showed up in town a few days before the explosion out to sea, asking questions and just generally making everyone nervous. They said they'd chased a rogue Ignurgist south past Whitefalls, and they'd heard rumor that he'd taken solace somewhere in the Grotto."

Nevin paced the room, his eyes watering from the smoke. "Ignurgist?"

"A particularly destructive and unpredictable kind of Wizard. It's said they have this perverse addiction to fire, often struggling to suppress the urge to burn everything within reach. Like they can't help themselves."

Hands on his hips, Nevin stared down at a small iron hasp set into the floor against the wall opposite the front door. He nudged it with a toe, but the hinged plate didn't budge. *Likely warped from the heat.*

"Just a cellar," Raiya said, answering his unspoken question. "Probably covers the entrance to a branch of the caves that run all throughout these hills. The locals sometimes use them to store food and dry goods."

He nodded absently, glancing at the shadowy figure occupying the corner of the room. It remained motionless, darker still than shadows it lurked within, watching him with unseen eyes.

Raiya continued her tale. "Rumor has it, the three mages chased the rogue Ignurgist to this cabin, but moments after they entered, the whole building erupted in flames. I could see the fires all the way from town. There's no way anyone could have survived, and the evidence suggests no one did."

He turned to face her, barely able to make out her lean form through the stagnant haze. "What evidence?"

She gestured to the melted pile of flesh in the center of the room. "Ignurgist."

She then pointed to the three lighter spots on the interior walls. "Three Wizards."

A low whistle escaped Nevin's lips. "Brutal."

Raiya danced in place. "Can we go now? This place makes my skin crawl."

Nevin finally nodded, crossing the ruined cabin to follow her out the door. The gaunt figure watched him go, only stepping off the wall to trail behind once he'd crossed the threshold and left the smoke-filled building in his wake.

He continually thumbed the rising blister on his finger as the two made their way west toward town. The burning sensation hadn't abated in the slightest, but Nevin was far more concerned with the gaunt figure following close on their heels. It hadn't once disappeared since he awoke on that chunk of wood several hours ago.

He wondered if he'd ever be alone again.

Chapter 49: Calibri Grotto

Calibri Grotto wasn't what Nevin had expected. Tales of the fishing village had placed it on a stony peninsula housing an elaborate system of caves, and while that information nearly described the full extent of his knowledge, what he assumed to be a simple fishing village ended up leaving him pleasantly surprised.

Though the beach continued westward, Raiya eventually shifted their path inland. The shores of the Sea of Calor disappeared below forty feet of sheer white stone after less than a mile of hiking, trading soft sand for coarse rock, and finally for patches of vibrant emerald mosses and broad-leaf grasses sporting a carpet of canary wildflowers. Scattered trees burgeoned with bright yellow fruits, and rollings plains swooped in from the north, their gentle vales decorated in deep greens and freckled yellows. A puffy cloud of bleating sheep drifted aimlessly through the verdant fields, unconcerned by their passing.

Nevin hadn't thought it possible for the ocean to seem more limitless than his view from the beach, but looking out toward the blurred horizon and finding it hard to separate sky from sea, he suddenly felt very small. The world stretched far beyond what his view from the crown of an apple tree belied.

The first signs of the region's namesake caverns appeared as a series of light-hungry holes, most barely large enough for a person to squeeze through, each sinking straight through the earth like an abandoned well. As they neared the town, Raiya began probing the grass with the butt of her spear as she walked and pointed out a few of the more dangerous holes, small enough to be obscured by weeds yet large enough to gobble up a careless leg.

A shiver ascended his spine as he imagined the sensation of rough stone scraping away the tender flesh of his leg before snapping his shin in twain. A lone traveler would likely not survive such a mistake.

He stepped closer to Raiya's side.

"Regular travelers of these hills know to be cautious and stick to established roads," she told him, adjusting their heading to avoid another of the barely visible holes. "Old men tell stories of careless children disappearing out here, or finding bones strewn about a hole, picked clean by wild dogs."

His eyes widened slightly at the image. "Have *you* ever found anyone out here?"

Her chin dipped in a small nod. "Two Fadings ago, actually. Said he'd been riding along the cliffs when the ground gave out beneath his horse. The sudden fall threw him clear of the hole, but his horse wasn't nearly so lucky. Other than a broken arm, a nasty gash on his forehead, and a bruised ego, he was fine. I set his arm, fixed it to a splint and led him back to town."

"But . . . what about his horse? Did he ever find it?"

She kicked at a loose stone, propelling the hapless rock into uncaring darkness. Silence marked its descent into oblivion. "He stayed with a friend of my father's for a few days to regain his strength. I visited him twice a day to check his arm and the wrappings on his gash, to make sure it wasn't getting infected. We talked to pass the time, about the town, about him, about me. We even discussed the weather."

She turned glistening eyes to the northern hills. "His horse never came up."

Such easy indifference confounded Nevin. Whenever a merchant had trotted into Elbin atop a palomino gelding or roan mare, he couldn't help but admire the connection the two shared, the level of cooperation necessary for such an easy partnership. That relationship seemed like it would engender a sense of closeness, friendship even.

A friend deserved better. Aidux deserved better.

He tried to focus more on the path before him and less on idea that the final vestiges of his old life had perished alongside the Misanthrope and her crew. The distraction came surprisingly easy. The last things he remembered before waking were the emotions; the overwhelming, thought-eroding depression and anguish, drowning him beneath their relentless downpour, washing away his identity and leaving only sadness in their wake.

Conversely, he now found it nearly impossible to feel anything but optimism. He knew he should feel bad about his inability to worry about his best friend and missing companions, but even *that* small measure of guilt lay outside his current emotional range.

Had that blue mist affected his emotions in some unexpected manner?

Still, the strange event on the ship couldn't be completely responsible for Nevin's high spirits. He could hardly turn his thoughts away from his attractive rescuer. In fact, he often found himself lagging slightly behind, attempting to keep her in his field of vision at all times.

Nothing about Raiya fit his traditional picture of women. The strongly patriarchal structure of Elbin found many of the town's women indoors, leaving the fathers and sons to tend to the pastures whilst the wives and daughters tended to the cooking and mending and general upkeep of the shops and houses. As such, the women had very pale, fair skin; a sharp contrast to the men's dark, leathery flesh.

Raiya, though, had the golden skin of someone who rarely saw shade, and unlike the harsh weathered look of a farmer's tan, Raiya's skin was uniform and effulgent, soft and clean.

It was often the uncomfortable warmth in his cheeks that told him he'd been watching her too closely.

Occasionally, Nevin found himself looking back at the shadowy figure trailing them in the distance. The scattered fruit trees left it few places to hide, but still it seemed draped in its own concealing darkness, as though the sun itself refused to look upon it too closely. He could feel it now always, watching him expectantly, waiting for something.

"What's wrong?" Raiya asked, following his gaze but seeing nothing. "You keep looking behind us."

Nevin shook his head and resolved to keep his eyes trained on the path before them. "It's nothing. I just keep thinking about that smoking house."

Finally, as their strides took them over a low hill, the scattered stone buildings of Calibri Grotto came into view. The rocky hills gave way to terraced steps, staggered foundations carved directly out of the granular stone. Each rectangular cutout held one or more buildings constructed from the same white-gray rock as the cliffs, and while some appeared to be made from stacked bricks, an equal amount seemed to be carved directly out of the hillside itself. The buildings supported a mixture of domed and tiled roofs, and nearly all possessed some sort of stone chimney exuding an unfamiliar charcoal-based smoke.

"What's that?" He pointed toward the north, where a substantial fissure cleaved through the earth. A man carrying a net filled with limp fish emerged from the hole and turned up a stone walkway bridging the gap across its middle.

"That? That's the entrance to our port." She grabbed his hand and tugged, pulling him behind. "Come on."

He craned his neck and stumbled after her. "Your port is underground?"

"Mmm-hmm," she said, quickening her pace. Nevin frowned, trotting to keep up. The two had enjoyed a casual pace until they had breached the town's edge, and Raiya now marched forward as if barreling through dangerous territory.

"I don't understand."

"The caves are what initially drew settlers to the area. Specifically, the area directly below the town—a spacious underground cove. When first discovered, it's said that there were so many fish crowded below the overhanging cliffs that you couldn't see the ocean floor. That's changed somewhat in the years since the town's founding, but the surrounding waters are still teeming with fish of all shapes and kinds.

"The opening back there is a ramp that descends into the belly of the town and the rear of that cove. This 'grotto' provides a natural shelter against inclement weather, allowing us to dock our ships with little fear of them being damaged by dangerous conditions. In addition, a number of storage buildings and other residences carved directly into the rock wall provide a safe place to take shelter during truly violent weather."

Raiya angled towards a switchback cart path that climbed up through the scattered buildings. Nevin marveled at the level of sophistication and detail evident in the fishing village's construction. Compared to Elbin, this town was of a different world entirely. Anywhere Nevin expected to see wood, he instead found stone.

Doors? Stone. Fencing? Stone. Flower boxes? Stone! Stone stairs connecting different sections of the meandering path, stone pillars supporting stone eaves covered in stone tiles. And nearly every piece of stone appeared to have felt the careful hand of a master craftsman. Not elaborate exactly, just perfectly shaped. Bricks fitting together tightly enough to deny the intrusion of a fingernail. Flawlessly squared stairs, each rising an equal measure above the previous.

A flash of color drew his eye. Raiya steered him up a set of wide steps that passed below a beautifully painted mural—a vibrant blue and silver fish emerging gracefully from a curl of water, its open mouth chasing a pair of detailed green dragonflies. The skillful use of color and shading made the water appear to glow as if lit from below, and both the fish and the dragonflies seemed to glitter metallically in the afternoon sun. Raiya paid it little mind as they passed, but Nevin couldn't look away.

"Who does all the stonework here? I've never seen such craftsmanship."

Raiya straightened, beaming. "That would be my father."

"Your father's a mason?"

"Oh no." She turned away from an approaching pack of weary fisherman and down a side path. Nevin thought he saw a half-wave of greeting from one before she adjusted direction. "He's our Shaper. One of them I mean."

Shaper? Nevin wasn't familiar with that term. "Is that some sort of artist? Like a stonecutter or something?"

"Druce? He doesn't have an artistic bone in his body." Raiya chuckled, a flummoxed look creeping across her face. "How do you not know what a Shaper is? Do you not have magic users back home?"

Nevin shook his head. "The Lancowl Barony is magic-free. Until a few days ago, I only knew of magic from stories."

"Oh." She pulled her ponytail over her shoulder and fiddled with the tip. "Let me see how to put this. Do you know what a Dabbler is?"

Nevin's silence spoke volumes.

"Okay, I'm no expert, but I'll do my best. When a mage first learns to use magic, he's taught how to use a small amount of each different element. As their training progresses, particularly skilled mages choose to focus on one element specifically. Like a blacksmith taking up gilding or weaponsmithing or bell-making. When a mage specializes, they become a 'Wizard'."

He scratched his neck. The stubble was starting to itch. "I thought all magic users were Wizards. There are other types?"

"Oh, definitely. More than I could name. Dabblers, Javeren, Animators, Sorcerers . . . not to mention the different classes of Wizard."

Raiya abruptly turned off the road and ascended one of the many staircases, avoiding a smiling elderly gentleman who was just about to cross their path. Despite his smile, Nevin noticed a distinct sadness in his graying eyes as he watched Raiya pass.

"Dabblers," she continued, the speed of their travel adding a breathy quality to her words, "are like a Wizard's opposite. Instead of honing their abilities toward a specific element, a Dabbler continues to study all of them, never really obtaining mastery of any one element, but often possessing a greater understanding of the relationships of all five."

"Okay, but what does a Shaper do exactly?"

"Well, a Shaper . . . shapes. Anything really. Jarell Nosbey, our first Shaper, particularly loved working with stone. With magic, he could mold stone like putty into any shape he could imagine. He could break a large block of stone into a collection of equal-sized smaller pieces, or he could combine those pieces into one solid block with no seams. Unlike a typical crafter, a Shaper doesn't really make mistakes, doesn't have excess unusable material, and can often build an item faster and more precisely than otherwise possible."

"That's amazing."

The path led by another of the colorful murals—a breathtaking depiction of an ocean sunset. He trailed a hand along the image's waxy surface, half-expecting an impossible heat to sear the hardened flesh of his palm, but the only heat he felt came from the raised blister on his index finger.

He thumbed the rough bubble of skin. His whole finger felt hot now, like the heat was spreading.

Raiya nodded. "Without Jarell, this town may have never been founded. Working stone by hand is a long, intensive process, and in the early days of Calibri Grotto, most people were too focused on cutting and hauling wood from the forests to the northwest, using that wood to build boats, or attempting to gather enough food through fishing and foraging to feed the colony. There wouldn't have been enough time or manpower to carve out shelter enough for everyone."

Nevin took another look around. With the majority of the buildings encircling the large fissure granting access to the port, the town proper likely only covered an area of just over a few square miles. Smaller settlements, farms most likely, were scattered throughout the hills farther north. A few hundred stone buildings altogether, but what amazed him was the sheer amount of completed stonework. Natural, unworked stone had almost ceased to exist within the boundaries of Calibri Grotto.

"He did all of this by himself?"

"For the most part. My father and a few others took up the mantle when he left."

Nevin shook his head in astonishment. He didn't know the amount of time and effort a group of masons would have had to put forth to accomplish the construction of a town like Calibri Grotto, but he didn't think it would be easy. Years, maybe. Decades even. That a single man had done the bulk of the work was more amazing still. He was beginning to wonder at the real reason behind Ishen's insistence on the troublesome nature of magic.

Raiya nudged him playfully with her shoulder and hooked her arm around his elbow. "Come on, Nevin. What are a few stairs to a warrior like you?"

"A tougher opponent I have yet to face," he huffed, grinning. Raiya stifled a giggle with the back of her hand. "So Shapers can make just about anything?"

"I assume anything they have material for and knowledge of."

"And they can make it faster than normal craftsmen?"

"Oh, definitely. Jarell could build a small house in a day or two, not including the roof. Well, with a few people to carry stone for him."

He scratched an itch hiding under the shoulder strap of his baldric. "Doesn't that take some of the work from those who can't use magic? I mean, if they can make *anything* with magic, better and faster than us normal folk, wouldn't that put traditional craftsmen out of business?"

Raiya beamed a huge grin at him. Combined with the growing fatigue in his legs, the smile almost knocked him off his feet. He couldn't help but return it. "What? What did I say?"

"Nothing. You just ask really good questions. It's nice to talk to someone that doesn't constantly ask me about . . ."

Her smile faded slightly as she trailed off, returning her gaze to the path ahead. "It's just nice. Other than my father, I don't really talk to anyone in town."

Nevin sensed there was more to it than that, but he didn't want to press her. After a moment, she answered his previous question. "You're right, though. I'm sure if Jarell had come to Calibri Grotto after it was already settled, his talents would have destroyed the careers of more mundane stonemasons. But have you noticed Calibri Grotto's complete lack of artistic touch?"

"I have. Except for these random paintings, the town is so bare, like it's waiting for people to move in and make a home out of it." Nevin trailed his hand along the slightly raised painting of a strange-looking shelled creature with one big and one small claw.

"The paintings do brighten up the town, don't they?" Raiya's eyes focused on something beyond the horizon, the tone of her voice haunted, wispy.

She trotted up a short staircase onto a landing that reached all the way out to the cliff's edge. A single building stood on the wide expanse of mossy stone, framed by a faded blue sky and stringy clouds clinging loosely to the horizon. A rectangular swatch of transplanted soil bore a small garden, arranged in meticulously spaced rows and paths. Various leafy and flowering vegetables swayed gently on the breeze.

Two stone storage bins guarded the house's rear door. A wide array of garden tools and jars of different colored liquids and burlap sacks crowded around the bins, exposed to the elements but arranged in a careful, deliberate manner. The tools were obviously well cared for, as not a hint of dirt lingered on shovel or trowel, and any speck of rusted metal had been diligently scoured away. A massive hewing ax leaned against the wall just outside the door, appearing out of place in a landscape with scant few trees.

"Now," Raiya began in a low voice, stepping up to the door and turning to face Nevin. "I have to warn you about my father. He's . . . well, he's a little intense."

Nevin cocked an eyebrow. "Intense?"

She nodded conspiratorially. "He'll probably ask you a lot of questions, and with that, I think you'll do fine. In fact, I think the two of you will have a lot in common."

She held up a finger. "Just don't touch his books."

He grunted his agreement. *From one Ishen to another.*

"I'm going to ask him if you can stay for a while, at least until you figure out what you're going to do, where you're going to go. All you have to do is convince him you aren't some sort of professional killer."

"It didn't take long to convince you. I'm sure I won't have any problem with him."

"Who said I was convinced?" With a playful smile, Raiya turned and pushed open the heavy door.

Chapter 50: Sage Druce

The sparsely furnished interior greeted them with the fragrance of mint tea, burning charcoal, and the tangy scent of paint in various stages of drying. Light, warm and red, flickered behind the grate of a cast iron stove. A door stood closed to each side of the short hallway guiding them into the house's neatly organized common room. A white linen cloth was draped delicately atop a square table, its tasseled edges almost hiding a set of stools sheltered beneath. Shelves arranged with an array of polished stone and black iron cooking and dinnerware lined the walls. The quiet droning of the ocean and the call of hovering gulls disappeared, replaced with the rumble and pop of boiling water.

All the windows save one were tightly shuttered. A ribbon of sunlight angled over the only clutter in the house—a collection of tiny mason jars presenting in all the colors of the rainbow and in between, stacked haphazardly around a tripod easel. Brushes thin and wide poked their frayed heads from a basket hanging from the easel's cross-member. A linen canvas waited patiently for someone to finish the image of a bonfire blazing beneath a starry sky. The paint was still glossy from recent attention.

A clear palm-sized nugget of polished crystal rested on the windowsill, throwing off wire-thin rays of multi-hued light across the walls of the room.

Raiya offered a hand out to the open room. "Make yourself comfortable. My father is probably reading in the other room. The written word is often louder to him than the spoken, so I doubt he even noticed us enter."

"Then I suppose it's fortuitous I chose this moment to break for tea."

The unexpected voice startled them both. A muscular man with streaks of gray in his wavy, chin-length hair silently pulled the hallway door closed behind him and folded his hands protectively over a leather-bound book held at his waist. A pair of thin spectacles sat low on his pointed nose, the glasses made to look even smaller against the backdrop of his bulging shoulders and broad chest.

Raiya leaned her spear against the wall and gathered the man up in hug. "Bet you didn't expect to see me back so soon."

He extracted himself from Raiya's arms and pushed his spectacles up his nose. "Well, I hear spontaneity is inherited from the mother's side of the family."

Raiya turned to her new companion. "Nevin, this is my father, Druce Callicade."

Nevin extended his hand, and Druce shook it slowly, his eyes unblinking as they searched the young man's face. Their intensity made Nevin nervous, as though the man attempted to read the truth of his life from his uncomfortable expression.

"Glad to meet you." He hoped her father hadn't heard his voice crack.

Raiya had. She elbowed her father and shot him a perturbed look. Druce ignored her, the whispers of a smile turning the corners of his mouth. "Have a seat at the table, Nevin. Do you like tea?"

"I do."

Ishen, Donald, and now Druce were all tea drinkers. Men of sophistication, of stature. Nothing at all like Dalen and his thirst for the sour apple wine.

Carefully drawing the tablecloth up, Nevin pulled three stools out from under the table and positioned them on all sides, taking the middle seat to avoid scraping the Sharasil against the nearby wall. Raiya joined him. She winked knowingly, as if urging him to relax.

Druce prepared three cups of tea and set them on the table with a small jar of honey and slices of a strange yellow fruit. He took a seat across from them, his muscular build appearing almost comical atop the narrow stool.

"We don't see many armed men in Calibri Grotto, Nevin. Our little village is far enough off the beaten path to keep us out of martial affairs. The sword on your back would generally give me cause for concern, but I trust my daughter's judge of character, and you don't carry it like a man hungry for blood."

Nevin grimaced internally. *Thirty seconds after meeting me, and he can already tell it's a sword. What took me so long to see it?*

The older man reached out to spoon some honey into his tea, but his eyes never left Nevin's face. "How old are you, if you don't mind me asking?"

He shifted uneasily in his chair. "Sixteen."

"A bit young for such a large, unusual weapon." His face hardened. "You're not one of those unsavory Origin Knights, are you?"

"I . . . I don't know what that is."

His ignorance caused the muscular man to brighten. "Would that we could all claim the same."

Raiya leaned forward. "I rescued Nevin from a piece of floating deck. He says he was on the ship that exploded two nights ago."

"The shipwreck?" Druce nearly choked on his tea. "I thought you looked a little worse for wear, young man, but compared to the bodies we've found washed up—"

"Daddy!" Raiya cut him off, nearly knocking her tea cup off the table. A tense hush descended over the room as Raiya stared at her father, while Druce sipped his tea and bored holes into the tablecloth with unblinking eyes.

Confused by their behavior, Nevin looked back and forth between them. "It's okay, you two. I saw the debris on the beach, the bits of shattered wood strewn through the sand and floating in the water. It's everywhere. With as much damage as the ship took, I figured out pretty quick that there were going to be casualties."

Druce looked up at him, then over to his daughter. Raiya chewed her lip before speaking. "But . . . some of your friends are missing. Aren't you worried?"

Nevin shrugged. "I mean, a little. But I survived just fine. I'm sure they're okay."

It was true. He couldn't bring himself to worry. Something told him they were fine, and they'd somehow find their way back together soon. He smiled to himself. He couldn't wait to hear all about Aidux's adventures.

Druce stirred his steaming cup of tea and searched Nevin's face. "Daughter, you were on the beach that night. Tell me again: what color was the light shed by the explosion?"

She wrapped her hands around her cup, but didn't drink. "Bright blue. Why do you ask?"

He took a sip and shook his head. "Just a curiosity. Been meaning to ask you again and it just came to mind."

He leaned over the table and changed the subject. "You're obviously on your way somewhere, but I'm more interested in where you came from."

Nevin cleared his throat and nodded. "Have you heard of Elbin?"

The man's eyebrows lifted slightly. "I have, though it surprises me to meet someone from there. You're a long way from home, young man."

Druce carefully sipped his tea. The steam painted his glasses with a white fog, but they were low enough on his face that it was obvious he didn't need them to see. Nevin supposed they were reading glasses.

"You do a lot of traveling? Walking from place to place?"

"Not really. Well, not until recently. Until a few weeks ago, I'd never left the village."

Druce appraised him quietly for a moment, musing on some hidden relevance within Nevin's answers. The young man squirmed beneath the scrutiny, thumbing the uncomfortable blister on the pad of his finger beneath the table. The small wound had only grown more painful as the hours slipped by, and he swore he could almost feel the heat of the burn creeping along the skin of his palm.

"Well," Raiya sighed, placing her hands flat on the table. "Nevin is going to need a place to stay for a few days. I thought I'd take him out and search the coast, ask some of the locals if they'd heard rumor of anyone washing up on the beach. With your permission, I hoped maybe he could stay here while we look."

She bumped Nevin with her shoulder. "And maybe steal some of your old clothes, since you hardly ever wear more than one outfit anymore."

Druce playfully flicked a glob of honey at Raiya, who raised her hands to shield herself from the sudden gooey onslaught. "I dress for comfort, not function. Long gone are the days when I've had a woman to impress."

Raiya shrugged, her bare shoulders nearly touching her ears. "I don't know, daddy. Every time I run into Maura Jane, she goes on and on about how you're in such good shape for a man of your age. Maybe it's time you invited her in for something more involved than a cup of tea."

He waved her off, hiding a grin behind his teacup. "Your mother was enough woman for one lifetime. I wouldn't even know what to do with a girl like Maura."

Raiya pointed over to the half-finished painting of a bonfire. "If it helps, I could paint you a picture."

"Oh, I think the last thing I want is a lesson on sex from my daughter. The fact that there's a boy in my house is enough cause for celebration."

All mirth disappeared from her face. "Daddy . . ."

Chuckling, he turned to Nevin. "Not once in her life has she shown an ounce of interest in the opposite sex, but the fact that she hasn't already skewered you with that spear of hers—"

"*Daddy*," Raiya interrupted threateningly. Druce pinched his lips together to hold back a smile.

"Drink your tea, Nevin," he said, gesturing to the untouched cup with a wink.

Nevin promised himself to ask Raiya about that 'skewering' comment at a later time. For now, he forced himself to change the focus of the conversation to Druce. "Raiya tells me you have a large collection of books. What do you read about?"

Druce reflexively pushed his glasses up his nose, frowning when he realized he couldn't see through them due to fog.

"I try to sample a bit of everything," he said, wiping his lenses with the aid of the tablecloth. "Though I don't have access to the sheer variety available before I settled here. Still, I tend to favor history, myth and legend, and the origin of names."

"Old stories were always my favorite too," he admitted.

"Truly? You learned to read in Elbin?"

Nevin nodded.

Druce seemed genuinely pleased. "A warrior *and* a scholar. I'm impressed. You and I have a bit in common there."

The older man stood and retrieved a small hickory box decorated with two silver hinges. From within, he produced a bulbous, hand-carved pipe and stuffed it with a pinch of sweet smelling tobacco. Druce dipped a finger in the pipe's bowl, his eyes twinkling faintly. The air around him vibrated curiously, and Nevin fought the urge to scratch his arms as a tickle spread across his skin. A thin line of smoke drizzled up from the now lit tobacco, and Druce puffed happily on the mouthpiece.

"Was that . . . ?" Nevin said, his words breathy and filled with wonder.

Druce nodded, puffing twice on the pipe. "Since I'm allowing you to sleep in my house and share my food, the least you can do is tell me your last name. As I've said, the origin of names has always fascinated me. Maybe I can enlighten you on some of your more obscure family history, if you're interested."

Nevin wasn't, though he was too polite to say it. "Probably not much to tell. My family have been apple farmers since Elbin was founded, and I think they took up their last name just before settling there."

"Mmm, of course," Druce gushed, chewing the stem of his pipe. "If I remember correctly, Elbin was founded by refugees fleeing the various religious wars. It would only make sense that they would want a fresh start, both geographically and anthroponymically."

Nevin's eyebrows reached for each other. "Anthropo—what?"

Raiya rolled her eyes. "He does that a lot. I can't have a conversation with him without asking him six times the meaning of some strange word he's used."

"Yes, but you learn something new every time we talk, do you not?"

Raiya pointedly slurped her tea, pretending to ignore him.

"Anthroponymy is the study of people's names. All I'm saying is that it's quite common for people starting a new life to take up a new name. Quite common, indeed. But, that may or may not be the case within your family. What is your last name?"

The tea was finally cool enough for Nevin to take more than a sip. "It's Walker. Nevin Walker."

Druce stared at him wordlessly. Nevin just shrugged. "I know, it doesn't really fit the image of an apple farmer."

"No, it certainly does not." He chewed idly on his pipe, staring through the ceiling at the heavens beyond. "Walker. Nevin Walker. 'The Walking Man'. I like that. Considering how far your feet have carried you away from home, 'The Walking Man' is a more apt moniker than would first appear. You just need the time to grow into it."

Raiya set her cup down. "You're about to run out of the room, aren't you."

It wasn't a question.

His eyes snapped back into focus as he hastily stood. "Yes, yes. You've made me curious about something, that's all. Something I need to look into."

He looked around like someone who had misplaced an item of importance. "Umm . . . help yourself to whatever food you can find, and . . . Raiya, can you show him how to erect the hammock stored beneath your bed? There a few extra blankets in your room too. I have something I need to . . ."

And with that, Druce shuffled down the hallway and disappeared back into the room he had emerged from upon their arrival.

"Your father is . . . odd." Nevin finished his tea in one gulp, leaving him with a mouthful of mint scraps.

Raiya scooped up their cups and placed them on a counter next to the stove. "Trust me, that was only odd because he said something before leaving. Sometimes he just leaves when I'm in the middle of a sentence. Or he is. But in all fairness, I guess the Sage of Calibri Grotto is allowed his eccentricities."

"Sage?"

She nodded. "His official title. He even has an honorary position on the town council, a position created specifically for him. Just goes to show how smart my father really is."

"I'm just happy to be treated with a measure of respect. Your father is a very nice man." He picked a fleck of mint off his tongue. "Odd, but nice."

While Raiya prepared the hammock, attaching it to a set of metal hooks driven into the house's stone walls and dressing it with two plump cotton comforters, Nevin pondered Druce's reaction to his family name.

The Walking Man.

The more he thought about it, the more it grew on him. It wasn't the most exciting title, but with how far his feet had taken him from his home in the Traagen Woods, Druce had been right about its appropriateness. How far had he really come? And far would he yet have to go to find his friends, to be free of the sword, to make a life of his own?

Chapter 51: Turmoil Revived

Something woke Raiya, some movement in the house. A door closing, maybe. A shift in pressure.

Rubbing her eyes, Raiya stretched, trying to banish the tightness sleeping in a real bed created in her muscles. She'd become so accustomed to falling asleep in the sand that nights spent tossing and turning in her bed often found her stiff and sore the next morning. With a groan, she swung her bare legs over the side of the bed and looked out the window.

The night sky was alive with twinkling lights, cloud-free and perfect, the kind of night that made sleeping on the beach all the more worth it. A soft whimper escaped her mouth as her feet connected with the cold stone. She high-stepped across the room, quickly shoving her protesting toes into a pair of slippers, and pulled a loosely woven robe on over her wool shift—all clothes she wore only when sleeping at home, and only because her father had given them to her as a gift. She figured such delicate clothing would quickly disintegrate after a few nights covered in sand, and she couldn't imagine what she would do if someone happened upon her in the middle of the night, and she was forced to defend herself in a piece of clothing that left more skin exposed than it covered.

Raiya shook her head. She had never understood why her mother only wore dresses. Walking around town wouldn't be so bad, but out hiking? Spearfishing the shallows? Sailing? Dresses just seemed silly to her. They were far too fragile for practical use. It amazed her how her mother could keep a dress in good form. No tears. No stains.

Raiya had owned exactly one dress in her lifetime. It had lasted a week. Her father hadn't bought her another since, but she'd never forgotten the look on his face the first time he saw her wearing it.

Inching her door open quietly, Raiya sneaked out into the hallway, pausing briefly next to her father's closed door and pressing her ear to the wood.

Only silence greeted her.

She frowned. Her father was a prolific snorer. Either he had just fallen asleep, or . . .

The faint red glow of a lit pipe briefly illuminated Druce's face. He sat at the table, watching Raiya as she shuffled down the hallway to stand before him.

"Are you alright?" she asked, rubbing an eye and yawning. "It's late."

"Mmm." The fragrant spice of tobacco smoke warmed her nose. "Just up checking on our guest, when I noticed he wasn't in his hammock."

Guest? The memory of sleep vanished and Raiya self-consciously drew closed the folds of her robe.

She'd almost forgotten about Nevin.

Leaning over the table, Raiya peered out through the only window in the room not tightly shuttered. Her father was right. Though she could only see part of it, the hammock was plainly empty—a bundle of loose rope swaying on the breeze. Nevin's sword wasn't where he'd left it either. Had he made off in the middle of the night?

Raiya hurried to the door, hoping he hadn't gone too far, hoping she could catch him and convince him to come back. There was so much about him she still wanted to know. Why was he on that boat? Why had he left Elbin? Who was Aidux? Why did he need a sword?

More so, she just wanted to talk to him more. The previous day had passed so quickly. It was exciting to make a new friend, one whom she shared so much in common, one her age, one so mysterious and . . .

Druce gestured off into the distance with his pipe. "On the bench."

Raiya scuttled back to his side and squinted out through the glass. Behind the cabin, chalky stone reached for the horizon for another fifty or sixty feet before dropping precipitously down into open waters. Small patches of fuzzy moss clung to the rock here and there, but the uneven ground was otherwise barren. About ten feet from the edge, a squarish slab of smoother stone rose parallel to cliff, just high enough to act as a makeshift bench of unworked limestone.

A shadowy figure sat off to one side, facing the night black Sea of Calor.

You know I'm right.

Nevin stared at his feet, pressing his forehead against the frigid pommel of the Sharasil to keep from tumbling forward off the stone bench. Cold seeped into his skull and crawled down his neck, leaving raised goose pimples behind as it conquered more and more of his flesh. Tears crystallized on flushed cheeks, but he didn't lift his head to challenge the gaunt figure leering down at him.

"Why won't you just leave me be," he mumbled, a puff of white fog materializing from his lips with each spoken word.

Leave you? Oh, you don't really want me to leave.

"I do, though."

You need me too much to send me away.

"Why?" he hissed, jerking his head up to look the shadow in its face, but he found nothing but blackness. "Why do you keep saying that? All you do is haunt me. You're nothing but a hallucination. You're not real. What good would come from acknowledging you, from listening to you, from giving you even a moment of my attention? Why would I need a thing like you?"

The shadowy figure glided closer, silently skimming across the craggy landscape.

Because you won't face. Won't see. Won't accept.

"So what!" He erupted from his seat, squeezing the Sharasil's coarse grip with both hands and ripping it through the empty air in front of him.

But the shadowy figure was already gone.

Furious, Nevin tossed his blade to the stone and collapsed back down on the bench. As per usual, the blade barely protested its violent dismissal with a dry thud, like knuckles rapping on a thick stone wall. He threaded shaky fingers through his tangled hair and tried to breathe through his anger.

In and out, Ishen would say. *Simple and easy. But what's easy to do, is also easy not to do.*

The warm air fought back the creeping cold, and a persistent breeze carrying the gentle lull of waves on stone soothed his waning frustration. Crying gulls could be heard even now, the hungry birds floating along on updrafts generated by the cliff's residual heat. At times, he thought he could pick out their white bodies against the backdrop of a lightless sea, but it could just as easily have been the white of cresting waves or even his overactive imagination.

Without the anger to hold them at bay, salty tears burned the corners of his eyes and Nevin buried his face in his hands and cried.

The soft sounds of sobbing stayed her hand as soon as she cracked the backdoor open.

"Nevin?" she whispered, cautiously peeking her head through the gap. The sobbing immediately ceased.

"Raiya?" said a shaky voice. "Is that you?"

Nevin sat on the raised stone bench, leaning forward with his elbows on his knees. Tears stained his cheeks, glistening weakly in Etro's pale glow. He straightened as she glided off the porch and sank down onto the bench next to him, returning her concerned smile with a weak one of his own.

Nevin wiped his face with the back of a hand. "Gods, I hope I didn't wake you. I was trying not to, I promise."

Raiya scooted closer and nudged him with her shoulder. His warmth felt good. "Don't be. I'm a light sleeper, and my bed is nowhere near as comfortable as the beach."

Relief flooded his eyes, washing away a measure of the pain she saw there. He stared out across the stone, out over the cliff's edge, out over the churning ocean some hundred feet below, and beyond the distant stars. Eyes hard and fixed on another place, another time.

"Do you . . . want to talk about it?" Her words were tentative, as if the very question would shatter him into a thousand jagged pieces.

He shrugged. "I don't know if I could explain it. I'm not even sure I know what 'it' is."

"Try."

Sighing, he nodded. "You know how, when you go into a dark room, at first you can't really see anything, but your eyes slowly become accustomed to the darkness and you can start to make out shapes and colors? You get used to the darkness, and it's like you forget what it's like to see light, and then even a dim candle seems bright?"

Raiya pulled her hair over her left shoulder and twirled the ends with her fingers. "If I spend enough time in the water, I can almost stop feeling it. It's like I'm weightless, floating on thick, warm air. Then, when I finally decide to get out, my arms and legs feel like they're filled with rocks. Kinda like that?"

"I wouldn't know. I don't know how to swim."

Raiya balked. "Wha . . . don't know how to . . ."

She waved away the matter with her hands. "We'll cross that bridge another time. Light hurts your eyes after you spend too much time in the dark. Continue."

"It's been a rough few weeks. Too much has happened. Too much has changed. A lot I've never had to deal with, a lot that *no one* should ever have to deal with. That night on the boat, it seemed like most of it was behind me. Like I was finally safe, at least for the moment. I walked up on deck, hugged my best friend Aidux, and completely lost it."

"You mean you cried? That makes sense. Sometimes tragedy needs time to sink in before we can really let ourselves feel it."

Nevin vigorously shook his head. "No, no. I mean, yeah, there was crying, but it was so much more than that. It was like I was drowning, choking on a flood of negative emotions. At first, I thought it was just like you said—the past week catching up to me. I let it happen, endured the pain, thinking that the feelings would pass on their own.

"But they just got worse."

A cold breeze whipped past and Raiya shivered. Pulling her robe tighter, she scooted into him. Nevin went rigid beneath her touch.

She didn't want him to move, so she urged him to continue. "Then what?"

Nevin shifted in his seat, but didn't pull away. "I can't exactly say. The emotions became so strong, so forceful that they pushed everything else from my mind. It got to the point where I didn't recognize where I was, who I was with. There was this weird blue mist . . . and then . . . nothing."

"Nothing?" she repeated.

"Yeah. I woke up on the beach after you rescued me, and things have been pretty good since." He didn't sound convinced.

"You say that like it's a bad thing. Nevin, I don't know what all happened to you before you got on that ship, but you survived a catastrophe!"

She laid a hand on his arm. "You don't know how lucky you are. Pieces of that ship have been washing up for days, and each piece was no bigger than a few feet long, barely a collection of nails and splinters. The fact that you survived with barely more than tattered clothing and shallow cuts is unbelievable, miraculous even!"

Nevin's troubled eyes connected with hers, and she squeezed his arm reassuringly. "I know you had friends with you, and you don't know what's become of them, but don't write them off yet. The sea is unpredictable. If I had chosen to believe like the rest of the village, if I had just accepted that everyone on your ship was dead, I may have never noticed you drifting along with the current. Braga has a way of doing things that we mortals can't possibly understand."

"That's just it, Raiya. Up until about half an hour ago, the fact that I could be the sole surviving member of the ship's passengers didn't bother me. I wasn't sad. I wasn't depressed. I wasn't even really that worried about Aidux and the rest of my friends. For some reason, it just didn't matter. It was like . . . like those emotions had ceased to exist for me.

"It's like walking into a pitch black room. At first, you strain your eyes, trying to find a glimmer of light, anything other than that endless, featureless darkness. And when you find it, even if it's just a candle, it seems so bright, so warm, to the point that, for a moment, you forget how weak it really is. As your eyes accustom to the new light, you suddenly realize that the darkness isn't really gone. It's still there, waiting for that candle to falter, waiting for the wick to burn out, waiting for that tiny moment so it can swoop back in and swallow you all over again.

"That's how I felt. I was lying there in the hammock, staring up at the stars, and it was like I could suddenly see the endless dark surrounding them, and everything just came rushing back in. Leaving home, all the fighting, the death, the explosion, that stupid sword . . ."

Disgusted, Nevin ran a hand through his hair and sighed apologetically. "I'm sorry, Raiya. I must sound like an idiot. I don't know what I'm thinking or doing."

"Don't say that," Raiya countered, taking his hand between hers. "I think anyone who has experienced tragedy is entitled to a little craziness. And if the worst thing you've done so far is throw your sword in frustration and shed a few tears, I'd have to say that you're handling your situation with bravery."

Nevin hung his head, and after a moment of silence, pulled away to put some space between them on the bench.

"And what if the worst I've done is kill people, Raiya? Would you think a murderer brave?"

Chapter 52: Opening Up to a Stranger

Murderer.

Nevin looked her dead in the eye as he said it, as if daring her to leap up from the stone bench and run back inside.

Curse you, Raiya Callicade, she thought, leaning away. *You saw a wounded bird and forgot to watch its talons.*

"What are you saying?" She gathered up the hem of her robe and crossed her arms, her hands balled tightly around the wispy fabric. "You told me you weren't the killing type."

"I—" A grimace flickered across his face and he cast his eyes to the stone. "This was a mistake. I never should have come here. My presence is putting you and your father in danger, and the last thing I want is for someone else to get hurt because of me."

Though her gaze never left his face, Raiya's eyes softened as her hand reached along her belly, pressing through the fabric of her nightclothes and down behind her belly button. She stretched her awareness out through her palm and into the swirling point of warmth beneath the skin of her taut stomach, a mass of energy that always felt far larger than the space containing it. The energy immediately reacted, reaching back with a soothing touch of reassurance, of safety, of concern from the troubled young man before her.

It was all the answer she needed.

Nevin moved to stand, but Raiya's surprisingly harsh tone gave him pause.

"Stop," she barked, clapping her hands together. "I invited you here because you needed help, and I don't regret that."

He shook his head. "You don't know everything, Raiya."

"Then I guess you'd better tell me." Her face smoothed into a stare of stern condemnation, and she almost thought she saw Nevin flinch. "You think

I'm letting you walk out into the night with little more than the rags on your back? No way. That ship don't sail. I will wrestle you back into that hammock and show you my rope tying skills, and trust me, young man, you do not want that. I've got more knots than a fish has scales."

Eyes wide with surprise, Nevin swallowed, but couldn't keep the grin from slowly parting his lips. "I think I could probably take you."

Her eyes narrowed and she leaned forward threateningly.

"You and what army?"

That got him laughing. He scratched the back of his head and nodded. "Okay, I give. You win. You and your father have been so kind to take me in, despite barely knowing me. I want to believe I left my problems back in Comelbough, but there's a chance of them following me even here."

"I don't understand."

He rubbed his clammy palms across the surface of his tattered pants.

"Then I guess I should start at the beginning."

Raiya shifted uncomfortably on the makeshift bench, the unyielding stone a poor substitute for a quality chair or even the sands along the beach. The thought of standing to flex her legs crossed her mind more than once, but she was afraid to interrupt the incredible tale spilling nearly non-stop from Nevin's lips. She found she had to close her mouth on more than one occasion.

Still, she could sense the young man wasn't being completely honest with her, could tell he was leaving out certain details of the journey that had led him to the Grotto. Nothing in those empty spaces of story caused the swirling warmth in her belly to tighten in alarm, so she quietly let him continue.

"And that's when I woke up to you." He twirled a finger before dropping both hands atop his knees with a dramatic slap.

Raiya was already absently nodding, her mind sifting through his tangled tale to set aside the chunks that didn't quite fit. "But you said you killed someone. That man in the clearing . . . he was still alive when you left."

"Not him," Nevin said.

"Who, Vincht? You can't know that. You blacked out. It's more likely this Theis or your Wizard friend killed him when they came to get you."

He shook his head and stared at his feet. "No, it was me. I don't understand how I did it, and I don't really even know how I know. But . . . I remember being there, in a way. I remember darkness, all around me, and a small circle of light. I'd been there before, back in Ishen's cabin when I first touched the sword. I stood there watching myself, like a ghost staring at that alley through a window in reality.

"The Sharasil . . . *changed* . . . shedding its hard metal exterior like a sheath of water and morphing into this burning shard of frigid light. Vincht raised his blade, but he was so slow in comparison. In the space of a breath I watched myself cross the distance between us and—"

He cut the air with the blade of his hand, the words dying in his throat. She didn't need anymore detail than that. The pained look on his face said enough.

"You could have just dreamed that, Nevin." She rested a comforting hand on his forearm, but he jerked away from her touch.

"It wasn't a dream!" He shoved to his feet, hands planted firmly on his hips as he paced around the circumference of the stone bench. "Okay, yes, I initially thought that dark, empty room was just the result of a head injury, a nightmare brought on by a concussion and stress. But I felt that same feeling when I crossed the tree bridge, and again in the alleyway. The feeling of having the world drop out from under you, of the ground leaving your feet. I said 'yes' and—"

He paused, shooting her a sideways glance before releasing a heavy sigh and dropping back down beside her. "It happened, Raiya. It was real. I decided I was going to kill that man, and I just . . . went away. And then I had to watch myself finish the job.

"But that's still not what I was talking about."

Raiya's frown enveloped her whole face. "Then who?"

"My—" He choked again, tears rolling freely down his flushed cheeks. His fingers, white-knuckled and trembling, gripped his knees. When she'd rescued him from that plank of wood just a few short hours before, his carefree attitude despite the tragedy he'd survived had made him seem mature for his years. Confident and self-assured.

But you're just a boy, aren't you, Nevin Walker? Just a boy faking his way through a life he didn't choose. And you're more afraid than you can possibly express. Raiya wiped a single tear from her own cheek and drew her robe tight around her midsection.

Nevin straightened, taking a deep breath to steady himself, a long exhale whistling softly through pursed lips. "I didn't have the best childhood. My mother died when I was very young, and the man who raised me hated me."

"You mean your father?"

He grimaced at the word. "He was never my father. He was a drunk who blamed me for killing his wife, and he spent his every waking moment making sure I knew how much he despised me for it. A father doesn't verbally abuse his children. A father doesn't piss on his kid's only blanket in winter, forcing him to choose between freezing to death or spending the night gagging from the stench."

She could practically hear his teeth grinding as he forced out the next sentence. "A father doesn't burn his child with a heated rod on the anniversary of his mother's death."

Tentatively, Raiya extended a comforting hand to his arm once more, and this time Nevin didn't pull away. Instead, he pressed his own hand to hers and squeezed.

"I learned how to deal with it. To avoid him when he was in one of his moods. To survive on my own in the woods. To ignore the pain, the bruises, the cuts and just live as best I could.

"I hated him, but I didn't want him dead. I just . . . I wanted to leave. I wanted to see the world, wanted to find a place for myself that wasn't all pain and fear. But I was stuck, so I made due. He wasn't the smartest man, and drunk more often than not, so the past year wasn't all that bad. I thought I'd outgrown him, outsmarted him.

"Turns out he'd just been quietly watching me. Waiting to find a way to hurt me more than he'd ever been able to before."

He looked at his feet again, grinding his boots against the loose flecks of limestone scattered out across the overlook. "I'd been sleeping in the barn for years, waking up before the sun to get my chores done. Dalen . . . that was his name. Dalen always slept in, so the mornings were often the best part of my day. I liked the quiet."

He flinched, and Raiya tightened her grip on his arm. "His boot woke me the morning all this started. A hard kick to the ribs. I was half-asleep, disoriented, confused. Still, it didn't take me long to realize he was already drunk on his feet. He must have been drinking all night.

"He said, 'You're a little sneak, you know that?' I tried to stand, but he clocked me here, right in the jaw." He rubbed just to the left of his chin. "Damn near knocked me out, but adrenaline kept me conscious, woke me up. I tried to get away, but I was already up against the wall. I'd learned it was better to run than to face him. I was stronger than him, bigger for sure, but he'd gone out of his way to teach me that fighting back would only make things worse for me in the long run.

"He tried to kick me but lost his balance. I scrambled past him toward the door but we got tangled up in each other. Dalen always kept this bronze canteen with him, a gift from my mother. It was the one thing of his I knew better than to touch, but somehow, as I rushed past him, my arm got caught in the leather strap and I ripped it free."

Nevin slurred his words as he grunted out Dalen's threats. "'Drop it, boy, or the next one's against your head.' For a second, I thought about keeping it. Though about running out the door and burying it somewhere deep in the woods where he'd never find it. But before I could decide, he said something else."

"What?" she whispered.

"He said, 'Then I'll go find that little friend of yours and put a blade right between those big, silver eyes of his.'"

Nevin cocked his head, his eyes unfocused and watery as he stared out across the ocean, like he could somehow see all the way back to that distant farmhouse from his past. His shoulders twitched, rising slowly at first, moving along with his breath, reaching higher and higher with each increasingly labored inhalation until his shirt nearly scraped his ears. His fists clenched and unclenched against his thighs.

Raiya lowered her eyes, fighting against the urge to reach out and hug him despite the awkwardness of barely knowing him.

After a moment, he stilled.

"For the first time since I could remember, I fought back. Not for me, not to save myself, but to protect someone I cared about. I reared back with that bronze canteen and swung it right at the side of that bastard's head. He dropped like a sack of apples. Blood literally pouring out of his face, and I . . . I just stood there, staring at him. He didn't move. I think I watched him for five or six minutes, but he never so much as twitched. So I ran."

She shook her head. "You don't know that you killed him. You might have just knocked him out, like the man in the clearing. And even so, he was threatening you and someone you cared about, and had shown himself to be the type of person to carry out those threats. You acted in self-defense."

"It doesn't matter. Elbin is gone and everyone in it, dead." He sighed. "Everyone but me and Aidux, that is."

Raiya didn't know how she'd feel if she was in his position. She'd never had to deal with the sort of terrible things he'd experienced as a child. Growing up, her parents were tough, but loving and kind. Her mother had shown her what it meant to care for those around her, and her father had taught her how to unapologetically love herself. Never once had they so much as raised their hand to her, so she couldn't even begin to understand the pain and confusion the young man beside her had dealt with on a daily basis.

As the minutes ticked by in silence, an idea struck her. *Maybe it was time for a lighter topic.*

"Hey, you wanna see why this area is named the 'White Crystal Shores?'"

"Sure," he said, his voice flat, thoroughly drained of all emotional content.

Raiya quickly glided back into the house. Her father no longer sat alone in the darkness, likely having watched enough of the situation to recognize she could handle things before returning to bed. She retrieved the object she was looking for from the window sill and hurried back to her place beside Nevin. She noticed he'd returned the sword to his side. It was propped against the bench at his hip.

"Here, give me your hands."

She gingerly placed a chunk of softly but strongly glowing crystal in Nevin's open palms. Squinting against the silvery light swirling beneath the crystal's highly polished surface, Nevin leaned forward in awe. To her delight, Raiya watched the light erase the trouble in his eyes.

"Is this what was sitting on the windowsill by the painting supplies?"

"Mmm-hmm."

"It's beautiful . . . what is it?"

"We call it 'Soul Quartz'. It grows on the shorelines near Calibri Grotto. Tiny flakes of Soul Quartz and sand mix together to form the White Crystal Shores. Sometimes you can find pieces about the size of your thumbnail in the sand, but pieces like this are far too big to wash up on shore."

Nevin turned it over in his hands. "How did you get this one?"

He didn't notice the smile wither from her lips. "Well, I was out diving one day, and I saw it poking up out of the sand about a hundred feet from the beach. I knocked it free with the butt of my spear, and it's been sitting there by the window ever since."

"It didn't seem like it was glowing yesterday."

Raiya tugged at the edges of her robe in response to a brief gust of chill air. "It only glows under certain circumstances, and even then, it's difficult to tell if it's glowing under direct sunlight."

He looked around. "So, what makes Soul Quartz glow?"

She shrugged. "Shaper Jarell thought it may have something to do with spiritual energy, though there's a legend that says if you place one in your window, it will begin to glow a few days before someone in the household will die."

Nevin flinched like he'd been struck by a whip. "Does that mean I . . . or your father . . . Oh gods, don't tell me . . ."

Raiya silenced him with a short laugh. "No, no, that's not why it's glowing now, though I appreciate your concern. I said it was a legend. Superstition, nothing more.

"There is, however, one thing that always causes Soul Quartz to glow." She pointed to his sword. "The presence of enchanted items."

"Magic, huh." Nevin shifted the blade back between his legs with one hand, holding the crystal with reverence in the other.

"But," she said, tapping the crystal with a finger. "I've never seen it glow this brightly before. Your sword must be very powerful."

Nevin's face hardened, losing the awe it held only moments before. He pressed the crystal into her waiting palm, closing her fingers around it.

"Yes, I'm sure it is."

Raiya mentally cursed herself. She'd finally managed to cheer him up, and one misstep had pushed his mood back into melancholy. Fortunately, it only lasted a moment.

Nevin nudged her with his shoulder and offered her a weak smile, as if sensing her unease. "So, who's the painter in the family?"

"That would be me," she answered, relieved.

"You're very good. How long have you been working on the one inside?"

"On and off again, for a month or two. It's almost done. I just need to make some more blue paint. Before I found you, I was planning on looking for some dyers' crook, a plant whose fruit can be used to make a wide variety of blues and purples. I have since been too distracted to search."

"Maybe tomorrow we could go for a hike and I can help you look. You know, to show you how much I appreciate being saved."

Raiya grinned. "I guess that means you're planning on sticking around?"

He shrugged. "You're still okay with having me around, after hearing my story?"

"For a little while at least. I don't want you to overstay your welcome, but it would be awful of me to just kick you out, knowing you have nowhere to go." She scrunched up her nose. "Especially in *that* outfit."

It was his turn to grin. "Thank you, Raiya. I don't know where I'd be without you."

"Uh, probably still floating around on a piece of broken wood."

Chapter 53: The Best Team

Maddox Blaine swayed lazily in the saddle with each step of his dappled bay, eyes closed and head tilted back. His clean-shaven cheeks elongated his already thin face, matching his lanky arrow-straight frame to a tee. He might have been persuaded to grow a beard in his younger years, but any hairs that sprouted from his chin now emerged stark white and clashed with the coffee-brown waves of hair falling carefree across his narrow shoulders.

Sighing with contentment, Maddox happily absorbed the warm afternoon rays of sunlight. The final days of the Waking were drawing swiftly to a close, and the growing warmth of each day signaled the arrival of the Tending, and the hottest months of the year.

Still, today was perfect. Not too hot, not too windy, and not a speck of dark, swollen clouds overhead to mar his high mood.

The five horses trailed a line of u-shaped depressions in the soft dirt on the road west, the brown earth yielding less and less to their iron horseshoes with each new mile. The cattails and white oak abundant in the marshes surrounding the road had steadily surrendered to elm, low-lying shrubs, and long-blade grasses. Behind them, a ceiling of featureless gray clouds extended as far as the peaks of the vaulted Granite Towers. A chorus of rock grouse called to each other from hidden perches, apparently just as pleased as Maddox at the beautiful Waking weather.

Still, the group hadn't moved far enough from the marsh to completely eliminate the sticky scent of damp earth, but Maddox was doing his best to focus his attention elsewhere.

"Enjoy it while it lasts, my friends," he said to the other four, an odd-looking group ranging in age, sex, and size. First, there was Gibbs, a gangly youth whose blonde beard was nearly invisible lest the sunlight catch his face at the right angle. Maddox had always thought Gibbs a cocky little bastard, far too self-assured for a man whose mother could lick him in a straight fight, but no amount of putting him in his place could curb the upstart's scathing tongue, and his quick wit and extensive knowledge had come in handy on more than one occasion.

Miles, a potbellied geezer whose occasional violent snore would cause his horse to jerk in surprise, trailed a few paces behind. The old man was about the toughest son-of-a-bitch Maddox had ever met, possessing an indefatigable constitution enviable by men a third his age. Miles credited his energy levels to his frequent naps, and with as often as Maddox caught the man sleeping, he was starting to believe him.

Beside Maddox rode Delia, a thickset beauty chewing the remnants of an apple core and layered in an abundance of black-dyed leather plates. Delia had the uncanny ability to see through bullshit, an invaluable asset to someone raising three children. Maddox had relied on her to keep the rest of the crew in line for years, as none of them were brave enough to cross her when the mom voice came out.

Maddox included.

The last, Maddox's son Arolde, posed vigilantly in his saddle at the head of the procession, idly stroking the night-black mane of his chestnut gelding. His younger clone ignored him as he addressed the group, in much the same manner as he'd ignored him since they set out that morning.

"In a few days," Maddox continued, "we'll be right back where we started —wet, cold, and wondering why in the name of the gods we ever bothered to return."

"Don't remind me," Delia groaned, chucking aside her spent apple, the naked core whizzing between him and the head of his horse. "I've been begging for any reason to leave town for over a month now. I need this vacation, Maddox, so try not to ruin it by constantly reminding me it's going to end sooner rather than later."

"Vacation?" sneered Gibbs, twisting back in his saddle. "Weren't you just in Garla Mill two months ago?"

"Pssh." Miles wiped the sleep-drool from his chin and tugged on his reins, as if attempting to correct some invisible heading miscalculation on his horse's part. To the beast's credit, it mostly just ignored him, protesting with a whinny and flip of its head. "Garla Mill ain't no vacation. Tick-tick-tick, day and night, nonstop. Don't know how them folk sleep with all those spinning windmills and their blasted ticking. It's little wonder the place is known for its whiskey."

Gibbs shot Miles a dirty look. "Windmills don't tick, you daffy twit. Their mechanisms convert smooth rotational energy along a perpendicular axis in an effort to turn a stone wheel for the purposes of milling grain or pumping water. If anything, the sounds produced by a properly functioning windmill would be akin to a ceaseless grinding or throaty burble."

Miles shook a fist at him. "There you go again with all them 'big city' words. Us simple folk got no use for them fancy words out here. You wanna say something, you just out and say it! Don't need you showin' me your 'diculars and swingin' round your axes and what not!"

"It's 'axis', you utter doorknob."

Maddox held his tongue. Getting involved in arguments between these two always turned out to be harmful to his mental health, but as a form of cheap entertainment, there wasn't much better.

Gibbs wasn't done. "Language exists as a method of delivering information, and specific words exist for a specific reason! Not all of us want to limit ourselves with a hundred word vocabulary."

"'Cabulary or not, them windmills tick! Mildred's cousin Lars spent a fortnight in Garla Mill hunting demperhogs last Fading, and said it took him nearly a week to get used to all the damn noise and get in a good night's sleep."

"Mildred's cousin . . ." Gibbs rubbed a bony hand down his face. "What are you on about now? Mildred's *your* sister, which means Lars is *your* cousin."

Miles wagged a finger. "*Half*-sister."

Gibbs looked about ready to explode. "YOU'RE TWINS!!!! She's literally you in a cheap wig!"

"Bah." The old man picked at his ear. "That's not the way I remember it."

The scrawny youth's face flushed so red, Maddox was surprised it didn't explode in a spray of hot blood. He cleared his throat. "You know, Delia did just come from Garla Mill. I bet she'd be willing to clear up this question of clicking windmills if you'd ask."

He could see her fists tightening on her reins out of the corner of his eye. She released a tense laugh and glared daggers at Maddox. "Don't you dare drag me into this. They're doing just fine without me."

"It's just as well," Miles mumbled under his breath, just loud enough for Gibbs to hear. "Don't need mama bear's input to know that windmills click."

The metallic twinge of a knife leaving its sheath rang out in the suddenly electric air, and Gibbs urged his gelding towards the old man. "That's it, ya old coot! I'm about to click this here knife—"

"GIBBS! Will you, for once, just SHUT UP?!"

Freezing in his saddle, Gibbs sheepishly lowered his eyes before the withering glare of Arolde, who had turned around in his saddle to face the mouthy young man. Gibbs maneuvered his horse back into position and slipped his short knife back in his hip sheath, hanging his head like scolded child. Maddox knew that wouldn't last long, a mile at best. Delia happily pondered the sky, while Miles went back to fiddling with his reins.

Maddox scratched at the scruff growing unchecked below his chin. "Well, well. He finally speaks. For awhile there, I was wondering if you were going to ride all the way to Calibri Grotto without a word to any of us. I dare say, now that I've tasted the sweetness of your voice, I don't know if I can stand another minute without it."

"Shove it, Maddox. I've got enough of a headache from listening to these two idiots. I really don't need your own special brew of sarcasm to make the pounding any louder."

Arolde turned back around, flicking the reins to urge his horse to speed up a bit. The rest of the party followed suit.

Gibbs gave a low whistle. "You gonna take that from him, Mads? If I ever talked like that to my old man . . ." He ran a finger across his neck and flopped his tongue out of the side of his mouth.

Maddox held his hands up. "Hey, I'm not leading this excursion. That honor belongs to the man at the head of the pack here. Just a visiting officiant."

"The boss must be gettin' daft, putting a boy in a man's place of power." Miles dropped the reins and reached out, pulling on his horse's ear. In response, the horse whipped his head around and bit him on the leg. "OW! Stupid animal! I'm the rider here! I give the orders!"

Maddox pointed a disapproving finger at the old man. "Careful, Miles. Talk like that can get a man in trouble. The boss may be open-minded, but he doesn't like it when people question his intelligence. You don't want one of the younger members here taking something you said out of context and relaying it back to him, would you?"

He cast a pointed look in Gibbs' direction.

"Now, now, you know I meant no harm by it," the old man said in response to Gibbs' sneer. "All I'm saying is I don't understand why he'd put young Arolde here in command, and still asked you to come along. It don't make a bean of sense. You're basically the boss' go-to-guy, his right hand. Why are you here if you aren't givin' the orders?"

"He's a spy." Arolde turned in his saddle again. "The boss isn't sure if I'm ready for leadership yet, so he sent Maddox along to make sure I don't do anything stupid, that I get the job done right."

"You can call me 'father' sometimes, son. Honest. I don't mind."

Arolde rolled his eyes and turned back to the road.

Gibbs smoothed down the unruly hairs of his fuzzy beard. "What's the boss want with some kid anyway? Nerrick or whatever. Or is it that big sword of his that he's after?"

Maddox waited a few seconds to see if his son would answer that question, then shrugged. "Kid's name is Nevin. And I don't know. Either way, we find one, we find the other, and he made it sound like they were both important in some way."

"And how's he know this 'Nevin' is in Calibri Grotto?"

The old man barked a raspy laugh. "How's the boss *ever* know what he knows? He just knows! That's why he's the boss!"

Maddox shook his head. "I don't think he *does* know exactly where this kid is. We aren't the only crew he sent out. Vox and Eden are out looking. Orlen's daughter, too."

Gibbs sat up straighter in his saddle. "Merissa's looking?"

It was Miles' turn to sneer. "Keep it in your pants, Gibbs. A girl like Merissa would never want nothing to do with a stick like you."

"I'll have you know that Merissa and I are very close."

Delia and Maddox shared a doubtful look.

"Yeah, close as in you follow her around like a lost puppy and she feels sorry for you on account of your lack of friends." Miles' laughter almost unseated him from his saddle.

"*Gibbs . . .*" cautioned Delia as the younger man's hand inched toward his knife again.

Miles wiped the tears from his eyes and continued. "Besides, I hear she's got an eye for ol' Arolde, though he seems just about as keen on her as she is in Gibbs . . ."

"Merissa's fine," Arolde barked, waving a hand dismissively. "She's just not very interesting."

Delia grunted. "Likely the very thing Gibbs finds attractive."

Maddox knuckled his smile. "There's a good chance we'll find this kid in Calibri Grotto. The boss doesn't send his best team out looking in the least likely places."

Arolde cursed. "Best team, my ass . . ."

"So, we reach the fishing village by this time tomorrow. Enjoy the weather while you can." Maddox closed his eyes again, and leaned back in the saddle. "I know I'll be soaking up as much of this beautiful sunlight as I possibly can."

Arolde looked back over his shoulder. "Don't let all the flapping jaws distract you from you vacation, *father*."

Maddox just smiled pleasantly.

"Will all of you *please* shut up for awhile?" Delia barked, but Miles was already asleep, and Arolde was back to ignoring them.

Chapter 54: Decisions

"Oh, stop whining, you big baby," Raiya teased, splashing at Nevin playfully. "That little fish is *not* going to hurt you."

"Little?!" Nevin shouted from the shoreline, the warm sea water barely washing over his bare toes. He'd somehow managed to lodge his oddly shaped sword firmly into the soft sands, a pillar of lusterless metal reaching up to the sky.

He liked the old clothes Raiya's father had loaned him: a sleeveless tan pullover and a pair of loose cotton breeches cut off just above the knee. They weren't the best clothes, but Raiya said he'd be much more comfortable hiking and foraging and learning to swim in these than in his tattered Elbin outfit. She'd forced him to leave his boots back at the house. For some reason, she told it would do him good to toughen up his feet, even though it meant listening to him constantly complain about rough surfaces and stickers, and practically slowed their travel time down to a snail's pace on anything but sand and smoothed rock.

Spending the last two days with Raiya in and around Calibri Grotto had lifted some of the considerable weight bearing down on his thoughts and emotions. He hadn't slept much after their heart-to-heart talk on the porch that night, but that wasn't to say he hadn't felt better.

In truth, the thoughts that kept him awake were not of his friends and the explosion that separated them. Mostly, he thought of her. Hanging a few feet off the porch in his hammock, blankets heaped atop his ankles, Nevin spent the remaining few hours before dawn replaying their conversations in his mind: their talks on the way into the village, the meeting with her father, and her most recent attempt to dispel his suddenly raging emotions.

Other than Aidux, he'd never known what it was like to have a friend. Even then, the lynx could never fully understand his life; cats just didn't have to deal with same problems as humans. With Raiya, he had developed a connection to another person like he'd never felt before. Not with Ishen, not with Aidux, and definitely not with his parents.

He'd never had so much fun in his life.

Walking barefoot through lush emerald fields and pastures, Raiya had taught him which herbs and wildflowers could be used to make specific colors of paint, and how picking them in different stages of growth or from different types of soil affects a pigment's shade and intensity. He found her knowledge of medical herbs rivaled even that of Ishen's. Nevin challenged her to a mock-sword fight using a pair of giant reed shoots they'd found in the shallows where the Mossalnag River met the shore. Afterwards, Raiya used the reed's tough leaves to wrap fish and wild potatoes for baking.

Little time was spent picking their way through the grasslands in comparison to the hours spent combing the beaches east of the town. Raiya never mentioned his friends, and he assumed she thought he stayed on the beaches in the hopes of spotting evidence of other survivors. There was truth in that assumption. He genuinely hoped to find signs that someone else had made it away from the shipwreck alive, but the main reason he preferred the prismatic sands of the White Crystal Shores to the green fields and hillsides further inland was far simpler.

Tender feet. But he wasn't about to tell *her* that.

It wasn't long before their beach strolls had evolved into swimming lessons. Actually, it began with Raiya tricking him into planting his sword in the sand, and then tackling and dragging him out into the frothy shallows. After an embarrassing amount of flailing and forcing an uncomfortable amount of saltwater through his nostrils, Nevin had finally learned enough to keep his head above the surface. Within the hour, he was adept enough that the lessons took on a more playful tone—fighting and splashing until they both collapsed on the shore.

He enjoyed his time in the water, and not just because it meant more time with Raiya. The burn on his right hand had grown more irritated with each passing day, and submerging it beneath the waves eased the near constant heat that had spread past his wrist. It was more annoying than anything, and he'd resolved to mention it to Raiya should it not start getting better soon.

Later that night, their stomachs full of baked fish and wild potatoes, Nevin and Raiya had fallen asleep beneath the stars. To his delight, the only dreams he experienced vanished like a light mist before the rising sun.

Raiya rolled her eyes. "Yes, little! That fish wasn't even as big as my hand. What's a fish that size gonna do against a scary swordsman like you?"

Hands planted on his hips, Nevin glared at Raiya through narrowed eyes, but his wide-lipped smile belied his ire. "That fish was *not* little. He was a vicious, big-toothed monster, and I swear he tried to take a bite out of my leg!"

"Oh, you mean it brushed you with its tail as it casually swam past."

"That is *not* what happened!" He turned, pointing out a tiny scrape on the back of his knee. "Look, look. You see this? See the teeth marks?"

Raiya covered her mouth in mock horror. "Oh my, I had no idea. You're lucky you made it out of the water alive, and with your leg mostly intact." The final part of Raiya's sarcastic retort was almost lost in a fit of hysterical laughter.

Nevin just smiled and shook his head. "You think you're *so* clever, don't you? Making fun of the injured. What if I came in there and took a bite out of your leg?"

"No, no, please don't!" she said between giggles. "I don't want that fish to come back and finish you off!"

"That's it!" Nevin slogged through the incoming waves after a rapidly fleeing Raiya. By the time he'd reached her position, Raiya's lean form and strawberry-blond hair had disappeared beneath the swirling blue water.

He was beginning to doubt her human heritage. Certainly his new friend was part fish.

The surface wasn't nearly still enough to make out an elusive swimming girl lurking somewhere beneath the froth and waves. He swatted at the water, sweeping his hand back and forth a few times before cursing his stupidity. He couldn't just clear away the water like a dust-shrouded window. He waded farther and farther from the shore, until the sandy seafloor vanished out from under him and he had to tread water to remain afloat.

"OW!!!" Nevin briefly disappeared beneath surface, reemerging with a giggling Raiya. "The heck!? Did you really just bite me?"

She offered him an exaggerated shrug. "I just wanted to make you even."

With her lips parted in a child-like grin, Raiya easily pulled free of his grasp and slipped back beneath the waves.

Nevin's mouth opened to call her back, but a sudden burning sensation swelled in his right hand. He flinched, flexing his tender fingers. He thumbed the raised blister on the tip of his index finger again. Something caught his fingernail this time, something small and sharp.

A splinter.

Hot agony barreled up his arm to the elbow, and the skin immediately flushed a bright, angry red. Sucking air, he cradled the arm to his chest, kicking his legs hard to stay afloat. Being underwater eased the searing pain, but only just.

He wiped his face and flexed his stinging hand. *Where did that come from?*

Fire ignited beneath his skin once more, but this time a torrent of bubbles boiled the water around him. Nevin screamed in pain, a brief cry cut short by a mouthful of ocean. He squeezed his eyes closed against the sting of salt water and sank like a rock, the pain erasing his elementary understanding of swimming and leaving him at the mercy of instinct.

His lungs burned in concert with the pain in his arm as he flailed about. A disconcerting lack of noticeable gravity turned up into down, down into up. If he started swimming in the wrong direction now, he might very well swim out to sea or knock himself cold on the bottom, and then where would he be?

He cracked his eyelids, hoping to glimpse the surface, but an impenetrable wall of roiling bubbles surrounded him like a cloak of death, and the salt in his eyes hurt almost as much as the flames searing their way toward his shoulder.

He squeezed his eyes shut, the effort gaining him nothing. He needed to do something, and fast. This pain was nothing, he told himself. Dalen had hurt him worse than this. Setting his jaw, Nevin wrenched his eyes wide despite the gritty burn and jerked his head around. Millions of tiny bubbles pored out of the inflamed skin of his right arm, spiraling around him in a chaotic, obscuring cloud.

He squinted through them. *Dammit.* Sand and grit kicked up by their horseplay had made it impossible to see.

His lungs ached for air, bullying his mind to overrule his instincts and allow the tiniest of breaths to sneak its way down his throat, to ease his suffering one way or another. With every passing second, that aggravated voice grew more and more insistent, and Nevin was beginning to see the wisdom in listening.

A darkness different from that which hung behind his eyelids closed in.

Just gonna sit there and let yourself drown?

He jerked his head in the direction of the voice. *I can't see anything! What do you want me to do?*

A shadowy presence glided closer, hovering just within reach. He didn't need to open his eyes to know it was there. He could sense it in his bones.

No decision is still a decision.

He could feel the sadistic grin spreading its pallid lips.

Or shall I offer my help again?

Nevin furiously kicked his legs, propelling him through the heart of the shadowy figure. The entity evaporated with an amused cackle.

Never again.

Arm pressed against his chest, Nevin slogged forward. There was no way to know if he'd chosen the right direction, but the voice was right. Doing nothing earned him nothing. Better to be wrong on his own terms than to fail by default.

The flames in his right hand exploded in a painful crescendo, and it took every ounce of his waning will not to suck in a lungful of water. He gripped his burning wrist with his good hand, his legs slowing.

The last bits of breath leaked through his lips, the larger bubbles mixing readily into the maelstrom surrounding him.

Chapter 55: A Sliver of Fire

An arm encircled his waist and pulled. Nevin opened his stinging eyes and was immediately relieved to see Raiya's face emerge from the cloud of bubbles. Within moments, he was gulping mouthfuls of air in between whimpers of agony.

Raiya heaved him ashore, digging her heels in the sand in an effort to pull him clear of the water. Nevin did his best to help, his wounded arm quivering against his chest. The searing pain had ceased its upward climb, but the flesh below his elbow felt raw, hot, and filled with holes. She dropped him on his back and knelt at his side.

"Blisters, redness, peeling." She frowned down at his wounded limb, hesitant to reach out and actually probe the inflamed skin. "Nevin, your arm looks someone doused it in burning lamp oil. What happened out there?"

Groaning, he shook his head. "It's not my arm, it's my hand! It feels like it's on fire."

She gingerly reached out and lifted the arm off his chest. Nevin winced at her gentle touch, but didn't fight back. All the hair below the shoulder was gone, singed clean off. The skin above his elbow was red and covered in tiny pus-filled blisters. Below his elbow looked much the same, but the blisters increased in number closer to his wrist, and many had already burst.

But it was his hand that caused his eyes to widen in fear. Deep ruts broke the skin where the intense heat had split the flesh like a charred sow, and the remaining skin was the color of fresh blood. A sliver of crimson light glimmered at the tip of his previously irritated index finger, and a thin stream of smoke spilled out from the light, vanishing almost instantly on the breeze.

"What *is* that?" Raiya leaned in, squinting.

"Just get it out!" He squirmed in the sand, blackness creeping in on the edges of his vision. His hand was ruined, he could already tell, but the only concern he had at the moment was being free of the unbearable heat radiating out from that infernal red light.

Raiya leaned in close, drawing the thin fillet knife he'd seen her use to clean fish from the sheath on her hip. The red light added a wicked gleam to its honed edge, and Nevin felt his eyes widen ever further as she dug its tip into the ruined flesh of his finger. Blackened skin crumbled painlessly away, with each twist of her blade leaving him with less and less of a finger.

Finally, she carefully extracted a smoking shard of red light. As soon as it was free of his hand, the glow flickered and died, leaving behind a mildly warm fleck of transparent crystal barely the width of a human hair.

Raiya put a hand to his chest and forced him onto his back. "You're in shock, Nevin, and right now that's protecting you from feeling most of the damage to your arm. You're not going to want to be awake when reality sets in, but with any luck, it won't come to that."

He returned an uncertain nod. Adrenaline was acting as a buffer between him and the pain, but he could already feel his heart beginning to slow, and the full extent of his injuries was becoming clearer. He was mere moments away from his whimpers shifting into uncontrolled screaming.

"This is going to feel a little . . . odd at first." Raiya trailed her fingers along his shoulder and down his wounded arm, before spreading them along the blistered and peeling skin of his forearm. Nevin winced, but didn't pull away. "I feel stupid saying this, but try to relax."

Nevin barked a laugh and wiped the tears from his cheeks. "Easier said than—"

An electric wave of energy rushed through his arm and out into the rest of his body, and Nevin arched his back in surprise. Warm tingles vibrated across his skin and down through his bones until he could feel every inch of his flesh respond. The undulating wave flowed over him again and again like a horde of tiny, buzzing insects, but as strange as the sensation was, it didn't hurt.

He looked up into Raiya's lidded eyes, and could just barely see a hint of lavender light swirling in the blackness of her pupils. He wanted to ask her what she was doing to him, but the electric tingles had robbed him of his ability to speak and placed him firmly at the mercy of whatever magic she was pouring into his ruined arm.

Within moments, his aches had vanished. The tender remnants of bruises and strains had quieted. His eyes discarded the sting of salt water and even the puffiness from crying subsided.

He looked down at his arm in disbelief. Blisters emptied and shrank before disappearing entirely. The glossy sheen of his skin grew more and more muted as the redness retreated.

Raiya closed her eyes and drew his blackened hand up between both of hers. A fresh wave of tingles danced up his arm, and flecks of charred flesh fell away, revealing unadulterated skin beneath. The electric tingles grew in intensity until he couldn't stand it any longer.

"Okay! Okay! That tickles!" he said, pulling his hand free from hers and laughing. He flexed his sensitive fingers and marveled at what he was seeing.

The hand looked and felt brand new. He could feel the warmth of the sunlight on his fresh skin, feel the wind threading through his fingers, feel the gentle thrum of blood moving just beneath the surface.

The young woman pulled her ponytail over her shoulder and slumped back on her knees, her feet splayed out beside her. "That does it," she said with a huff. "Any more and I'll need a nap."

"You healed me!" Grinning, Nevin sat up and thumbed the missing tip of his index finger where the glowing shard had been buried. Unlike the rest of his hand, the finger was glossy and shriveled, and ended abruptly in a shrunken nub. He'd lost nearly half an inch of flesh and bone, and he doubted he'd be getting it back.

Might make things awkward for a bit, but I'm no stranger to performing with injuries. Dalen made sure of that.

She reached out and grabbed his hand, giving it a once over herself. "I'm sorry, Nevin. It's not a perfect process, but I did what I could."

"Sorry?" He shook his head and beamed at her. "Raiya, you're amazing! Why didn't you tell me you could use magic? I mean, your dad can, so I should have suspected it might run in the family, but *never* would have had expected you to—"

The blackness lurking at the edges of his vision returned, and Nevin's head swam.

"Whoa, take it easy." Raiya reached out to steady him. "The healing process takes a lot out of you. Most people with wounds like yours pass out afterward."

Nevin focused on his breathing, driving the encroaching darkness back with each exhale. After a moment, his light-headedness faded, and he offered Raiya a reassuring smile. "I think I'm okay. Just caught me off guard is all."

He blinked at her. "What was I talking about?"

Raiya scrunched her nose in amusement. "Let's get you to your feet."

"Oh, that's just mean."

After ensuring he wasn't going to collapse as soon as she let him go, Raiya raised an open palm and presented the tiny sliver of red crystal to him. "This is what was in your finger."

He peered down at it quizzically. "What do you think it is?"

She tugged on the tip of her ponytail. "While I've never seen it myself, I'd guess this to be a sliver of Ignocite."

"Ignocite?" Something about the word sounded familiar, but he couldn't place it.

"A form of Orlicite. There's five altogether, and Ignocite is solidified Ignolis energy."

His blank look inspired her to extrapolate.

"Sorry. I forget you come from a place with no magic. Ignolis is fire, kinda. Still, I'm less worried about what it is and more concerned with where it came from. Do you think maybe it's a remnant of whatever happened to the ship?"

He must have shaken his head a little too quickly for her taste, because she planted her free hand on her hip and shot him a withering stare. "This is magic, Nevin. Magic in a stable, physical, portable form. Magic had something to do with whatever happened on that ship. A great magical explosion. Sounds to me like something fire would be really good at."

"Maybe, but I think the explanation is a little more proximate than that."

"Proximate," she repeated, lips pursed. "Now you're just showing off."

He knuckled a smile. "I just mean I think the cause is a bit more close to home." He pointed back over her shoulder to the faint wisp of black staining the otherwise cloud-free sky.

It took her a second to figure out what he meant. "The burning cabin?"

He nodded, holding up his stubby finger. "I touched the wall. At the time, I thought I'd just burned myself, but over the past few days, I couldn't help but feel like I had a splinter, and my hand felt inflamed and sensitive. I think whatever event killed the four people in that cabin and scorched the interior also embedded hundreds of tiny shards of Ignocite in the walls. If they are small enough, you wouldn't even be able to see them beneath the soot. It might also explain why the walls still burn."

She shook her head. "It doesn't work like that, Nevin. Orlicite is entirely inert until acted upon by an injection of both intent and will. In fact, they are almost indistinguishable from normal gemstones unless you really know what to look for."

"Then how do you know that's Ignocite?"

"I mean, the burned flesh, smoke, red glow . . . kinda gave it away."

Nevin cleared his throat and glanced sheepishly at his feet. *That was a stupid question.* "Okay, but . . . if it really *is* Ignocite, you said that cabin's been burning for days. Can you just will it to burn and walk away? What keeps it from stopping?"

Raiya's mouth closed just as quickly as it opened. "You've got me there. That's probably a question for my father."

It wasn't his only question. Too many aspects of the situation didn't add up. Why had the shard in his finger been mostly inactive over the past few days, even while the ones buried in the cabin's interior walls still smoldered? And why had it suddenly ramped up its output today? What was different, and what had changed?

Nevin ran his thumb around the shriveled edges of his stubby finger, weary from a day of searching the beaches and playing with Raiya and drained by the magical repairs she'd made to his hand and arm. He dreaded the walk back into town, knowing that making the journey by meadow meant irritating his tender feet, and choosing to spare them by walking through the sands meant losing even more of his limited energy to the shifting, uneven ground.

His questions would have to wait. Nevin walked over and yanked his sword free from the sand. "Let's head back. I could use a nap, and I'd like to pick your father's ear."

Chapter 56: Avoiding Harm

Raiya knew something was different as soon they set foot in town.

Their westward trek along the rim of the chalky white cliffs chased the fading sun through the darkening lapis sky. The diminishing daylight had brought life to the streets of Calibri Grotto. Leather-skinned men and women carrying stringers of colorful fish trudged between houses, offering nothing more than a weary smile and nod to other villagers as they passed. A mule-drawn cart filled with bins of charcoal rolled along the serpentine streets, occasionally stopping to make a drop off or visit with a customer. A young woman watered a flower box filled with pink and red variegated tulips.

On any normal day, Raiya could expect an uncomfortable reception from the townspeople. Pity-filled stares regarding her from street-sides and doorways, endless conversations concerning the wisdom of her father and the similarities she shared with her mother, and condescending queries into her lack of interest in the town's male population. They watched her closer than a shark in the shallows.

After dealing with it for so many years, Raiya didn't realize how much she'd taken their undeviating responses to her presence for granted. It had become an integral—if undesired—facet of her reality.

And when the attention of every single person in town suddenly shifted from her to her new companion, an uncomfortable heaviness in the pit of her stomach alerted her that the scales of reality had shifted.

Maybe it was just curiosity—a new face in a small community. Maybe it was the sight of the massive blade mounted across his back. Maybe it was the simple fact that she had finally taken an interest in male companionship.

Either way, she found the shift in attentions unnerving.

Nevin seemed to notice it too. "Do I really look that silly in your father's clothes?"

Raiya scrunched up her nose. "I don't want to say 'yes', but those pants aren't very flattering."

He smiled absently. "You think you're so funny."

She clapped her hands together excitedly. "Since we headed back earlier than expected, I didn't have a chance to catch us dinner. Luckily, I just so happened to bring a few shils with me, so I thought we might pop by a few vendors and buy the necessary ingredients for a special dinner. I'm thinking potatoes, wild onions, a little rosemary . . ."

Nevin, though, wasn't really listening.

"I haven't gotten this much attention since . . ." His words and feet trailed to halt on the final step of a curved stairway.

She squeezed around him, tugging on his arm as she passed, but Nevin didn't budge. "Come on. We'll pick up some food and head back. I'll whip us up a tasty meal and you can relax. And don't forget! Daddy did promise to get you some proper clothes while we were gone. Who knows? Maybe he found you something in a delightful checkered print."

Her encouraging smile went entirely unnoticed. With a furrowed brow and distant eyes, Nevin's countenance had taken on a cautious edge.

"Is something wrong?"

He didn't look at her for a long moment, choosing instead to stare out over the twisting townscape like a hunter spying the movement of some camouflaged prey. Tugging on her ponytail, Raiya followed his gaze, but the late hour had turned out the populace in force, and she couldn't pick out anything noteworthy. She searched the swirling warmth in the pit of her stomach, but that afternoon's bout of healing had left it nearly out of reach of her mental probings.

"Nevin?" She reached out and gently brushed his arm with her fingers.

That soft touch seemingly brought him back to life. A thin smile touched his lips as he folded into a weary lean. "Sorry about that. I think I'm just more worn out than I thought."

"I told you. I'm still surprised you didn't pass out."

"I may still." He scratched the back of his head. "I think . . . would you be mad at me if I headed back early? Met up with you after?"

Raiya wanted to tell him no, to tease him until he relented and accompanied her into the lower part of town. She inadvertently dropped her gaze to his scarred finger. She couldn't help but feel somewhat responsible for his lasting injury, if only because she didn't possess the training or power necessary to completely regenerate missing flesh.

He must have caught her looking because he folded his hands together behind his back. "Just don't take too long, okay? I'm starving, and I'm afraid of what your father might ask me if I'm left alone with him."

Raiya rolled her eyes. "I wouldn't worry about that. If he isn't futzing around in the garden, I doubt your arrival would even cause him to lift his nose from his book. You remember the way?"

He nodded, looking back the direction they were headed. "I can manage."

"Okay," she said finally. "I shouldn't be more than ten minutes behind you, so don't get too comfortable. I'm putting you to work chopping onions as soon as I get back."

"I've never looked forward to crying more."

Raiya turned to leave, but Nevin grabbed hold of her hand and pulled her back, threading his fingers through hers. Something in his tone of voice set the fine hairs on her neck standing on end, but the unexpected closeness of his body interrupted her ability to think clearly.

"If I haven't said it yet," he said softly, a breathy quality to his words that brought an uncomfortable warmth to her cheeks. "I wanted to thank you for everything you've done for me. Nursing me back to health, giving me somewhere to stay, saving me from burning Orlicite. Meeting you was the best thing that's happened to me for as long as I can remember."

Raiya chewed her lip as she searched for an appropriate response, but the best she could muster was a forced 'sure'.

Her face flushed seven shades of red. *Stupid!*

Nevin released her hand and trotted off down the path toward home. For some unknown reason, Raiya wanted to chase after him, forgoing her dinner plans for whatever her father had squirreled away at home, but her muted instincts failed to sway her.

A collier in charge of delivering Calibri Grotto's unique form of grass-derived charcoal and a frail-looking woman in an atrocious floral parka stood side-by-side at the rear of a mostly empty cart. An attractive older woman in a darker leather plate folded her arms and quietly fumed as her potbellied male companion jabbered to the engrossed collier and parka, gesturing wildly with his hands as if describing some large object. The two villagers didn't appear to have any idea what he was talking about, which only served to fuel the old man's growing frustration.

Nevin hadn't recognize either, but something about their presence and body language set off alarm bells in his exhausted mind. A pair of wolves in sheep's clothing, lurking right out in the midst of the flock.

It was time to leave, and he had to leave *now*.

He immediately regretted misleading Raiya. She would no doubt be furious with him once she figured out his ruse, but he couldn't risk subjecting her into his problems. Not with how kindly she and her father had treated him over the past few days. Not with how violently his pursuers had treated him over the past few weeks. He didn't want to hurt anyone, but he definitely didn't want any hurt because of him, either.

As he darted down the winding path, Nevin glanced back at the two strangers. With one hand stabbing in his direction, the old man frantically yanked on the woman's arm like a lumberjack trying to uproot a full-grown oak.

Not good. Nevin broke into a run, darting between houses and up staircases, strategically choosing paths that reduced his visibility. As certain as he was that those two were after him, he also knew that there was little chance of them following once he made it out of sight. Bare feet left no discernible trail on hard stone, and Nevin flew through the town like a man on fire.

By the time he burst through the front door of Raiya's house, his legs and lungs burned from the strain. Druce lounged at the dining table, cocking an eyebrow over the top of a well-read sheet of vellum. A stream of pipe smoke drizzled from his partially open mouth. Nevin leaned back against the closed door, masking his fatigue with a small wave and a smile.

"There he is. The Walking Man himself." Druce carefully foldedthe sheet of vellum into a small square before tucking into his shirt. "Where's your beautiful guide."

"She's off buying dinner." Nevin strolled down the hallway as casually as his racing heart would allow, eyes pouring through the room in search of some excuse to feed his host. "Sent me back early to see if I can get the stove going."

Druce raised his eyebrows and nodded, rising from his stool with a throaty groan. "Her fish-stuffed potatoes, I hope. Been some time since I've had the pleasure of those."

Nevin nodded. "Come to think of it, she did say something about potatoes and wild onions."

The well-spoken scholar rubbed his hands together like an excited child, but as Nevin entered the dining room, Druce reached out and stopped him with a firm hand to the shoulder. "Just a moment, young man."

He quickly glanced at the back door, then forced a questioning smile. *A minute might be too long, Druce.*

"My daughter insisted I have something made for you, and my tailor had it delivered not but an hour ago."

"Tailor?"

Druce gestured to the table, to a pile of dark clothing folded neatly and bound together with twine. "Durable travel clothes are a necessity if one plans to operate outside the bounds of civilization, and while the simple outfit I gave you has been adequate in the short-term, my daughter helped me concoct a more long-term solution."

Nevin hesitantly untied the twine and examined each piece of the outfit in turn. A chocolate leather vest with a high rounded collar and vertical ribbing. A crimson shirt with long, double-cuffed sleeves. A wide braided belt colored to match his shirt. A pair of straight-legged chocolate buckskin pants. The pants were ribbed across the knees for durability. The outfit, while built for longevity, possessed an ostentatious flair that struck Nevin as unnecessarily showy.

He scratched the back of his sweat-drenched neck. "This is . . . for me?"

Druce nodded, brushing his chin-length hair aside with the stem of his pipe. "I couldn't, in good conscience, allow you out into world in the rags you arrived in. Call it the curse of fatherhood. You see a young one in need and your mind won't stop chattering until you make it okay."

A hot rush of shame filled his cheeks with blood. "These are really nice clothes, Druce."

"But?"

"But I can't pay you for this."

Druce waved him off. "As the 'Sage of Calibri Grotto', my needs are well-taken care of. Much of whatever money comes into my possession gets converted into new reading material. And as my daughter absolutely refuses to let me spoil her, it pleases me to no end to meet someone who is both in need of and worth the effort. So let's just call it a gift, from one good man to another."

His smile faded. "A good man, huh. I'm not so sure."

Nothing felt further from the truth.

"That uncertainty is often a telling feature of good people." A warm hand squeezed his shoulder. "Tell me. Do you know what it is that makes a good man good?"

He didn't want to say, certain that his own definition of what it meant to be good would immediately disqualify him from the title.

Druce continued without awaiting an answer. "Good isn't a measurement of deeds done, pure thoughts, noble intent. These are the results of goodness, but not goodness itself. Even still, evil men are just as capable of good deeds and thought as good men are capable of actions many might consider evil.

"No, what makes a person good lies in their possessing that terrible capacity for harm, but in their wisdom abstaining. One cannot be good without being capable of evil, of violence."

Nevin balked at such nonsense. "See, that sounds crazy to me. How can you call someone who hurts people good? Someone who kills people?"

The hand on his shoulder tightened and Druce peered down his pointed nose and into Nevin's eyes. "The tragedy of living occasionally calls for the sword. Is it evil to protect your family? Your lover? Your friends?"

"I . . ."

His eyes softened. "Yourself?"

Nevin looked away, unable to bear the weight of Druce's gaze any longer. "Good people don't choose to hurt other people. I don't want to hurt anyone."

"Even if it means losing your own life?"

His fists vibrated against his sides. "I don't want to hurt *anyone*."

"Even if it means those you care about will be? If you have the means to protect them but you choose not to, how is that any different from you hurting them? If they die due to your inaction, are you not complicit in their deaths?"

His eyes glistening and his mouth slack, Nevin was a statue of uncertainty. Like a cancerous growth, pain had accompanied him throughout his childhood, but with that tumor finally excised, he could move forward into a life free of disease.

Druce's words left him torn. Could the power to act be divorced from the responsibility to do so? He wasn't so sure, but he knew he'd never allow himself to become like the man responsible for so much of his suffering. Where did heroism cross the line into villainy?

A slow, knowing smile spread across Druce's face. "Think on it a bit."

There will be time enough for that on the road.

Druce popped the pipe back into his mouth and took an empty pull, the bowl having gone cold while he talked. Rolling his eyes, he set it down on the table. "You know, I might just have a few turnips squirreled away in my dry box. A smoked turnip would make a fine side dish to a stuffed potato."

"You don't have a root cellar?" Nevin asked offhandedly, his mind already detached from the conversation as he mapped escape routes through the town.

Losing pursuers in between buildings and along the many serpentine pathways and winding staircases was one thing. Once his trek took him through open countryside, consistently breaking line of sight would be next to impossible, and in any of his outfits—new or old—he'd stand out against the backdrop of greens and grays like a blot of ink on white paper.

He looked out the window, his eye briefly catching on the hunk of Soul Quartz twinkling naturally in the fading light. A dark frown colored his face. A good hour of day remained, so he couldn't even count on the veil of night to mask his escape.

Druce shoved his feet into a pair of soft boots. "None of the houses above the port have root cellars. The soil layer is quite thin in town, and tunneling through solid limestone is a daunting task even for a Shaper. To be honest, the only reason the outlying homesteads have cellars is because they've commandeered a section of the caves where it breaches the surface. And that's only the ones brave enough to deal with the occasional wandering Chuurik."

Something clicked in his brain, and Nevin straightened.

"The caves. They all connect."

"I suppose it's possible, but you're guess is as good as mine."

Nevin snapped his fingers. "I almost forgot. Raiya wanted me to ask if you'd pick some fresh rosemary from your garden."

"Mmm. A fine idea. You get to work on that fire and I'll get the rest."

"Druce?"

The broad-shouldered man turned back one final time, and Nevin swallowed the lump in his throat. "Thank you. For everything. I won't forget it."

Though he couldn't be sure, Nevin thought he detected a hint of sadness in the small smile Druce returned. "Well. Work on putting aside that harmless streak, and we'll call it even, okay?

"Now then." He clapped his hands. "Rosemary is one thing, but . . . maybe I'll give you some thyme as well. Yes . . . plenty of thyme, indeed."

As soon as the door closed behind the man, Nevin leapt into action.

Chapter 57: Independence

Raiya propped her spear up against the wall and kicked the door closed behind her, hurrying down the hall with an armload of groceries. Druce sat hunched over the table, idly chewing on the stem of his unlit tobacco pipe as he poured over the contents of a yellowed note. The fine vellum was covered in dark circles, and had adopted a waxy sheen from handling. The faint impression of a crumbled wax seal had dyed a red-shaped blob into the back of the letter, just above some barely legible writing.

A sudden avalanche of root vegetables across the tabletop startled Druce from his trance, the pipe falling from his lips with a clatter. Spent tobacco spilled out across the limestone floor.

"I didn't hear you enter," he said, a slight quiver to his voice.

"Do you ever?" Raiya rolled her eyes playfully. "Sorry to startle you."

He shrugged, a weak smile causing his spectacles to slide down his pointed nose. "No, no. I was just . . ." He nodded down to the vellum letter.

"Who sent you a letter? It looks ancient." She gathered the loose vegetables in a pile at the center of the table, pushing aside an empty buckskin knapsack to make room. *Wonder what that's doing out?*

Druce pulled off his spectacles and rubbed an eye. "Something an old friend wrote me, someone I haven't seen in a long, long while. Someone I doubt I'll ever see again. Some wisdom to help me through a rough moment in my life."

"Oh, well done," she said, offering the man a painfully slow round of applause. "That's the most exceptional non-answer you've ever given me."

She craned her neck as though she might be able to sneak a peek, but Druce reflexively tilted the letter away. Still, she managed to glimpse the other side of the paper, and though she couldn't make out any of the words, she could tell the paper on that side bore none of the hallmarks of wear, almost appearing as though it had never seen the light of day. "Can I ask what it says?"

"What it says?" Druce peered down into the letter like the sheet of vellum was a window into another world.

With a sigh, his shoulders rolled forward, but Raiya couldn't tell if it was a sigh of relief, or of resignation. He placed the letter face down on the table and took off his glasses. "I know you don't want to believe it, daughter, but your mother—"

Raiya held her hands up and took a step back. "Stop. I don't care."

But Druce talked over her. "Your mother was a wonderful woman, and one who loved you and I far more than either of us could ever hope to understand. She loved me more than I deserved, but that was her way. She cared about people, all people, even strangers, in a way that instantly made you fall in love with her. She saw in people who they really were, despite appearances and defense mechanisms and lies. She could look at you, and just *know*."

A trait that her father had accused her of inheriting on more than one occasion. Raiya crossed her arms tightly beneath her breasts. "Oh, I remember. I remember all the people who sought her out, hoping she might fix them or someone they loved. I remember her vanishing for days at a time as she traveled to some distant town to help someone she'd never even met. I remember begging her to just spend some time with me, but she always had more important things to do."

Druce nodded morosely, his gaze trained on the empty knapsack she'd shoved up against the wall. "I was angry at her for a long time, too. And losing her . . . well, that was almost too much, but from the way you tell it, her death almost cost me you as well. For years, I couldn't reconcile my unwavering love for your mother against the fury of her passing and her actions on that final day."

"Why are you telling me all this?"

"The letter," he said quietly, lifting it to his face. "Something in it reminded me of her, made me think that maybe I've been judging her too harshly these many years. That maybe we both have."

She vehemently shook her head. "You weren't there. You don't get to say that."

"Maybe," he said softly. With a quick twist of his hands, her father ripped the letter in twain and stood. He started to leave, but paused beside the table, turning to appraise the small pile of vegetables so he wouldn't have to look at her. "It's just . . . you're so much like her it scares me. Headstrong, independent, empathetic. I look at you and sometimes all I see is her."

"Don't," she said, her voice cracking.

"I'm just proud of you. You have so much to give, and you don't hesitate to do so. That young man is lucky you were the one who found him."

He paused, turning to her with a sad smile, and pressed a finger to his lips as if trying to stem the tide of words flowing from his mouth. "I don't know that Nevin could survive without you."

Nevin. Eager to change the subject, Raiya uncrossed her arms and looked around. "Where *is* Nevin? He should have been back before me."

Druce nodded, finally bending over to retrieve his fallen pipe. "He was here a moment ago. Asked me a bunch of questions about root cellars and how the outlying homesteads use the caves to store food. Last I saw him, he said he was going out to the garden to get some herbs for dinner."

Her eyes narrowed. Something in his words bothered her, a hollowness to his tone, but she couldn't put her finger on it.

"Root cellars?"

Druce nodded absently, stuffing his pipe with a fresh pinch of tobacco and lighting it with a flash of Ignolis from his fingertip. "He was acting a bit odd though, breathing heavily and sweating. I didn't think much of it at the time."

Raiya frowned, the swirling energy in her gut tightening uncomfortably. She squeezed past her half-finished painting and peeked out the back window, but the hammock and stone bench were both empty. His belt pouches had disappeared from beside the back door as well.

But it was the empty windowsill that tied her gut in knots.

The Soul Quartz was gone.

"Water always settles at the lowest point."

Raiya shot Druce a quizzical look. "What's that?"

Her father puffed on his pipe. "The part of the letter that reminded me of your mother. It's a quote from Bormuud's treatise on talent and power and its relationship with civic responsibility. Any time I grew irritated by her unflinching commitment to the less fortunate, she'd recite a section of that text until I gave in. She rarely made it far enough to get to the line about water, but if I remember correctly, it's an analogy about accepting the natural order of things and allowing the universe to drive you toward your proper position rather than fighting against our intrinsic nature."

She was only half-listening to his explanation, her mind piecing together the puzzle of Nevin's disappearance. His behavior in town had struck her as strange, like he'd seen something in the crowd of townies he didn't like. Druce said he'd been out of breath, like he'd been running. Had someone come looking for him, someone unfriendly, and had Nevin decided not to stick around and wait for them to find him?

If that was the case, his questions about root cellars and the missing Soul Quartz told her everything she need to know about how he planned to get away. She bristled, silently cursing his rashness.

She only hoped she could catch up to him before he got too far ahead.

Muscular arms wrapped around her unexpectedly, and Druce pulled her tight against his broad chest. "Think I might take a walk," he said. "Check on the state of that retaining wall I put together for Donna Corven. She owes me a good meal anyway."

Chuckling, Raiya wrapped her arms around his waist and squeezed. The warm hug invigorated her, its soothing energy spreading throughout her body. The swirling tangle knotting up her insides bloomed like a field of Waking wildflowers, stealing away her anxiety and replacing it with the certainty of purpose.

When he released her, Raiya smiled up at her father's haggard face. She'd never thought of him as old, but looking up into his tired eyes, she couldn't help but see the face of a man in the twilight of his life. Something was different, she couldn't tell what, but as she planted a kiss on his cheek, she hoped he knew just how much he really meant to her.

Druce winked, popping his pipe back in his mouth and taking an empty pull. Rolling his eyes, he shoved a finger in the bowl as he disappeared down the hall, the faintest wisp of fragrant smoke hanging about in the air behind him.

"Goodbye, father," she whispered, wishing she had the time to explain.

Raiya took a breath, her gaze quickly settling on the empty knapsack and collection of vegetables scattered across the table.

With a reassuring nod, the young woman snatched up the pack and began stuffing it with food.

Nevin wrapped his hands around the swollen belt pouch and squeezed, fighting to smother the light peeking out and threatening to give away his presence in the dark. He'd nearly burst the seams of the undersized pouch when he shoved the irregular hunk of glowing Soul Quartz inside, and it was protesting its captivity by bleeding clear white light out of every imperfection present in its modest construction.

He really needed to find some bigger pouches.

He craned his neck around the narrow bend in the stone tunnel, listening for the sound of boots on wood as his pursuers combed the decimated cabin for any sign of their quarry. In the dark of the sunken cave, the stone magnified even the smallest of sounds, and Nevin struggled to catch any evidence of movement over the deafening sound of his heart shoving blood through his ears.

Light peeked through his fingers, forcing Nevin to press his body against the damp stone in an effort to smother it with his stomach. The light winked out.

The seconds stretched into minutes as he waited, unwilling to move for the fear that the cellar would magnify any errant sound he made and summon his pursuers down the hidden shaft like a limestone horn. With any luck, the incessantly smoking walls within the cabin above would dissuade them from lingering too long, and he'd made sure to break off the iron ring used to lift the cellar door before disappearing into the darkness beneath the floor.

In the growing twilight and surrounded by smoke, he doubted anyone who didn't know it was already there would be able to locate the underground entrance, but he also didn't want to give them a good reason to look.

A soft creak froze the breath in his throat. Slowly, Nevin tilted an ear up the narrow corridor and prayed he was imagining things.

A faint cough, followed by a number of quick steps. His hand reflexively left the pouch at his waist and wrapped around the coarse stone grip of the Sharasil hanging over his right shoulder.

Someone was up there.

He wanted to fade back into the heart of the cellar, putting as much distance between himself and the trapdoor as possible, but foolishly hadn't made time to access the state of the underground room before hastily snuffing his one light source, and if he moved the wall now, he'd be hard pressed to keep the poorly contained Soul Quartz from splashing light all over the place.

He didn't trust the local carpenters' ability to fashion gapless floorboards.

The footsteps grew louder, then ceased altogether. Someone coughed again, a dry sound that irritated his sympathetic nerve and made him ache to clear the non-existent hitch in his throat. He rubbed his throat, struggling to suppress the urge, but each breath only served to strengthen the itch, morphing the annoying tickle into the need to cough.

Just don't think about it. Just don't think about it.

A wry chuckle pierced the silence, the first sound that hadn't echoed off the limestone walls.

How's that working out for you?

Nevin's teeth protested his overly clenched jaw. *Shut up.*

Don't be so sensitive. The shadow chuckled again. **Want me to handle our little guest? You know what I want to hear.**

Nevin shook his head. *I already told you, never again, so stop asking!*

Aww, so ungrateful. I kept us alive, did I not?

You killed someone!

Even without being able to see it, Nevin could feel the derision emanating in waves off the gaunt shadow. The voice discarded its trademark condescension in favor of a touch of frustration and obvious disappointment.

Perhaps that 'sage' was wrong about you.

Shame warmed his cheeks as he thought back to he and Druce's final conversation. Why was he so opposed to self-preservation, even in the face of unquestionable evil? On the one hand, maybe Vincht had gotten exactly what he deserved, but on the other, death meant no do-overs, and didn't everyone deserve the chance to become a better version of themselves?

A memory of flame and screaming flashed through his mind's eye, and Nevin had to shake his head to clear the taste of smoke from his mouth.

The trapdoor shuddered as if struck, and Nevin sucked air in surprise. Moments later, the trapdoor shuddered again, followed this time by the groan of splintering wood. He stepped back from the wall, the light from the Soul Quartz leaking out to glisten along the damp walls of the narrow stone shaft leading up to the door.

He pulled the Sharasil free of its baldric and lifted it protectively before him, little more than an awkward metal club in untrained hands.

Just say the word . . .

Nevin set his jaw, prepared to do anything but that.

White light flooded the tunnel as the trapdoor was yanked upward, and a lithe, shadowy figure extended a glowing pole into the throat of the cellar.

A familiar feminine voice barked down at him, and Nevin's cheeks warmed with blood once more.

"Nevin Walker, words cannot express how pissed I am at you."

Chapter 58: A Lack of Quality Blades

Reclining against the wall outside Calibri Grotto's one and only inn, a single-story stone building unimaginatively labeled Bluff Lodge, Maddox Blaine scratched fervently at the itchy stubble growing unchecked beneath his chin. Not since misplacing his favorite razor some three days prior to leaving on this search-and-retrieve mission had Maddox enjoyed a decent shave, and while he strongly considered just breaking down and buying a new one, the scruffy appearance of nearly every man in town suggested a patent lack of quality blades available. He almost thought it worth scraping away the sensitive skin of his neck with a dull knife if it meant a measure of relief from the incessant itching.

He took a deep breath and groaned for the forty seventh time in so many minutes. As much as he agreed with his son's decision to separate their five member team into three smaller groups to better search the town, standing watch over the inn left him with a growing boredom.

Maddox was a doer, a man of action. He hated waiting for something to happen, hated waiting for someone else to make a move. He understood the need to have a lookout posted at the inn—this 'Nevin' may very well seek out lodging, and the building's position along the main thorough-fare meant more foot traffic than anywhere else in town—but that didn't mean Maddox wanted to be the one left in limbo.

For the first time in a decade though, the mantle of leadership rested on another's shoulders, and as proud as he was of his son's new position of responsibility, he hoped the boy would soon get over the agitation engendered by his father's unwelcome presence on his first command mission. While it was true the boss had only placed Maddox there to ensure the boy was ready to lead his own team, Arolde hadn't seen things in such a pragmatic light. He viewed his father as some sort of threat, and wasted no time making sure he knew his rightful place.

Maddox couldn't fault him. Growing up in his old man's shadow couldn't have been easy on the boy: held to a higher standard than other members of the organization, expected to show up earlier and stay later, to know more and learn faster, to consistently give one hundred and ten percent, and all those other irritating platitudes. No one had cut his son any slack on mistakes made, even when doing so was a necessary part of turning him into a wiser, more experienced leader.

In a way, Maddox suspected Arolde hated him in some small way. And though he was also certain that hate paled in comparison to how much the boy loved him, knowing this didn't make dealing with his son's spite any easier.

Maddox cracked his neck and sighed. "Here comes the spiteful lad now."

"That near-sighted wrinkle box didn't have a clue," Gibbs spat, throwing his scrawny arms about as he fought to keep up with Arolde on the steep stone path. "Blind enough to feed a rain cloud if it grumbled at him."

Arolde clenched his jaw and walked faster. "He gave us the name and location of a resident who was seen with this kid. Even if he's off his rocker, it would be stupid not to check it out."

"Come on. It's a waste of time. That old man served us a slice of dementia pie. This 'sage'," he emphasized, quoting the air with his fingers, "likely only exists in that twisted, decaying mind of his. Probably invented it all just to make you happy, because you reminded him of his grandson or something. It doesn't even make sense."

Maddox dipped his head to hide a smirk. He'd bet a gold shil his son had grown to regret his choice of teammate for the day.

Knuckling his forehead, Arolde came to a stop before his father. "Gibbs, the gods know I'm going to regret asking, but what about it doesn't make sense?"

A balmy ocean gust blew a tangle of greasy hair across Gibbs' face. He slapped it aside and held up a finger. "There is no way there's more than one or two books in this entire town—probably being used as doorstops at that—let alone the hundreds supposedly owned by this mythical sage. A collection of that size would cost more money than this town is worth.

"Besides," he continued dramatically, extending a second finger. "You think any of these *yokels* even know how to read? What good would it do them? You can't read a fish out of the water."

Maddox rubbed his chin, pretending to carefully consider the weight of Gibbs' argument. "He has a point, son. Still, Gibbs . . . you don't suppose this sage could have . . . I don't know . . . moved here from another town maybe?"

Gibbs laughed, a squealing, breathy noise that reminded Maddox of an upset sow. "Why would any man with enough shils to afford that many books move out to *this* hole?"

Maddox threw his hands up in mock defeat. "Well, I'm convinced. What do you think, son? There any merit to Gibbs' theory?"

A hateful stare told Maddox that his little game was having the desired effect, and this time, he couldn't hide the impish smirk spreading across his face. Though his son might not see it just then, Gibbs was useful in his own ways.

As a form of guilt-free psychological warfare? The kid was golden.

Gibbs didn't wait for Arolde to answer. "Here's what's gonna happen. We'll stand here until ma'am and the geezer get back. We'll march ourselves over to that house, knock on the door, and some toothless widow will answer the door. She'll invite us in for tea, and waste our time telling us all about her three hundred children and grandchildren, going on and on about how they never visit anymore and how lonely her life has become, until old Miles starts feeling sorry for her and decides to do whatever it takes to give her life a little bit of excitement, culminating in an awkward moment for the rest of us when he takes her by the hand and leads her into the bedroom . . ."

"By all the gods in the Numen, you idiot, will you *please* shut up!" Arolde yelled, slapping his hands over his ears. He looked on the verge of retching. Based on the mental picture Gibbs had painted in his mind, Maddox could sympathize.

The mouthy lad shrank back, holding his palms up apologetically. "I'm just saying, I think we're wasting our time here. We've spoken to half the town, and no one seems to know this kid. He's not here. Maybe he did come into town, but caught one whiff of discarded fish guts and decided to high-tail—"

"We found him! He's here!" Waving one hand frantically over his head and cradling his heart with the other, Miles burst up the hill, wheezing like a worn-out bellows. Delia jogged leisurely behind him.

Arolde stepped between Gibbs and his father, making a point to shove Gibbs out of the way. "What happened?"

Miles loped to a stop before Arolde, sagging forward over his knees and coughing. He stank of sweat and woodsmoke.

Delia spoke first, her stern voice somewhat rougher than usual. "We were talking to the charcoal vendor—"

"And this nice lady with the most beautiful flowered parka," interjected Miles between gasps.

Arolde twirled a finger. "What did they say? Had they seen the boy?"

He shot a cold look at Gibbs, who quickly averted his eyes. "Or did they say anything about a sage, a man that owns a lot of books in a house on the southern edge of town?"

Delia shook her head. "No."

Gibbs puffed up like rooster in a henhouse.

Miles cracked his back and straightened sharply. "I'll handle this, woman! You never let me do the talkin'!"

Delia waved a conciliatory hand at him, her palm stained black with soot. "Oh, by all means then, handle it."

"What did they say about the boy?" said Arolde, trying to keep them on topic.

Miles nodded, then shook his head. "Yeah, no, they hadn't seen him."

Arolde looked confused. "Okay . . . what *did* they tell you?"

The potbellied man scratched his neck with soot-stained fingers. "Nothin' really. They didn't much know what we were on about."

Arolde stared at Miles for a moment before closing his eyes and massaging his temples with his thumbs. Turning to look at his father, he whispered, "Explain to me why you've put up with these idiots for so many years."

Maddox, smirking like a petulant child, just shrugged. "They're horribly entertaining."

Miles dismissed their aside with an annoyed wave. "No, no, no. Those people had nothing to do with it. I just happened to look away while I was talking to them, and there he was, plain as the nose on your face, true to your description right down to the huge sword dangling between his shoulder blades."

"Fantastic. Where is he now?"

Miles exchanged an uneasy glance with Delia.

Arolde took a step toward them. "You followed him, yes?"

Maddox squeezed his lips together to keep from chuckling.

Miles shrugged. "Well, he sorta got away from us."

Delia held her hands up. "Don't look at me. You know I can't keep up with Miles. Man runs like he's on fire."

Gibbs sneered. "You spooked him, didn't you, you goofy old fart."

The old man bristled. "This town's a maze! Whoever put in all these maddenin' stairs oughta get dragged out into the brush and skinned! We managed to follow him to house out on the cliffs, but no sooner did we arrive did he burst out the back door and dash off into the wilderness."

Delia pointed at her soot-stained palms. "Go on. Tell them about the house."

"Don't rush me!" he spat, stomping his feet. "Ma'am here was laggin', but I managed to follow him into the ruins of this old shack. Whole place was chock-full a smoke, just bleedin' out the walls like they was slowly 'vaporatin or somethin'. Well, he musta 'vatorated too, cuz he weren't nowhere to be found! Cursed house ate him up, I swear it!"

"See, Arolde?" Gibbs chirped, clearly proud of himself. "Old people and dementia go hand-in-hand!"

Red-faced and teeth bared, Miles lunged at Gibbs. Arolde shot an arm out as he flew past, catching the fuming old man by his collar. Lucky for Gibbs, Maddox thought. As out of shape as Miles looked, Maddox had never met anyone who could throw a punch quite like him. One of his victims once likened it to being struck by a runaway cart.

"Knock it off, both of you." Arolde yanked Miles behind him and pushed the two apart. Smirking, Gibbs stuck his tongue out at the old man. Miles knuckled his palm and seethed. "Delia? That all sound right?"

She nodded, her layered leather armor creaking its agreement. "Far as I saw, the kid ran right at that cabin and vanished soon after. Might be that he ran through and out, might be that he hid somewhere inside. All's I know is we couldn't see much of anything with all that smoke, and I had to drag Miles out of there before he had a heart attack."

"Bah!" The potbellied geezer tossed his hands overhead. "Weren't nothin' but a bit a heartburn on account of that grouper salami I had for breakfast. Stuff had enough pepper in it to scare off a wolverine."

"Enough. Where about is this smoking cabin you found?"

Miles described their eastern flight out of town and into the lowlands, gesticulating more and more dramatically as the story progressed. Arolde listened carefully, quickly realizing the cabin's telltale pillar of smoke would soon be impossible to see against a backdrop of stars. Luckily, the twin rings of Etro were already glowing brightly in the eastern sky, bathing the shadowed countryside in muted blues.

When Miles had finished, Arolde gestured to the south. "Delia, take Miles with you back to that house on the cliffs and see if you can't get some more information out of whoever lives there. I want to know how long this kid's been here, who he's been talking to, anything that might help us figure out where he might run off to."

The stocky brunette raised a fist to her chin in salute and grabbed Miles by the back of his shirt, prepared to drag the protesting old man along behind her to keep him from pouncing on Gibbs. "I'll keep these two in line."

"Meet back here in an hour." Arolde turned to Maddox. "Help me get the horses ready. I've got a different job for you."

Maddox nodded, pushing off the wall and striding toward the stables beside his son.

"I'll just wait here," Gibbs called out to them as they walked off, but neither paid him any mind.

"I don't know how you can stand these people," Arolde began, waving off an eager young stable boy. "It's one thing working beside them. It's quite another trying to lead them."

Maddox grunted. "Now you see why I've asked so much of you these past few years. Worst came to worst, you were the person I could depend on most."

"I get that." Arolde wiped the sweat from his neck. "Which is why I need you to find a wing scribe and see if you can get a message back home. Tell the boss we've found the kid, but we spooked him and don't know if we can get to him before he leaves town.

"After that's done, I need you to head towards Whitefalls. Set up a checkpoint at the river crossing. And be discrete."

"Anything else?"

"Yeah, take Gibbs with you."

Maddox grinned. "He making you crazy?"

"No thanks to you." Arolde paused at the stable gates, crossing his arms and turning to face his father. He appraised Maddox wordlessly, his jaw moving like he wanted to speak but was unable to form the proper sounds.

Maddox scratched his fledgling beard. The excitement had made him forget all about the itching. "Anything else?"

Arolde bowed his head and sighed. "Just make it quick. The kid caught us flat-footed. We need to get ahead of him."

"I'll make sure it gets done." Pride swelled in his chest. Arolde had grown into a capable leader. He only hoped the process hadn't done any lasting damage to their relationship.

Arolde lifted his water skin to his lips and took a long tug, wiping away a thin line of some red liquid that had stolen out the corner of his mouth. "This team . . . I always knew they weren't the sharpest blades around, but now that I'm seeing things from your shoes . . . How in the blazes did we ever become the boss' best team?"

Chuckling softly, Maddox placed a comforting hand on his son's shoulder. "Some things in this world are more important for success than brains or brawn."

Arolde snorted. "Like what," he said flatly.

Maddox squeezed the young man's shoulder and winked. "Like Fate."

One day after the explosion . . .

Chapter 59: The Shadow and the Pain

Blackness stole the world away. Drifting weightlessly along on an invisible current, Theis surrendered himself gratefully into the darkness and silence.

It only lasted a moment.

Shimmering blue eyes vaulted open and a scream of pure, unrestrained agony tore from his throat. His chest quivered as it attempted to squeeze every ounce of air from the deepest reserves of his lungs. Echoes resounded from all sides, mocking his pain with their twisted facsimiles.

Salty water splashed through the opening of his cowl, filling his mouth and muffling the final gurgles of the scream, sending him into a fit of coughing that flashed bright, white-hot pain down his right side with each body-shaking hack. Wave after wave crested across his face as his feet struggled for purchase on the sandy beach. Another hot flash of pain stole his breath as his back dragged across the abrasive soil, but at least he was out of the water. He sucked air through clenched teeth as he fought to gain control of himself.

Reaching up to cradle his burning shoulder, his gloved fingers bumped something hard protruding from a ragged, bloody wound just above his right armpit. *Wood*, he thought. He couldn't tell how bad it was, but it felt as though the wooden spike pierced all the way through.

"*Khek.*" He slumped his head back. A hand's width away from death, maybe less. A hand's width, and he would have never woken up.

Too bad.

Trying not to move his head too much, Theis took in his surroundings. A thin beach wrapped around the interior of a confined cove, a sparkling white swatch of crystalline sand butting up against a cloudy stone cliff, rent with rugged clefts and fissures and reaching for the darkened sky. The beach disappeared below swirling blue waters long before it escaped the walls of the cove. Bits of dusky blue-green lichen clung to the undersides of ledges and pocks, havens from the driving wind that occasionally whipped along the beach. Fog blanketed the area, condensing considerably just outside the cove's curved walls.

Theis reclined below a gathering ridge, an abutment joining the cliff with a partially submerged slender pillar. The overhang sheltered a portion of the beach that disappeared into a large, shadowed breach in the cliff face. Bits of splintered wood floated in the water at his feet.

Searching the soupy fog for signs of the wrecked Misanthrope, Theis wondered how long he'd been out, how far he'd drifted from the site of the accident. Though he'd been left temporarily blinded by the sheer density of the unexpected Pool, Theis knew that the powerfully sickening vibrations of magic had been the root cause of the accident, the wreck.

An explosion. Like something had ignited the highly volatile energies of the Pool. A distant memory struggled to make its presence known, a memory he would rather stayed forgotten, but he forcefully shoved it back into the darkness from whence it came.

Theis ran his tongue across the front of his teeth, remembering the way the Pool had felt on his tongue as the boat moved deeper and deeper into its heart. Slick, like lamp oil, but otherwise tasteless.

Figures. A Somnalis Pool over the ocean. Water on water.

Water. The waves must have washed him up on shore, and from the beach's composition, he guessed he must be somewhere along the length of the White Crystal Shores. The Delphine continent.

Theis reached up to probe the mutilated flesh surrounding the jagged wooden spike. It must have been his shoulder's collision with the beach which spurred the agony that roused him from his temporary coma. He pressed around the insertion site and then looked at his gloves. No fresh blood at least.

As he lifted the edge of his cloak, wanting to pull it away from the wound, the movement ushered in a hot wave of nausea. Swallowing back a throat full of bile, he released the cloak and twisted his neck for a better look.

"Oh, *Khek.*"

To his unfortunate surprise, the wooden spike had not only pierced his shoulder, but had managed to cleave right through his cloak as well. Gritting his teeth and holding his breath, Theis pinched the edge of the cloak near the spike and softly inched the fabric up its length.

This time, Theis retched in his mouth. Cradling his stomach with his good hand, Theis fought the need to empty his already empty stomach all over his chest. Wave after hot wave washed over him, turning his guts into a twisted pile of slithering snakes.

Panting through the unfamiliar pain, Theis scooted up the beach and rested his back against the rough cliff, leaning on his good shoulder for support. The pain and nausea didn't stop, feeding off itself as his muscles twitched and lurched against the wooden intruder.

"Good time for a bad idea," he huffed through clenched teeth.

Unable to stand it any longer, Theis wrapped his gloved fingers around the spike, sucking air into the deepest corners of his chest in preparation for the scream he knew would follow. He only hoped the pain would send him back into unconsciousness.

With every ounce of his remaining strength, Theis wrenched at the spike, drawing it from the wound at an excruciatingly slow pace. He opened his mouth, his jaw quivering in silent agony. The nausea disappeared, replaced by the feeling of his intestines being shredded by shards of jagged metal.

Time drew the seconds out to the width of spider silk. Fresh blood poured from the wound, draining the little warmth his body contained. Pain distorted his vision, barely holding back the darkness that threatened to swallow him whole before he could finish the job.

The spike ripped free with a wet spurt of hot blood, and Theis' silent scream finally erupted in a wail that resounded long after the pain returned him to that peaceful sea of darkness.

Hours passed. Days maybe, he didn't know. His awareness faded in and out with the crash of breaking waves. Each time he awoke, his shoulder felt a little better, until the pain was reduced to little more than an unpleasant simmering. At some point, he woke to find he had slid down the wall and onto his back.

Once, during the night, as he stared through lidded eyes at the underside of the ridge blocking his view of the sky, Theis thought he felt something crawling around on his chest near the wound, something small and awkward, but he hadn't the strength to check. In his haze, he pictured a tiny green crab scuttling about his torso, snipping away any loose bits of flesh, taking advantage of a singular opportunity to feed.

It wasn't until he woke up again later that he realized how stupid all of that sounded, how much he sounded like the boy he'd taken as his charge.

Nevin wouldn't have thought it stupid. Nevin would have thought the crab was interesting, tried to befriend it, maybe even tried talking to it.

Foolish child. How had he survived this long in the world? He couldn't fight, he knew nothing of magic, and he'd never even left his hometown. He had no real world experience aside from what he'd read in books, and the words of watchers were no substitute for the actions of doers. Nevin was both useless and infuriating in equal measure.

And yet . . . here he was, lying in a dried puddle of his own blood, fading in and out of consciousness, stuck in a cove that required either swimming or spelunking to escape, and the thing that occupied his thoughts was some random kid he'd picked up halfway across the world, some kid he'd probably never see again, some kid who was most likely rotting on the lightless bottom of the Sea of Calor.

But what pissed him off the most though, was how much he hoped that the kid had made it out okay.

Eventually, the afternoon sun peeked over the edge of the ridge, rousing Theis from a world hanging precariously between waking and dreaming. He squinted against the sudden brightness, and before he could remember the considerable wound in his shoulder, he lifted his right hand to shield his eyes.

Only, his arm didn't move.

Cringing, Theis scooted back against the wall and sat up. A tiny hermit crab lifted its pincers in surprise before ducking back into its conical shell. Tugging at the edge of his hood with his good hand, he craned his neck to get a better look at the wound. A dark crust sheathed the hole in his flesh and coated much of his right torso. He could feel more of the scab grinding against his cloak between him and the wall.

The pain had nearly faded entirely, and the nausea was nothing but an unpleasant memory. That was to be expected.

What he hadn't expected was the complete lack of feeling in his arm.

Furrowing his brow, Theis focused his efforts, urging the limp appendage to listen. A frustrated growl built in his throat, rumbling past quivering neck muscles and clenched teeth until morphing into a defiant bellow that drowned out the rush of ocean wind and subtle drone of crashing waves.

Panting, he collapsed. Not even a twitch. As he peered down at his limp fingers, it was like looking at a mannequin's hand. Below his shoulder, there was nothing. No sense of weight or pressure. His mind knew better, screaming at the lifeless arm to do something, to prove it still belonged to him.

Nothing.

A swordsman without his sword arm . . . Things would have been easier had the blast just killed him.

Theis spent a few minutes scouring the rest of his body for undetected wounds, but it appeared his shoulder had been the only unlucky victim. He doubted any of the smaller pieces of flying debris could have made it through his cloak, but even the areas not protected by the sturdy leather bore no serious trauma.

Grunting through the stiffness that glued his bones together, Theis slid up the cliff wall and stood on shaky feet. Dizzying motes of light danced before his eyes. He gripped his swimming head with a hand to keep it from floating away.

A spark of hope glistened in the darkness of his thoughts. He had survived the explosion with but one major injury. Could it be that Nevin had survived as well? Maybe the boy had somehow found his way to shore. If he still had the sword, Theis might be able to track him. People tended to remember seeing things like that, and Nevin would leave a trail of rumors wherever he went.

Theis took a few hesitant steps into the shadows beneath the ridge and looked around. The recession delved into the rock wall, widening as it pushed farther and farther into the cliff face. A bottomless pool glowed faintly in the darkness, casting dancing lines of greenish light on the cavern's glistening walls and stalactite-encrusted ceiling. Black splotches marred the weathered floor below groups of sleeping bats. The fresh scent of the ocean was replaced with the stink of stagnant water.

Theis nearly lost his feet as he stepped from the gritty sand onto the deceptively slick cavern floor. His balance was still compromised. In truth, he needed a few more days to properly heal before traveling, but if Nevin really was alive, he may not have a few more days.

Cursing his foul luck, Theis shuffled forward and into the throat of the Grotto.

Chapter 60: Tentacles and Teeth

The man in black knelt at the brink of a luminescent pool, returning the curious stare of a translucent yellow fish with bulging eyes and glowing skin. Below, the pale green of the pool faded into an obscure darkness, revealing none of the lonely yellow fish's kinsmen.

Like Theis, the fish was alone, lost in a maze of endless corridors.

The fish didn't flee into deeper waters as Theis straightened. Instead, it wriggled closer, nuzzling the motionless surface with its whiskered snout.

The man in black cocked his head. As an experiment, he paced around the circumference of the pool, careful not to slip on the lichen-encrusted stones. Wherever he moved, the fish followed, swimming sideways to keep up.

Theis knelt back down, extending a single gloved finger out to the pool. The fish nipped at it with strong, leathery lips. He shook his head in amazement. "Is it my eyes? Do you like my eyes, little one?"

Talking to the fish stirred up thoughts of Nevin. With a snort, Theis slapped the water, spraying frigid droplets all down his front. The fish had disappeared long before the waters returned to normal.

With a dejected huff, the man in black sat on his heels and carefully folded his cloak behind his right shoulder. The wound was unchanged—a throbbing depression filled with dry, crusted blood. The pain was bearable if annoying, only truly bothering him when he had to bend forward to avoid a low ceiling, or when he had scraped it against a protrusion jutting from the wall in a particularly cramped section of the cavern.

Had there been any life to these caves other than glowing fish and himself, his pain-filled scream would have driven them out.

The brief rest did him good. The ceaseless trek over uneven terrain wore on his already weary muscles, and he still hadn't regenerated the pints of blood lost to the ocean and beach. Not to mention the limp sausage of an arm tucked into his belt to keep it from flopping around as he moved. His time spent in the cave had done nothing to restore the lack of sensation in his sword arm.

Time had become just another featureless decoration within the endless black. The seconds ticked by with every beat of his heart, a sound he hadn't been able to ignore since he set foot in this cursed hole. Without the sun, there was no telling how much time had passed. It could have been days. It could have been only a few hours. He really had no way of knowing.

He supposed it didn't matter. With this injury, he couldn't move any faster than a cautious shuffle without tempting a fall. And since exacerbating his shoulder would only prove to lengthen his stay in the cave, he much preferred to escape the tunnels without a further loss of his own blood.

As he stared into the luminescent pool, a glint of white light shimmered briefly on its placid surface.

The man in black jerked into a half-crouch, his bright blue eyes searching the distant shadows. Nothing moved.

As the seconds passed, Theis began to question his sanity. Darkness had a way of playing tricks on a person, the visual deprivation driving the mind to create false sensations of light and color and movement where none would logically exist.

There, again. Nearly fifty feet away, within the squat opening of another corridor. A faint pulse of soft white light, building and fading in waves. It appeared to float, drifting from side to side as if born aloft by undetectable air currents. He couldn't make out its source; the light wasn't half as bright as candlelight and it hung just beyond the range of the pool's illumination.

As the light continued to wax and wane, Theis cautiously stood and circled around the edge of the pool. The light continued, unfazed. Whatever it was, it had no fear of him.

Alarm tickled the back of Theis' mind.

He froze mid-step, straining his eyes against the fog of darkness to locate the source of the feeling. Had it not been for the luminescent pool shining up into his mask, forcing his eyes to ignore the room's shadowed nuances, he would have little trouble discerning who—or what—controlled the light.

To his surprise, the danger sense directed him elsewhere, warning him of something else, something hidden, something off to the side.

He jerked his head to the right in time to see a strange creature sink into a crouch. Six spindly legs angled out from a mass of milky flesh, watery skin having never known the warm caress of the sun. A mass of tentacles jutted from each side of its wide, dagger-filled maw, a writhing mustache that terminated in pairs upon pairs of chitinous pincers. Eight holes penetrated its skin in two rows running the length of its pronounced spinal column. The thing had no eyes, but a single filament protruded from its ridged spine, dangling in the air before it like a carrot on a stick.

A crab-like monstrosity, swollen and twisted to nightmarish proportions. An Aberrant.

The creature's toothy mouth parted in a chirping hiss, and a faint white light sparked to life from within a strange crystalline growth covering the filament's tip.

Clever, he thought. *One distracts while the other sneaks around behind.* The man in black reached for his sword as the crab beast scuttled towards him on silent, pod-like feet.

Only, his sword arm didn't respond.

A rush of panic sent him to the ground in a somersault, rolling over his shoulder away from the charging creature. It skidded past him, coming to a stop against the far wall, half of its bony legs pressed up on the vertical rise of stone. Theis overshot his roll, stumbling forward and barely catching himself with his one good arm.

A glowing filament emerged from the dark corridor a few feet from his head—he had rolled right into the other creature's patient grasp.

Tentacles sliced through the air before his face, ruffling his hood. Behind, a trilling hiss signaled the renewed charge of the first attacker.

Theis launched free of the stone floor, leaping over slashing tentacles and onto the back of the surprised creature before him. Bone cracked beneath the heel of his boot as he propelled himself past the squealing beast, stumbling as his feet transitioned from soft, springy flesh to unforgiving stone.

The uninjured monstrosity scuttled over his writhing, complaining companion, catching Theis by the ankle with a grasping pincer and jerking him from his feet. The man in black landed flat on his chest, driving the wind from his lungs with a yelp.

Bulbous feet skirted his body, pressing down on the hem of his cloak, pinning him to the ground. Tiny claws scraped at the smooth leather covering his back, and tentacles wrapped around his neck, choking him as they pulled his head towards the creature's salivating maw.

He tensed his neck against the constricting tentacles and tried to push over onto his back. His cloak was caught, trapped beneath the creature's strange feet, and Theis couldn't put enough force behind his efforts without slamming his bad shoulder into either the creature or the ground.

A warbling chitter sounded from behind his head, and the faint white light shining from the creature's dangling lure intensified threateningly. Particles of dust and stone danced against the surface of the floor, a growing vibration lifting them into the air around him.

The itching in his mind vaulted into overdrive, and a threatening blue film washed over his vision.

Drawing a knee to his chest, Theis planted a foot against the stone and shoved, arching his back into the creature and launching them into a nearby wall. The chittering ceased, and the crab-beast unwound its tentacles from his neck with a wail of confused pain that echoed through the endless tight corridors.

Theis spun away, drawing his thin blade underhanded as he moved. He rotated the blade over the back of his hand, caught it right-side up and buried it in the beast's gaping maw.

"Chew on that," he grumbled, yanking the blade free with a wet splurch.

Theis flicked the ocher blood from his blade and carefully returned it to its scabbard. Tentacles flailed and twitched as the beast collapsed, vomiting steaming, viscous fluid through impotent fangs.

Good hand resting on his knee, Theis propped himself up as he tried to catch his breath. *You stupid, stupid man*, he thought. Had his good arm not been out of commission, those crab-beasts wouldn't have even increased his heart rate. Had he not instinctively reached for his sword with his injured arm, the fight wouldn't have lasted more than a few seconds.

Trying to ignore the swimmy feeling in his head, Theis pulled his cloak tight and soldiered on. Where there were two of these creatures, there were likely to be more. If the scent of fresh blood didn't draw further attention to him, it was likely the dying squeals of their kin would.

He warily traversed the winding halls of the grotto, pushing himself harder than he would have liked, but not as hard as he felt the situation necessitated. Occasionally, he found himself leaning against the wall, the brief rests preventing the light-headedness from becoming unbearable. He slipped only once, as that was all it took to remind him why he continually struggled to keep his feet.

Following the gradually rising slope of the corridor eventually led Theis into a grand vaulted hall. Clustered quartz formations grew from the walls and floor like wayward barnacles. Scores of stalactites and stalagmites pierced the open air threateningly, a thick coating of lichen and mineral-laced dew coloring their surface with dusky greens and powdery whites. Monolithic columns held sky and surface apart, ensuring plenty of room for a vast underground lake. Unlike the previous bodies of water, the dark surface of the motionless lake was black as pitch and bereft of any obvious life.

The hall was still, silent. A tomb undisturbed until his blasphemous arrival.

Theis slipped between the hulking pillars. His eyes searched the darkened walls for exits, finding multiple openings leading in different directions.

He couldn't ignore the heavy sense of foreboding eating at the back of his mind. The itching hadn't subsided since his encounter with the creatures some time ago, and the constant weight of impending danger was beginning to wear on his psyche.

When a series of tightly-packed stalagmites forced him to bear towards the shore, a thin haze of azure light painted a film across his vision.

He stopped suddenly, loose rock and quartz fragments grinding audibly beneath his boots. All the weariness and pain of the last few days vanished beneath a wave of heightened awareness and renewed energy.

He took a hesitant step forward and to the side, edging towards an opening in the line of stalagmites. His view of the hall adopted a decidedly more opaque shade of blue. The man in black backpedaled until his vision cleared.

A Pool? he thought, squinting. Likely centered over the lake. Visions of his final moments on the Misanthrope flashed through his mind's eye.

Visions of Nevin.

"*Khek*," he muttered, louder than intended. The curse resounded off the hard walls of the hall, the echos folding in on themselves in a building cacophony that hardly resembled his initial outburst.

In the distance, something stirred beneath the lake's glassy surface.

Theis held his breath.

The previously calm waters erupted in a tangle of twisted forms, writhing and clawing at one another like a ravenous swarm of locusts. The shore lit up like the night sky as a horde of crab-beasts emerged from beneath the churning waters in frenzied droves. A chorus of hissing trills cried out in desperation, hungry from the scent of blood.

A brighter, more insistent glow sparked in the darkest depths of the lake, and a voluminous mass crested with a wail that shook the walls, breaking free a number of the larger stalactites and bringing them crashing down into the lake and shore. The writhing carpet of tentacles and teeth stilled, their pulsing filaments extinguishing like candles before a gust of wind.

The lake boiled as the new creature hauled itself onto the shore, treading carelessly on any unfortunate crab-beasts that couldn't scuttle out of the way fast enough. The fleshy giant tasted the air of the hall with an ocher tongue, searching for the intruder whose presence had summoned it from the deep.

But Theis was already gone.

Chapter 61: Stone-Eating Worms

"This doesn't make any sense," Nevin grumbled into the darkened corridor of slick limestone, the weak glow of the outstretched Soul Quartz succumbing to the curtain of darkness no more than twenty paces on either side of him. His fingertips grazed the sword hanging from his back, oddly comforted by the Sharasil's familiar chill.

Two equally confounding tubular paths split the winding corridor before him in twain, neither displaying an indication of measurable progress through the region's namesake caverns. Displaying a waxy luster and slick with colorless slime, the smooth limestone gave the impression of some insect's inside-out shell, like he and his companion had trespassed into the belly of a monstrous beetle and found its intestines to be just as resilient as its armor.

"Told you we should have gone the other way."

Behind him, Raiya's condescending tone trod across his thinning nerves. Standing at the dead center of the oddly roundish tunnel, the fingers of one hand thrummed on her hip as she leaned into her spear. Though the sun-shy limestone seemed to exude an aura of cold, Raiya displayed no signs of being affected despite her sleeveless top and calf-length pants. Her own Soul Quartz shined out overhead, fitted snugly within a y-shaped nook beneath the blade of her spear.

"And I told *you* to go back home."

The butt of her spear thumped against the stone floor. "Say that again, Nevin Walker. You say that one more time and I will take back the Soul Quartz you stole from my father's home and leave you in the dark to be eaten by Chuurik." The emphasis she placed on that final syllable bore all the weight of a slamming door.

"The heck is a Chuurik," he mumbled, tugging at the collar of his new leather vest. The red-and-black ensemble Druce had put together for him still possessed the rigidity of untempered fabric, needing a few days of wear before its inflexible hems didn't chaff his neck. Still, he silently praised the man's name for the gift, as the ribbed leather offered a measure of protection against the cave's ceaseless chill. More importantly, though, Nevin thought it made him look dashing.

Not that his companion had taken the time to notice.

After a few moments of awkward silence, Raiya waved a hand and spoke, a trace of resignation stealing the harshness from her tone. "Why?"

"Because . . . because these are my problems." Nevin spun around so quickly he nearly lost his balance on the damp floor. "Because I'm the one stuck with this stupid sword. I'm the one being chased. If you'd seen what they did to my home, Raiya—"

"Stop," she snipped, cutting him off. "You've already made all that abundantly clear. I meant, why doesn't this make any sense?"

He blinked. "Oh. Right."

He scratched the back of his head, gesturing first back the way they came and then to the pair of corridors that spurred his initial outburst. In truth, he relished the opportunity to talk about anything other than Raiya's indefatigable irritation with him, and the confusing nature of the Grotto's layout was a far more immediate problem as it was.

"Well, I don't have the first hand knowledge of the Grotto that you do, but I did spend some time studying the area back at Ishen's cabin." He paused, walking over to rest a hand on the damp wall. "This is limestone. Beneath the surface, this whole region is basically solid limestone up until just short of the Brennan River to the north."

"Is a geography lesson really appropriate right now?"

He ignored her snark. "Due to its relative softness, limestone is well-known for having cave systems. People used to build shelters in existing caves to hide out in when the weather turned or to defend from invaders. These caves have been studied extensively, and scholars are actually very familiar with the way they form, how they're laid out, the features, the dangers.

"And this . . ." He swiped a hand around the circumference of the tunnel and shook his head. "I don't think it's natural."

For the first time in hours, the mask of irritation slipped from Raiya's face. "How could you possibly know that?"

"Limestone caves are cut by running water. Rain, ocean tides, rivers. It takes time. A lot, actually. Decades. Hundreds of years, maybe. It's an uneven, chaotic process. The flowing water eats away at tiny imperfections in the rock, wearing it down, wearing it smooth. Its weight bears down on weak points in the stone, eventually breaking through to fill-in smaller cavities. Each time this happens, the system expands in size.

"If I'm remembering correctly, there's two types of caves: wet caves and dry caves. Wet caves are an active process. Water is still moving through them in some form or another, continuing to grow the system. Rivers can sometimes run for miles underground before joining up with another leg or washing out to sea. Whole lakes have been discovered hidden in the bowels of the earth."

With a flat look, Raiya sank cross-legged to the floor and pulled her pack into her lap. Nevin took the action as a tacit approval of his long-winded explanation and continued.

"Dry caves are different. Rivers sometimes shift course. They find an easier path or dry up or get dammed. They call it 'cooked' when a cave goes dry. It means they are done growing, they're 'cooked'. Parts of a wet cave can be cooked if the water that made them has moved on to other legs."

Raiya fished a raw potato out of her pack and took a bite. "Other than a few standing pools of water and a general humidity, I'd say this cave is pretty well cooked."

"That's the thing." He eyed her potato, but kept his hunger to himself. "I'm pretty sure none of these tunnels have ever seen a drop of moving water. Natural caves are rarely walkable for long stretches, and more often than not, explorers find themselves on their bellies in order to make any sort of progress. Stone doesn't erode evenly, and it definitely doesn't form in long, round tunnels like these. It's more likely the Grotto is the product some gargantuan, stone-eating worms than it is of some natural process, and believe me when I say that the prospect of running across such a worm down here scares the shit out of me."

Craunch. The young woman pulled her strawberry blonde braid over her shoulder and loudly, obnoxiously chewed her potato. Raw as it was, Nevin still felt his stomach groan in anticipation.

Her eyes never leaving his, Raiya popped the final bite into her mouth and cocked her head. "Why don't you just leave it?"

"Leave it?" He shook his head, a hand floating unconsciously to his belt. "Leave what?"

She pointed to oblong metal object mounted to his back. "The sword. These people looking for you? If you ask me, they won't be able to find you if you get rid of that giant target. It is impossible to hide in a crowd with that thing sticking up over your shoulder. And without it, what reason does anyone have to chase you? You'd be free."

His fingertips brushed the unusually cold metal, and a puff of mist chased his every word. "Raiya, no, I'm trying to tell you there's something wrong with the caves—"

He ducked as what looked like an onion sailed past where his head used to be. Produce scattered in all directions from her overturned pack as Raiya shoved to her feet. "Just leave it, Nevin!"

"I don't—"

"I've spent years exploring the Grotto. I probably have more experience in these caves than anyone else alive, and not even I have ever been this far in. You couldn't ask for a better hiding place. Just take it off, lay it on the ground, and we can both turn around and leave before something worse comes along."

He had to admit, she had a point. These caves were a tomb, and while they may be easy to enter, the chances of someone up and stumbling upon the blade this far into the system was practically zero. Even if someone knew he'd abandoned it down here, it could take years of intensive search to navigate the labyrinthine tunnels, and what would give his pursuers any reason to suspect he'd left it behind?

That would be like leaving your own arm behind.

A shadowy figure materialized out of the dark, appearing even blacker than usual beneath the cold glow of the Soul Quartz. It crowded against him greedily, and Nevin felt his fingertips unwillingly fan out across the surface of the Sharasil until every inch of the flesh of hand clutched at the freezing metal. His finger bones creaked beneath the strength of his grip, and had the sword been capable of it, he was sure it would have been rattling in its harness.

"How are you . . ." he muttered, a thick cloud of fog billowing out from his lips.

A deep crease painted his brow as he tried to open his hand, but it wasn't his to control. He shot the shadow a defiant look. Somehow, he was fully aware of the wide sneer peeling its invisible lips away from its invisible teeth.

But it doesn't really feel like your arm anymore, does it?

"Nevin?"

He jumped at the sound of his name, and the shadow winked out of existence, returning to him control of his hand. He held it against his chest, flexing warmth back into each finger in turn.

The shadow had never done that before, taken control without him inviting it in. It had always wanted his verbal agreement, wanted him to cede control of his own free will.

Had something changed since his fight with Vincht? Had that one moment of weakness opened a door he couldn't so easily close?

"Are you okay?" she asked, taking a concerned step toward him.

He cleared his throat and nodded. "Yeah, I just . . . I thought I heard something."

"What do you mean?" Her tone sharpened. "What kind of something?"

"I don't know. Probably my imagination."

She immediately closed the distance between them and stared intently up into his startled face. "Seriously, what did you hear? Was it behind us or in front of us? I was stupid to yell at you. I shouldn't have done that."

Her insistent tone gave him pause, but it also highlighted some of her comments in the last few minutes. She had kept trying to persuade him to turn around. She had threatened to leave him to be eaten by . . . something he couldn't remember the name of. She'd also expressed her desire to turn back before something worse came along.

"Raiya, why didn't you argue when I said the caves weren't natural?"

Her mouth opened, but nothing came out. Instead, she looked warily in both directions before bending down to scoop wayward vegetables back into her deflated pack.

But Nevin wasn't letting her off that easy. "Did you already know there was something weird about these caves?"

"No!" she hissed. "Not in so many words."

Bending over the help her clean up her mess, it was his turn to whisper. "Are the worms real? By all the souls in Obolvia, tell me I didn't drag us down into a giant stone-eating worm den."

"Ugh, there's no such thing as stone-eating worms." Making a sour face, she tossed aside a slime-covered turnip. "Okay, I'm *pretty* sure there's no such thing as stone-eating worms."

"Then what the heck made these tunnels?!" he shout-whispered, shaking a handful of potatoes at her.

She straightened, huffing a strand of wavy hair out of her face. "Look, there may have been rumors of some weird, sightless creatures living in the caves, and there may have been whispers that these creatures could melt stone with their screams—"

"The WHAT you tell me?"

"—but I've been exploring down here for years and I've never once run across anything scarier than a spider, so I was *mostly* sure they were just old fisherman tales meant to scare children away from playing in the caves."

Nevin swiped a clammy palm down his face, the action only serving to amplify his incredulous expression. "So you're telling me we're . . . I don't know . . . *miles* inside a decidedly unnatural cave system with no exit in sight, and there is an increasingly probable possibility of us running into some sort of screaming monstrosity capable of melting stone, and you didn't think it pertinent to bring it up until now?!"

With a strained smile, the young woman shrugged. ". . . yes?"

"Just how mad at me were you?"

"What do you mean, 'were'?"

Nevin grabbed her hand as she reached for a crumpled scrap of vellum. "That's not even the worst of it. I came down here assuming these caves were a naturally occurring phenomenon. They existed at a higher elevation than the ocean, which means they should have been made by water flowing down through the rock from the surface. That means water has to enter from somewhere, and we should be able to follow the caves up until they breach the surface somewhere.

"But if these caves were made by some stone-melting creature, it means they don't follow any natural rules. It means there may be no rhyme or reason for their design. It means there may very well not be an exit farther in, and every corner we round could lead us right into the middle of some monster's den."

Chapter 62: The Freedom of Choice

"Okay, now you're just being dramatic." Raiya rolled her eyes and tried to pull her hand away, but Nevin held fast. "We can just turn around and go back the way we came. Imagine if you'd just listened to me in the first place."

"It's not that simple."

"I told you these caves go on for miles. I told you how easy it was to get lost down here. I told you these things more than once, but you didn't want to listen."

"That was before I knew the cave was carved by screaming monsters! I might have made different choices had that information been made available to me."

Her face hardened. "Let go of my hand."

Heat bloomed in his cheeks. "I'm serious, Raiya."

"So am I," she said flatly. "Let go of my hand. Right now."

With a disgusted sigh, Nevin tossed her hand aside and stood. "Look, I'm sorry, okay? I didn't have a lot of time, and I panicked. No one else needs to get hurt because of me, especially those who went out of their way to care for and protect me. I can barely stand knowing I'm the only survivor of the massacre back in Elbin, and none of that had anything to do with me.

"Theis? Aurnia? Aidux?" He held up a finger for each of his missing companions. "Helping me may have gotten them killed for all I know, and there's nothing I can do about that now. But you and your father? These people will kill you to get to me, all because I let you help me. That's something I could prevent, so I made a choice."

Raiya retrieved the crumpled bit of vellum and sat back on her heels, peering down at the darkened swatch of paper without really seeing it. "I'm not mad at you. I mean, I am, but that's not the point. You chose to leave. You didn't have to, but like you said, you had a choice and you made it.

"Me? I don't like having my choices being stripped away. I don't like people deciding my outcomes for me. I don't like being victim to other people's decisions, not when I'm perfectly capable of making up my own mind about something, and definitely not when the person deciding for me is someone I care about."

He shook his head. "But you barely even know me."

"Not the point! *I* get to decide my level of involvement in my own life. Not you. Not the townspeople. Not my father. Not my—"

Her voice caught, and she turned her head to the side to hide her frustration. "You didn't 'let' me help you. You needed help, and I made a choice. Did you 'let' me pull your unconscious body out of the ocean? Did you 'let' me heal your wounds while you slept? Those were things you 'let' me do?

"You don't get to take away my agency like that. I saw someone in need of help and I did something good. I helped you. I fed you. I healed you. I invited you into my home."

She wiped her cheeks, all the fire gone from her speech. "And then you left and took any choice I had in the matter with you."

"I—"

Nevin was taken aback. He hadn't thought of it like that. Here he thought he was doing the noble thing by leaving before her involvement ended up getting her hurt, but was that really his choice to make? Ishen's disappearance still bothered him, and not just because of the mystery surrounding his empty cabin. His old mentor had left without warning, and to some degree, Nevin was angry with him for doing so.

A shy smile finally cracked his lips, and he couldn't help but chuckle.

Still leaning back on her heels, Raiya practically shook with anger. "Are you really laughing at—"

Nevin sank to the stone and pulled her into a tight embrace. She yelped in surprise and tensed up, but once she realized what was happening, he felt her lean arms wind around his sides to squeeze him back.

"I'm sorry," he said softly. He could still smell the ocean on her braid, clean and salty and inviting. "I should have said something."

"Yes, you should have." The slip of vellum crinkled against his leather vest. "But I'll get over it."

"Good, because it's gonna take some serious cooperation to get ourselves out of this pickle."

She pushed him back with a sour expression. "I can't stand pickles."

"Look, I'm all for heading back, okay? You've convinced me. But here's the thing." Nevin strode through the tunnel until the Soul Quartz's light illuminated the split in the corridor and then turned to face her. "This isn't the first split we've come across. We've passed dozens of connecting tunnels, and each time I made a choice about which way to go, I did so under the assumption that the cave had been formed by natural forces."

"You keep saying that, but I don't know what that means." She smoothed the wad of vellum against her leg in the hopes of pressing out the wrinkles.

"It means I assumed these tunnels were formed by water passing though on its way to the ocean. That would mean there's some sort of logical consistency to its layout, and I thought if we just headed inland, we would eventually find our way out the other side.

"But if something else made it, it's possible we'll just head deeper and deeper into the earth and never find our way out. All these tunnels look basically the same. No stalagmites. No mineral formations. Just featureless stone. Even if we turned around now, I don't know that I'd even been able to recognize the tunnels we've been through."

If Raiya was listening, she wasn't showing it. While he had explained their situation, she had hefted the head of her spear over her shoulder in such a way that the Soul Quartz shined directly down onto the scrap of flattened vellum stretched between her fingertips. She mouthed its contents to herself, her expression incomprehensible.

"What is that?"

"A piece of a letter. My father must have put it in the bottom of my pack. Why would he . . ."

She squinted into the darkness surrounding Nevin, reaching up to block the cold light of the Soul Quartz with her hand. Frowning, he followed her stare, but all he saw was another lightless tunnel.

Raiya materialized by his side, grabbing him by the hand.

"Come on," she whispered, leading him along the right fork in the tunnel. "I almost missed it, but there's some light down this way."

"Another one of those glowing pools?" He didn't want to get his hopes up, but he had to say it. "Or possibly a hole in the ceiling?"

She squeezed his hand reassuringly. "It's worth a look."

The unremarkable passageway angled sharply skyward after less than a hundred feet, discarding the tight corridor for open space after a brief lichen-infested ramp. Nevin bolted up the incline ahead of her, hoping the momentum would prevent him from slipping and earning a mouthful of stone for his efforts. He then grabbed Raiya's extended spear and hauled her up behind him.

When Nevin turned around, he immediately stepped in front of his companion protectively, his hand flying back to the coarse stone grip of his sword.

The rumors were at least half-true.

A peculiar creature with gray flesh, spindly legs, and writhing tentacles loomed over a pool teeming with glowing yellow fish. The fish crowded together at the surface, mesmerized by a pulsing white crystal dangling over the water at the end of filament growing from the creature's head. At the end of its twitching tentacles, a pair of pincers snapped in barely restrained anticipation.

"Raiya," he whispered out of the corner of his mouth. "What was that word you used? The thing you threatened to let eat me?"

She grabbed a fistful of his shirt and pulled him close. "Let's just go back. Preferably before it sees us."

Nevin was inclined to agree, but before they could retreat, a distant wail shattered the uneasy silence, echoing from every direction at once like a herd of pigs being slaughtered. Raiya's fingers dug painfully into his taut bicep. To their credit, neither uttered so much as a whimper at the sudden, unnerving cry.

It didn't matter. As the wail died away, the creature's twitching tentacles jerked in their direction. It arched its back and snorted. Scuttling around on bulbous, fleshy feet, the creature's wide mouth parted in a sinister grin, dripping thin strings of milky drool and threatening them with a low, hissing trill.

A chorus of similar trills joined in from beyond the limited range of the Soul Quartz's light.

Nevin swallowed and popped his sword free from its clasp. "Too late."

Chapter 63: A Good Man

Nevin hastily dropped the Soul Quartz at his feet as he brought the Sharasil to bear.

Swallowing the rocks in his throat, Nevin unwillingly opened the door to a rush of cold fear. The clamoring thud of each heartbeat pounded in his ears, drowning out the insistent hissing of the approaching monstrosity. His eyes darted from shadow to shadow, trying to pinpoint the creatures that had yet to reveal themselves.

He must be losing his mind. Who did he think he was? Theis? He couldn't fight a literal monster, not with a blunt stick of metal. He should be running, sprinting back down the corridors as fast as his legs could carry him.

Haven't you already proven the value of that move?

An uncomfortable chill washed over him. His hands twisted around the sword's coarse grip, but he couldn't tell if it was his own nervous tension, or the shadow's hunger for control.

"No."

Nevin focused his intent until his fingers responded to his mental directives and relaxed.

The creature hissed, its crystalline lure flaring impatiently. With a chirping trill, it gave in to its hunger and charged.

He breathed in through his nose and honed his focus to a razor's edge. He was so tired of running, tired of being chased, tired of giving in to fear and surrendering his freedom to those with the desire to do him harm.

He couldn't stand to be helpless any longer. He had to make a stand. He had to fight back. He had to be willing to kill.

Druce's voice filled his head. *The tragedy of living occasionally calls for the sword.*

He emptied his lungs and raised the Sharasil before him.

Call for the sword.

But nothing happened.

Nevin's eyes stretched wide. "Wha—"

A lithe form stepped protectively in front of him, and its shining steel blade vanished beneath the pallid skin of the creature's writhing face with a wet squelch and a squeal of inhuman agony. The glowing filament flickered wildly, and the stone beneath their feet cracked and split.

Raiya's arms shook from the adrenaline. The crab-like monstrosity collapsed in a heap and slid off her spear, a strand of ocher goo bridging the gap between the tip of her weapon and the creature's mortal wound.

"Nicely done," he said wondrously, stepping up beside her.

Raiya's face was ashen as she stared at the still twitching corpse. Her mouth worked but no sounded emerged. Folding an arm across her roiling stomach, she covered her mouth with the back of her hand in the effort to keep from vomiting.

Nevin's eyebrows reached for each other, not quite understanding her reaction. It wasn't the creature she was staring at. It was the blood. Thick as tree sap and reeking of tangy metal, the viscous goo oozed from the wound in the creature's face, inching slowly down the length of her spear. Raiya watched with horror in her eyes as it trickled ever closer to her white-knuckled fingers.

As confident and self-sufficient as Raiya appeared to be, Nevin had never really considered the fact that she was still just an innocent teenage girl, and he was now watching that innocence die.

White light swept through the chamber as more dangling filaments blinked to life, washing over four more crouching monstrosities, each creeping silently forward on bulbous feet. He had barely a moment to register their presence before one of them sprang into action.

Nevin glanced at Raiya, but the young woman's eyes hadn't lifted from her assailant's corpse. Thick tears gathered on her eyelids, glimmering weakly in the Soul Quartz's cold light.

Druce's voice once again emerged from the shadows of his mind. *Is it evil to protect your family? Your lover? Your friends?*

Nevin didn't wait. Extending the Sharasil protectively before him, he shoved Raiya backward and stepped up to meet his attacker head-on.

Yourself?

A tremor shook the sword, rippling up the length of the storm gray metal like a rock dropped in a still pond. Beginning at the grip, the lusterless metal momentarily bulged outward before collapsing in on itself, the area behind the ripple morphing until the full length of the sword had changed into a smooth, glossy plane the color of burnished pewter. Six thin lines of seething white light angled intricately along the width of the revealed blade, striking out from the strange circular indentation in its midst to feed the sword's sparking white edge. Running from the tip, across the front of the hilt guard, and into a blazing white shard at the pommel, the blade's single edge appeared to be constructed of electric glass.

Nevin stepped into a thrust, but a claw-tipped tentacle slapped his blade astray before it reached its target. The unexpected defense sent the sword high, and the seething tip just clipped the creature's dangling lure. With a flash of light and a high-pitched squeal, a fleck of darkened crystal broke right, while the thrashing beast jerked left. The lure flickered and flashed, and the air before its quivering maw seemed to twist beneath the influence of some unseen force, and as the creature scuttled away, jagged cracks sprang into existence along the adjacent wall and dust rained from the ceiling.

"What the—" Nevin muttered, awe-struck, before the beast regained its senses and charged him once more.

The young man turned into his opponent, drawing the blade around his rotating body as he sidestepped the mass of spindly legs and gnashing teeth. He brought the sword low and across, and the blazing edge caught two of the creature's legs, severing them at the joint in a spurt of blood.

Before the creature could retreat, Nevin followed the glowing blade around once more. Shifting into the narrow space between them, he angled the sword towards the stone and arched the blade's stroke into a vicious uppercut.

An unnatural chill drove any hint of warmth from the room, freezing the breath as it left his mouth and coating the ragged edges of the creature's torn flesh with frost as the sword ripped its body asunder. Raiya whimpered softly in surprise at the brief and terrible loss of heat.

Then, just as suddenly as it appeared, the cold abated.

The other creatures didn't hesitate, skittering across the floor as one.

Nevin turned sideways and pushed Raiya towards the ramp, allowing the sword's tip to descend to the floor. An intricate webbing of frost burst into existence wherever the blade touched stone.

"Move! We have to go!"

Raiya offered a small nod before awkwardly sliding down the ramp, using her spear to brace her descent. Nevin feinted at the hissing beasts with a wild slice, forcing them to pull their charge up short. Clawed tentacles clacked in frustration. Yawning mouths oozed thick, yellow saliva.

When he looked over his shoulder to see if Raiya had reached the bottom of the ramp, one of the deceptively spry creatures lunged beneath his blade, slamming into his knees and wrapping its tentacles around his thighs. Teeth scraped his buckskin pants.

Had the blow not knocked him off-balance, Nevin would have quickly sheathed his blade in the creature's ridged spine. Instead, he had to fight to keep his feet. He flexed his thighs away from the onslaught of teeth, hoping his flattened muscle would prevent the slather-coated daggers from tearing into his flesh.

Such a thing wouldn't save him from the other creatures. As unsteady as he was, if this one managed to drag him back into the room, it wouldn't be long before his companion found herself searching for a way out of the caves alone.

Nevin held his breath and stopped fighting to remain upright. Bending his knees, he launched himself into the air, taking the surprised creature with him. The pair slammed into the stone ramp, sliding down through the dusky lichen in a tangle of flailing limbs and sharp exhales and clenched teeth. As the creature fought to free its tentacles, Nevin drove the sword between his legs. The seething blade cleanly severed both tentacles just below their clacking pincers. He squeezed his eyes shut against the spray of hot blood.

When he opened his eyes, he was lying on his back at the bottom of the ramp and the creature was impaled through its face on the end of Raiya's spear. A scowl of determination had replaced her vacant look, though her hands still trembled.

At the top of the ramp, the two remaining creatures flashed their crystal-tipped filaments and hissed threateningly. They squeezed side-by-side through the narrow opening, shifting position until half of their legs skittered along the wall above their heads.

The young woman ripped her spear free with a wet splurch and yanked Nevin to his feet. "Come on!"

"Wait! The Soul Quartz!"

She dragged him down the darkened corridor, shoving her spear tip ahead of her to light the way. "Leave it! Your sword's doing fine without it."

Raiya bolted ahead of him, and Nevin reluctantly followed. He draped the burning blade back over one shoulder, careful not to graze the blazing white lines with his cheek or ear. He couldn't imagine how he'd gotten the blade to change, but he prayed to the gods that he didn't accidentally undo it before they could escape.

The fork in the corridor flashed by as their feet carried them around a bend in the hallway. Despite their many legs, the creatures lagged behind, quickly disappearing back beyond the reach of their light. He briefly entertained the idea that maybe they would stop chasing them once enough distance separated them, but he and Raiya couldn't keep up such pace on the slick floors for long without risking injury.

"What in the Numen was that horrible noise?" Nevin asked between breaths. "It sounded like it came from everywhere all at once."

"I don't know," she answered without turning. "But it sounded like one of them."

"It sounded huge!"

Just as the sound of their hissing pursuers faded into the distance, Raiya came to a skidding halt as the corridor abruptly terminated into thin air. A semi-circular ledge overlooked a sheer drop into another, much larger corridor running perpendicular to their path. Nevin came to a stop beside her.

"Whoa," he marveled, gazing out into the precipice. The murmur of running water called up to them from the darkness below, though they couldn't see its source. "This definitely isn't the way we came."

"Exactly why I came this way." She shook her arm loose and knelt at the edge. "You said caves like these are often carved by moving water, right?"

"Yes, but haven't we established that's not the case with these caves?"

She stretched her spear down below the lip of the drop off. The shimmer of water returned the glow of her Soul Quartz. "It doesn't matter. Running water is about the best thing we could come across."

"What? Why did you think that?" He could hear the creatures approaching, their hissing trills growing louder and louder with each passing breath. Stepping between Raiya and the approaching threat, Nevin brought his seething blade to bear.

Raiya tossed a stone off the cliff. A deep bloorp resonated off the walls, and a self-satisfied smile crawled across her face.

"Because," she began, rising. "Water always settles at the lowest point."

"That doesn't—"

With a wink, Raiya jumped backward off the cliff and disappeared into empty air.

Chapter 64: Chitter and Shake

Theis stumbled along, barely pausing when the craggy walls on either side narrowed so drastically he had to turn sideways to fit. The horde of hissing creatures drew uncomfortably close, his weakened state having allowed them to outpace his escape.

The ceiling brushed the hem of his cowl, with another step forcing him to splay his legs in order to sink low enough to thread the gap. Another sliding step found his chest wedged between the two walls, his thick leather cloak the only thing keeping the rugged stone from grinding painfully against his sternum.

A harsh glow bloomed behind him, and Theis could now pick out the individual plodding slaps of bulbous feet on moist stone. Something else as well, something larger among them, something with mass enough to rain dust from the ceiling as it approached. He could hear it, too, wading through the midst of the clacking, hissing horde, and he didn't need his instincts to impress on him the need to be elsewhere when it arrived.

Safety lay just on the other side of this narrow gap in the tunnel.

Theis rested his mask against the wall and took a number of short, rapid breaths. With a forceful exhale, the man in black emptied his lungs and crammed his body deeper into the gap.

For a moment, he inched through the opening, his cloak catching intermittently on minor extrusions in the stone. His wounded shoulder passed through the narrowing and into a larger space, and Theis cocked his head, craning his neck until he was sure nothing with tentacles awaited his arrival.

Then, as his body forced its way into the gap's narrowest point, all forward progress suddenly stopped.

With his legs splayed out in an awkward squat, his boots struggled to find traction on the damp stone. He reached overhead with his good arm, feeling about for the rim of the gap but finding it out of reach.

Theis cursed his foolishness. Had he just been turned the opposite way, he could have used his left hand to pull himself the rest of the way through, but as it was, the only arm in any position to help him hung like a bad thief in the afternoon sun.

His lungs burned for the need of fresh air, but Theis taxed them further, huffing every last wisp of breath remaining in the deeper parts of his chest out through his mask's mouth slit.

He pushed with his good arm. His body shook. His chest ached.

Darkness of a different sort descended across his vision.

Suffocation is such a pathetic way to die.

A massive bulk collided with the narrow fissure behind him and a squeal like a chorus of frightened pigs filled the cavern from end to end. The force of the blow jettisoned him free, slamming him shoulder-first against the uneven stone floor.

A long moan poured from his lips. Something had torn loose in his wounded shoulder like the ripping of wet paper doused in lamp oil and set ablaze.

Gloved fingers clawed at the stone. His instincts screamed at him to stand, to ignore the pain, to press forward with every ounce of life he possessed. The warm light of his soul agreed, spreading out from the darkness behind his thoughts to suffuse his body with the tingle of spiritual energy.

"Easy for you to say," he groaned. A gloved hand returned from beneath his cloak coated in fresh blood.

The unseen bulk slammed against the narrow gap once more, but as a fetid wind stole around him, Theis felt something more substantial nudge his boot.

A needle-nosed pincer half the length of his body snaked along the floor through the gap, mere inches away from snatching him by the ankle and dragging him away. Theis kicked it aside and struggled to his feet. The pincer clacked its claws and felt around for him blindly.

The snapping pincer jerked back into the gap as the unseen bulk shifted. The momentary gap allowed a single crab-beast the chance to sneak past, but it soon became wedged between the narrow walls just as Theis had before. Spindly legs and flailing tentacles scrabbled against the vertical stone for purchase. To Theis' amusement, it only served to wedge the creature tighter.

Content with his momentary safety, Theis took in the room. Something about this space was different. None of the limestone walls possessed the smooth, almost melted look of the rest of the tunnels. Tapered pillars coated in a slimy film supported the domed ceiling, waiting for the younger stone projections to catch up and share the burden. Shallow pools of milky water rippled weakly from the turmoil caused by the horde's violent pursuit.

But it was the murmur of flowing water that drew his attention.

"That's new." He squinted into the murky black, barely able to pick out the deeper darkness of another passageway on the far side of the domed room.

Squeals of irritation morphed into one continuous chitter, causing the itching in the back of Theis' mind to return. He turned in time to witness the stuck creature dangle its glowing lure mere inches from its maw, the white light vibrating in time with the ebb of its vocalizations.

Undulating rings of force grew out of the flickering lure, distorting the air as they passed. Wherever the rings touched the fissure, flecks of stone quivered and broke free. An uncomfortable pressure washed over him, and it was almost as though he could feel his teeth rattling in his skull.

After a moment, the edge of the fissure slowly peeled back like the hot wax of a burning candle. The rings expanded in size as they crept through the still air, and as they grew closer, a faint blue film washed over his vision.

The itching in his mind intensified.

Just in time, Theis leapt backward, splashing through a shallow pool. His cloak, however, was not so lucky. The rings caught the nubuck's hem, fraying the resilient fabric wherever the two connected.

He rubbed the tattered edge between his gloved fingers. He didn't want to think about what effect those rings would have had on his flesh.

A harsh glow framed the stuck beast, and its chittering immediately ceased. It froze, but only for a moment, before each of its multifarious tentacles fumbled against the lip of the fissure. A desperate squeal accompanied its fruitless attempts to free itself.

A deeper chittering sounded from the far side of the fissure, and the itching in his mind vaulted into overdrive.

"Raiya!"

Nevin dashed forward to grab the young woman before she could leap off the cliff, but his fingers caught only air. He skidded to a stop at the edge, his boots raining crumbs of limestone out into the abyss.

It was too late. She was already gone.

A resonant bloop preceded a barely noticeable smattering of smaller plerps that were rapidly swallowed up in the former's echoes. He shuffled back an inch or two so as not to send more rocks sailing down on Raiya's head. After a moment, the cold light of a Soul Quartz rose from the depths of a milky pool of barely moving water. Raiya breached the surface with a sharp gasp.

"Braga's tits, that's cold!" she cried out, paddling one-armed toward shallower waters.

Nevin followed her progress, sidestepping along the cliff's edge to remain above her. "Are you nuts? You could have killed yourself!"

"Not at all." Raiya crawled up the gradual incline, straightening only once the water reached no higher than her knees. "You better hurry up and do the same. I won't be able to protect you from down here."

"Protect *me*?" Huffing with mild annoyance, he looked back to see just how much time he had before the scuttling beasts caught up to him. White light crept along the walls of the tunnel, but he couldn't yet see his pursuers.

"Okay," he said to himself, peering uncertainly at the transformed blade. "What do I do about you, though? Can you just change back? Will I be able to bring you out again if I need you? I don't know how comfortable I am jumping into water with you looking all . . . angry."

Almost on queue, the metal surface of the blade expanded with a soft sucking noise and the seething edge was once again hidden beneath a harmless facade. Darkness rushed in, and his ears rang in the unexpected silence. He hadn't realized how much noise the blade was making until it was contained.

Two dangling lures turned the distant corner, and Nevin set his jaw.

Now or never, I guess.

His stomach rose up his throat as the world disappeared beneath him, and the sudden shock of frigid water nearly choked the life from him. The impact ripped the blade from his shocked fingers. Luckily, his feet quickly found the bottom and Nevin shoved himself upward, breaching the surface with a cry. He wiped at his eyes and frantically looked around for Raiya.

She crouched on the shore, pointing at something in the pool with him. "Is that normal?"

Amazed, the young woman could only stare as the Sharasil somehow floated, bobbing up and down on the ripples created by Nevin's plunge. An inch-thick halo of ice surrounded the blade, but whether the ice was responsible for keeping it afloat or if buoyancy was but another of its mysterious qualities, he didn't particularly care at the moment.

Shivering uncontrollably, Nevin dragged himself ashore, plucking his sword from the water as he passed. One good thwack against the wall was all it took to shake it free of the ice.

"We need to get moving," Raiya urged through chattering teeth, not waiting for his agreement to turn and head up the slight incline in the tunnel. "It's already cold enough down here without being wet, and you won't last long if you don't keep your blood pumping."

"Me? What about you?"

Short one light source, Nevin hurried to remain in close proximity to his companion. Hunks of raw limestone littered their path, and they had to weave through pointed stalactites as they walked. A clear stream trickled along a shallow depression in the corridor, but there was evidence a much larger volume of water once flowed through the chamber.

"This is different," he said, reaching out to trail his fingers down an impressive sheet of curtain-like flowstone. "This is nothing like what we've seen before."

Raiya nodded. "I think you were right. When we got to that cliff, I could hear a difference in the way sound moved through the cave, and I realized I was hearing water underneath it all. And that made me think of something my father said to me right before I left."

"Water always settles at the lowest point?" Nevin returned the Sharasil to its spot on his back and ducked beneath the jagged end of a broken stalactite.

Again, she nodded, her lips curling in a self-satisfied smirk. "If what you say is true, we can't trust the layout of the caves. But flowing water *has* to come from somewhere, and if water always settles at the lowest point, we should be able to follow moving water upward to its source."

Hugging his chest, Nevin prayed she was right. Time had lost all meaning in the blackness of the grotto. He couldn't tell if hours or days had passed since they had entered, but he knew he wanted nothing more to do with the endless twists and turns of unchanging limestone. The prospect of escape got his heart pumping in a way that facing off against frightening crab-beasts couldn't match.

A scream of animalistic fury echoed from all directions, and Nevin nearly tripped over Raiya as she jerked to a halt. She reached back for him, threading her hand into his and pressing her shoulder to his chest. Their combined warmth felt good.

The scream continued in agitated bursts. Beneath their feet, the floor shuddered, its vibrations building in intensity until the two had to shield their eyes from falling debris and crouch to maintain their balance. Behind them, a stalactite broke from the ceiling and crashed to the floor, sending bits of jagged stone flying in all directions. Nevin wrapped his arms around Raiya protectively, feeling the stone pepper his leather vest and hair.

"What *is* that?" Raiya's voice trembled slightly as she spoke.

"A better question is, where is it coming from?"

The vibrations slowed, then ceased altogether. Raiya pulled free of his embrace to wave her spear tip back and forth, scattering the shadows like startled crows. "I can't tell. All this stone just amplifies sound. It could be miles away. It could be fifteen feet from us."

She gestured upstream with the glowing gem. "Let's just go. The faster we get to the surface, the faster we can stop worrying about it."

He really didn't like that idea. "And if we run into whatever it is? What if it's waiting upstream?"

Raiya shot him a stern look. "We're not getting anywhere just standing here. If we run into it, we'll deal with it. Until then, keep your eyes open."

Nevin shivered. "I don't think I'll ever be able to close my eyes again after this."

Chapter 65: A Sea of Flesh

"That sounds like trouble," Raiya breathed quietly, her spear point tilted back the direction they'd come from. Nevin would have agreed with that assessment had he been paying attention, but the problems lying before them troubled him more than those on the way.

Following the shallow stream had lead them to another of the milky pools, the larger underground pond spilling its contents down several side tunnels. It was toward one of these adjacent tunnels that Raiya now directed her attention, as what sounded like a hungry swarm of crab-beasts clamored their way.

Water burbled around their feet, clear and clean and warmer than it had any right to be. The rank smell of decaying plant matter subtly intruded on the stormy scent of petrichor. Both spoke of the welcome influence of the outside world, but if escape lay nearby, it was hiding behind a wall of jumbled stone.

Time had choked the corridor in front of them with tightly fitting boulders, remnants of an unstable ceiling from ages past. Water colored many of the dusky stones several shades darker than that of their companions, seeping through imperfect cracks in the lofty pile to gather into a stream that delved fearlessly into the heart of the grotto.

Nevin regarded the stone blockade with a hint of anger. Following moving water toward its source had seemed such a good plan, until it wasn't. Now, with the prospect of facing down what sounded like an entire army of crab-beasts, their gamble had quite literally put their backs against the wall.

He swiped a hand along the chalky surface of an oddly discolored boulder. Unlike the muted mustard-color found nearly everywhere else in the cave, a lusterless black film coated a section of the boulder's surface. Other rocks scattered within the jumbled blockade bore similar markings.

Nevin moved to wipe his palm on his breeches, but instead lifted his finger to his nose and sniffed. An acrid scent stung his sinuses.

Sulfur?

"There," Raiya said, pointing up the rockslide to a squat opening in the wall to the left of the rubble's apex. At merely five feet high, he couldn't tell if the pinched opening was a tunnel to another room or simply another section of this room partially filled in by chunks of fallen limestone.

His jawed flexed as he considered the hole. If it was a dead-end, he and Raiya would be as good as trapped. Then again, the narrow entrance would at least afford them some protection from becoming surrounded, and they'd both proven their ability to fight back against small numbers of the beasts.

Raiya didn't wait for him to make up his mind, using her spear to steady her gait as she ascended the uneven stone ramp.

Moments later, Nevin ducked through the low opening behind Raiya, squinting into the murky blackness of the rubble-strewn cavity in an effort to pick out any dangers that might be lurking in the shadows. He thought he'd heard something upon entering, a shifting of the fine scree making up the floor, but the cavern was silent now.

Anxiety playing tricks on his senses, he thought, but still something nagged at him, a faint pressure in the back of his thoughts that wouldn't cease.

Raiya froze, a small cascade of rock tumbling into the corridor's throat. She hesitantly extended her spear forward, the meager light of the Soul Quartz peeling back the layers of darkness shrouding the path ahead. As the light crawled forth, piles of larger dusky rocks emerged against the far wall, revealing the corridor to be a dead-end.

One of the rocks shifted, unfurling like a coiled snake and lashing out with a single, gleaming fang.

Without hesitation, Nevin jerked Raiya behind him and brought his blade up defensively.

The Sharasil blazed into lethal action, dropping its harmless facade in a blink and illuminating the small chamber in harsh, blue-white light.

And just in time to deflect the downward cut of razor-sharp blade.

Twin blue orbs winked into existence from within a drooping leather cowl, their fine motes vibrating excitedly at the sight of him.

"About time you . . . figured out that sword," said Theis weakly.

The man in black huffed his telltale snort before collapsing to his knees, his own blade clattering to the floor beside him.

"Theis!" A boyish grin spread his lips wide as he marveled at his disheveled companion's unexpected appearance. In the harsh light, a fine coating of limestone dust on his nubuck cloak had given the man the appearance of stone, but there was no mistaking those dazzlingly blue eyes. Nevin hastily knelt at the man's side, but a gloved hand caught him in the chest before he could get too close.

"Care . . . ful," he groaned, stretching the syllables of the word across a pair of strained breaths.

"You know this man?" Raiya joined Nevin in a crouch, casually nudging the warrior's discarded sword out-of-reach farther down the ramp with the butt of her spear.

"He was with me on the ship."

A million questions ran through his mind. Had he seen their other companions? Where had he been, and how had he survived? Was Aidux okay?!? He wanted desperately to grab the man by the shoulders and shake out some answers, but he recognized that safety needed to be his first priority.

"He's hurt." Raiya gently moved the man in black's hand off Nevin's chest, earning the young woman a withering look from the stoic warrior. If she noticed, she didn't react, reaching across his body to carefully peel back his leather cloak.

Strings of gore bridged the gap, and Raiya involuntarily winced at the sight. "Gods, he's covered in blood. I don't even know how you're still conscious, let alone capable of swinging a sword."

Theis glanced past them. The plodding of bulbous feet and hungry chitters were growing increasingly close, mere moments away from swarming the bottom of the rock slide without. "Being awake . . . helps when . . . you're trying not . . . to get eaten."

Nevin rolled his eyes. "Come on, help me get him to the back of the room. We're gonna need the space to move around if those crab-things come after us."

Theis grabbed him by the arm as Nevin moved to stand, his fingertips biting almost painfully through the stiff fabric of his shirt despite the man's apparent weakness. He shook his head toward the opening. "Something else . . . with them. Something big. Can melt . . . stone . . . with its voice."

His eyebrows reached for one another, unsure how seriously he could take the man in his current state. Blood loss and fever could be spinning figments in his mind, delusions of—

The fingers surrounding his forearm wrenched tighter, and Nevin nearly yelped in pain. The motes in his eyes trembled furiously as Theis glared up at him. "Wipe that doubt . . . off your face . . . boy. My mind will . . . always be sharper . . . than my sword."

Visibly swallowing, Nevin fixed his face and nodded.

"Come on," said Raiya, gently prying his hand from Nevin's arm. With their help, Theis repositioned himself against the wall, sitting with his wounded arm drawn across his lap.

Nevin placed the man's curved blade at his side. "Just in case."

Awash in white light, the chamber without overflowed with the hungry trills of their pursuers. A trumpeting squeal shook the walls of their hiding place, the fine scree dancing in place while a few of the more precariously perched boulders framing the entrance broke free to tumble down the ramp. Nevin and Raiya covered their ears, but Theis could only wince and groan.

The chittering horde went deathly silent. Nevin's fingers tightened around the pommel of the Sharasil, and he carefully slid into position between his two companions and the room's squat opening. The seething hiss of his exposed blade seemed deafening in the sudden silence, and Nevin realized they were likely only moments away from being discovered.

A solitary threatening trill made his heart pound against his sternum, and a dangling lure crested the top of the boulder-strewn ramp.

The events that followed happened far quicker than he thought possible.

First, a dark figure emerged from the lighter blackness within the small chamber with a derisive chuckle, pressing up against his back. A pair of clammy hands crawled up his tense shoulders. To his horror, his hands and feet began moving of their own accord, shifting the blade into an offensive position and stepping forth to challenge the approaching beast.

You're not ready for this. Let me handle it, boy.

Fighting back against the invasive presence, Nevin's toes curled as he dug in his heels.

The shadow persisted, and the edges of the scene softened and pulled away, stranding Nevin at the center of a growing circle of white light afloat in an endless sea of nothing.

Give into me as before, and I will save you once again.

Nevin cast about for a view of his two companions, but nothing existed beyond the confines of the circle of light. He squeezed closed his eyes and shook his head to clear the shadow's influence from his mind. When he opened them, he could barely make out the walls of the cramped space through the blackness surrounding him.

Damp fingers inched along his collar-bone until he felt them digging painfully into the meat of his chest, frozen daggers in search of his heart.

Do not trouble yourself with protecting the impotent. You killed your friends when you chose to hide away in this cave like a coward. You only need hide but one more time, boy.

Breath tickled his ear.

Step aside and survive. Give up and live.

The shadow was right. He had run from Elbin, run from Comelbough, run from Calibri Grotto. Each time he had run, he'd survived. But each time he'd run, he had left something terrible in his wake. Fire. Destruction. Death. Raiya had been dragged into his mess because he had refused to face his pursuers head-on, and now, both she and Theis might pay the price for his cowardice.

Did he possess the skill necessary to protect them both? He'd managed to kill one of the creature's already, and now he was mentally prepared for more. But would that be enough?

He'd escaped death at the hands of Vincht with the shadow's help before, its domination of the learned swordsman proving its competence with a blade. But would it fight to protect his friends, or would it readily sacrifice their lives in an effort to safe-guard his own?

There was only one way to ensure they had the best chance of leaving the caverns unharmed.

He set his jaw and shrugged off the shadow's embrace. The room slammed into focus as Nevin leveled his seething blade at the hissing monstrosity ducking beneath the squat opening.

With a derisive chuckle, the shadow faded back into the darkness and left him to his fate.

Pincers clacking, a pallid tentacle whipped through the air. His sword flashed and the tentacle sloshed to the stone, slithering about like a startled snake and spewing ocher fluid across the wall. Nevin kicked the surprised creature in its eyeless face, the force of the blow ejecting the unexpectedly light monster out of the room and into empty air.

Nevin grabbed the lip of the opening to steady himself on the uneven stone and froze at the sight awaiting him below.

A writhing sea of slimy flesh and glowing filaments bucked and roiled at the foot of the ramp, jostling for the right to rush Nevin's hiding space and feast on its occupants. The anxious monsters readily trampled their smaller kin in their haste, and sharp squeals of pain and rage sounded from various points all around the flesh-choked chamber. A number of the more impatient beasts crowded around an injured member of their group, unabashedly tearing hunks of pallid flesh from the helpless creature and slinging fluid from their flailing tentacles.

At the center of the horde, an over-sized matriarch presided over the chaos, easily twice as tall as its minions and caked in the drying blood of those unfortunate enough to be crushed beneath its careless mass. A crystal-encrusted tendril swept an arc through the air before it like a searchlight, the strength of its harsh white glow stinging Nevin's light-weak eyes. It barked a resonant, trumpeting cry, and the sea of writhing flesh spasmed in response.

Almost as one, the horde turned to face him.

Nevin did the smart thing and ducked out of sight.

Chapter 66: Trust Me

The Sharasil ripped through another of the overeager beasts, and a flash of cold light briefly stole all trace of warmth from the cramped chamber, making the cave's natural chill seem downright balmy in comparison. Another pallid corpse joined what would have been over half a dozen others clogging the ramp leading up to the squat opening in the cavern wall, but as each creature fell, its lifeless form was hurriedly snatched up and dragged back beneath the sea of flailing tentacles to be ripped to pieces in a cannibalistic frenzy. Patches of yellow fluid drooled off the sides of the piled stone, making it increasingly harder for the creature's bulbous feet to find purchase as they clambered up the ramp.

"Kill them . . . in the gap," said Theis, pawing at the ground beside him in search of his sword.

Raiya knelt down at his side, her spear extended protectively in case any of the strange creatures managed to slip past Nevin. So far, none had even come close, but with their seemingly endless numbers, Nevin suspected it was only a matter of time.

He shook his head, feinting with his seething blade to drive back two more. "I'm trying to keep them *out* of the room!"

"Clog . . . the entrance . . . with their bodies." Theis rested his head against the wall and breathed, fighting the urge to press on the grisly shoulder wound hiding beneath a layer of tattered nubuck and congealed blood.

Nevin fed his blade to another snapping maw, and the resulting blast of cold scared its surviving companion back down the ramp. In its haste, one of its bulbous feet became wedged between a shifting pair of large stones. With a cry of fear, the creature yanked at its trapped limb, but Nevin could tell it wasn't going to be able to free itself easily.

Then it did something strange.

Drawing the lure close to its quivering maw, the creature stilled—a low, continuous trill building up in the base of its throat. The cold light of the lure flickered in time with the sound, and the air ahead of it twisted and warped. Small rings of force rippled out from the dangling crystal, and wherever they touched the stone, the rock crumbled away.

In a handful of seconds from start to finish, the creature had freed itself, and without a moment's hesitation, it snagged the limp body of its fallen comrade in its teeth and disappeared back down the ramp to feast.

Nevin gripped the rim of the opening and leaned out over the rocky ramp to search the shadowed limits of the larger chamber. Even if Theis had the strength to move, escape in these circumstances would be practically impossible. A number of smaller corridors branched off of the larger chamber like the legs of a spider, but dozens of chittering beasts stood in their way, and he had no way of knowing if any of those corridors even went anywhere.

A curious tentacle earned the edge of his blade, and the creature squealed in pain and retreated. Maybe Theis was right. Maybe he should pull back a bit and kill them as they followed. It would only take three or four of their awkward corpses to bar any further assault, but by the way they eagerly fed on their own kind, he doubted an edible wall would last long enough to make any kind of difference.

A blackened chunk of fallen stone amid the chalky yellow drew his gaze, and once again, the acrid scent of sulfur tickled his nose. He struggled to place why that small detail bothered him, but instinct pulled his eyes down the ramp to the wide channel of eroded stone and the burbling stream of water that had no hope of filling it. The riverbed cut through the heart of the chamber, spreading wide enough that it nearly brushed the walls on either side.

His eyes widened, and the pieces of an idea suddenly fell into place.

"I think I have a way out of here," he said, ducking back into the room. He kicked at the loose scree carpeting the floor until he spotted a rock about half the size of his fist. He picked it up and nodded to himself, satisfied with its weight.

Raiya eyed him warily. "I feel like there's a 'but' hidden in that statement."

Smiling awkwardly, Nevin half-shrugged. "The line between brilliant and stupid is often drawn by the outcome."

"Oh, that *really* doesn't make me feel better."

Theis chuckled. "I've seen . . . what chases us. I'm good . . . with stupid."

With an apologetic look at his female companion, Nevin stepped out of the opening and heaved the stone through the air.

And right into the middle of the horde of crab-beasts.

The stone caught the over-sized matriarch right below her dangling tendril, eliciting a chirp of annoyance. The massive beast snorted and bared row upon row of jagged, sword-like fangs, then lurched a few steps forward and screamed. A puff of rancid wind buffeted him, and Nevin clapped a hand to his mouth and nose.

You've really done it now.

"Come on," he whispered, ignoring the shadow's taunt. The matriarch huffed and stomped, but didn't advance. Scowling, Nevin raised his sword in a challenge and screamed. "Come on, you coward! Come get me yourself!"

Tentacles blossoming around its mouth like a carnivorous flower, the massive beast screamed in response. Dust and pebbles rained down from the ceiling, and the writhing sea of pallid flesh shrank to the outskirts of the room in a bid to not get eaten.

The matriarch lumbered forward, pounding its bulbous feet into the stone as it picked up speed. The fine scree danced underfoot with each of its steps. A faint high-pitched ringing accompanied the piercing light of its lure, and with a grim look of determination, Nevin squeezed the grip of the Sharasil with both hands and faded back into the opening.

The pounding of his heart was almost immediately overridden by a cry of frustrated blood-lust.

"Did you just do what I think you did?" Raiya screamed over the noise, her spear shaking in her hands.

"Trust me!" he called back, trying to hide his faltering confidence.

A mass of stark-white flesh pressed up against the opening, but the squat fissure was far too narrow for the bulky beast to bully its way through.

Nevin swung his sword, but the wall of flesh leaned away, its saliva-coated teeth gleaming in the light. The hot stink of rancid fish flooded the chamber, and Nevin coughed into his elbow.

To his infinite displeasure, the beast's glowing lure was nowhere in sight. He'd have to wait for the right moment.

A dozen snake-like tentacles dug at the rocks piled up against the opening, attempting to widen the fissure. Nevin cut through the closest.

"No you don't!"

The creature lurched away before ramming its face against the gap, chomping and slathering and squealing with barely restrained agitation. Nevin's swing broke a tooth, and the beast retreated once more.

"Look out!" Raiya cried in warning. Two tentacles, each thicker around than his waist and fitted with a chitinous pincer, darted through the opening. The young woman lunged forward, her spear tip deflecting one before it could get at him. Still off-balance from his last attack, Nevin missed the other as it shot into the room and clamped onto the meat of his leg. Bone pierced leather, and Nevin cried out in pain, grabbing at the needle-nosed pincer as warm blood flowed down his thigh.

Theis struggled to stand, but collapsed onto his side. The other tentacle snapped at Raiya, keeping itself between her and Nevin. He brought his sword down, trying to break the pincer's hold on his leg, but the bony carapace extended farther up the tentacle than his blade could reach, and it merely bounced harmlessly off the surface.

His heels ground against the scree as the tentacle pulled him forward, inching him toward the massive beast's hungry maw. Theis grabbed him by the ankle, but even their combined weight wasn't enough to counteract the creature's strength.

He brought his ineffective blade down again, the seething edge leaving behind little but a thin coating of frost for his efforts. More of the smaller tentacles returned to the gap, digging at the pile and shifting rocks about.

"Attack this one!" Raiya screamed, shrinking back into the cave and forcing the snapping tentacle to follow. As it did, the fleshy portion of the pale appendage crawled into reach, and Nevin saw his chance.

The glowing white blade cut through its flesh like an oar through water, and the creature and all its tentacles recoiled from the opening and screamed. For a moment, Nevin thought it would drag him out with it, but just as it jerked his legs out from under him, the pincer biting into his thigh let go and retreated. He landed hard on his back with a groan.

Raiya gave him no time to catch his breath though, grabbing him by the arm and hauling him to his feet. "This is a weird plan you've got here."

He rubbed his leg. "It's a work in progress, okay?"

Theis groaned, and Raiya rushed to get him back against the wall while Nevin kept an eye on the opening. The severed pincer twitched open and closed occasionally, squirting out a stream of grisly fluid with each involuntary spasm.

"I'm alright," Theis grunted, feebly pushing her hands away.

Raiya hefted her spear and crowded up against Nevin. Shoulder to shoulder, the two peered out the opening at the grumbling monstrosity, their racing heartbeats pounding in sync with one another.

"Good thinking back there," he said, nudging her with his shoulder. He winced, trying not to put too much weight on his wounded thigh.

She nudged him back, but didn't pull away. "That thing's eventually gonna make it in here, and when it does—"

The opening brightened as the creature's dangling lure finally descended into view.

"It's not gonna make it that far, I promise."

His jaw tightened. *One way or another, it was definitely not going to come to that.*

A pale hand ran its fingers down his forearm, coming to rest atop his wrist.

Now or never, boy.

He shook it free. "Get off me," he muttered, not quite to himself.

Raiya pulled away. "I'm sorry?"

Crap.

"I . . . I meant get back. Get to the back of the room and keep an eye out for falling rocks. I have a feeling things are about to get hairy."

Raiya searched his face in silence, then, with a shallow nod, she faded back to crouch at Theis' side.

The mass of pale flesh leaned closer toward the opening, and a low, throaty trill drowned out the dozens of chittering beasts without. Its sword-filled maw parted, and the dangling lure pulsed, slowly building and fading in time with the creature's resonant trill.

Swallowing the fear-shaped rocks in his throat, Nevin darted for the hole.

Focus blocked out everything that wasn't important. The cold vanished. The hungry horde faded into obscurity. The electric hiss of his blade quieted. His aches, his wounds, his worry all fell away, crumbling with each purposeful stride across the scree.

The stones beneath his boots danced from the creature's efforts, but Nevin ignored them. An uncomfortable pressure wrapped itself around him, but still he pushed forward. His vision wavered, but all he could see was the cold light of the crystal-encrusted lure hanging just beyond his reach.

At the rim of the meager chamber, he planted his foot and ripped the Sharasil through the fetid air with all his might. The blade arced a shining curve toward the dangling lure. One solid blow was all he needed, and after that, all he could do was pray.

His wounded leg gave out beneath him, and Nevin's focus shattered.

Instead of stopping, momentum carried him out of the opening and toward slather-coated teeth. Worse still, the extra reach would likely bury his blade in the beast's shoulder.

And then it would gorge itself on his corpse.

Hands took hold of his leather vest and forestalled his momentum, and the Sharasil sliced through the air and struck true. The lower half of the dangling crystal exploded in a hundred glittering shards, and the surprised beast reared to the side, screaming and bucking and sending rings of undulating force deep into the blocked tunnel.

Hands yanked him back into the smaller chamber, and as the light from his sword vanished, he tumbled to the floor in Raiya's arms.

"You could have told me what you were planning!" she said over the noise, dragging him along as she scooted farther away from the opening. Barking a laugh, he started to say something smart when the floor itself began to shift beneath them.

Clambering to their feet, they backpedaled to the rear of chamber, plugging their ears against the ear-splitting grind of hundreds of tons of limestone repositioning itself into the void created by the creature's stone-melting voice. Cries of pain and surprise could be heard in the spaces between crumbling rock, but soon it too was replaced by an undefinable roar.

A hot, wet wind swirled through the opening, choking the room with an impenetrable cloud of sticky rock dust. Coughing, the trio covered their mouths with their arms as best they could, and, with no other choice but to wait, hunkered down against the wall together.

Finally, the dust settled enough for a warm orange glow to filter through, and Nevin came to his feet.

Raiya grabbed his hand. "Wait, where are you—"

"It's okay. It's safe now, I think." He offered her hand a reassuring squeeze. "Stay here with Theis."

Waving aside the thinning haze, Nevin picked his way across the unstable scree and cautiously poked his head out to assess their situation. Shaking his head in disbelief, he turned a tired smile back at his two companions.

"So," he began, rubbing his injured thigh. "Do you want the good news or the great news first?"

Chapter 67: To Answer Your Question

Escaping the grotto had been easy once the sudden influx of water died down enough to reveal a broken path of flattish rocks peeking out through the surface of the churning, murky river. Panicked trout and perch writhed fruitlessly against the current, flashing streaks of momentary silver and yellow within the frothy water before being swallowed up by the darkness of the grotto. Other than treading upon the damp and sometimes slick rocks, the three battered travelers didn't even have to get their boots wet as they emerged from the thirsty gullet of the cave and onto the rocky shores of a swiftly receding pond.

Few words were spoken as the party sought out a suitable campsite for the evening, more out of unabashed wonder at the forgotten beauty of the surface world than general weariness. A burnished orange sunset cast a pleasing glow over the countryside, painting the sky in vibrant layers of dwindling intensity and imbuing the willow trees' lazy tendrils with an ethereal delicateness, as if the faintest breeze could uproot and loft them up into the faintly bespeckled heavens.

Hidden frogs gurgled hesitantly from the moist silt and cat-tails, complaining at the loss of their leisure spots in the shallows of the pond. Crisp, fresh air carrying the light scent of flowering dogwoods replaced the heavy mustiness of the cavern. And warmth, *gods* the warmth.

Nevin brushed aside the oval leaves of a willow as he guided the weary man in black toward its watery trunk. Theis extracted his arm from Nevin's shoulder and sank to the ground without a hint of complaint. His glowing eyes bore no hint of their usual fire, having faded to a deep violet barely brighter than his dilated pupils.

Theis didn't act much like a man in pain. Aside from his lethargy, the man was no different than usual. Quieter, if that was even possible.

Raiya ducked through the willow's drooping branches and appraised the level space beneath the shelter of her limbs. With a happy sigh, she plopped her pack onto the short grass and shoved her spear deep into the loamy soil.

"No rocks. No limitless black. No creepy tentacle monsters trying to eat us." A tired smile split her lips as she tugged her strawberry-blonde hair over her shoulder, idly running her fingers through its tangled ends. "This tree could be on fire, and I don't think I'd be any less happy."

"I second that." He rubbed his jaw, dislodging flakes of grime crusted on the fine hairs of a few days growth.

What I wouldn't give for a bath.

"How's your leg doing?" She knelt down beside him and began poking around without waiting for an answer.

"It hurts."

"We can't have that," she said, rubbing her hands together before resting them atop the twin puncture holes in his new leather pants. The awkward tingle of magic immediately spread throughout his leg and within moments, the pain disappeared.

Raiya hopped to her feet and planted her hands on her hips, leaning over to examine her handiwork. "Better?"

He nodded, resting a hand on her shoulder to steady himself as a brief wave of dizziness set him off-balance. "That did the trick."

"Good, because I saw a rotting log about thirty yards back. If you'll work on gathering wood, I'll go find some stones to line a fire pit and refill our water skins. And, if we're lucky, maybe I'll find a couple of fish for dinner."

He groaned, rubbing his eyes. "Why does it take so much effort to just relax?"

Propped against the tree trunk, Theis watched silently as Raiya made a circle of rounded river rocks and Nevin stacked slender pieces of rotten wood against each other in a cone shape, moving only when Nevin requested the wide skinning knife he kept hidden in his boot. By the time Nevin had shaved a stick of wood down to a pile of tinder, Raiya had returned with three good-sized trout she'd found trapped in a shallow pool.

"Aberrants," Theis mumbled as the young woman maneuvered the prepped fish onto a wide stone she'd placed in the center of the fire pit.

She glanced up at Nevin, a concerned look on her face. She spoke quietly enough that only Nevin should have heard. "Probably time I take a look at him."

Theis weakly cleared his throat. "Not necessary, girl."

Raiya pulled her pack across her knees and rooted around inside. "I don't promise it will be pleasant, but I can definitely guarantee its necessity. Who knows what diseases lurked in that cave, especially considering the existence of those monsters—"

"Aberrants," he repeated, cutting her off. "Products of a Pool. Unnatural, and generally very dangerous."

"A pool?" Nevin rubbed at the drying splotches of yellow blood coating his new outfit. Now he really wanted a bath. "Like a pool of water?"

"A Pool of magic."

Nevin had no idea what a Pool of magic was, but he wasn't about to press Theis for information. While he was fairly sure the man in black would just ignore him if he felt the need, Nevin didn't want to assault him with an array of questions.

"Aha!" Raiya exclaimed, yanking a large pouch from the folds of her pack. The stiff leather pouch was fitted with a long shoulder strap and a brass clasp holding it closed. The leather was a deep, chocolate brown and possessed an unusual matte finish. Extracting herself from beneath the backpack, Raiya maneuvered herself to Theis' side.

The man in black eyed her suspiciously. "What, exactly, do you think you're doing, girl?"

She slipped the pouch's strap over her shoulder and clicked open the clasp. "You can call me Raiya."

Nevin scratched at his neck. "I wouldn't count on it."

She ignored him. "And I suppose you're the legendary Theis Bane?"

"*Infamous* Theis Bane."

"Word has it you're dead."

"Word has it that I'm a demon-in-the-flesh, too. That I devour the souls of my victims, keeping me eternally young and fueling my unholy strength."

He closed his eyes. "Only an idiot believes everything they hear."

"True," she conceded. "Alright then, Infamous Bane, now that the introductions are out of the way, where exactly are you bleeding from?"

The violet glow returned through narrowed lids. "Why?"

Raiya reached for the edge of his cloak, but the man in black quickly deflected her grasping hands. She sighed. "If you are wounded as badly as I think you are, ignoring it will most likely kill you."

"When I ignore things, they tend to leave me alone." His gaze shifted to Nevin. "Though I have recently encountered some exceptions to that rule."

The young man just rolled his eyes.

"This, and myself, are two of those exceptions," she said, her voice dropping effortlessly into that stern, mothering tone she'd used on Nevin when she thought he was being foolish. "If I don't clean and dress your wound, it will likely get infected, and in your weakened condition, it wouldn't be long before nothing short of magic would be able to prevent a long, agonizing death."

He snorted. "A Wizard wouldn't even know what to do with me, and I don't get infected. Leave me be. I'll heal on my own."

"Don't be ridiculous." She swatted away his protesting hand and gingerly peeled the leather cloak away from his right side.

Theis' eyes widened and jumped from violet to bright blue.

"Gods . . ." Raiya covered her mouth as the full extent of his injury filled her round eyes. The cloak lifted away from his side with a wet, sticky slurp. His entire right torso and arm was caked with dark blood in various stages of clotting, making it nearly impossible to determine the source of the mess. Darkness trailed down his pants leg, disappearing beneath the top of his calf-high boot. Streamers of red drooled from the underside of the cloak before snapping and staining the grass in irregular crimson stars.

So much blood . . . Nevin didn't know how Theis could remain conscious with that much misplaced life fluid, let alone walk and talk. The man's strength was unreal. Either Theis had an indomitable will or . . . he didn't know. Much about him was unusual. The man in black clothed himself in secrets as thick and resilient as his leather cloak, and wrapped just as tightly.

"What happened to you, Theis?" Nevin motioned towards the wide swath of blood. "Did those creatures—those 'Aberrants'—did they do that to you?"

"No, this one I brought upon myself."

"Shoulder?" Her gentle poke elicited a threatening growl from beneath the drooping cowl. She smiled apologetically. "I take that as a yes."

Theis' words came in a low hiss. "Dammit, girl! Do you even know what you're doing?"

"Nevin, pass me my water skin before you check the fish."

He did as he was told, tossing the bulging water skin at her feet, then shifting his attention to dinner. He scooted the sizzling fish around the steaming rock, flipping each one individually with a thin stick, careful not to accidentally fling them into the open flame.

"Braga can be a very fickle patron," she began, emptying the contents of her canteen onto Theis' decimated shoulder as she spoke. "But as god of the sea, he's the only patron we lowly fisherman have. Our prayers often include requests for clear skies, a calm, steady wind, and a bounty of fish.

"But mostly though, we pray that Braga's mood remains agreeable."

A distant smile curved her rosy lips as she picked at the farthest edges of his scab, patiently working her way to the wound's epicenter. "There are times I can remember waking at sunrise, marveling at the day's perfection, a true gift to Braga's faithful. Cloudless skies, warm breezes, crystal-clear waves . . . absolutely beautiful. A fisherman could ask for little more. Some of those days, that perfection would stay the many hours, never seeming to end, yet passing quicker than one could ever hope."

The smile vanished. "Other days it seemed like Braga began the day so well just so he could take it all away, to intensify by contrast the anger that boiled just beyond the horizon. You can't imagine how quickly those blue skies can disappear, choked with rain-swollen thunderheads and clusters of green lightning. Water as smooth as glass erupting into thirty foot swells. White rain sweeping into town like a curtain, so thick and heavy that those without shelter have to fight to keep from drowning on their feet."

"There a point to this story, or are you just trying to bore me into unconsciousness?" Theis tried to push her away again, but Raiya effortlessly shoved his hand aside.

"The fishing boats leave just before dawn, heading miles out into the Sea of Calor. These boats aren't built for speed; they're built to facilitate the catching and hauling of fish. When a storm materializes like that, they often don't have time to make it back to port before the worst hits. Most don't even try. It's better to be out on the open ocean when the wind and waves kick up than to be caught among the submerged rocks and cliffs along the shore.

"I've seen boats come back with shattered masts, holes bigger than your head punched in their hulls, listing along at a precarious angle, fisherman clinging to rope and railing to keep from sliding off the nearly vertical decks and into the churning water. It's always amazed me what those boats can go through and still not sink.

"Most of the fisherman, however, are not so resilient."

Raiya softly brushed away bits of clinging scab with her fingers, then wet the area again with her water skin. She offered the remnants to Theis, but the swordsman refused, wordlessly turning his head aside. Cinching the mouth of the skin closed with her teeth, the young woman turned her attention back to her work.

"Few people in town know much of the healing arts. Their general theory for simple wound treatment consists either of dipping it in the ocean or rubbing dirt in it. Or they just simply ignore it. Of course, if any of these treatments worked, then the wound wasn't significant enough to merit attention. At least most were wise enough to seek out those with the means to help them when an injury proved more serious, as was common after a storm.

"My—" She paused, her voice breaking. Theis shot her a curious look, but didn't interrupt.

After a calming breath, her fingers started moving again and she continued. "My mother was one such person, trained in the knowledge of herbs and the workings of the human body. She dedicated her life to serving those in need. In return, the people provided her with nearly anything she needed, free of charge."

Theis shifted uncomfortably as her fingers inched ever closer to the source of the blood. "Now you're going to tell me she taught you everything she knows."

Raiya nodded. "When I was old enough, yes. Whenever a storm hit, I'd stand at her side in the port below town, waiting for boats to return, waiting to offer our skills to the wounded. She taught me how to recognize the severity of an injury, how and with what herbs to treat it, and what actions would be necessary to ensure it heals properly. Over the years, I've tended to wounds ranging from broken bones to severed limbs, treated various maladies, and even performed the duties of a mid-wife on two separate occasions.

"So, to answer your previous question," she said, flashing Theis a bright smile. "Yes, I do know what I'm doing."

Theis squeezed his eyes closed. "Next time, cut the long-winded story short with a simple 'yes.' Save me the effort of ignoring you."

Chapter 68: Face It

Sticking his tongue out the side of his mouth, Nevin carefully scooped each trout off of the cooking stone with a pair of sticks and transferred the crisp, steaming fish onto another flat rock Raiya had left outside of the fire. Despite his lingering distaste for fishy smell, the three trout smelled delicious.

"Theis, what . . ." Squinting intently, Raiya picked at the tattered fabric revealed by her cleaning. "Your skin. It's so . . . Are these scars?"

Nevin craned his neck around the young woman, trying to see what she was talking about, but Theis grabbed her by the wrist and shoved her hand away from his shoulder.

"Does it matter? Either treat the wound or go away."

Raiya delicately pried his fingers off of her wrist. "Your skin is covered in them. How did you get so many scars?"

"Been fighting a long time."

"But they look like burns." Nevin could tell she wasn't just trying to pry; her words rang with genuine concern.

"All mistakes have consequences," he said grimly, shaking his head. "Now do whatever you're going to do before I lose my patience."

Nevin rustled through her pack and produced an assortment of vegetables, shoving them on the end of a stick. A few minutes in the fire would give Raiya time to finish with Theis, and give the fish time to cool.

Raiya pulled a chalky black stone about the size and shape of a goose egg from her first-aid pouch. Pock-marks and tiny holes covered nearly every inch of its surface, and by the way it shuddered in her open palm from but a breath of wind, Nevin got the impression it weighed practically nothing.

"This," she began, nodding to the stone, "is 'pumice'. It's a highly abrasive type of stone we sometimes find on the beaches near town. It's good for buffing away dead skin, a side effect of spending large amounts of time in the ocean. I use one almost every day. It can be painful at first, but your skin gets used to it fairly quickly."

Nevin caught himself eyeing the smooth, hairless skin of her bare legs. He swallowed hard and forced his attention back to the fire. *Must be a side-effect of all that scrubbing.*

Raiya continued, enunciating each word carefully, as though explaining something important to a child. "What I'm about to do is not going to be pleasant, but if I don't clean the debris from the wound, it *will* get infected."

"Hold on a second," said Nevin, confused. He extended the hand with the partial missing fingertip, a remnant of his encounter with the splinter of Ignocite a few days prior. "Why even go to all this trouble? Can't you just heal him like you did me?"

"That takes magic, so that wouldn't . . ."

Frowning, she glared down at the man in black. "You mean you've been running around with him for weeks and he doesn't know?"

Theis shrugged. "Never came up."

She nearly punched him in the shoulder, but caught herself at the last second with a resigned sigh. "Nevin, Theis is a magic eater. Most kinds of magic have exactly zero effect on him."

"Wait, that's a thing?!"

"*One* thing." Theis extended a single finger. "Me. The only one."

"Which means I have to do this hard way." She shook the hunk of pumice at the man in black, who immediately straightened reflexively. "Nevin, it might be a good idea to talk to him while I do this. Help keep his mind off the pain."

Nodding, Nevin wiped a hand down his face and yawned. The day's stress-level was beginning to catch up to him. He foresaw himself lying face-down in the dirt within the hour, and it couldn't come too soon.

Theis' eyes lit up like the rising sun when Raiya began scrubbing, but Nevin tried to keep him distracted by filling him in on the events prior to their reunion in the grotto. Raiya hauling him ashore, the smoking cabin, meeting Druce, learning how to swim and about different plants.

The man in black occasionally interrupted, urging him to 'get on with it', but otherwise sat perfectly still, his blazing eyes frozen on the younger man's face. Nevin told him about the men in town, how they had recognized him and tried to chase him down, but he was too quick, disappearing through the alleys of Calibri Grotto.

"Echoes of Vincht?" Theis forced through clenched teeth.

Nevin shrugged. "Who else could they be? As soon as they spotted me, they stopped what they were doing and gave chase. I've never been outside of Elbin. No one knows me. I don't have any telltale scars or other distinguishing features. You couldn't really describe me to someone and honestly expect them to be able to pick me out of a crowd. That old man *must* have recognized the sword, and the only person I know that could have done that is someone connected with Vincht."

"Or someone associated with Ishen."

His mouth twisted in thought. His old mentor's serendipitous escape from Elbin coincided perfectly with the arrival of men seeking the Sharasil, a mysterious artifact that Theis had put Ishen in charge of protecting. But if the man *had* desired the sword, wouldn't it have made more sense to just take it with him?

He bowed his head and sighed. *Too many questions.* "I didn't stick around to find out. As far as I'm concerned, I can't afford to take chances on strangers. Not right now."

He nibbled on a piece of fish as he continued his tale, explaining how helpful Druce had been, how Raiya had basically shamed him into letting her come, and finished with the battle with the tentacled creatures and how the sword changed in his hands. Raiya took a break during this last part, interjecting her point of view between mouthfuls of fish and roasted onion. Theis didn't respond when Raiya suggested he wait to eat until after she was done scrubbing his shoulder.

"Well," Theis said, sliding forward and crossing his legs beneath him. "If I'm to have the rest of my shoulder's flesh scraped away, I prefer you get to it now and have it done."

Raiya dusted off her palms and rinsed her fingers with a splash of water. "There isn't much left to do. I was just about to apply a poultice."

Theis shook his head. "Haven't done the back yet."

"The back?"

"Wound goes all the way through."

She scooted over to his side, drawing the cloak back as she moved.

"Gods, there's just as much . . . What did this?"

"Piece of wood about the length of my forearm."

"I can't believe how close it is to your shoulder blade," she mumbled, lightly brushing the prickly scabs with her fingertips. "A piece of wood? Are you sure? I can't find so much as a splinter back here."

"Of course I'm sure," he snapped. "I'm the one who yanked it out."

"You *yanked* it out?!" Raiya nearly fell over backward. "Are you insane? That could have killed you!"

Theis sighed. "But it did not. Now, can we please get on with it?"

Raiya nodded, attempting to shame the man in black with her judgment stare. She poured the remaining bits of water from her water skin over the blood-choked pumice stone, washing out the bits of sticky skin that clogged the stone's multifarious pores. A pool of red threaded through the short-bladed grasses around the willow's base, inching along as if weeping up from tree's roots.

After a few minutes of scrubbing, Raiya set the pumice aside and withdrew a few more supplies from her first-aid pouch. She applied a mixture of powdered herbs to a bandage before soaking it in water and wrapping it loosely around Theis' shoulder.

"All done," she said quietly, standing up. "Now, if you'll both excuse me, I have a date with a bar of soap."

She winked at Nevin. "And you're next, stinky."

Groaning happily, he mouthed a 'thank you' and watched her brush aside the drooping limbs and disappear into the night.

After all they'd been through recently, Nevin couldn't help but feel apprehensive about her being alone this close to the cave. Who knew if those creatures would venture out into the open air? And what was stopping them, now that the rock slide had been swept away? She didn't even take her spear.

"What's your plan here, boy?"

Nevin's teeth squeaked against one another, his jaw flexing with irritation. *Still with the 'boy'.* "That's the second time you've asked me that question now."

"Means you should be better prepared to answer it."

"You'd think." He snapped a twig between his fingers and tossed it into the flames. "Honestly? With Aurnia missing, I don't really have a lead on what to do with the sword. I'd head to Vadderstrix like she originally planned, but that was only a stop on the way to her ultimate destination, so I'm not sure how much good that would even do."

He hugged his legs to his chest and rested his chin on his knees. "I don't know how to explain it, but . . . the more I think about it, the more I believe you and I weren't the only ones to survive the wreck. I have this weird feeling in my gut whenever I think about Aidux. Like he's out there somewhere, like he survived the wreck just like you and I did.

"Maybe they *both* survived, and if I can find them, then I still might be able to get some answers."

Closing his eyes, Theis took a moment to center himself. When he spoke again, his words sounded fuller, more focused. "I recognize this country, though it's been many years since I've been this far west. There should be a road about an hour or two to the east. It isn't very well traveled, but it does connect Calibri Grotto to one of the region's major thoroughfares."

He reopened his eyes, the discolored motes slowly orbiting his depthless pupils. "Be a good place to part ways with your new friend."

Nevin shot the man a dark look. "I didn't ask her to come in the first place, and she's capable of making her own decisions. But you and I would both be dead without her, so don't be so quick to dismiss her."

"Her assistance—and yours, for that matter—wasn't as necessary as you seem to think."

Hot blood flushed his cheeks crimson. He hardly noticed his breath turn to fog as his hands pulled the Sharasil into his lap.

"You're so full of it, Theis. Actually, you know what? You may have saved me back in Elbin, and I let you lead me around with little to no faith in who you were or what you were about. But whether you want to admit it or not, I saved *you* this time, so it's my turn to make the decisions for awhile. And until Raiya wants to leave, I say she's welcome to stay."

"This isn't some casual cross-country hike, boy. This is real. This is dangerous. If she stays, she's likely to get killed. Having her around is a liability. Can't protect the both of you."

Nevin lifted the blade out in front of him. "I'm not entirely worthless. Neither of us are. She killed her share of those creatures, too. You should be grateful for the help."

He dropped the blade back into his lap and ran a hand through his hair. "Besides, what makes you think you can protect me all the time? Where were you when I washed up on shore? Where were you when I was chased out of town? Where were you when I was attacked by monsters in the caves?"

Theis leaned forward, his voice low and ominous. "I've been there when it mattered, boy."

"It doesn't matter if you've been watching over me my entire life, Theis. You aren't infallible, and now you've only one good arm to rely on!"

The man in black closed his eyes and sighed. He straightened, pulling his wounded arm into his lap and folding his hands, one atop the other. His cloak obediently followed the movement, sliding slowly back into place and encasing him in a fortress of matte-black leather.

"Send her away, Nevin. For her own good."

Disgusted, Nevin could only shake his head. "She'd be flattered to know you're *so* worried about her."

The silence between them stretched thin, the quiet interrupted only by the distant chirping of hidden frogs and the crackle of fire. Nevin glared into the wavering flames, trying to ignore the feeling of the man in black's eyes boring into him and only partially succeeding. As the minutes ticked by, he wondered how much of the heat in his cheeks came from sitting so close to the fire, and how much came from the anger burning in his chest.

Had Nevin not been so irritated when Raiya finally returned, he might have stared. In the firelight, her bronze skin practically glowed, and her hair's strawberry undertones rose to the surface. She threaded her fingers through the tips of her wavy hair in attempt to dislodge any stubborn tangles, pausing to look hesitantly between the two men.

"Am I . . . interrupting something?"

Nevin finally turned back to the man in black. "It's nothing. He's just being more stoic than usual."

The swordsman mumbled something under his breath, and though Nevin couldn't make it out, he sensed it was something insulting.

A slimy lump of soap landed in his lap. "Your turn," said Raiya with a smirk.

A bath sounds fantastic. "We should try to get some rest. We got lucky in the grotto, but there are still people out there looking for the sword, and I don't want to be exhausted if and when we happen across them."

"Why don't we just head back home? I doubt they would look for you in Calibri Grotto again, and even if they do, we know enough about the caves to stay hidden for some time."

"Some of us could," the man in black grumbled.

Nevin shook his head. "I've already searched everywhere in and around the Grotto. Aidux and Aurnia are out there somewhere, I'm sure of it, and if I ever want to figure out the Sharasil and regain some semblance of control over my life, I have to find them."

"Damn your fool head, boy."

Uttering a string of incomprehensible expletives, Theis shoved to his feet. "Wanting something to be true doesn't force reality to rewrite itself to please you. Everyone but you and I died on that ship, and if you don't want to become a corpse, you'd better pull your head from your ass and face facts."

Beneath Nevin's curled fingers, the blade wavered, white light blazing to life as it shed its innocuous travel form and adopted the deadly edge that had viciously ended the lives of so many Aberrants not but a few hours earlier. It flickered back and forth between the forms a hundred times with each thundering beat of his heart. In his fury, the generally cold blade felt warm on his skin, and a haze of crimson colored his vision, staining its pulsing white glow a faint shade of red.

Theis' blue eyes grew ever more vibrant as the two stared intently at one another. Leaning back on her hands, Raiya regarded the scene in silence, afraid that even the slightest movement would devolve the fragile tension into violence.

The blade stilled, but the hot fury still raged through his veins.

"You're a real bastard, Theis." Anger overshadowed the pain hidden behind his words.

"I promised to keep you alive, not to coddle you, not to be your friend. Don't care if you like me, so don't expect me to pad the truth with pleasantries and reassurances. They are dead. You are not. Face it."

A cruel whisper sounded from beyond the drooping branches. ***But you won't face. You won't see. You won't accept.***

Nevin swallowed the lump in his throat. "Just get away from me," he whispered. He turned to the blazing fire, hiding his face from his companions before they could spot the tears welling up in the corners of his eyes.

No one moved. Finally, he heard the grass crunch beneath the soft leather of the swordsman's boot as he took a half-step towards him. When the man spoke, his voice had traded the harsh certainty for a more hesitant tone.

"Look—"

Nevin spun around, tears speeding down his cheeks. "*I said go away!*" he screamed, his voice cracking. A pair of startled doves lit from some hidden branch above, their wings beating the air like wet sheets of cloth.

Theis answered the outburst with his tell-tale snort before striding out into the night air, and thankfully out of his sight.

Raiya knelt at his side, placing a comforting hand on his tense forearm. He could feel her beside him, quietly searching for the right words, but before she could speak, Nevin cleared his throat and spoke.

"I'm gonna go clean myself up. Don't want to ruin these fancy new clothes so soon after your father gave them to me."

Without another word, he left her there, watching him walk away with a concerned look painted across her face.

The cool air soothed the residual heat left on his skin from sitting so close to the campfire, but it did little to ease the inferno that blazed just beneath the surface. Theis was wrong. Hope was all he had to hold on to. His two companions had to be alive. Somewhere.

And why not? He'd survived the wreck, and Theis was mostly fine. All the evidence told him that those below deck had caught the worst of it. The two bodies that had washed up on the shores near Calibri Grotto had both been crew members of the Misanthrope. Raiya had said those bodies were shredded beyond recognition, yet Nevin had escaped with little more than scratches. Surely, Aidux and Aurnia had escaped the worst of it.

As he shed his clothes in the grass near the water's edge, Nevin finally allowed himself to really cry. With tears running down his neck and bare chest in rivulets, his mind whispered a silent prayer for his missing friends, calling on the name of any god he could remember, any god that might hear.

The prayers rose up into the twinkling night sky, touching each star individually as they spread across the heavens.

He only hoped someone was listening.

Just out of sight of the campsite, Theis whipped his thin, curved blade free of its scabbard with his one good hand and took his anger out on a low-hanging branch, cleanly separating a three foot wisp of diaphanous leaves and mottled wood from the greater portion of an innocent willow.

The man in black slammed his blade home and dropped to his knees in the grass before the tree's twisted roots. He yanked his cloak tight around his muscled form and closed his eyes, turning his focus inward, forcing his wild breathing into deep, measured droughts.

He tried to picture three stars on a black background, each one shining brightly above the other in a stacked line. He tried to imagine the bottom star lending its light to the middle, tried to imagine the middle directing its enhanced glow to the top. He tried, time and again, to hold that image steady in his mind's eye, to block out the distant frogs, to push aside his anger, to ignore the burning in his wounded shoulder.

"*Khek*," he finally sighed, opening his eyes after too many minutes of failure.

For the first time in his too long life, Theis couldn't meditate.

He wanted to believe the problem revolved around the unfamiliar pain that had invaded the upper portion of his torso, that the uncomfortable sensations were too alien to ignore, but he knew better than that. The pain was little more than an inconvenience, a gnat buzzing around the fringes of his cowl.

He tried to convince himself that the problem was Nevin, that the boy's incessant idealism and naivety were more than he could stomach, but he knew his attitude was only partially responsible for his inability to concentrate. As Theis had already clarified, he could really care less what the boy thought of him; it wasn't his place to inspire warm, fuzzy feelings. His was the place of the protector, and one didn't have to like their protector for him to do his job well.

Though he was loathe to admit it, the problem was more internal than external. More specifically, Theis was angry at himself.

What had he been thinking? There was sound logic in Nevin's hope for their companions' survival. Aurnia was no ordinary old woman, and the lynx . . . well, the lynx was special in more ways than one. If an unremarkable kid like Nevin could survive a blast like that . . .

Part of him agreed with the boy, agreed that they *should* be looking for the other two, but some other part of him vehemently opposed that course of action. The worry was not with being unable to locate them. No, the world was large enough that two people could search for one another for an entire lifetime and never locate each other.

The crux of his worry rested firmly on the possibility of actually *finding* one of them.

Theis slammed his fist into the ground, narrowly missing an exposed root. What if they found Aurnia, but not Aidux? What if she had found the cat floating lifelessly in the ocean, shredded by flying bits of razor-sharp wood?

As much as he tried to tell himself he didn't care what the boy thought of him, Theis didn't know if he could stand knowing with one hundred percent certainty that *his* presence had caused the death of Nevin's best friend, and nearly killed the boy as well.

He shook his head and slammed his fist into the ground again. No, it would be better if he didn't know. The boy would be fine with that hope still burning in his heart. Better that neither of them knew the true fate of the old woman and his pet cat.

Better that no one else knew that his presence had nearly killed the first person he'd felt some connection to in more than a decade.

Moments after the explosion . . .

Chapter 69: Vilum Fever

Aurnia was flying.

As the world brimmed with the blue tingle of unhinged magical energies, a powerful wind erupted from a point over the deck of the Misanthrope, lifting her from her feet and flinging her out into the night like a Fading leaf. Doubled over, the rushing air spun her over until she could see the dark waters of the Sea of Calor passing by at a frightening speed. Wind nipped at the wispy material of her yellow dress, threatening to tear it from her trim form.

Her mind worked the problem with unnatural speed. At this rate and angle of travel, she would strike the surface like a flat stone, skipping painfully through the waves until her broken form was cast beneath the stygian depths. If she did nothing, the fall could very well kill her.

As a Wizard, she knew better than most how unforgiving water could be.

Taking hold of her flailing limbs, Aurnia shoved back her anxiety and reached for the warm spark of light glowing faintly in the darkest corners of her mind. An unfamiliar thickness slowed her, as if the search found her wading into a deep pond. The warm light spread through her until she could feel her soul vibrating in the tips of her fingers and toes.

She made it no further than that.

Before she could focus her intent to weave a cushioning shield, the winds abruptly reversed direction on her, recalling the previously expelled energies and erasing her concentration as they propelled her into a violent mid-air cartwheel.

Though the change reduced her forward momentum to a safer speed, she still crashed into the water at an odd angle. The impact torqued her spine, jerking the connected muscles in unnatural directions. Deep in her lower back, something pulled free. Tangy brine rushed into her open mouth and choked a pain-filled scream to silence.

An eternity came and went in the brief seconds it took her head to emerge into the balmy night air.

"Foolish woman," she cursed herself between ragged coughs, each of which sent bolts of agony radiating up her spine. "Never lose concentration. Never!"

Disgusted with herself, Aurnia spat. The taste of salt lined her mouth so thoroughly that she knew no amount of spitting would rid her of its tang. She did it again anyway, enjoying the momentary relief it provided.

Blinking away the brine, she looked around, confused. Where was the Misanthrope? In fact, where was *anything*?

Reminiscent of her final night in Comelbough, the night sat obscured behind a milky fog in all directions. She tread water, turning slowly about so as not to aggravate her back. Aurnia rubbed her eyes and looked again.

Nothing. No ship. No blue light. No companions.

Just fog.

A weight pressed down on her chest. Who knew how far from shore she was? What if the ship was out there right now, floating off without her? Would the survivors even search for her, or would they just continue on, leaving her to find her way ashore in the dead of night with a strained back? How long could she tread water before some hungry fish made a meal of her?

Aurnia squeezed her eyes shut hard enough that white splotches colored the inside of her eyelids. "Hush yourself," she whispered, trying to take control of her raging emotions. "It's just the Pool talking. You are a Wizard. There is no obstacle too great in this world that you cannot overcome."

She could sense it in her mind, the buttery feeling that coated every thought, overriding logic and replacing each conclusion with one tainted by doubt, fear, and sorrow experienced by those who linger too long in a Pool, or who enter a particularly dense Pool. Though not permanent, she would have to maintain careful control of her thoughts until the fever wore off, else she may suddenly decide that the best solution to her problem would be to slip quietly beneath the waters and drown.

Images of Nevin kneeling on the deck, clutching his head and sobbing uncontrollably, lingered in her mind's eye as she tried to figure out what to do next. *Full-blown Vilum Fever.* She heard stories about people caught up in the effects of a fully actualized Vilum Fever, and in nearly every instance the victim died, sometimes taking others with them as they lashed out in fits of unfathomable terror or fury.

If the blast hadn't killed him, the fever definitely would. The sword was gone, and with it, all hopes of finding out why—

She huffed in frustration. The fever talking again. Pessimism was one of the trademark symptoms of a Vilum Fever stricken by a Somnalis Pool.

A strange noise carried on the breeze flipped her focus to the external.

Ignoring the pain in her lower back, Aurnia sucked air, filling her lungs to brink of bursting and held her breath. The added buoyancy lifted her head clear of the waves, granting her ears an uninterrupted taste of their surroundings.

There, again. It sounded like a small child, plaintively calling out to something in the darkness.

She shook her head. *A child? It couldn't be. Captain Williams ran a tight crew. Surely he wouldn't have allowed his men to bring children on a smuggling run.*

Again, and louder this time. She could almost make out what it was saying. The fever told her the sound was probably the cry of some deceptive Aberrant, meant to draw her into a trap so the beast could devour her, but logic told her that if she didn't do something, she would die just as easily from exhaustion.

"May Fate be good to me." With that muttered prayer, Aurnia began a slow and careful paddle off in the cry's direction.

She tried not to think as she swam, tried not to give in to the fears scratching at the inside of her skull, tried to avoid fueling their insistent whispers with musings of her companions' fate or the violent behavior of the Pool, but while no amount of wondering would give her insight into the current state of her three companions, the Pool's reaction gnawed at her more than the fever.

Aurnia spat out a mouthful of seawater. No sailor worth a tick would knowingly sail into the heart of a visible Pool, and Captain Williams hadn't mentioned anything about a Pool when she proposed travel through the Calorthian Void. Strange as it may seem, that meant the Pool wasn't visible until they were already in its midst.

She'd never heard of such a thing. Either a Pool was visible, or it wasn't. Pools grew denser over time, and even an invisible Pool would one day adopt a specific color in accordance with its element, but not even the most learned members of the College of the Faithless knew how long that could take, and it most certainly wouldn't occur instantaneously.

And the explosion? She didn't even know where to begin with that.

After an eternity of paddling, a dark shape emerged from the fog like a great carnivorous fish breaching the surface to swallow the sky. The sight gave her such a start that she wrenched her back trying to swim backwards.

"By all the souls in Obolvia . . ."

A specter of her former self, the Misanthrope floated lifelessly, surrounded by islands of shattered wood and sheets of torn canvas. Two of the ship's towering masts lay back across the rear portion of the deck, the other extended over her stern. The way they were snapped off near the base and cracked in multiple places gave them the appearance of massive brown caterpillars squiggling off the ship in fright. The area she had confused for fish teeth was centered just below where she imagined herself standing just before the blast. A gaping hole nearly twenty feet across cut a jagged v-shaped crevasse into the heart of the Misanthrope, stopping only a few feet shy of water level. The edges were warped, curled outward.

She was amazed the ship still tread water, and more capably than herself. She needed to find stable ground, get dry, and soon. If there was any chance of finding others while they still lived, she would need to act fast.

If they still lived.

Before she could choose a suitable piece of driftwood to act as her lifeboat, the sound returned again, much closer than before. Close enough that she could finally make out the single word it kept repeating, yelling in its boyish tenor.

"*Nevin!*"

And that's when she saw the lynx.

Perched atop a piece of deck no larger than a wagon wheel, Aidux had his butt in air, bobtail twitching furiously, his right front paw gingerly swiping at the water in an attempt to circle the wreckage, but his efforts merely spun the island of wood in place. With his golden brown fur matted and dyed nearly black by his time in the ocean, Aidux appeared a shadow of his former self, a wraith plying the waters in search of wayward souls.

"*Nevin!*" His desperate call was muted by the cottony fog.

"Aidux!" she breathed, grateful to see someone she recognized.

The cat froze, one paw extended inches above the water's surface, his silver eyes as big as saucers as he stared at her in obvious surprise, surprise that only lasted a second before his stubby tail set to twitching again and he nearly toppled off his narrow perch in frantic excitement.

"Aurnia! Aurnia! I can't find Nevin! I've been calling and calling and calling and calling and . . ."

"I could hear you," she managed, overwhelmed by the lynx's sudden onslaught of words. "I wouldn't have been able to find the ship without you."

Aidux bobbed his head up and down and pulled his lips back over his teeth in a snarl. She thought he meant it to be a smile, but the expression just came out frightening. "Oh good. I'm glad *someone* heard me. I called and called and no one answered. Then I fell off my board and it took me *forever* to crawl back up on it—"

He stopped mid-sentence, leaning ever so slightly in her direction before he spoke again.

"You . . . you haven't seen Nevin, have you?"

She shook her head sadly. "But if I can get out of this water and up onto one of the larger pieces of debris, I'll see what I can do to find him."

His ears perked up at that, flinging droplets of saltwater over his shoulders. "There's one big enough for both of us behind me."

Within minutes, Aurnia and Aidux were huddled together in the center of what appeared to be a large triangular portion of the Misanthrope's starboard hull. The lynx watched her anxiously as she arranged herself in a cross-legged position across from him. The buttery sensation caused by the Vilum Fever had all but faded now, leaving only a growing fatigue to cloud her focus.

Aidux shifted nervously, rocking their makeshift lifeboat. "Now what? How are we going to find Nevin? Can I help? What do you want me to do?"

"*You* don't need to do anything," she whispered, closing her eyes and trying to will the tension from her muscles. "Aside from sitting still."

The cat's ears wilted, but he consented to her request.

Aurnia took a deep breath, cringing when the effort sent her lower back into a brief spasm. She adjusted her breathing accordingly, and soon forgot all about the pain, the weariness, her drenched and slightly chilly clothes, the gently rocking sheet of wood, and the talking lynx sitting a foot away, his wide silver eyes boring into her face as if somehow trying to strengthen her focus with his. The outside world disappeared, replaced with brilliantly gleaming white-hot light of her soul, shining out from the confines of the deepest parts of her mind.

As she drew her soul through its ethereal channel and felt it wash over her entire body, weaving the spell from her reserves of Vellis and Somnalis felt like a wrestling match. She had gotten out of practice. Other than the battle with the soldiers of Comelbough a few days before, she could hardly remember the last time she had found herself using some of the higher forms of magic in stressful situations.

She pushed the thoughts aside. Nothing could mar her intent if she expected this to work properly. First, though, she needed a medium.

She opened her eyes, staring at the empty space between her raised palms. Aidux cocked his head, looking back and forth quizzically between her hands. "I don't think now's a good time for a hug, Aurnia."

"Hush." A brief glimmer of blue light sparked between her palms before quickly being replaced by a steadily ballooning ball of azure liquid. The amazed look on Aidux's face nearly made her smile.

She knew scrying on Theis would be a waste of energy. If he still lived, he was on his own, something he was more than used to. She wasn't worried about him in the least, either. The man seemed indestructible, a vagrant soul cast into the world of form.

Nevin would not be so indestructible. She doubted the boy would last half a day before the fish got him.

Nevin had the blade, the key that unlocked the door barring the answers to her questions.

Nevin was the only person that mattered.

Nevin.

A burst of color rippled out from the center of the azure sphere, spreading varying degrees of blue through its mass. Strangely, the color grew and then faded with each passing ripple, never forming into a distinct picture.

She frowned. *What is it doing?*

After a few more frustrating moments, Aidux leaned over to the side of the rippling sphere, gazing at Aurnia apologetically. "Is your crystal ball broken, Aurnia?"

Aurnia released her hold on the spell and the ball of water collapsed with a splash at their feet. "Crystal ball?"

"Nevin says witches always have crystal balls in the stories. He told me all about them. They use them to spy on people. I didn't see anyone in your crystal ball though. Is it broken?"

As confused and annoyed as she was at her spell's failure, Aurnia couldn't stop the smile from broaching her lips. She wiped her hands together, brushing off the thin layer of Gluph deposited on her skin from the casting.

"I don't know what's wrong. While a scrying spell is not one I would recommend a novice Wizard to attempt, it is well within my capabilities to manifest properly. A hundred times I've cast this spell, and never have I seen it act so strangely."

The lynx scooted closer. "Does that mean . . . Is Nevin . . ."

Aurnia instinctively placed a comforting hand between the cat's tufted ears. It felt strange, humanizing a lynx, but she got the weird feeling that Aidux was more human than cat. "You can't scry on the dead. Attempting to do so would garner no result at all. The sphere would remain exactly so, unchanged by my efforts. No, this was something different, almost like something was interfering with the spell. Your friend is still alive, I'm sure of it."

She wondered if the Pool was having some lingering effects on her spell casting, effects other than the Vilum Fever.

A deep crease darkened Aurnia's brow. Where *was* the Pool? Why could she not feel it, not see it? Had the ship floated outside its borders?

Aidux glanced back to the wreckage of the Misanthrope. "In there, maybe?"

Aurnia pursed her lips. "Maybe, but I don't know how safe it would be for us to be walking around in there."

Aidux stood up and faced the boat. "We have to try. Some of those sailors could be in there, too injured to move. And Theis might be somewhere on the boat also, waiting for us to come and rescue him. He's too stubborn to call for help, Aurnia."

She snorted. *The cat knows him well.*

Staring at the wreckage, Aurnia suddenly wished she'd focused her elemental sub-specialty in Sharlis instead of Somnalis. Knowledge of the subtle intricacies of spirit magic could have served her quite splendidly in this situation. A simple life probe could instantly tell her whether or not exploring the decimated Misanthrope would be a worthy endeavor. Unfortunately, a 'simple life probe' was not so simple for a Wizard of her specialties.

"I'll go," said the cat, holding his head up high. "I'm far more dexterable than you are. The ship won't even know I'm there."

"That word is 'dexterous', my friend," she corrected. Aidux cocked his head, mouthing the word soundlessly over and over again. "And no, you won't. If someone *is* alive over there, I can do much more for them than drag them into the water with my teeth. You're going to stay here."

"But, can't we can search it twice as fast together?"

"Yes, and the boat will fall apart twice as fast with both of us tromping through its remains." She reached into the folds of her robe and extracted a tiny cube-cut yellow gemstone, placing it at Aidux's feet. "I'll need you to keep an eye on this. If it falls in the ocean, you'll be the one paddling us to shore."

The lynx scrunched up his nose and pawed at the stone. "What is it?"

"A magical focus. You know that ball of water I had floating between my hands?" He nodded. "I wrapped it in a cocoon of Vellis, of wind. The wind held it together. I'm going to do the same to the ship."

"But it's so *big*," he whispered reverently. "And wind isn't very strong. How can air hold something like that together?"

Smiling, she softly poked his shiny black nose. "Wind is stronger than you think. Just ask the trees."

Dropping back into a state of relaxation, Aurnia left the lynx's questioning look unanswered as her soul once again expanded to fill her expectant body. This time though, before she formed the intent that would wreathe the Misanthrope in a stabilizing cocoon of wind, Aurnia urged her soul out beyond the boundaries of her skin and into the Vellis Orlicite.

The tiny square gemstone lit up a golden yellow in response.

Invisible cords of braided wind encircled the creaking Misanthrope, tightly binding the remaining pieces together. The ship's complaints were fervent but brief. A steady wind belied the spell's apparent cessation, continually feeding the protective shell of air.

Before she withdrew her soul, Aurnia reached into the back of her mind to the source of the warm light and broke off a sliver of the spark. Pain, like ten thousand tiny cuts slicing her skin, radiated out from the base of her skull. She did her best to ignore it—such was the price of persistent spells. She carefully directed the spark into the heart of the Orlicite and released her mental grip on her soul. With her soul's absence, the shadows quickly returned to the corners of her mind, but the Orlicite still shone brightly.

Her stomach growled angrily. She would need to do something about that if she expected to cast many more spells tonight.

Aidux adjusted his position until the Orlicite rested in a small nook between his massive paws. "Now what?"

Aurnia carefully slid off the slab of wood and back into the inky waters. "Try to stay near the ship. I shouldn't be long."

With a soft shove, she pushed off towards the Misanthrope, leaving the talking lynx to watch over the Orlicite.

Chapter 70: The Stench of Wet Lynx

Aidux never was any good at understanding the passage of time.

Sure, the sun rose, the sun set, the stars came out, the pretty blue moon appeared in the eastern sky. He understood morning, noon, evening, and night. He got the whole breakfast, lunch, and dinner thing too, although he never got why humans limited themselves to eating at only certain parts of the day.

What if he didn't catch anything at dinner time? Was he supposed to give up and wait until breakfast, to go to sleep hungry?

So when Aurnia said she shouldn't be long, Aidux got a little nervous.

The lynx rested his chin on his outstretched legs, staring down into the golden yellow glow of the magic thingie Aurnia had asked him to keep an eye on.

What had she called it? A focus? It was pretty, like a never-ending sunrise.

A low grumble tickled his throat. How long was 'long'? He didn't know. Whatever it meant, Aidux was sure that if Aurnia wasn't going to *be* long, then she would probably return a little bit before however long was supposed to be.

But . . . when would *that* be? Did that mean she would be 'short'? If so, how long is short?

Aidux cocked his head. If long is long, and 'long' is long, but short isn't long, then how could 'short' be long?

Aidux buried his head in his paws. His brain hurt. As much as he loved words, sometimes they made less sense than time.

Each time the creak of wood emerged from the fog, the cat's ears flattened nervously against his head. He hoped Aurnia was okay. He really liked her. He didn't want to think about the ship falling apart with her in it. Bad things happened to people when heavy things fell on them.

Cats, too. A tree had fallen on his brother once. Well, not a whole tree. Just a limb really, and the limb didn't even have any leaves on it at the time, but Mixin had squealed like a baby pig when it happened.

He didn't think Aurnia would squeal like a baby pig if the ship fell on her, and he didn't think it would be nearly as funny if that happened either. Not funny at all. The ship was much bigger than a tree limb, even without leaves. Who knew how bad *that* would hurt.

Aidux licked his nose. The continuous wind kept tickling his nostrils. At least it was drying him off. He really didn't like the smell of wet cat. Wet dog was worse, wet fox even more so, but he couldn't just walk away from wet cat smell. Mostly because it was him that stank, and he couldn't walk away from himself, although he thought it might be really useful if he could.

The ship groaned angrily, followed by a number of violent splashes. Aidux whined. He wished she would hurry. If Nevin wasn't on the boat, then they had to hurry up and get to looking around. Being surrounded by all this water couldn't be safe.

He remembered one of the fish the sailors had caught the day before—a 'swordfish' they called it. It was the scariest thing he'd ever seen. While he loved the taste of a good fish, he didn't like knowing there were fish out there big enough to eat *him*.

Did lynx taste good to fish? Probably. Maybe that's why he didn't see many lynxes out on the open ocean. All the swordfish ate them. He hoped they wouldn't eat Nevin. Or Theis, for that matter, but definitely not Nevin.

Aidux self-consciously scooted closer to the center of his life raft.

Time passed at an unknown rate, but Aidux eventually spotted Aurnia's pretty head bobbing in and out of the water toward him. She swam like him, though with only one arm. He needed to tell her how much easier it was when she used both arms.

He searched through the fog behind her, but no one else followed. His ears wilted.

Aurnia hefted a sopping burlap sack onto the plank before hauling herself up, whimpering painfully.

Aidux sat up straight, his tufted ears alert. "What's wrong? Did you hurt yourself on the ship?" He sniffed. She smelled like blood.

She shook her head. "I hurt my back when I was thrown from the ship."

Aidux whined softly. "Nevin? Theis?"

Again, she shook her head, never taking her eyes off of the burlap sack. "Not there, Fate be praised, otherwise I seriously doubt either of them would be alive right now. All of the sailors are dead. Mutilated. I could hardly tell they were human."

"I don't understand. How were the sailpeople hurt so bad but we're both okay?" He remembered a bright flash of blue light before being tossed up in the air, but he hadn't gotten so much as a splinter from the explosion.

"Being on deck helped, I imagine, but I also just managed to get a spell off at the last second to protect us from the blast. A cushion of wind powered by that little gemstone."

Frowning at the omnipresent fog, she squished some of the seawater from her soaked dress. "As fortuitous as that may have been, it's likely this fog was also the result of that spell. There's a reason why casting while inside a Pool is discouraged."

Aidux nodded. "That makes sense."

It did not.

"What's that?" he asked, nudging the bag with a paw. It felt hard, like a rock.

"I think . . ." she began, patting it hesitantly, "I think this may be the reason the Pool reacted the way it did. I think this may be the reason the ship exploded."

Aidux lowered his head and sniffed. It smelled like flour. Wet, salty flour. That can't be right. Flour wasn't scary at all.

"Can I see it?"

"Later." Aurnia waved her hand over the pretty yellow gem. The light within blinked out and the air around them stilled. Aidux mimed her, waving his paw back and forth above it, but the light didn't come back. Maybe he was doing it wrong.

She plucked the gem up and stood, groaning as she straightened her back. With the gem held out before her, Aurnia turned to the Misanthrope. The golden yellow light returned. His ears perked up again. Maybe she was going to fix the ship so they could use it to find Nevin.

The plaintive moan of straining wood split the air, so loud the sound hurt his ears. Aidux's mane stood on end. He didn't like this.

Behind a curtain of fog, the damaged ship broke in half and collapsed into a hundred separate pieces, falling to the water in a rain of wood and metal. Aidux gripped the plank with his claws as a wave rocked their raft. Aurnia bent down to steady the burlap sack, dragging it closer to the center of the plank with one arm.

Aidux rubbed his aching ears with his paws. "Why'd you do that for? I thought you were gonna fix it!"

The woman squeezed the lightless gemstone tightly between her hands. "That ship was far beyond the ability of magic to fix. Maybe if I was a Shaper, but it is more useful to us in this condition than otherwise. Besides, that explosion may have been visible for twenty to thirty miles or more, and I'll not have scavengers out here picking clean the remains of Captain Williams and his ship. These men gave their lives to the sea. May they find peace beneath her waves 'til Obolvia come."

Aidux peered apprehensively down at the dark water lapping at their raft. "Now what? I . . . I don't wanna swim."

He couldn't do that. The swordfish would get him.

"Patience, Aidux. Patience."

Aurnia held her empty hand out over the water, still as a log. The lynx yawned. He was tired of being patient. They needed to go, needed to find Nevin. How were they going to find him now, with only a tiny piece of driftwood supporting them?

Wayward bits of the shattered Misanthrope slowly begin drifting toward them from all over, carried along on currents hidden just below the ocean's surface. Aidux backed away from the edge as a ten-foot long board nudged the raft, then forced its way up on top. Another strangely shaped piece from the rear of the Misanthrope butted up at the rear of the raft. Aurnia scanned the wreckage, looking for something, and then moments later a long coil of rope floated over, scooting up next to the ten-foot long board. A wide swath of canvas soon joined them. Aidux was beginning to feel crowded, but he wasn't about to ask what was going on.

Aurnia ushered him to the edge of the raft and moved the sack next to him.

"Do *not* let this fall in the water," she said sternly before turning to the raft's center. She waved her hand, and a thin gash opened up beneath her palm as the wood fell away, disappearing below the raft. She twirled her finger, and the ten-foot long board stood straight up and slipped firmly into the gap. She twirled her finger again, and the ragged swatch of canvas floated up and over the top of the board, and in one swift motion, impaled both ends on the erect board.

Aurnia picked up the rope and ran a finger across its width at about the midway point. There was a soft 'fffft', like breath between clenched teeth, and the rope fell away, cut cleanly in two. She tied one part of the rope around the lowest section of canvas where it met the wood, but when she realized she couldn't reach the top section, she turned out to the ocean and waited as a crate floated over and onto the plank. Standing on the crate, she finished securing the upper half of the canvas, then hauled the strange looking piece of wood aboard, letting it drag the water behind her.

Aidux blinked. "Did you just build a boat?"

She smiled. "I may not be a Shaper, but I have a few tricks of my own."

"What's a Shaper?"

She placed the gemstone on the crate, and it soon came to life again, the golden light summoning forth the constantly swirling wind. The canvas snapped taut and billowed outward, and Aidux had to dig his claws into the raft to keep from falling out as the entire construction lurched forward. Aurnia shifted the strangely shaped board, and the boat turned in the opposite direction.

"Are we gonna sail around? Look for Theis and Nevin?"

Aurnia stared solemnly ahead, watching the horizon. "Not in this fog. I'm afraid our chances of finding them so long after the wreck are very slim."

The lynx lay down, resting his chin on his paws. "Then . . . what are we going to do?"

"The shores of the Delphine continent aren't far. We should reach it before sunrise. Unfortunately, the currents in this area are highly unpredictable. If Nevin really is floating out there somewhere, he could wash up any number of places."

"Can't you just keep using your crystal ball to find him? Maybe it will work now."

Aurnia barely nodded. "Maybe. I'll keep trying. If it doesn't start working though, it would be wise of us to have a backup plan. An old friend of mine lives on the Delphine continent. He might be able to help us."

Taking the drawstring of the burlap sack in his mouth, Aidux curled up at the bow of their make-shift boat. Maybe he would get some sleep. A nap sounded amazing, and morning would be there when he woke up. If he could stop worrying about Nevin. If he could stop thinking about massive cat-eating swordfish.

If he could somehow learn to ignore the stench of wet lynx.

Chapter 71: Discomfort in Fen Quarry

Aidux mrowed impatiently and shook the continually accumulating water free of his dark, twisted mane. His golden-brown fur clung to his skin, pulling the truth of his size from the lie of his otherwise deceptively fluffy coat. Fat droplets clung to the tips of drooping whiskers before growing too cumbersome for the wiry hairs to support, their brief absence sending the whiskers bobbing skyward until more droplets could descend to replace them.

Ignoring his complaint, Aurnia hugged a sopping-wet flour sack tightly to her chest as though worried it might blip out of existence should she loosen her grip. He wondered if she, like him, was starting to forget what being dry felt like. Long strings of chestnut hair were pasted to her pale cheeks, and her wispy yellow dress clung to every inch of her lithe form, yet she never made an effort to pluck the strands from her face or adjust her outfit. She seemed almost comfortable in the rain, at ease, like the way slinking through the low ferns blanketing the woods around Elbin made him feel.

Had made him feel. He missed his woods. There were all sorts of good hiding places among the trees, places the rain could never get to, places he could curl up in and nap until the storm passed and not have to worry about wet paws.

Aidux released a resigned sigh. At least the cobbles weren't muddy. Muddy paws were worse than wet paws. All the sticky goop and tiny rocks crammed between his toes, forcing him to finally stop somewhere and clean them with his tongue to prevent the grit from rubbing away at the tender flesh until it opened a sore. And once that icky muck coated his mouth, there was almost no getting rid of the taste.

After assembling that makeshift boat using her magic nearly two days before, Aurnia had given him the go ahead to take a nap, and he had gratefully fallen asleep with a warm ocean wind in his face. Given enough time, he knew the wind and rising sun would dry him out, but sometime just after sunrise, the boat had suddenly stopped, ejecting him headfirst from his perch and into the swirling currents of a broad river. He had barely the time to get his eyes open before finding himself underwater.

Again.

In their eastward trek, the pair had only enjoyed about half a day's walk before the clouds opened up in a gentle but near-constant drizzle that, even now, showed no sign of relenting. As much as he ached to abandon the road for shelter, Aidux knew it would take more than a brief respite to dry out his matted fur.

Besides, every time the urge to stop popped into the back of his mind, he quietly reminded himself that each second not spent walking was another second that Nevin was out there, somewhere, alone and possibly injured. He wanted to get to wherever Aurnia was leading them as swiftly as possible, and if she could continue forward without the need for rest, then so could he.

The cobblestone causeway narrowed as it approached an ornate wrought-iron gate set into the opening of a ten-foot high wall constructed of irregular granite blocks. Chunks of mildew-stained stone dotted the empty approach, fallen from their perches atop the aging wall's crown and ignored long enough for the muddy ground to slowly begin swallowing them up.

The iron gate suffered from a similar neglect, its wiry balusters speckled in orange rust and mangled like a cage that had failed to contain some captured monstrosity. It clung tenuously to the wall from only one of its three mounting points, standing only by virtue of its leading corner being buried in a foot of soggy earth. A gold-plated 'O' decorated the center of the gate, its gleaming surface marred by a wealth of gouges and warped into a dented bean shape. The gate stood open, and Aidux wondered at the last time it had been closed.

"Nearly forty years later, and the man still hasn't made the time to get it fixed." The way she mumbled it struck Aidux less like an astounded observation of another's laziness, and more like the wonder of child-like amazement, as if leaving the gate in such a state of disrepair was somehow a good thing. A praise-worthy oversight.

As they passed between the twisted gates, the tight fitting cobbles fell away, replaced by murky puddles and an old gravel path meandering through muzzle-high weeds and feral crabapple trees. Their tangled, twiggy branches were bereft of greenery, presenting instead with delicate tufts of pure, white flowers, granting the illusion of a snowy Languor in the dwindling days of a balmy Waking.

Aidux deftly skirted a pair of discarded pruning shears, rusted firmly shut from years of exposure to the damp climate. He wondered how someone could leave a tool outside long enough to reach such a state, but by the look of the rest of the courtyard, he doubted anyone had assumed responsibility for taming the neglected greenery for many seasons. Strangely, he didn't notice the rotten husks of fallen crabapples anywhere; it seemed that someone had at least taken an interest in claiming those before they went bad.

"Don't worry," Aurnia reassured him, responding to his quiet whine. "We'll not have to deal with this rain much longer."

Aidux nodded wordlessly, leaving her assumption uncorrected. His whine had nothing to do with the ceaseless rain, his tired paws, or even the steady ache that had taken up residence in each of his complaining joints. The apple trees had reminded him again of Nevin, and of how far their journey to find him had taken him away from the last place they had been together.

The trees parted, revealing a grand two-story mansion. Discolored water spots crept up its mottled walls, advancing ahead of a thick layer of sticky mud that clung to the foundations like an unkempt beard. The shrill creak of rusting hinges accompanied every gust of wind, complaints voiced from window shutters whose warped planks had torn them free from their moorings. Candles flickered through lofty arched windows, glowing feebly behind the white glaze of mildew like moonlight reflecting in the milky eyes of an aging deer. Starlings flitted nervously about beneath exaggerated eaves, alighting on one of the countless nests tucked away from the rain long enough to berate the two travelers before hopping back into the air.

Aurnia hiked her dress up around her calves as she stepped up onto a broad, covered porch. He leapt up after her, sighing with relief when he emerged into the dry air below the overhang. Three rocking chairs unwillingly shared in his discomfort when he paused to shake his matted fur, spraying them with a cloud of smelly water.

"Feel better?" Aurnia said sarcastically, pausing before a pair of massive oak doors to straighten her dress. Aidux noticed that the imposing doors didn't match the rest of the mansion's state of decay.

"Not surprisingly, no."

He trotted up beside her, nose hanging inches away from the door as he waited for her to open it. The smell of burning wood greeted him like an old friend, and he wanted nothing more at that moment than to plop down in front a fire and bake away the day's incessant rain from his matted fur.

A soft wind swirled around him, and a warm mist enveloped the porch. Aidux jumped back a step, hackles raised despite their sodden state, but the mist faded just as swiftly as it had appeared.

He looked up at Aurnia in confusion, wanting to ask her if she had seen it too, but the words froze in his throat.

The woman was completely dry, and looked as radiant and composed as the day he'd met her in Comelbough.

As surprising as his companion's mysterious transformation was, what surprised him the most was the new smell permeating his nasal passages, overpowering the acrid bite of wood smoke and flavorless rain—fear, both sickeningly sweet and burning all at once. The hair on his mane rose another half an inch.

He looked around, wondering where the unpleasant smell was coming from. It wasn't something he had expected to encounter here, in the middle of a new town, standing on some stranger's porch. His keen eyes hadn't spotted any animals hunkered down in the tall grasses, and the starlings were far too small to exude such a powerful scent. Bigger animals could, like dogs and cats and people, but aside from Aurnia and himself, Aidux couldn't detect anyone else—

He blinked. Aurnia. He was smelling her now not because the two of them had recently found their way out of the rain, but because her scent, much like the state of her hair and dress, had suddenly changed.

Before, her scent had resembled a breeze through an alpine meadow. Clean. Refreshing. Uncomplicated.

Now though, the generally calm and focused woman stunk with the cloying odor of nervous fear.

"Aurnia?" he whispered.

"Celine?"

The breathy exclamation came from behind, startling Aurnia so fiercely she nearly dropped the flour sack. Arching his back in alarm, Aidux whipped around and backpedaled until his rear end rested against the sturdy doors. A cautious growl filled the expansive porch as the pair stared down their unexpected visitors.

Two men stood in the midst of the gravel path. She didn't recognize the man in the back, little more than a child on the brink of adulthood. A thick head of coffee-brown curls lay flat against his forehead and neck, and his exceptionally narrow frame seemed almost emaciated with his damp clothes plastered to him like a second skin. A natural downward curl of the lips gave him an aura of almost perpetual irritation despite the curious glimmer in his dark eyes.

But it had been the familiar man in front that spoke her second name and woke the butterflies in her gut.

"Blake," she managed, mentally cursing her inability to speak the name without a noticeable quaver in her voice.

At just over six feet tall, Blake Osmund's penetrating stare met her eyeline almost perfectly from below the porch despite the obvious hunch to his rounded shoulders. His stark-white hair fell about his creased face and ears in waves, the aged-deepened wrinkles in his furrowed brow almost hiding an old, jagged scar. A worn leather poncho protected him from the bulk of the downpour, matching its owner's wrinkles with its own impressive share of rucks.

Setting his jaw, Blake shook his head and marched right past her. "You have absolutely otherworldly timing, woman," he grumbled, shoving the double doors wide to disappear inside, the younger man jogging to keep up.

Aurnia's breath whistled through pursed lips. *That could have gone a lot worse.*

A cozy fire warmed the smoke-stained brick hearth opposite the mansion's foyer, casting a flickering orange glow across the two worn leather sofas and low tea table resting in the midst of a vaulted parlor. A crystal chandelier sparkled dimly overhead, a combination of dust and soot marring what would otherwise be a breathtaking work of art. The tasseled area rug covering the scratched hardwood floor suffered similarly, its detailed pattern obscured by years of muddy boots and neglect. Cobwebs long abandoned by their eight-legged owners clung tenuously to the spindles of a pair of twin spiral staircases. The wrap-around second balcony lurked beneath a veil of shadows.

To Aurnia, everything was exactly as it should be, exactly as she remembered it, but that familiarity only served to exacerbate her nervousness.

"Wow," Aidux whispered, shaking the water from his toes and gazing reverently about the parlor. "It's even bigger on the inside."

Aurnia hardly heard him over the din of her thoughts. *How long has it been? How many years since I've found myself standing in this foyer?*

Far too many, she knew. The world had passed beneath her feet more than once since that day, and it didn't surprise her to realize that, though her travels had brought her near Fen Quarry on many occasions, never did her feet find themselves walking the mining town's rain-slick streets. There was always a good, sound reason for her avoidance: travel was faster by ship, movement through the pass was restricted due to heavy snow, and even the need to remain inconspicuous had pushed her into the tangled, swampy wilds outside of town.

And yet, as soon as she had realized that Nevin and the sword were beyond her means to locate, the image of Blake had popped unbidden into her thoughts, answering her silent call for help. It had seemed so right at the time, but now that she stood here, Aurnia was suddenly beginning to question the wisdom of that first instinct.

"Um, Aurnia?" Aidux said, pawing softly at the fabric covering her knee.

"Mmm?"

"Do I need to stay here with you, or can I go lie down in front of the fire?"

Aurnia shot him a queer look, but the cat merely peered up at her with wide, questioning peepers. Something in those eyes told her it wasn't permission he was seeking. Aidux could likely sense her discomfort.

She offered him a conciliatory nod. "Go ahead. We have nothing to fear in this house."

Aidux licked the rain from his black nose before quietly padding through the sitting area to curl up before the crackling fire. It was only a handful of seconds before thin lines of steam lifted free of his tangled coat to vanish in the still air of the parlor. The lynx purred in contentment, resting his tired chin on equally tired paws.

A two-way door at the edge of the parlor swung inward. Wiping his hands on a dingy towel, Blake appraised the pile of cat lounging before his fireplace as he entered the room. He'd shed the worn poncho in exchange for a creme tunic that fit more snugly about his midsection than she remembered. Aidux perked up an ear at the creak of the door, then lifted his head to regard the man curiously.

"You adopting stray, carnivorous animals now? A guard cat?" He shot her an uneasy look. "It *is* tame, right?"

Aidux was staring at her now as well, waiting. "Go on," she urged, knowing that an explanation was no substitute for the real thing.

The cat stretched, arching his back and fanning his toes out against the irregular stones paving the floor around the hearth before he stood. Blake leaned ever-so-slightly backward as Aidux approached, but to his credit, the man didn't move an inch when the lynx reached out and pressed a paw onto his thigh in greeting.

"Hello, Mister Blake. You can call me Aidux. I'm a lynx. I don't know about the whole 'tame' thing, but I don't eat people. Well, not unless they deserve it, and I try to ask permission first."

Blake cleared his throat a few times as he searched for his voice. "Permission, you say? From whom?"

"From Nevin," he answered in a proud, matter-of-fact tone. "My bestest friend."

"Nevin?" The older man rubbed at the discolored gouge on his brow with the back of a finger. She supposed the move was similar to the way some men stroked their beard or scratched their heads when caught up in troubled thoughts. The motion had always left her feeling uneasy, dredging up memories of events better left hidden in the shadows of her mind.

Blake reached down and took Aidux's paw in his hand, shaking it in the same manner as he would any other human. The action struck Aurnia as silly, but Blake always did have a way with people that not even the most powerful Vellurgists could rival.

"Well, Aidux, feel free to drop the 'mister' and call me Blake. I've never been one for silly titles."

"Sounds good." The cat looked between he and Aurnia. "So, the two of you are friends?"

Straightening, Blake pursed his lips and nodded, almost reluctantly.

"It's just . . . we walked a long way and she said *nothing* about you."

"Oh, I don't doubt it, my furry friend. That woman has more skeletons in her closet than a forgotten battlefield."

The man's playful wink was met with a look of utter confusion. "Closets? Humans are so weird. I normally just *leave* the bones when I'm full."

Hanging the dingy towel across his shoulder, Blake retrieved a wooden mug from a serving station beside the two-way door and filled it with some dark wine from a glass decanter. Having finished his introductions, Aidux happily returned to his spot by the fire. Aurnia still hadn't moved from the house's foyer, quietly awaiting her host to warm up to the idea of her presence.

He sipped at the wine, but didn't turn, and when he did finally address her, all of the tenderness he'd displayed with Aidux had vanished. "Of all the days you could choose to show back up, Celine . . ."

She wrinkled her nose at the second use of her middle name. "It's been a long time since the days I let you call me that. Things have changed considerably between—"

Blake slammed his fist onto the server hard enough to topple the glass decanter. Wine drizzled off its surface in a crimson waterfall. The sudden racket brought Aidux to a half-crouch, his round eyes darting to and fro.

"I'll call you whatever I damn-well feel like, *Celine*," the man growled through clenched teeth. "Now, are you going to tell me why you're here, or I am going to have to start guessing?"

Her lips pressed together in a thin, hard line, Aurnia took a moment to gather her shattered composure. The knots tangling up her stomach tightened uncomfortably. This was exactly what she had feared, why she had always avoided coming back here, even for a brief visit. She had known that coming here wouldn't be easy, but the journey had given her two whole days to mentally prepare herself for the reunion. And still, it had only taken a single outburst for her defenses to waver.

It was disheartening to know that, even after so many years apart, Blake still had the same level of power over her.

"This was a mistake," she said, clutching the flour sack to her chest. "It's obvious I've caught you in the middle of something important. I came here hoping to obtain your brother's help with a bit of a magical problem, so if you'll point me in his direction, I'll do my best to stay out of your way."

Blake slapped the dingy towel over the spilled wine and hung his head. "What do you want with Myron?"

"I need his help with a ritualized scrying spell. I've become separated from a young man I was traveling with, and it is imperative I find him."

"Imperative," he repeated with a wry chuckle. "Our lives must seem so simple beside all the important matters you always find yourself caught up in. Makes it easy for you to just show up wherever and whenever you want and demand we all put our own problems on hold until you can get a handle on yours."

Her brow furrowed in thought. Blake had never been the type to surrender to emotion, and her brief objection to the use of her middle name was hardly deserving of such a heated rebuttal, their own personal histories notwithstanding. Anger dripped from his every word like venom, but instinct told her that she wasn't the reason for his mood.

Something else was wrong. This was not the man she remembered.

"Blake, has something happened?"

Wine pooled around his boots like spilled blood.

"Myron's dead."

By the way he spoke the words, like he was trying to reign in an explosion, she didn't imagine his baby brother's death was from natural causes. "How?"

"He was murdered."

Chapter 72: The Contents of the Vault

Concern overcame trepidation, and before she realized what she was doing, Aurnia had crossed the parlor to stand at Blake's side. He stopped her with a trembling hand, stepping back before she could get too close. A mixture of rage and despair warred in his troubled eyes.

"Don't," he said softly.

Aurnia stilled, hurt flickering briefly across her face before she forced her expression into one of cold indifference. She set the flour sack on one of the leather sofas and folded her hands together in a downward steeple, giving the man a moment to compose himself.

"Tell me what happened," she said, unconcerned with the sharpness of her tone. "Leave nothing out."

Blake may not be happy to have her there, especially considering the timing of her arrival, but Myron had been a good man and a kindred spirit, and Aurnia wasn't about to allow their personal issues to stand between her and the truth of his death.

With a resigned sigh, the white-haired man idly rubbed the scar on his forehead and nodded. Eyes on the floor, he paced around the edge of the parlor as he spoke.

"Despite his skills as a Shaper, Myron never shared my endless fascination with Orlicite. He understood their usefulness, of course, but rarely did any of his duties require an investment of magical energy great enough to employ an Orlicite, and I wasn't exactly eager for him to be seen around town with one of our personal stock."

Aurnia sank gracefully into the sofa beside the flour sack, draping a protective arm across the bag's hidden bulk. "I always suspected your little hobby would bring you nothing but trouble. If the College ever got wind of the sort of power you keep within reach . . ."

He waved off her objection. "Preparing the estate to deal with a Trine was one of Myron's first major goals. Like you, he thought my collection would eventually be my undoing, but instead of fighting about it, he went to great lengths to help me safeguard it."

"Probably realized how futile it is to argue with you once you've set your mind to something."

The muscles along Blake's jaw rippled with tension. "Are you going to sit there and make snide comments or are you going to let me tell my story?"

Aurnia held up her hands apologetically. "Go ahead."

"Thank you." He wiped the sweat from his face. "Where was I?"

"You didn't want Myron to be seen with glowing rocks," said Aidux, happy to help.

"Yes, that." Blake nodded, rewarding the cat with a scratch between his tufted ears. "Maintaining order in a province is a game where new pieces are constantly being added to the board. A leader has to know the opposing pieces just as well as he knows his own. He must pay close attention to the field of play. And above all, he must trust his own pieces and sometimes allow them to play themselves.

"Magic, though . . . magic is a piece with no rules, no limitations, and sometimes . . . sometimes it's actually the kid who can't stand to lose so it just knocks the board off the table and refuses to clean up the mess. Firestorms. Tornadoes. Earthquakes. That's the sort of danger that Orlicite brings to the game.

"*People* can be led, be reasoned with, bargained with, coerced, threatened, and—only as a last resort—removed from play. But one hunk of Orlicite in the wrong hands has the power to make the game unplayable for everyone. Fen Quarry barely survived the last time a single 'glowing rock' was turned against it. That one crisis was enough to teach me to fight to keep these stones out of circulation in the hopes of preventing the next crisis from finishing us off."

Aurnia already knew all of this, had actually been there to witness that one crisis firsthand, but she kept her mouth shut and let him vent. He was setting the stage for a greater point, she knew, and if any part of Myron's death had something to do with Orlicite, she wanted to absorb every word of his story.

"Though Myron never seemed interested in *using* Orlicite, he'd occasionally ask for permission to study them in the vault. It struck me as little more than a bit of curiosity, a way to pass the time almost. After a . . . minor . . . accident nearly took out the estate's foundation, he spent the next few years building a series of reinforced rooms and shoring up the vault's defenses in his spare time.

"That all changed two years ago."

Blake set his mug atop the mantle and leaned back against the hearth, crossing his arms. "Myron came to me one afternoon in an excited frenzy, waving a tattered leather book around and talking like his teeth were on fire. I never got the specifics of where he'd come by it, but he didn't hesitate to tell me over and over what it was supposed to be—the field journal of some dead Wizard named Rheus Lar."

"Preposterous," Aurnia said, practically snorting the word. "Myron could be a bit dense at times, but he never struck me as naive. Rheus Lar's field journal. Of all the ways to scam someone out of a few shils . . ."

"What's a Rheus Lar?" said Aidux.

"Not a what. A who. Myron claimed he was one the more celebrated researchers at the College of the Faithless, back in its early days." Blake shrugged. "Before he fell out of favor and was basically banished."

Aurnia shook her head. "Not one of. The. Rheus Lar was the preeminent magical researcher for the College, not to mention one of its founding members. The very first High Velyr."

The cat's eyes widened in awe. "He sounds really important."

"More than the College would like to admit. In fact, without his research into the nature of the soul channel and the intentional manifestation of spiritual energies, magic users like Myron wouldn't even exist. Try as they might to minimize their connection to the man, the College will never succeed in erasing his legacy. A gold-plated stain on the pages of history."

Blake twirled a hand impatiently. "Regardless, Myron was convinced of the journal's legitimacy. According to him, being forced out of the College didn't stop Rheus' research. Instead of lab work, Rheus took his theories to the field, seeking out Pools of magic all over Stragus in the hope of uncovering the reasons behind their development.

"Myron eventually came to the conclusion that Orlicite wasn't merely a byproduct of the Pools, but could actually be the seed which drives their growth. What began as curiosity and excitement soon changed into a full-blown obsession. He barely slept anymore. He shunned his duties as a Shaper. He'd disappear for days on end, sometimes showing back up with strange injuries, burns and bruises."

"Where do you think he went? Didn't he live here with you?"

Blake nodded. "I'm getting to that. I eventually assigned him a caretaker out of worry—a pretense created so I could have someone keep an eye on the man—but Myron was smart. He didn't even need magic to slip a tail whenever he wanted, so I never could determine where he would vanish to.

"Yesterday morning I awoke to find both Myron and his caretaker missing . . . along with almost my entire collection of Ignocite."

Her eyes twitched a hair wider, the slightest crack in her emotionless facade. "Myron loves this town, and as far as I remember, he doesn't have a violent bone in his body."

"Agreed."

"And I have a hard time believing he'd sell them. His brother is the de facto ruler of Fen Quarry. He wants for nothing."

"True."

The supple leather creaked beneath her as she leaned forward. "But . . . you said Myron was murdered, so you already know all this, don't you?"

Blake's measured nod did nothing to affect the weight of his stare. "And it's so much worse than you've hit on yet."

Worse than the loss of a brother, coinciding with a handful of arguably the most destructive form of Orlicite going missing? "I think it's time you got to the point."

Strumming his fingers on his elbows, Blake dipped his head as he continued. "We scoured Fen Quarry all day yesterday, but came up with nothing. I sent riders along all major roads out of town, but as of this morning, none of them had found any evidence he'd left the area. We expanded our search to the northern wilds today, and a little over an hour ago we stumbled upon Bennig in the swamps."

"Bennig?"

"His caretaker." Blake picked up his mug and downed its contents in one swallow. "The man was covered in burns, his skin literally melted in places, but nearly every burn showed signs of healing. He could barely hold his head up when we found him, but he pointed us toward a house hidden deeper in the marsh before . . ."

"Before what?"

Clearing his throat, Blake continued as though she hadn't spoken. "I had my men carry Bennig here while the rest of us scouted the house. We were cautious in our approach, but the windows were dark and the door stood open. It was quiet, and the air carried this gut-churning stink I didn't recognize at first.

When it dawned on me I was smelling burned meat, I rushed into the house, praying to every god I could name I was wrong."

Her heart ached for him in that moment. "Myron."

The word 'yes' formed on his lips, but his voice betrayed him, and the only sound that escaped was a faint hiss across his teeth. A furry paw spread across his thigh.

Blake offered Aidux a weak smile and, wiping his eyes, he continued.

"Someone had wrapped a chain around my little brother's ankles, hanged him by his feet, and set him on fire. And the only reason I could even identify him was because his head was the sole part of him they didn't burn."

Rubbing her thighs through the thin fabric of her yellow dress, Aurnia suppressed a shiver. Burning to death was a horrible way to go. Someone wanted Myron to suffer.

"What of the Ignocite? You searched the house, yes?"

"Gone."

"How much, Blake? Tell me it was only a few small pieces."

The man avoided her focused gaze. "Twenty-one assorted carats."

"Twen—" she choked out, coming to her feet so quickly she nearly overturned the tea table. By comparison, the tiny Vellicite she'd obtained from Donald back in Comelbough would have barely measured higher than a carat. She cast a nervous glance at the flour sack and pondered the implications of so much Orlicite reaching the hands of the wrong kind of people.

A flicker of realization brightened his stormy eyes. "I . . . I think this is the part of my story where I ask for your help."

Aurnia balked. "*My* help? I came here, against my better judgment, because I needed Myron's help. Without him, I'm back to square one, and I don't have the time or the resources to help you hunt down—"

"Celine, hear me out."

He reached out and grasped her hand between both of his. The tenderness of his touch roused feelings in her chest she'd long since buried. "Whatever you need—men, money, transportation—I'll provide it. I know you wouldn't be here if it wasn't important, if you had any other choice in the world. I just . . . I have a bit of a magic problem, and with Myron gone, I don't have a Wizard anymore."

She searched his face, how the years had deepened the wrinkles on his cheeks and forehead, had dulled the twinkle of his eyes, had hardened his expression in the sobering way that only a lifetime of leadership could. She pretended to weigh his offer, but the truth was, Blake *was* uniquely positioned to help her in every way she couldn't help herself. No one else had the manpower, the resources, the connections, and the willingness to help her locate Nevin and the missing sword like the man standing before her.

She couldn't afford to tell him no, no matter his request.

Finally, she offered him the smallest of nods. "What do you need of me?"

"We locked Bennig in the cellar."

Aurnia cocked her head. "Why would you do that? It sounded to me like he needed a doctor, not a jail cell."

"Bennig is the only one who can give me answers about what happened out in that swamp, and frankly, I'm not entirely sure he wasn't somehow partly responsible for what happened to Myron. But that's not why I locked him up.

"I locked him up because he started glowing."

Chapter 73: The Caretaker

Aurnia clung tightly to the bulky flour sack with one hand and the folds of her wispy yellow dress with the other as she carefully descended the narrow staircase. The pitted steps glistened weakly before the flickering glow of Blake's lantern, the smell of burning oil mixing with the stale air and hinted essence of decay. The lantern's feeble light failed to touch the deepest reaches of the staircase, giving the impression that the three were traveling not into an unkempt wine cellar, but a system of natural caves hidden deep beneath the manor. If not for the rhythmic plink of dripping water and the squick of each footfall, the silence would have weighed as heavily as the stone overhead.

Despite Blake's desire for answers, the man had recognized her weariness from the road and had taken the time to feed and water both she and her furry companion before ushering her into the bowels of the manor. As a Wizard, she required little in the way of sustenance, so rejuvenation had come in the form of a handful of sweet biscuits and a warm apple-blossom tea. The cat had torn into a heaping bowl of raw mutton like it might up and run away at any moment.

Now, as the three of them silently descended into darkness, the stirrings of worry and uncertainty began working their knots in her gut. According to Blake, Bennig's skills were of an entirely mundane nature, so he should not have been able to generate a spontaneous glow of his own accord. Another Wizard could have temporarily enchanted one of his possessions to emit light . . . but to what end?

"Blake," she began, keeping her voice low so as to reduce the echo in the cramped stairway. "Did you search Bennig for the source of the glow when you brought him in?"

"Of course I did," Blake grumbled, a bit harshly. "I may not be a Wizard, but I'm fully capable of using Soul Quartz to detect magical energy. None of his possessions displayed anything out of the ordinary."

Ignoring the sharpness in Blake's response, Aurnia's mouth twisted in thought. If nothing he carried was capable of generating light, that meant the glow had to have been coming from the man himself. Could Bennig have hidden a secret talent for magic from everyone who knew him for years without being discovered?

"Bleck," Aidux grumbled, flicking a blob of goop from his paw. "I hate that later I'm going to know how that tastes."

Aurnia sighed. "You realize your presence here isn't really necessary, Aidux."

"I'm here to help finish this quick so we can get back to finding Nevin." The lynx flicked another blob of slime from a paw and whined softly, a sound that reminded Aurnia like a small, lost child. "Why do humans have so much stuff if they can't even keep it *clean*?"

"I didn't used to come down here often." Blake reached out and brushed aside a sticky cobweb, sending a small, brown spider clambering hastily for the ceiling. "The collection of fine wines and other trophies of affluence were my father's love, not mine. He would come down here on a daily basis, to fawn over the 'treasures' he had so painstakingly accumulated over the years, to add another to his collection, or to retrieve a bottle of wine for mother and him to share over dinner. Aside from a few choice servants, no one else was allowed down here, not even mother and I.

"I never developed much of a taste for wine, and I sold or gave away most of father's ridiculous collection long ago, so until Myron began converting some of the abandoned mine shafts that run beneath the manor to a specialized vault, I was content to forget this part of the estate even existed."

He ran a finger along the wall, revealing a much lighter-colored stone beneath the layers of grime and mildew. "Still, you might have a point."

The stairs leveled out onto a brief landing that terminated before a rusty iron door. Years of neglect and a shifting foundation had warped its rectangular shape into a twisted parallelogram, like a door in the fun house of some traveling carnival. Considering the dangerous nature of the items stored behind it, Aurnia found the mental picture disturbingly ironic.

From floor to ceiling, rows of diagonal lattice wine racks lined the walls of the cellar, brimming with the multicolored wax-coated heads of hundreds of green-glass wine bottles. Tattered flaps of rotting tags hung precariously from too few of their slender necks, vestiges of a poorly maintained system of vintner and age identification. Another such rack split the cellar neatly in twain, its construction carefully designed to mask the location of an unsightly support pillar. The mildly astringent scent of vinegar tickled her nose.

A modest tasting table jutted out from one wall. A single, half-finished bottle of Lysivian Pinot sat uncorked next to an empty fluted lamp. The sight of the bottle stirred up unpleasant memories for her, memories of her most recent visit to the manor some years before, a day she had played over and over in her mind whenever the day's silence had given her time for regret.

Aurnia shifted from one foot to the other uncomfortably. Everything was exactly were she had left it. Maybe a few bottles were missing, she couldn't really tell, but the room was otherwise untouched.

"Well? Where is this captive of yours?" she asked, staring into the darker parts of the room where the meager lamp light couldn't quite reach.

Aidux took a big whiff of the stale air before sneezing. "Yuck. All I smell is rotten fruit. You could be hiding an army down here and I'd never know."

Blake gestured to the left wall with his lantern, a wall entirely composed of lattice wine racks. "I put him in the vault."

Aurnia nearly stumbled. "The vault? You put him in the *vault*?"

He ignored her, silently counting each bottle of wine with his free hand as he passed. Aidux shot her a queer look, then padded off after him.

So, that was it then. Blake's decision to lock Bennig away in the vault could only mean one thing.

He had already judged, convicted, and decided his sentence.

The man was as good as dead.

Blake's hand stopped on a relatively unremarkable red-capped bottle of Lake Helsted Port, coated in what appeared to be a thin veneer of dust. With a quick twist, a shove, and a sharp click, Blake activated the hidden switch and a false wall swung quietly outward, revealing the opening to a secret chamber. A strong glow spilled into the previously shadowed room.

"Everyone in," Blake said flatly, reaching out to turn the bottle immediately above the hidden switch as he waved his two companions past.

White light bloomed along the high walls of the hidden chamber as they entered, emanating from five rhombus-shaped quartz gems that glowed in reaction to their presence in the vault. A solid, windowless iron door sat flush with the wall beneath all but one of the light crystals—two on the left wall, two on the right, and one at the far end of the hall. The closest doorway was a simple arch that led into a side room, and Aurnia thought she could hear a faint melodic humming coming from within.

Blake wasted little time, striding deeper into the lengthy corridor without waiting for her to take it all in. The salt-and-pepper granite walls were unnaturally smooth, the remnants of a quarry cut by an accomplished mason and extracted by laborers sometime during the founding of Fen Quarry. Myron had likely come behind and magically filed off any harsh edges in his effort to convert the space.

She shook her head in amazement. A stone fortress, naturally protected from every angle but the one hidden in the depths of Blake's wine cellar. Genius.

"Myron did far more down here than I ever would have asked," said Blake as if responding to her unspoken wonder. "Unfortunately, the extent to which he modified these old mines exposed how little effort he put into his job as Fen Quarry's Shaper."

"A few rooms fitted into an existing space? I think maybe you're too hard on your brother."

Blake paused before the open arch, his shoulders slumping beneath an invisible weight. "This is merely the entrance. His vault occupies almost the entirety of the ancient quarry, and when that wasn't enough, I fear he cut additional rooms directly out of the raw stone. I have yet to explore the whole of the complex that lies beneath the house I grew up in."

Taken aback by his admission, Aurnia looked upon the vault with fresh eyes. Myron was but one man of average magical talent. How much could he have really accomplished on his own?

The humming abruptly ceased when the three entered the smaller side chamber, a multipurpose room designed to function like a combination study, lounge, and center for vault operations. A plush burgundy carpet covered nearly every exposed inch of granite floor, soaking up stray sounds before they could resonate off the hard stone all around. A rectangular table was pushed up against the far wall beside a barred iron door. Mud-stained clothing and an assortment of personal objects lay in separate piles on its surface. A simple desk watched both doors, and an older woman quickly rose to her feet and waddled out from behind it to eagerly reach for Aurnia's hands.

"Can it really be you?" Aurnia couldn't help but return the uninhibited grin plastered across the woman's face, and happily let herself be drawn into a tight embrace. "You left in such a hurry, I never got the chance to say goodbye!"

"Hello, Laura. It's good to see you, too."

Holding Aurnia at arms length, Laura adjusted her oval glasses and looked her up and down. As caregiver for the Osmund household, Laura had been with the family since just after Blake was born. Initially brought on at ten years of age as an older playmate for the growing young man, the tomboyish woman had eventually served as an almost fatherly stand-in for the oft-ignored heir to the Osmund name, and had readily adjusted to her new position once Blake took over after his parents passed away. Her simple outfit fit rather loosely, as if she'd lost weight and had forgotten to update her wardrobe.

"Oh," she said in surprise, running her hands down Aurnia's arms. "Not a single wrinkle in that beautiful face. It's as though you've stepped right out of my memories and walked through that door."

"That's very kind of you, but the years have taken their toll in less obvious ways, believe me."

Laura's hand covered her mouth, her eyes glistening behind her thin spectacles. "Myron would often say the same thing."

Aidux opened his mouth to speak, but Blake stepped impatiently between the two women, cutting their reunion short. "Tell me of Bennig. Any changes to his condition since Wells and Vera brought him in?"

"Not really, no." Laura retrieved a stoppered glass bottle from the front pocket of her knee-length leather apron and held it up for everyone to see. A thick purple film coated the glass, but the bottle was nearly empty. "I've been giving him regular doses of highly concentrated valerian extract. Breathing has been steady, heartbeat . . . weak, but regular. His skin is flushed and hot, but there have been no other obvious complications from his wounds."

"Nothing strange?" He rubbed his scar. "No more glowing?"

Aidux broke away from the group, cautiously approaching the barred door with his ears up and his head low. Laura watched him without comment, having seen stranger things than a tame lynx while working for the Osmunds.

"Not that I have seen, but I've only been checking in on him in half-an-hour increments." She gestured to the door. With no window into the room beyond, Aurnia knew the man locked within could have gone through any number of physical changes and they would be none the wiser.

Aurnia cast Blake a dark look, plucking the nearly empty glass bottle from Laura's still outstretched hand. "You aren't particularly concerned with Bennig's well-being at this point, are you now?"

"No," he said, refusing to meet Aurnia's stare. "I'm really not."

Her soul tickled the back of her mind. Something about this situation wasn't quite right. She'd never seen him so worked up. Despite the terrible loss of his brother, his treatment of Bennig seemed so out-of-character. On the one hand, every action he had taken made sense given the situation, but on the other hand, she detected an undercurrent of anger woven into each of his decisions, a callous disregard for the human side of the equation.

This wasn't how the Blake she knew would handle this.

With a quick squeeze of his forearm, Laura returned to her place behind the desk. Aurnia though, turned her attention to the clothes carefully spaced along the surface of the table. Setting the nearly empty vial on the tabletop, she focused her intent, her hand alighting briefly on one item at a time. Breeches, a linen tunic, a pair of mud-caked boots, a small pouch containing a meager amount of shils, two wooden bracelets, a braided iron ring. Nothing reacted, each piece utterly devoid of any magical signature.

A small glimmer of white light caught her eye. She picked up a sliver of Soul Quartz, an uncut wafer of transparent crystal no larger than her thumb. As she lifted it to her face, the glimmer of white light within brightened.

A poor man's magic detector.

"Aurnia . . ." said Aidux quietly, his nose mere inches from the sealed door. Focused as she was, Aurnia failed to notice the apprehensive edge to her name.

"This all he had on him?" Slipping the Soul Quartz into the folds of her dress, she joined Aidux by the door. Blake nodded. "And you found nothing of interest at the house, I'm assuming?"

He shook his head, taking a small, three-prong key from a hook beside the door. "Nothing worth mentioning."

"And you want to know whether Bennig is somehow responsible for your brother's death—"

"Or if he can point me in the direction of who is."

She folded her arms beneath her breasts. "You should stay out here, Blake. You're in no state of mind to handle this, and if there really is some sort of magical influence involved, you'll just get in my way."

The man was already shaking his head before she finished speaking. "Not going to happen. You don't get to cut me out of this just because I'm a little angry."

"A little?" She put a hand to his arm, but he pulled away. "You wouldn't be human if you weren't upset, but you're like a tightly wound spring. One misstep and you'll explode."

"I'm fine."

"You're not—"

"I'm fine!" he yelled, slamming his fist into the face of the iron door. A dull thrum filled the room. Laura flinched at her desk, her palms and eyes glued to its polished surface.

Aurnia's eyes never left his face, though Blake refused to look at her. He shook his throbbing hand, the first two knuckles leaking blood down his fingers. She slowly reached out him, laying his shaking hand across her open palm and gingerly placing her other hand on top. Blake's jaw tightened in response, but he didn't pull away.

"You're not fine," she said quietly, urging her soul down through her arm and into his injured hand. "Your brother just died. You're not supposed to be fine."

After a moment, Blake retracted his hand and wiped it across his pants. Fresh, pink skin had filled in the shallow cuts on his first two knuckles. "You're not going in there without me. End of discussion."

Aurnia pursed her lips, weighing the value of arguing with him further and sensing the futility in that. "Very well. But I do the talking, and if things get out of hand, you defer to me. Do I make myself clear?"

Blake stepped past her and Aidux, the lock clicking beneath the turn of the key. He rested a hand on the iron bar stretched across the face of the door. "We'll cross that bridge when we come to it."

A sour expression colored her face. "You know I hate it when you say that."

Chapter 74: Focus on the Fear

An uncomfortable heat burst through the opening as Blake wrenched the iron door open. Aidux slipped inside before she could stop him. With a resigned sigh, Aurnia followed him in, hearing Blake draw the door closed behind them.

A single chair occupied the far wall of the otherwise austere chamber. There, a bruised and burned man sat bound, each appendage wrapped tightly in rope. His head hung limply to the side, a swollen goose-egg just behind his left temple. Hideous burn scars decorated his skin like spilled paint, each waxy mark presenting in various stages of the healing process.

The worst of the wounds spread out across his chest, a crisscrossing mess of raised crimson lines and swollen blisters on the verge of bursting. He'd been stripped down to his nightclothes, his flushed skin glistening with sweat in the light of the glowing quartz hanging just overhead. Whether he was feverish or just reacting to the room's unexpected warmth, Aurnia couldn't be sure.

"Blake Osmund!" she admonished, a hand flying to her slack mouth. "Have you gone mad? This is no way to treat—"

"He's alive and breathing. That might be more than he deserves. Laura is quite capable, and we checked him in the field. Despite how it looks, most of his wounds are superficial, and none are life-threatening."

She planted her hands on her hips. "And that lump on his head?"

Blake turned a small stoppered vial over and over in his hands. The word 'hartshorn' had been scribbled across its label. "I did what I had to. He kept getting louder and louder, and I didn't want to give our position away to anyone else who might be involved. But I didn't hit him until he started glowing."

Aidux stared quizzically at the bound man with his head cocked slightly to the side, his nostrils flaring wildly as he absorbed the room's scents. His ears twitched. The tilt of his head increased, and he took a small step forward, a low growl building in his chest.

"Hush, Aidux." Aurnia stooped to set the bulky flour sack on the floor. Following the cat's unflinching stare, she nearly stumbled backward in surprise when she found what he was looking at.

Bennig blinked in her direction, the glazed look in his eyes fading rapidly as he flexed his arms and legs against his bonds.

"Where's Myron?" he demanded, his voice displaying a firmness that Aurnia would not have expected from someone with his injuries emerging from an herb-induced unconsciousness.

Blake's expression hardened. He returned the small vial to his vest pocket as he spoke. "That's a question I seem to be asking *you* a lot lately."

"Control yourself, Blake," she admonished.

Bennig craned his neck as he looked around. The strained movement caused one of the swollen blisters crossing his chest to burst, spilling clear fluid down his belly. "This isn't our cabin. How did I get here? Why am I tied up?"

"What do you mean 'our cabin'?" Blake said, speaking before Aurnia could take control of the conversation. "That little house in the swamp?"

The bound man's eyes jerked forward, his cracked lips playing at the thought of a smile. Aidux's low growl returned. "Myron was right. And here I thought you were just playing the fool for your brother's sake."

"I am no fool!" His lips peeled back in a hateful sneer, Blake started toward the bound man, but Aurnia grabbed him by the arm and jerked him back to her side.

"Have you lost your wits?" she asked, corralling him toward the door with a finger to the chest. Blake's unblinking eyes burned into Bennig, utterly ignoring the sharp nail digging into his breastbone. Tiny beads of sweat bled from his open pores to steal down his cheeks and drip from his beardless chin.

The tickling in the back of her mind became an incessant itch as her soul scratched away at her thoughts. She wiped a hand across her forehead, looking down at fingers literally drenched with perspiration.

How is it so hot in here?

"Where's Myron?" Bennig repeated, an insistent edge to his tone. He flexed his arms against the ropes encircling his wrists, the strain bursting another of the swollen blisters cutting down the center of his chest. The raw flesh connected strangely, as though split apart and rejoined improperly.

"He's *dead*." The white haired man tried to sidestep her, but Aurnia wasn't about to let him past. It took most of her strength to keep him in place, and she didn't know how much longer she could contain him.

"Blake, look at me." He refused, practically snarling at the man sitting not fifteen feet behind her.

"Dead?!" Bennig jerked against his bonds, but the ropes held tight. "That lying bastard!"

"Blake, *look at me.*"

"He said he wouldn't kill him! Not if we gave him the stones!" The chair rattled against the floor as the man wrenched and bucked, but the ropes held.

Blake grabbed her by the shoulders, and with a feral grunt, tossed her aside like a discarded plaything. Aurnia barely managed to keep her feet. Vaulting across the room, he reared back and slugged the man across the jaw. A thin line of blood hit the floor beside Bennig.

"Don't lie to me, you bastard!" he screamed, shoving an accusatory finger in the man's face. "You did this. This is your fault!"

Bennig just screamed back. "They held me there in case he didn't come back with the stones. He hung me by ankles . . . burned me all over. He tortured me out of boredom!"

"LIAR!" He struck him again, but if the assault affected him, the man didn't show it.

"They made me leave, told me to come get you. They said they wouldn't hurt him if I came back with you."

"WHO?" Blake wrapped his fingers around Bennig's throat. The bound man's eyes widened.

Bennig barely managed to speak a single choked word before Blake's hands cut off his air.

"Valhurst."

His cracked lips parted in a crazed smile.

A sickly red aura enveloped him. Aurnia's soul screamed in warning.

Knowing she wasn't strong enough to pry the raging Blake away from Bennig, Aurnia did the first thing that came to mind. She brought her hands together in an interlocking c-shape to compact a mote of Vellis. A ball of tightly compacted air actualized in the small space between the two men. Wrenching her hands apart, the ball exploded outward with enough force to send both men careening towards the nearest wall.

Without warning, the itching in her mind tore her thoughts back to that fateful night on the deck of the Misanthrope, surrounded by the blue glow of the Pool, and the terrible depression that followed as the result of steeping herself in its unconstrained power.

With a feral roar, Blake shot to his feet to charge back across the room. Bennig lay helpless on his side, chuckling softly to himself as he struggled against his bonds.

Forgive me, Blake.

Planting her feet, she stepped up and slapped her palm against his chest, channeling air into the space between him and her hand. The tiny ball of air expanded forward in a burst, and Blake lost his feet and sailed backward into the iron door once more. As soon as his heels touched the ground, she yanked her hand back, and another quick burst of wind knocked his legs out from under him, dumping him unceremoniously on his rear.

His stunned look only lasted a moment before his face twisted in unrestrained fury. He tried to come to his feet, but Aurnia was one step ahead. She lashed out again with her palm, this time without magical intent, and struck him square in the space just below his breastbone. Blake's eyebrows raised in surprise as the air rushed from his lungs and he found himself struggling to convince them to pull in more.

"Focus on that feeling," she urged, leaning in close. Blake clawed at his chest, but her strike had paralyzed his diaphragm, and there was little he could do but wait it out. "Ignore the anger and feel the helplessness, the fear."

Aidux's ears perked up. "Fear?" he mumbled.

Mouth working like a fish out of water, Blake's glare bore a hint of betrayal. She held his face in her hands and nodded. "You're suffering from Vilum Fever. The uncontrollable rage you're feeling is a symptom. You have to keep telling yourself it isn't real, that it's just a part of the sickness. It's the only way to keep it from taking control of you."

The hatred swirling in his brown eyes nearly broke her heart.

It's the fever, it's not him. He's sick.

"Aurnia . . ." Aidux growled, backing up to her side.

"Blake," she said, her tone insistent. "You have to get control of this, or else I'm going to have to do something much worse. This anger isn't real. You are so much stronger than this. But you have to focus."

He blinked, a deep furrow of concentration forming on his brow. With a strained nod, he closed his eyes and relaxed. After a moment, his diaphragm followed suite, and he gulped in mouthfuls of the heated air.

"I'm . . . sorry," he managed between breaths.

"Aurnia!" Aidux pawed at her shoulder, his claws catching on the fabric of her dress.

"*What?*"

The lynx crowded up against her, his silver eyes never straying from Bennig. "I could tell something was off as soon I stepped into the room. His smell is all wrong. I was looking for something I thought didn't belong, when I really should have been looking for something that wasn't there at all. The guy is sweating like a hen in a fox hole, but he has absolutely no fear. None at all.

"But that's not even the worst of it! He's cooking from the inside out. I can smell it. It's like . . . he swallowed some fire but it didn't go out!"

"Swallowed fire?"

Bennig's chuckle had escalated into a full-blown, body-shaking cackle. Rivers of steam poured off his bright red skin, each droplet of fresh sweat evaporating as it emerged from his pores. At this point, the red aura had grown so dense that she could hardly make out the back wall of the room through its violent haze.

With a roar of psychotic glee and a blast of scorching air, Bennig burst into flames.

Chapter 75: The Cinder in the Cellar

The conflagration that was Bennig grew in size and intensity until none of them could bear to look at it. Smoke and ash and the stink of burning flesh choked the air, making every breath burn like the fire before them. Sweat erupted from every pore on their bodies like leaks in a failing dam. Bennig thrashed and strained against his bonds as the inferno quickly ate through the thick ropes and turned his chair into sticks of charcoal.

His shirt pulled over his face, Blake reached for the lever that would open the door and let out the poisonous smoke.

"No!" Aurnia screamed over the roar of the flames, grabbing his wrist just in time to stop him. "The fresh air will only feed the fire! You open that door and we all die!"

"I don't open this door and we die anyway!"

The lynx pressed up against Blake's shoulder, his head low to the ground where the smoke was still relatively thin, a frantic look in his watery eyes.

Bennig squealed in mad delight and burst his bonds, sending flaming splinters of chair and burning strands of rope to all corners of the room. He stood with his arms stretched out wide, the orange flames eating at the floor and walls, but doing little more to him than turning his clothes to ash and blistering his skin.

Looking at him was like staring into the face of the sun.

"I'm going to find him, Blake!" Bennig screamed. The inferno expanded, turning the far end of the room into a writhing curtain of fire that seethed from his rapidly blackening body. "I will make him pay for what he did to me, for what he did to Myron. I will make him suffer like he made me suffer, like he made my Myron suffer!"

Aurnia scuttled back against the door. *The mania has completely taken over. The man's lost his mind.*

Blake grabbed her arm, placing his face next to her ear. "Can't you blow him out or something?"

If only it was that simple. As she already told him, introducing a large influx of air would only exacerbate their problem. For a small fire, too much wind would smother the flames, but she doubted she could produce enough wind force using her internal reserves of Vellis to overcome a fire this size. Such an effort would most likely form a flashfire, an explosive burst of Ignolis that would instantly activate the dormant fire energies inside everyone and everything in this room. They would all burn alive in the span of a single breath.

She wished she understood how this was happening. No man possessed Ignolis reserves extensive enough to power such a blaze, and his body was taking far too little damage for the flames to be feeding on him anyway. Something else was fueling Bennig's transformation, and the same thing was most likely causing his Vilum Fever.

An Ignocite would do the trick for the first part, but she had never heard of any Orlicite causing Vilum Fever. They were magical energy made stable. Besides, she couldn't fathom how Blake would have missed finding that on Bennig during his detainment. That was not a detail the Blake she remembered would miss.

If only the Vellicite Donald had given her hadn't shattered, she thought, cursing her luck. A strong enough blast of wind *might* be enough to put out the fires, but could just as easily earn her a quick and agonizing death. Aurnia suddenly wished she was a Grolurgist. Dumping dirt on an open flame was the surest way to smother it. Water was a close second, but there wasn't enough water in all three of them combined to do more than turn the sealed vault into a deadly sauna, and she didn't have . . .

Her eyes shot to the flour sack lying on the floor. Like it or not, it was time to find out the answer to the question she'd been too afraid to ask since the night of the Misanthrope's destruction.

It was time to find out if that huge chunk of unworked mineral really was the largest piece of Somnicite she had ever seen.

Bennig raised his arms skyward and howled like a madman. The flames pulsed and grew, inching closer and closer to their side of the room. The copper fixture mounted to the wall drooped and melted, sending its glowing crystal tumbling to the floor.

Aurnia spun on Blake. "The moment he stops burning, I want you to open that door!"

Blake grabbed hold of the lever. "What are you going to do?"

"Something I hope doesn't end up killing us anyway." She stretched across the floor, grabbing the flour sack's drawstring and pulling it into her lap. "I'm going to clear the air! When I do, take as big a breath as you can and hold it!"

Both Blake and Aidux looked at her like she was crazy, but at least they nodded. Closing her eyes, she called her soul into the furthest reaches of her body, letting its warm light wash away all fear and doubt. She steeled herself against the unpredictable. Casting a spell into an unworked Orlicite could have devastating consequences. Instead of any sort of plan, she would have to focus on raw elemental power.

Her eyes flew open, and a sphere of faultless air appeared around each of them, driving the smoke and ash up and away. She sucked in, filling her lungs to the point of shaking, hoping that Blake and Aidux had done the same in the small moment she'd given them.

With no time to waste, Aurnia reached out and grasped at nothing with both hands, drawing her fists into her chest and sucking every ounce of breathable air wafting about the room into a tight, distorted ball that floated inches from her face. The sudden change in pressure made her ears pop. The flames surrounding Bennig faltered, but only momentarily.

Fate be with me.

She ignited her intent, sending it barreling through the block of blue mineral hidden in the flour sack and into the swirling ball of air before her. The flour sack flared with a dazzling blue light, powerful enough to drown out Bennig's crimson corona and cloak the room in the fully-realized brilliance of Somnalis.

Time stood still.

The ball of air floated motionless before her like a bump in the fabric of reality. Blake and Aidux hugged the wall, their faces frozen in horrified anticipation. Her heart paused mid-beat.

Time came crashing back.

A wall of the purest azure water erupted from the core of the shimmering ball of air, slamming into her with the force of a tidal wave. Luckily, she didn't have far to go before she hit the wall. She absorbed the blow with a grunt, and poured more effort into growing the wave.

It didn't take much. The water bullied Bennig against the wall, quickly rising to his waist. Dense clouds of white steam replaced the smoke, but still the fire raged. Her heart thudded in her chest as the water climbed, rising higher and higher with every tense second. Her lungs burned from the strain of holding her breath.

Bennig was awash in a cloud of orange bubbles. Somehow, even through the mass of water, she could still hear him laughing. Aurnia held her intent with a resolve of iron, knowing that if she released the spell too soon, Bennig's magical inferno would just regenerate, and then he'd be on top of them.

They only had one shot at this. She just had to hold on.

The strain clawed at the walls of her soul channel, ripping into the ethereal conduit with a growing fervor.

The seconds ticked away, and with each one lost, a layer of orange bubbles peeled away to reveal a smaller, more compact reaction. Then, just as quickly as the inferno began, the bubbles died, revealing the blackened remnants of limbless human body floating harmlessly before them.

Bennig had completely burned himself out.

Blake wrenched on the lever, and the door flew open, dumping a torrent of magically-generated water in the entry room. Aurnia let go her soul and curled into a ball, letting the current drag her from the vault alongside Blake and Aidux. The older man tumbled head over heels. Aidux paddled up stream to no avail.

Once the river of water stilled, Blake helped Aurnia to her feet, brushing the tangled strands of hair from her face as he checked her for injuries.

She waved him away, hiding an appreciative smile with the back of her hand. "I'm more than fine, thank you."

Aidux high-stepped through the lingering water and jumped up onto Laura's desk.

"Not that I don't appreciate you dowsing Mister Firebreeches in there," he said, shaking the water from his matted fur. "But I don't understand why you insist on soaking me every chance you get. Don't you know cats *hate* water?"

He looked around, confused. "Hey, where's Laura?"

Blake poked his head out into the hall, finding it clear. "Looks like she took a break after we got here. Woman's practically a ghost."

He ran a hand through his stringy white locks. "What was all that about in there? The man was cracked. And the fire? How in the name of the *gods* can a man burn with such intensity and still be standing? Still be *laughing*?"

The woman in yellow straightened her dress as she waded through the calf-deep water. It was already destabilizing. In a few minutes, the only evidence of the water's existence would be the chaotic mess of furniture the flood had managed to dislodge from their places along the walls. Even their clothes would be dry.

"I have a suspicion," she said, re-entering the vault. The cube-shaped room was bathed in the shimmering reflections cast by the single lantern construct glowing beneath the water's surface. A film of umbral soot blanketed the far half of the room, baked into the stone beyond any ability to cleanse. Already, the water had receded to just above the round bones of her ankle.

Blake followed her in. "And this water? Are you hiding a Somnicite from me?"

You have no idea, she thought. "If you will calm down and take a breath, I'll answer all of your questions in a moment." She halted in the center of the room, counting the seconds as the remaining few inches of water steadily vanished.

"Aurnia, Aurnia!" Aidux exclaimed, dashing headlong into the room. "The water's gone! See, look! My fur's even dry! And cleanish too!"

"Indeed." She searched the now unobscured stone floor, finally locating the remains of Bennig shoved into the corner. The fire and subsequent flooding had reduced his body to little more than a charred mass of tissue, presumably the upper portion of his torso. The scent of roasted human flesh was faint, but enough to irritate her gag reflex.

Her face twisted in disgust, Aurnia gingerly reached into the pile of overcooked Bennig and withdrew a red gemstone no bigger than her pinkie nail.

She squeezed it in a shaking fist. Just as she suspected. *Ignocite.*

Aidux had taken to Blake's side, the older gentleman idly scratching the lynx's fluffy head as he waited patiently for Aurnia to explain the tumultuous events. Looking at the man's haggard expression, she doubted if he was currently in a state of mind capable of recognizing the full implications of Bennig's transformation and the message it carried.

"Here's the cinder that started the fire," she said, pressing the Ignocite into the palm of Blake's hand. He held it up to his eye between two fingers, tracing his gaze along the gemstone's meticulously executed facets. An array of flickering spots of crimson light danced along the contours of his face.

He gave a solemn nod. "I recognize it. It's one of mine, alright."

Aidux strained his neck as he peered up at the gem. "Oh, that's really pretty. It looks just like the glowy yellow rock you had on your magic boat. I think you called it a focus?"

She nodded. "Just like that one, this is Orlicite. Specifically Ignocite, a highly condensed reservoir of elemental fire."

Blake turned the gem over in his hand. "The spell's reaction makes sense now. A trilliant cut is one of uncontrollable power, of unchecked growth. Only a small measure of energy needs to be injected through this Ignocite for it to react, but the outcome is entirely out of the Wizard's hands.

"Look, here." He pointed to the heart of the gem. "See the tiny triangle in the deepest part of the stone? See how its shape mirrors exactly the shape of the gem as a whole? Look at the facets extending out from the center here. Each one looks like a beam of light, long and straight and growing wider as it closes in on the outer edge. Then, just before it reaches it, it begins overlapping with its neighbors, creating the illusion of hundreds of even tinier triangular facets."

She saw it just as clearly as he described it. The man had become quite the Orlicite expert in the years since she'd been away. Blake handed it back to her. "Bennig had this?"

She nodded, and the gem disappeared beneath the folds of her dress. "I found it in the remains."

He crossed his arms defensively. "No, that can't be. I searched him thoroughly, head to toe. If he'd been in possession of an Orlicite, I would have found it. You know me, Celine. That's not something I would have missed."

"You misunderstand," she said, cocking an eyebrow. "I didn't say I found it *on* the remains. I said I found it *in* the remains."

Aidux shrank away in exaggerated horror. "Wait, what do you mean, *in*? Like what, he swallowed it or something?"

"It's possible, but considering what we know and what we've seen here today, I don't think that's the case. Whoever sent him out to find you must have suspected you would search him. He probably didn't know exactly when you'd come, or how long it would take until the conditions were right to spring his trap, so he had to engineer a way for Bennig to maintain constant possession of the Orlicite. Had he swallowed it, the stone would have just passed through his body's digestive system over a couple of days, and then he would have had to reswallow it."

Aidux made a face. "That's not something I want to think about."

Blake stroked the gouge on his forehead with the back of a finger. "That bright light that appeared to come from his chest just before he started to burn. Now that I think about it, that light is exactly the kind of reaction you'd get from an Orlicite that's currently being used as a focus."

"Precisely. I believe that whoever set this plan in motion used him as a mule to transport and deliver this nasty little magical concoction by implanting the Ignocite inside his body."

"That makes sense," he said absently. "I did find a fairly fresh scar on his chest when I searched him. Someone had cauterized the wound to sterilize and seal it closed. But why was he acting so crazy? It was like he didn't even notice he was being roasted alive."

Aurnia nudged a charred arm with her toe."I believe he was suffering from a particularly potent bout of Vilum Fever."

Blake and Aidux looked at one another, confused.

"What's 'Vilum Fever'?"

Chapter 76: The Three Loci

Aurnia pursed her lips in thought.

"Forgive me, Blake. While you may have extensive knowledge of Orlicite, I often forget how truly little you know about the workings of magic itself."

Explaining such things so soon after the three of them nearly lost their lives felt odd, but Aurnia thought it might give Blake some time to get his head right, and give her time to work through the problem of a Vilum Fever without an appreciable source.

"There are three major centers of energy within the human body. One here," she explained, holding her palm over each area as she spoke, "just below the belly button. One here, over the heart. And one here, between and just above the eyebrows. These spots are Loci—Aqum, Vilum, and Cohim, respectively. Out of each Locus is born a specific aspect of human behavior, and that Locus is responsible for the growth and maintenance of those behaviors.

"The most primitive Locus, the Aqum Locus, gives rise to our basal instincts, the inborn laws of survival granted us by our parents. Here, in the chest, the Vilum Locus controls the formation of emotion. Emotion is constructed on the foundation of instinct, reacting to situations based on our subconscious expectations in order to grant us the additional power necessary to physically and mentally survive dangerous situations.

"Finally, we have the Cohim Locus, the center of logic and conscious thought. It is this Locus that provides man with free will, or the ability to break the chains of emotion and instinct to pursue an outcome beyond the immediate. It is initially the weakest of the Loci, but it possesses a nearly infinite amount of potential for growth."

She held a hand over her heart. "Out of the three, the Vilum Locus is the most powerful and unstable, capable of asserting such dominance over the Aqum and Cohim Loci that a man—out of anger, fear, or love—will sometimes place himself in mortal danger for seemingly incomprehensible reasons. Such is the power of the Vilum Locus that a man can burn to ash without recognizing the danger he is in."

Blake rubbed his own heart, painfully aware that the sickness she was describing still had some sway over his own emotions. To his credit, the man was attempting to logic his way out of the hole his Vilum Locus had dug.

And succeeding brilliantly, she thought.

"So, this Vilum Fever, this is a corruption of the Vilum Locus? A magical infection that sends it into overdrive?"

"So it is believed. Not much is known about its true methods of attacking the Loci. The only thing we really know for sure about it is that it is often contracted through extended contact with a Pool of elemental energy, and its symptoms manifest a specific set of emotions based on the Pool's elemental make-up. In Bennig's case, and to a lesser degree yours, that would be anger and extreme mania."

He shook his head. "No, that's not right. I would know if there were any Pools of interest in or around Fen Quarry. Every few months, Myron and I would take a walk through the countryside, looking for any signs just in case one finally gains enough density to become visible. I refuse to be caught with my pants down when Orlicite starts growing right under my nose."

"And yet," Aurnia countered, "the only known source of Vilum Fever is a Pool of magical energy, though, unless Bennig has a wide enough soul channel to grant him magical potential, I don't understand how he could unknowingly happen upon a Pool dense enough to cause Vilum Fever.

"Then there's the issue of your own fever. For you to be affected like you were, you would have most certainly had to have spent some amount of time in a Pool of noticeable density."

Aidux circled Blake's legs before sinking onto his haunches with a sigh. "Locusts, Pools, magic rocks . . . too much for a cat to take in."

Blake snapped his fingers. "The Orlicite."

Aurnia frowned. "No, Orlicite are stable forms of elemental Pools. Possessing an Orlicite can in no way affect the bearer's Loci."

"Under normal circumstances, you'd be right." He gestured toward the hallway and the unexplored remains of his underground vault. "I've been secretly collecting Orlicite for years, hiding it down here to stifle the violent campaigns run by the men who seek it out. In my younger days, I would often spend hours at a time studying the stones. Sometimes we'd test how specific cuts affected simple spells. And not once did either I or my brother suffer from any sort of extreme emotional state like this Vilum Fever you describe."

She gave him an exaggerated nod. "Like I said, by themselves, Orlicite are rather harmless, inert."

"Bear with me. The cut of an Orlicite helps shape and direct the spell flowing through it. A fire that size would have required the consumption of an amazing amount of Ignolis, so the gem was cut to magnify the extraction of the elemental materials as the spell aged. The reason Bennig himself wasn't instantly consumed was because the flames manifested around him rather than on him. It was the heat that blackened his skin. The heat and sheer volume of Ignolis energies passing through his body to power the spell."

Aurnia's eyes went wide. "You think that the liberated energies of the Orlicite flowing through him created a circumstance similar to being steeped in the unstable energies of a Pool."

He snapped his fingers once more, the sharp crack of flesh echoing in the hollow room. "Exactly."

She leaned back against the wall and stared at the ceiling, lost in thought. It made sense, in theory. Bennig wakes, causing the spell to activate. The spell grows, gradually pumping more and more Ignolis through its carrier until it becomes strong enough to ignite the very air. Doing so requires a fair amount of Ignolis, so, for the first few minutes, the spell goes unnoticed, evidenced only by a mild case of Vilum Fever. Once the blaze actualizes, the fever prevented Bennig from recognizing the danger of the spell, even allows him to ignore the pain it must be causing him, turning him into a living weapon incapable of fear.

The perfect assassin.

"Gods," she groaned. Things were much worse than she thought.

It was Blake's turn to frown. "Now what?"

She took a deep breath. "The man who set this whole thing up . . . this Valhurst character . . . he has to be an Ignurgist. Generally speaking, dealing with an Ignurgist is preferable to dealing with any other type of Wizard. They tend to be rash and direct, flaunting their powers like a child with a toy sword. They love to watch things burn. They are literally mesmerized by flames, obsessed to the point that they sometimes turn even their most prized possessions to ash. Dealing with an Ignurgist is dangerous, but any Wizard capable of thinking laterally can outsmart even the most intelligent Ignurgist.

"But this man is something else. Whoever he is, he can plan ahead, strategize, and even perform feats of magical assembly that I can only fantasize about. Setting a trap in an Orlicite, and one implanted in a person's body? He has an intimate knowledge of the capabilities of Orlicite that rivals some of the brightest minds within the College of the Faithless. He managed to set a brilliant trap, and without your Wizard, one you couldn't have possibly escaped."

Blake held up a finger. "But, thanks to you, I did escape. You handled it."

Her eyes settled on the flour sack resting just inside the doorway. "It seems he couldn't plan for every eventuality."

He followed her gaze. "I think it's time you showed me what you're keeping in that sack, Celine."

Aidux perked up, his curiosity engaged at the thought of finally learning the contents of the sack that she valued so greatly. Aurnia smoothed her dress before standing. "I think you're right."

She gingerly lifted the sack by its drawstring. It was much lighter than the size of its contents belied. Reaching into the bag, she wrapped her fingers around the object and drew into out into the light for all to see.

The crystalline sphere was roughly the size of a grapefruit, tapered slightly at the top like a stylized teardrop. Despite a lack of polishing and an array of jagged ridges, the surface of the massive gemstone was as clear as a mountain stream and a deep cobalt blue. It glimmered with a layer of false moisture, granting the illusion of a raindrop frozen in mid-descent.

Blake stared, slack-jawed and eyes popping out of his head, at the largest Orlicite either of them had ever seen.

Aidux wasn't nearly so impressed. "Huh. Another pretty rock, only bigger and blue. If these things are so rare, why the heck do we keep finding them?"

Aurnia pressed the impressive stone into Blake's shaking hands. "This is how I created all that water so quickly. Without it, we never would have made it out of this chamber alive."

Blake's voice trembled with reverence as he spoke. "Celine, do you have any idea what this is, what the value of such a thing is? This . . . this is a *Prime* Orlicite, the existence of which has only ever been theorized. This makes largest known Orlicite—the crown jewel of Calo'Brae—look like a bauble in comparison. Nations would mobilize entire armies if there was but a rumor this really existed. Old allies would immediately turn on one another."

He looked at her like she was a complete idiot. "And you've been carrying this around in a *flour sack*?! Are you *insane*?!"

She started to answer, but Blake just cut her off. "No, no. That's not even the worst of it. An Orlicite of this size, uncut, and you cast through it. *You cast through an uncut Orlicite, Celine.* You could have killed everyone in Fen Quarry!"

Her expression darkened as she glared daggers at Blake. "I'm no novice Wizard, Blake Osmund. You'd do well to remember who you're talking to. Would you rather I'd have done nothing? Let Bennig turn you and I and the cat into a pile of smoking ash? Would that have made you happy?"

Like a scolded child, Blake's gaze dropped to the side. "I'm sorry. Of course, you're right. It's just . . . this is absolute insanity. You can't be carrying this around with you everywhere you go. If the wrong person got their hands on this . . ."

He trailed off. "I don't even want to think about the potential devastation and loss of life this thing could cause."

Her voice lost its edge. "That's the other reason I came to you, Blake. This was the only place I could leave this and be sure that it would be safely kept out of improper hands."

With a heavy sigh, Aurnia extracted the Orlicite from Blake's grasp and replaced it in the flour sack.

The man's eyes narrowed suspiciously. "What do you mean 'was'? What are you doing, Celine?"

"Listen," she began, hefting the sack over one shoulder. "I know you're going through a rough time right now, and I feel for you. I really do. But that's no excuse for being stupid. You know how dangerous it is to keep such a large collection of Orlicite in one place, and only a handful of your most trusted companions even know of its existence. Yet, here you are, using your hidden vault as a prison to hold a man you suspected in the death of your brother.

"Tell me, Blake, what would have happened had he escaped? What if he had killed you and looted the vault? You think Fen Quarry would be safe once word got out that so much Orlicite had been discovered in one place? You think people would just write it off as a fluke, or would they come in here in droves with their magic and their weapons and their complete lack of morals?"

She hated herself for saying it, but it needed to be said. "Have you forgotten what happened to your parents?"

His cheeks flushed with shame, but he didn't answer.

Aurnia shook her head. "I can't leave this with you. Not while you're still healing from your loss. You aren't thinking clearly. For now, the Orlicite stays with me."

She turned to the door. "Come, Aidux. I tire of the stale air down here."

The lynx nodded, pressing a comforting paw to Blake's thigh before plodding off after her.

Before she could leave, Blake finally found his voice. "Wait."

Aurnia paused. A warm hand gently took her by the shoulder and turned her around. Blake slid his hands down her arms until her held her by the elbows, dipping his gaze to stare down into her honey-brown eyes. Looking up at him, she could feel years of defenses cracking, could feel the fluttering of forgotten emotion tickling her stomach, could feel the dormant love she'd once had for the man before her stirring in the dusty recesses of her heart.

Feelings that made her ashamed of the life she'd chosen.

As if sensing the change in her demeanor, Blake withdrew his hands, folding them awkwardly behind his back. "I made you a promise. You came to me for help, and instead I asked you for yours. You've upheld your end of the bargain. Let me take you upstairs, and you can tell me your story over tea. I promise to devote everything I can to help solve whatever problem you have."

Hugging the bulky flour sack to her chest, Aurnia nodded in agreement and stepped out into the hallway.

It might take all you have to offer and more to find the sword.

Chapter 77: Cowardice

His thumbs hooked into the small gap between his black leather pants and the braided belt encircling his hips, Nevin paused at the edge of a pair of well-worn cart ruts cutting across the countryside like parallel scars. The broad leaves of vibrant short-blade grasses and bright yellow dandelions reached out in all directions, except near the packed brown soil of the ruts. Here the grass leaned away, shunning the scars as if worried their proximity would lead to a similar fate. The sweetly pungent dogwood and drooping willows had faded from their path not long after sight of the emptied pond vanished behind the gently rolling hills, replaced with scattered collections of squat bushes and dusty white boulders.

Chewing his lip, Nevin faced a troubled expression first to the north, searching the open, empty road before him, then reluctantly back again to the south. The head turning was reflexive. He wasn't really looking for anything, didn't really see the road, the grass, the collection of ominous clouds that grew ever darker as they crowded together farther east.

She's better off far away from here.

The shadowy figure materialized at his side, its cold hand crawling up to perch on his shoulder.

A short walk home to a life free of cave-dwelling beasts and the machinations of power-hungry men.

Nevin shrugged him off. "I didn't ask for your opinion."

And yet you keep needing it. The broken swordsman was right, and you know it.

He could feel the heavy gaze of the shadowy figure, boring into the back of his head. There were words in that gaze, words that the figure had yet to speak, words that Nevin didn't want to hear, but now that the time had come to make the decision, he found those words impossible to ignore.

Theis had made his thoughts on Raiya's continued assistance painfully clear the night before, and the ensuing argument had made for an especially tense morning. Nevin had set out from their camp almost immediately upon waking to scout the surrounding countryside and ensure none of the cave beasts had ventured beyond the grotto. A valid reason to make himself scarce, but secondary to his desire to avoid the man in black.

And now his own personal hallucination seemed to agree with the man.

Nevin could feel his jaw tighten. "What do you care? You're not even real."

I'm real enough, boy. Keeping her around will eventually get her killed, and you aren't strong enough to survive knowing your cowardice caused another friend's death.

"My cowardice?!" He spun on his heel, thumbing his chest aggressively with each use of the word 'I'. "I chose to leave Calibri Grotto. I was going into the caves alone. I was the one who stood between them and that giant creature, and I was the one who got us out of those caves in one piece!"

The figure's pale lips peeled back in a knowing sneer. ***Such a brave one, you are.***

"Don't mock me."

Honesty, then. A single finger reached skyward. ***If you aren't a coward, why then have you not asked the girl what SHE wants to do? Afraid of the answer she may give?***

"I—"

Shaking his head, Nevin frowned. Their situation was dangerous, but Raiya could take care of herself. She had already proven that against the Aberrants of the grotto. Besides, coming along had been her idea, and she'd practically shamed him into accepting that decision. She was like to pull the same shenanigans a second time if he even mentioned separating now.

He turned back to the road, rubbing a hand along the fine growth decorating his chin. The young woman had made a strong point about being allowed to make her own decisions, though. Was he being selfish by not asking what she wanted? With the seriousness of Theis' injury and her concern for Nevin's safety, he suspected her natural need to play caretaker might drive her to go along with whatever he decided, but was that truly in her best interest?

Maybe the shadow—and for that matter, Theis—was right. So many had already lost their lives in pursuit of the mysterious sword mounted to his back and bound to his presence. Did he really have the right to quietly pull her along into what might end up killing her in the long run?

He was doing it again. Just like he'd done in Calibri Grotto, he was making her choice for her by not saying anything. Only this time, he had no delusions of nobility. He was afraid she might choose to leave him to face his fate alone.

A cold hand pressed itself over his own, forcing him to reach down and caress the dented metal object bound tightly to his hip.

Just because you choose to ignore it, doesn't mean wasn't always there.

A finger poked him playfully in the ribs, jerking him away from his inner drama. Raiya stepped to his side, bumping him with her shoulder and shooting him a beaming grin. Her strawberry-blond braid was draped over her shoulder, long enough to brush the bare skin just below where her sleeveless green shirt stopped short above her rib cage. She leaned lightly on the smooth ash pole of her fishing spear.

Looking into her vivid emerald eyes, alive with intelligence and concern, Nevin couldn't help but think how beautiful she was.

She nodded to the north. "This road eventually leads to a three-way crossroads. To the northwest lies Alcara, a militant town straddling the border between this kingdom and the lands of Rothsfel. My father told me that relations between the Curlidges of Rothsfel and the Van Lubbicks of Tichoor have never been cordial, but things have been decidedly worse in recent years. As such, Alcara is always full of soldiers from both sides of the dispute. Doing anything quietly in that town is next to impossible.

"Fen Quarry lies to the east, and controls the only pass through the Granite Thrust for miles. If you're wanting to make your way on to Vadderstrix or even Faulk, you'll want to take the eastern fork into a trading outpost called Whitefalls. We could probably be there in just over an hour if we walk fast."

"Mmm-hmm." Nevin barely heard her, his eyes playing across the tan skin of her flawless face. He didn't want her to go. He needed her. Her presence made the task of carrying the sword bearable.

"Nevin?" she said, her cheeks flushing five shades of crimson. "Are we going, or we just going to stand here looking at each other all day?"

Eyes going wide, Nevin dipped his head and knuckled a smile. He looked around, but she was alone. "Where's Theis?"

Raiya rolled her eyes. "Pouting. He didn't like how roughly I was changing his bandage so I told him to stop being a child, and let's just say the man has a firm grasp on colorful language and leave it at that. He isn't far behind."

He glanced back the way she'd came in search of the man, but instead of the surly warrior, the shadowy figure watched him in the distance. Nevin chewed his lip, offering the figure a defeated nod that a normal man wouldn't be able to see at this distance, but knowing full-well the shadow would.

"Raiya, I need to ask you something."

She bumped his shoulder once again. "Yes, you look nice in your fancy new outfit. A little out of place, maybe, but very handsome."

An involuntary grin spread across his face. "Thanks, but, you said something to me back in the cave. You told me . . . you said that you get to decide your level of involvement in your life. You were mad at me for leaving you behind without saying anything, without giving you the choice to help me or leave me to my own devices."

He took her hand in his, rubbing his thumb along the ridge of her knuckles. "I heard you, Raiya, back in the caves. I don't want to take away your choice by not—"

"Nevin, I'm okay. Whitefalls is literally just around the bend. Besides, Theis could keel over at any moment, and I want to be there to see it when it happens."

She cleared her throat. "I mean 'if' it happens."

A part of him knew he should press the issue with her, that he should go out of his way to ensure she knew what she was getting herself into, but the part that wanted the young woman around proved stronger. Reluctantly, he closed his mouth and nodded, but in the background, the shadowy figure was shaking his head.

Coward.

Raiya smacked him with her ponytail. "Let's go fetch the grump."

As the two turned from the road, she glanced over her shoulder in the direction of home. Nevin thought he saw a hint of sadness in her eyes when she looked back at him.

Have I really made the right choice?

A narrow signpost stood askew in a small circle of grass, its base rotten to the point of crumbling. Theis surmised the post would fall beneath the weight of a fierce look, should he stand with the wind at his back. Three pointed lengths of scrap wood each bore the name of a different locale, all directing the viewer toward a separate set of dark brown cart ruts. The words looked to have been burnt into the wood by a blind man; he wouldn't have known their message had he not already been familiar with the surrounding territory.

Nevin and his little friend had been quiet for some time now, though they hadn't used any of that extra energy to close the considerable distance between he and them. *Fine by me.* Nevin's current stretch of youthful foolishness was more than Theis could contend with. He had kept his opinion to himself after the previous night's argument, had given the boy the choice of sending the girl home or asking her to follow. Theis thought the young man had earned that much, but that was based on the assumption that he would at least make the smart decision.

Infuriatingly, he had not.

Theis rubbed at the linen bandages covering the tender wound penetrating the meat of his shoulder. The wound had sapped his strength and left him on the brink of exhaustion. Only his constant anger kept him going now.

At least he wasn't in any pain. The herbs in his poultice had left his shoulder almost as numb as the useless arm hanging from it. The girl knew her way around a first aid kit, he'd give her that.

He struggled to see what it was about her that made Nevin so adamant to put her in harm's way. Being an adequate healer was almost all she had going for her. And her personality was just irritating—upbeat and polite had no place among warriors. He supposed she was somewhat physically attractive, in an immature sort of way, but if Nevin hadn't shown any sort of reaction to a woman as attractive as Aurnia, then a slip of a girl like her had no chance of turning his head.

There was something between them though, invisible and intangible, and while Theis didn't understand it, he knew exactly where it would end.

It would end with her dead. On that day, Theis wouldn't hesitate to tell Nevin how stupid he had been for not listening.

"Khek," he spat, cracking the knuckles of his good hand. None of this would have mattered if not for him. Nevin would never have met her if not for the explosion, an event Theis readily ascribed to the curious behavior of magic around himself.

Who knows, he mused. *The boy might have even been free of the sword by now.*

Maybe that's why he was so angry. Not angry with Nevin. Still angry with himself. Theis hadn't so much as said a word to either of them before reaching the road, too frustrated to even coordinate breaking camp.

The boy's careful avoidance of him had said everything Theis needed to know concerning the previous evening's confrontation. He doubted Nevin's irritating penchant for frivolous conversation would bother him for some time to come. Strangely, he wasn't sure how much he would welcome the silence.

Discomfort and alarm tickled the back of Theis' mind.

His shadow-filled cowl jerked to attention, blue eyes bursting with an intense azure light. Turning in a slow circle, Theis scanned the surrounding grasslands, the bushes, the rock hills, the horizon. His ears strained to hear through the quiet breeze, the distant roar of falling water, the hidden buzz of flying insects. His nose disregarded the sickly sweet aroma of blooming flowers, the unpleasant stench of drying manure, the scent of distant thunderheads.

There's nothing.

He squinted his eyes against the sun and looked again. More nothing. The low hills and squat bushes offered scant sanctuary for predator and prey alike, and Theis saw no sign of sentient life aside from his two young companions.

The feeling in the back of his mind faded, but only slightly. He was missing something, but couldn't imagine what.

The pair finally caught up with him, coming to a stop next to the barely erect signpost. Nevin leaned forward and brushed a hand across the top-most sign like he was trying to read by touch. The wood creaked morbidly.

"Whitefalls Trading Post, that way," he said matter-of-fact, pointing to the east. He stood up straight, blocking the high sun with an outstretched hand. "What's that sound? Is that the river?"

Theis clenched his teeth in mild annoyance. "It's a waterfall."

He nodded thoughtfully, ignoring the bite to Theis' retort. "That would make sense, given the outpost's name. If I remember my geography correctly, three separate tributaries converge somewhere in this area; the Mossalnag to the northeast, the Erlept Flow to the north, and the Brennan to the west. The Mossalnag is the only one of the three that originates entirely in this kingdom, so that name applies to the resulting river that continues southward, eventually spilling into the Sea of Calor just outside of Calibri Grotto."

"Oh sure," Raiya began, making a show of rolling her eyes. "But can you name seven species of fish that live in each river and carefully describe their spawning rituals?"

Nevin scrunched up his nose and gave her a playful shove. "I don't remember ever reading anything about a waterfall. If these hills are any indication, it can't be all that impressive."

The uncomfortable feeling in the back of Theis' mind wouldn't fade, and Theis was beginning to get nervous. Spinning on his heel, the man in black strode off in the direction of Whitefalls. "Enough talk."

While they both immediately followed, the girl ignored his request for silence. "Actually, the falls are quite a sight. Whitefalls benefits not only from the trade its location brings to the town, but also as a tourist destination. I hear there are some very nice inns within sight of the falls."

The next few minutes passed in silence, and the path adopted a mild downward slope as it slowly wound along the northern perimeter of a lopsided slab of limestone, protruding from the grass like a massive book being balanced on the corner of its binding. The roaring continued to grow, quickly consuming the less intrusive sounds of nature until Theis could no longer hear his companions' feet scraping along the surface of the road.

The falls were the first thing they saw as they rounded the limestone slab. A torrent of froth and water spilled out into the warm air, millions upon millions of gallons careening down a sheer white cliff. An ever-shifting cloud of sparkling mist pervaded the scene, obscuring a clear view of the two-hundred foot wide curtain of white water. The falls bulged in some places, as if portions of the river were more ambitious, more impatient in its bid to reach the distant sea.

The waterfall tumbled into the limestone mouth of a wide gorge, a thirsty crack descending nearly a hundred feet into the earth. Log and white stone buildings closely lined the far edge of the gorge like awed onlookers anxious for a glimpse of the natural wonder. Fingers of gray smoke wriggled free of narrow chimneys, and hungry gulls paced the slanted roofs.

But it was what lay in between them and Whitefalls that awoke the distant memory of why Nevin had never left the Traagen Peninsula.

A long bridge stretched across the gorge, wide enough for two horse-drawn wagons to fit side-by-side. The surface of the bridge appeared to be made of interlocking wood panels resting on a web of rope. Dozens of thick poles buried in the stone stood sentry-like on either side of the bridge, with more rope extending out from each to brace different sections of the wooden path. Two taller poles supported the bridge's handrails in a parabolic arch of rope links.

The sheer amount of rope weaving through the construction seemed excessive, but Theis couldn't argue with results; the two hundred fifty foot long bridge suffered from almost no sag, and hung practically motionless, unaffected by the air displaced by the constantly flowing wall of water.

Theis spun around just in time to see the color drain from Nevin's face.

Chapter 79: The Price of Freedom

Nevin froze mid-step, swaying side-to-side as the mist-rich wind darted around him. Then, reversing his momentum, the pale young man took three quick steps back up the slope. A pair of shadowy hands stopped his retreat, crawling up his back to grip his shoulders with a firmness that belied their ephemeral nature.

What's wrong, boy? Found something else to be afraid of?

"I . . . I d-don't . . . *do* bridges," he stuttered. "Not over gorges. I c-c-can't."

The young woman, apparently oblivious to her companion's alarming change in countenance, covered a small smile with her hand. Theis wanted to slap her. "Aw, don't tell me you're afraid of heights. If you want, I can hold your hand the whole time, and just as long as you don't look down . . ."

"*Raiya*," Theis barked with enough force to make her jump. His boiling eyes never left Nevin's ashen face. "Shut. Up."

Swallowing, Raiya nodded obediently.

Theis inched forward. The boy looked up at him, confused. "Nevin . . ."

He cut him off, frantically waving his hands. "I know! We'll go south, cross the river at ground level. Raiya taught me how to swim. We don't have to take the bridge. It's okay. I'm a really good swimmer."

Theis shook his head. "Not that good. The Mossalnag is swollen by melting snows and rainfall. You wouldn't make it halfway across before the current drags you underwater."

Nevin took another step back, and the shadowy figure welcomed his retreat, wrapping its arms around his chest and pulling him into a frigid embrace.

I can get us across. I can free you from this fear.

"We'll find some reeds. Bundle them together. I could hold on to them as I swim. They'll keep me above water. I won't drown."

The man in black pulled his cloak over his right shoulder, pointing to the bandages encircling his arm. "And what of me? I won't be able to follow you without both of my arms."

Nevin spun on Raiya with such intensity the young woman flinched in surprise. She looked at him with confusion, failing to comprehend how something so seemingly innocuous could engender such metamorphic terror. Uncertainty reflected in her glistening eyes. In this moment of vulnerability, he'd become a stranger once more.

"Raiya, you could cross here, with Theis. If you'll just wait for me . . ."

It was her turn to shake her head. "No, Theis is right. The current is too strong. You'd be swept out to sea again."

She reached out to comfort him, but Nevin retreated another step. The shadowy figure rested its chin on his shoulder, grinding it cheek against his own and grinning like the fiend it was.

I can take all the scary things away. You know what to say.

His breathing accelerated until his chest heaved with every panicked draft. "Please, Theis. You don't . . . you just don't understand . . ."

The man's eyes deepened to a dark, swirling violet. "I understand better than you know."

He turned back to Raiya, turned to beg the young woman not to force him to do this thing, to save him from himself and offer him a way out, but the words never left his mouth.

Because Raiya wasn't looking at Nevin. With a furrowed brow, Raiya was staring at something behind them, and Nevin suddenly realized he could feel the earth thumping through the soles of his boots.

A tingle of discomfort and alarm screamed from the deepest recesses of his mind.

The look on Raiya's face told Theis everything he needed to know about the rapidly approaching horsemen.

In his weakened state, Theis wasn't confident in his ability to face off against three warriors of unknown skill and training. And Nevin . . . Nevin was in no frame of mind to fight *at all*. In his desperation, the boy would strike recklessly, pressing after his opponent like a cornered beast, and like a beast, he would most likely find himself impaled on the spear points of his hunters.

Seems like everything is against us.

Out of the three of them, only Raiya possessed both a level of health and mental clarity befitting combat, but Theis was not about to place their fate in the battle-green hands of a fisherman. Not when some semblance of sanctuary lay only a short distance across the gorge. He sincerely doubted their pursuers would continue to engage them within the town's borders. Not in the daylight, at least.

Unfortunately, with the seconds rapidly evaporating with each thundering hoof beat, the time to reason with the hysterical Nevin had run out.

Tightening his fingers around the leather-wound hilt of his sword, Theis decided that the only way to get Nevin across that bridge without fighting him the whole way would be if he was unconscious.

As his weight shifted to his lead foot, Nevin followed Raiya's gaze back over his right shoulder. Theis steeled his resolve and took a half-step forward, silently inching his blade free of its mahogany scabbard beneath the shadows of his cloak.

One swift strike to the boy's temple once he turned back around, and then a quick sprint across the bridge. He hoped he had enough strength left to make that run with Nevin's limp body draped over his one good shoulder.

"Yes," said the boy under his breath, barely loud enough for Theis to make out over the roar of water.

When Nevin turned around, the look in his eyes froze Theis in place.

It was like looking into the eyes of a completely different person.

The wild look of desperation had vanished, replaced by a hawk-like intensity, his penetrating glare laying Theis' intentions out in the open like a mile-wide banner. His chest barely moved as he quietly drew shallow, measured breaths, expelling a thin mist with each exhalation.

With one hand behind his back, Nevin squeezed the rounded scabbard of his sword in a white-knuckled fist.

Before Theis could take hold of his surprise, Nevin jogged past his two surprised companions, breaking into a flat-out run as the ground leveled off before the bridge.

Swallowing back an uneasy feeling, Theis followed.

An endless plane of curious absence stretched out before him.

Breath rushed into Nevin's lungs and his eyes fluttered open, coming into focus as the absence withdrew, leaving him standing alone in the center of a shimmering circle of white light. His bare toes curled against the familiar coarse white stone beneath them.

The same as the blade's grip. I'm back inside the sword.

The sudden transition away from reality had temporarily stripped him of his mounting anxiety, resetting his emotions to a state of neutrality. His breathing was calm and even, his skin dry. Still, the memory of terror remained, and Nevin caught himself rubbing his chest to comfort his previously racing heart.

"Hello?" he called into the empty, knowing he wasn't alone in the curious space.

The darkness at the edge of nothing coalesced, and a shadowy figure stepped right up to the rim of his little island of light. He could barely see it, a lighter blotch against a backdrop of impenetrable black, but it was there.

Snapping fingers summoned a floating rectangle of what looked like curved glass. A moving image appeared within, a translucent picture of the bridge spanning the massive gorge. As Nevin watched, the bridge drew closer at increasing speeds, though something about its movement gave him the impression that time flowed different here, like the seconds passed somewhat slower out there than they did within the sword.

"Let's hurry this up," he said, surprised at how little the image bothered him, especially with the knowledge that what he was seeing was still happening to his body back in the real world.

The shadowy figure turned to pace around the limits of the circle of light. "And why is that?"

Nevin shivered at the voice's similarity to his own. "I don't want to be here any longer than I have to. Just get us to the other side and put me back."

"Put you back?" The figure paused, turning. It sounded somewhat amused, entertained by its own feigned ignorance.

"You know what I mean. Back in my body." A pair of lofty wooden pillars briefly framed the floating image as his body took its first steps onto the bridge, and Nevin almost thought he could feel the wooden support beams passing on either side. A difference in pressure almost, a change in the low background hum of the empty.

"That's not how things work, boy."

Nevin turned, but the figure had vanished, fading back into the blackness from whence it came.

"What do you mean, that's not what I—"

"You think you can just . . . pass the unpleasant aspects of life onto someone else without consequence?"

The words echoed all around him now, a chorus of mocking shadows, each speaking slightly out of time with the next until Nevin found himself inundated by countless layers of his own voice.

"Avoid responsibility? Shun the true nature of things in the hope that someone might come along and save you from yourself?"

"It's not like that! I just needed a little help."

"Help?" Footsteps circled his position, slowly winding closer and closer, growing louder with each plodding thud. Nevin held his breath, expecting the shadows to part at any moment and the mysterious figure to finally emerge into the light and reveal himself to have been Dalen all along.

"You didn't want help. You wanted to run. You thought you could hide away and let me do your dirty work, and for what? A few moments of freedom? The sensation of flesh containing what little remains of me?"

"I don't understand. You said you could help me!"

The voice continued, ignoring his outburst. "You hid from your troubles, came to this place of your own free will, traded control of your physical body to some . . . .'fiend', as you call me. Not once, but twice. Twice you have given yourself to me, and now you think you can just come and go as you please?"

The footsteps stopped just beyond the edge of revelation, the echoing chorus fading until but a single, confident voice commanded his full attention.

"Without responsibility, there can be no freedom. By giving up one, you've lost the other."

A circular metal object flew out of the darkness, skidding across the stone to rest at his feet.

Shocked, Nevin looked down at Dalen's tarnished canteen, and its two deep crevasses stained with fresh blood.

"And all because you've refused to see what's been in front of you all this time."

Chapter 79: Exposition

"*Mrrrroooooow,*" Aidux groaned, arching his back and fanning his claws out against the cherry wood planks before flopping unceremoniously onto his side. "I am *so* sore. I've got hurt in places I didn't even think *could* hurt. Like the tips of my ears. How the heck are the tips of my ears sore?"

"Probably because you slept on them," Blake said, chuckling. "And how can you be sore anyway? It's not like you've been walking around much. You spent the entire trip to Whitefalls asleep in the back of my cart. On your back."

The lynx adjusted, grimacing. "Yes, but, I was sore before we left. I was sorta hoping a good, long nap would make me feel better."

He stretched again. "Must have been all that rain. I'm not a young cat anymore, ya know."

Aurnia pinched the bridge of her nose. The two's constant banter had grated on her nerves all morning. "Blake, what makes you so sure they'll come through here and not head north to Alcara? Or just cross the river to the south? Or take a boat out of Calibri Grotto? Or any number of other possibilities?"

Blake's smile faded. "Once again, Celine, I have this under control. Just try to be patient."

Aurnia straightened in her chair and shot the man a withering look. "I'm serious, Blake. We traveled all night to get here, and we've been sitting inside this inn of yours all day now with no further information regarding the sword. I'm starting to wonder if your people really know what they're doing."

Blake closed his eyes and took a bit of goat cheese from his plate, chewing it slowly to let his annoyance with Aurnia's jab fade before he answered. A warm glow suffused the inn's common area, light trickling in from a series of broad windows that encompassed the rectangular building, granting a clear view of the manicured garden out front as well as the yawning, mist-cloaked chasm and voluminous wall of rushing water spanning the horizon behind. None of the room's circular tables or skinny bar stools were occupied at the moment, as Blake had politely requested the innkeep to close up and take the day off.

Once the last few overnight visitors had left that morning, the three travelers had the building all to themselves, but the incessant silence marred only by the occasional frivolous comment by Aidux or Blake had only served to heighten Aurnia's simmering anxiety.

Blake finally opened his eyes, but he didn't look at her as he spoke. "You may be well-traveled, and you may have spent some time in my province many years ago, but this is my home. I know its hills and mires and roads and towns far better than you could ever hope to, so when I say that, out of all the places this young man is like to go, he will most likely come through here first, I know what I'm talking about.

"Now, when and if someone learns something new, they will come let us know. In the meantime, please, just try to relax." He motioned to the cup of hot ginger tea resting untouched on the lavender tablecloth before her.

Aurnia swallowed her words and reached for her tea, but in her frustration, she missed the handle, sending the teacup tumbling across the table to shatter on the floor, raining hot liquid down on the innocent and guilty alike.

Aidux and Blake stared at her in silent surprise. Her cheeks flushed a hot, bright red and her eyes dropped to the tea stain inching steadily toward her feet.

"Look, I know I've been rather abrasive—" she began, but at that exact moment, a strange feeling erupted from the back of her mind, cutting off her apology mid-stream. The warm light of her soul burned into her consciousness a feeling of alarm, like a lighthouse on a foggy night. Her eyes and mouth went wide as she tried to acclimate herself to this new and unpleasant sensation.

Blake stood, immediately recognizing the sudden shift in her expression for what it was. "What's happened? What do you sense?"

Aurnia grabbed the flour sack and hefted it over one shoulder as she rose. "Something's coming."

"It's good to see you again, Sandy," said Maddox, planting a firm grip on the old goat farmer's calloused hand. "Maybe this time those soldiers will give you a fair price for such handsome animals."

A chorus of bleating shouted their agreement from the bed of Sandy Jameson's wagon. The old man tipped his straw hat and nodded, offering him a toothless smile. "I doubts it, but I appreciate the thought. Take care."

"You too, Sandy. Peddis by your side."

As the two mules strained to pull the overloaded wagon over the lip marking the cusp of the bridge, Maddox resigned himself back into his seat, an old chopping block marred by deep gouges. It wasn't the most comfortable of seats, but it kept him wary, kept him vigilant.

After a brief yawn, Maddox reached again for the spyglass.

Gibbs kicked a pebble, sending it tumbling haplessly into the gorge.

"Hey Mads," he mused, pointing in the distance. "Do the falls look weird to you?"

"Weird?"

"I don't know. Different?" He swooped a hand in a descending arc. "Not as full, maybe. You think Rothsfel is going through a bit a dry patch this year? The Brennan running a mite shallow?"

Maddox gave the falls a cursory glance and shrugged. "Looks the same to me."

Gibbs hung his head and groaned. "This is soooo boring. We've been staring at this bridge for, like, *forever*. Nothing is happening. How much longer do we have to do this for?"

"Until we find this kid or Arolde comes back."

Maddox held the spyglass to his eye and tried to see over Sandy's wagon as it headed over the gorge, attempting to ignore the grating sound of Gibb's voice. As an outside observer to his team's internal communication, Maddox had always found the kid's personality to be somewhat humorous, if a little inflammatory. Yet now, without the other members of his team present to entertain Gibbs, he was quickly relearning just how annoying the kid could actually be.

Squinting into the eyepiece, Maddox leaned forward, focusing his gaze on a hazy group of travelers approaching the town from the far ridge. "Look, Gibbs, if you're so bored, why don't you go find us something to eat. Walk off some of that boredom. Give me a little peace for half-an-hour."

"Yeah, okay, fine." He shuffled over to the stump and started riffling through Blake's pack. "But you're paying this time."

"Help yourself," he mumbled, shaking his head in amazement.

With a smirk, Gibbs trotted off down the street, a handful of Maddox's shils jangling in his pocket.

Maddox shot to his feet, waving frantically at Gibbs as he tried to steady the spyglass with one hand. There, in the distance, a girl and a boy with what looked like a large sword grip protruding over one shoulder, raced across the bridge as if the god of death himself was on their heels.

His sharp inhalation whistled against slightly parted teeth. Moments behind, a black splotch glided through reality, a shadow with two vibrant blue spots for eyes. The shadow moved with inhuman grace, yet Maddox got the distinct impression that it was damaged somehow, wounded.

Impossible. Over a decade had passed since the last sighting of the infamous swordsman. Many considered him dead, his incessant pursuit of challenging opponents having brought him a battle even he couldn't win.

Yet here he was, a ghost in the world of form.

"Gibbs!" he exclaimed, lowering the spyglass and spinning on his heel. "Forget the food! They're here! Go back to the inn and . . ."

But Gibbs hadn't gone far, as Blake and Aurnia were already hustling up to the bridge, the golden-furred lynx trotting along behind them.

Raiya slid to a halt beside Nevin. She had to brace herself against the haft of her spear in order to keep from stumbling to her knees, a fall that would have undoubtedly peppered her kneecaps with painful splinters. The rumble of the approaching horses sent tremors through the floating bridge, making her stomach churn uneasily.

Fear wracked her body with uncontrollable tremors, terror born of a sense of entrapment coupled with concern for Nevin's safety and the unusual locale of their inevitable confrontation with his pursuers. Raiya had never been so afraid in her life. She didn't understand it. How was this any different than facing those disgusting creatures back in the grotto? How was this any different than being trapped in that cramped hole while the mother-of-all Chuurik tore at the meager opening with both tooth and tentacle?

"We can't stop here, Nevin!" She had to yell over the deep roar of water as it careened over the edge of a hundred foot drop. A fine mist tickled her throat with each heaving breath, leaving her on the cusp of a fit of wet coughs that never arose. A dark sheen coated the twisted web of ropes and wood panels under their boots, creating treacherous conditions for hastily crossing the yawning chasm. She had no idea how Nevin had managed to stop so suddenly.

Theis skidded to a stop behind them, his thin sword hanging loosely from his one good hand. His azure eyes vibrated with agitation, the tiny motes dancing excitedly around the lightless void of his pupils.

"There," he said, pointing toward the far side of the bridge with his blade. Raiya's gaze followed the glistening length of metal, squinting through the haze of prismatic mist.

Her breath caught in her throat. At the farthest reaches of her sight, just on the other side of a double horse-drawn wagon, a group of indistinguishable people spread out at the foot of the bridge where suspended wood met solid rock.

Waiting. Watching.

There was nowhere left to run. They were surrounded.

Theis calmly turned back the way they came, squaring off against the now cautiously approaching riders. Nevin, frowning, watched them as well, his hand reaching over his shoulder in search of his sword hilt. He mumbled something incomprehensible beside the onslaught of water and shook his head.

Raiya edged closer to his side. "We're trapped, Nevin. What are we going to do?"

Nevin jerked away, his wild eyes staring at her like he'd never seen her before.

"Stay back!" Theis screamed, leveling his sword at the shirtless rider.

Nevin slid his awkward blade free of the baldric. The storm gray metal drew along the smooth, damp surface of the leather strap as he pulled it over his shoulder, silent as a shadow on a starless night.

Raiya's hand flew to her mouth, but it wasn't able to contain her frightened gasp. The haunted, far-off look in Nevin's unfamiliar eyes terrified her more the men closing in from all sides.

With a flash of white light, Nevin summoned forth the blade's lethal edge.

Arolde jerked his chestnut gelding to a halt, signaling for Miles and Delia to do the same. He had no idea who this dark swordsman was, but he wasn't about to incite the wrath of an unknown warrior by crowding him.

"Stay on your horses," he said to his companions without turning.

"Are you sure?" asked Delia. "What if he . . ."

She extended her hand in a thrusting motion. Miles snorted in agreement.

Arolde dismounted, resting his hand on the only weapon in his possession, a long knife with a hilt made of elk antler. "Pray that he does not."

Taking a calming breath, Arolde held his hands up in supplication and slowly approached the dark warrior's raised sword. Upon first glance, Arolde had thought the swordsman to be the boy's captor, as Maddox had made no mention of him in their briefing. But all three seemed equally disturbed by his group's sudden appearance, and neither the boy nor the girl made a move to escape the swordsman while his back was turned.

That meant he had to be protecting them from the perceived threat of Arolde, Miles, and Delia. He only hoped he could convince him otherwise before he ended up with a sword buried in the meat of his gut.

"Swordsman!" he screamed over the din of the waterfall. "I don't know who you are, but if you are protecting this boy, then you and I are on the same side! Lower your blade and speak!"

The man's sword lowered slightly, and it was then that Arolde's gaze locked onto a pair of fiery blue orbs burning beneath his mahogany mask. The eyes narrowed slightly, and the man took three steps forward, faster than Arolde could shift his weight to his rear foot in surprise.

The hair on the back of his neck stood tall and stiff. He had heard stories, little more than campfire tales spun to scare the arrogance out of childhood bullies, but he'd never believed they were true.

But maybe they *were* true. The man before him could be none other than the Theis Bane of legend.

Arolde felt as if the cold hand of death itself had brushed his soul.

Chapter 80: Rising Action

"Get that thing the hell away from me."

Nevin backpedaled from the dented canteen, confounded by its appearance in a place where nothing else from the real world had followed.

A chuckle echoed all around him from the darkness. "Something wrong?"

"Don't act innocent. You're the reason this stupid canteen keeps following me around, the reason why every time I leave it behind it somehow reappears when I'm not paying attention. You've been torturing me since that day in Ishen's cabin, taunting and insulting and . . . and . . ."

Through the floating glass display, he could hear Raiya's panicked breathing and the electric hiss of the exposed Sharasil. But worse still was the image's apparent lack of forward progress, the rapid blur of interlocking wooden panels beneath his body's feet having come to a dead stop.

"What are you doing?" Nevin asked, shocked that the entity controlling his body was no longer in motion. "They're right behind us!"

"In front of us, too."

A hand jabbed in the direction of the floating glass. The appendage's brief appearance aroused uncomfortable feelings in the pit of Nevin's stomach, feelings of familiarity, of an understanding hanging just beyond the grasp of an addled mind. "These people are far more coordinated than I thought. While you were lost in the caves, they were setting a trap. One you walked right into, I might add."

Nevin squinted at the image, but the figures standing at the far end of the bridge were too blurry to make out. Maybe there were three. Maybe there were ten, he couldn't tell. One thing was certain though, they were spread out across the mouth of the bridge, and the only way out was through.

"This can't be real," he said, turning to approach the last place he'd seen the figure at the light's edge, searching the darkness for any sign of its presence.

If it was out there, watching him, weighing his words, he couldn't tell. "We're right outside a town. They won't try anything with all these people watching."

"Oh? Are we talking about the same people who burned down an entire village and the forest around it in order to find the sword?"

"That's not—" Nevin stumbled over his words, his fists shaking against his thighs. "This is crazy! We can't just stand here and wait for them to come to us. You have to do something!"

"Do . . . something? Just what would you have me do?"

It was taunting him again, and Nevin knew it, but he couldn't figure out why it felt the need to continually antagonize him. Now that it had received exactly what it always wanted, still it sought to aggravate him. To what end?

"I don't know!" Nevin tossed his hands up in exasperation. "Why are you making this so difficult? What do you want me from me?"

"I want you to stop running and accept some responsibility!" The words resounded with such ferocity that Nevin slammed his palms against his ears and shrank back from the edge of the circle.

The scuffed toes of a pair of boots inched into the light. "You're so afraid to be honest, to admit the existence of your own darkness, and you'll do anything to escape a situation where you're forced to confront that part of yourself. You're terrified by what you might learn.

"Your fear is what called me. That fear is *always* what brings me out, but even here, hidden away from the dangers of the world, you're not even man enough to ask me to fight to save you and your friends."

An arm pierced the darkness, leveling an accusatory finger. A white linen shirt covered a tanned stretch of lean muscle, the cuff rolled up just below the elbow. "Whether it's my will or yours that swings the blade, it's still your hands that get drenched in blood. Closing your eyes and running away won't put out the fires that consume your life."

A flash of hot orange light.

"Fires? What are you—" Nevin shook his head, pain lancing through the back of his skull. Blinking, he rubbed at the spot, surprised to feel the roughness of a scab grinding against his fingertips. The acrid stench of woodsmoke permeated his nostrils.

The canteen vibrated against the stone floor, rocking and turning and spinning until its motion forced it up onto its edge. It continued to spin, glinting in the weak light and slinging blood droplets in an ever-increasing halo of red around it.

"But I—like you, young man—am not interested in fighting. Fighting invites the prospect of death, and I'm only interested in survival."

Like the surface of some stygian lake, the darkness rippled aside and the voice's owner stepped into the light.

"And I don't particularly care who gets hurt to ensure that happens."

Theis lurched to a halt, gritting his teeth against the adrenaline driving his heart into a hard gallop. The shirtless rider jerked back a step, but his hands never went to the knife resting at his hip.

He raised his blade again. "You must think me the worst kind of fool. You and your men have us surrounded, and you want me to think you a friend?"

Theis barked a weak laugh. "I'd sooner kill you and take the chance that you were trying to help than give in to such an obvious ploy."

The younger man violently shook his head in disagreement. "You don't understand," he yelled. "Aurnia sent us. We aren't here to fight!"

The tip of Theis' blade wavered as he tried to process what he thought the shirtless leader had said. Adrenaline and exhaustion had an uncanny knack for altering how the ear translated the spoken word. Combined with the cacophonous deluge within spitting distance to his right side, Theis recognized how easy it would be to mistake a garbled challenge for a tentative declaration of peace.

Especially when the mistake played upon his most unexpected hopes.

Checking over his shoulder to be sure the other group of men hadn't advanced within charging distance, Theis took a few hesitant steps forward.

"Say again?!" he called, straining his voice to its limits.

The shirtless man cautiously advanced, holding his empty arms wide and repeated himself. "We aren't your enemies! We were sent by Aurnia to find a boy by the name of Nevin Walker!"

A drop of water fled down the length of his curved blade and leapt onto the suspended planks at his feet as his sword arm relaxed to his side, but he didn't yet replace it in its scabbard. Neither the two men nor the armored woman had drawn weapons, and they didn't move like they were looking for blood. In fact, the older man and his stocky female companion seemed almost confused by his aggressive response.

Still, the itching in the back of his mind wouldn't abate. Something wasn't right, something he wasn't seeing.

"How do you know Aurnia?" he said, taking another step closer to the trio.

The shirtless man shook his head. "We don't. She's a friend of our boss."

"And who is your boss?"

"Blake Osmund, mayor of Fen Quarry and lord of the Tichooran lands west of the Granite Spires."

Theis blinked. That was a name he hadn't heard in many, many years, but so many things suddenly made sense.

Nodding, Theis moved to sheath his blade, but an abrupt change in the shirtless man's demeanor halted his arm.

With wide eyes, the man stared over Theis' shoulder. His mouth moved erratically as he failed to put words to warning.

The itching in the back of his mind vaulted into a terrified wail.

Blake threw his arms out to both sides, blocking the forward advancement of his four companions.

He couldn't believe what he was seeing.

"Oh, gods, *NO!*" he screamed, watching in abject horror as the young man stepped up to the waist-high support rope running the length of the massive bridge and prepared to raise his sword overhead.

"Wait . . . is that Nevin?" Aidux cocked his head and padded forward.

Blake reached down and grabbed him by the scruff of the neck, attempting to pull him back. "Everyone off the bridge *now!* That crazy kid is about to cut the ropes!"

Aidux lunged forward, breaking Blake's grip on his mane. The older man reached for him again, but the golden lynx was a blur of feet and fur, dashing forward to take his place at his best friend's side.

"Nevin, no!" Raiya screamed.

For Theis, the world moved through thick molasses as his head worked its way around, inching through space at a snail's pace, the hem of his hood colliding spectacularly with every speck of water floating through the air.

His sword arm followed behind, both a hair's breadth and an eternity behind his searching gaze. He saw Nevin's sword careening towards the rope long before he thought to block it, yet his blade still rose just in time to deflect it away. The force of the impact sent a shock wave radiating up his arm.

With a speed that Theis had never thought him capable of, Nevin lashed out with an open palm, slamming into the center of his chest with the force of a thunderbolt. The blow froze his lungs and made his heart skip a beat. Theis crumpled backwards, his sword spilling from his open hand.

As Theis clutched his chest, Nevin looked down at him, the faintest traces of a smile on the corners of his mouth. His swollen pupils had completely swallowed his irises, lending an otherworldly quality to his gaze.

He didn't know how it was possible, but the man standing over him was not Nevin Walker.

"Who . . . or what . . . are you?" Theis managed, struggling to regain his breath.

The faint smile disappeared, and when the young man spoke, the blood in Theis' veins froze solid.

"I'm someone who can survive the fall."

With a quick turn and a grunt of effort, the man that wasn't Nevin Walker heaved his glowing sword and split the bridge's support rope in twain.

Chapter 81: Conflict

Nevin stumbled away from the strange figure as it stepped into the circle of light, finding its new appearance far more unnerving than the undefined shadow that had chased him since Ishen's cabin.

"You—" he choked out, fumbling around a tongue gone numb from shock. "Why do you look like me?"

The scowling face *did* look like him, but only in a twisted, dream-like sort of way. Where his hair was short, his other's was long and fell about his rounded shoulders in thick waves. A thin layer of dark scruff coated the lower half of his face, even possessing the narrow bald spots that ran vertically along either side of Nevin's mouth. Two pairs of deep brown eyes stared into one another, but where Nevin's quivered with surprise and trepidation, his other's were steady as a falcon's in search of a meal.

A shadowy doppelganger, and a dark reflection of everything Nevin could be, but wasn't.

An electric hiss and the ring of metal cried out from the glass panel, and a tremor rocked the tiny island of light.

"What was that?" he asked, returning to the display in time to see his hand strike Theis in the chest.

His other just shrugged. "The swordsman doesn't want me to cut down the bridge. An understandable objection."

"Cut the bridge? Are you trying to get us killed?"

"Quite the opposite."

His twin stepped up to the display beside him, arms folded across his chest. "You may not remember, but the sword floats in water, and though the drop might be far, we're standing over the deepest part of the river. Everyone on the bridge falls with us, but we're the only one to survive. We escape and kill all our pursuers in one decisive blow. The perfect solution."

"The perf . . . But you'll kill Theis and Raiya, too!" Nevin lunged for the man, but the man moved with a preternatural speed, latching onto his wrist and twisting until Nevin found his face pressed flat against the floating display. The ethereal glass was cold against the tender flesh of his cheek.

"You wanted my help, which means you accept my solution." His arm wrenched further, eliciting a cry of pain. "You think you could do better? Go out there and protect them from the bad men? Play hero with your sword and save the day?"

His chest tightened until it hurt to breathe, and he ground his forehead into the glass as he shook his head in resignation. It was one thing to watch it happening from a distance, detached from the situation by a thin sheet of glass and protected from his paralyzing fear by a curtain of darkness.

"I can't," he mumbled, a thick stream of tears trickling down the glass display. "The bridge—"

His other jerked him back, sending him tumbling across the coarse stone floor before coming to a rest on his side. When he lifted his head, the man was crouched before him, his hard eyes brimming with sadness. With pity.

"The bridge isn't why you ran. It's just another excuse to stay a coward. No, you ran because of the people chasing you."

"The horsemen?" Nevin pushed himself up on his elbow. He could barely remember the moments before transitioning into this space, but he did remember turning, remembered seeing three riders bearing down on them. Something about two of them seemed familiar, as though he'd come across them recently.

An old man and an armored woman. He nodded. "I saw them in Calibri Grotto. They're the reason I left."

"And now they're here, and you want to keep running. But at some point Nevin, you have to stop and face your fears, because if you don't fight to solve your own problems, then you might not like the solution that someone else comes up with for you."

He gestured to the glass display in time for Nevin to watch in horror as the glowing white Sharasil sliced through the braided support rope and the island of light dropped out beneath him.

"Brace yourselves!" Blake screamed, wrapping a protective arm around Aurnia's shoulders.

The southern support rail snapped with a wet thwack, and the bridge shuddered and groaned like a ship on stormy waters. Blake and Aurnia dropped into a huddled crouch, while Maddox unsuccessfully tried to catch a flailing Gibbs. Sandy's mules bucked nervously, but it was the goats that complained loudest, crashing repeatedly against the slated walls of the wagon in a mad attempt to be free of their mobile prison.

In a feat of providence, the remaining network of rope somehow managed to sustain the wooden behemoth. A shock wave rippled through the tension strands fanning out from the sides of the bridge to different locations along the ridge, sending puffs of rock dust into the moisture-laden air.

They didn't have much time before the boy finished what he started.

"Get your men off the bridge," Aurnia said, shrugging off his embrace and pushing to her feet. "I'll try to buy us some time."

Blake ran a hand through his sodden white locks. "Dammit, Celine, what have you gotten us into? You didn't tell me this kid was crazy!"

Aurnia slowed her breathing and reached into the deeper parts of her mind, embracing the warm light of her soul. "Just do as I say and get your men off the bridge."

It was like he didn't hear her. "Can't you just put him to sleep or something? Freeze him in place?"

"Not with Theis right in the middle of things."

Blake frowned. "Why would it matter if—"

"Because Theis is a magic eater!" she barked, the final thread of her already frayed patience snapping. "Now go do your job so I can do mine!"

His jaw clapped shut, a brief look of embarrassment flashing across his face. With a small nod, he turned to Maddox and Gibbs.

"Help me get that wagon off the bridge. Preferably before the ground drops out from under us."

Aurnia ignored the exchange as she called up the winds, moving her arms in slow circles to focus her intent. A horizontal vortex of mist swirled about her, growing in size until the driving winds encircled the section of bridge beneath her feet. Her arms drew smaller and smaller circles until the vortex formed an ever-tightening noose of air that supported the entire suspended causeway.

Without the help of an Orlicite, Blake knew her solution wouldn't last. Hopefully Theis would get control of the situation before her strength failed.

"Arolde?" Maddox gasped in surprise, the spyglass shaking in his hands. "That's my son over there!"

Blake grabbed Maddox by the arm. "He'll be fine! He's closer to the other side than this one."

Maddox tried to shrug free of Blake's grip, but the older man held fast. "It was your idea to make him leader of this mission. I trusted him because I trust you. It's time we see what that trust is worth."

With a resigned nod, Maddox wrenched himself free and pulled a grumbling Gibbs to his feet, and the three men dashed toward Sandy's wagon.

A blast of cold mist whipped across the planks as Theis struggled back to his feet, and a haze of blue washed over his sight.

He snorted. *Seems the old woman has made it here, as well.*

"Nevin!" he screamed, but the boy's attention seemed distracted by the sudden onslaught of wind. He squinted past a stupefied Raiya, searching for the source of the disturbance. A golden streak of lynx was quickly closing the distance behind the young woman.

Theis spun to the shirtless rider. The man looked nearly as confused as Raiya. "You say you're here to help?"

The shirtless man blinked, then nodded.

"Then get the girl out of here. I don't know if I can stop him, and things are going to get much worse before they get better."

"But you're . . . *you*, and he's just a kid! How can he be better than you?"

Theis bent over and closed the fingers of his good hand around the hilt of his sword. "I'm not practiced at sparing my opponent's lives."

The pot-bellied old man leaned forward in his saddle, shoving at his mount's head when it turned to nip him in the leg. "What's the plan, Arolde?"

The man called Arolde tossed the reins of his horse to the woman. "Take my horse and go back the way we came. I'm going to try to get to the girl."

With a quick nod, the old man wordlessly jerked his horse around, following his female companion back to stable ground.

Theis readied his blade and advanced on Nevin.

"Right then. Let's see how good you really are."

Lunging forward, Theis leveled the flat of his blade at the back of Nevin's head, hoping to catch him unaware. Arolde broke into a sprint at nearly the same instant, using the distraction to slip by unnoticed.

Even with his back turned, the boy sensed the coming attack, ducking beneath the blade at the last instant. He twirled on one heel, lifting the massive blade in a vicious uppercut, but Theis let the momentum of his own attack carry him safely to the side.

The sudden flurry of movement broke the spell over Raiya. At the sight of the shirtless rider racing towards her, she made a move toward the distant ridge.

Theis aimed the dull edge of his blade at Nevin's knees, but instead of allowing himself to be tripped, Nevin somersaulted over the attack, rolling across the planks towards the other side of the bridge.

Theis realized his goal too late.

Coming smoothly to his feet, Nevin brought his sword down on the other supporting rail, and the world violently lost all stability.

Raiya knew she was dead as soon as the floor dropped out from under her. In a few moments she'd crash into the churning waters of the swollen Mossalnag and drown, or miss the water entirely and land on an unforgiving pile of jagged rocks. Either way, she wasn't long for this world.

And to think, not an hour before, she had stood beside the road that would lead her back home, back to her father, and had chosen instead to continue on a journey that had nearly claimed her life on more than one occasion.

In hindsight, she wished she had chosen differently.

Despite her premonition, the bridge abruptly stilled its descent, sending Raiya into a painful forward roll. Her spear slipped from her grasp, but it didn't go far, clattering along beside her as she tumbled. Bits of wood scraped and clawed at her skin, tearing gashes too shallow to bleed.

To her surprise, something soft and wet slammed into her, and the two collapsed in a tangle of limbs.

"Are you okay?" she said, rising to her knees.

"I'm fine, but I have to get to Nevin!"

Raiya nearly choked. Lying between her arms was the largest cat she had ever seen, all matted fur and pointed teeth and round, silver eyes.

"You can . . . you . . ." she stuttered.

Aidux rolled his eyes. "Yes, I'm a talking cat. It's weird, I know. Now, can you please get off me? I have to get to Nevin before Theis kills him."

Raiya's hand crept towards her spear, her fingers wrapping around the comforting wood. "He's not trying to kill him. Something's wrong. Theis is just trying to stop him from destroying the bridge and killing everyone on it."

The bridge shuddered again. Aidux pressed his paws to her shoulders and shoved her aside. "Then maybe he'll listen to me."

Raiya shook her head. "That's not Nevin. I don't know who that is, but that is definitely not the boy I pulled from the sea a week ago."

Aidux whined softly, a sound that reminded Raiya of a crying child. "But . . . I can't do *nothing*. He's my bestest friend!"

Behind her, the shirtless rider was on his knees, one hand pressed against his bleeding forehead. "Look, if we don't get off—"

With a series of successive snaps, a handful of tension ropes succumbed to the increased strain, and the bridge lurched again, this time dipping off to one side.

Raiya hurtled feet-first toward the abyss.

Chapter 82: Climax

Her eyes watering from the strain, Aurnia pushed her focus to the limit to steady the vortex of wind, only briefly allowing the bridge to list northward.

She hadn't been fast enough. From her position near the ridge, the bridge had only tilted enough to slide her a few inches to the side, but farther up, the wagon that Blake and his men were desperately trying to back off the bridge had caught air and shattered both wheels along one side when it landed. Not everyone had immediately reappeared after the violent collision, but she couldn't look.

She didn't have the attention to spare.

Everyone needed more time, but she could feel her soul channel beginning to contract, cutting into the necessary flow of spiritual energy. If she continued with her current strategy, she didn't know if it would be enough to keep the bridge aloft when the next array of ropes gave way.

Gritting her teeth, Aurnia reached through the light in her mind to slice off a sizable chunk of the ethereal conduit and attach it to the continued execution of the spell. Pain, like hundreds of razors sliding across her tender skin, radiated out from her skull, persistent and sharp and wholly unpleasant. She screamed through clenched teeth, clutching her aching head with trembling hands. Never before had she tied off a spell so powerful, and now she was paying the price.

Tears stinging her eyes, she sank to her knees, a trembling hand pulling the flour sack into her lap. All she had to do was get the next spell going and she could untie the other.

She just needed to focus. The pain in her skull would be nothing in comparison to what was in store for her if she miscalculated now.

Breathing through the stinging pain, Aurnia gingerly removed the imperfect azure sphere from the bag and held it at arm's length. She wasted no time, focusing her intent to a deadly acuity, and propelled it into and through the uncut Orlicite.

A bright light welled up from within, and her world was drowned in blue.

Claws digging into the wooden planks, Aidux leaned back against the weight of the terrified girl, his teeth clenched tightly around the shaft of her spear. She looked up at him with wide, pleading eyes as she dangled over the precipice.

Aidux had barely gotten to her in time.

"Please," she mumbled through a thick stream of tears. "Please don't let go of me."

The lynx arched his back and pulled, but despite the adrenaline flooding his muscles, he just didn't have the strength to lift an entire person by himself.

He flexed his toes against the rim of the wooden panel, but each time he took a breath, he inched further from safety.

He squeezed his eyes closed and held his breath and wrenched on the spear with everything he had. He couldn't give up. Not when the person he was trying to save had done the same for Nevin.

A shadow blotted out the sun, and another pair of hands took hold of the spear on either side of Aidux's head.

"Alright, cat," said the shirtless rider, planting his feet. "Let's do this together!"

The lynx heaved with all his might, and with the added help of the stranger, the girl regained her place on the bridge beside them. She immediately flung her arms around his furry neck, shaking uncontrollably.

"Thank you," she whispered, planting a kiss on his tufted ear.

The shirtless rider grabbed her by the hand and hauled her to her feet. "You're happy, the cat's happy, everyone's happy. Save the gratitude for solid ground. We've got about thirty seconds to sprout some wings or book it off this bridge."

The incessant roar the waterfall spiked in intensity, overwhelming the furious sounds of battle not more than thirty feet behind them. Aidux stared in wonder as the waterfall itself bubbled outward like the flow had suddenly increased ten-fold.

The shirtless rider shoved her and Aidux out ahead of him. "Let's go, you two! Move it!"

With a final look over his shoulder, Aidux surrendered the fate of his friend into the hands of the man in black, and the three of them sprinted toward safety.

Theis backpedaled, barely escaping the reach of a lethal thrust. The man that wasn't Nevin smirked, but didn't advance. Theis used the time to catch his breath. The wound in his shoulder screamed for attention, and the man in black's will was beginning to crack. He didn't have much energy let, but Nevin wasn't even breathing hard.

His mask concealed a scowl. *Youth.*

The roar of the tumbling water multiplied in volume, and the vertical column of frothing river bulged outward. Both combatants turned to stare, momentarily forgetting the other existed.

The hundred foot tall bulge jerked free of the torrent, hunching forward, feeding on the constant supply of water. It throbbed and pulsed in regular intervals, breathing deeply in its first moments of life. When the unnatural hump descended out of view beneath the bridge, the causeway shuddered once again, dipping another foot into the gorge as the vortex of wind holding it aloft died away.

Theis stumbled sideways, sinking the tip of his blade into the wooden planks in an effort to steady himself. Another thud rocked the bridge, and the entire construct jerked skyward.

A massive tower of roiling water climbed into view beside the bridge, supporting the structure along a pair of lithe, flowing arms. The cobalt haze obscuring the man in black's vision waxed nearly opaque.

The aqueous apparition bore the distinctly feminine visage of Aurnia.

Theis lunged, again taking advantage of Nevin's presumed distraction, but the boy sidestepped his attack using little more than his peripheral vision and countered with the width of his glowing sword. Theis crumpled onto his back with a grunt, sliding across the slick planks before grinding to a stop.

"Stop it!" Nevin screamed from his knees, resigning himself to the floor after losing his feet to the room's erratic movements for the third time.

"Stand up and make me!" His doppelganger screamed back at him. "Get up and fight! Beat me down! Take back control of your body, of your fate!"

Helplessness burned his throat as he cried. He knew full-well the futility of the man's request. "I can't. You're so much stronger than me."

"And so you won't even try? Something challenges you so you just avoid it? Is that who you want to be? Just another coward that blames everyone but himself for the sorry nature of his life?"

"It's not fair! These bad things . . . why do they keep happening to me?" Nevin slapped himself in the chest. "*To* me, not *because* of me. I didn't ask for any of this! I didn't want to be afraid of heights. I didn't want that ship to explode. I didn't want everyone I knew to die, to get murdered by someone looking for a sword I was forced to carry."

He squeezed his head with trembling hands, as though the painful thoughts threatened to burst his skull lest he hold them in. "I didn't want to lose Ishen. I didn't want to lose Aidux. I don't want people getting hurt because of me, and I definitely don't want to hurt anyone else."

The man squatted before him, tilting Nevin's chin up until their eyes met.

"You don't want people to have to feel the same things Dalen made you feel, do you?"

A wave of shame washed over him, and Nevin tried to pull away, but his other wouldn't let him.

"Are you really going to let the detestable actions of the man who raised you taint every waking moment of the rest of your existence? He wanted to hurt you, and so he did. He wanted to torture you, and so he did. He wanted you to be miserable because he couldn't control his *own* pain, couldn't manage his *own* shortcomings, couldn't handle the responsibility of rising above his *own* misfortune and disaster to protect those who couldn't do so for themselves."

A hand gently cupped his cheek, and the man's voice softened.

"He wanted to break you, but did he succeed? Are you really going to let him have the final say? Are you willing to sit there and let him win?"

Pain lanced through the back of his skull.

Trees flanked him on either side. The heat of the flames warmed his face, and smoke burned his unblinking eyes.

"Are you just going to watch as everyone you care about dies?"

His fingers crawled to the back of his head, where the strange scab from earlier had vanished, now an open wound seeping warm blood down his neck.

The brightness of the flames made the barn's darkened portal seem like a hole in reality, and though his eyes were already stretched to their limits, he felt them widen further when the shadows within began to shift.

"What . . . what is this?" Nevin barely managed to get the words through lips that felt too big for his mouth.

"Not choosing is still choosing, Nevin. The choice to not help your friends, to not help yourself, is no different than the non-choice you made the day this all started."

The images evaporated, and Nevin's gaze jerked up to meet the hardened expression of his other.

"The day you made no choice is the day you killed Dalen."

Chapter 83: Revelation

"But it was an accident!" Nevin frantically shook his head, the sharp pain in the back of his skull ebbing in and out with the rapid pounding of his heart. "That's not . . . I didn't—"

His other shot to his feet, circling the crouched young man as he shouted. "Why can you still not accept responsibility for what you've done? After everything I've said?"

"He said he was going to hurt Aidux and I . . . I just . . . I just reacted. I didn't want to . . ." He gripped his throbbing head.

Laughter, coming from inside the house. He didn't look, knowing no one could see him from where he stood in the trees.

"He landed on some tools and . . . and I . . ." Stretching his jaw, Nevin fought to speak through the pain. "His head was bleeding, and his chest was bleeding, and he wasn't moving and I was scared and there were . . . there were voices outside. Someone was coming, so I grabbed my pack and ran through the house to hide.

"There wasn't a choice to make! I was scared, but I didn't mean to hit him so hard. He attacked me while I slept, nearly broke my ribs, and threatened the one person I care about. I fought back. I reacted! So what!"

Anger cleared the strange images from his thoughts and brought strength to his voice. "It's not like he hasn't done the same to me! I put up with his abuse for years, and I'm not going to feel bad that, for once, he had to suffer in my stead."

"There! There it is!" His other exclaimed, clenching his fists in triumph. "Now we're seeing the real you, the you you've forgotten, the you you've buried beneath layer upon layer of fear and regret and trauma and denial. Bruises, cuts, scrapes, lost sleep, hunger, uncertainty, shame . . . all of this made you angry, made you resentful, filled you with hate.

"And for good reason! You said it yourself. You didn't ask for this. You were just a child. How dare some grown man treat you with such disregard, such contempt. And it was only getting worse. The better you got at avoiding it, the crueler he became in return. It was only a matter of time before another tragedy found its way to the Walker household.

"Admit it." His other stopped circling and faced him down, his feet planted just beyond Nevin's knees. "You wanted Dalen to die."

"I didn't," he said, without an ounce of conviction to his words.

"You did!"

"No!" he cried, but even he didn't believe himself.

"Who are you lying to, boy? You've earned your darkness, so own it!"

"STOP IT!" he screamed, leaping to his feet to grab his other by the collar. He shoved him back against the floating display hard enough to crack the glass. His voice wavered with barely restrained emotion as he screamed his truth into the face of the man that looked like him, screamed the truth he'd been avoiding, the truth he was afraid to admit.

"YES! I wanted him to suffer! Is that what you want to hear? You want me to tell you that I wanted him to feel everything he's made me feel over the years? That I wanted him to know what it was like to be unable to save himself like I was unable to save myself from him? That I wanted him helpless and scared and hurt and I wanted him to die so I could *finally* be free of him?

"Is that what you want me to say? Do you want me to say that, in some very dark and terrible way, there's a part of me that's no different from the horrible man that raised me? The man I left bleeding out on the floor of the barn? The man I kill . . . the man . . . the man I—"

Hot agony lanced through his skull once more, and it was all he could do to keep his feet. He gripped the sides of his head. The pain wouldn't stop, wouldn't diminish, wouldn't let up and give him even the briefest respite.

But then . . . something strange happened. An unexpected pair of arms wrapped themselves around him and squeezed, holding him aloft and preventing the pain from tearing him to pieces.

"You're almost there, Nevin," his other whispered into his ear. "You're finally ready. Take responsibility for what you did, for the choice you made. Let yourself remember so all of this can end."

"It hurts so much . . ." he managed, feeling a wetness spreading from the gaping wound in his skull. "Please . . . just make it stop hurting. I can't take it anymore. I'll do anything to make it stop."

"Then face what you've done. Push through the pain and see the darkness you've hidden away from yourself. Accept who you really are, Nevin. Accept yourself and be free."

Sobbing into the shoulder of his other, Nevin nodded, willing to do anything to escape the fire burning through his skull.

A gentle hand stroked his hair.

"Open your mind and remember."

A warm, white light washed away the agony, and Nevin felt the world fall out beneath him.

Leaning on the tip of his blade, Theis pushed up to his knees, feeding on the magical energies he was siphoning off of Aurnia's watery avatar. He panted from exhaustion and rolled his wounded shoulder. A probing glove came away dotted with blood.

"I have to do this, Theis." Nevin stomped at the interlocking wooden panels making up the floor of the bridge and dragged the hissing tip of his blade along its surface, searching. "It's the only way."

The man in black pulled his limp arm across his lap without releasing his grip on his sword. "The only way to what? Look around. This isn't an ambush. These people aren't trying to hurt you. They're trying to help, and you're about to kill them."

The young-man-who-wasn't glanced up and chuckled. "With all that blood staining your hands, it's odd to hear you so worried about me getting a little on mine."

"It's not the same and you know it. I kill when I have to."

"Really?" Nevin cocked his head in mock confusion. "All those men who came in search of the sword needed to die, did they? And all those soldiers in Comelbough, too? The ones just doing their jobs? You couldn't have wounded them and made your escape?"

"It's not that simple," Theis growled. Using his blade for leverage, the man in black rose to his feet. Water slid free of his cloak as he straightened, painting a halo of moisture on the boards around him.

"It never is with you, is it? Always have to be right, no matter the consequences, no matter who it hurts."

Nevin gripped the sword with both hands and set his feet. "Like father, like son, I guess."

"Like fath—" The words crumbled on his lips, and his sicklesque blade fell from slack fingers. *That's not possible.*

The young man winked in his direction. "See you at the bottom, Theis."

Nevin lifted the seething blade overhead, his swollen pupils trained on the precise spot where four wooden panels adjoined.

Shaking off his surprise, Theis lunged forward. If Nevin managed to cleave through that point in the bridge, no amount of magic would be able to hold it together.

The Sharasil's edge came down hard and fast, and Theis realized he was too far away to stop it.

The soft morning light played on Nevin's shoulders through the shifting canopy behind him, dancing at the call of an easy breeze laden with pine sap, cedar, and a hint of apple from the nearby groves. Reaching ferns scraped at his pant legs, just tall enough to hide the dented bronze canteen hanging from his wrist by a thick leather strap.

It's that morning again. After I fought with Dalen. I don't remember this, though. Is this what happened after the wheelbarrow?

The young man stood motionless at the edge of the trees, looking not off into the woods quietly awaiting his company, but back the way he came. Back into the modest homestead where he'd spent his childhood hiding from the man who raised him. Back into the rundown farm where he'd been forced to work for days without a proper meal. Back into the barn where he'd spent so many cold Langour nights with naught but a ratty blanket and a pile of dirty straw to keep him warm.

Back to the place where Dalen was about to die.

No, this isn't right. I have the canteen at this point, which means Dalen is already dead.

Flames crawled along the walls of the barn like a swarm of hungry insects, eating their way up the rotting walls to spread out across the pitted roof. The men who lit that fire laughed to one another from inside the nearby hovel, partly obscured from sight by a copse of balsam firs.

The young man knew he was safe from view where he stood, but not for long. Biggan and Widge would notice him soon enough. He needed to go, to find Aidux, to find Ishen, to warn them both of what was to come, of the men sweeping through Elbin with an intent to harm.

But he didn't move. He didn't budge as he stared into the darkness of that barn. He didn't so much as twitch when a bloodied hand broached the shadows and dragged a crumpled form out into the soft morning light.

Though his eyes were already stretched to their limits, Nevin could feel them widen even further.

"Boy!" came a raspy cry, spat from the cracked lips of the monster named Dalen as he fumbled for purchase on the rain-loosened dirt. Cuts and swollen bruises marred his barely recognizable face from his encounter with the men now tearing his hovel apart, wounds partially staunched by a crust of grime and straw. He huffed as he dragged himself along, his other arm angled unnaturally beneath him. Lines of pink spittle drooled from his slack mouth. Most of his rotten teeth were little more than bloody stumps.

Dalen was alive. I didn't kill him!

The wounded man barely made it halfway out the door before his broken body gave out.

"You just . . . gon stand there . . ." His head slumped to the ground as he tried to breathe, struggling to be heard over the roaring fire creeping up behind him. A wet cough wracked his body and left the dirt near his mouth red and glistening with blood.

"Gon stand there . . . watching . . . or you gon . . . help?"

The fear of what Dalen would do to him if he didn't pull the man to safety turned Nevin's insides into a nest of worms, and after a moment of indecision, he felt his weight shift to his toes.

"Move yer ass . . . boy . . ." Dalen craned his neck, casting a hateful scowl across the open space. "Know better . . . than to make yer . . . daddy wait."

Nevin's weight shifted to his heels.

No . . . I wouldn't have . . .

He took a slow, deliberate step back. He shook his head, feeling a heat building in his chest, growing stronger with each breath, a fire stoked by years of mistreatment and abuse that yearned to taste the air of freedom.

"You're no father of mine. You're nothing but a worthless drunk."

The rickety barn groaned beneath its own moldering stature, weakened by the hungry flames and a lifetime of neglect. The roof shifted first, peppering the sodden earth with hunks of smoldering wood. Dalen feebly shielded his head, but a number of fiery daggers pierced his soiled tunic and lodged themselves deep in the meat of his back. The whole structure listed forward, and Nevin could feel his lips curling up in self-satisfied smile.

"You're never going to hurt me again."

The last thing he saw before he turned and sprinted into the woods was a final, pleading look from the doomed old drunk, as the terrible weight of his sins came crashing down on him in the form of old, rotten barn.

"I . . . I left him to die." Nevin sputtered, opening his eyes to find his face held in the comforting hands of his other. Flexing his toes against the cool, coarse stone, he rubbed his wrist where the thick leather strap had bit into his flesh, but found only smooth, unadulterated skin.

His other stepped back, but kept hold of Nevin's shoulders. "You made a choice."

"And that's so much worse." Wiping the blurriness from his swollen eyes, Nevin shrugged free of the man's grasp. "I didn't kill him. In the barn, during our fight. I thought the canteen had accidentally killed him, but he survived. He survived to be tortured by those two soldiers. He survived to pull himself out of the barn. An accident is one thing, but a choice?

"I didn't kill Dalen, but that doesn't mean his death isn't my fault. I had the chance to pull him to safety. I had the chance to be the bigger person. I had the chance to be a hero—"

"—and instead, you discovered your humanity. You discovered you're fallible. Weak. Capable of terrible, monstrous things."

Nevin looked away. "Of evil, you mean."

"Yes, even of evil. We're all capable of evil. We're all capable of making selfish, deplorable, seemingly unforgivable choices, but most people can't accept their own darkness. They can't understand the breadth of their potential. They aren't strong enough to see themselves as anything but good, honorable people, and anything that challenges that notion has the power to cripple their psyche."

His other gestured to the metal object at their feet. "Just look at what it did to you. You were confronted with your own evil, but rather than succumb, your unprepared mind saved itself by forgetting, by suppressing the memory of that choice and moving forward like it never happened."

Nevin picked up the tarnished bronze canteen, and as he did, a flood of images filled his mind. Where he remembered leaving the flask behind inside the fallen silver maple, he had actually tied it to his belt. Later, as he crept through Ishen's cabin, he had felt it banging against his leg, but rather than deal with its unwelcome presence, his mind had protected him by dropping it on the ground and forcing him into the study. During a nightmare in the upper reaches of the Traagen, he had reached for it in his sleep, waking to find it resting atop his chest.

Every time he thought he'd gotten rid of the thing, his mind had quietly manipulated him into keeping it and changed his memory so he'd be none the wiser. The canteen hadn't left his side since he'd retrieved it from the tree.

A grim reminder of the choice he had made, but wasn't yet prepared to face.

Nevin shook his head. "Why now? Why would my mind choose this moment to let me remember?"

"Because you're finally strong enough to face it. But more importantly, because you were willing."

Nevin turned to the cracked glass display. An image of Theis greeted him, the man in black leaping through the air toward him at the edge of his field of view. A gloved hand reached out, and the man's eyes burned brightly enough to completely illuminate the shadowed interior of his cowl. The image barely changed as he watched, so taut was the passage of time in the strange realm hidden within the sword.

"I have to go back. I have to fix this, before it gets any worse."

His other stepped up beside him, leaning out to touch the broken display. A tiny spark flashed beneath his finger, and the jagged crack stitched itself back together with a crystalline tinkling.

"Nothing is keeping you here. It never really was. Just say the word, and your body is yours once more."

He placed his hand on the image of Theis' frozen form. "Do you . . . do you think they'll forgive me?"

"In time." He flashed an encouraging smile. "Despite all your flaws and whether or not you believe it, you *are* a good man. Or at the very least, you're trying to be. They'll grow to see it just as plainly as I do."

He swallowed the lump growing in his throat and nodded.

"I'm ready."

Chapter 84: Falling Action

"Go!" Arolde yelled to the young girl and the over-sized lynx. "Don't stop until you reach land!"

Neither of them looked back at him as they ran, charging into the herd of goats, the cat snarling and nipping at their legs to help drive the creatures onward.

Sandy lifted Maddox free of the overturned wagon, easing the wounded man's arm around his neck help take the weight off of a bloody foot. Gibbs was already dragging the two mules away from the wreckage, cursing the animals for their lack of urgency every step of the way. Wincing from the pain, Maddox caught Arolde's eye, a look of boundless relief passing over his strained face.

"In Peddis' holy name, Arolde. I was afraid you weren't going to make it."

Arolde ducked beneath his father's other arm to take some of the weight off the aging goat farmer. "What happened to you?"

Maddox shrugged as best he could with both arms lodged behind the men's necks. "Wrong place, wrong time. I'm lucky Sandy here is built like a horse beneath those baggy clothes, otherwise I might still be trapped beneath that wagon."

Frowning, he tried to search the bridge behind them. "Delia? Miles?"

Arolde nodded. "Safe. Though they might be stuck together for awhile."

"Oh, Delia's gonna love that." He winced as his bloodied foot caught briefly on the spot where two panels connected.

When they reached the end of the bridge, they found Blake kneeling beside a woman in a gauzy yellow dress, his quivering eyes glued to her face. The woman sweat constantly flowing rivers of disappearing water and shivered uncontrollably, her nearly vacant pupils the size of a grain of sand. Her fingers clung to a glowing crystal teardrop, shining with a radiance that painted her surroundings in varying shades of blue.

Arolde thumbed over his shoulder. "She the one responsible for that?"

Blake nodded, running a weary hand over the scar on his forehead. "I don't know for how much longer, though. The Orlicite hasn't been properly prepared to handle a spell this complicated, let alone one of this magnitude."

He raised a hand like he wanted to reach out and touch her, but couldn't decide whether to brave the water pouring from her skin by the gallon. "I can't let this go much longer. I think it's killing her."

Aidux padded up beside them. "She can't stop now! If the big water lady stops holding the bridge up, both Nevin and Theis will fall in the gorge. And Nevin doesn't know how to swim!"

Arolde squinted through the mist, trying to make out what was happening on the far side of the gorge. Though he didn't want to say it aloud, Arolde didn't much care what happened to one of the greatest professional killers in history, or the young man that had gotten them all into this mess.

I'm not going to make it.

Feet became inches as Theis sprinted headlong toward the crazed young man about to tear the world from out beneath them, but his speed was no match for the falling blade. He stretched the fingers of his one good hand until the joints ached, shoved his arm out until his shoulder complained, pumped his legs faster and harder but the blade proved faster still.

Is this what helplessness feels like?

Of all the enemies I've faced, is it my lot to finally be killed by a friend?

The electric hiss of the Sharasil ceased as the blade collapsed in upon itself and the mysterious sword tumbled soundlessly from the young man's hands.

The man in black bore Nevin to the ground, the pair skidding along the moisture-slick surface of the bridge like a flat rock on a still lake. Nevin wrapped his arms around the wounded swordsman protectively, turning himself as they fell to make sure the swordsman stayed at the top of the pile.

Theis didn't wait for them to stop sliding. Rolling off the boy's chest, he stumbled to his feet and raised a fist. Nevin brought his hands up in defense but didn't stand. "Theis, wait! It's me. Wait!"

The man in black hesitated, fist clenched to the side his cowl, a nearly opaque blue film coating his sight. "It's you?" he asked, nearly out of breath.

Nevin nodded, swiping a hand through his sodden chestnut waves. He looked around, the deep brown of his eyes no longer swallowed by his overactive pupils. "The men who were after us, where did they go?"

"They're not after us. Aurnia sent them to find us." His shining eyes narrowed suspiciously. "You really don't remember?"

He shook his head and stood. "Only bits and pieces. I wasn't very focused on what was happening about here."

"Out . . . here?"

Nevin stared up at the giant aqueous shape of Aurnia barely managing to hold the bridge aloft. It shuddered beneath the strain, shedding water with every violent spasm that sent tremors rippling down the bridge and through the remaining tension ropes.

Looking out over the expansive gorge and witnessing the devastation wrought by his own hand, the young man displayed none of the debilitating terror the mere sight of the bridge had engendered just minutes before. Only a mild apprehension glimmered in his focused eyes, but whether it was the result of some lingering fear or the recognition of the part he played in the bridge's destruction, Theis could only guess.

A question for another time.

Nevin fumbled at his belt, frantically looking for something that clearly wasn't there, before spinning around to scan the surface of the ruined bridge.

"Lose something, boy?"

"I think so," he said, an unexpected smile blooming on his face. "For the first time, Theis, I think it's actually gone."

Confused but not interested in a discussion, the man in black retrieved his dropped sword, and Nevin quickly followed suite. "You sure you're good?"

Nevin clicked his sword into the hasps on his baldric. "Better than, but I'm sorry for what I put you through."

"Save it," he said, jogging toward the eastern shore of the gorge. "You're gonna have a lot of apologizing to do in about five minutes, so don't waste it on me."

Blake watched helplessly as the cloaked swordsman and the young man he'd been sent to find charged toward his group. Only a small stretch of bridge separated the pair from salvation.

And yet there was still time enough for it all to fall apart.

"Just a little longer, Celine," he whispered. He brushed a soggy clump of golden hair from her ashen face, the fear of what might happen if he touched her discarded before the situation's increasing desperation. "It's almost over. Just hold on a little longer."

A seemingly endless supply of water poured down Aurnia's convulsing body in a nearly unbroken sheet of ephemeral liquid. Looking at it, Blake couldn't figure out how she was getting air.

If she was even breathing.

Aurnia's eyes slammed shut. The light emanating from the Orlicite fluttered. A tremor shook the bridge.

Her head dipped forward, and the blue light dimmed. The bridge shook and shivered as the tower of supportive water struggled to maintain cohesion.

"Almost there," he prayed, resting his head against hers. He could hear her whimpering quietly beneath the droning hum of the sustained spell. The sound made his heart ache.

Theis and Nevin finally raced past the abandoned wagon. Blake slipped his arms beneath Aurnia's legs and behind her back.

"Everyone's safe," he said. "Let it go."

The light fluttered faintly for a moment, and then extinguished completely. Aurnia slumped against Blake as he rose, unconscious. In the distance, the aqueous apparition shuddered dramatically before collapsing in a shower of mist and rain.

The final remaining tension ropes rent apart and the bridge buckled in the center, ripping apart in two spectacular waves of twisted rope and square wood panels. The gorge swallowed the debris like a hungry bird, mouth agape and eager for more.

A crowd of Whitefalls natives watched the event in horror, muttering and gasping to one another and peering at the strangers responsible for the display with a mixture of anger and concern. Theis crouched over the discarded Somnicite, securing the priceless artifact in the folds of his cloak.

Blake's voice bore only a hint of strain from carrying the woman in yellow when he spoke. "Everyone head to the Warbler. There is food and drink enough for all, and we all need to rest. The sooner we get out the public eye, the better, though I'd bet a whole case of saffron mead a Trine has already been dispatched to investigate today's events."

A scowling Arolde dashed through the group and punched Nevin in the jaw. He reared back for a second swing, but an agitated lynx quickly jumped to his friend's defense, and Arolde—not interested in wrestling a pissed-off cat—

raised his hands and backed away.

Nevin rubbed his stinging face, but Blake spoke up before anyone could respond to the attack. "Arolde, I don't care where you go. Leave if you must, but pull something like that again and I will personally make sure you spend the next year mucking out pig runs all over Fen Quarry. Do I make myself clear?"

Arolde tossed his hands in the air and nodded, wisely choosing to keep his mouth closed.

"Gibbs," Blake continued, his hard gaze still leveled on Arolde. "I'm taking Celine to the inn, so I need you to send for a healer. I don't think Whitefalls has a dedicated Shaman, so just find whoever you can. Maddox, you'd do well to come with me so we can tend to that foot."

Before Gibbs could even nod, the girl with the strawberry-blonde hair raised a hand and stepped forward. "No need to send for a healer. I can fulfill that role."

Blake looked her up and down. Though Wizards rarely appeared anywhere close to their true age, this one looked especially young. "And what am I to call you, young lady?"

"Raiya Callicade, of Calibri Grotto."

He nodded in greeting. "Then follow me, Raiya of Calibri Grotto. It looks like you've got your work cut out for you."

He looked at each of them in turn, coming to a stop when his gaze met Nevin's. Something about the young man struck him, itched at the back of his mind like a cut on the roof of his mouth, but as Aurnia shivered in his arms, Blake realized he had more important issues to attend.

"Let's go, everyone. We all have a lot to talk about."

With a series of nods and murmured agreements, the motley crew moved southward as a singular entity.

Chapter 85: A Simple Farm Boy

Draped in a thick woolen blanket, Aurnia stared into her nearly empty plate and carefully replayed the events that each of her companions had recounted to her over dinner, mentally weaving the threads of plot into a complex tapestry depicting the previous six days from multiple viewpoints. Most fit perfectly, lending Aurnia a clearer understanding of how all involved parties had made it to Whitefalls in such a timely manner.

But it was the snags that bothered her. Like a loose thread dangling from the hem of a sleeve, she picked at them relentlessly until her thoughts had exacerbated the problem into a tangled mess of imperfect theories and speculations.

She scraped her teeth along the juicy flesh of a crab apple—one of Blake's personal stash from his home in Fen Quarry. She couldn't remember the last time she'd been so ravenous. Along with a decreased need for sleep and extended lifespan, an experienced Wizard benefited from an almost complete independence from food. The limitless spiritual energy of the Numen sustained her, pouring through her supernaturally widened soul channel to fulfill the requirements of life more efficiently than water and air and rest.

Still, like any muscle, the strength of a person's soul channel waned after periods of overuse, reducing her to the status of a mere mortal. Casting through the uncut Orlicite had overextended her. Now, she could barely even feel the warm light of her soul, could barely sense it sparkling feebly at the end of the narrowed tunnel of her soul channel, and her hunger had returned with a vengeance.

No morsel of food was safe.

More concerning though, was the palpable sense of wrongness marring the feel of her soul channel. A thinness of the protective membrane encircling the ethereal conduit almost, and an uncomfortable proximity to things of neither the physical nor the spiritual realm. Things having no claim on either, yet hungering for both.

She drew her blanket around her shoulders and shivered. A warm hand rubbed her back, and Blake leaned in close.

"Are you okay? If this is too much—"

"I'm fine," she said, forcing her pale lips into a thin smile. Blake hadn't so much as left her side since she awoke in one of the Warbler's private rooms, making sure she had whatever she needed to regain her faculties after the events some hours before. He'd initially been hesitant to allow her to join the others in the common room below, but her dogged insistence had eventually won out, and with his help, she'd managed to find herself a somewhat comfortable table near the bar to enjoy a rejuvenating meal.

And to listen as the others tried to piece together the events of the previous week.

At the edge of the Warbler's common room, Blake lounged against the bar not far from her side, nursing a glass of local brandy and gnawing on an apple of his own. Raiya sat on the raised hearth, poking idly at the fire with a cast-iron rod. The gaunt young Arolde stood before a line of windows overlooking the gorge, hands planted on his hips as he scowled at a team of men traversing the canyon on a suspended platform. The older Maddox shared her table, flexing his previously wounded foot under the table and picking at the remains of a roasted quail.

As for Nevin, the misplaced apple farmer had taken a seat near the stairs, his hands wrapped around the strange blade standing upright between his knees. Twin streams of chill mist exited his nostrils with each fall of his shoulders. The cat watched him curiously from atop a nearby table, cocking his head when one of the tiny clouds drifted too close. Theis stood on the stairs above them all like a macabre gargoyle, constantly surveying the room and all its inhabitants like there might be an enemy hidden among them.

Aside from Theis and Aidux, each of the room's occupants had pointedly chosen a vantage point opposite Nevin, and were doing everything in their power not to look at him. They had all heard his story, his explanation of what had led to the events on the bridge. And as tough as it was to accept so incredulous a tale, Aurnia had a feeling those who took him at his word saw more in him to fear than those who did not.

It vexed her how her entire world revolved around a simple, unimpressive farm boy.

Arolde audibly huffed, shaking his head and taking a sip from a limp waterskin. The man in black's cowl jerked in the youth's direction and his shining eyes narrowed beneath the cover of his mahogany mask.

"Something on your mind, boy?"

"I said 'horseshit'," he barked, backhanding the air beside him as he turned to glare at Nevin. "You expect us to believe some . . . ghost or something took over your body, and decided the best way to keep you alive was to drop you a hundred feet into churning waters and hidden rocks? That's what you're telling us?"

Nevin withered at Arolde's sudden animosity, his fingers tightening further around the blade of the Sharasil.

Maddox rubbed his thumb against the arch of his bare foot. "I'm sorry, but I have to agree with my son on this. I personally find the idea of some body-possessing entity a mite hard to stomach. I'd sooner believe that fear led you to make some irrational decisions, and you're so embarrassed by what you did that it's simply easier to act like it wasn't your choice than to admit to any wrong-doing."

"Let's get something straight," Theis interjected, swooping down the stairs to stand at Nevin's side. "We've spent the greater part of this evening detailing our individual experiences during the past week, and while some of what has been said tonight borders on the improbable, I don't much care if you believe it or not. Stranger things have happened. You're standing in a room with a man who eats magic, a talking lynx, and a Wizard capable of bending an entire waterfall to her will. A Wizard, I'll add, that you each owe your lives to."

Aurnia raised an eyebrow. This wasn't his usual morose indifference. Theis was actually coming to Nevin's defense. Curious, but she decided it would be best to keep her mouth shut for the moment.

Arolde rolled his eyes. "Only because this one's a few logs short of a cord."

He took another swig from the deflated water skin. Aurnia noticed a hint of red drizzling from the corner of his lip before he wiped it away with his sleeve.

"Let's take it down a bit," said Maddox, attempting to rise from his chair. He though the better of standing when his weight shifted to his still tender foot.

"Not until he owns up to what he did." Arolde strode out into the middle of the floor toward Nevin, coming to a stop when Aidux leapt to the floor between the two young men, hackles raised and a faint snarl peeling back his lips. The cat's expression paled in comparison to the hateful one decorating Arolde's contorted face.

"I'm just saying what everyone's already thinking. Had he not lost it and clipped the bridge, we'd all be halfway to home by now. Instead, you nearly lost your foot, your Wizard nearly drowned in magic water, and the rest of us barely made it here alive!"

Nevin scooted forward in his chair. "I know it's hard to believe. I wouldn't I'd believe me if I hadn't witnessed it firsthand, but I'm telling the truth."

Arolde kicked a chair in disgust. "Oh, come on! Just own up to it. Or do you really think we're that stupid?"

"Don't talk to him like that." said Raiya, tossing the poker to the floor. It clattered to a stop beneath a neighboring table. "What makes you think you know anything? You don't know him."

"And you do? You only met him a week ago! What makes you the expert?"

Blake held up his hands. "I think we all need to calm down. We've all had a tough day, and I—"

Jumping to her feet, Raiya skirted the tables and advanced on Arolde with a raised fist. "I trust him more than I trust a jerk like you!"

The distinctive ring of metal drowned out the fighting as Theis ripped his sword from its scabbard and took a purposeful step forward. Arolde backed away, nearly tripping over the fallen chair. Raiya took the hint, returning to her spot by the fire, but her glare never left Arolde's crimson face. The rest of the room froze, hanging on a razor's edge.

It was Aurnia who finally broke the silence. "Theis is right."

She pushed her plate aside and folded her hands on the polished tabletop. "We aren't here to point fingers at one another. In-fighting serves no one. Each of us chose our level of involvement in the previous week's events. Nevin, however, hasn't been afforded the luxury of such choice. He is here because he was driven from his home, pursued by the sort of men who would kill to obtain that which only he can carry.

"He is a prisoner of Fate, and that sword is his cell. For as long as he carries it, he will have more enemies than allies, so it rests on others to protect him. Theis made it quite clear that we are not to discuss the probability of his claims, and in that, I wholeheartedly agree."

"Amazing." Shaking his head, Arolde glared at Nevin and shrugged. "Looks like you've got everybody fooled."

Picking up the fallen chair, he slammed it back into place before sweeping past Blake at the bar. His elbow caught a number of loose bottles as he disappeared through the swinging door, sending them to the floor with a crash.

"Sorry about that, Blake." Maddox offered their leader a pained expression as the older man bent over to clean up the scattered bottles.

Aurnia tucked a strand of hair behind her ear. "We have vastly more important issues to discuss. I've spent the last few hours turning each of your stories over and over in my mind, scrutinizing the inexplicable elements and formulating theories for the explosion on the Misanthrope, and more importantly, what I've come to realize about the sword."

Theis snorted, slamming his blade home in its scabbard. "Theories for the explosion? You can keep those to yourself. I already know what caused it."

Aurnia tapped a fingernail on the tabletop. "Oh? And what makes you so sure you're responsible?"

He extended a gloved thumb towards his mask. "These eyes aren't just decoration, old woman."

Nevin shook his head, confused. "Wait, you think *you* caused the explosion? Because you can absorb magic? Wouldn't it make just as much sense that the sword had something to do with what happened?"

Aurnia wiped a hand along the empty tabletop, searching for the simplest way to explain what even she didn't fully understand. "With each passing day, the use of magic becomes more and more prevalent. Kings and queens acquire the services of Wizard and Dabbler alike in order to ensure the security of their nation. Shapers are replacing the common craftsman in towns and cities all across Stragus. The College of the Faithless scours the world, and not just for those with the inborn capability for magical talent, but for those capable of being invested with the skill to call upon their soul. They are literally making Dabblers of common men and women.

"Magicians understand more about the way our world functions than ever before. Though they may not know everything, fewer and fewer mysteries remain to be cataloged. Things that were once thought to be unique are now only considered rare, sometimes even commonplace."

She held up a finger. "Theis, however, is an anomaly without precedent. In all the annals of history, never before has anything been written of one who possesses the capability to absorb and nullify magic."

"A magic eater," Blake said thoughtfully. "That's what you called him on the bridge today."

Aurnia nodded. "Aside from Theis, a few complex magical constructs, and a special type of magician called a Javeren, nothing in the known world can directly unravel a fully formed spell. But unlike the second two, Theis doesn't merely dismantle the bonds of intent holding a spell together; he actually absorbs the constituent elements as well. Among the Wizarding community, those eyes of his are far more famous than his combat prowess.

"On the night of the explosion," Aurnia continued, "the ship happened to pass through the middle of a naturally occurring magical phenomenon, a collection of pure, unbound element called a Pool. Little is known about why a Pool forms, but everyone agrees on their dangerous, volatile nature. Physical mutations, corrupted spells, and even an emotional affliction called Vilum Fever —all are threats when encountering a Pool."

A flash of understanding raced across Nevin's face, but he remained silent.

Aidux, however, did not. "Oh, oh! Maybe that's why you were crying so hard that night! You know, right before everything turned all blue and shiny. You had that fever thing."

Nevin knuckled his forehead. "Yes, Aidux. Thank you." He cast a sheepish glance at Raiya, but the young woman quickly looked away.

"So, Theis thinks the explosion was his fault because of the way magic reacts to him?" he asked, eager to change the subject.

"Yes, and quite erroneously, I should say."

Theis snorted. "Pompous old . . ." he muttered.

Aurnia hid a smug grin behind a delicate hand. "Theis absorbs magic, removing it from the environment. It wouldn't make sense for the Pool to react violently to having a portion of its mass siphoned off. A dam doesn't suddenly break apart when you release some of the pressure behind it."

She hefted a leather pack onto the table, undoing the buckles as she spoke. "A dam breaks when the load behind it becomes more than it can bear."

From the folds of the pack, Aurnia extracted a cobalt crystal sphere, larger than her balled fist and shaped roughly like a frozen tear. The warm firelight filtered readily through the massive gem, casting puddles of the most vibrant blue effulgence upon the awe-struck faces leaning into admire it.

Chapter 86: Older Than Creation

"Is that what I think it is?" said Nevin with all the wonder of a small child.

Aurnia caressed the Somnicite's unworked surface with a finger. "While searching for survivors, I found this in the bowels of the sundered Misanthrope, directly below the epicenter of the explosion. I had suspected Captain Williams to be a smuggler during our initial negotiations, but I never could have guessed that his hidden cargo would be as valuable and dangerous as something like this.

"This is a Prime Orlicite, an especially potent form of Orlicite that, until last week, I had assumed only existed in the theoretical musings of starry-eyed Wizards. You see, Orlicite generally don't come in sizes larger than a walnut, with the largest one I've ever heard of being a Grolicite being used as the centerpiece of the Rothsfellian crown jewels.

"Orlicite are repositories of elemental energy that greatly magnifies a Wizard's ability to control and manifest its particular element. Larger Orlicite lend greater power, but like all power, it is not without a price . . ."

She sighed, her thoughts briefly turning to her diminished soul channel and uncomfortable feeling of wrongness. "Don't let the stable crystalline structure of an Orlicite fool you. It's only one step removed from the dangerous unpredictability of a Pool. The larger and denser the Pool, the more dangerous and immediate are its effects. The same can be said of Orlicite.

"I believe," she said, folding her hands together in a steeple formation. "That by suddenly introducing a Prime Somnalis Orlicite into a Pool of identical makeup and sufficient density, it instantly increased its density exponentially, resulting in a cascade effect that, to put it quite simply, 'breached the dam'.

"What made our situation so dangerous was that only the oldest and densest of Pools are visible to the naked eye, and only an amateur would knowingly sail into a visible Pool. That meant our Pool wasn't initially visible. It only became visible once exposed to the Prime Orlicite.

"Captain Williams and his crew had no way of knowing the danger they were sailing into, and it cost them their lives. I believe we only survived because we each happened to be on deck at the exact moment of the explosion. It was the shrapnel that killed the crew, the flying bits of wood and metal, not the explosion itself."

Theis half-drew his blade and slammed it back into place. "Doesn't really matter. It won't happen again. You said you had some ideas about the sword. It's time we got some answers."

"The sword," she said, drawing the word taut as she returned the Orlicite to the worn leather knapsack. Nevin watched her expectantly, perking up for the first time since they'd arrived. If nothing else, what she had to tell them would serve to take some of the heat off of the boy, though she suspected Theis would have little love for what she was about to admit.

"Well, for starters," she began, bracing herself. "I haven't exactly been honest with you."

Theis stood still, his blue eyes burning into her.

"Go on."

"You don't exactly seem surprised."

He snorted derisively. "I've met you."

Aurnia folded her arms beneath her breasts. "The truth is, when I came to Comelbough in search of you, I didn't exactly know what I was looking for. A weapon, yes, but the letter I'd received told me little more than to seek you out, that what you were holding would help me find what I was looking for."

"What were you looking for?" asked Blake, refilling his empty cup with a generous pour from the brandy bottle.

Her lips parted in response, but she paused and simply shook her head. "A question for another time. My point is, up until you and Nevin showed up with the sword, I had no idea what to expect. It wasn't until later that I began to understand what we might be dealing with, even though I still didn't fully recognize the significance of the item in your possession."

Nevin pulled the sword across his lap and peered down at it curiously. "So . . . what is it?"

"When I was a child being raised by the Empyrians, I eventually reached an age where the clergy would accept me as an acolyte. Once they realized I had the potential to grow into a potent Wizard, I was elevated to a special rank within the church that would pair well with my need to travel back and forth between Volludon and the College of the Faithless for training.

"Both organizations saw the benefit of using my station within the two groups as a way to curry favor and inform on one another, so as the years passed and I proved myself a valuable asset, I was slowly drawn into some of the more secretive circles within each.

"And that's when I learned about the Gyrfalcons."

Nevin frowned in thought. "A rare, over-sized version of the common falcon. White and gray, and said to be found far from civilization, especially on the colder slopes of the highest mountains."

Smiling, she nodded. The breadth of the young man's knowledge never ceased to catch her off guard. "But in this case, the Gyrfalcons were a covert operation ensconced deep within the upper echelons of the Empyrian hierarchy. The high priests didn't mean for me to discover their existence, but as my skills in magic grew, so too had my ability to suss out and reveal that which others sought to keep hidden.

"From what I learned, the Gyrfalcons possessed but one directive: to conceal the existence of and prevent access to an artifact said to have existed before the creation of the world."

"Before the creation of the world?" Aidux cocked his head. "I think you mixed up some words there."

She held up her hands. "I'll admit, I initially didn't understand it myself. But now I had a thread, and so I started pulling. From what I could gather, members of the Gyrfalcons were split into teams of elite warriors with exceptional survival skills and sent out into the world with . . . a copy, if you will, of the original item.

"Their task was to constantly remain on the move until a certain number of years had passed, and only then would they be allowed to return to Volludon in order to submit their charge into the hands of the next group, continuing the cycle. None of the teams knew if they were carrying the actual artifact or the copy, as each facsimile had been imbued with a number of magical abilities and safeguards to fool any potential thief."

Theis rolled his wounded shoulder. "If nothing else, this is at least a far better story than the crap you fed us back in Comelbough."

Aurnia ignored him. "I didn't have much to go on at the time. However, during our boat ride, I remembered a bit of gossip, if you will, from the time I spent in the Empyrian capital over a decade before. The Gyrfalcon teams change out every eight years or so to keep their members fresh and at peak performance, and one of the teams had failed to return in time to retire their charge. The church's leaders were caught between the need to solve the problem and their intense desire to keep it under wraps, and in their fervor, I managed to finally get hold of a description of the artifact in question."

Her eyes turned to the mysterious weapon draped across Nevin's lap. "I wonder what they would do if they learned it had found its way in the hands of some nobody apple farmer."

The young man rested a palm atop the storm gray metal. "Is the real thing? Or just a decoy?"

"That I don't know. I think the next step will be to get it to Fen Quarry where we can examine it more closely. Blake has the facilities necessary for an in-depth investigation, though our priority will revolve around figuring out a way to safely sever your connection to it."

Wood squealed against the polished floor as Nevin quickly stood. "I . . . I need some air."

"There's a bench out in the courtyard," Blake said, gesturing to a door on the wall adjacent to the bar.

Nevin nodded wordlessly before weaving through the common room furniture, his hip bumping chairs and tables in his haste. Aidux hopped down from the table to follow him, but a firm word from Blake stopped him mid-stride.

"Let him have some time to himself, Aidux. That boy has more weight on his back than a plow ox in the early months of the Waking."

Ears drooping, the lynx skulked over to Blake's side, where the older gentleman was more than happy to scratch between his tufted ears.

Aurnia wiped her hands across the surface of the table. "I need to rest," she said, the excuse only a half-lie. "I think that will be enough for tonight."

Blake nodded in agreement, tossing back the remnants of his glass before reaching for the bottle. "I want everyone to remain in town for now. We've all been through quite an ordeal, and a bit of rest would do us good. In the meantime, Celine and I will discuss our options.

"Maddox, I want to thank you and your team again for your help. If you could spend tomorrow sending messages to the other teams to let them know they can return home, I would be very grateful." He put a firm hand on the man's shoulder to keep him from standing, placing the bottle on the table beside him. "Maybe have a drink or two to help numb that foot before you go."

With a grateful chuckle, Maddox patted his friend's hand and reached for the stoppered bottle of brandy.

"Raiya," Blake continued, straightening. The sudden mention of her name jarred the young woman from her private thoughts. "Why don't you come over here, have a drink with me?"

"Alcohol?" The girl scrunched up her nose. "I've only ever had it once. Scotch, I think. Awful stuff."

Blake chuckled, waving her over. "Scotch is a drink of old, refined men, both of which I am not. I bet if we look, we can find something we'll both enjoy."

With a final bite of her crab apple, Aurnia rose from her chair with a throaty groan.

She realized she actually felt like the old woman in Theis' mind.

Chapter 87: Worthy

Resting on a pine-slat bench positioned at the end of a meandering path of softly rounded river stones, Nevin Walker bent the tines of a purloined pewter fork and leaned over the stalwart ironwood box that he finally had the time to tinker with. He carefully inserted a pointed tine into the scratched keyhole and set to work, if only to distract himself from the stress of the day's events and the effects his mistakes had had on those he cared for.

Occasionally, he would pause to study the cloud-spotted night sky. The clean perfume of blooming roses brushed the back of his throat with each breath. Meticulously manicured bushes displayed their dark blossoms beside the twisting gravel path, artfully designed to present the illusion of flowing water. Coated in a thin veneer of mist, the multi-hued river stones glistened like a single moment in the life of a mountain creek, stolen away and placed in the garden for all to enjoy.

Overhead, the tiny pinpricks of distant stars winked in and out of existence as puffy clouds hustled across the heavens like sheep late for a routine shearing. The clouds jostled together as they moved east, agitating the herd so thoroughly that angry flashes of yellow and orange electricity regularly burst forth from the cluster as a result of their agitation.

Despite the distant show of lightning, Nevin heard only the measured poundings of hammer on nail and the equally rhythmic shouts of men as they heaved against a tangled web of rope. Though the construction camp lay on the far side of the Warbler and was thus beyond his sight, he could still make out the mass of rope straining beneath the cover of the ethereal mist swelling up from within the gorge.

For all the noise they made, it sounded to Nevin as though the citizens of Whitefalls had abandoned the idea of rebuilding their bridge, and now attempted to draw closed the very jaws of the canyon itself.

He enjoyed the momentary peace, whether unearned or not, before setting back to work on the box.

"What day is it?"

Despite his focus, the unseen speaker hadn't caught Nevin by surprise. In some indescribable way, he had the sense his inescapable doppelganger was somewhere out there all evening . . . watching . . . listening. Just as he had been for the past few weeks.

A faint smile tilted the corners of the young man's lips, and he moved the Sharasil from the seat beside him and propped it up against his leg. "Tharsun, I think. Been hard to keep track."

"No, I meant the date." The familiar figure emerged from the darkness and casually sank down on the bench beside him, the sword the only thing keeping their knees from touching. Gone were the ever-present shadows and the unnaturally pallid skin, with the entity now presenting itself as Nevin had seen him during their last encounter within the sword—as a dark reflection of himself.

"Twenty . . . second of Veet?" He shrugged. "Give or take a few days."

His other mimicked his pose, reclining back into the seat and resting a hand on the Sharasil's enshrouded blade. While the skin on metal contact caused Nevin to expel breaths laden with chill mist, no such cloud appeared on the lips of his other, not even when he spoke.

"Rough day." It wasn't a question.

Nevin nodded. "Could have been worse."

"Almost was."

With an annoyed sigh, Nevin went about adjusting the bend on his single-tine lock pick. "I notice you're still here."

"And more so than ever, from what I can tell." He tugged at the wrist of his rust-colored doublet, offering his wardrobe a complicated expression. "A little dated, but it will do."

"Sorry I didn't imagine you a more fashionable outfit," Nevin said dryly, fumbling with the lock. The tip of his tongue poked out the side of his mouth.

"I happen to think I look rather dashing. The two of us make quite the pair. Or we would, if anyone other than you could see me."

His other thrummed his fingers against the Sharasil. "I should be congratulating you, by the way. Against all odds and despite your own expectations, you actually survived to see your seventeenth birthday. By the skin of your teeth, but you made it."

Nevin's head jerked to face his companion. "You can't possibly . . . That was years ago, years before I touched the sword. I was alone when I said that."

He nodded. "You *were* alone. Standing out among the balsams, kneeling over Frieda's grave in the hours before sunrise. It was the last time you visited her, I believe."

The man shrugged uncomfortably beneath the weight of Nevin's stare. "You were worried Dalen was escalating his treatment of you, and that if you didn't figure a way off the peninsula soon, he was likely to cross a line that would end with you getting fed to the neighbor's pigs. You told her, that at the rate his abuse was progressing, you didn't expect you'd live long enough to see your seventeenth birthday."

When the flabbergasted young man didn't respond, his other continued. "Look, this thing we have, this connection, it's more than just being able to see and hear one another. Your entire life is . . . well, when I think about it, it's almost like I've been there for all of it, standing off in the shadows, observing. Unable to intervene, to interact, or even to look away. And the longer we're connected, the more . . . intimate my knowledge of your life becomes."

"That's . . ." Nevin began, struggling to form words.

"Intrusive, yes." His other rubbed his neck and looked off toward the inn. Candles shined out from the first floor windows, and the silhouettes of the rest of his party occasionally darkened the foggy glass. "I can't argue with that."

Nevin gazed despondently toward the garden door. He doubted anyone would come check on him, and without access to opposable thumbs, even Aidux would be unable to visit. He couldn't blame them. In spite of the supernatural explanation of his actions and the heartfelt apology that had followed, he had seen the skepticism in their eyes, had heard the judgment in their tones.

He suspected he could fall asleep out here among the roses, and no one would spare a minute to make sure he was okay.

"You said something else," said his other, measuring his words as though an improperly placed emphasis might shatter the fragile peace within the quiet garden. "Out there, kneeling beside Frieda's grave. It was the last thing you said before you walked away, never to return. Do you remember?"

Looking out over the gorge, Nevin pressed his fists against his thighs and stayed silent. He didn't want to remember, didn't want to think about his life in that place anymore.

"You were . . . fourteen, I think, and had just come off a particularly bad fight with Dalen. He'd caught you sneaking food from the house, and the bastard had wrenched your arm so hard you couldn't lift it for a week. He told you, he didn't care if you starved as long as you starved where he couldn't see you.

"It made you think of Frieda. She was always fussing over you to make sure you ate. She'd stuff you full of bread and cheese before sending you off to your chores, or she'd bring you morsels of jerky while you worked the orchards.

"That's why you were at her grave that morning. You wanted her to know that you hadn't been eating very well, that Dalen barely fed you, and you said a prayer at the foot of her grave, somehow hoping your words would reach her in the afterlife and she'd come help. Do you remember?"

Nodding, he swiped an arm across his nose and sniffed. "I was a fool. The dead can't hear the living, and things never get any better."

"Maybe, but you asked anyway. That's the whole point. Do you know what that means? What that says about you?"

He shrugged, fighting the burn building in the corners of his eyes. "That I was a stupid kid?"

"It means you knew that Frieda loved you. Dalen treated you terribly because *he* was terrible, but not because you were somehow unworthy of love. And you understood this, on some unconscious level, because before she died, Frieda's love left a mark on you that you never forgot.

His other leaned forward, resting his forearms across his knees. "Looking through your memories, I can easily see that Frieda was good people. Bad taste in men, but otherwise good.

"And them?" He pointed toward the garden door. "They're good people, too. They'll forgive you, in time. They're just a little raw right now, but tomorrow is another day. But most of all, you're worthy of their forgiveness."

Nevin wanted to believe him, wanted to think he hadn't somehow ruined his relationships with Aurnia and Theis and Raiya, or destroyed any chance of these newcomers ever trusting him, but he couldn't stop thinking about how angry that Arolde kid had been.

He flexed his jaw, feeling the tightness where the young man had punched him beside the ruins of the bridge. The others were sure to feel similarly, and were probably far better at burying their mistrust and dislike beneath a thin veneer of civility.

"I hate that you know so much about me," Nevin said, wiping his eyes and returning to his tinkering. "Yet I know practically nothing about you. What are you? Are you a ghost? Are you the sword? And why, in the name of all that's good, do you look like me?"

His other scratched at his beard. "Doesn't really seem fair, does it?"

"I'm getting used to life being unfair," he grumbled, feeling the lock's inner mechanisms shifting beneath his focused probing.

"That's adulthood for you."

"Then give me something." Nevin cranked on the makeshift key in frustration before slouching back onto the bench. "Anything! Even the playing field a little."

"And ruin this thing we've got going here?" With a sly wink, his other leapt to his feet and headed back toward the shadows from whence he arrived.

"So . . . that's it, then? Our entire relationship consists of you being privy to the entire breadth of my existence, and all I get from you is . . ." He dragged a palm across his forehead, incredulous. "Antagonism and evasive wit?"

A soft chuckle shook the man's shoulders.

"Your box is open."

Nevin glanced at his lap, surprised to see that last twist of the fork had successfully released the internal clasp on Ishen's box, and a narrow gap now darkened the space between the fitted lid and its unimpressive yet structurally reinforced base. He ran his thumb along the rim of the box, pursing his lips thoughtfully at the idea of finally glimpsing its contents—contents he fully expected to be Ishen's last message to him before his old mentor had vanished into thin air.

Taking a deep breath, Nevin nudged the lid, but it didn't budge. He pressed harder, grasping the sides with both hands and shoving his thumbs against the recalcitrant panel of ironwood until a crescent of white colored his nails from the pressure and his arms shook with the strain. When he realized that no amount of forcing would get the job done, his breath hissed through clenched teeth and the box dropped back into his lap.

"Zerik," said a voice from the shadows, the single word enunciated with a gentleness that somehow magnified its importance.

Nevin shook the throbbing from his fingers. A sharp indention crossed the pad of both thumbs.

"What's that? Is that your name?"

His other's response echoed out from the ether, fading closer toward silence with the cessation of each word.

"Figure you've earned that much."

Rolling his eyes, Nevin picked up the ironwood box up with one hand, the pewter fork with the other. He jammed the handle into the crack and twisted.

The soft metal warped beneath the strain, but with a satisfying click, the lid popped free.

His hands shook as he lowered the box into his lap. Staring down at his prize, he refused to even blink, worried that the enigmatic container would find a way to vanish should his attention slip for the slimmest of moments. He rubbed his thumbs against the tips of his fingers, keenly aware that each pass only served to spread the perspiration leaking from his anxious palms.

"Alright, Ishen," he whispered, turning the box sideways and tilting the lid back like the cover of some forbidden book. "I think its finally time you gave up your secrets."

Chapter 88: Reason Enough

"Theis."

The silky voice of the woman in the yellow dress quietly called up to him as he ascended the stairs. He briefly considered ignoring her, but the knowledge that the Warbler's upper story had only one exit—the stairs beneath his boots—changed his mind. A woman like Aurnia was as tenacious as she was beautiful, and he doubted a simple wooden door would be enough to stymie her plans for confrontation.

He stopped without turning. "I thought you were tired," he said, a hint of mocking bite to his words.

"And I thought you were the type who only cared about himself." Dress hiked up just below her knees, Aurnia took each step with the careful attention of a woman on the verge of exhaustion, slipping around his dark form to stand in his way. From this distance, he could clearly see the dark bags bunched below her eyes and the pallor of her sunken cheeks.

"Caring about myself? You're one to talk. You look at Nevin, and all you see is the sword."

"Oh, don't act so self-righteous. We both know there's nothing remotely special about that boy. Had I the ability to separate him from the blade when we first met, I would have left him with Donald and never looked back."

Theis reached out with his good arm to push her aside, but the woman caught him by the wrist, advancing on him until he could feel her warm breath through his mask.

She glanced over his shoulder, but Blake and Raiya were deeply entranced in quiet conversation. Nevertheless, her voice was little more than a forced whisper.

"Why *are* you still here, Theis Bane?"

His eyes narrowed. "What are you talking about?"

"Exactly what it sounds like. Why did you get on the ship from Comelbough? Neither Nevin nor myself asked you to come with us, so why did you?"

His gaze rested on her fingers wrapped around his wrist, but if she noticed, Aurnia didn't loosen her grip. "Woman, you barely had strength enough to lift the cat. As humorous as it would have been to watch you try, I doubt you could have gotten the both of them on that boat without my help. Besides, the Lancowls and I share an unpleasant history, so staying in Comelbough wasn't necessarily in my best interest."

"Oh, please. I may have doubted the meat of your infamy before, but you proved that day that a swordsman of your caliber would have little to fear from the Lancowls of the Lesser Delphine."

Theis jerked his wrist free of her grasp. "You know nothing of combat, Wizard. You throw puffs of wind and sprinkle raindrops on your enemies. You think that somehow makes you a capable warrior? Fighting groups of well-armed men is like throwing dice against the ebon form of Khek himself. One wrong step, one improperly timed breath, one compulsory flinch, and you'd be dead.

"Fine, but why are you *still* here?" She flicked a delicate hand toward the front door of the inn. "Nothing is stopping you from leaving. Your obligation has been fulfilled. I never intended for you to accompany me out of Comelbough, let alone follow me all the way to Fen Quarry."

Theis snorted. "And just what makes you think your desires mean anything to me?"

It was her turn to regard him suspiciously. "How *did* you know where to find the sword?"

A sly smile formed beneath the cover of his mahogany mask. "Just as soon as you tell me the real reason why you're so damned interested in it yourself."

Aurnia's poignant stare was all the answer he had expected to get.

He shrugged. "That's what I thought."

Aurnia closed her eyes, washing away all trace of emotion from her face until it assumed the look of polished stone. When she opened them again, he could feel the ice in her gaze. "Keep your secrets, if it suites you. Regardless of your reasons, you are of little use to me in your current condition."

She extended a crooked finger and pressed firmly on his cloak where it covered the tender portion of his shoulder. His eyes flared violently as hot pain radiated down his arm and up his neck and skull, but he didn't move to stop her.

"Let's get something clear, *Theis*. We're finished. You couldn't even stop a child from cutting apart a bridge. What good will you be when Fate sends real danger against us?"

With smug smile, Aurnia turned away, sweeping up the stairs like a yellow ghost.

Beneath the cover of his cloak, Theis willed the fingers of his dead hand into a loosely clenched fist.

"I'm not going anywhere, *Aurnia*."

THE END

Epilogue

Many days before the explosion . . .

https://wp.me/PeibPA-YC

About the Author

Brandon Carter was born, raised, and has never escaped for more than brief stretches of time from his home in Oklahoma City, Oklahoma. Luckily, he likes it there. He has a first name, but it's not important, and likely never will be. He's married, has dogs on occasion, and has held north of 30+ different jobs in his lifetime. He is currently a bartender at Oklahoma's largest bourbon bar, and has been so for more than 6 years. Did I mention he's old? Like . . . 41, and is quite grateful to have survived this long.

No, his wife didn't write this. He's just pretty sure no one will actually read it. Is that enough? This third-person thing is getting weird.

HEY! Before you go, drop over to Amazon and give 'Sparking the Inferno' a quick review! You don't even have to write anything if you want, just give it a star rating. As an indie author, your reviews help tell Amazon to promote my works, leading to greater success and more books. If you REALLY want to help, drop over to Goodreads and do the same! Thank you for being here!

PATRONS

The creation of this book was funded almost entirely by a growing list of Patreon supporters of various levels. Without them, this project would not have been possible. Here are all my upper tier supporters. Thank you for believing in me and helping me get this far!

EVERYMAN HEROES

My Everyman Heroes are the cream-of-the-crop, my top tier backers, and those that supported me at this level did so knowing there was very little extra I can give them. They have made an undeniable impact, not just on this project, but on my life in general. I am beyond grateful for their generosity and blind-faith in my abilities, but I continue to strive to live up to the love that they have shown me. They are as follows, listed in order of the amount of time they've been a supporter.

Karen Mize, Thank You.

DARK WARRIORS

My Dark Warriors are the front-line fighters to my cause, the ones always sacrificing of themselves to make sure I have everything I need to be successful. They, like my Everyman Heroes, have earned a permanent place in my books in one form or another. Their attention and support has directly shaped the story I tell, and without them, the books I release would be very different animals, indeed. They are as follows, listed in order of the amount of time they've been a supporter.

James Sandmann, my first Patron!
Donald Justice
Laura Schile

WIZENED MENTORS

Jenya Golubeva
Anonymous 1

TALKATIVE FELINES

Able Ardo
Kevin Coker

Thank you to all my Patrons for your continued love and support! If you want an early view of upcoming chapters or thoughts on the writing process, consider becoming a patron yourself. Go to www.patreon.com/CircleOfOrigin and sign up today, or head to https://CircleofOrigin.blog to stay up-to-date on the series.

Made in the USA
Columbia, SC
08 October 2023

23958126R00350